HUNTERS

Created and edited by **PAUL MAYBURY & JOSH TIERNEY**
Hunters outfit design by **AFU CHAN**

Plot by **PAUL MAYBURY & JOSH TIERNEY**

Design and Layout by **PAUL MAYBURY & MIKE KENNEDY**

LION FORGE buño

ISBN: 978-1-942367-63-5
Library of Congress Control Number: 2018931326

10 9 8 7 6 5 4 3 2 1

HUNTERS

-THE JOURNEY-

JOSH TIERNEY - MIGUEL VALDERRAMA

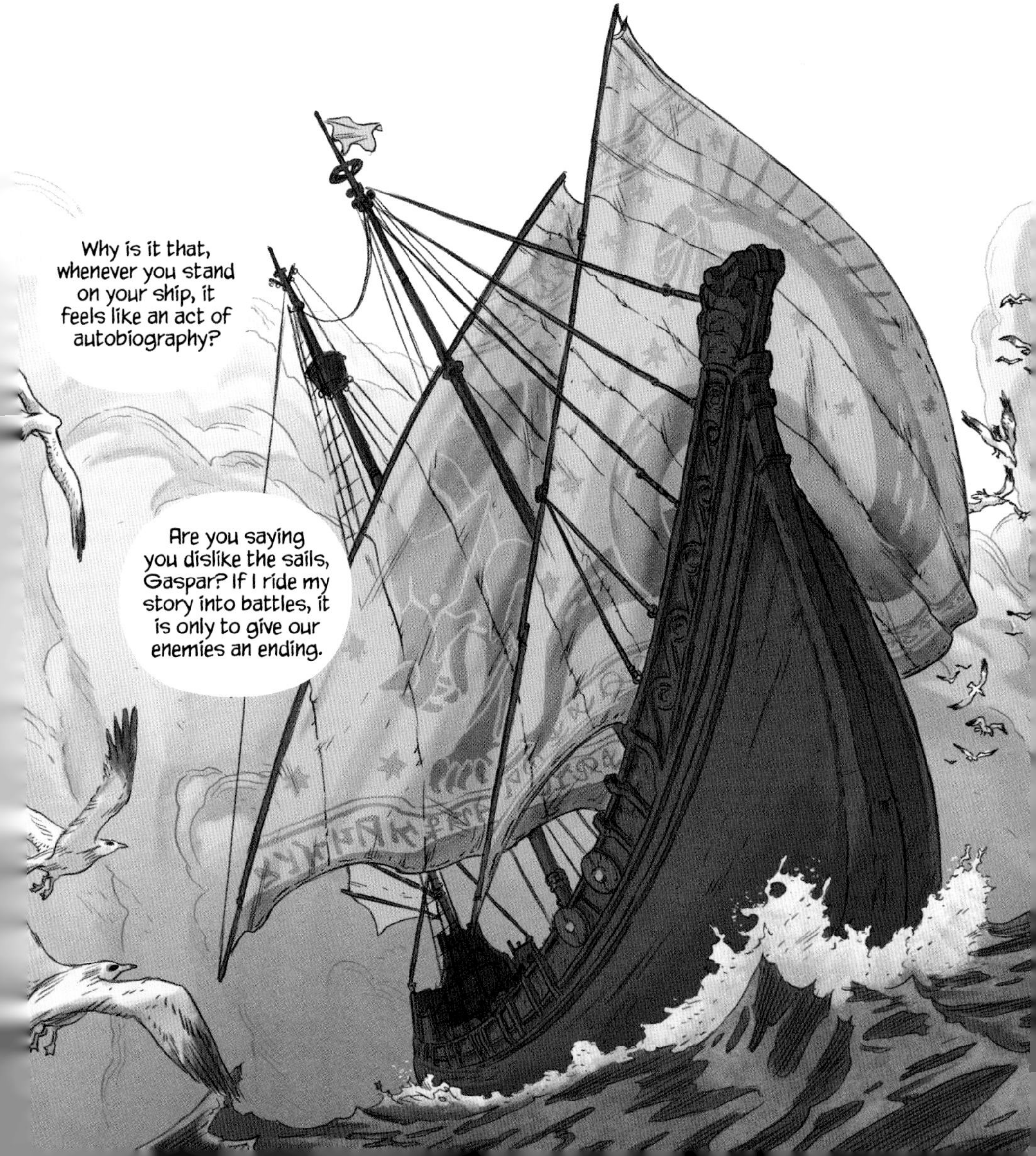
Why is it that, whenever you stand on your ship, it feels like an act of autobiography?
Are you saying you dislike the sails, Gaspar? If I ride my story into battles, it is only to give our enemies an ending.

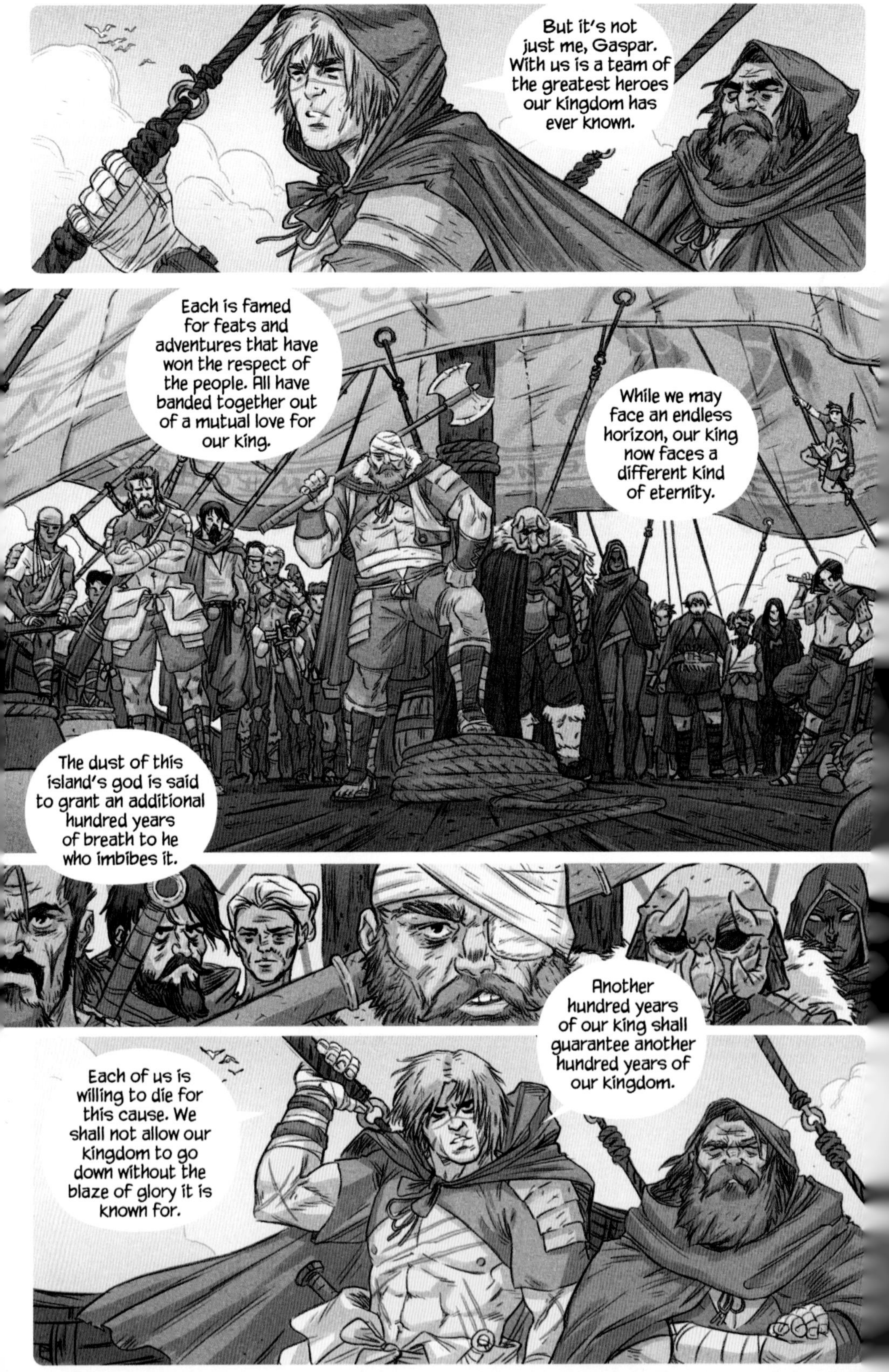
But it's not just me, Gaspar. With us is a team of the greatest heroes our kingdom has ever known.
Each is famed for feats and adventures that have won the respect of the people. All have banded together out of a mutual love for our king.
While we may face an endless horizon, our king now faces a different kind of eternity.
The dust of this island's god is said to grant an additional hundred years of breath to he who imbibes it.
Another hundred years of our king shall guarantee another hundred years of our kingdom.
Each of us is willing to die for this cause. We shall not allow our kingdom to go down without the blaze of glory it is known for.

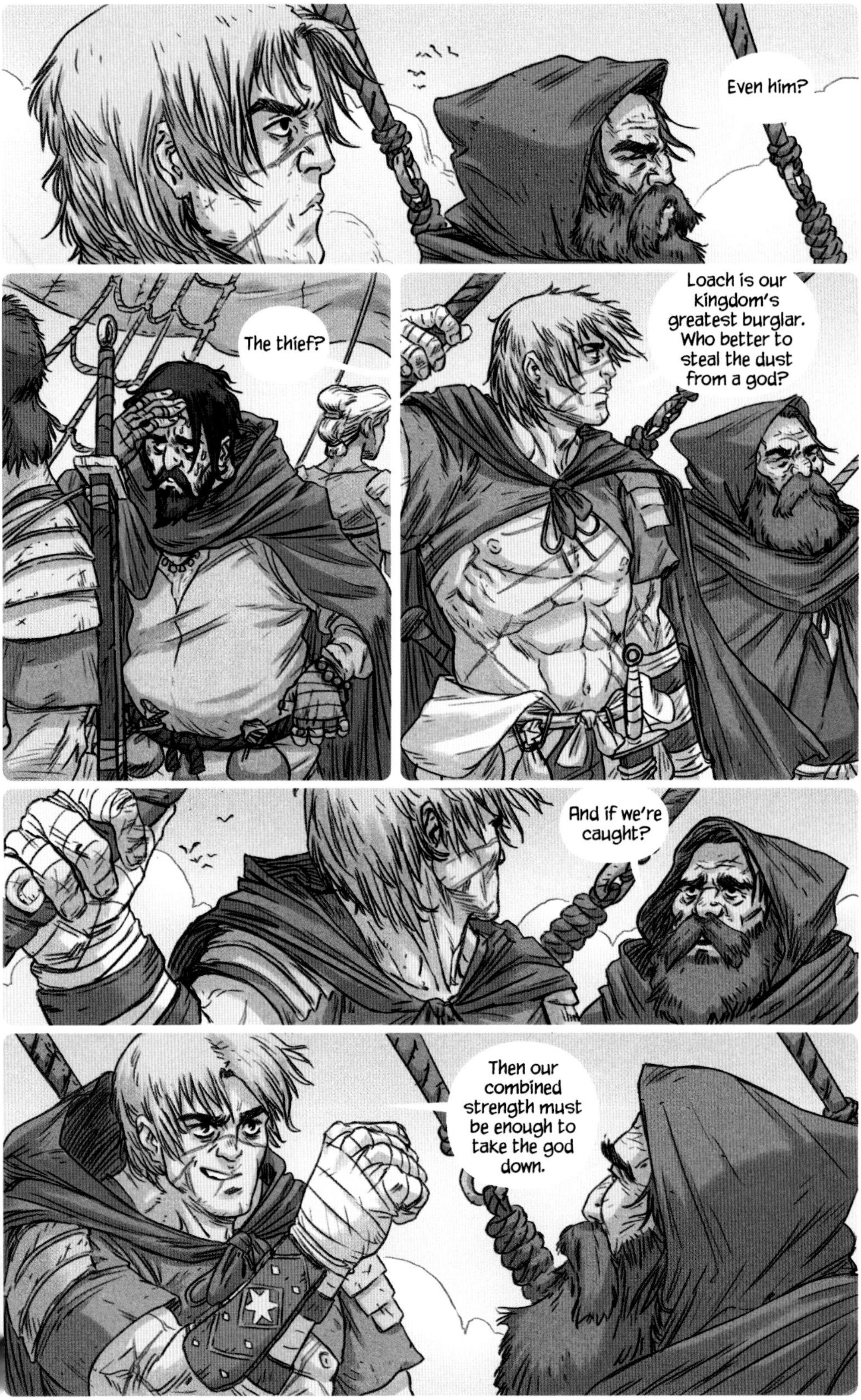
Even him?
The thief?
Loach is our kingdom's greatest burglar. Who better to steal the dust from a god?
And if we're caught?
Then our combined strength must be enough to take the god down.

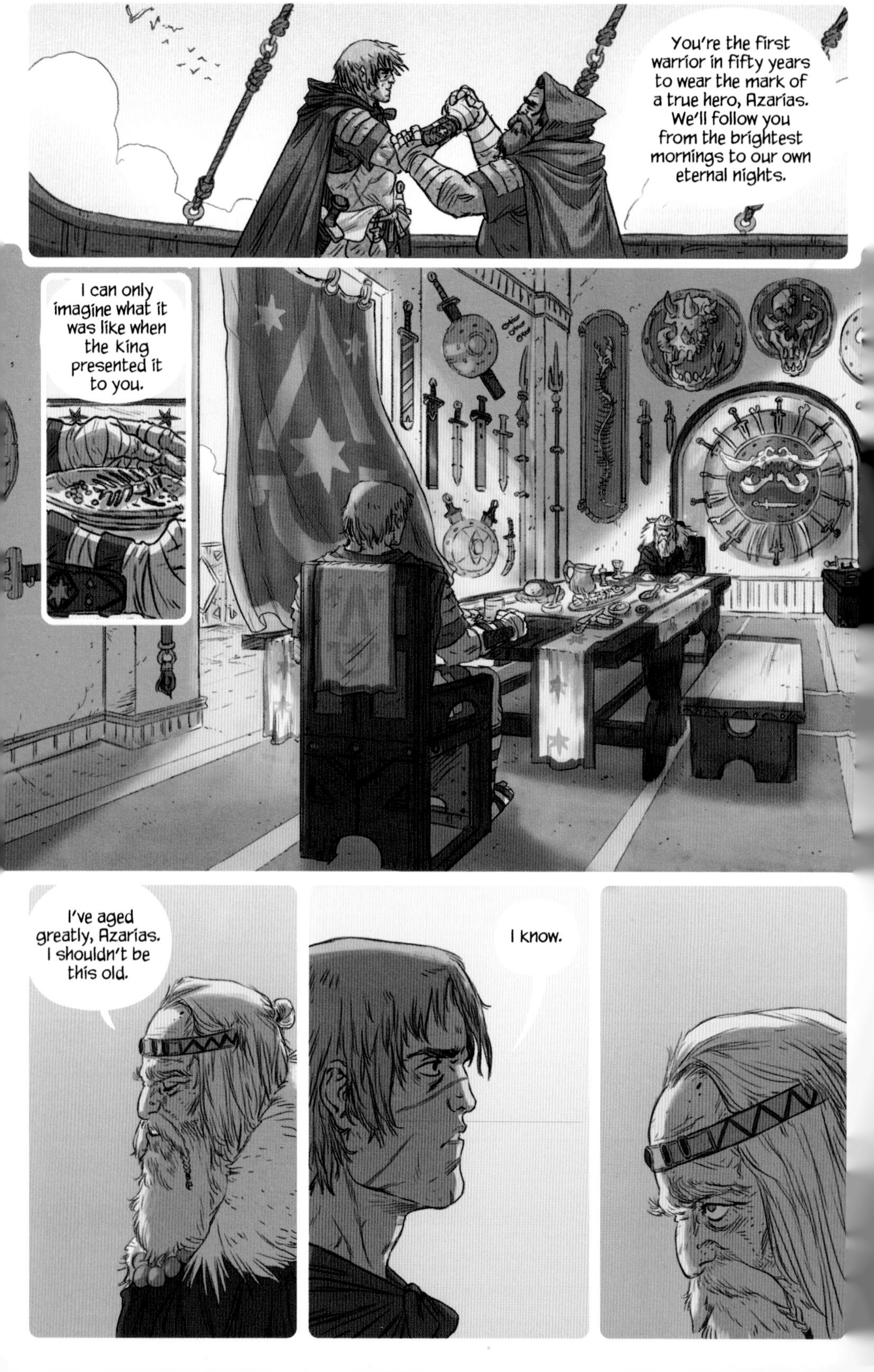
You're the first warrior in fifty years to wear the mark of a true hero, Azarias. We'll follow you from the brightest mornings to our own eternal nights.
I can only imagine what it was like when the king presented it to you.
I've aged greatly, Azarias. I shouldn't be this old.
I know.

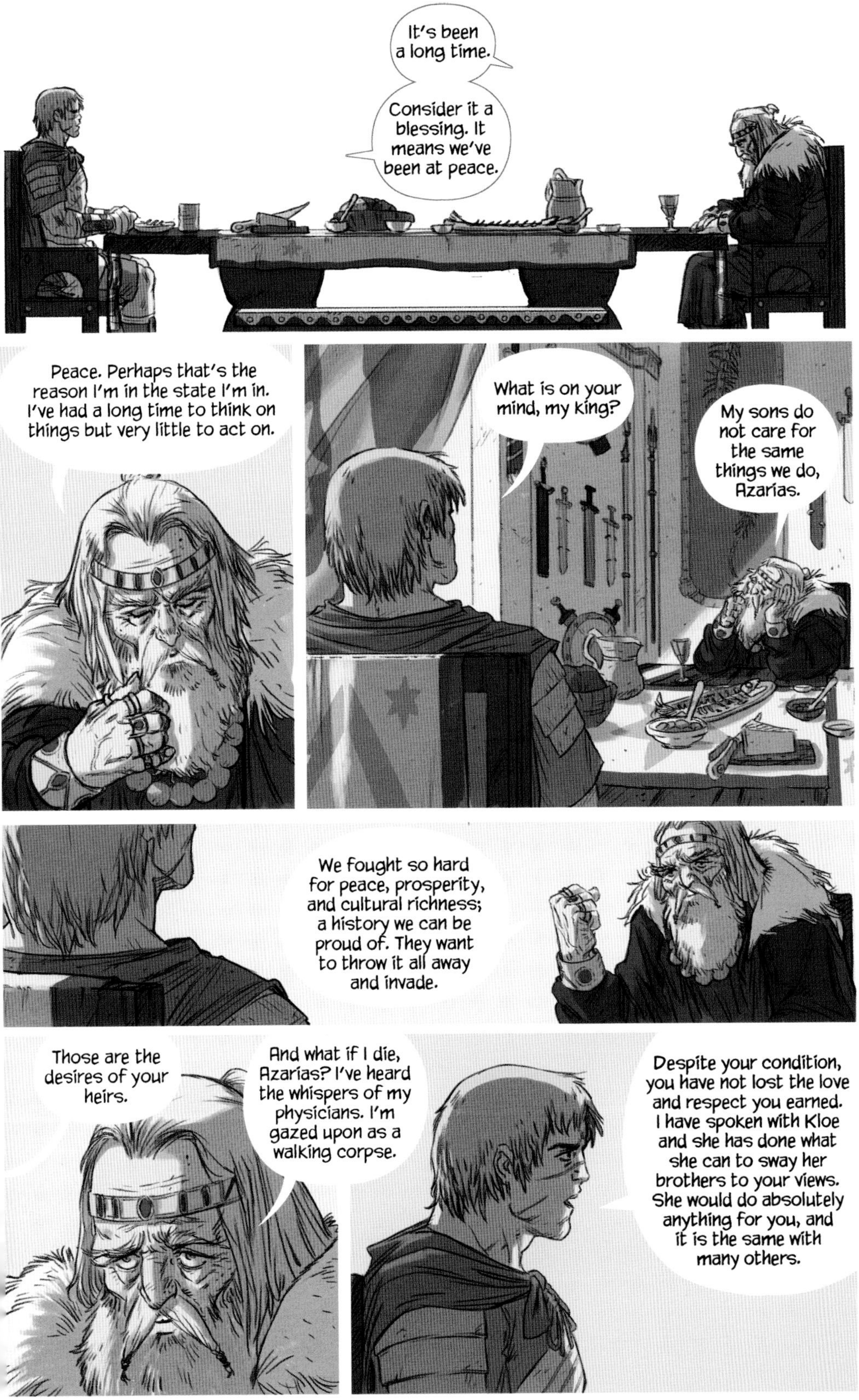
It's been a long time.
Consider it a blessing. It means we've been at peace.
Peace. Perhaps that's the reason I'm in the state I'm in. I've had a long time to think on things but very little to act on.
What is on your mind, my king?
My sons do not care for the same things we do, Azarias.
We fought so hard for peace, prosperity, and cultural richness; a history we can be proud of. They want to throw it all away and invade.
Those are the desires of your heirs.
And what if I die, Azarias? I've heard the whispers of my physicians. I'm gazed upon as a walking corpse.
Despite your condition, you have not lost the love and respect you earned. I have spoken with Kloe and she has done what she can to sway her brothers to your views. She would do absolutely anything for you, and it is the same with many others.

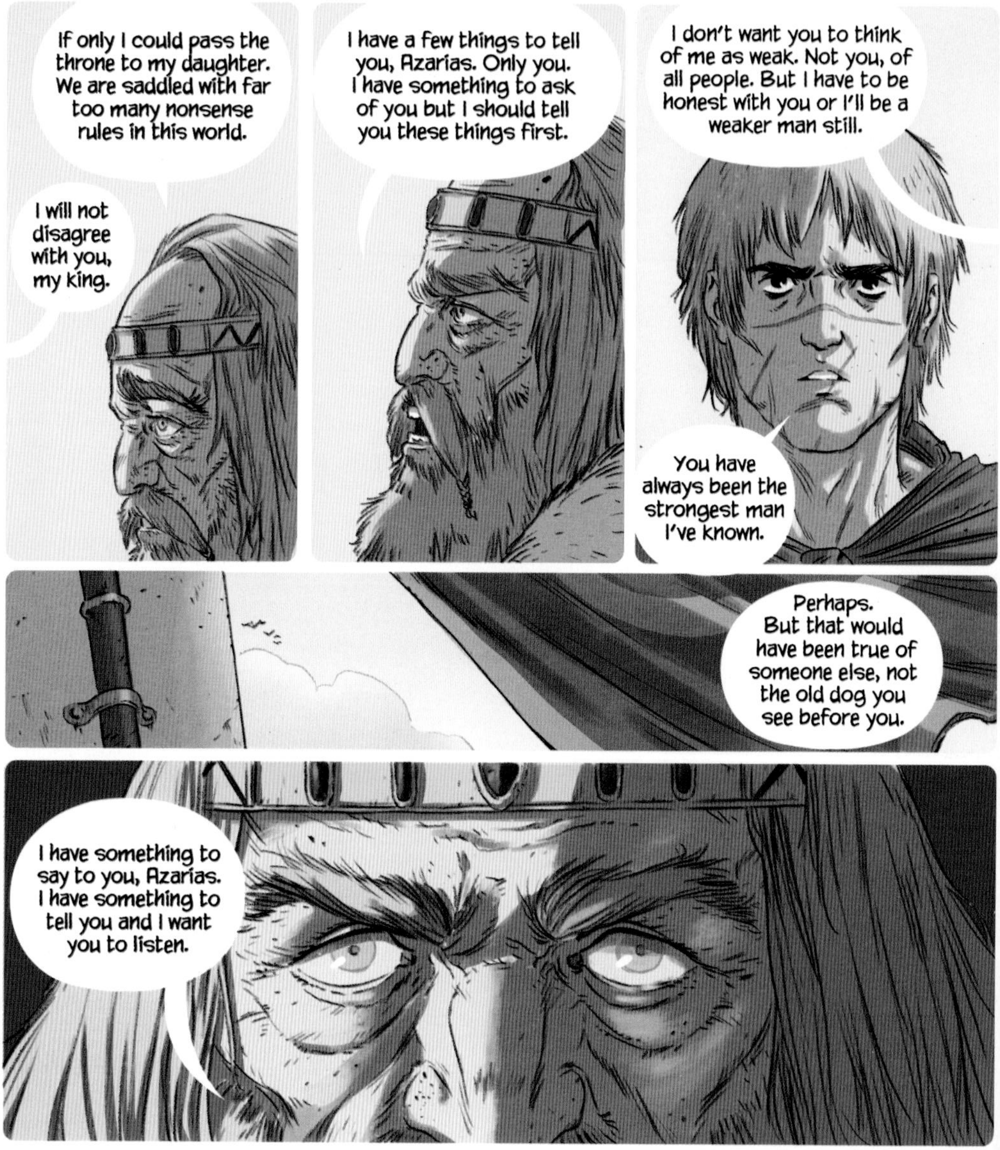
If only I could pass the throne to my daughter. We are saddled with far too many nonsense rules in this world.
I will not disagree with you, my king.
I have a few things to tell you, Azarias. Only you. I have something to ask of you but I should tell you these things first.
I don't want you to think of me as weak. Not you, of all people. But I have to be honest with you or I'll be a weaker man still.
You have always been the strongest man I've known.
Perhaps. But that would have been true of someone else, not the old dog you see before you.
I have something to say to you, Azarias. I have something to tell you and I want you to listen.

It was the last great war.

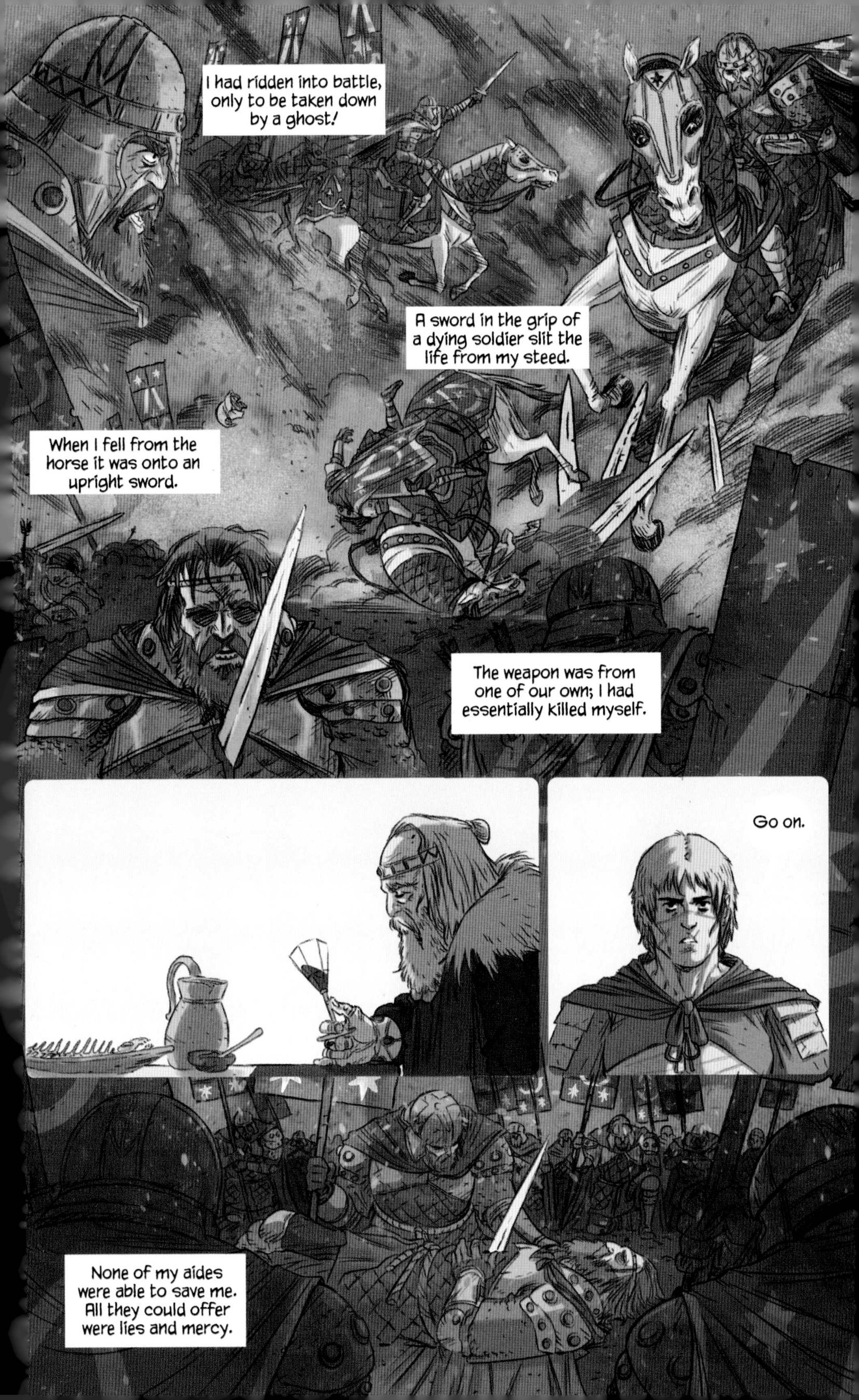
I had ridden into battle, only to be taken down by a ghost!
A sword in the grip of a dying soldier slit the life from my steed.
When I fell from the horse it was onto an upright sword.
The weapon was from one of our own; I had essentially killed myself.
Go on.
None of my aides were able to save me. All they could offer were lies and mercy.

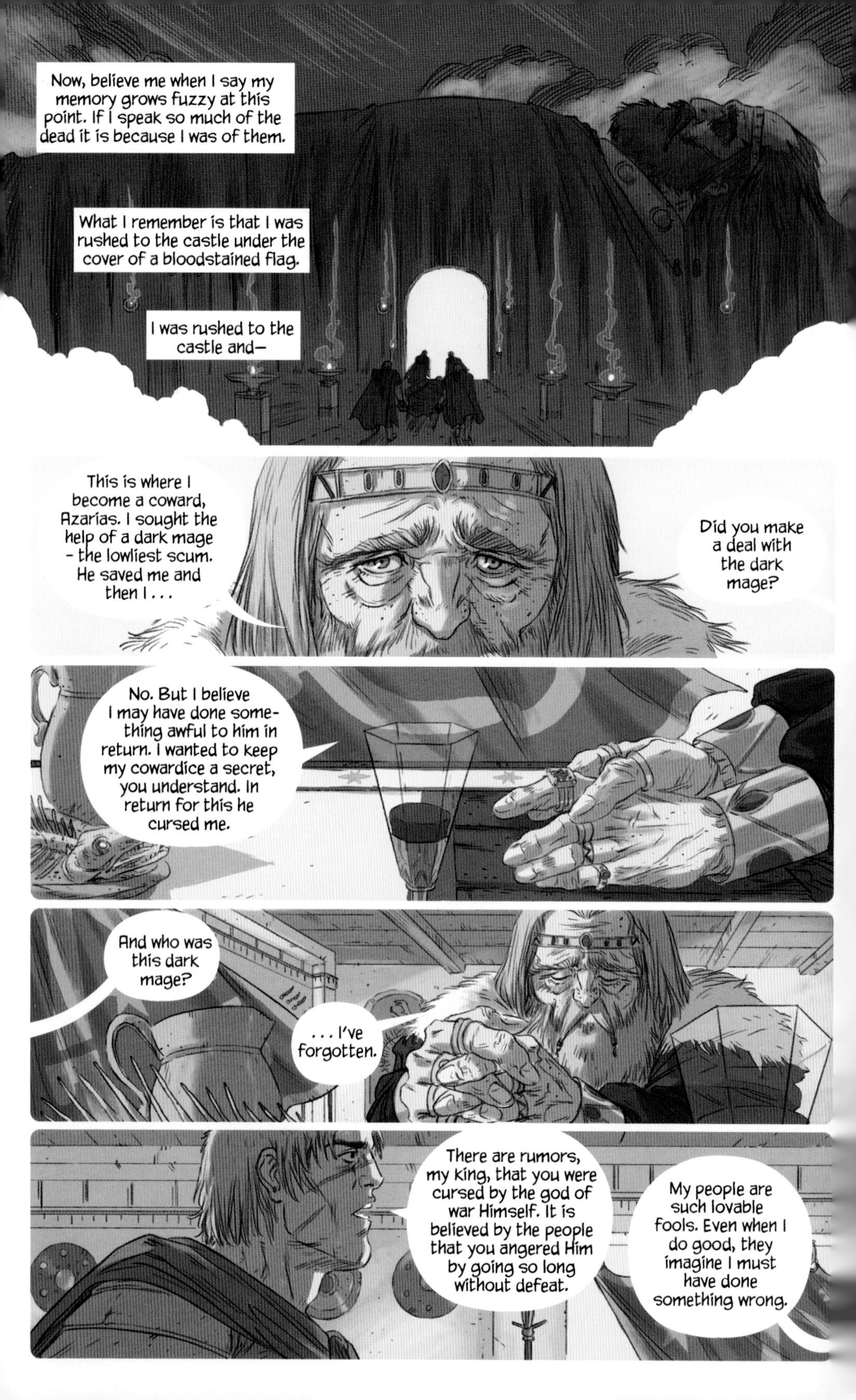
Now, believe me when I say my memory grows fuzzy at this point. If I speak so much of the dead it is because I was of them.
What I remember is that I was rushed to the castle under the cover of a bloodstained flag.
I was rushed to the castle and—
This is where I become a coward, Azarias. I sought the help of a dark mage - the lowliest scum. He saved me and then I . . .
Did you make a deal with the dark mage?
No. But I believe I may have done something awful to him in return. I wanted to keep my cowardice a secret, you understand. In return for this he cursed me.
And who was this dark mage?
. . . I've forgotten.
There are rumors, my king, that you were cursed by the god of war Himself. It is believed by the people that you angered Him by going so long without defeat.
My people are such lovable fools. Even when I do good, they imagine I must have done something wrong.

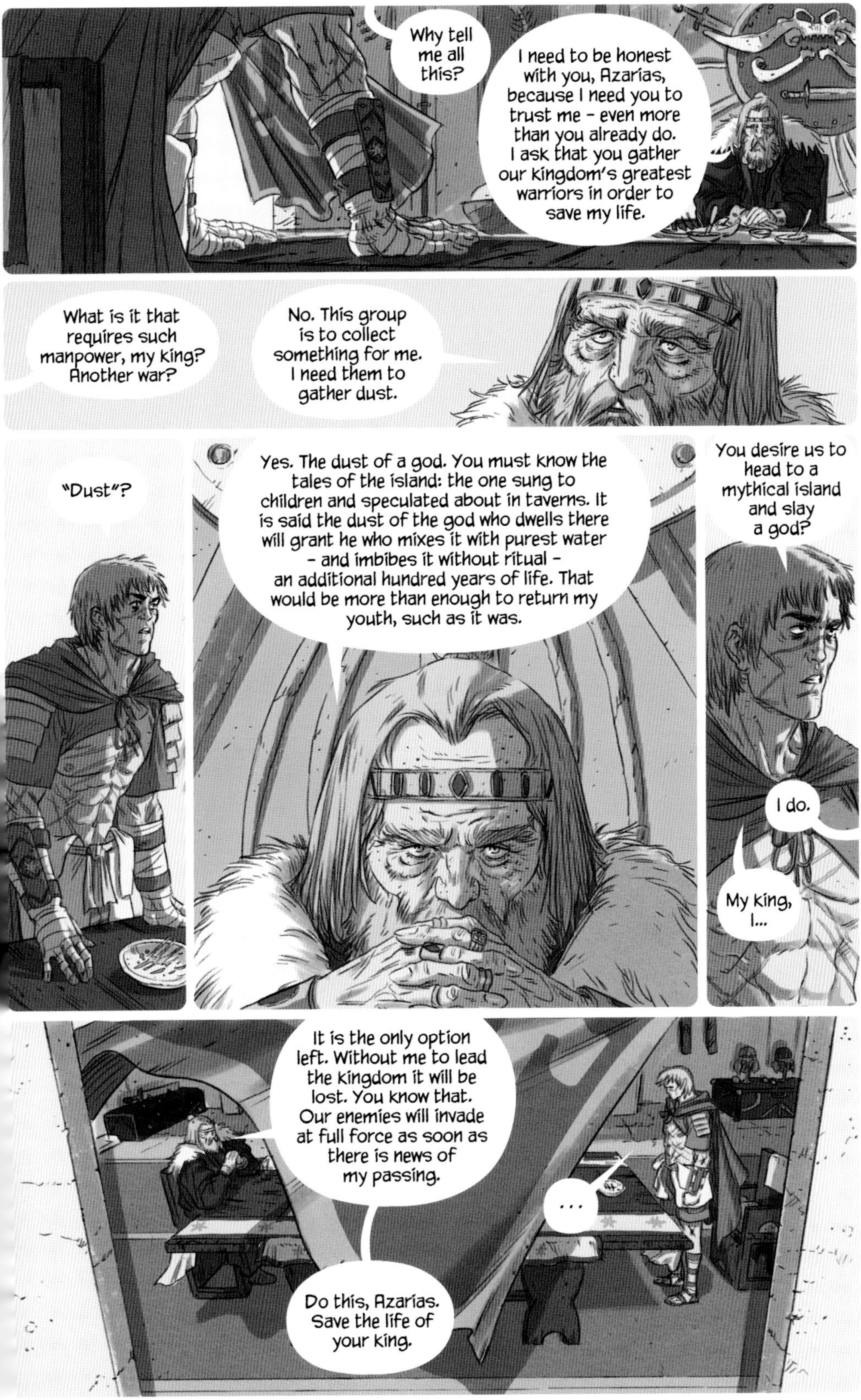
Why tell me all this?
I need to be honest with you, Azarias, because I need you to trust me - even more than you already do. I ask that you gather our kingdom's greatest warriors in order to save my life.
What is it that requires such manpower, my king? Another war?
No. This group is to collect something for me. I need them to gather dust.
"Dust"?
Yes. The dust of a god. You must know the tales of the island: the one sung to children and speculated about in taverns. It is said the dust of the god who dwells there will grant he who mixes it with purest water - and imbibes it without ritual - an additional hundred years of life. That would be more than enough to return my youth, such as it was.
You desire us to head to a mythical island and slay a god?
I do.
My king, I...
It is the only option left. Without me to lead the kingdom it will be lost. You know that. Our enemies will invade at full force as soon as there is news of my passing.
...
Do this, Azarias. Save the life of your king.

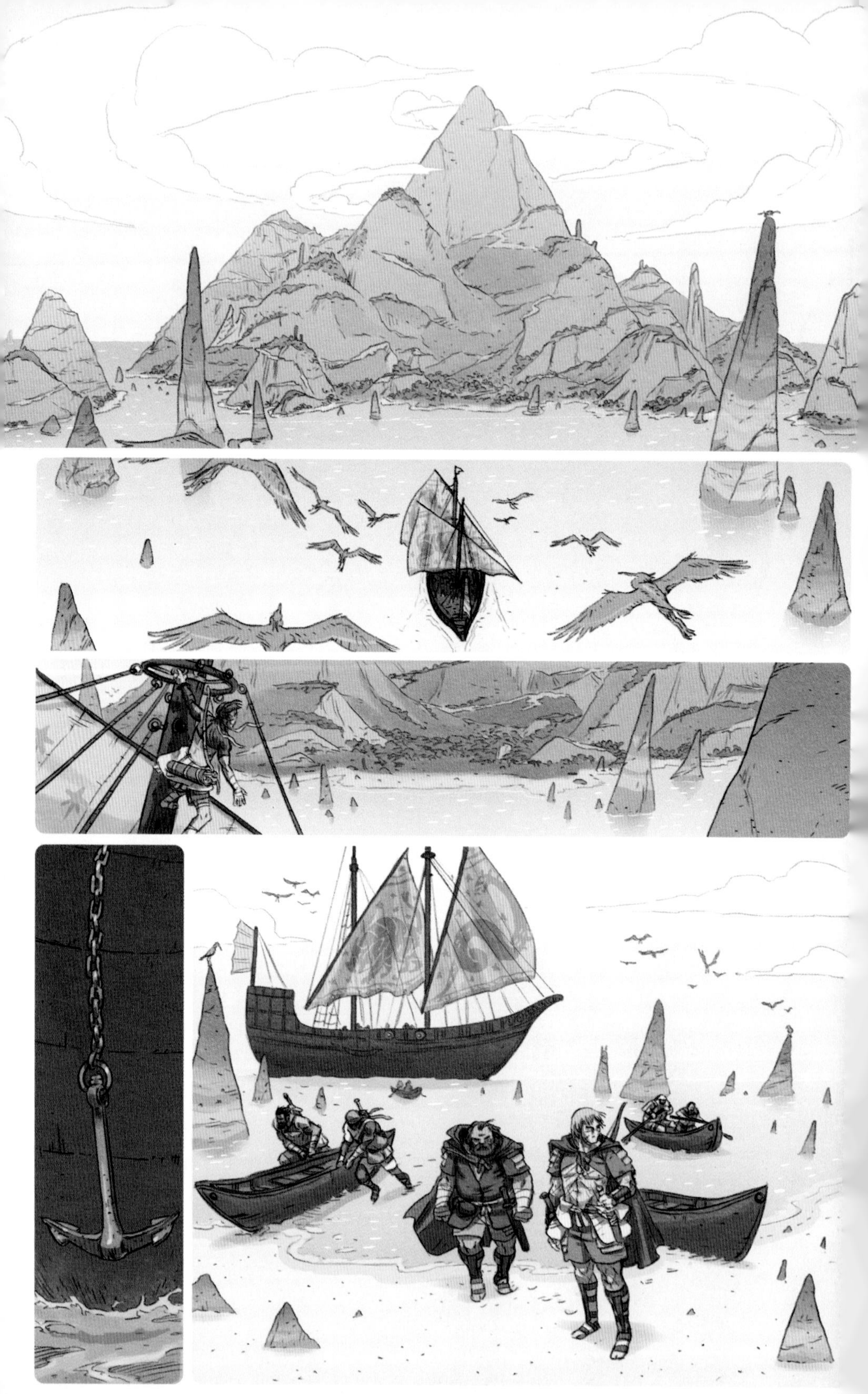

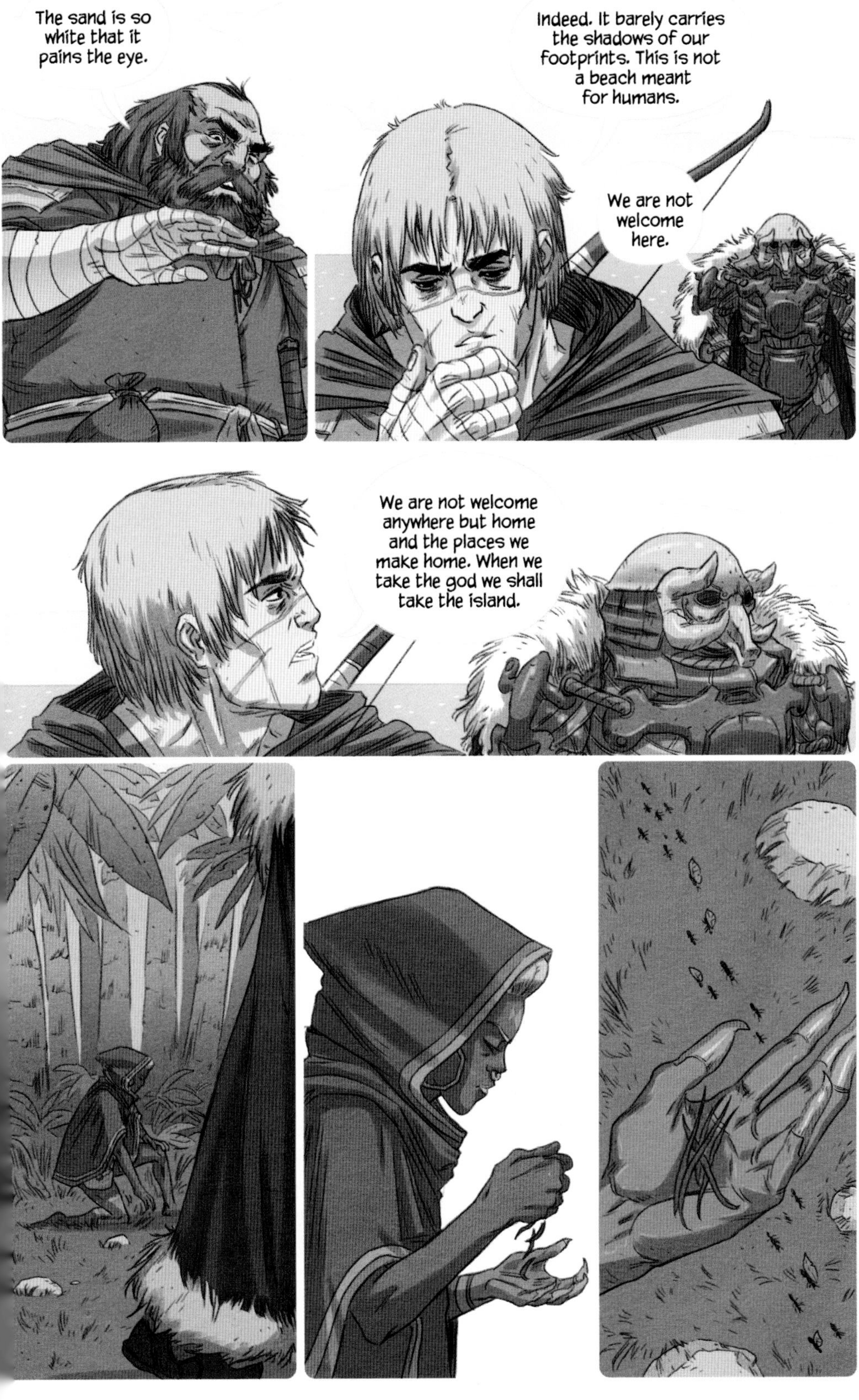
The sand is so white that it pains the eye.
Indeed. It barely carries the shadows of our footprints. This is not a beach meant for humans.
We are not welcome here.
We are not welcome anywhere but home and the places we make home. When we take the god we shall take the island.

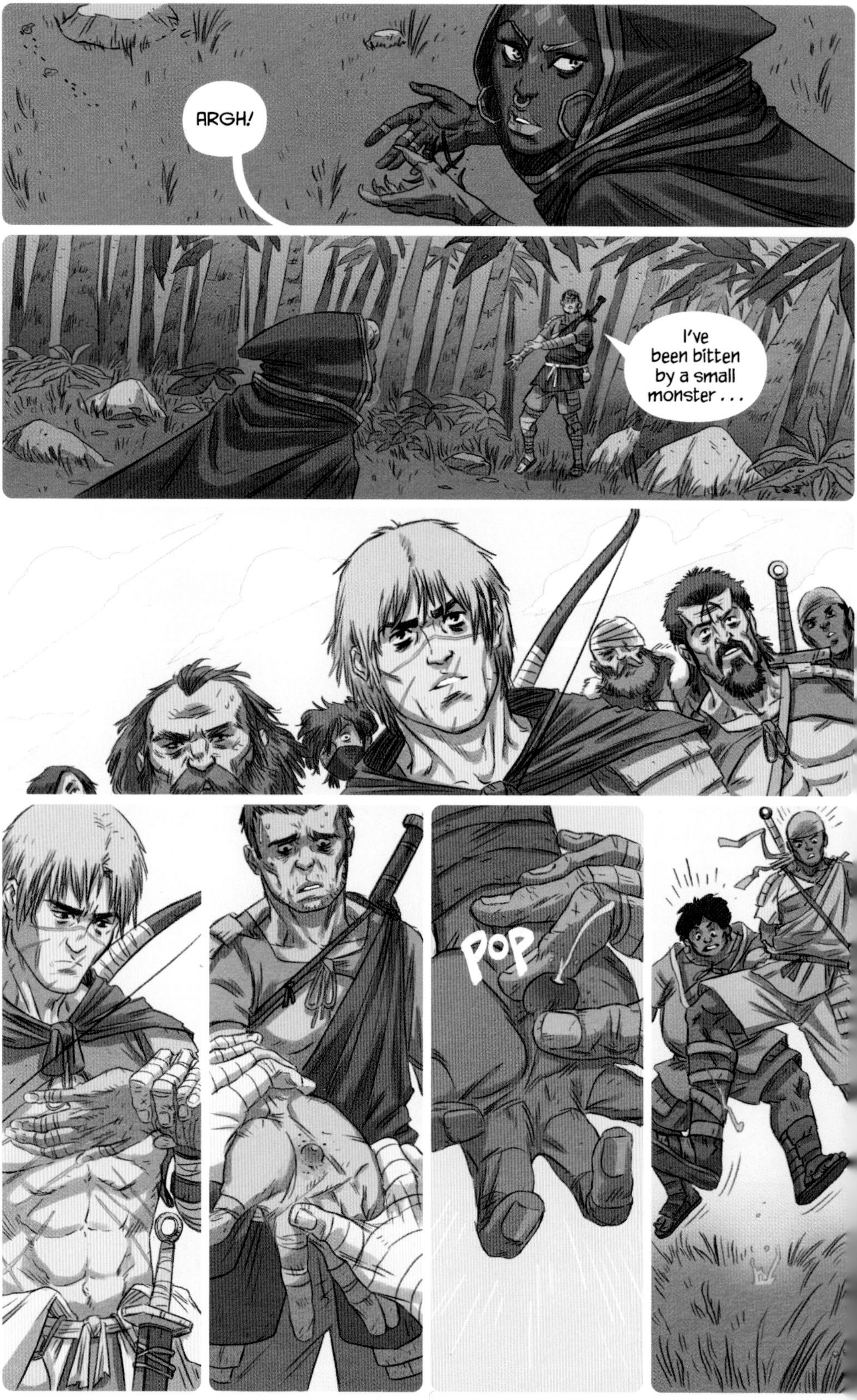
ARGH!
I've been bitten by a small monster . . .
POP

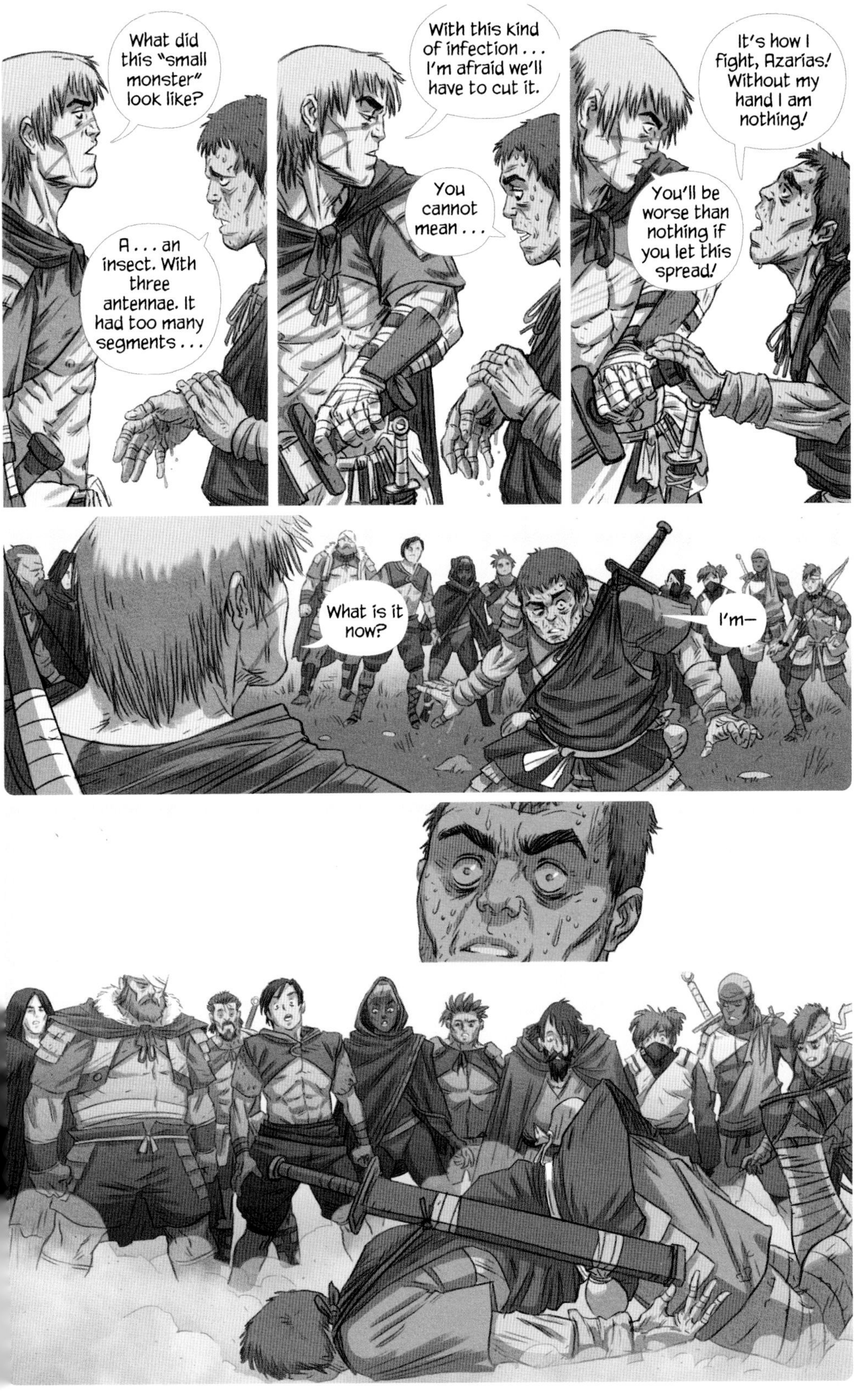

What did this "small monster" look like?
A . . . an insect. With three antennae. It had too many segments . . .
With this kind of infection . . . I'm afraid we'll have to cut it.
You cannot mean . . .
It's how I fight, Azarias! Without my hand I am nothing!
You'll be worse than nothing if you let this spread!
What is it now?
I'm—

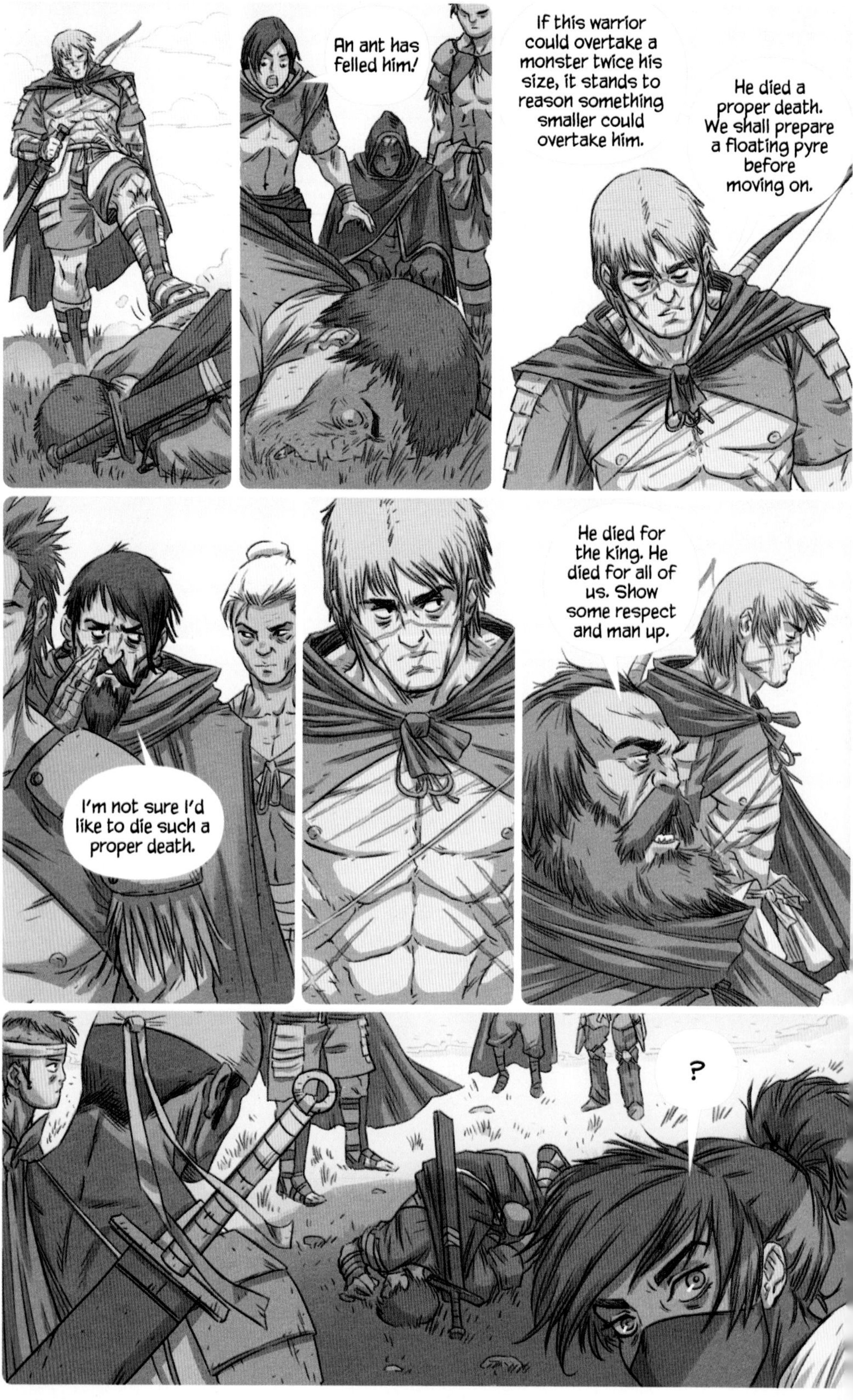
An ant has felled him!
If this warrior could overtake a monster twice his size, it stands to reason something smaller could overtake him.
He died a proper death. We shall prepare a floating pyre before moving on.
I'm not sure I'd like to die such a proper death.
He died for the king. He died for all of us. Show some respect and man up.
?

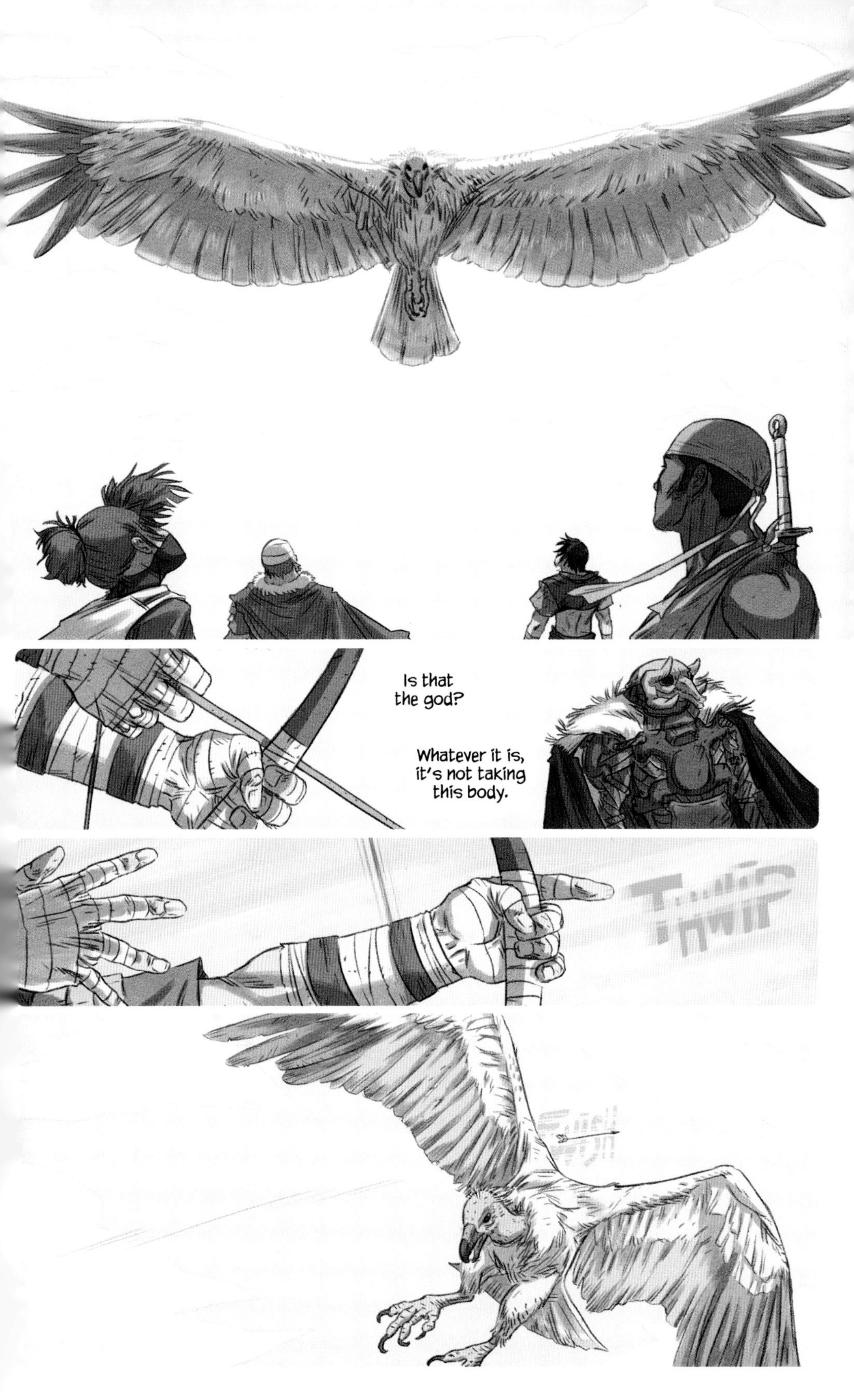
Is that the god?
Whatever it is, it's not taking this body.

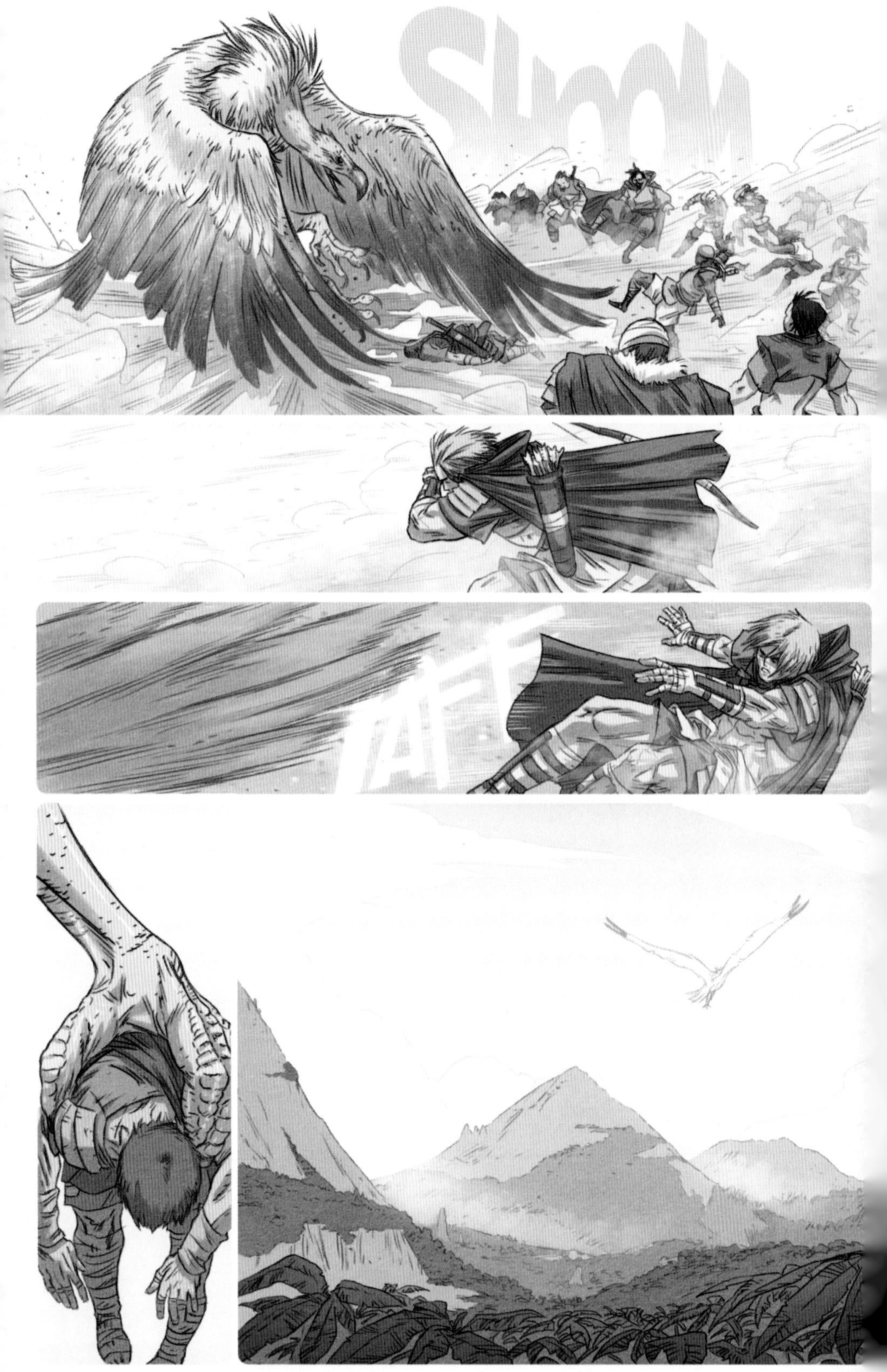
SHOOM

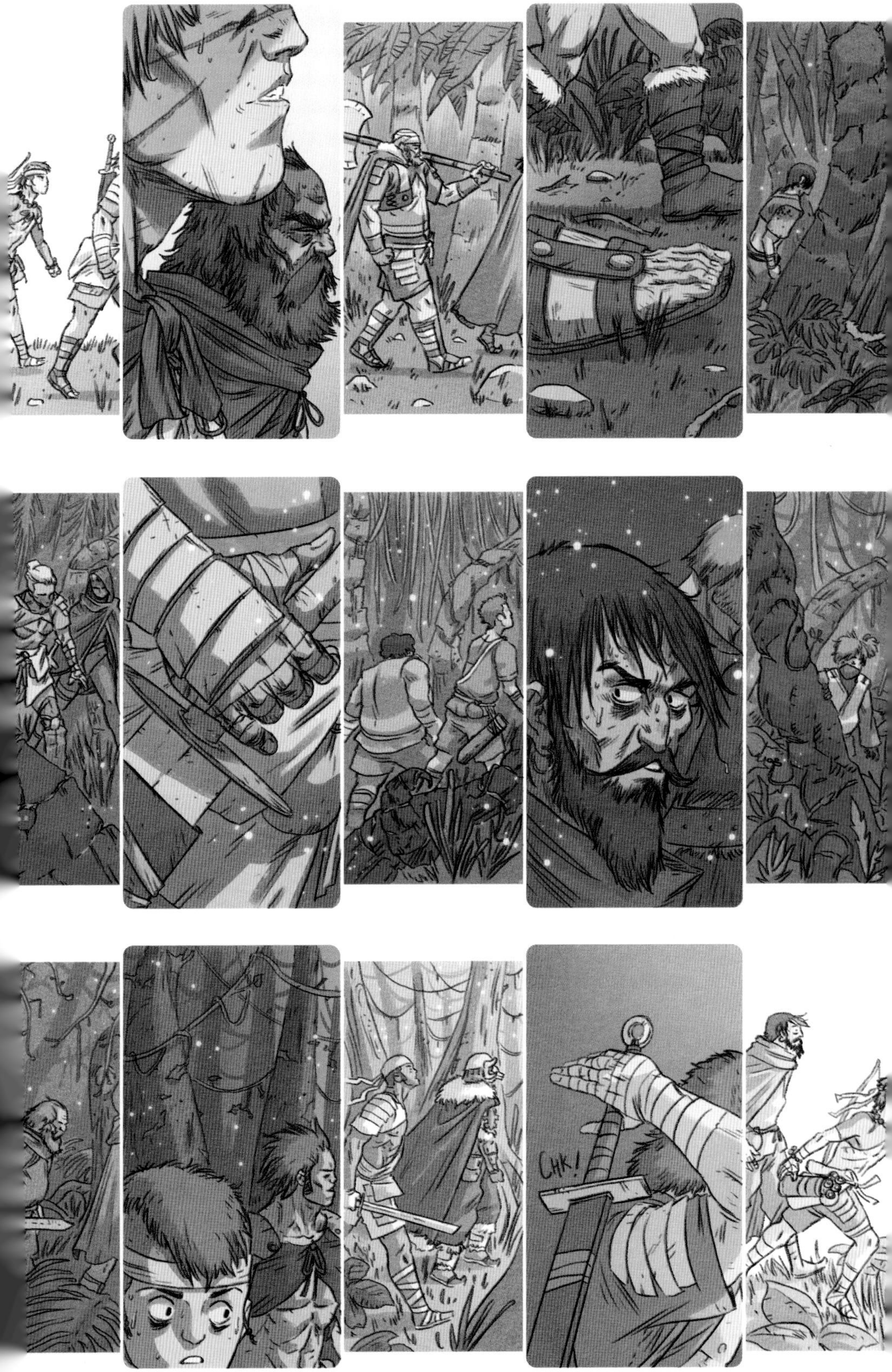
CHK!

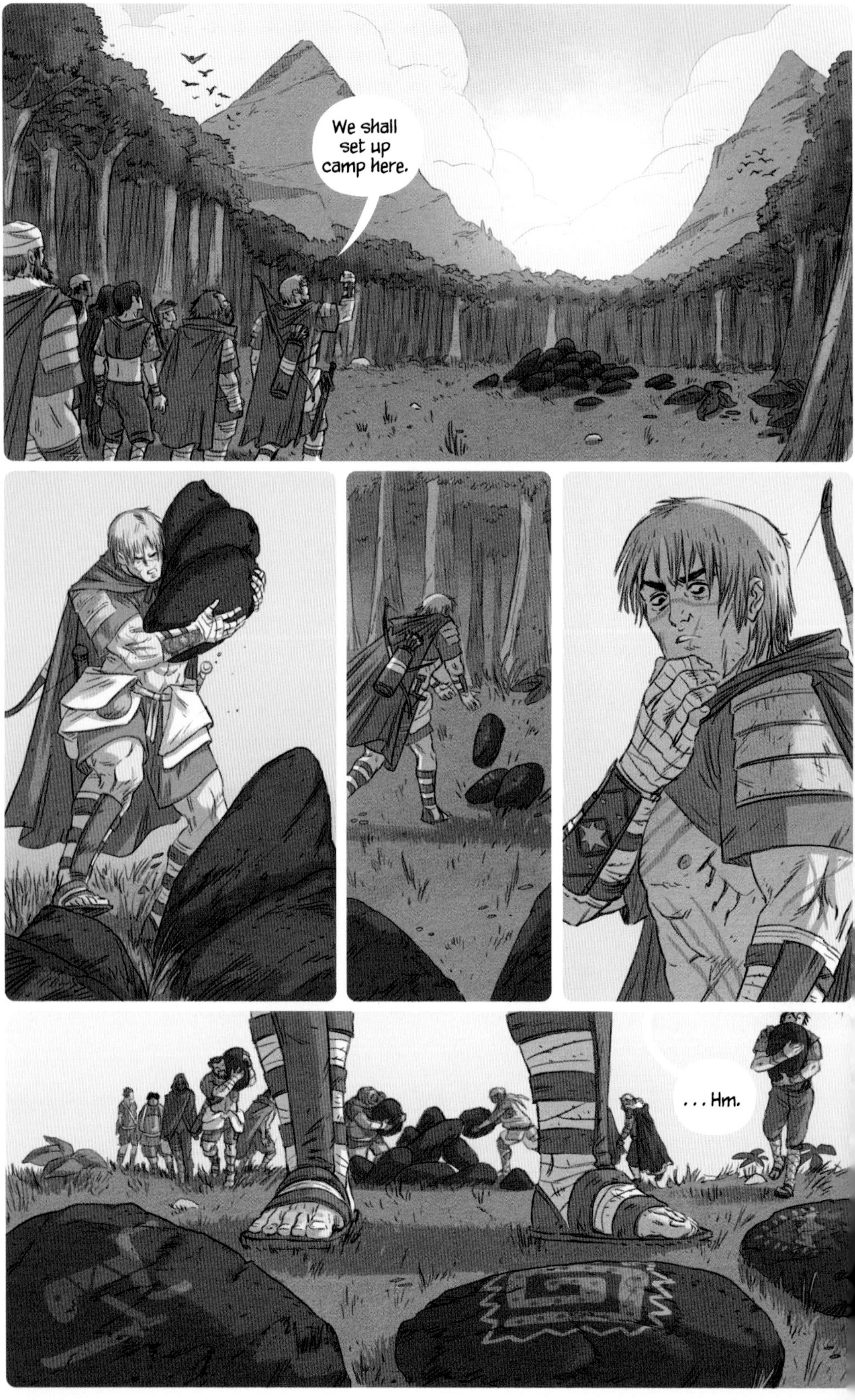
We shall set up camp here.
. . . Hm.

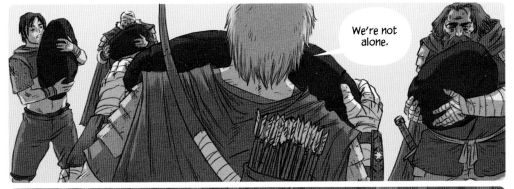

We're not alone.

Bring the stones back here. It's possible we'll learn a thing or two about the island.

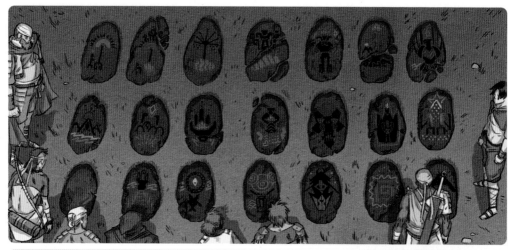

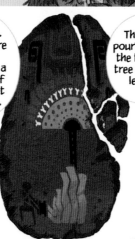

If read left-to-right . . . this manlike figure is lugging a bucket of fire to a great tree, one of a type we have yet to come across.

The figure is pouring fire onto the tree and the tree falls to ash, leaving . . .

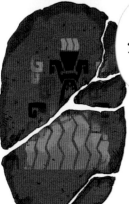

. . . leaving behind the shape of some beast. The beast is wearing a crown.

Another manlike figure comes from behind the beast and the two men overpower it, removing the crown.

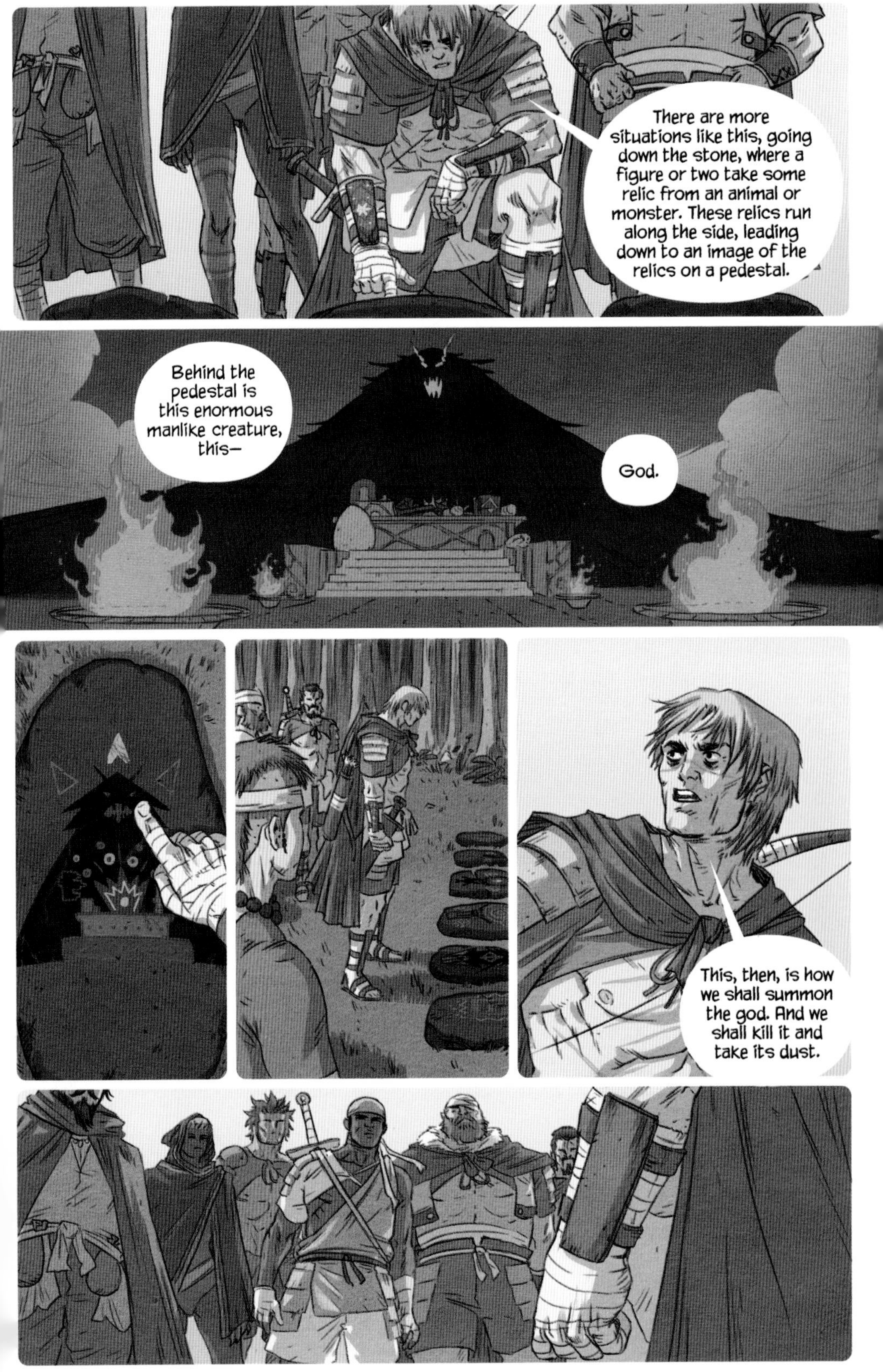
There are more situations like this, going down the stone, where a figure or two take some relic from an animal or monster. These relics run along the side, leading down to an image of the relics on a pedestal.
Behind the pedestal is this enormous manlike creature, this—
God.
This, then, is how we shall summon the god. And we shall kill it and take its dust.

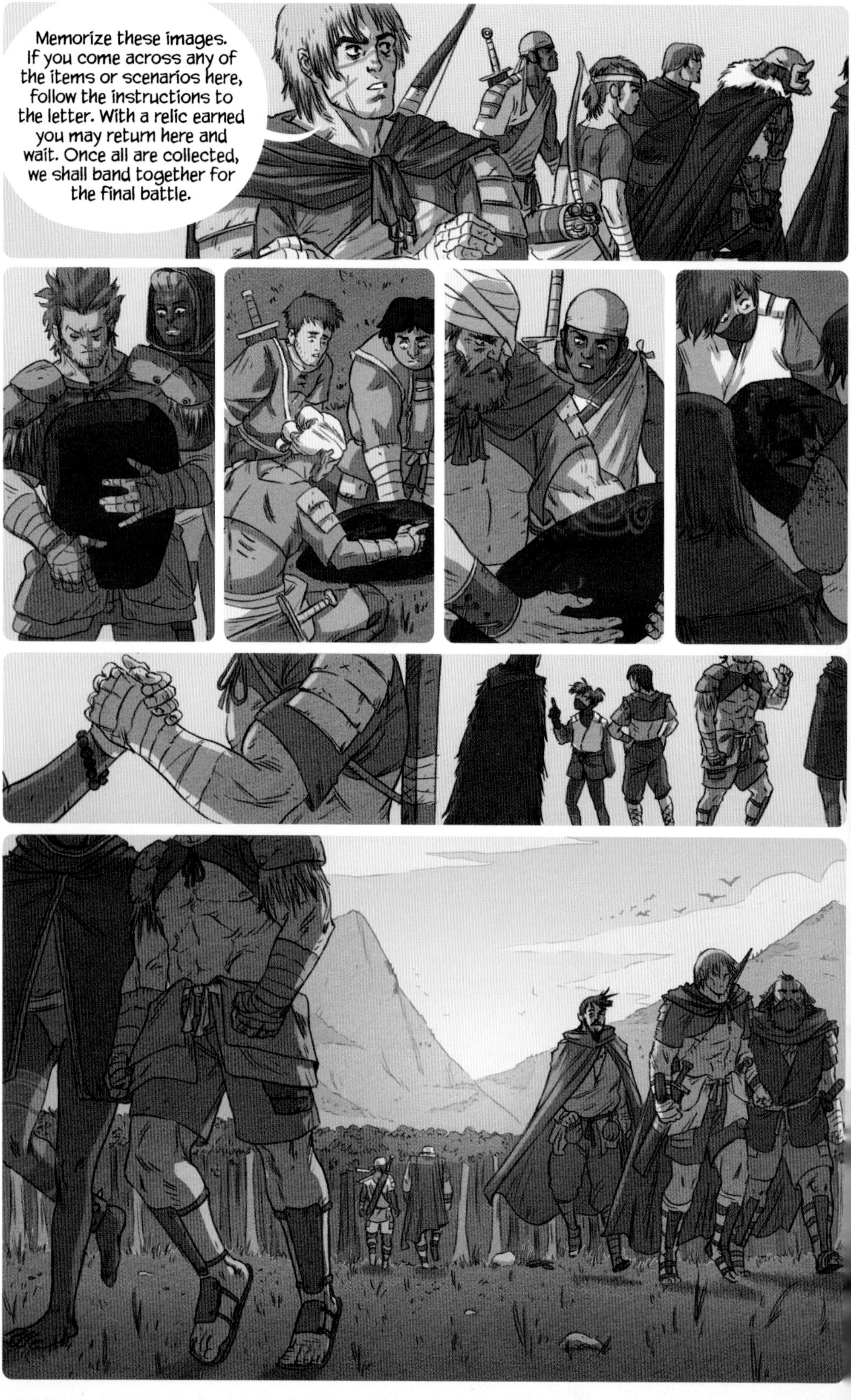
Memorize these images. If you come across any of the items or scenarios here, follow the instructions to the letter. With a relic earned you may return here and wait. Once all are collected, we shall band together for the final battle.

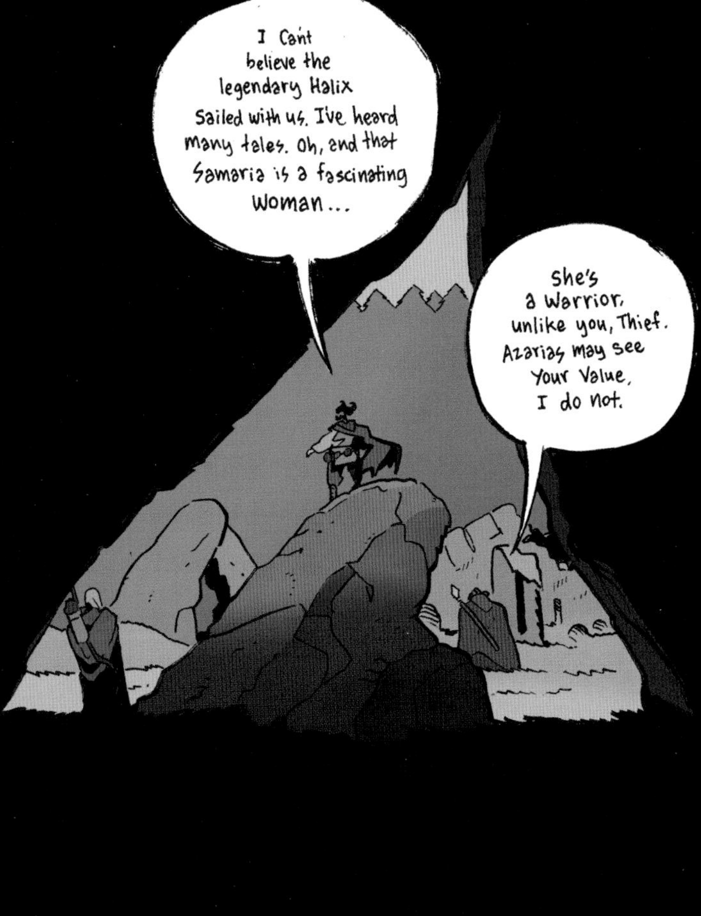
I Can't believe the legendary Halix Sailed with us. I've heard many tales. Oh, and that Samaria is a fascinating Woman...
She's a Warrior, unlike you, Thief. Azarias may see Your Value, I do Not.

Vulture

PAUL MAYBURY 2018

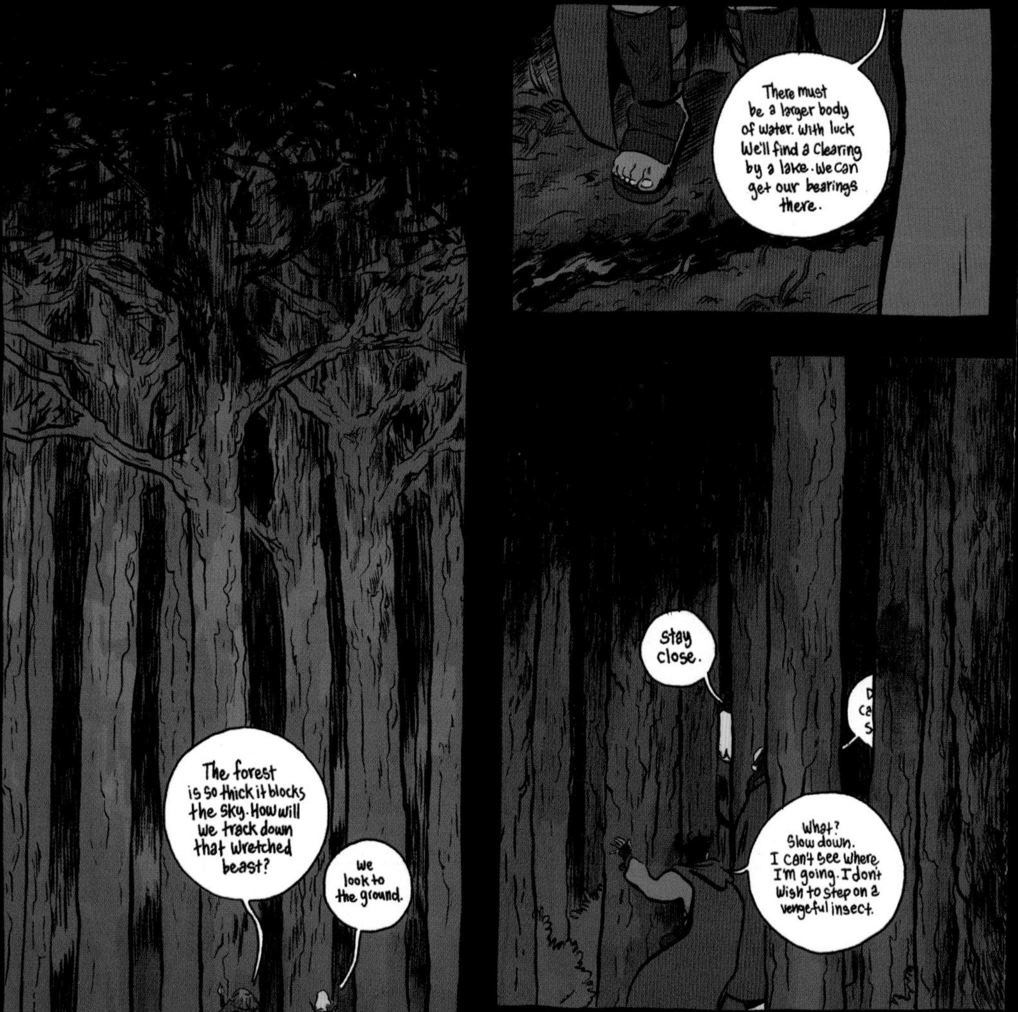
The forest is so thick it blocks the sky. How will we track down that wretched beast?
We look to the ground.
There must be a larger body of water. With luck we'll find a clearing by a lake. We can get our bearings there.
Stay close.
What? Slow down. I can't see where I'm going. I don't wish to step on a vengeful insect.

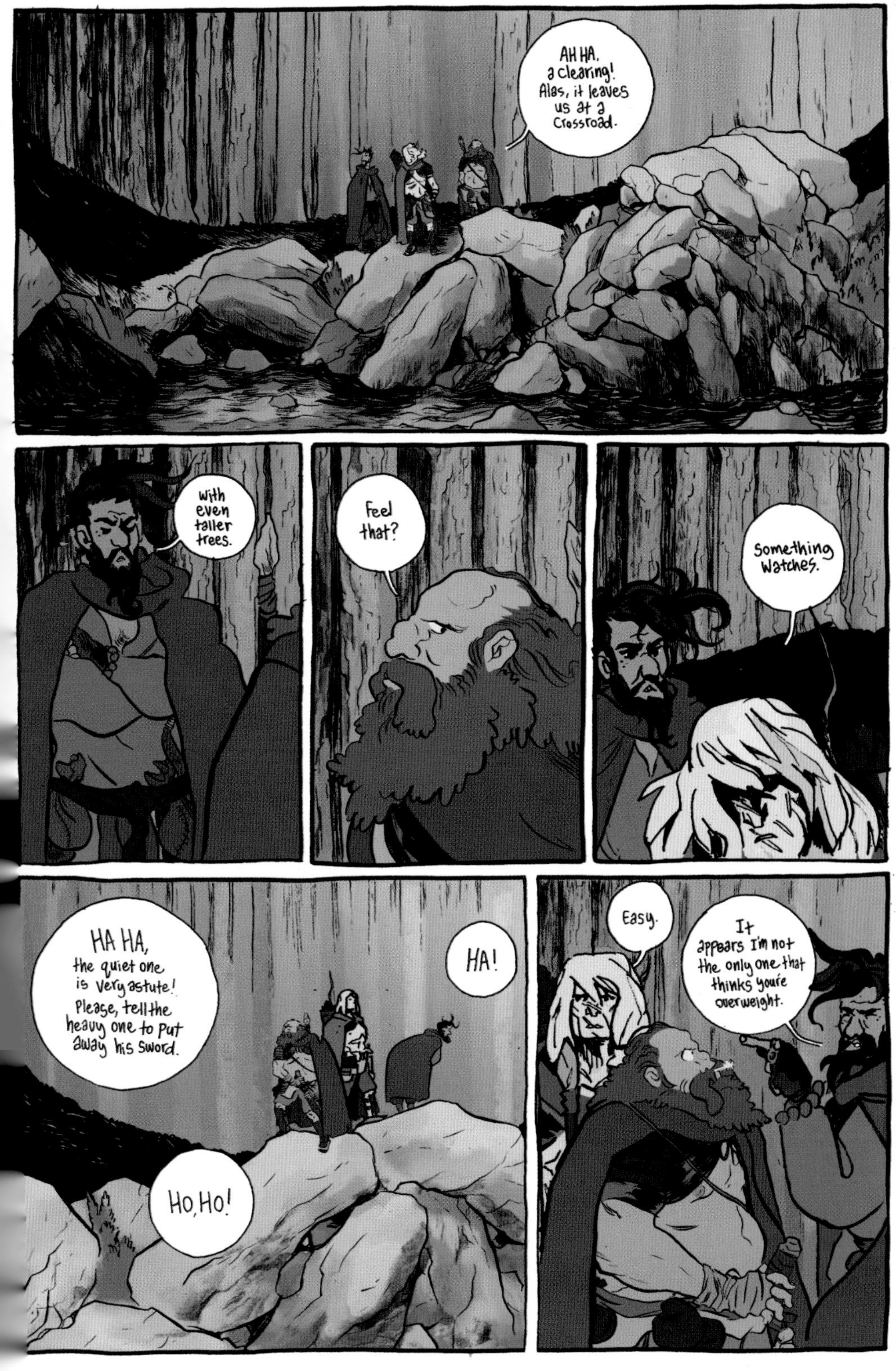
AH HA, a clearing! Alas, it leaves us at a crossroad.
with even taller trees.
Feel that?
Something watches.
HA HA, the quiet one is very astute! Please, tell the heavy one to put away his sword.
HA!
Ho, Ho!
Easy.
It appears I'm not the only one that thinks you're overweight.

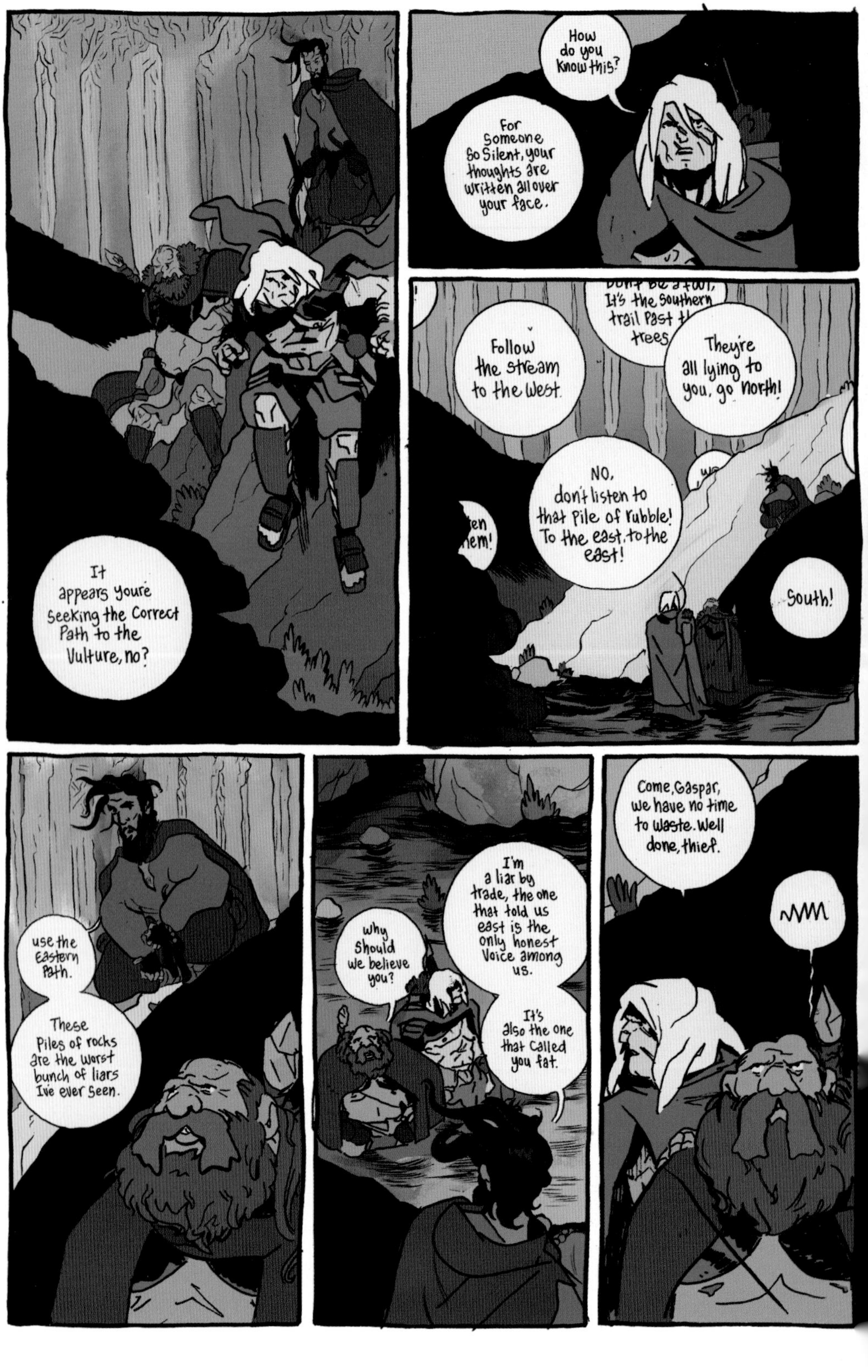

It appears youre seeking the Correct Path to the Vulture, no?
How do you know this?
For Someone So Silent, your thoughts are written all over your face.
Follow the stream to the West.
It's the southern trail Past
trees.
Theyre all lying to you, go north!
NO, don't listen to that Pile of rubble! To the east, to the east!
South!
use the Eastern Path.
These Piles of rocks are the worst bunch of liars Ive ever Seen.
why Should we believe you?
I'm a liar by trade, the one that told us east is the only honest Voice among us.
It's also the one that called you fat.
Come, Gaspar, we have no time to waste. Well done, thief.

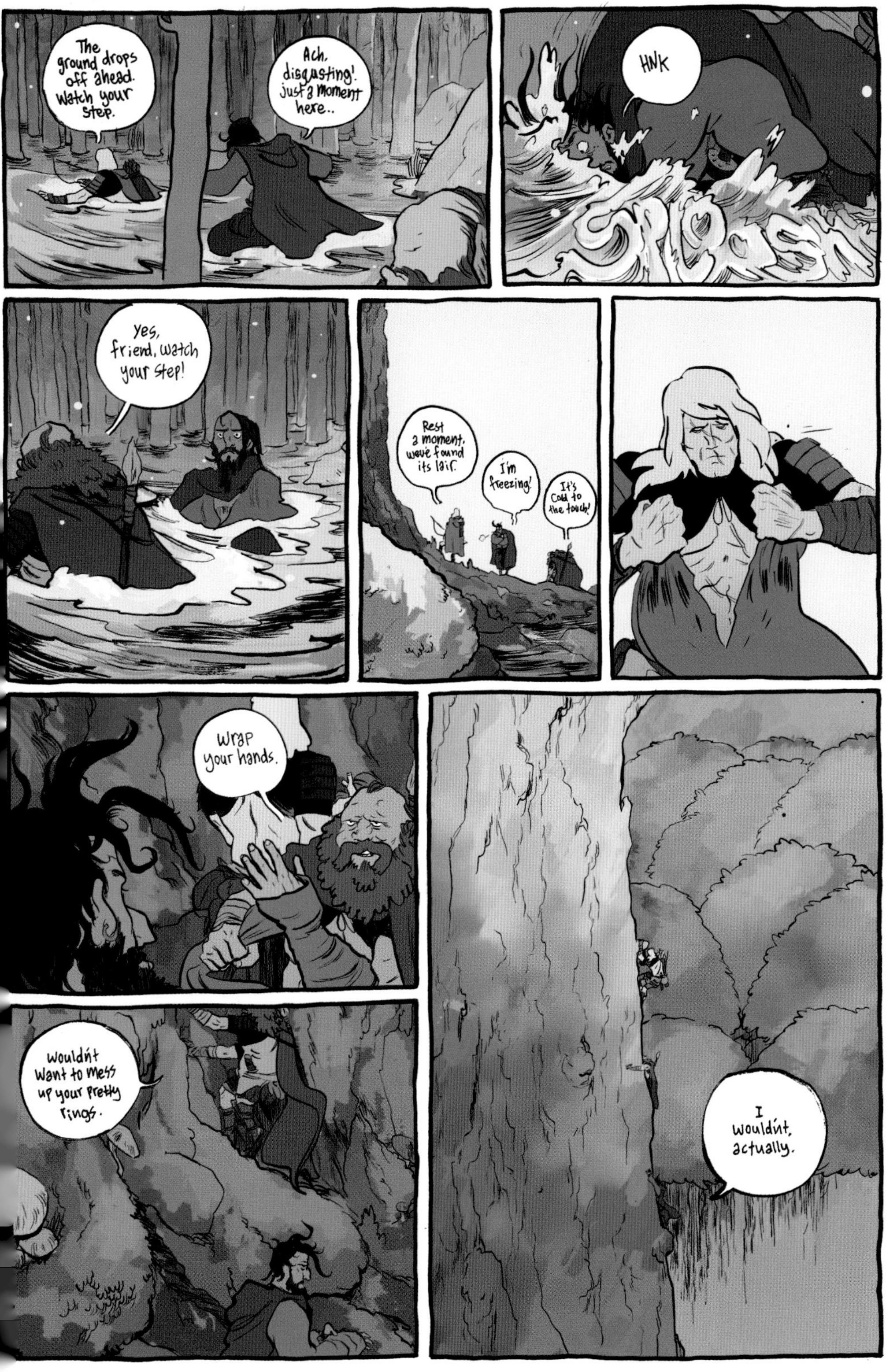
The ground drops off ahead. Watch your step.
Ach, disgusting! Just a moment here..
HNK
SPLOOSH
yes, friend, watch your step!
Rest a moment, we've found its lair.
I'm freezing!
It's cold to the touch!
Wrap your hands.
wouldn't want to mess up your pretty rings.
I wouldn't, actually.

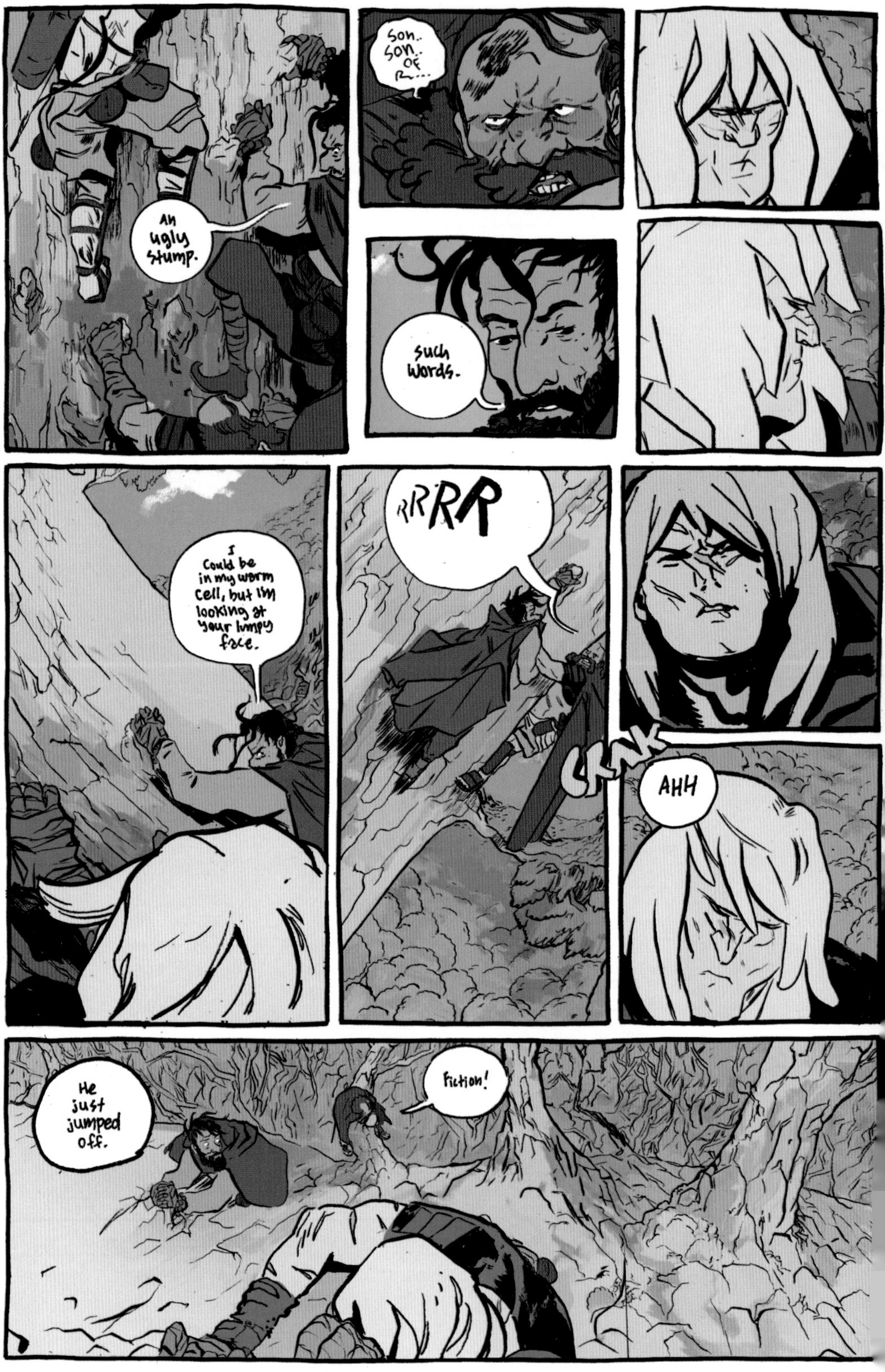
An ugly stump.
Son.. son.. of R....
Such words.
I could be in my warm cell, but I'm looking at your lumpy face.
RRRR
CLNK
AHH
He just jumped off.
Fiction!

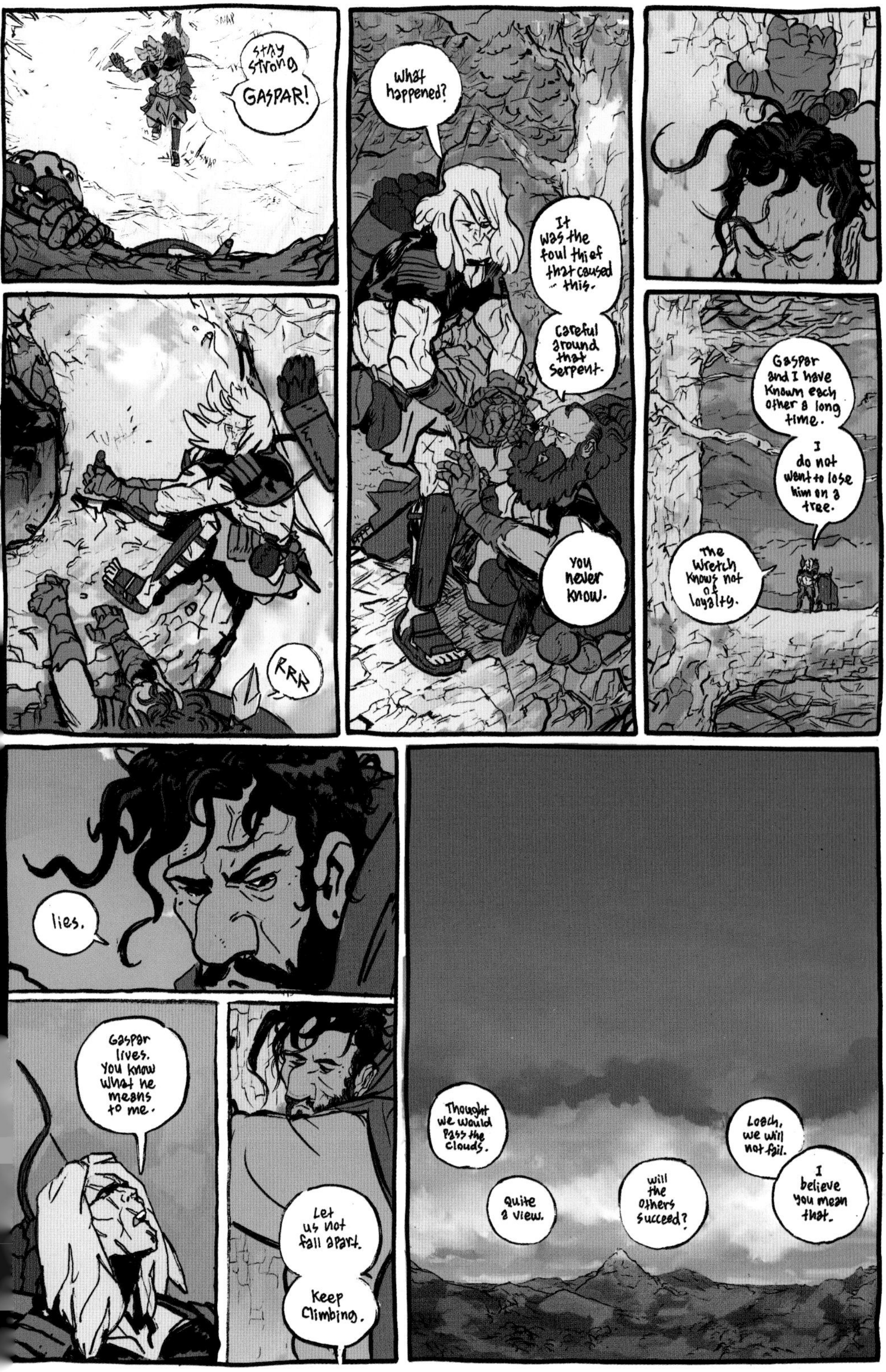
SNAP
Stay strong
GASPAR!
SNAP
What happened?
It was the foul thief that caused this.
Careful around that serpent.
You never know.
RRR
Gaspar and I have known each other a long time.
I do not went to lose him on a tree.
The wretch knows not of loyalty.
lies.
Gaspar lives. You know what he means to me.
Let us not fall apart.
Keep Climbing.
Thought we would pass the clouds.
Quite a view.
Will the others succeed?
Loch, we will not fail.
I believe you mean that.

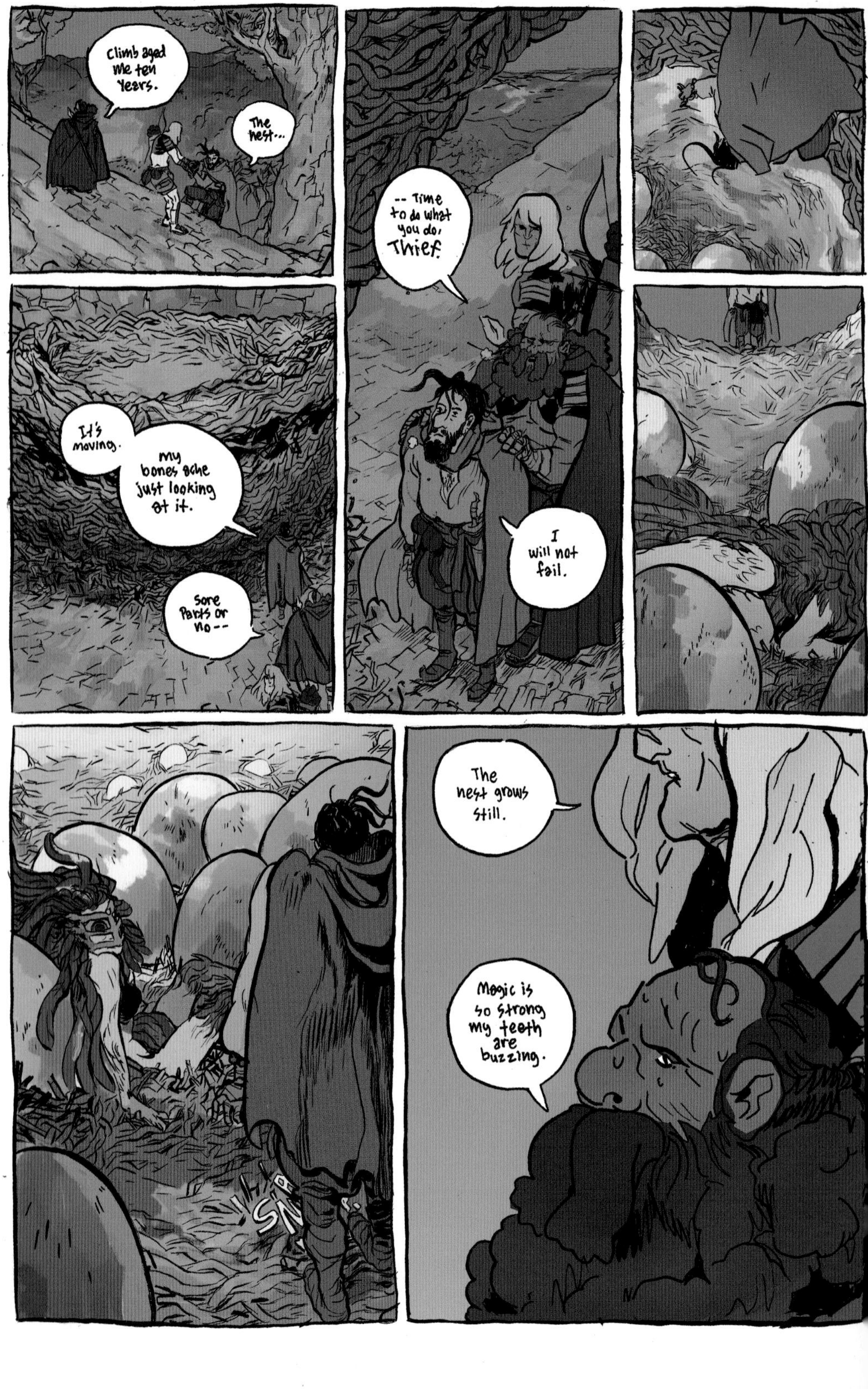
Climb aged me ten years.
The nest...
-- Time to do what you do, Thief.
I will not fail.
It's moving.
my bones ache just looking at it.
Sore parts or no --
The nest grows still.
Magic is so strong my teeth are buzzing.

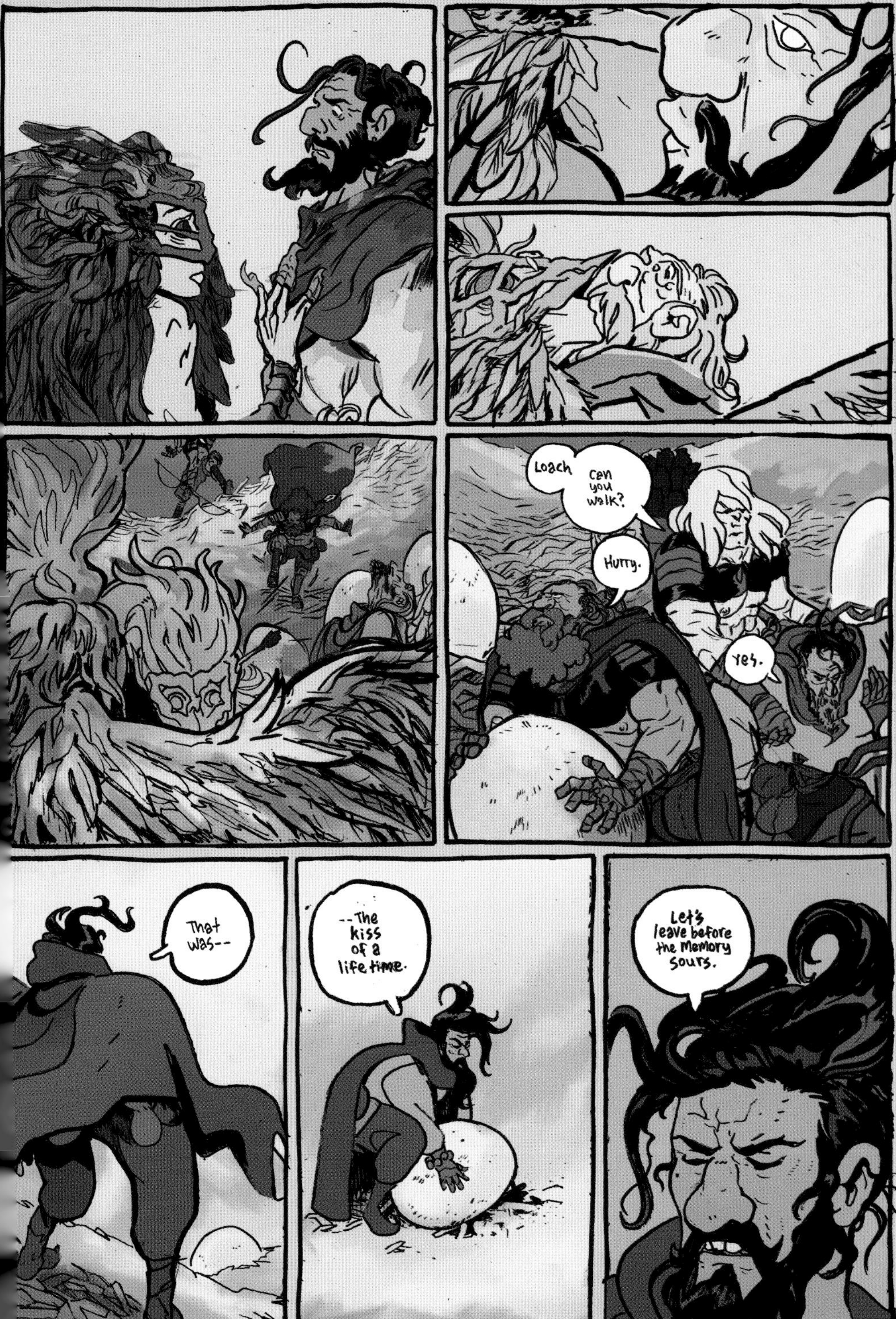
Loach
can you walk?
Hurry.
Yes.
That was--
--The kiss of a life time.
Let's leave before the Memory sours.

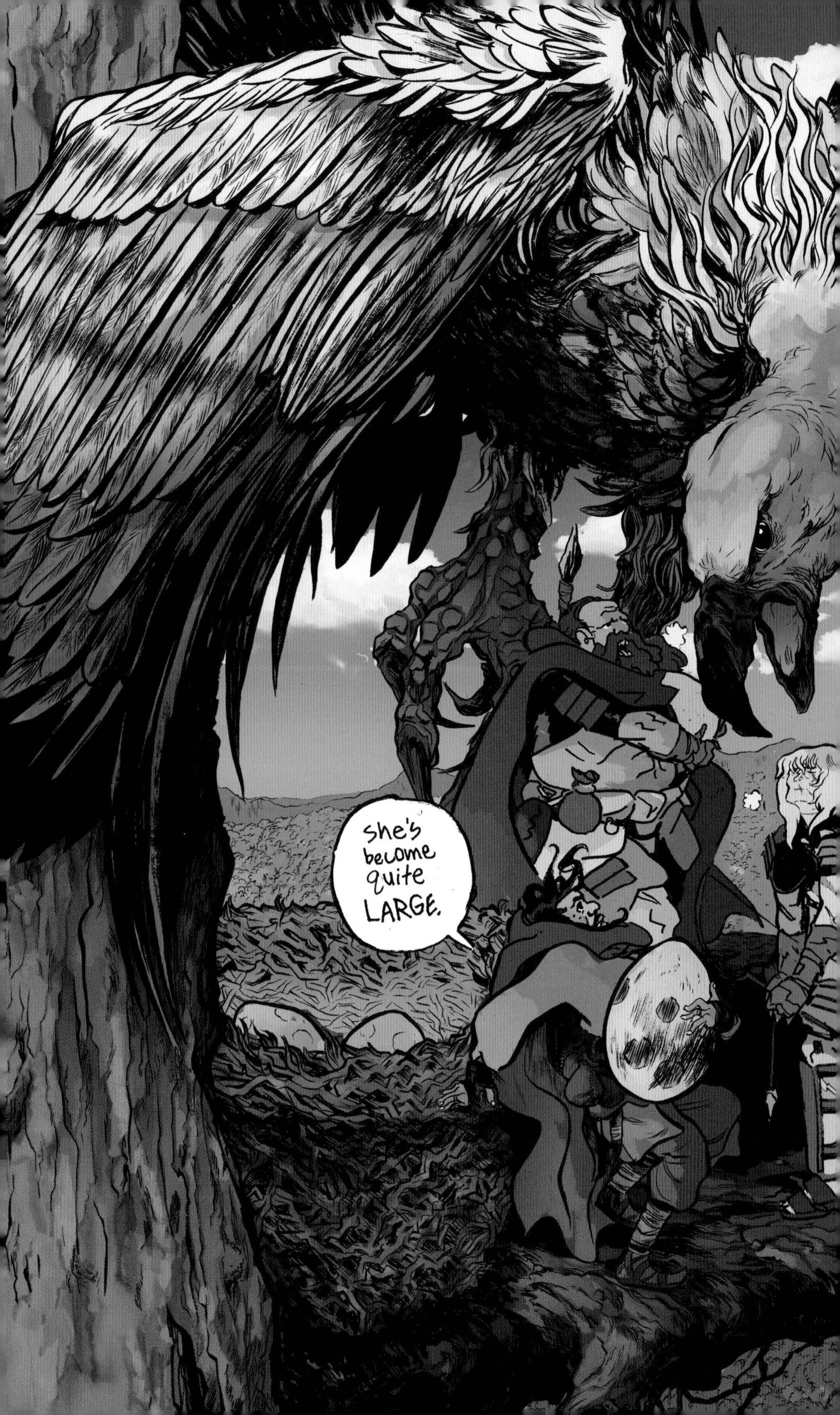
She's become quite LARGE.

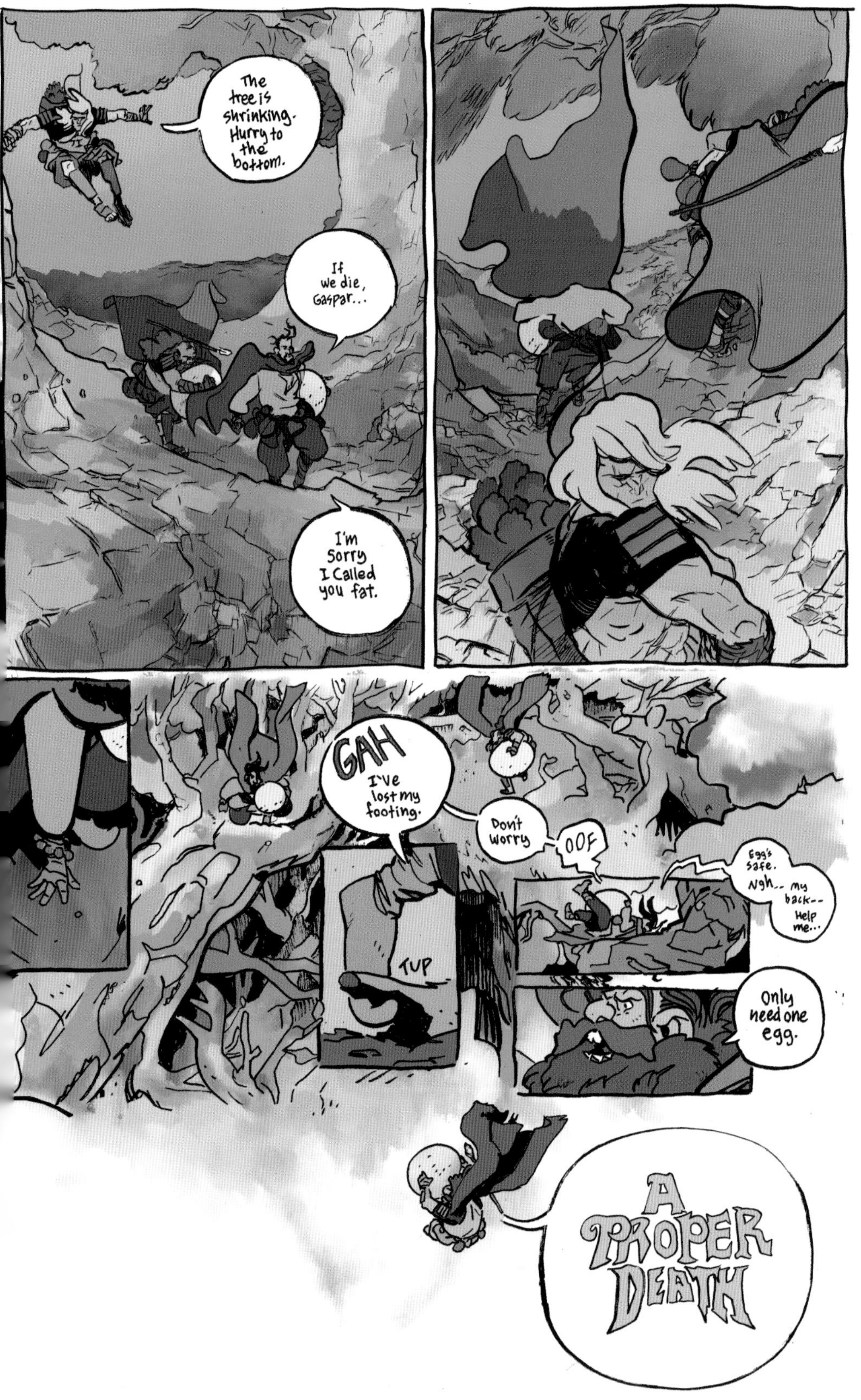

The tree is shrinking. Hurry to the bottom.
If we die, Gaspar...
I'm sorry I called you fat.
GAH
I've lost my footing.
Don't worry
OOF
TUP
Egg's safe.
Ngh.. my back--
Help me...
Only need one egg.
A PROPER DEATH

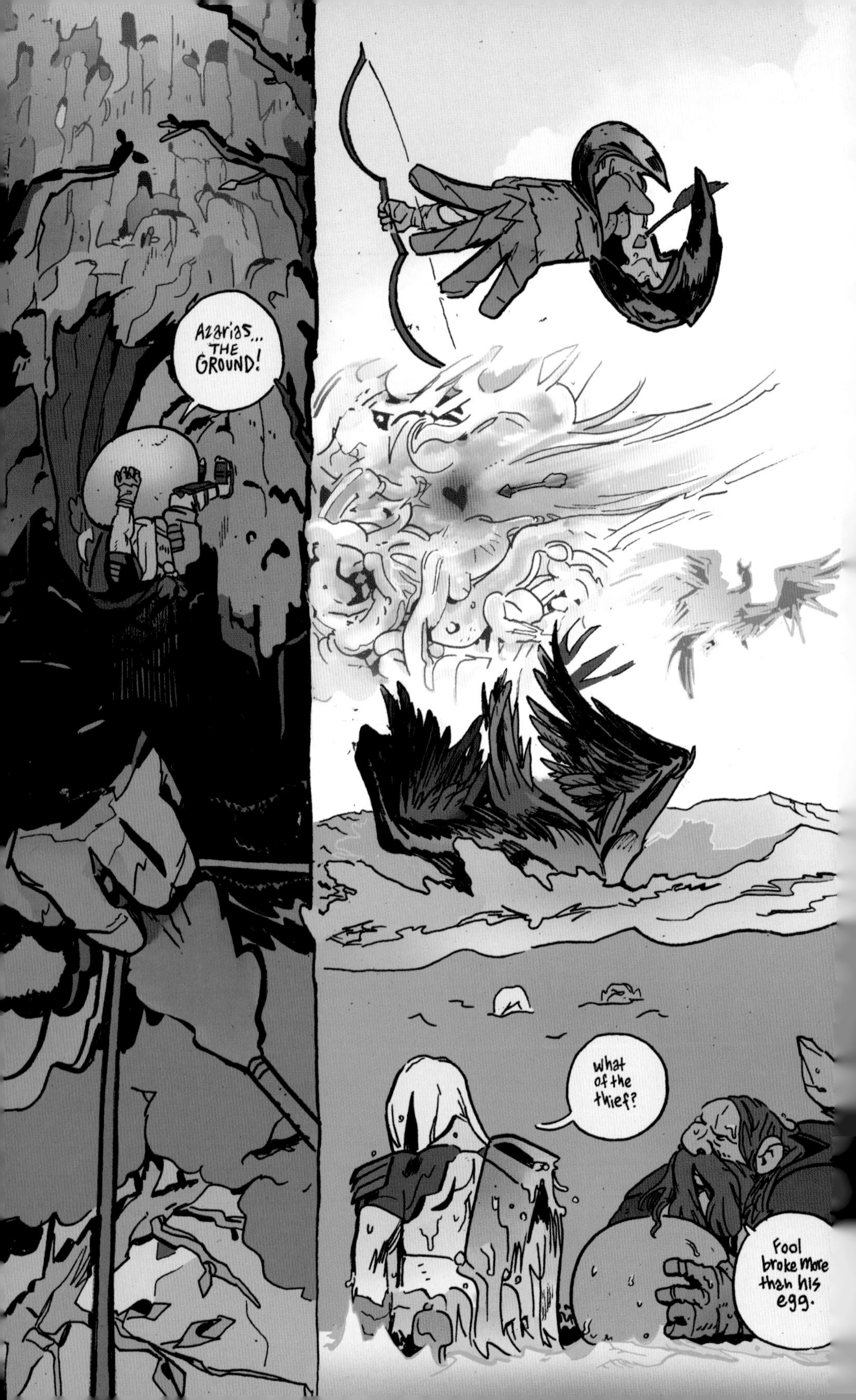
Azarias... THE GROUND!
what of the thief?
Fool broke more than his egg.

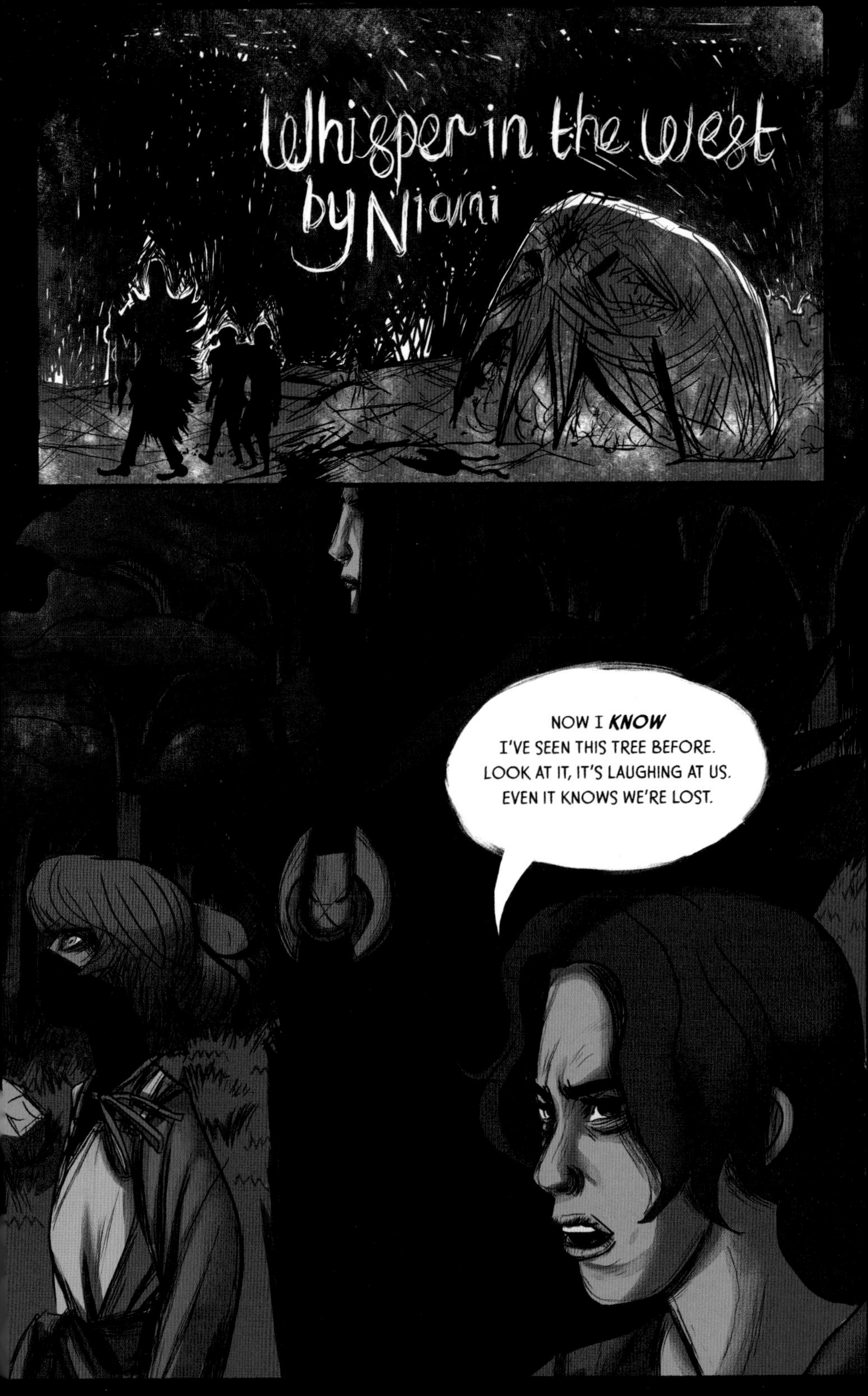
Whisper in the West
by Niami
NOW I KNOW I'VE SEEN THIS TREE BEFORE. LOOK AT IT, IT'S LAUGHING AT US. EVEN IT KNOWS WE'RE LOST.

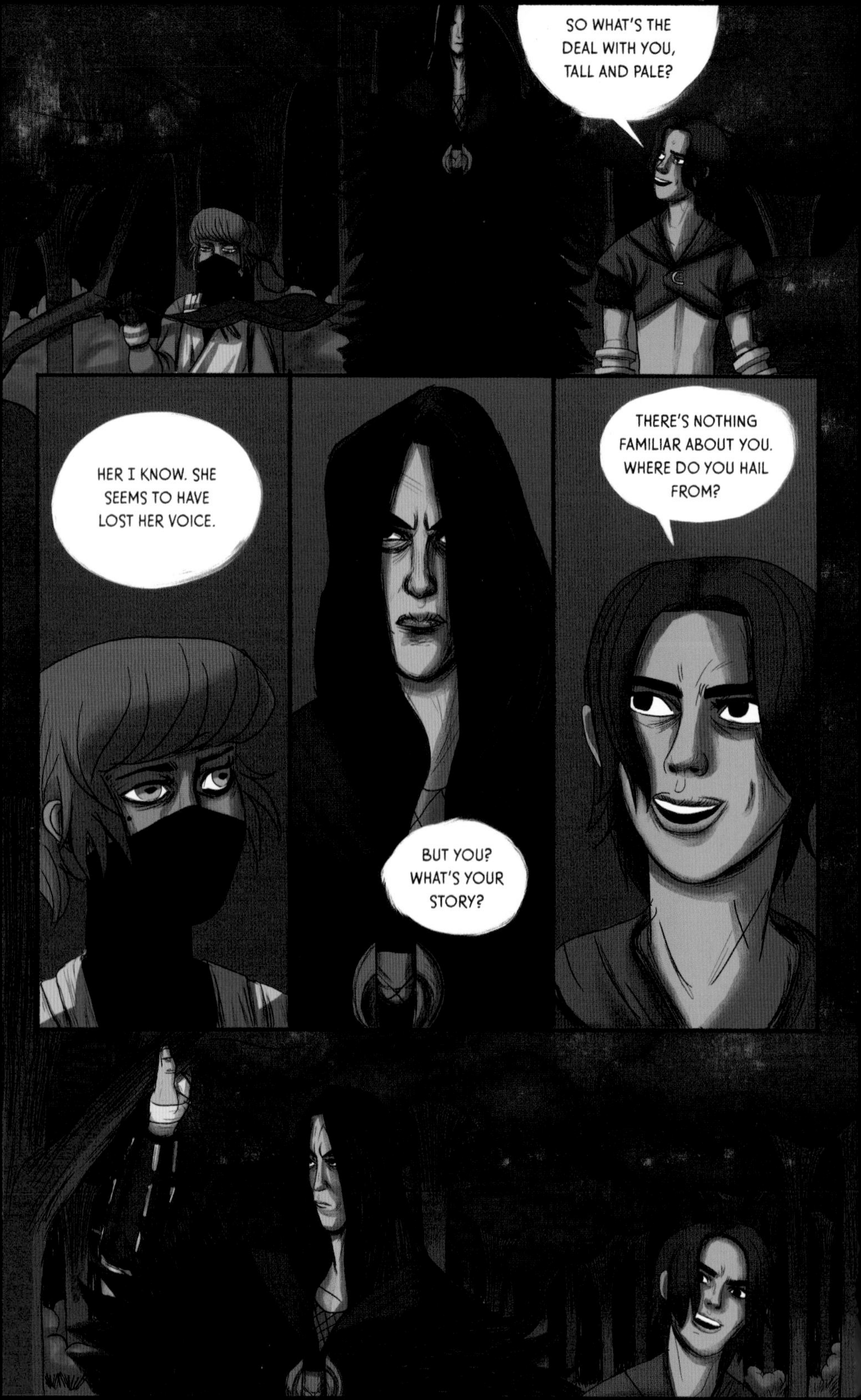
SO WHAT'S THE DEAL WITH YOU, TALL AND PALE?
HER I KNOW. SHE SEEMS TO HAVE LOST HER VOICE.
THERE'S NOTHING FAMILIAR ABOUT YOU. WHERE DO YOU HAIL FROM?
BUT YOU? WHAT'S YOUR STORY?

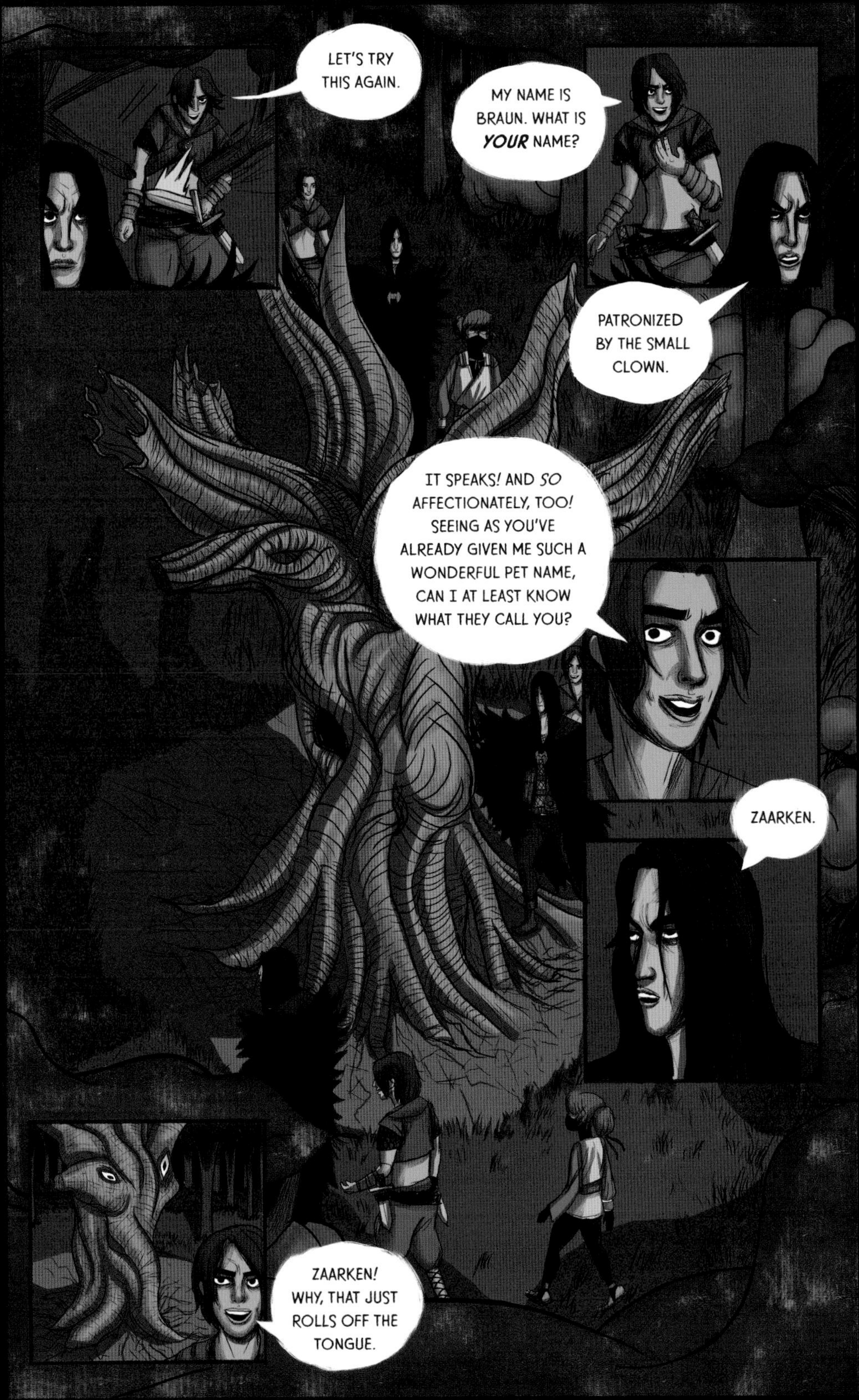
LET'S TRY THIS AGAIN.
MY NAME IS BRAUN. WHAT IS *YOUR* NAME?
PATRONIZED BY THE SMALL CLOWN.
IT SPEAKS! AND *SO* AFFECTIONATELY, TOO! SEEING AS YOU'VE ALREADY GIVEN ME SUCH A WONDERFUL PET NAME, CAN I AT LEAST KNOW WHAT THEY CALL YOU?
ZAARKEN.
ZAARKEN! WHY, THAT JUST ROLLS OFF THE TONGUE.

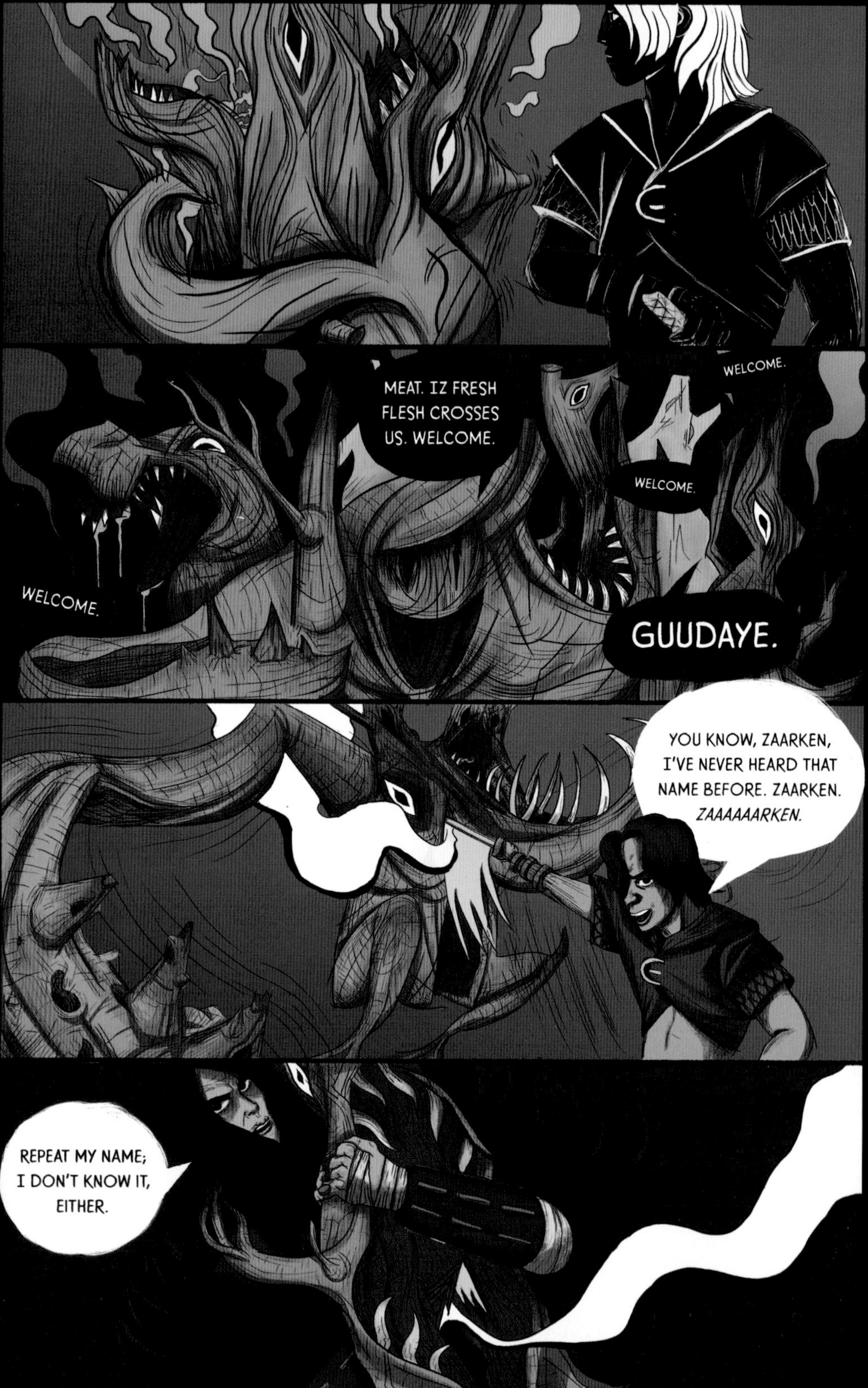
MEAT. IZ FRESH FLESH CROSSES US. WELCOME.
WELCOME.
WELCOME.
WELCOME.
GUUDAYE.
YOU KNOW, ZAARKEN, I'VE NEVER HEARD THAT NAME BEFORE. ZAARKEN. *ZAAAAAARKEN.*
REPEAT MY NAME; I DON'T KNOW IT, EITHER.

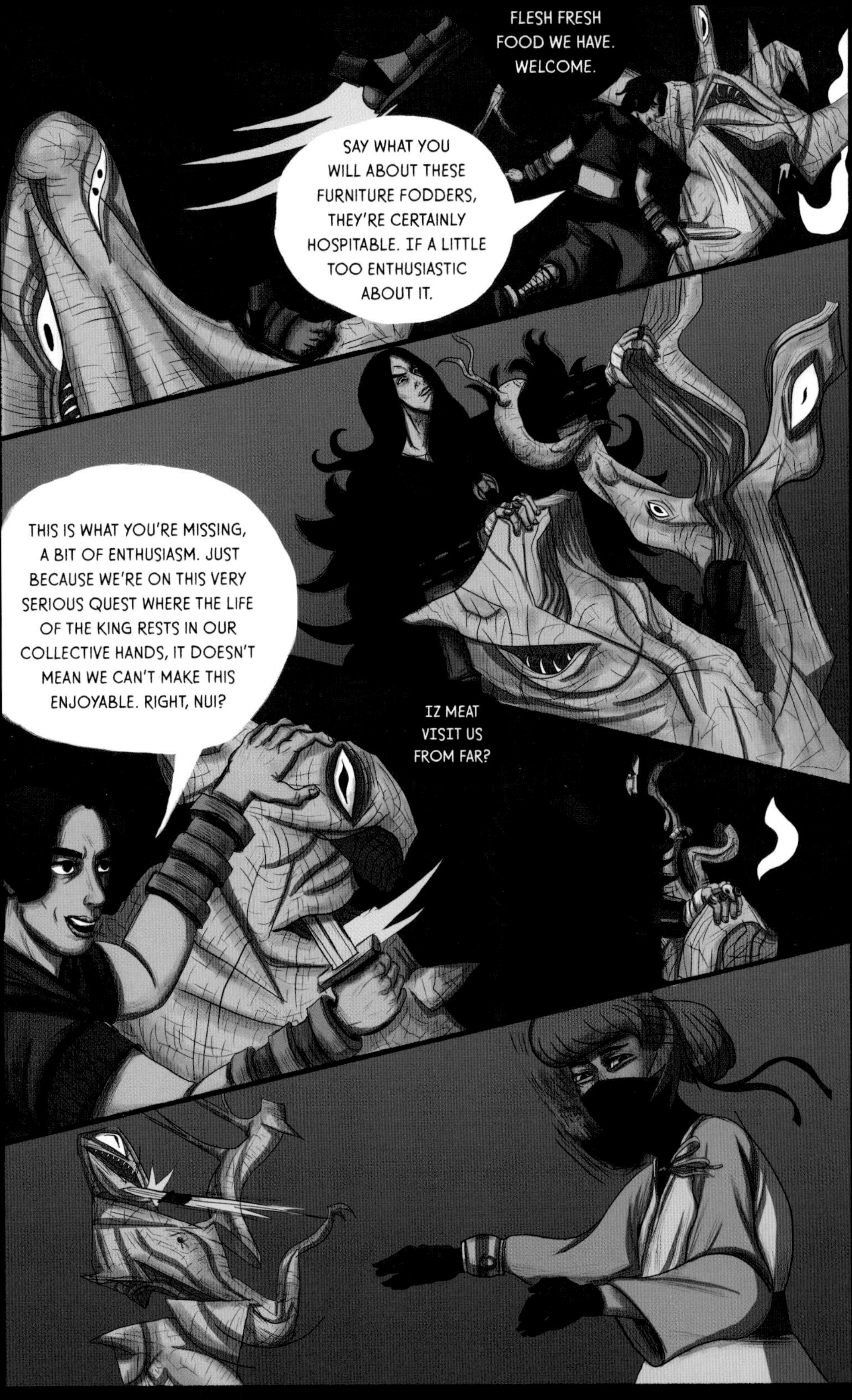
FLESH FRESH FOOD WE HAVE. WELCOME.
SAY WHAT YOU WILL ABOUT THESE FURNITURE FODDERS, THEY'RE CERTAINLY HOSPITABLE. IF A LITTLE TOO ENTHUSIASTIC ABOUT IT.
THIS IS WHAT YOU'RE MISSING, A BIT OF ENTHUSIASM. JUST BECAUSE WE'RE ON THIS VERY SERIOUS QUEST WHERE THE LIFE OF THE KING RESTS IN OUR COLLECTIVE HANDS, IT DOESN'T MEAN WE CAN'T MAKE THIS ENJOYABLE. RIGHT, NUI?
IZ MEAT VISIT US FROM FAR?

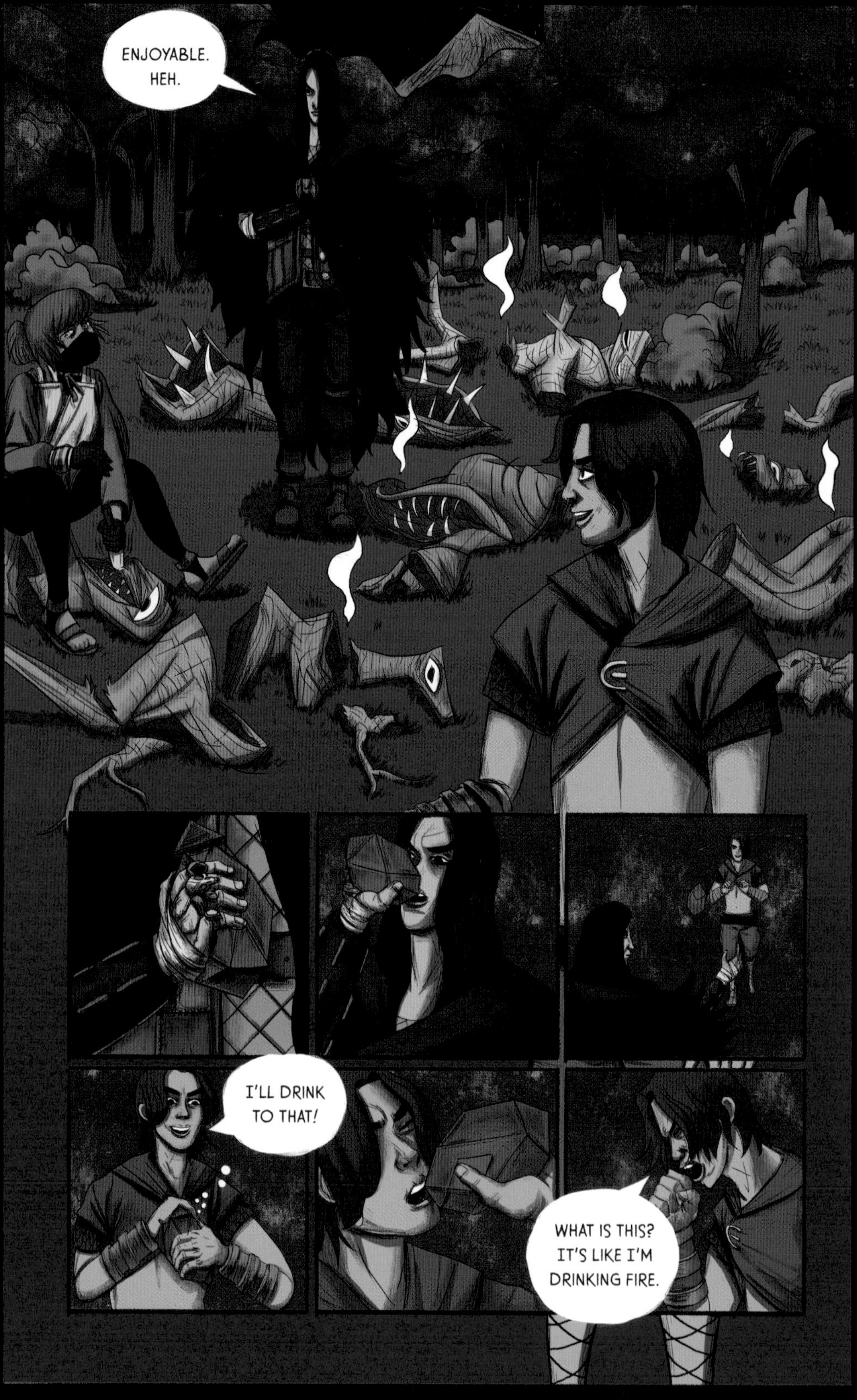
ENJOYABLE. HEH.
I'LL DRINK TO THAT!
WHAT IS THIS? IT'S LIKE I'M DRINKING FIRE.

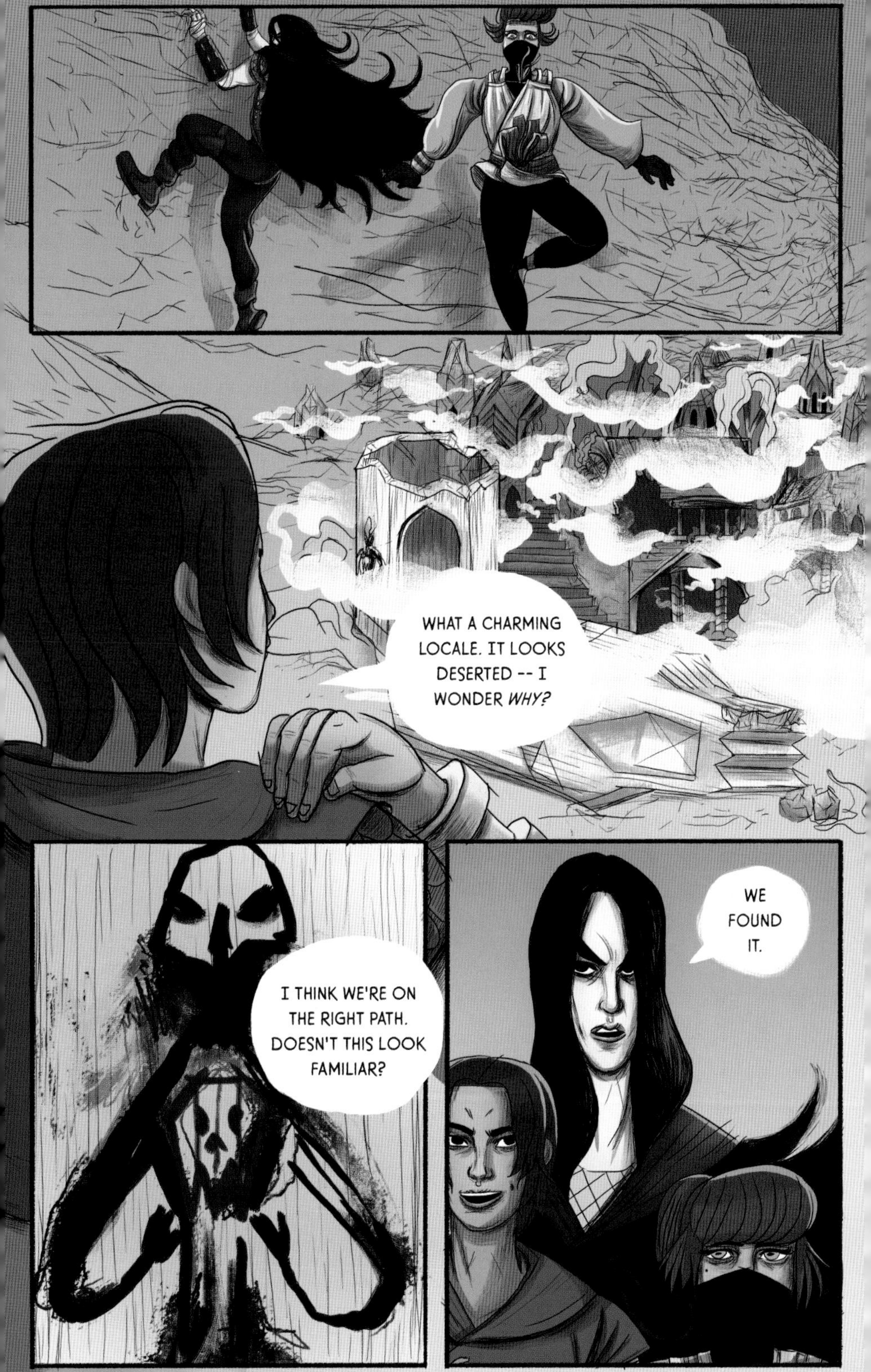
WHAT A CHARMING LOCALE. IT LOOKS DESERTED -- I WONDER *WHY?*
I THINK WE'RE ON THE RIGHT PATH. DOESN'T THIS LOOK FAMILIAR?
WE FOUND IT.

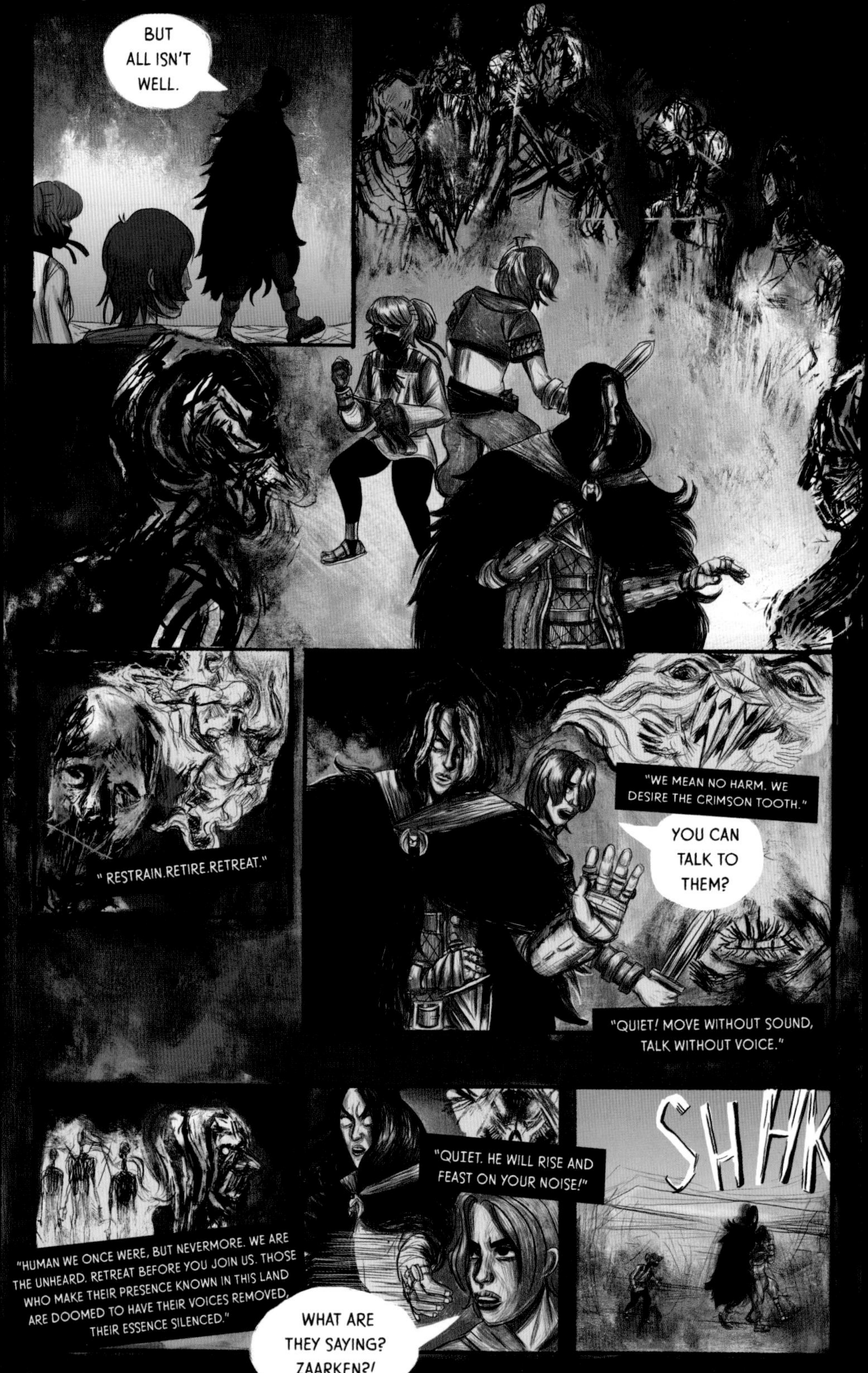
BUT ALL ISN'T WELL.
" RESTRAIN.RETIRE.RETREAT."
"WE MEAN NO HARM. WE DESIRE THE CRIMSON TOOTH."
YOU CAN TALK TO THEM?
"QUIET! MOVE WITHOUT SOUND, TALK WITHOUT VOICE."
"HUMAN WE ONCE WERE, BUT NEVERMORE. WE ARE THE UNHEARD. RETREAT BEFORE YOU JOIN US. THOSE WHO MAKE THEIR PRESENCE KNOWN IN THIS LAND ARE DOOMED TO HAVE THEIR VOICES REMOVED, THEIR ESSENCE SILENCED."
"QUIET. HE WILL RISE AND FEAST ON YOUR NOISE!"
WHAT ARE THEY SAYING? ZAARKEN?!
SHHK

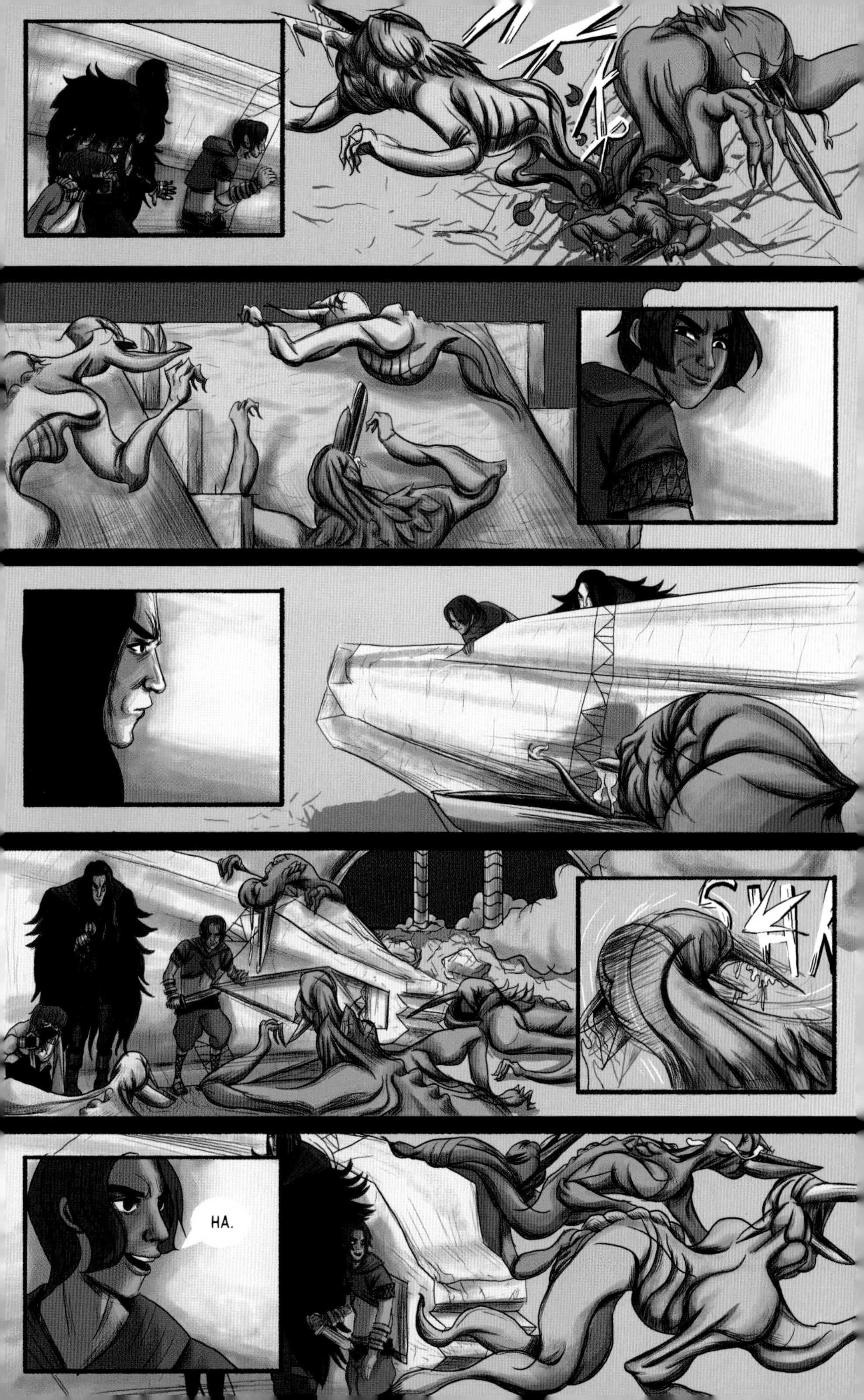
HA.

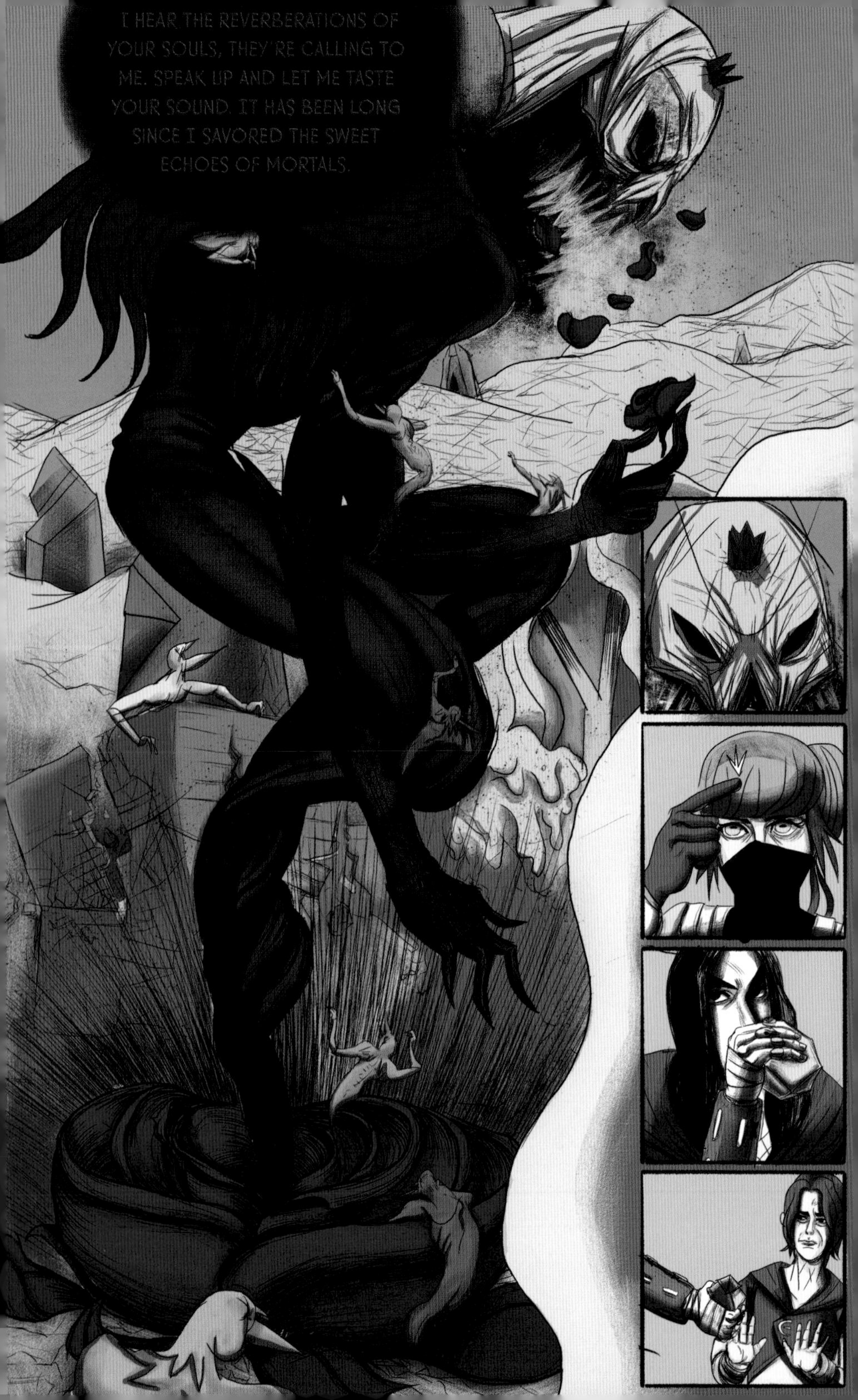
I HEAR THE REVERBERATIONS OF YOUR SOULS, THEY'RE CALLING TO ME. SPEAK UP AND LET ME TASTE YOUR SOUND. IT HAS BEEN LONG SINCE I SAVORED THE SWEET ECHOES OF MORTALS.

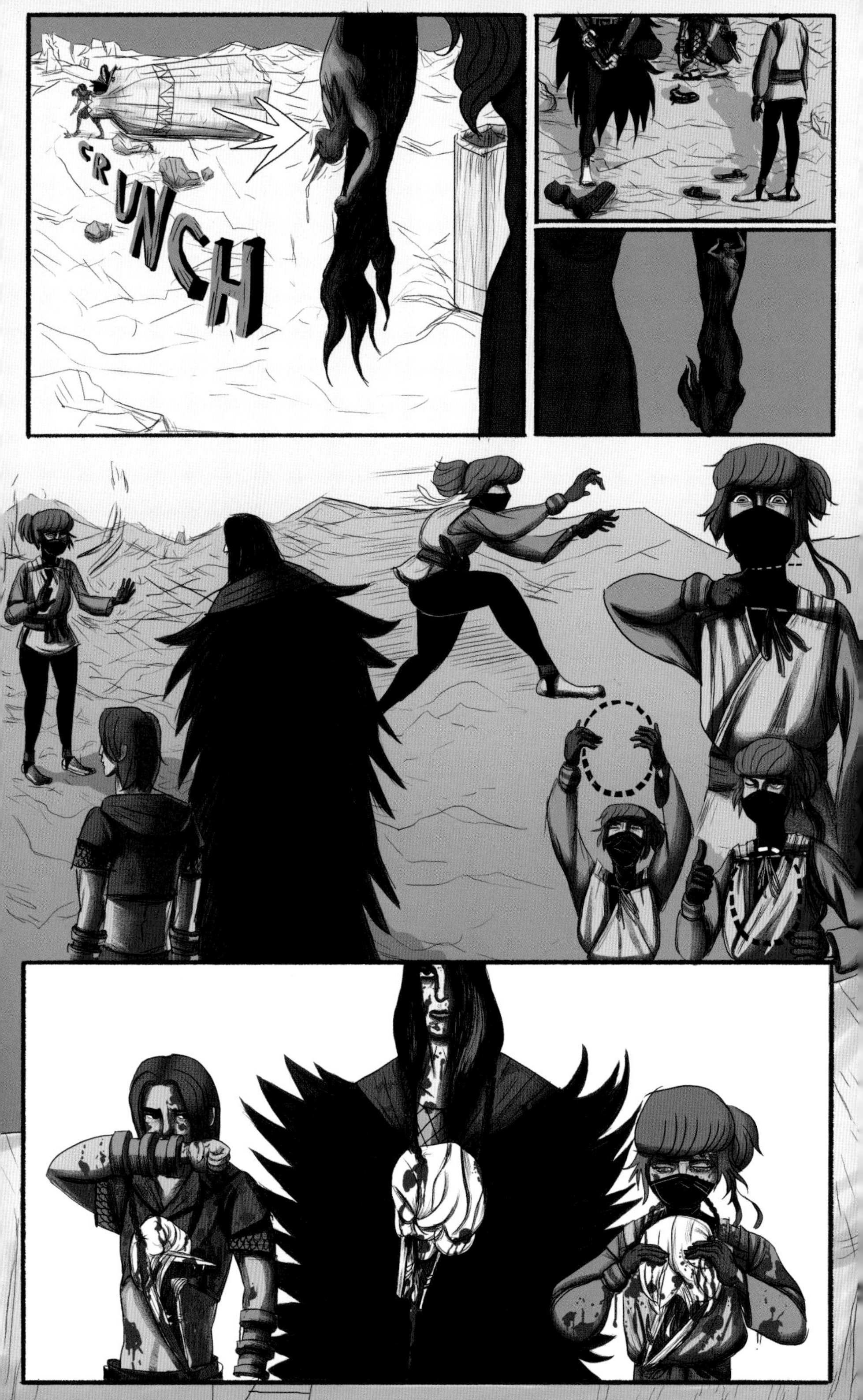
CRUNCH

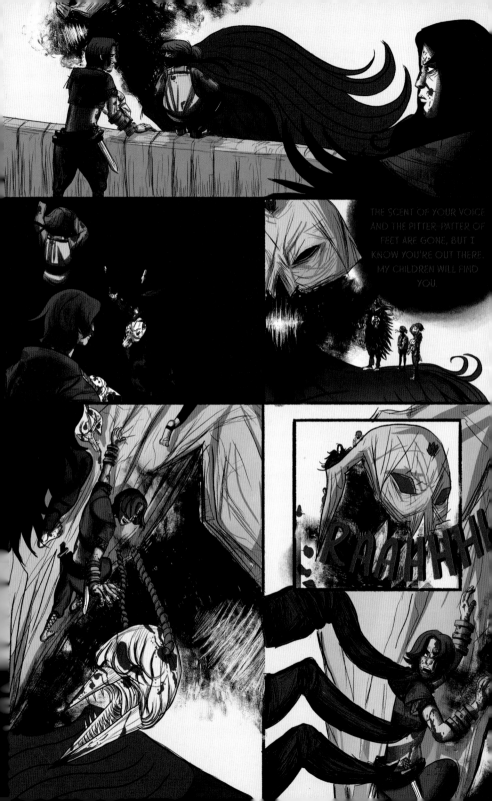

THE SCENT OF YOUR VOICE AND THE PITTER-PATTER OF FEET ARE GONE, BUT I KNOW YOU'RE OUT THERE. MY CHILDREN WILL FIND YOU.

RAAHHHH!

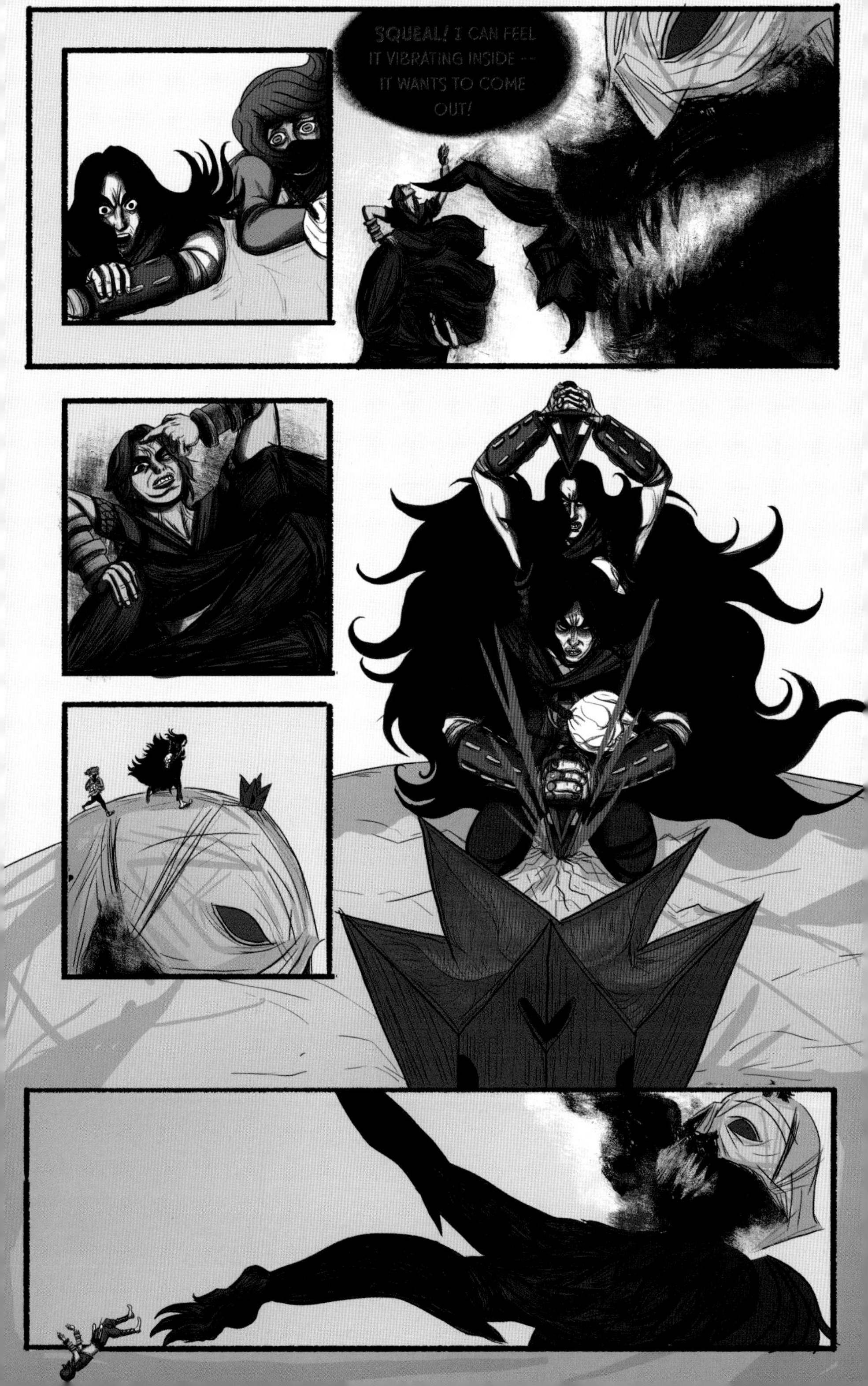
SQUEAL! I CAN FEEL IT VIBRATING INSIDE -- IT WANTS TO COME OUT!

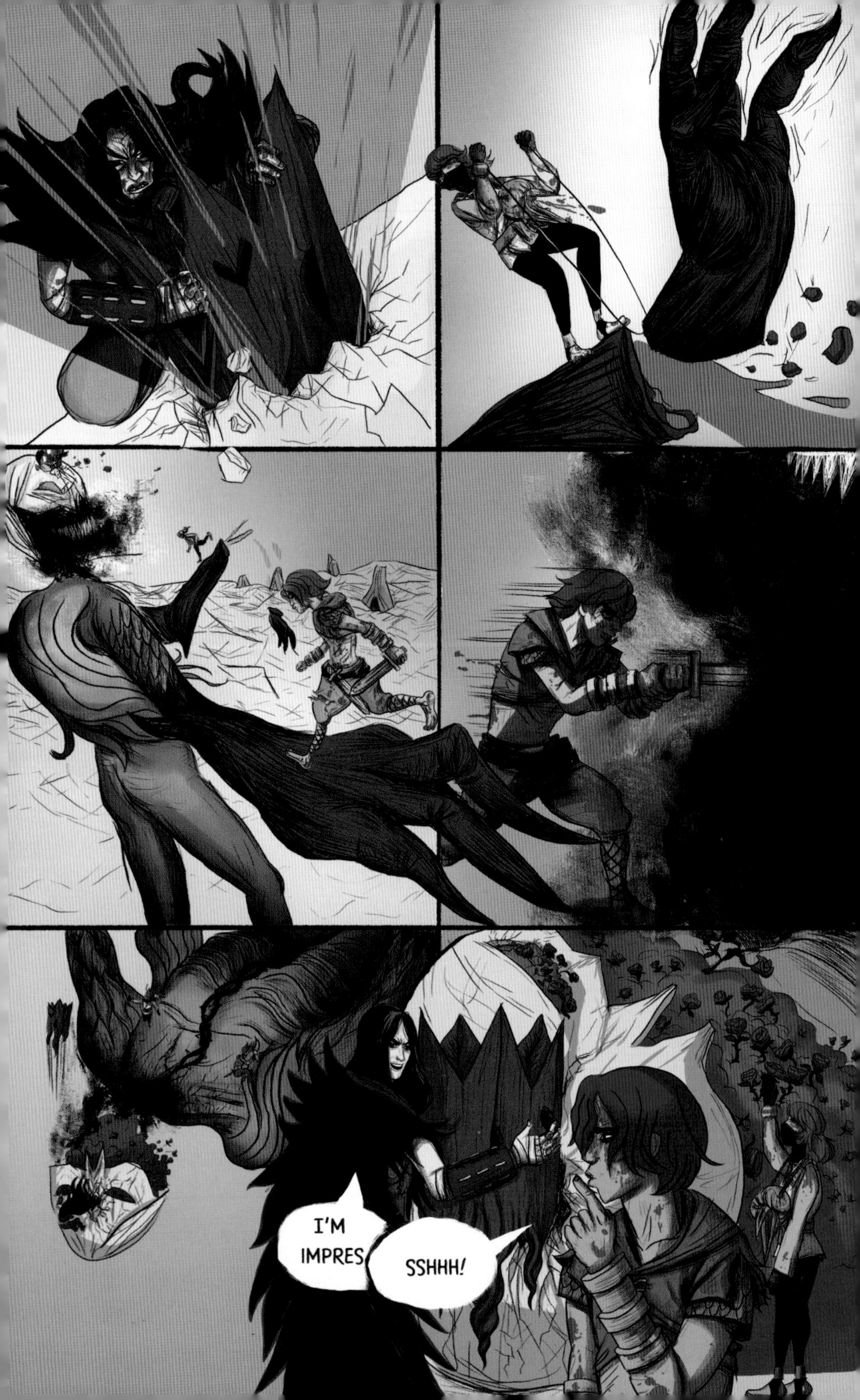
I'M
IMPRES
SSHHH!

Full of Wind

BY JOSH TIERNEY & JARED MORGAN

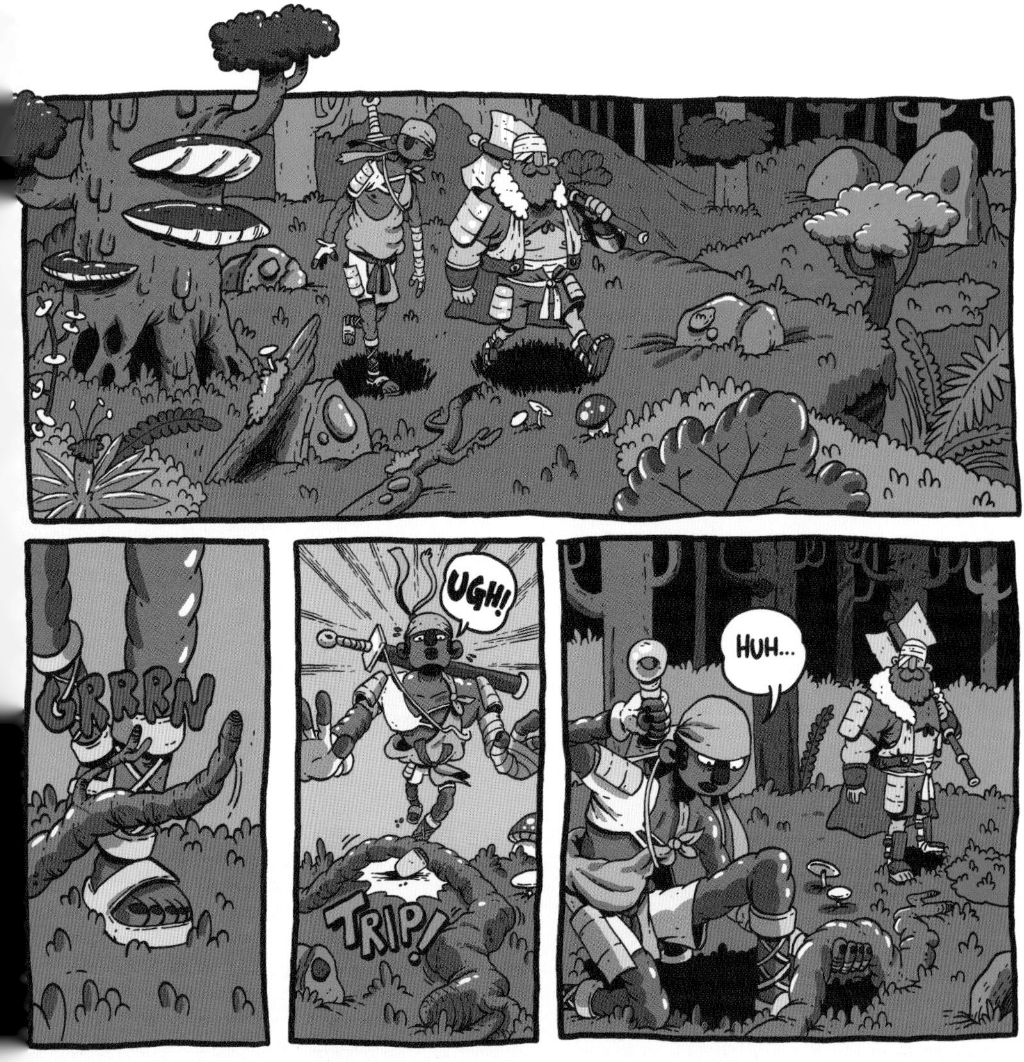
GRRRN
UGH!
TRIP!
HUH...

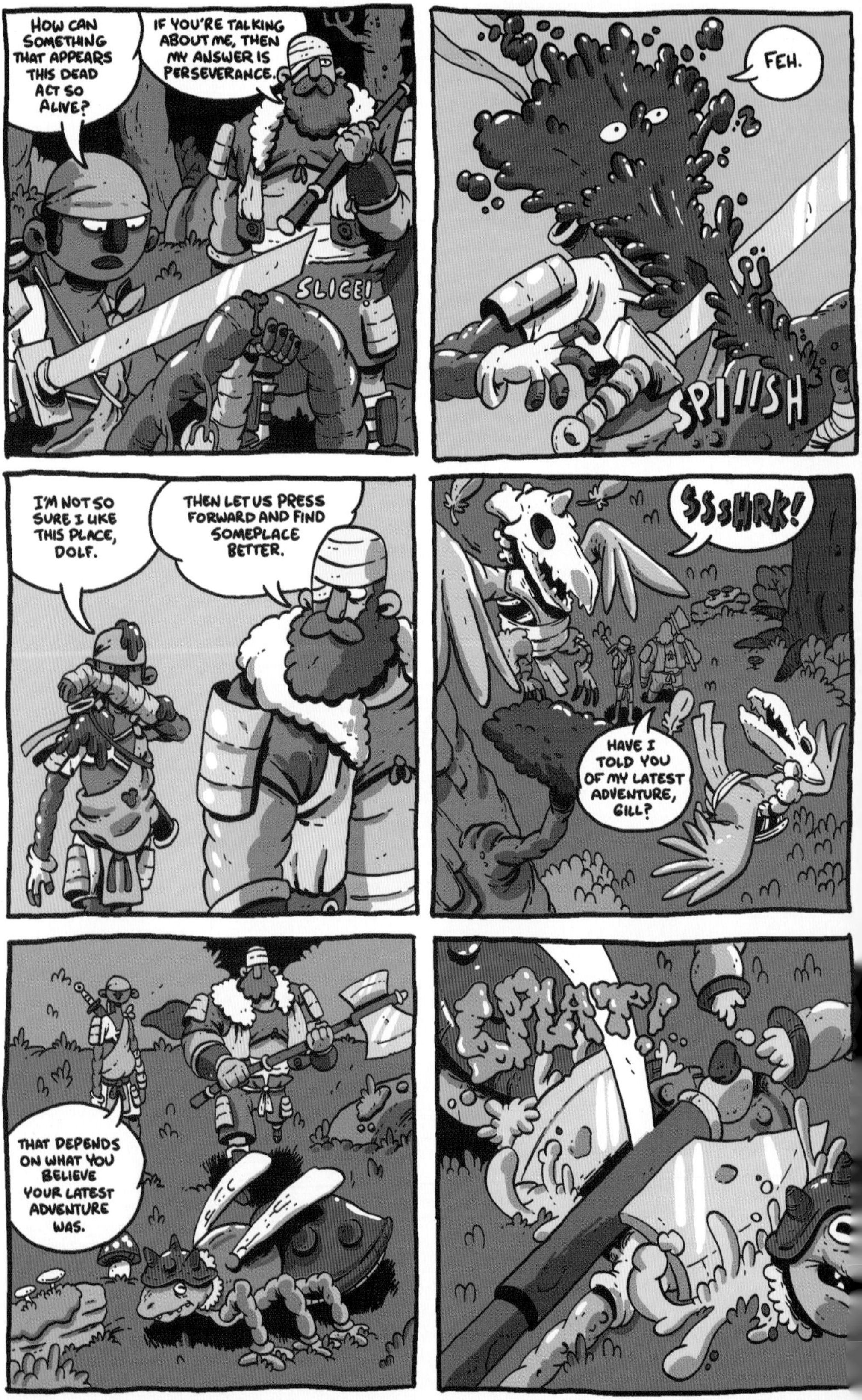
HOW CAN SOMETHING THAT APPEARS THIS DEAD ACT SO ALIVE?
IF YOU'RE TALKING ABOUT ME, THEN MY ANSWER IS PERSEVERANCE.
SLICE!
FEH.
SPIIIISH
I'M NOT SO SURE I LIKE THIS PLACE, DOLF.
THEN LET US PRESS FORWARD AND FIND SOMEPLACE BETTER.
SSSHRK!
HAVE I TOLD YOU OF MY LATEST ADVENTURE, GILL?
THAT DEPENDS ON WHAT YOU BELIEVE YOUR LATEST ADVENTURE WAS.
SPLAT!

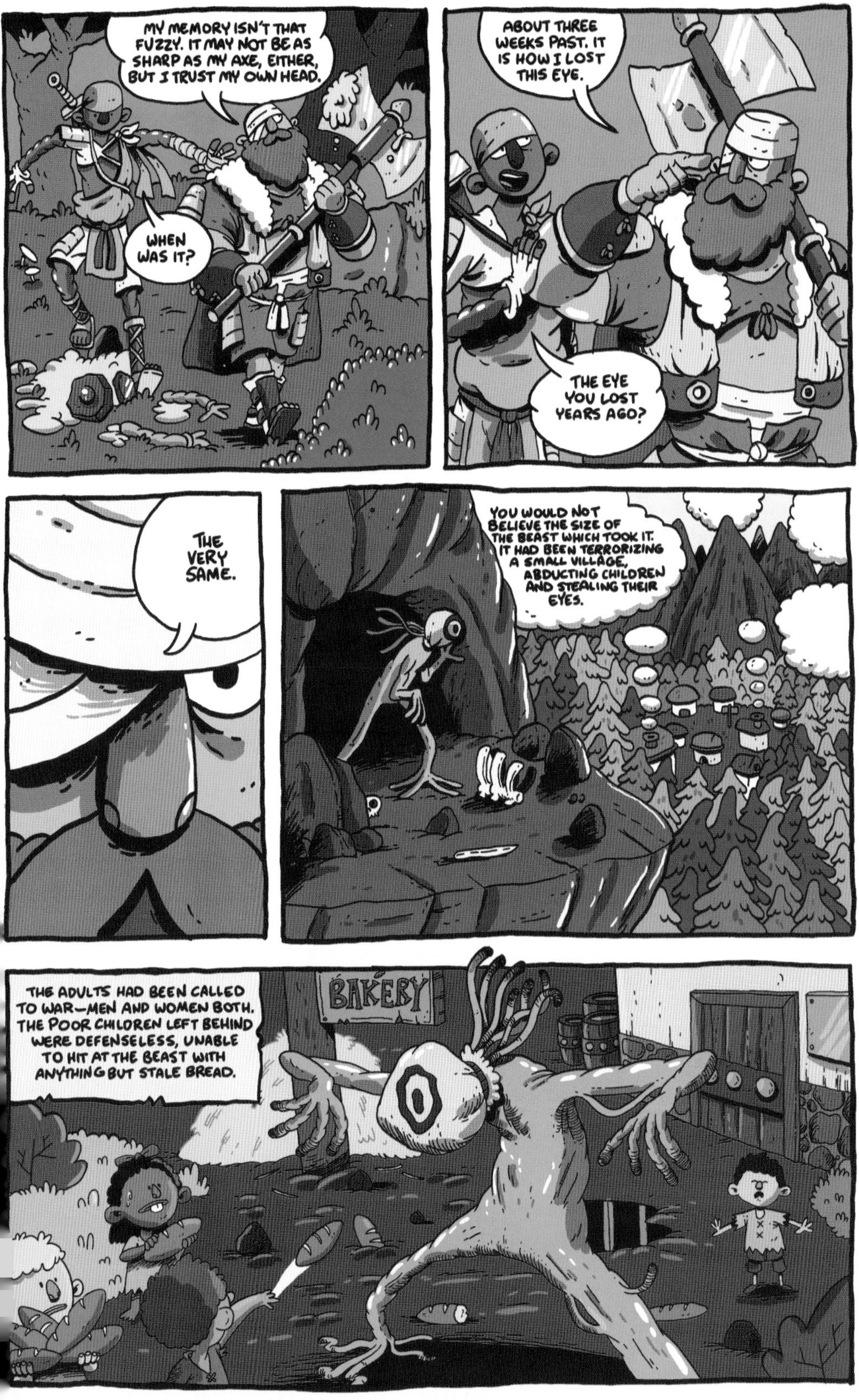
MY MEMORY ISN'T THAT FUZZY. IT MAY NOT BE AS SHARP AS MY AXE, EITHER, BUT I TRUST MY OWN HEAD.
WHEN WAS IT?
ABOUT THREE WEEKS PAST. IT IS HOW I LOST THIS EYE.
THE EYE YOU LOST YEARS AGO?
THE VERY SAME.
YOU WOULD NOT BELIEVE THE SIZE OF THE BEAST WHICH TOOK IT. IT HAD BEEN TERRORIZING A SMALL VILLAGE, ABDUCTING CHILDREN AND STEALING THEIR EYES.
THE ADULTS HAD BEEN CALLED TO WAR—MEN AND WOMEN BOTH. THE POOR CHILDREN LEFT BEHIND WERE DEFENSELESS, UNABLE TO HIT AT THE BEAST WITH ANYTHING BUT STALE BREAD.
BAKERY

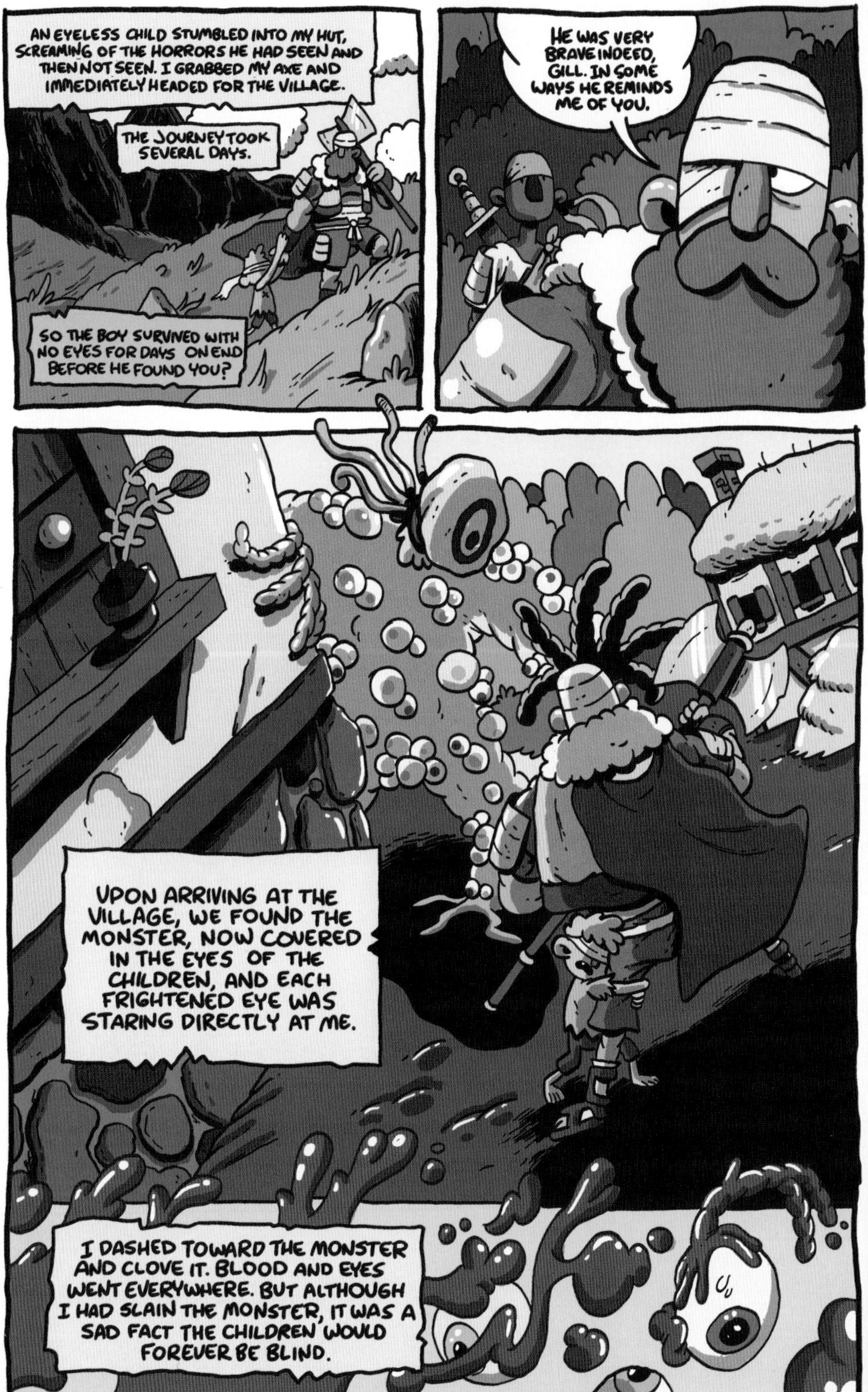
AN EYELESS CHILD STUMBLED INTO MY HUT, SCREAMING OF THE HORRORS HE HAD SEEN AND THEN NOT SEEN. I GRABBED MY AXE AND IMMEDIATELY HEADED FOR THE VILLAGE.
THE JOURNEY TOOK SEVERAL DAYS.
SO THE BOY SURVIVED WITH NO EYES FOR DAYS ON END BEFORE HE FOUND YOU?
HE WAS VERY BRAVE INDEED, GILL. IN SOME WAYS HE REMINDS ME OF YOU.
UPON ARRIVING AT THE VILLAGE, WE FOUND THE MONSTER, NOW COVERED IN THE EYES OF THE CHILDREN, AND EACH FRIGHTENED EYE WAS STARING DIRECTLY AT ME.
I DASHED TOWARD THE MONSTER AND CLOVE IT. BLOOD AND EYES WENT EVERYWHERE. BUT ALTHOUGH I HAD SLAIN THE MONSTER, IT WAS A SAD FACT THE CHILDREN WOULD FOREVER BE BLIND.

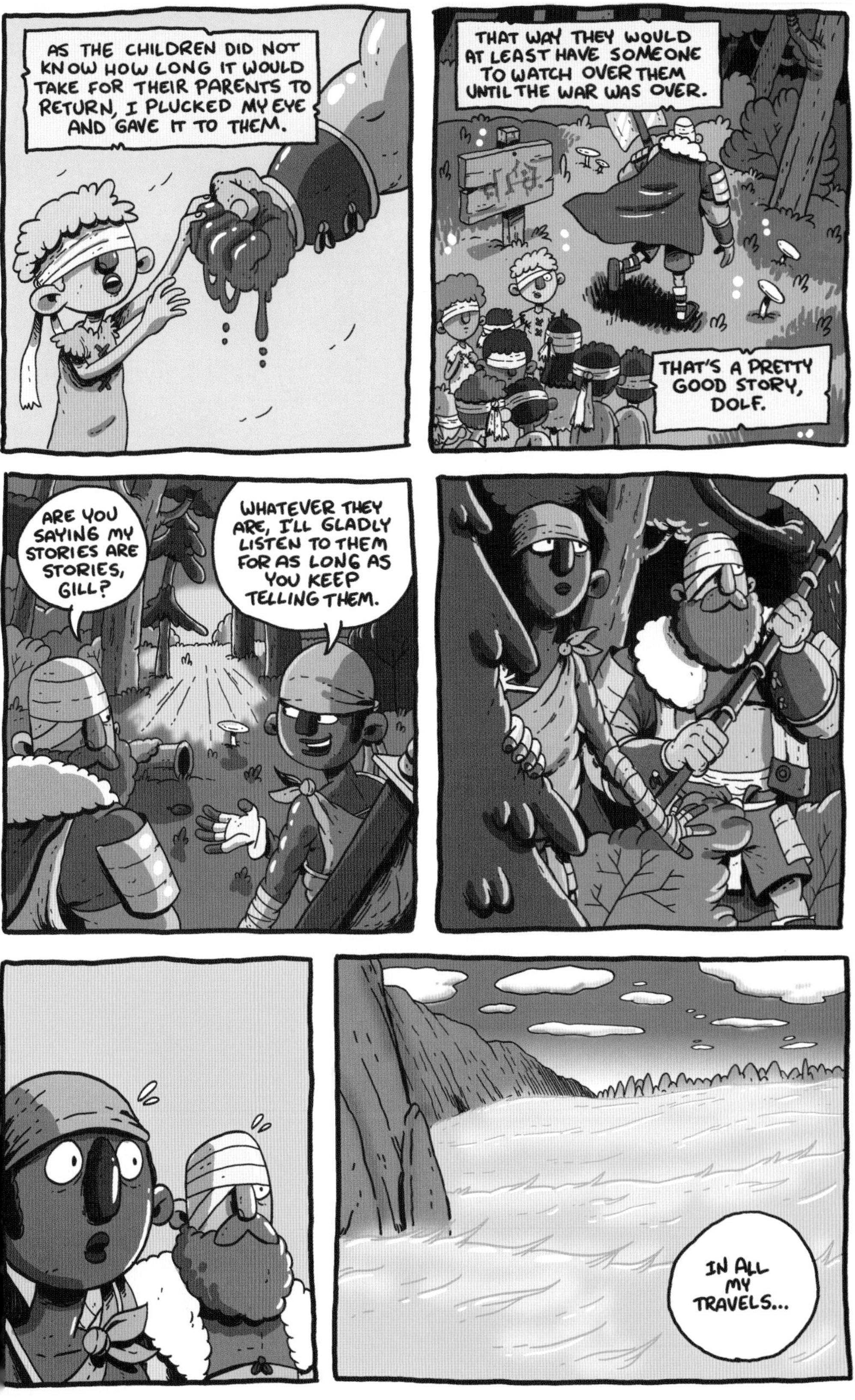
AS THE CHILDREN DID NOT KNOW HOW LONG IT WOULD TAKE FOR THEIR PARENTS TO RETURN, I PLUCKED MY EYE AND GAVE IT TO THEM.
THAT WAY THEY WOULD AT LEAST HAVE SOMEONE TO WATCH OVER THEM UNTIL THE WAR WAS OVER.
THAT'S A PRETTY GOOD STORY, DOLF.
ARE YOU SAYING MY STORIES ARE STORIES, GILL?
WHATEVER THEY ARE, I'LL GLADLY LISTEN TO THEM FOR AS LONG AS YOU KEEP TELLING THEM.
IN ALL MY TRAVELS...

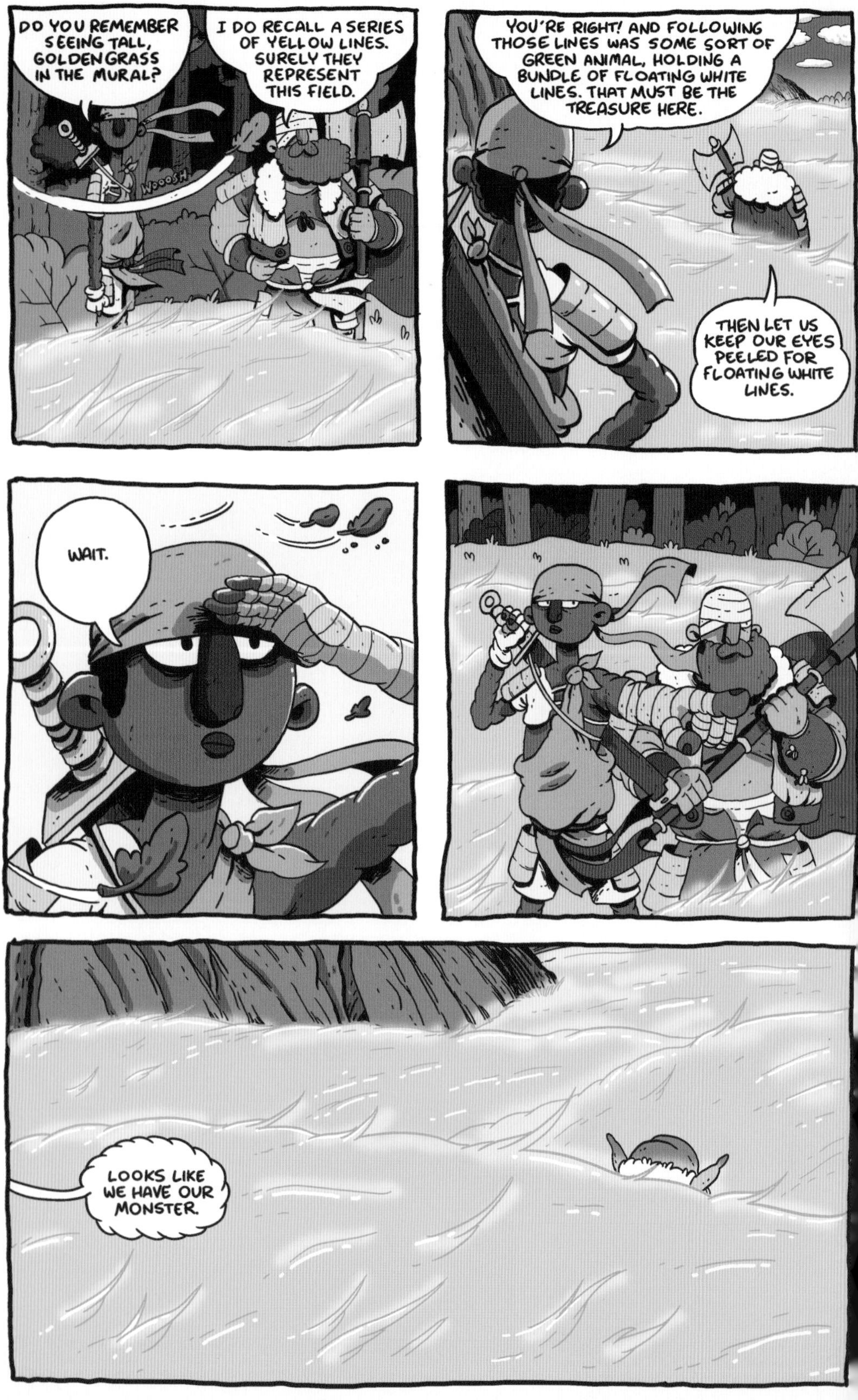
DO YOU REMEMBER SEEING TALL, GOLDEN GRASS IN THE MURAL?
I DO RECALL A SERIES OF YELLOW LINES. SURELY THEY REPRESENT THIS FIELD.
WOOOSH
YOU'RE RIGHT! AND FOLLOWING THOSE LINES WAS SOME SORT OF GREEN ANIMAL, HOLDING A BUNDLE OF FLOATING WHITE LINES. THAT MUST BE THE TREASURE HERE.
THEN LET US KEEP OUR EYES PEELED FOR FLOATING WHITE LINES.
WAIT.
LOOKS LIKE WE HAVE OUR MONSTER.

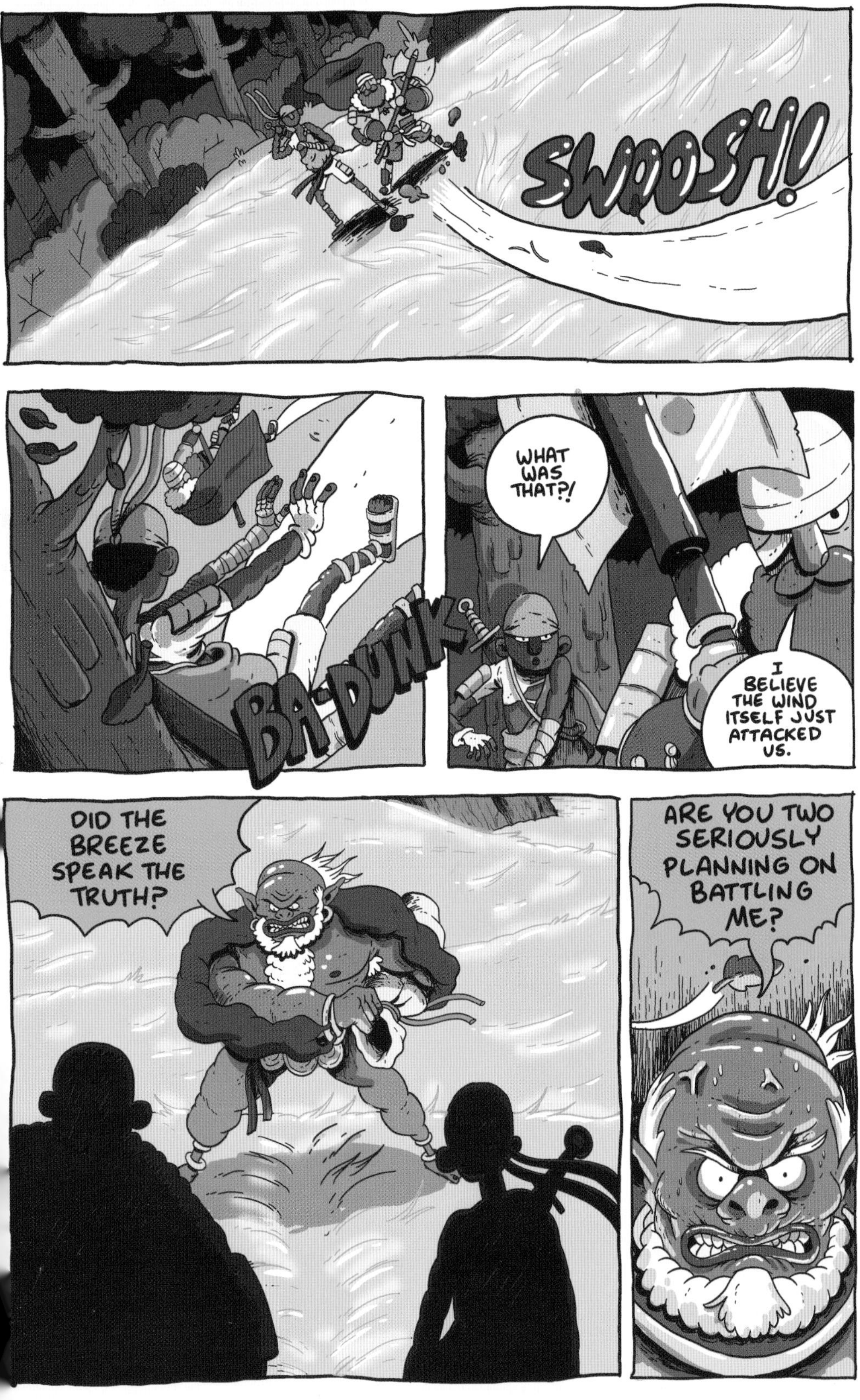
SWOOSH!
BA-DUNK
WHAT WAS THAT?!
I BELIEVE THE WIND ITSELF JUST ATTACKED US.
DID THE BREEZE SPEAK THE TRUTH?
ARE YOU TWO SERIOUSLY PLANNING ON BATTLING ME?

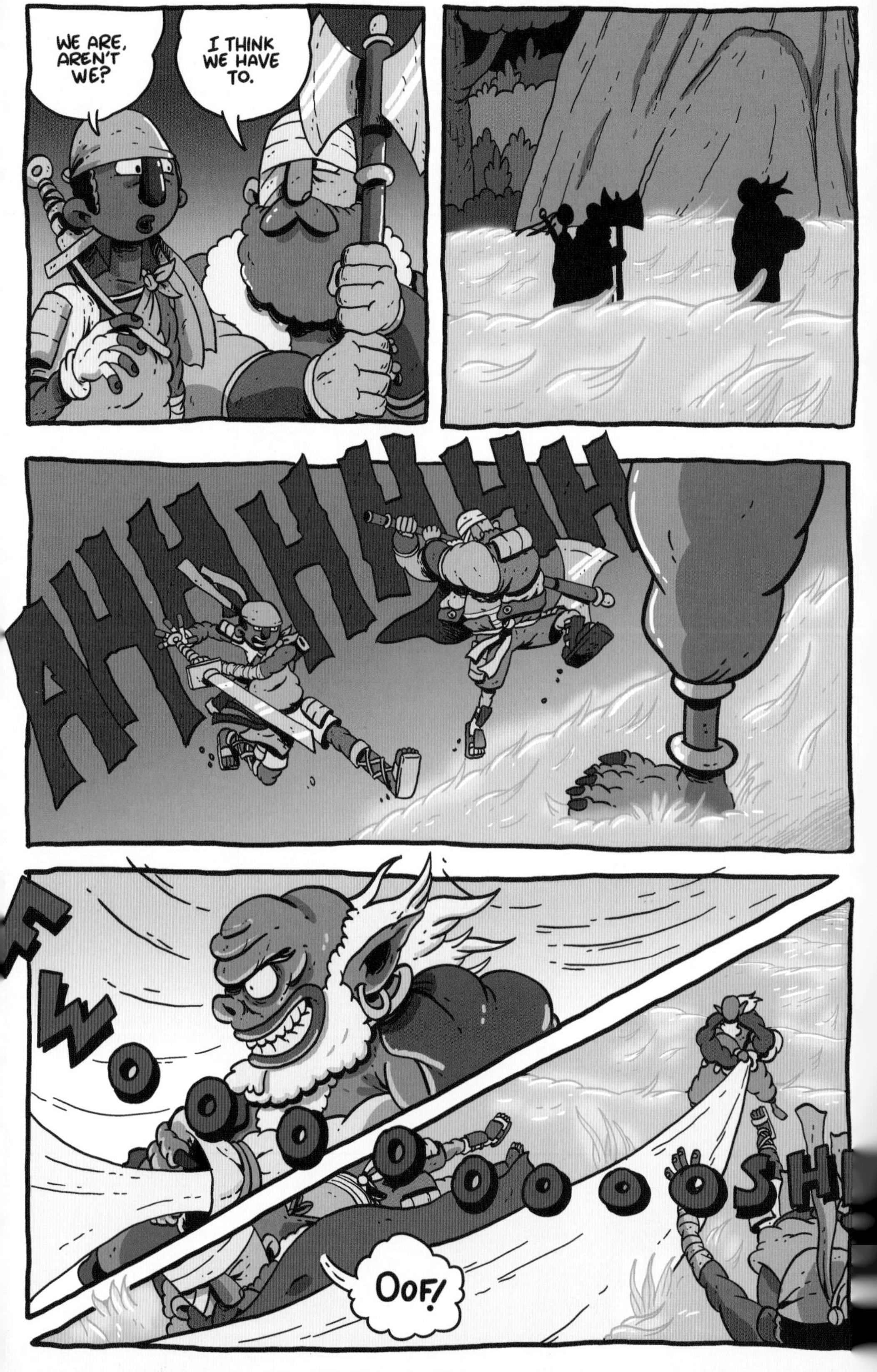
WE ARE, AREN'T WE?
I THINK WE HAVE TO.
AHHHHHHH
FWOOOOOOOOSH
OOF!

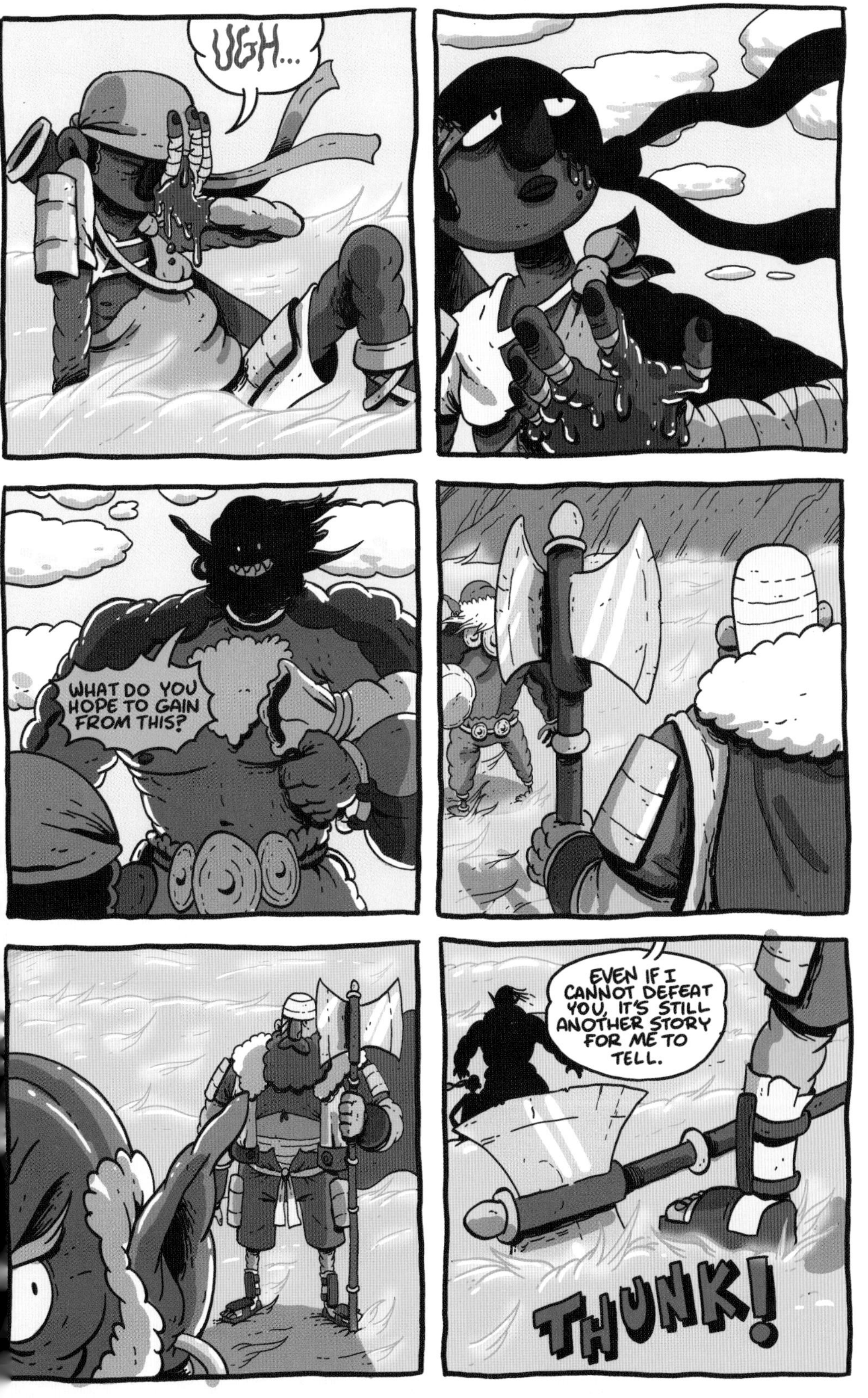
UGH...
WHAT DO YOU HOPE TO GAIN FROM THIS?
EVEN IF I CANNOT DEFEAT YOU, IT'S STILL ANOTHER STORY FOR ME TO TELL.
THUNK!

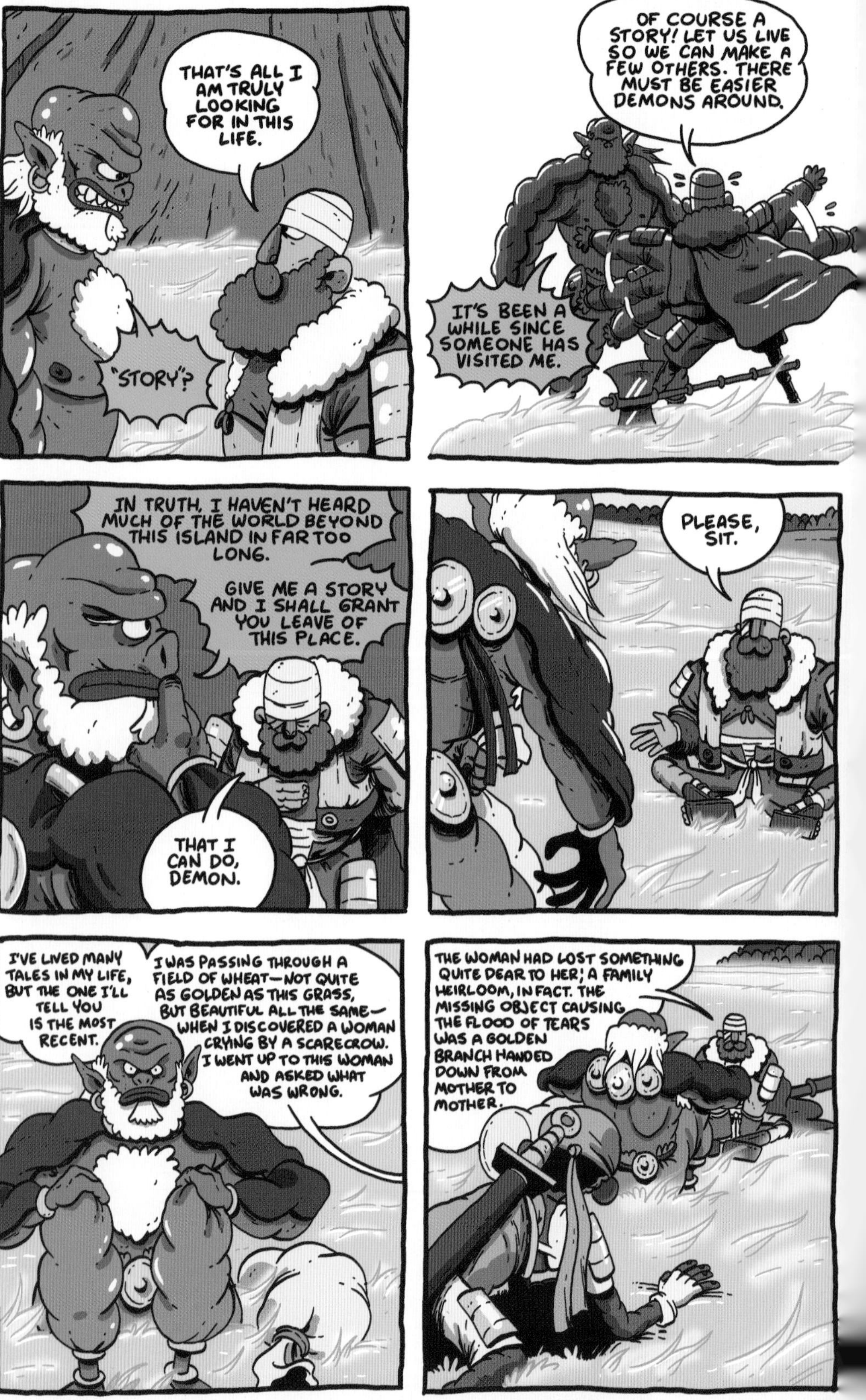
THAT'S ALL I AM TRULY LOOKING FOR IN THIS LIFE.
"STORY"?
OF COURSE A STORY! LET US LIVE SO WE CAN MAKE A FEW OTHERS. THERE MUST BE EASIER DEMONS AROUND.
IT'S BEEN A WHILE SINCE SOMEONE HAS VISITED ME.
IN TRUTH, I HAVEN'T HEARD MUCH OF THE WORLD BEYOND THIS ISLAND IN FAR TOO LONG.
GIVE ME A STORY AND I SHALL GRANT YOU LEAVE OF THIS PLACE.
THAT I CAN DO, DEMON.
PLEASE, SIT.
I'VE LIVED MANY TALES IN MY LIFE, BUT THE ONE I'LL TELL YOU IS THE MOST RECENT.
I WAS PASSING THROUGH A FIELD OF WHEAT—NOT QUITE AS GOLDEN AS THIS GRASS, BUT BEAUTIFUL ALL THE SAME—WHEN I DISCOVERED A WOMAN CRYING BY A SCARECROW. I WENT UP TO THIS WOMAN AND ASKED WHAT WAS WRONG.
THE WOMAN HAD LOST SOMETHING QUITE DEAR TO HER; A FAMILY HEIRLOOM, IN FACT. THE MISSING OBJECT CAUSING THE FLOOD OF TEARS WAS A GOLDEN BRANCH HANDED DOWN FROM MOTHER TO MOTHER.

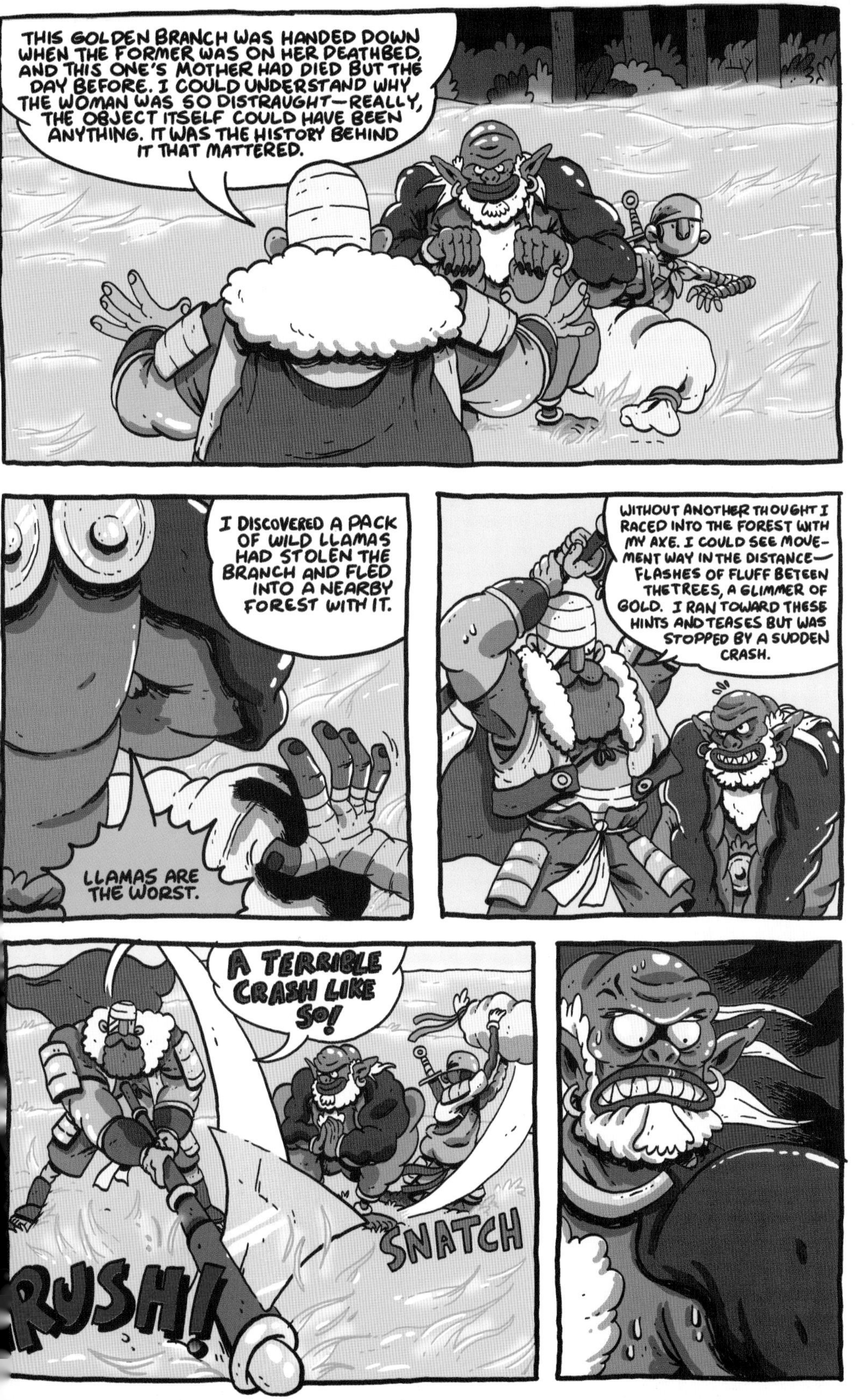
THIS GOLDEN BRANCH WAS HANDED DOWN WHEN THE FORMER WAS ON HER DEATHBED, AND THIS ONE'S MOTHER HAD DIED BUT THE DAY BEFORE. I COULD UNDERSTAND WHY THE WOMAN WAS SO DISTRAUGHT—REALLY, THE OBJECT ITSELF COULD HAVE BEEN ANYTHING. IT WAS THE HISTORY BEHIND IT THAT MATTERED.
I DISCOVERED A PACK OF WILD LLAMAS HAD STOLEN THE BRANCH AND FLED INTO A NEARBY FOREST WITH IT.
LLAMAS ARE THE WORST.
WITHOUT ANOTHER THOUGHT I RACED INTO THE FOREST WITH MY AXE. I COULD SEE MOVEMENT WAY IN THE DISTANCE—FLASHES OF FLUFF BETEEN THE TREES, A GLIMMER OF GOLD. I RAN TOWARD THESE HINTS AND TEASES BUT WAS STOPPED BY A SUDDEN CRASH.
A TERRIBLE CRASH LIKE SO!
SNATCH
RUSH!

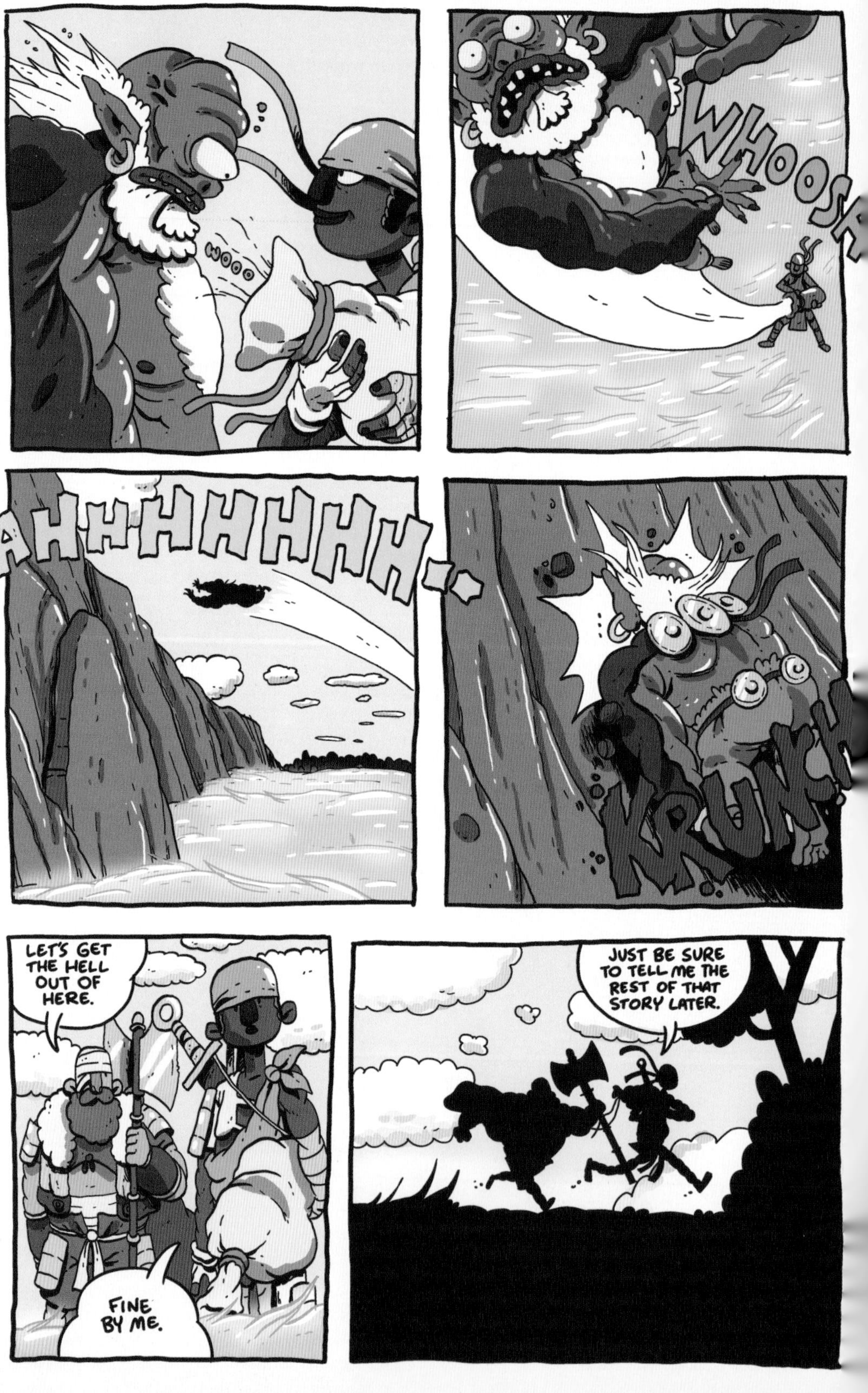
WOOO
WHOOSH
AHHHHHHHH..
KRUNCH
LET'S GET THE HELL OUT OF HERE.
FINE BY ME.
JUST BE SURE TO TELL ME THE REST OF THAT STORY LATER.

A GARGANTUAN EXPERIENCE

CARLOS & MIGUEL VALDERRAMA

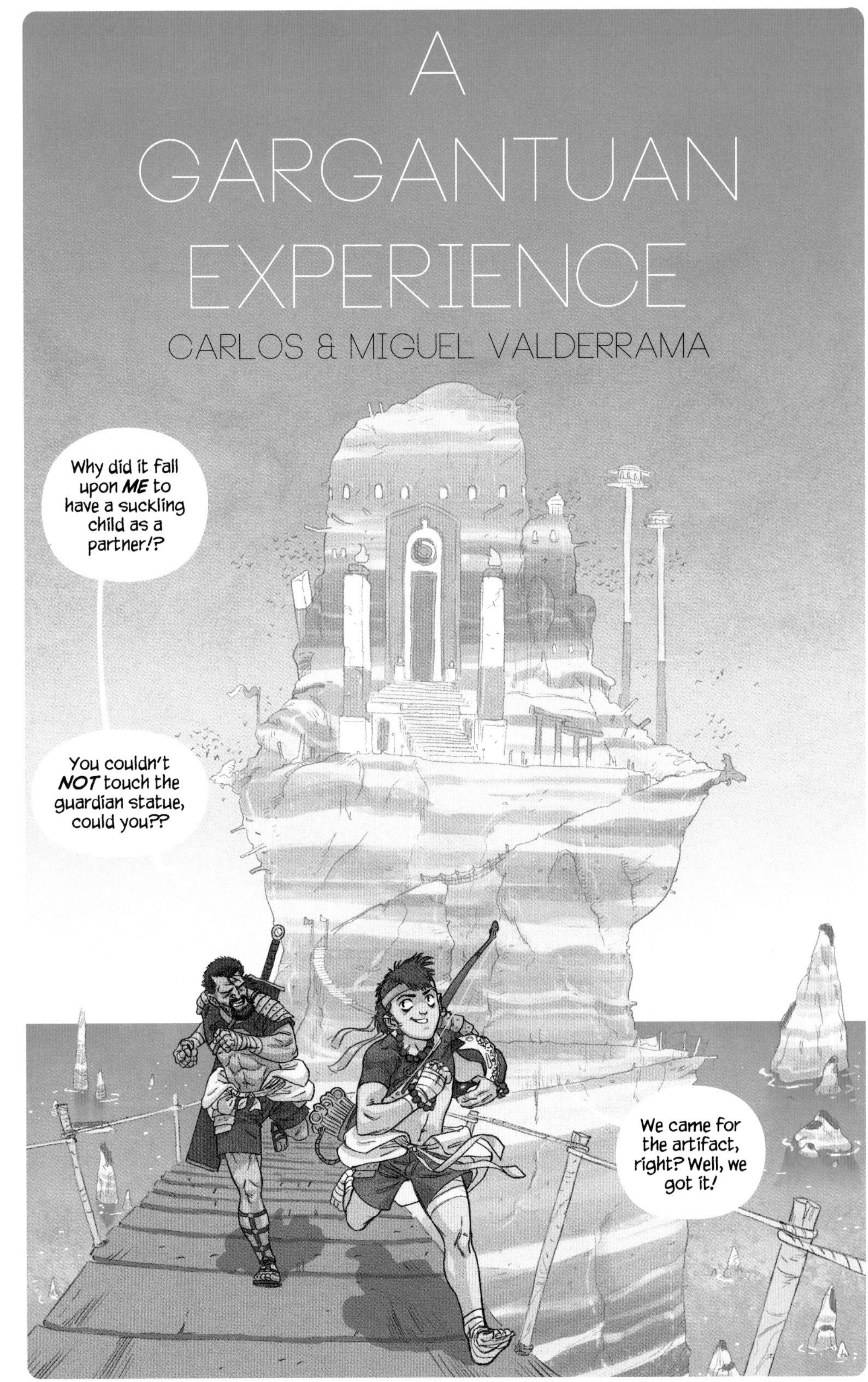

Why did it fall upon *ME* to have a suckling child as a partner!?
You couldn't *NOT* touch the guardian statue, could you??
We came for the artifact, right? Well, we got it!

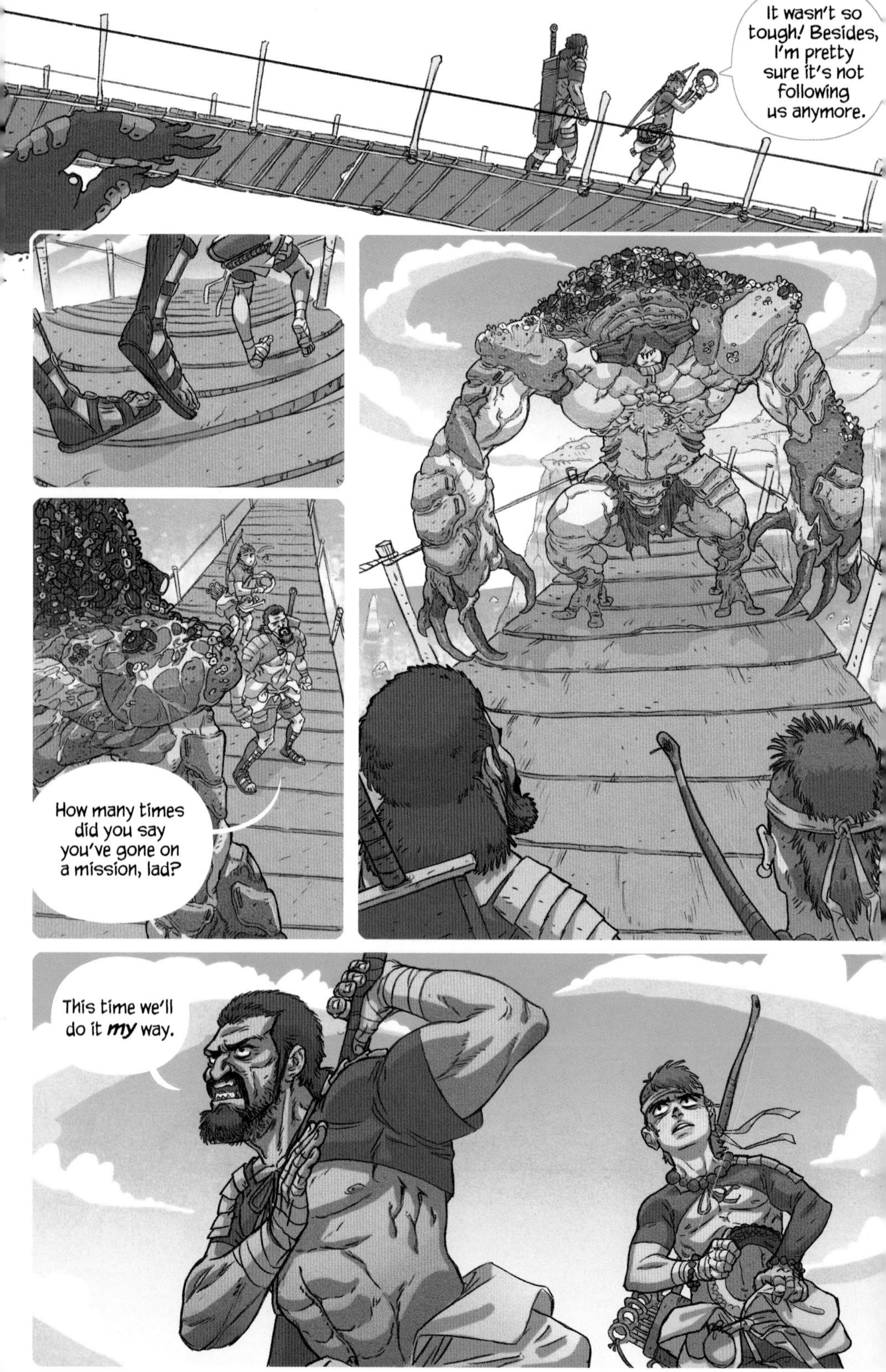
It wasn't so tough! Besides, I'm pretty sure it's not following us anymore.
How many times did you say you've gone on a mission, lad?
This time we'll do it ***my*** way.

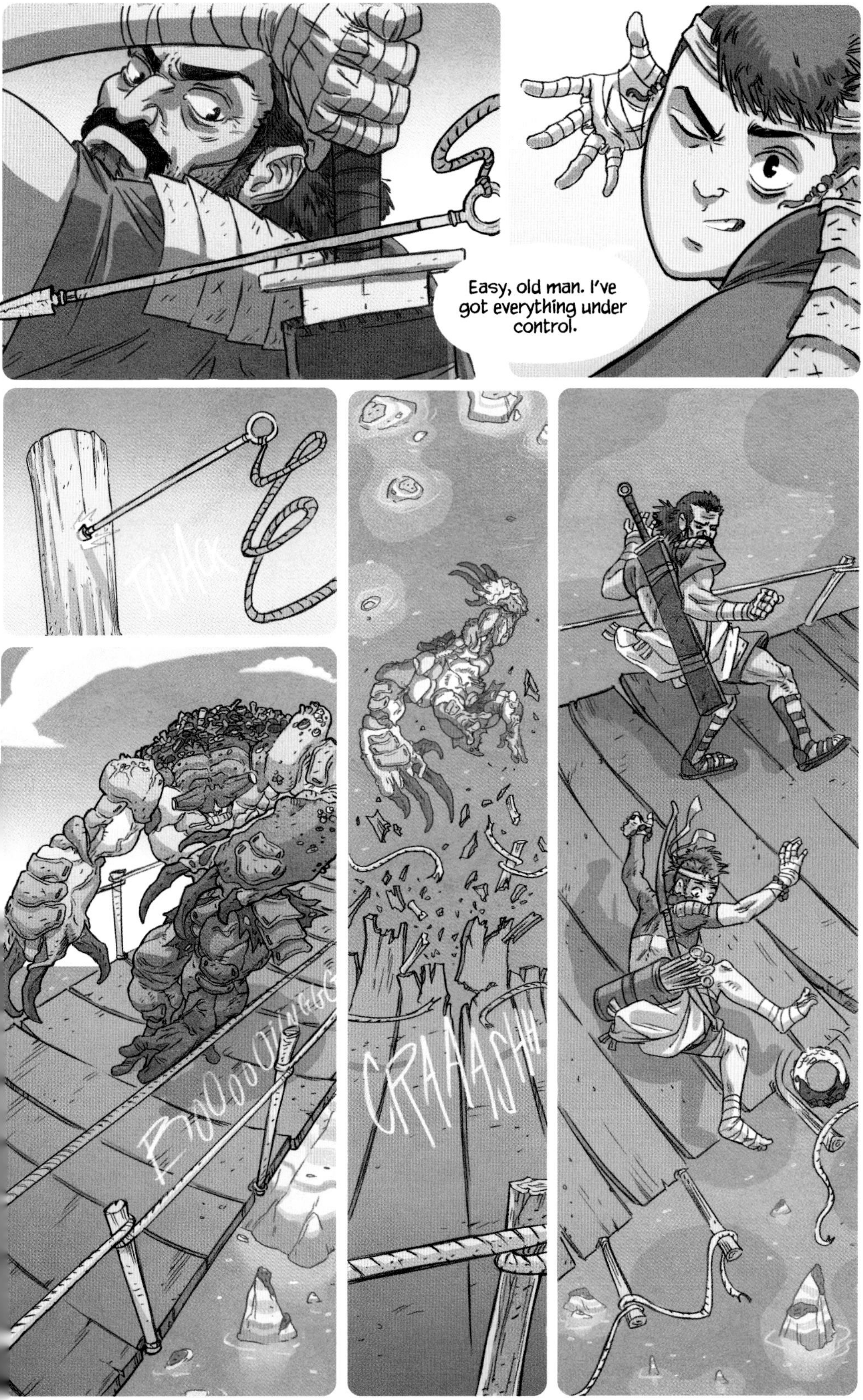
Easy, old man. I've got everything under control.
THHACK
CRAAASHH

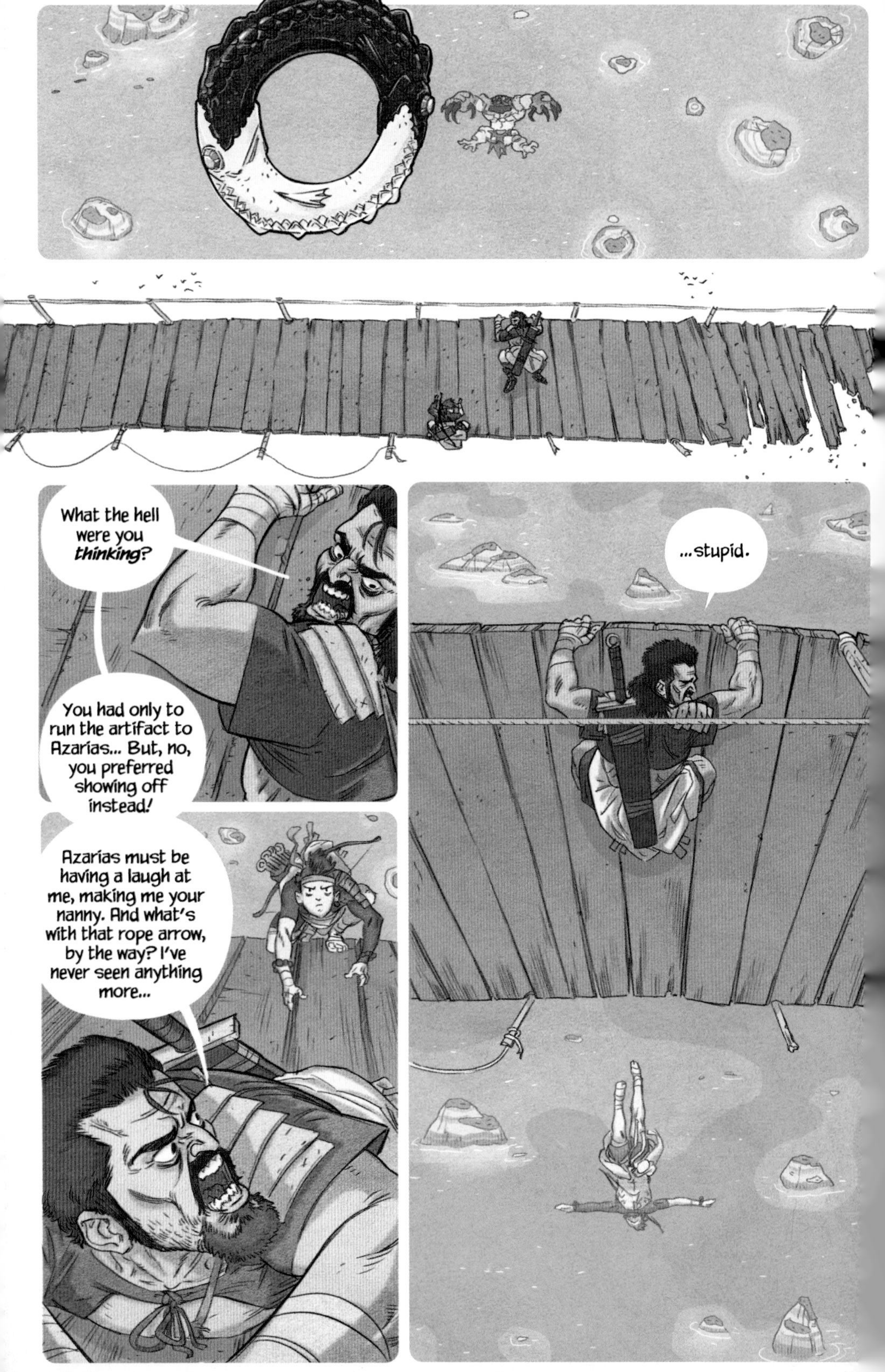
What the hell were you *thinking*?
You had only to run the artifact to Azarias... But, no, you preferred showing off instead!
Azarias must be having a laugh at me, making me your nanny. And what's with that rope arrow, by the way? I've never seen anything more...
...stupid.

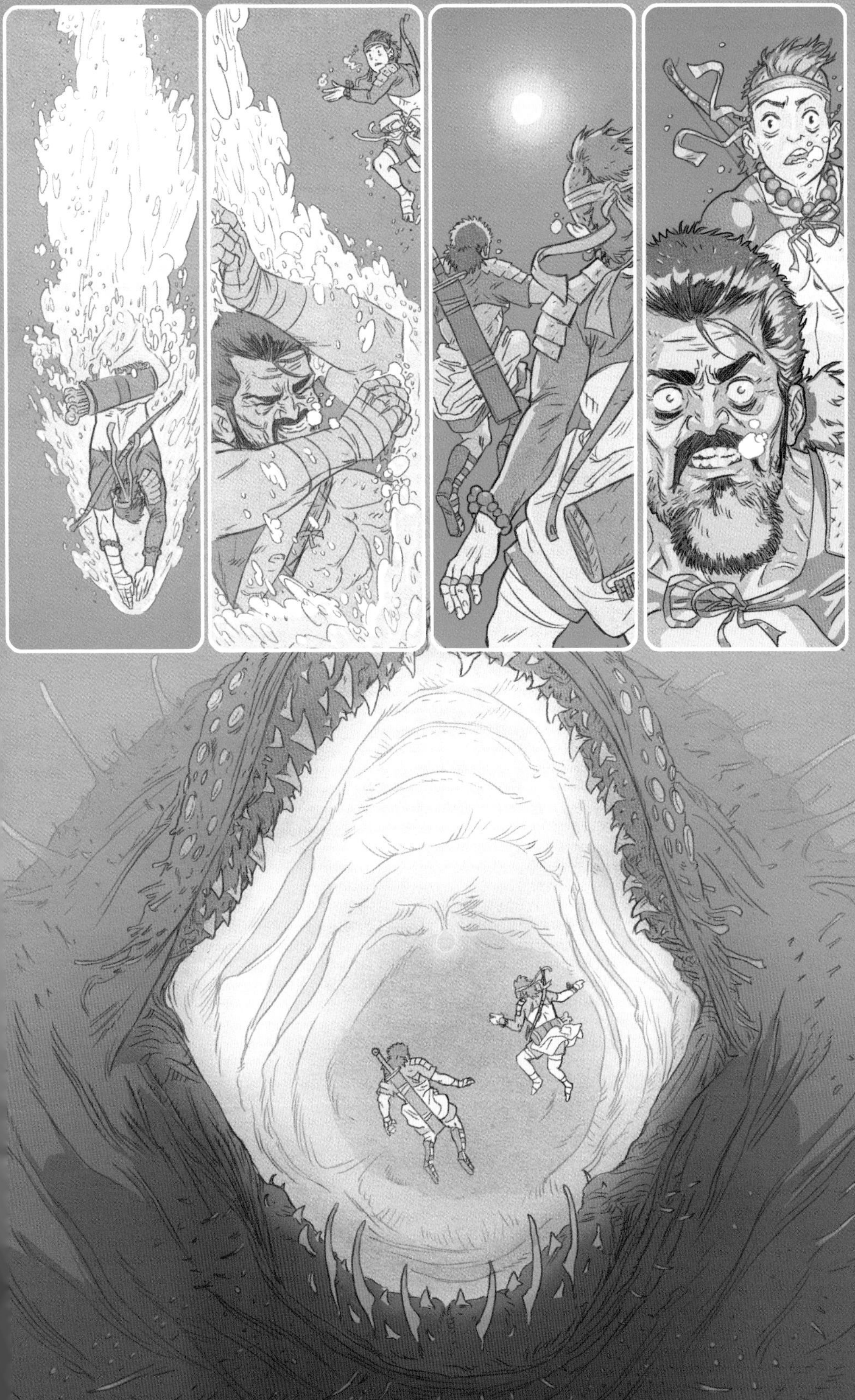

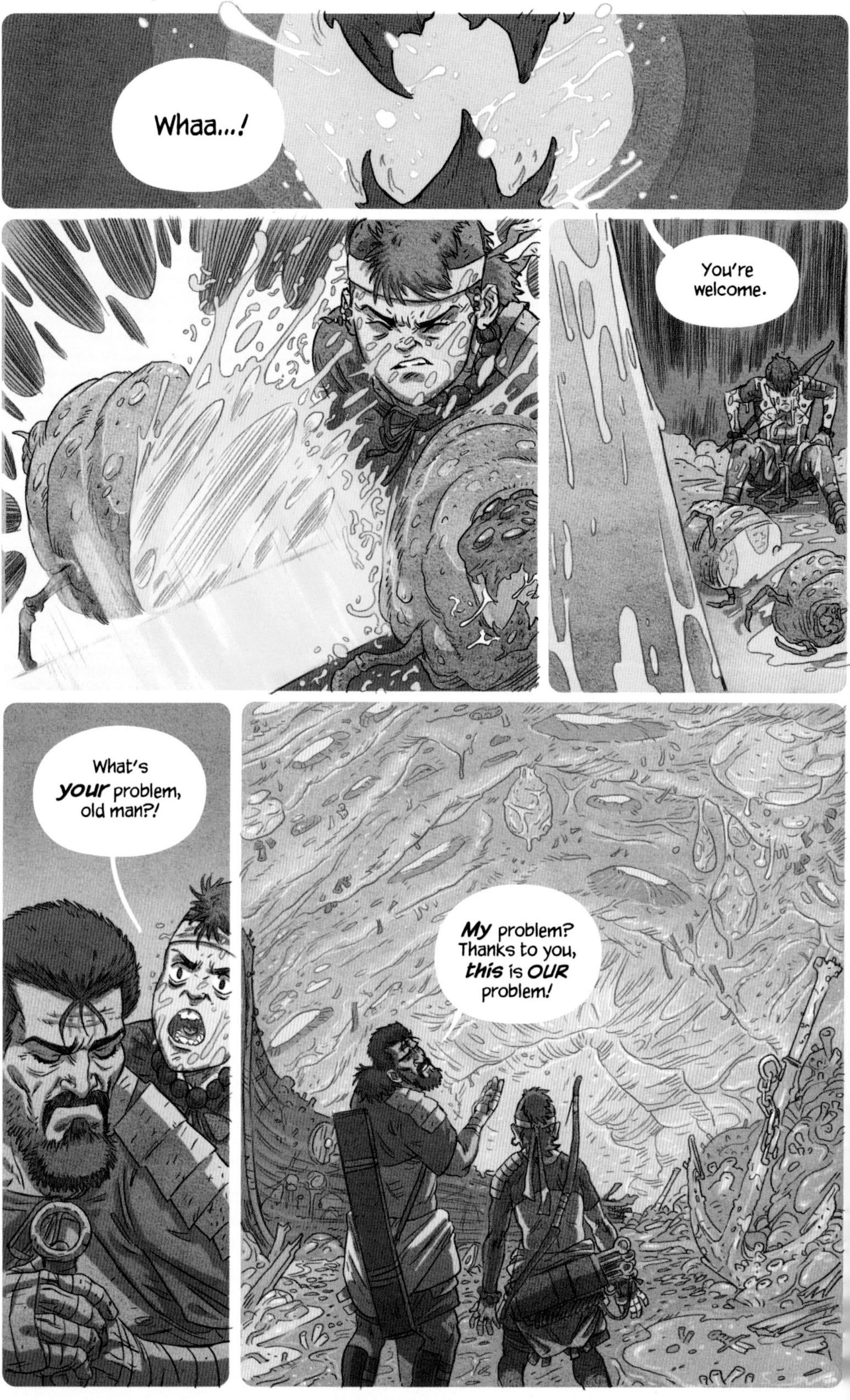
Whaa...!
You're welcome.
What's *your* problem, old man?!
My problem? Thanks to you, *this* is *OUR* problem!

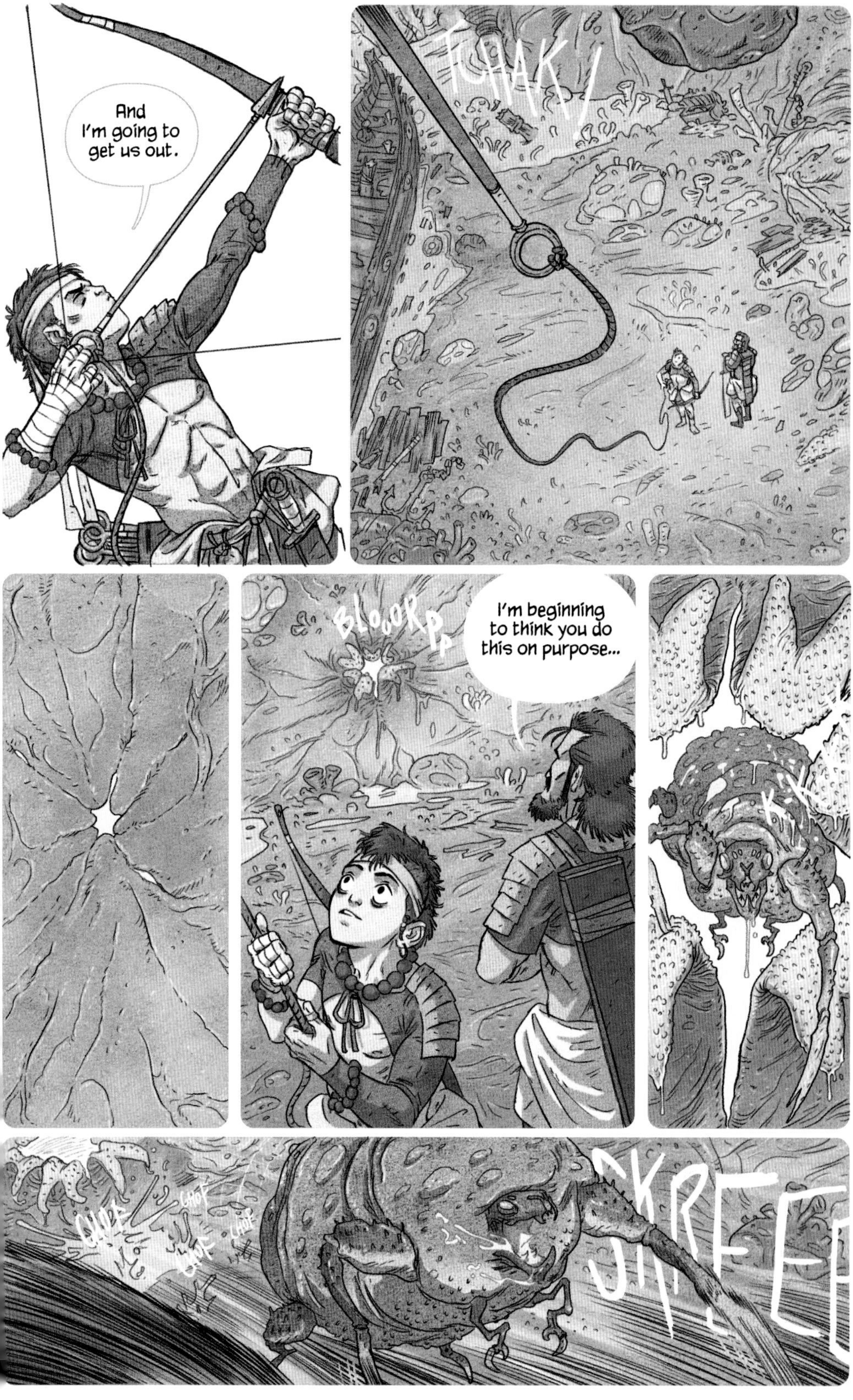
And I'm going to get us out.
I'm beginning to think you do this on purpose...

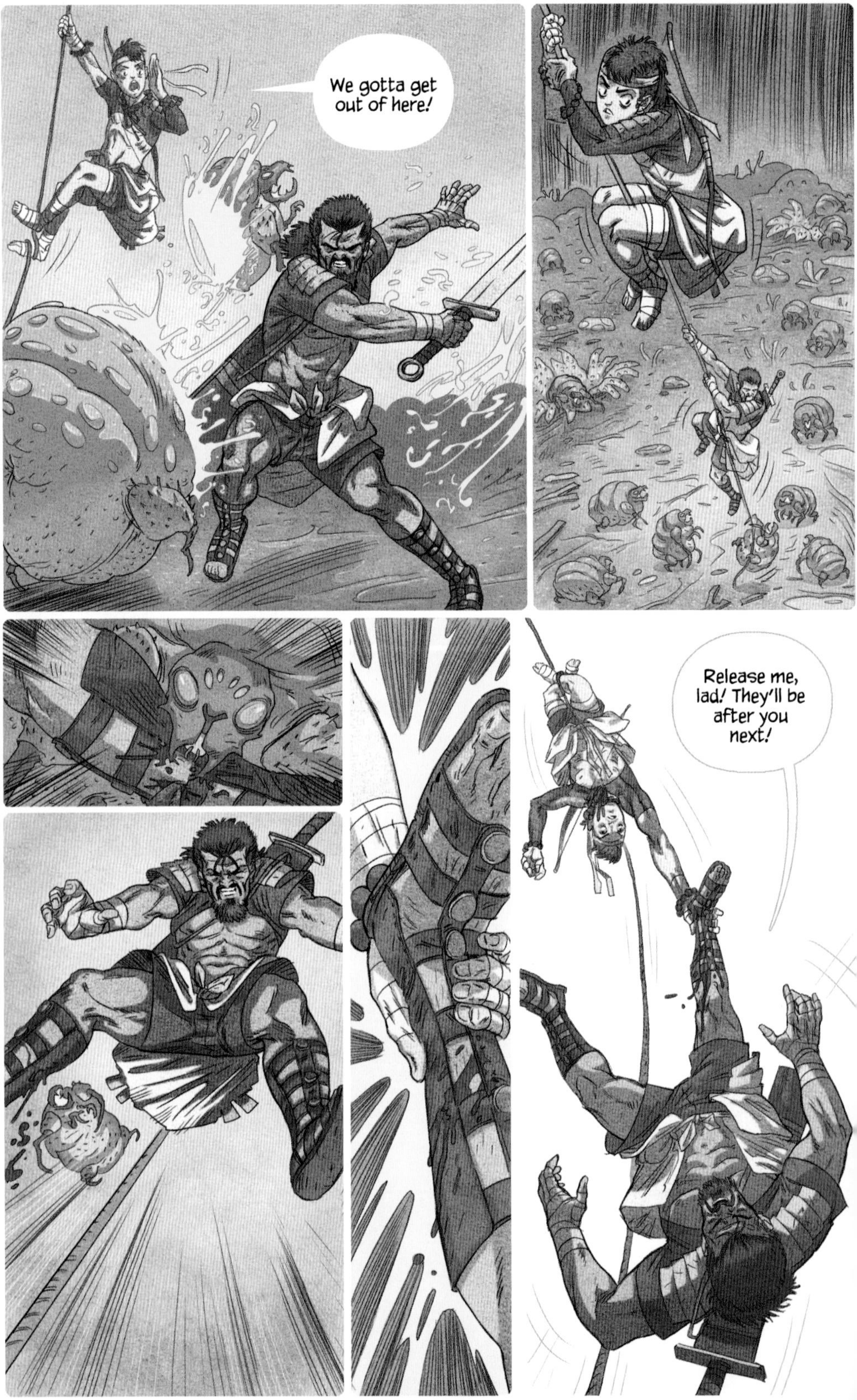
We gotta get out of here!
Release me, lad! They'll be after you next!

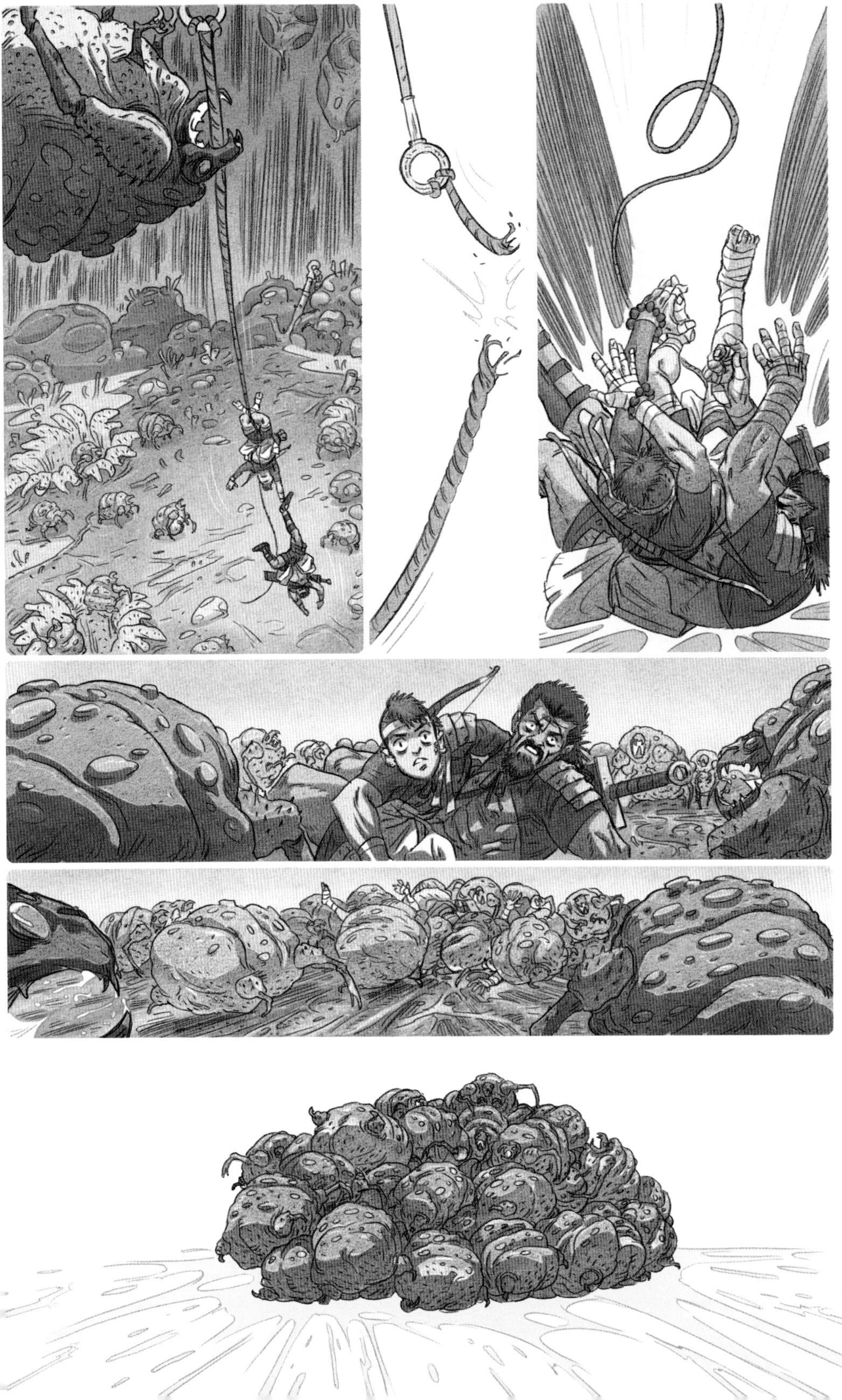

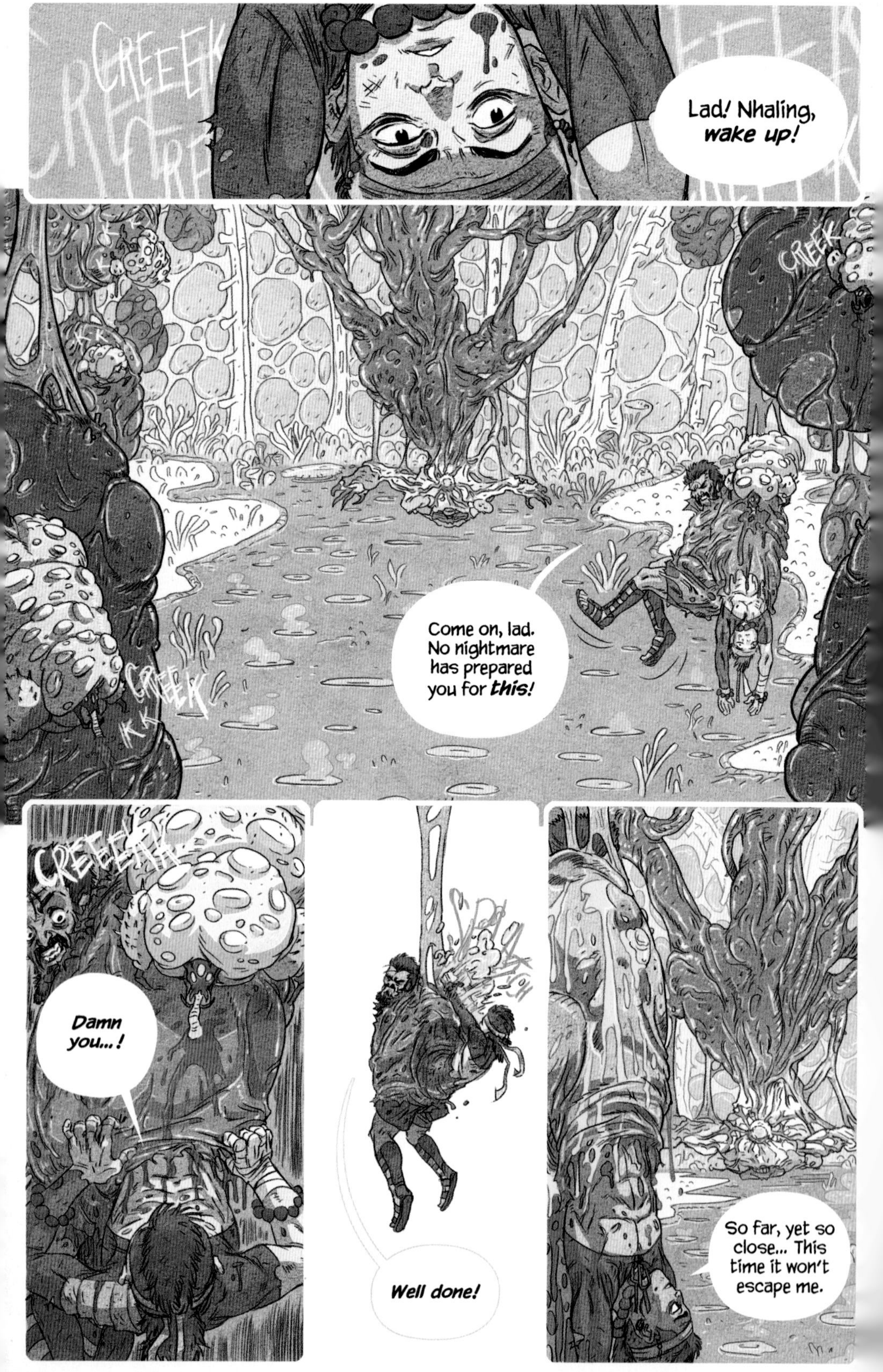
CREEEK
Lad! Nhaling, *wake up!*
CREEK
Come on, lad. No nightmare has prepared you for *this!*
CREEEK
CREEEEK
Damn you...!
Well done!
So far, yet so close... This time it won't escape me.

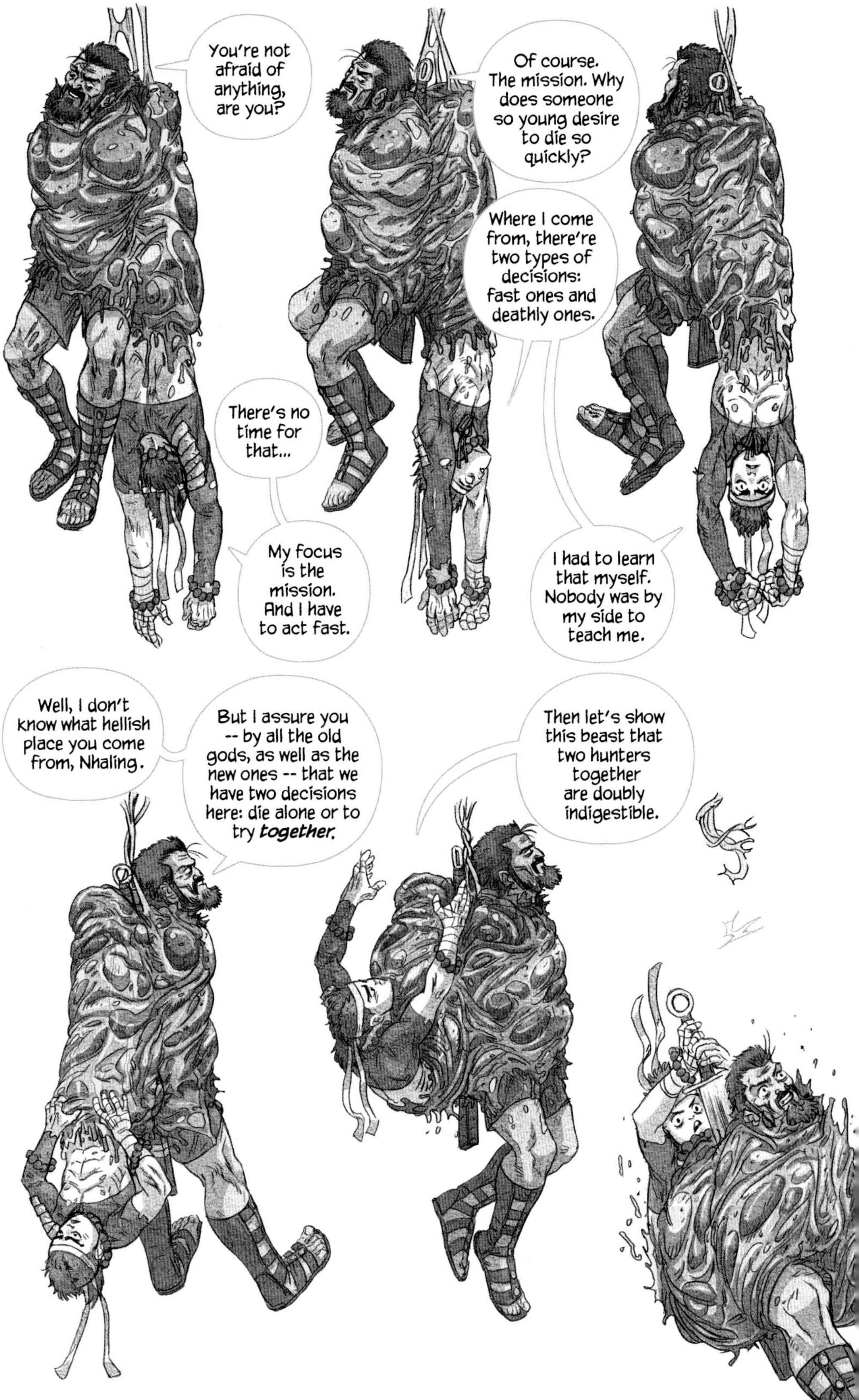

You're not afraid of anything, are you?
There's no time for that...
My focus is the mission. And I have to act fast.
Of course. The mission. Why does someone so young desire to die so quickly?
Where I come from, there're two types of decisions: fast ones and deathly ones.
I had to learn that myself. Nobody was by my side to teach me.
Well, I don't know what hellish place you come from, Nhaling.
But I assure you -- by all the old gods, as well as the new ones -- that we have two decisions here: die alone or to try *together*.
Then let's show this beast that two hunters together are doubly indigestible.

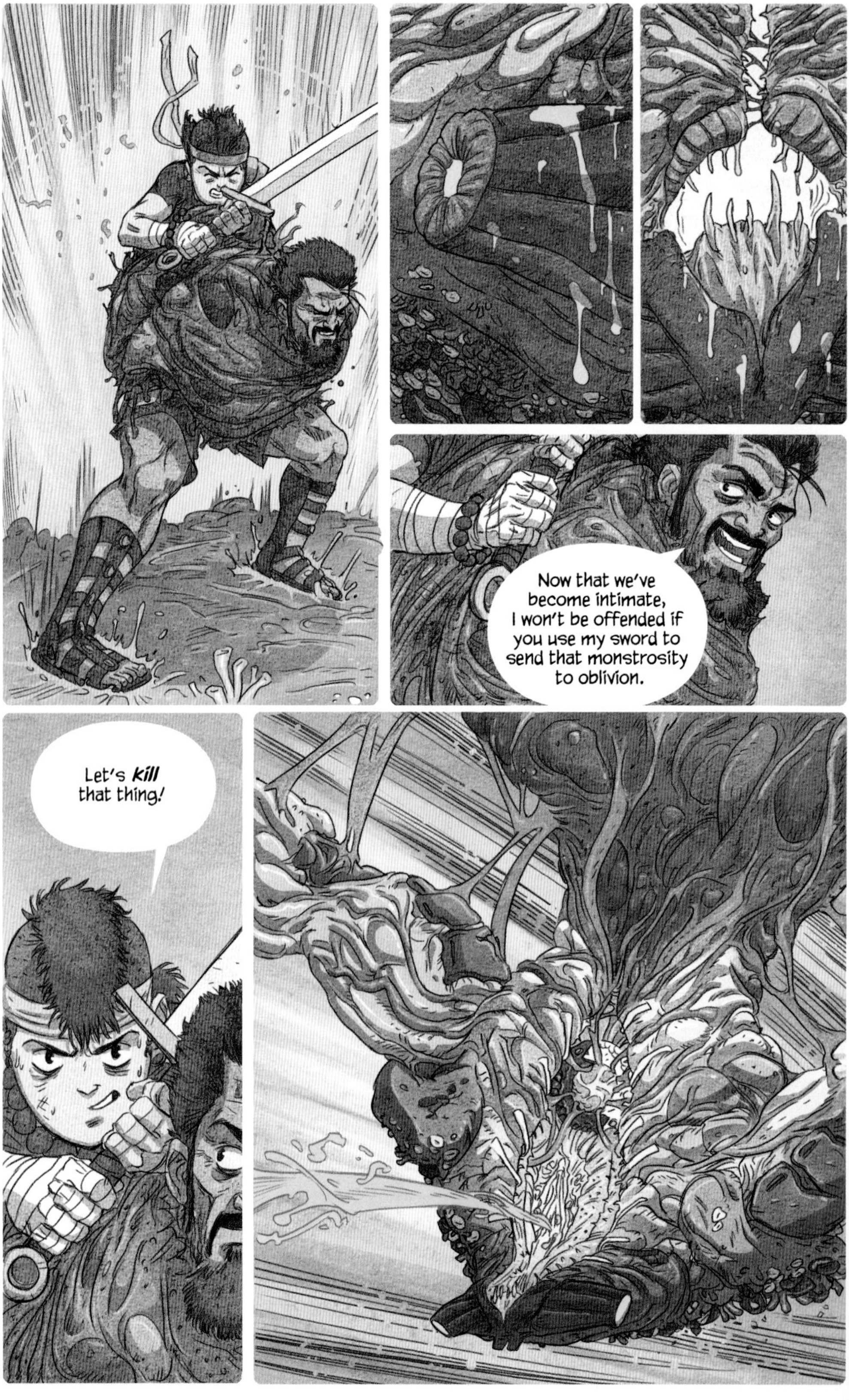
Now that we've become intimate, I won't be offended if you use my sword to send that monstrosity to oblivion.
Let's **kill** that thing!

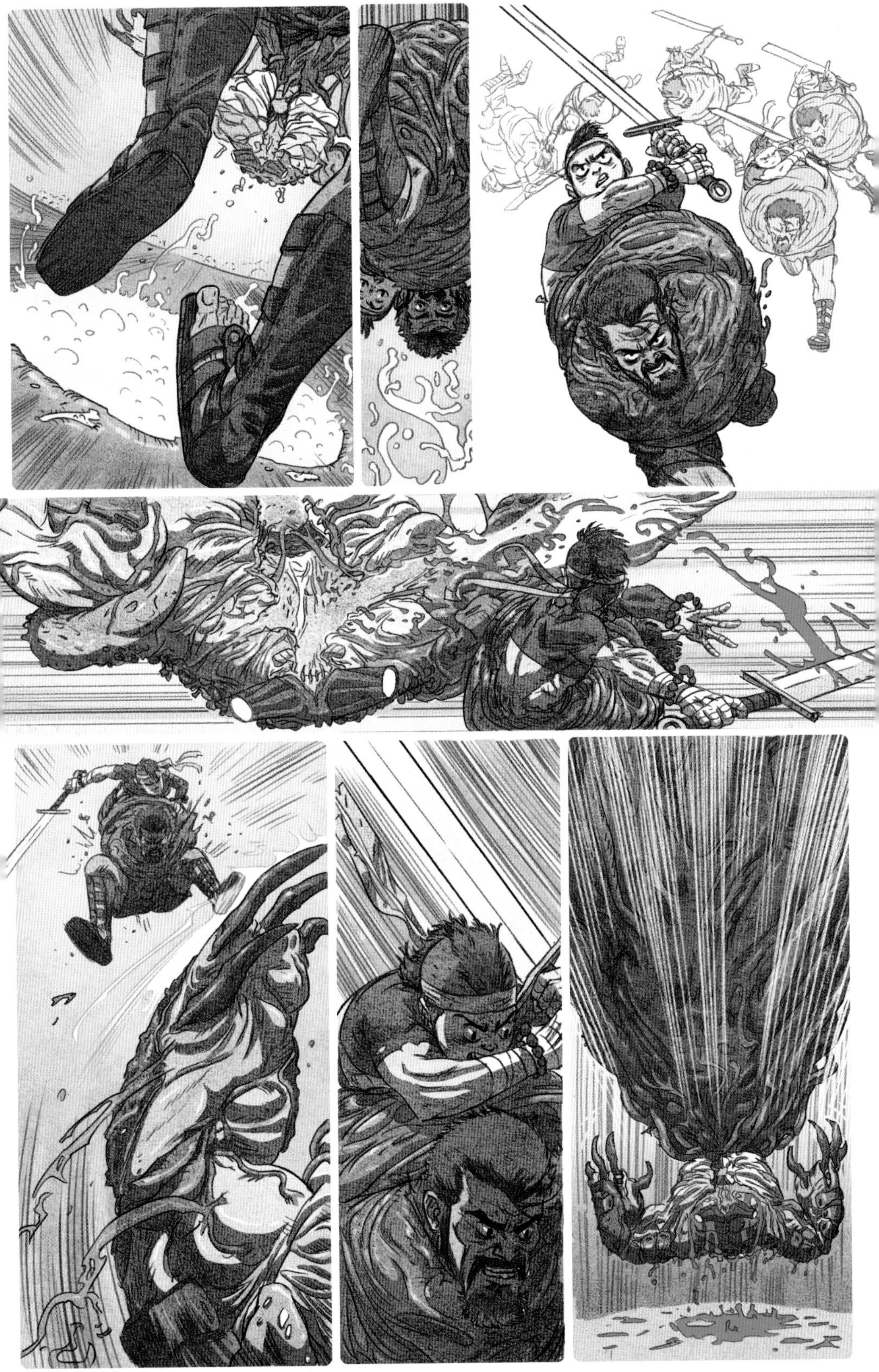

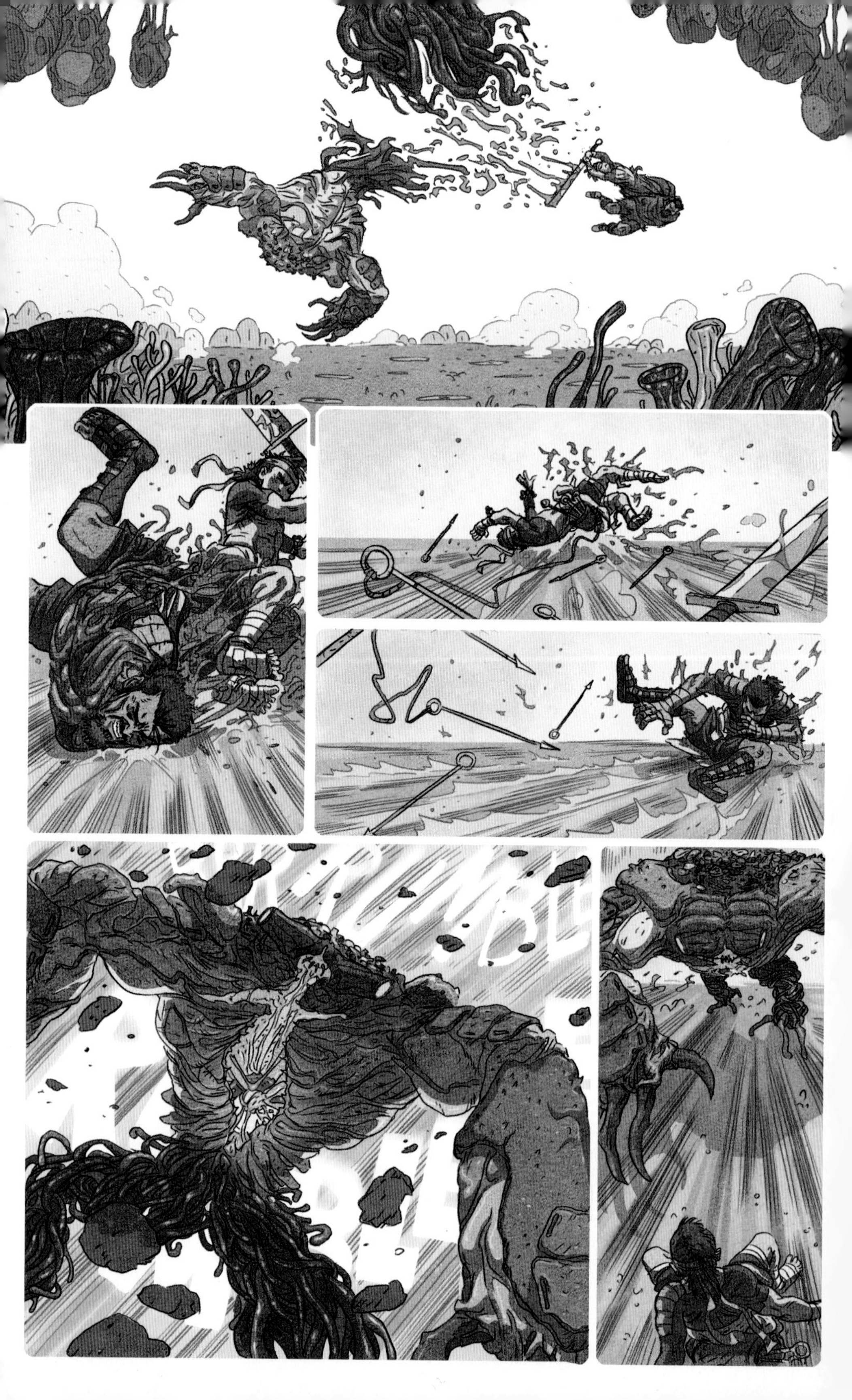

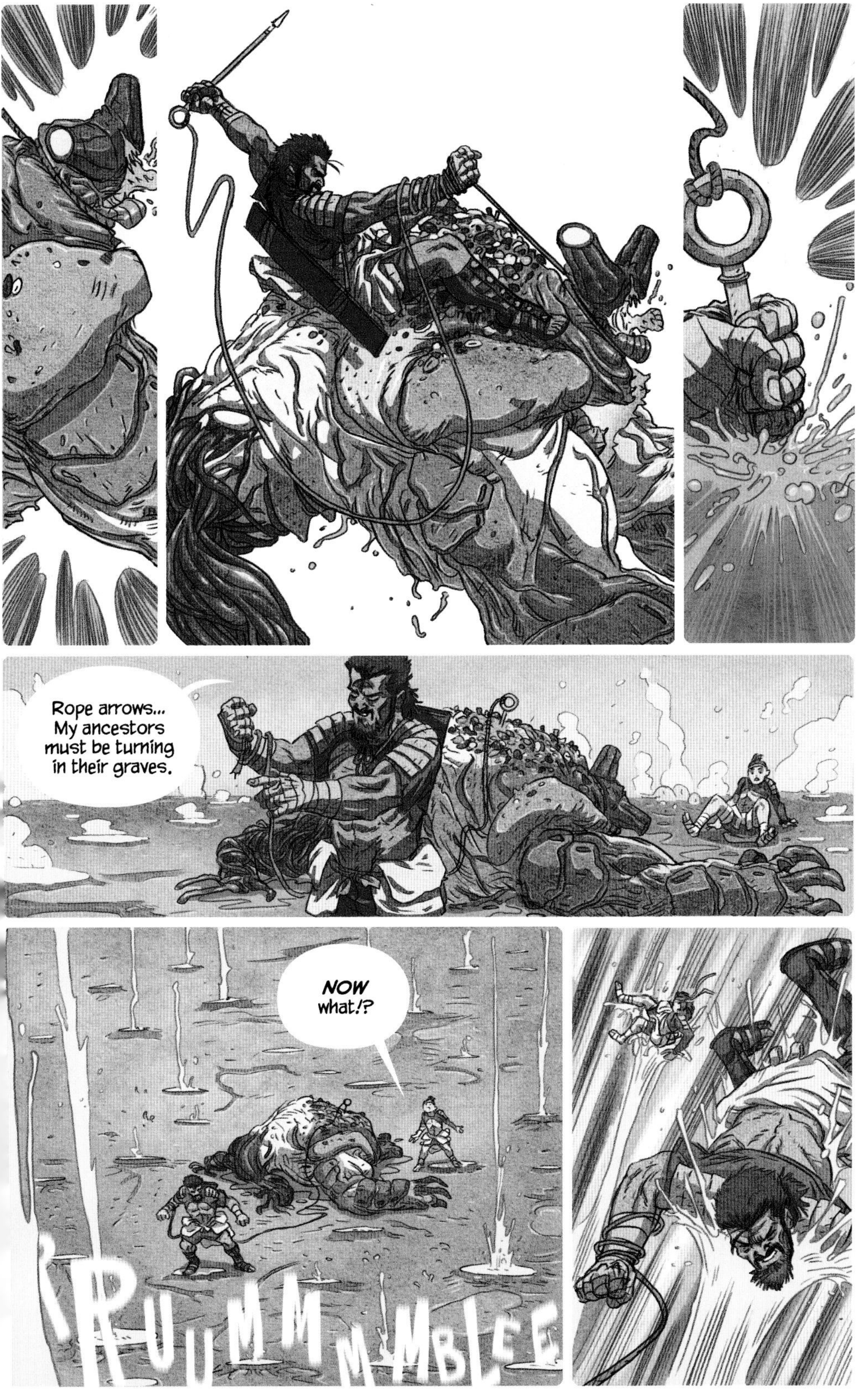

Rope arrows... My ancestors must be turning in their graves.
NOW what!?
RRUMMMMBLEE

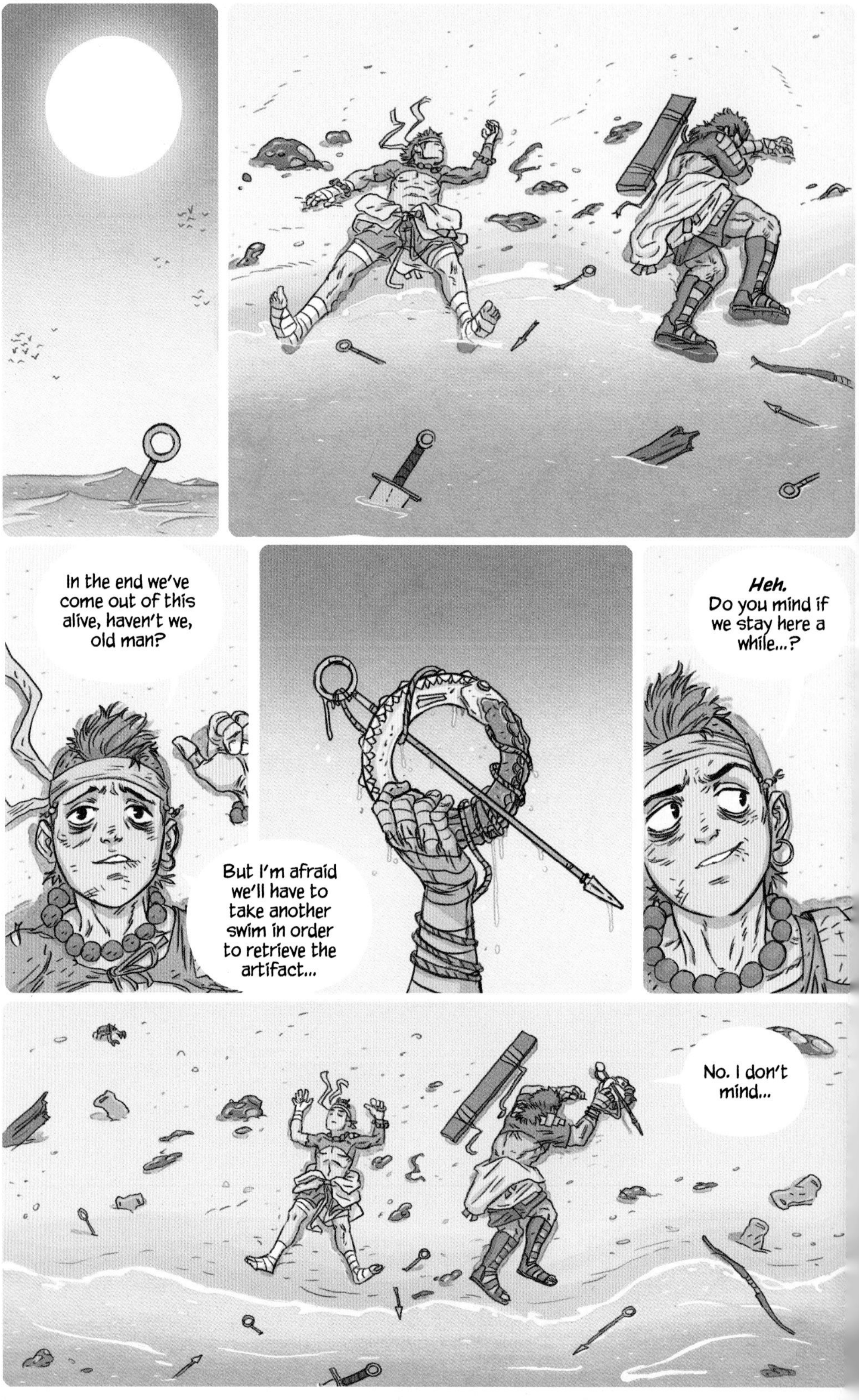
In the end we've come out of this alive, haven't we, old man?
But I'm afraid we'll have to take another swim in order to retrieve the artifact...
Heh. Do you mind if we stay here a while...?
No. I don't mind...

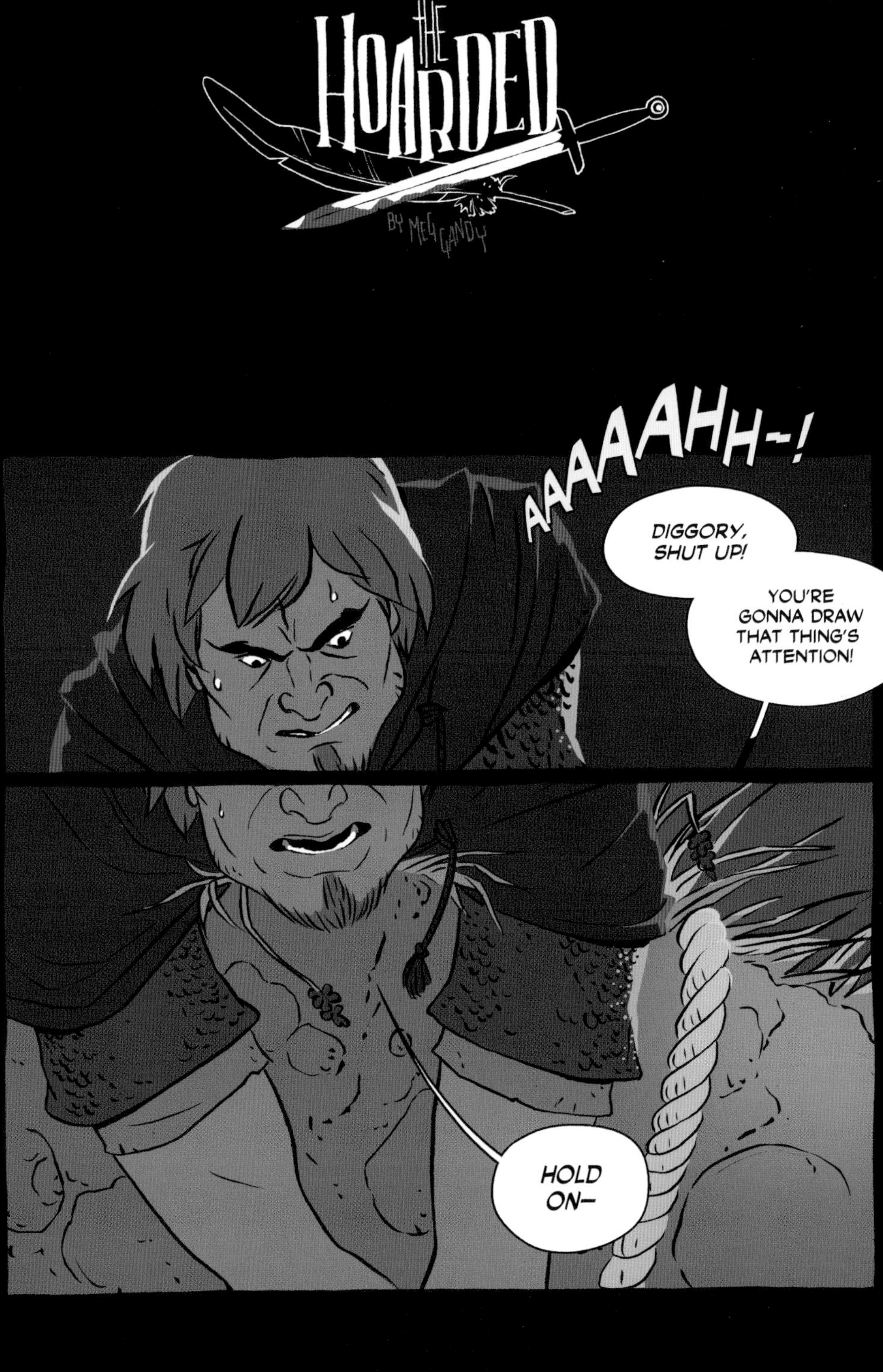
THE HOARDED
BY MEG GANDY
AAAAAHH-!
DIGGORY, SHUT UP!
YOU'RE GONNA DRAW THAT THING'S ATTENTION!
HOLD ON—

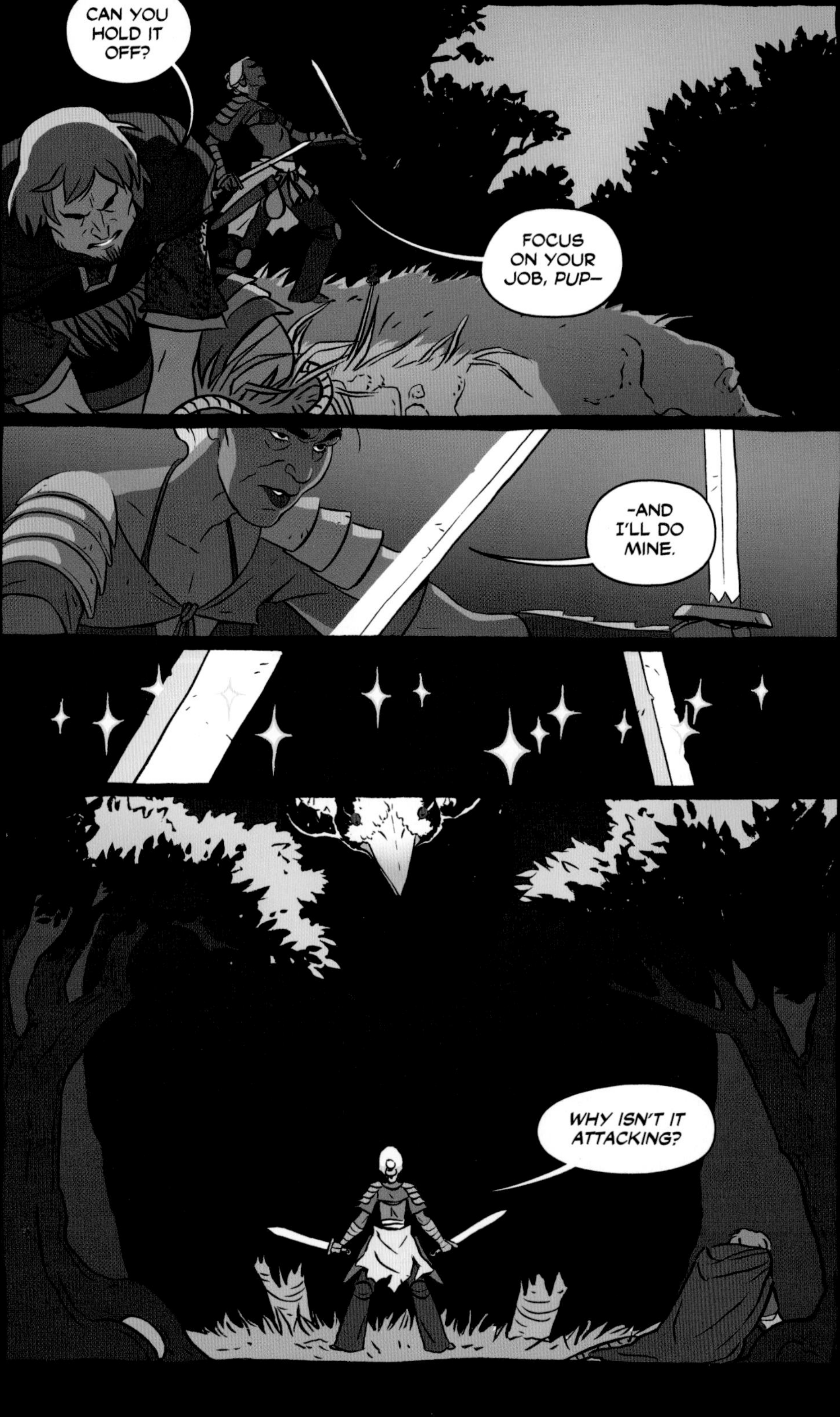
CAN YOU HOLD IT OFF?
FOCUS ON YOUR JOB, *PUP*—
-AND I'LL DO MINE.
WHY ISN'T IT ATTACKING?

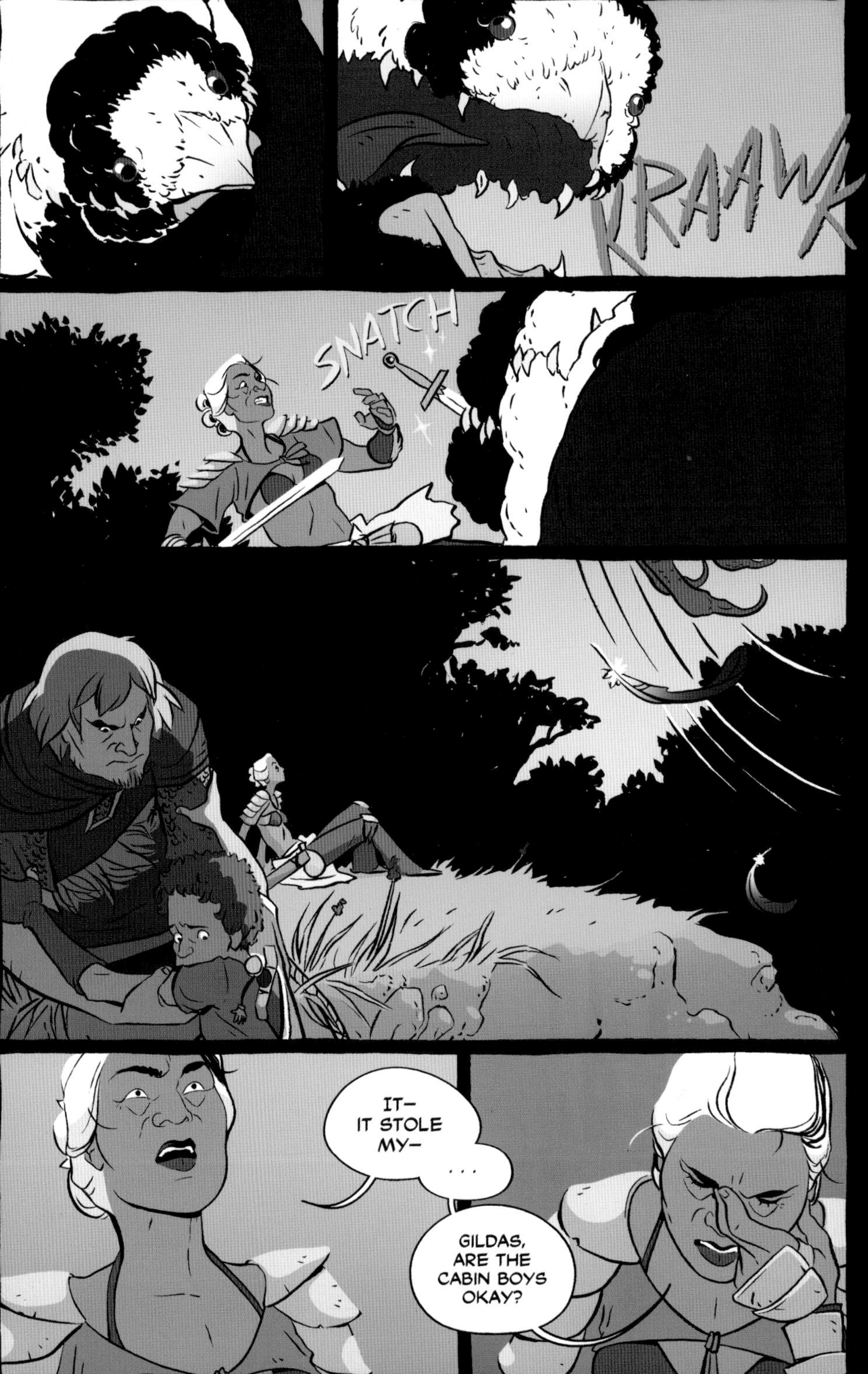
KRAAWK
SNATCH
IT—
IT STOLE
MY—
. . .
GILDAS, ARE THE CABIN BOYS OKAY?

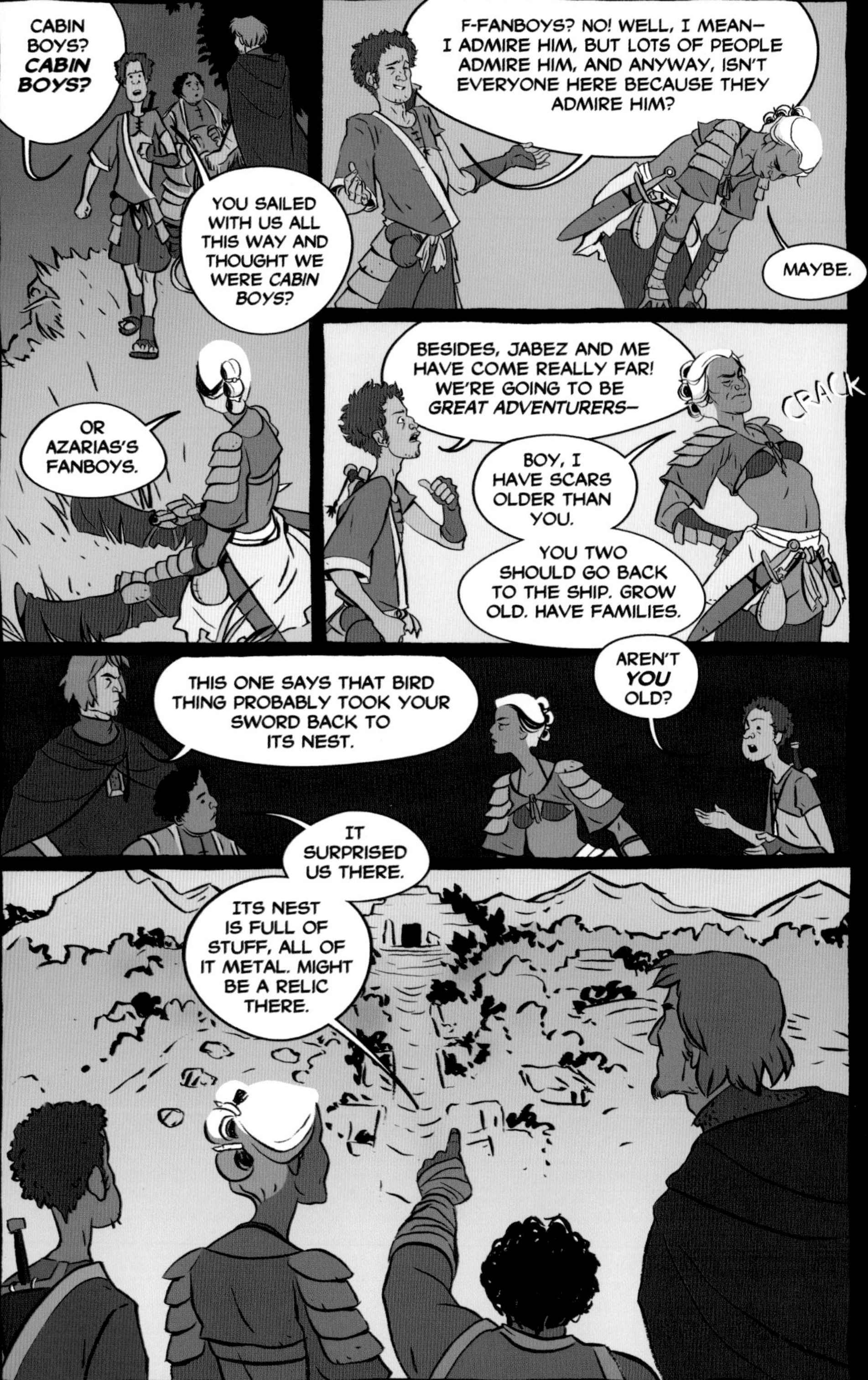
CABIN BOYS? *CABIN BOYS?*
YOU SAILED WITH US ALL THIS WAY AND THOUGHT WE WERE *CABIN BOYS?*
F-FANBOYS? NO! WELL, I MEAN— I ADMIRE HIM, BUT LOTS OF PEOPLE ADMIRE HIM, AND ANYWAY, ISN'T EVERYONE HERE BECAUSE THEY ADMIRE HIM?
MAYBE.
OR AZARIAS'S FANBOYS.
BESIDES, JABEZ AND ME HAVE COME REALLY FAR! WE'RE GOING TO BE *GREAT ADVENTURERS*—
CRACK
BOY, I HAVE SCARS OLDER THAN YOU.
YOU TWO SHOULD GO BACK TO THE SHIP. GROW OLD. HAVE FAMILIES.
AREN'T *YOU* OLD?
THIS ONE SAYS THAT BIRD THING PROBABLY TOOK YOUR SWORD BACK TO ITS NEST.
IT SURPRISED US THERE.
ITS NEST IS FULL OF STUFF, ALL OF IT METAL. MIGHT BE A RELIC THERE.

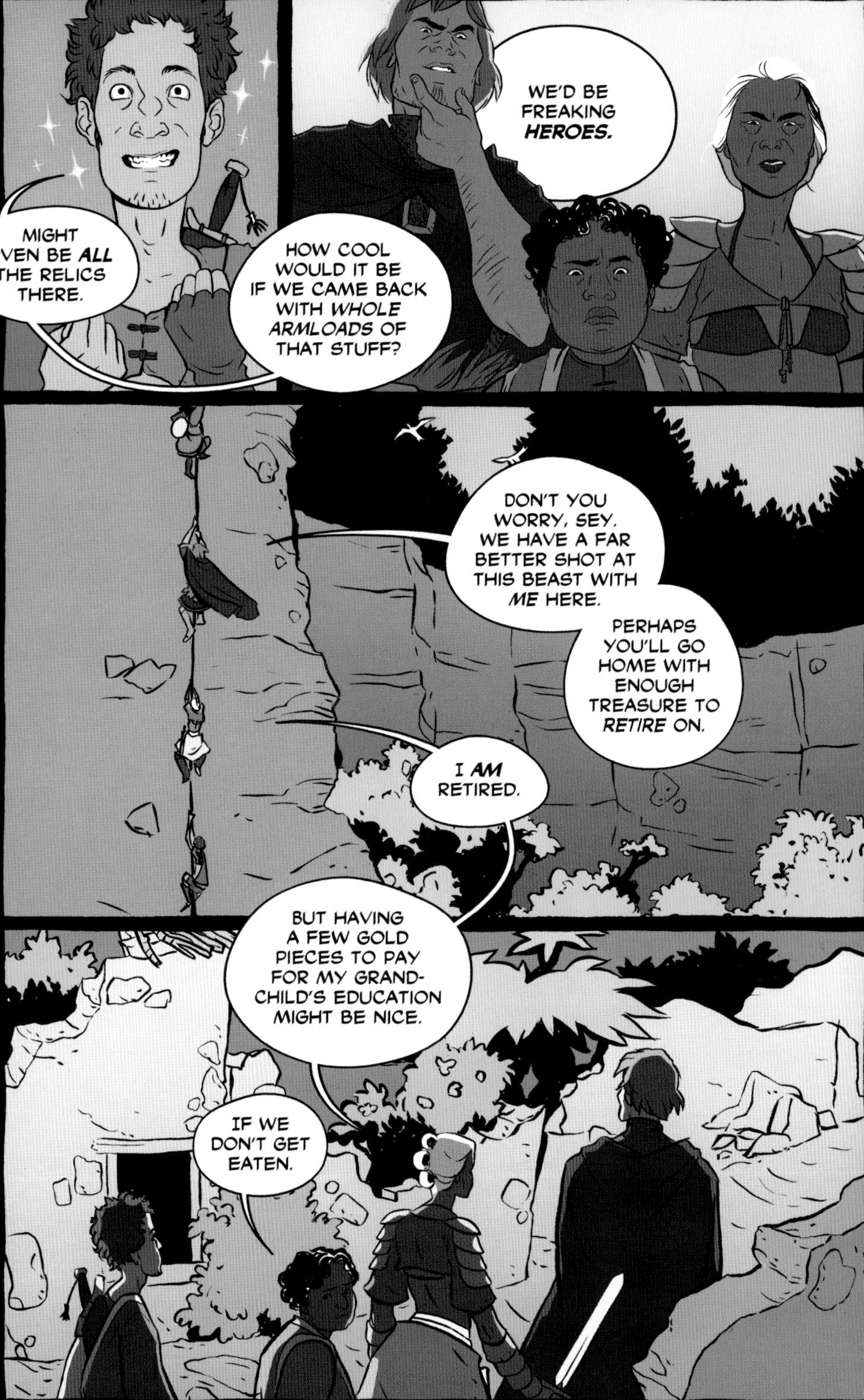
MIGHT EVEN BE *ALL* THE RELICS THERE.
HOW COOL WOULD IT BE IF WE CAME BACK WITH *WHOLE ARMLOADS* OF THAT STUFF?
WE'D BE FREAKING ***HEROES.***
DON'T YOU WORRY, SEY. WE HAVE A FAR BETTER SHOT AT THIS BEAST WITH *ME* HERE.
PERHAPS YOU'LL GO HOME WITH ENOUGH TREASURE TO *RETIRE* ON.
I ***AM*** RETIRED.
BUT HAVING A FEW GOLD PIECES TO PAY FOR MY GRAND-CHILD'S EDUCATION MIGHT BE NICE.
IF WE DON'T GET EATEN.

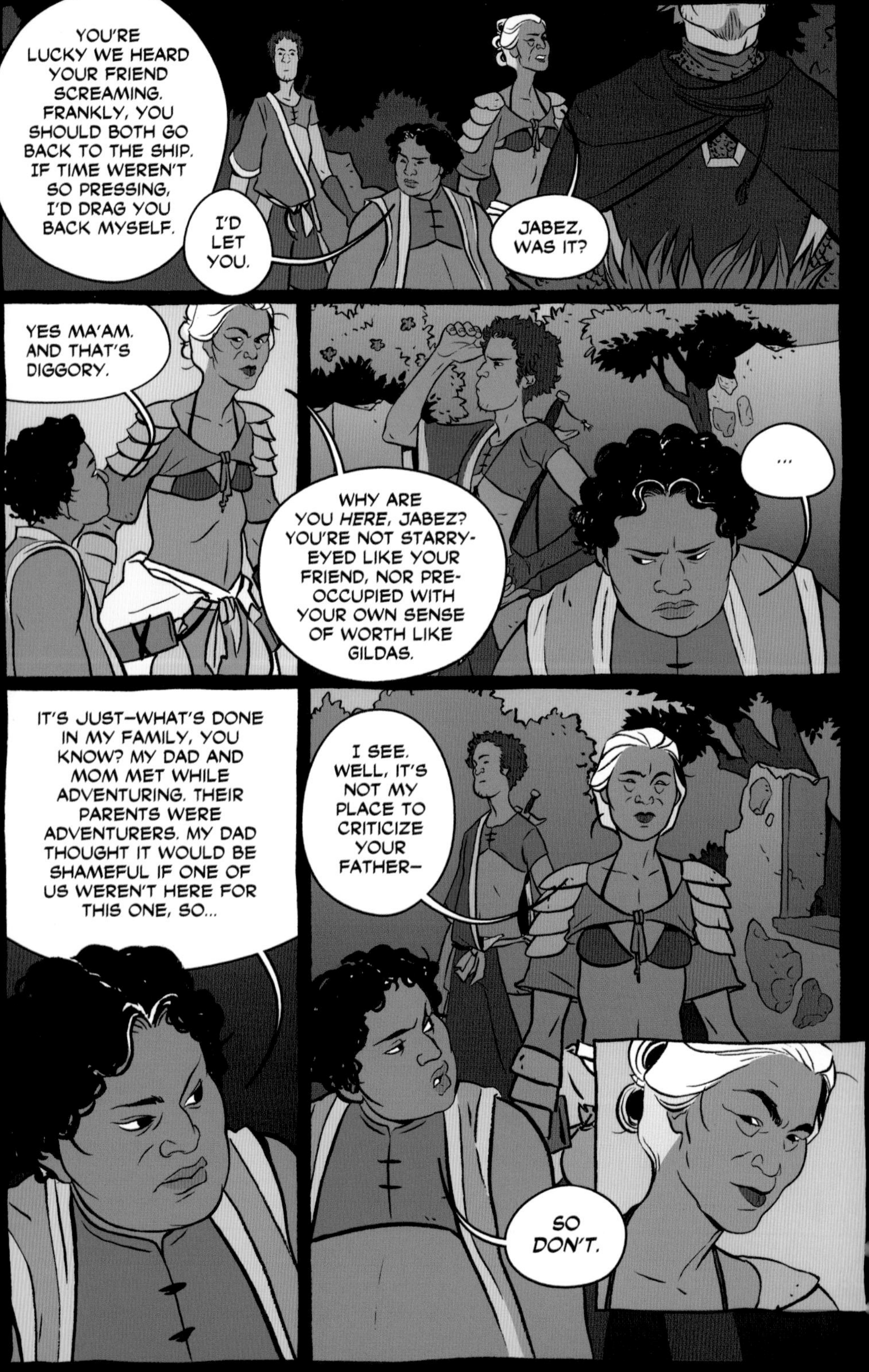

YOU'RE LUCKY WE HEARD YOUR FRIEND SCREAMING. FRANKLY, YOU SHOULD BOTH GO BACK TO THE SHIP. IF TIME WEREN'T SO PRESSING, I'D DRAG YOU BACK MYSELF.
I'D LET YOU.
JABEZ, WAS IT?
YES MA'AM. AND THAT'S DIGGORY.
WHY ARE YOU *HERE*, JABEZ? YOU'RE NOT STARRY-EYED LIKE YOUR FRIEND, NOR PRE-OCCUPIED WITH YOUR OWN SENSE OF WORTH LIKE GILDAS.
...
IT'S JUST—WHAT'S DONE IN MY FAMILY, YOU KNOW? MY DAD AND MOM MET WHILE ADVENTURING. THEIR PARENTS WERE ADVENTURERS. MY DAD THOUGHT IT WOULD BE SHAMEFUL IF ONE OF US WEREN'T HERE FOR THIS ONE, SO...
I SEE. WELL, IT'S NOT MY PLACE TO CRITICIZE YOUR FATHER—
SO *DON'T*.

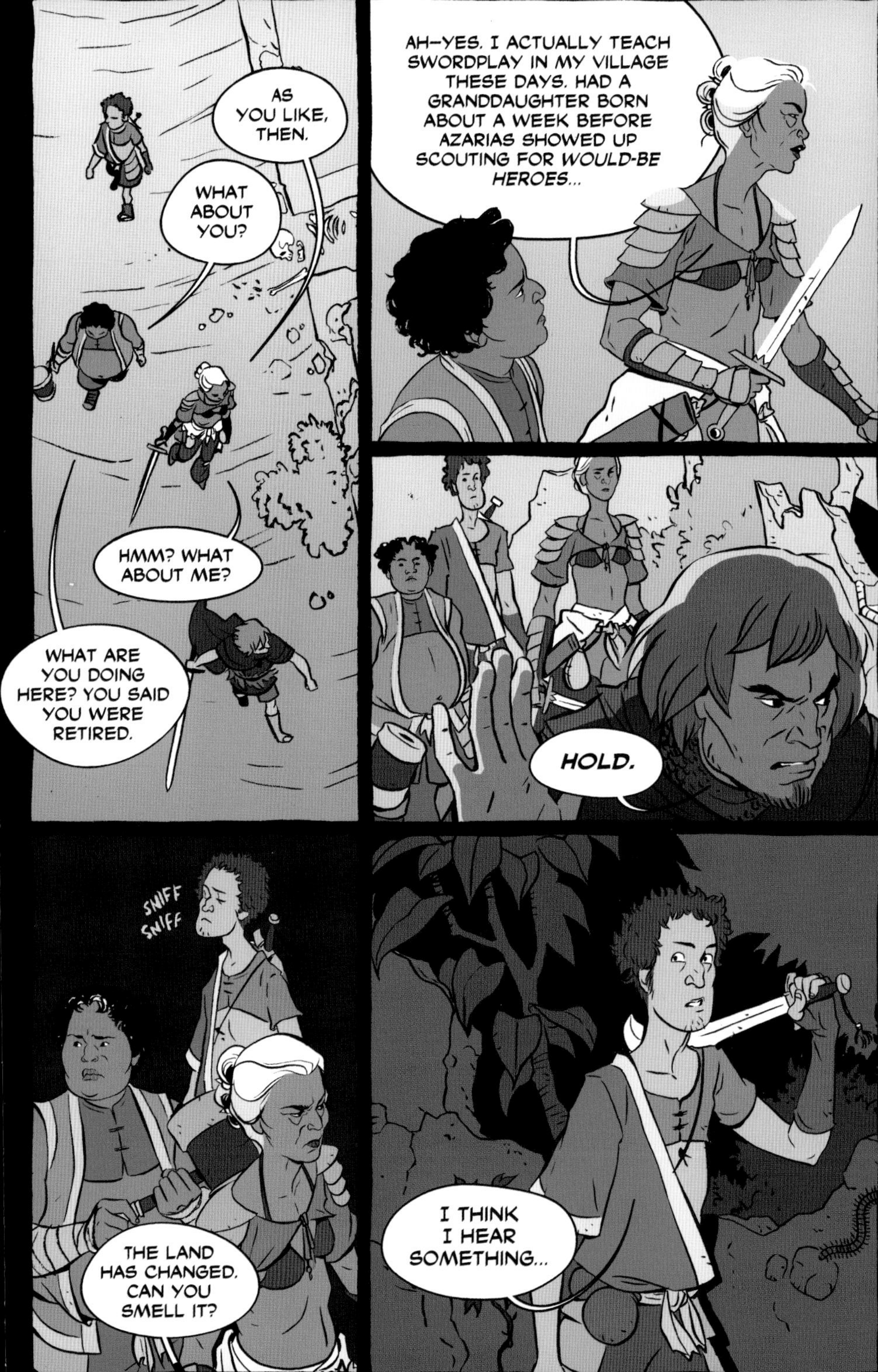
AS YOU LIKE, THEN.
WHAT ABOUT YOU?
HMM? WHAT ABOUT ME?
WHAT ARE YOU DOING HERE? YOU SAID YOU WERE RETIRED.
AH—YES. I ACTUALLY TEACH SWORDPLAY IN MY VILLAGE THESE DAYS. HAD A GRANDDAUGHTER BORN ABOUT A WEEK BEFORE AZARIAS SHOWED UP SCOUTING FOR *WOULD-BE HEROES*...
HOLD.
SNIFF SNIFF
THE LAND HAS CHANGED. CAN YOU SMELL IT?
I THINK I HEAR SOMETHING...

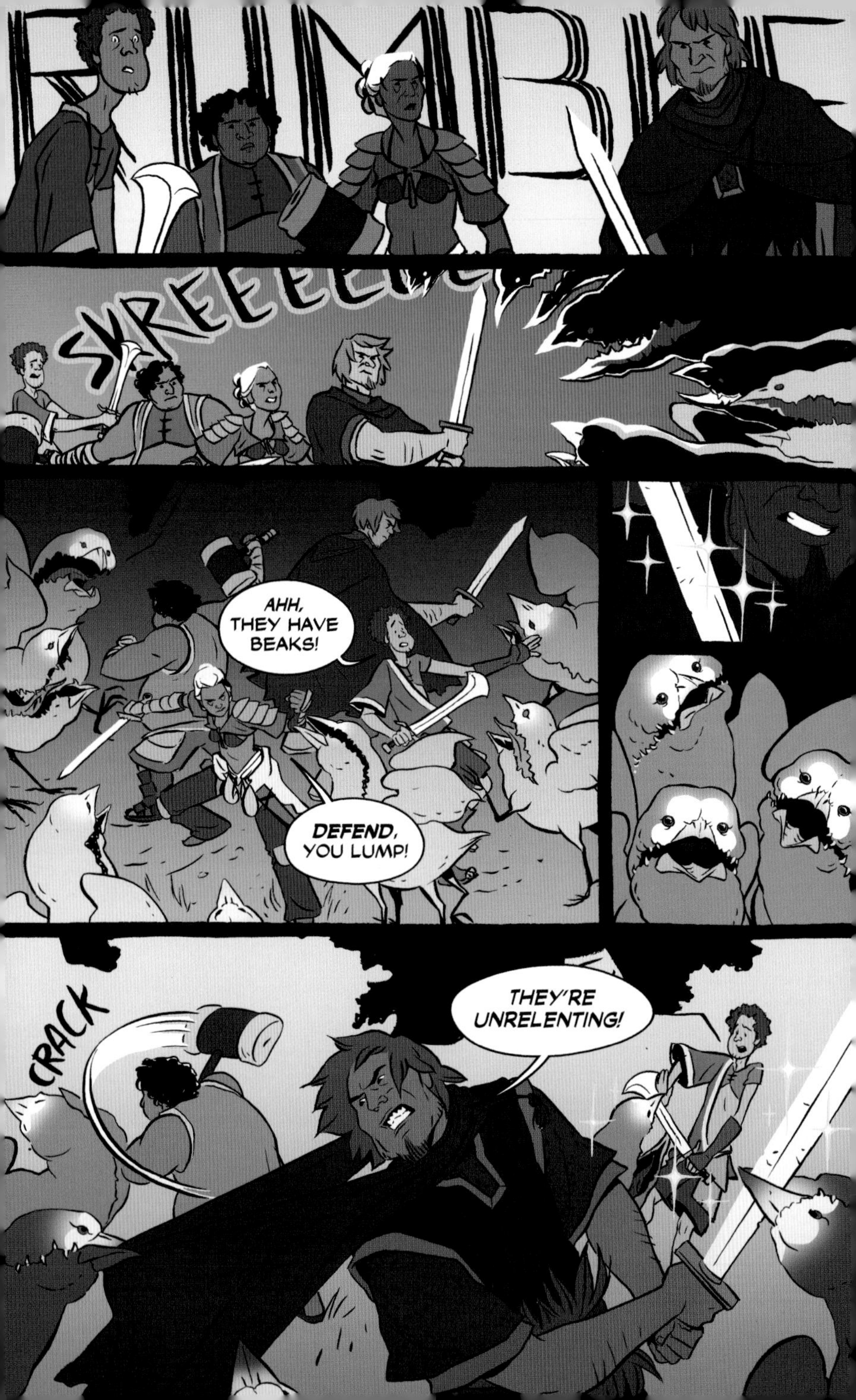
AHH, THEY HAVE BEAKS!
DEFEND, YOU LUMP!
CRACK
THEY'RE UNRELENTING!

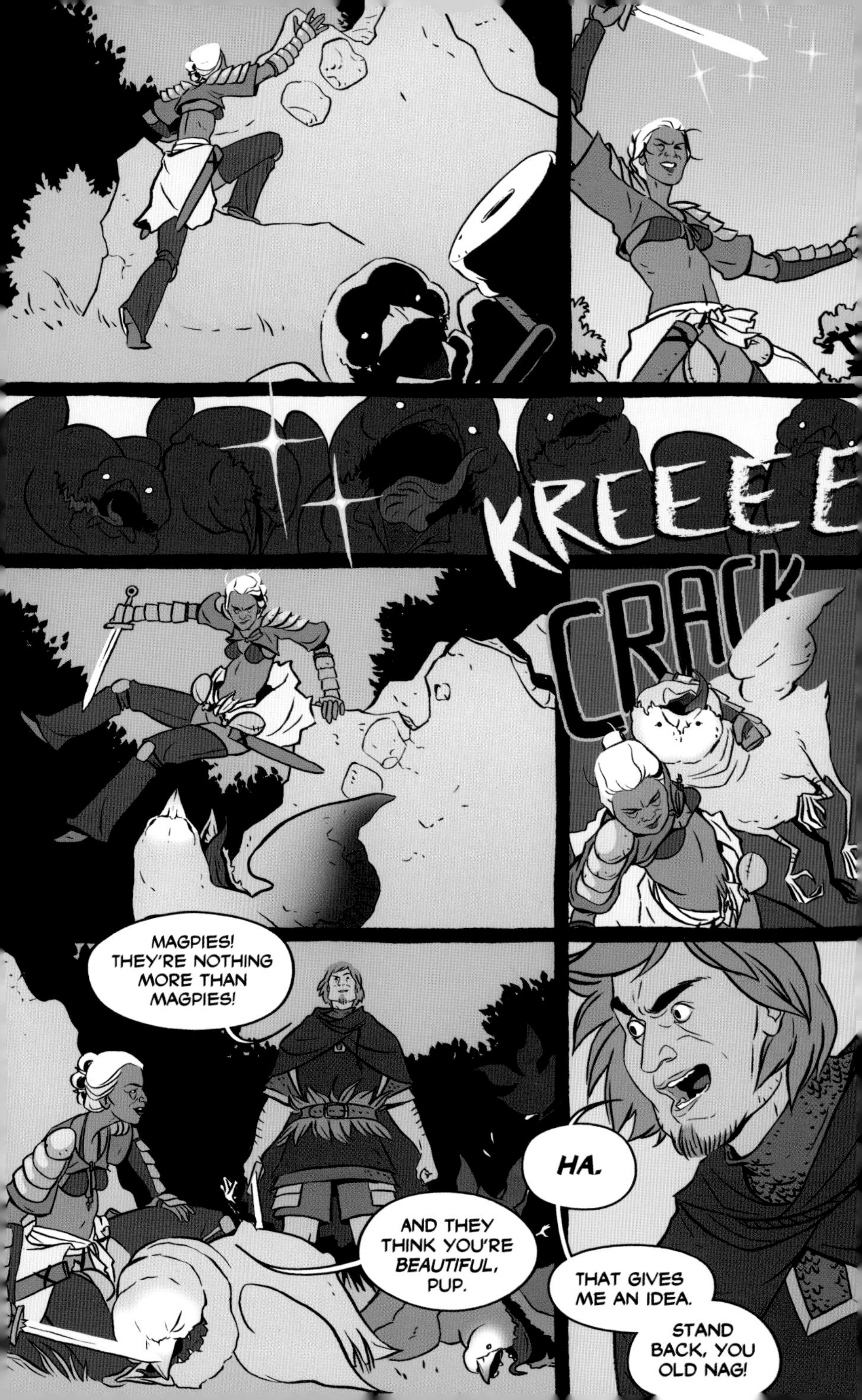
KREEEE
CRACK
MAGPIES! THEY'RE NOTHING MORE THAN MAGPIES!
AND THEY THINK YOU'RE *BEAUTIFUL*, PUP.
HA.
THAT GIVES ME AN IDEA.
STAND BACK, YOU OLD NAG!

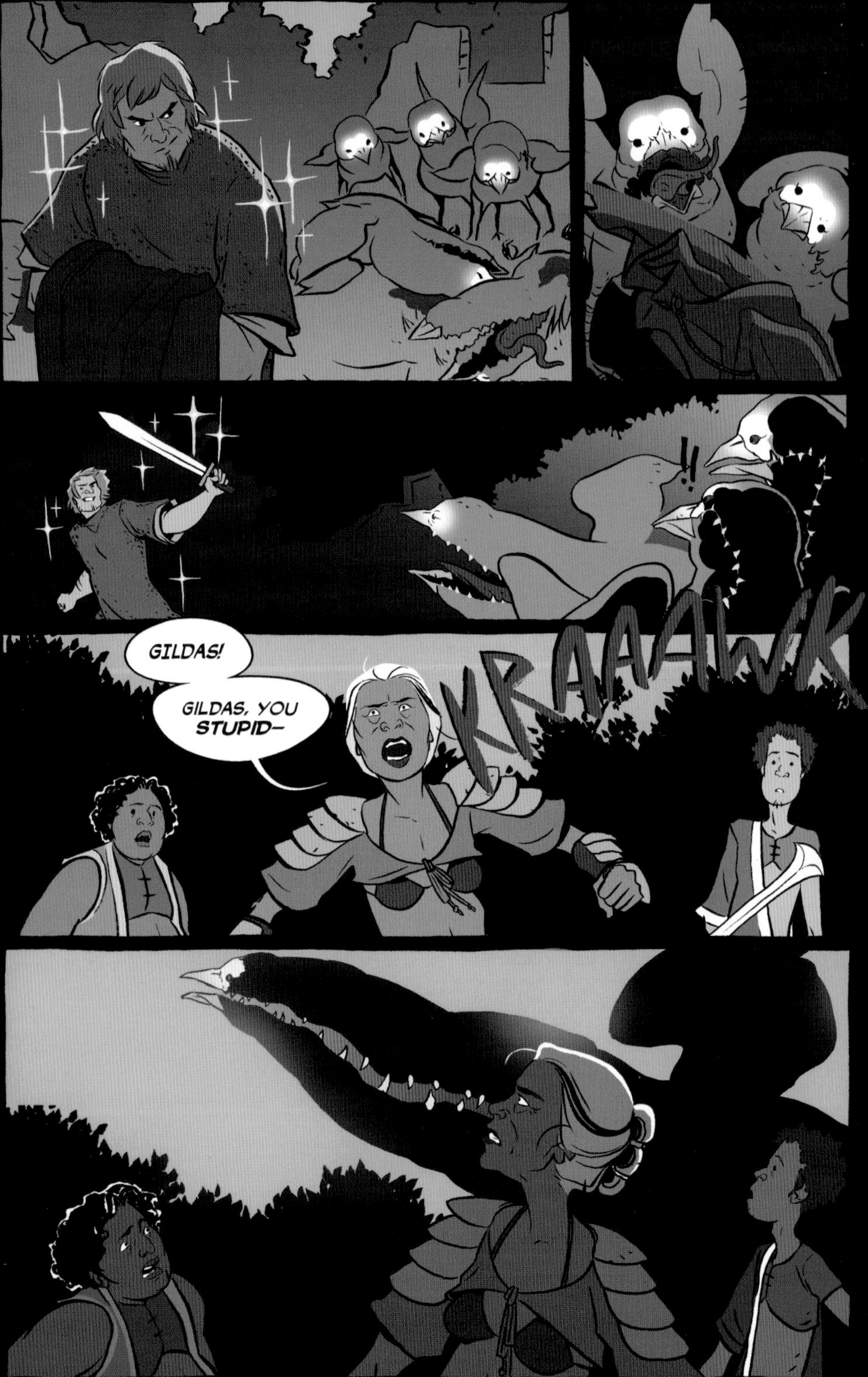
!!
KRAAAWK
GILDAS!
GILDAS, YOU STUPID—

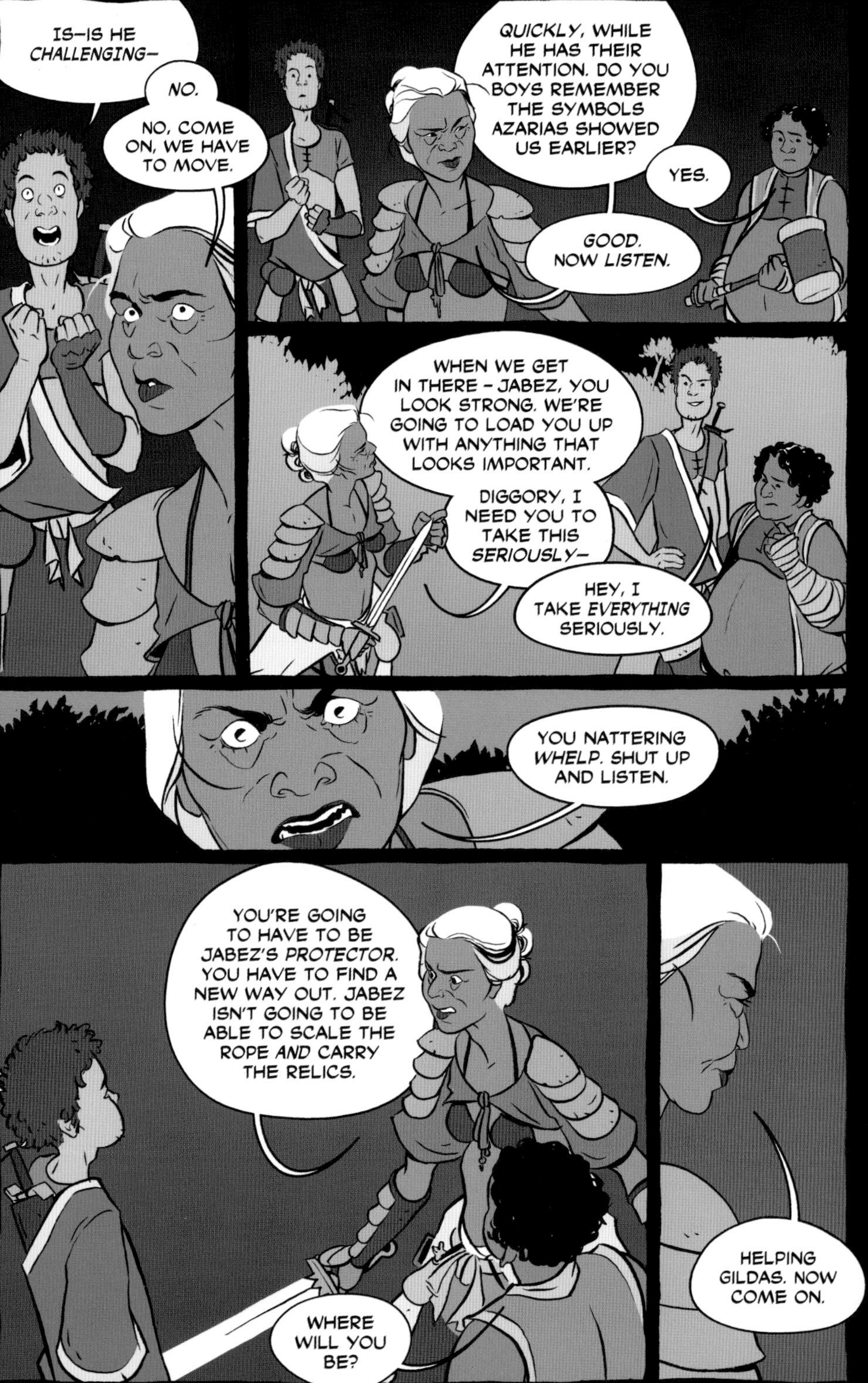
IS—IS HE CHALLENGING—
NO.
NO, COME ON, WE HAVE TO MOVE.
QUICKLY, WHILE HE HAS THEIR ATTENTION. DO YOU BOYS REMEMBER THE SYMBOLS AZARIAS SHOWED US EARLIER?
YES.
GOOD. NOW LISTEN.
WHEN WE GET IN THERE – JABEZ, YOU LOOK STRONG. WE'RE GOING TO LOAD YOU UP WITH ANYTHING THAT LOOKS IMPORTANT.
DIGGORY, I NEED YOU TO TAKE THIS SERIOUSLY—
HEY, I TAKE EVERYTHING SERIOUSLY.
YOU NATTERING WHELP. SHUT UP AND LISTEN.
YOU'RE GOING TO HAVE TO BE JABEZ'S PROTECTOR. YOU HAVE TO FIND A NEW WAY OUT. JABEZ ISN'T GOING TO BE ABLE TO SCALE THE ROPE AND CARRY THE RELICS.
WHERE WILL YOU BE?
HELPING GILDAS. NOW COME ON.

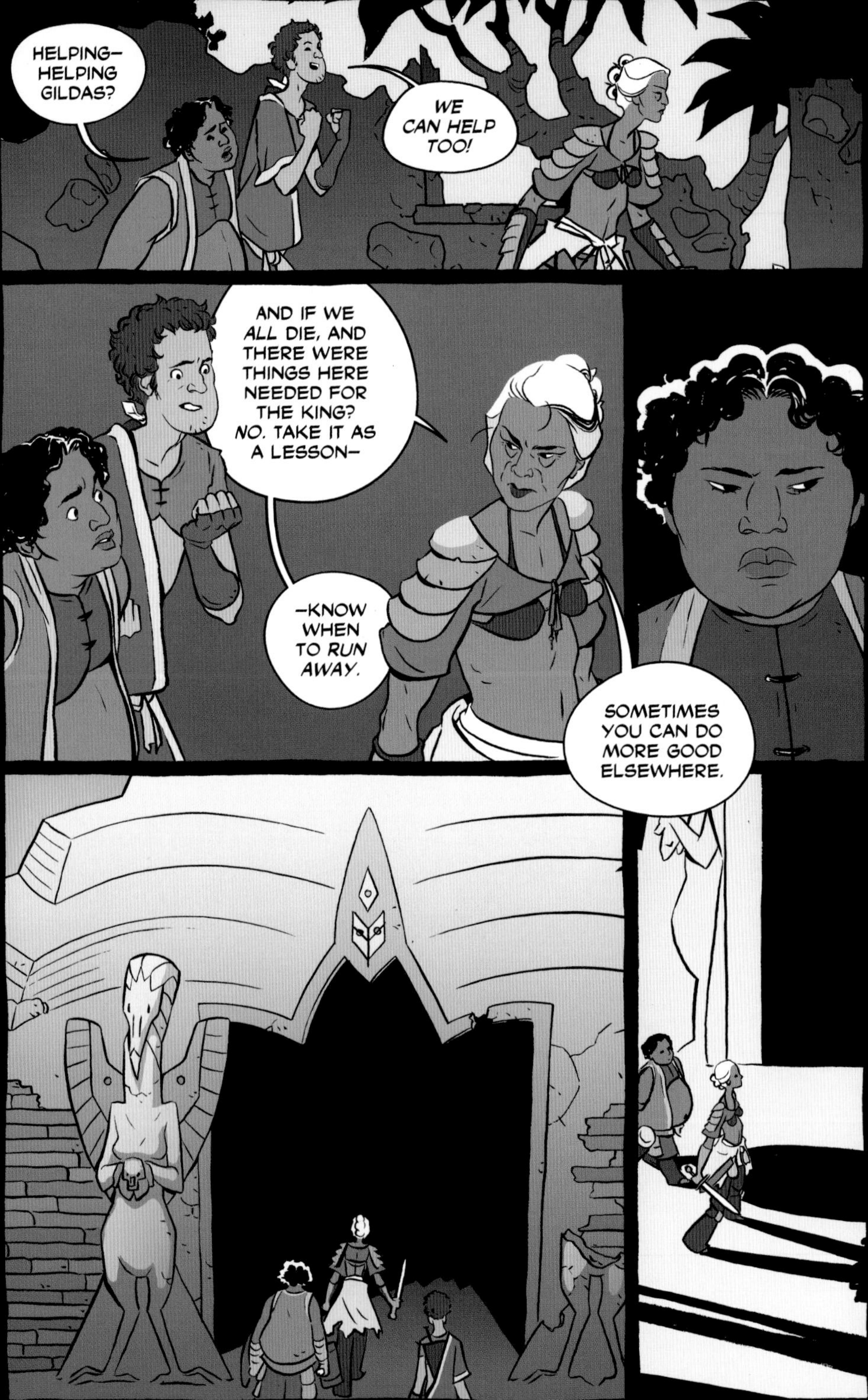
HELPING— HELPING GILDAS?
WE CAN HELP TOO!
AND IF WE ALL DIE, AND THERE WERE THINGS HERE NEEDED FOR THE KING? NO. TAKE IT AS A LESSON—
—KNOW WHEN TO RUN AWAY.
SOMETIMES YOU CAN DO MORE GOOD ELSEWHERE.

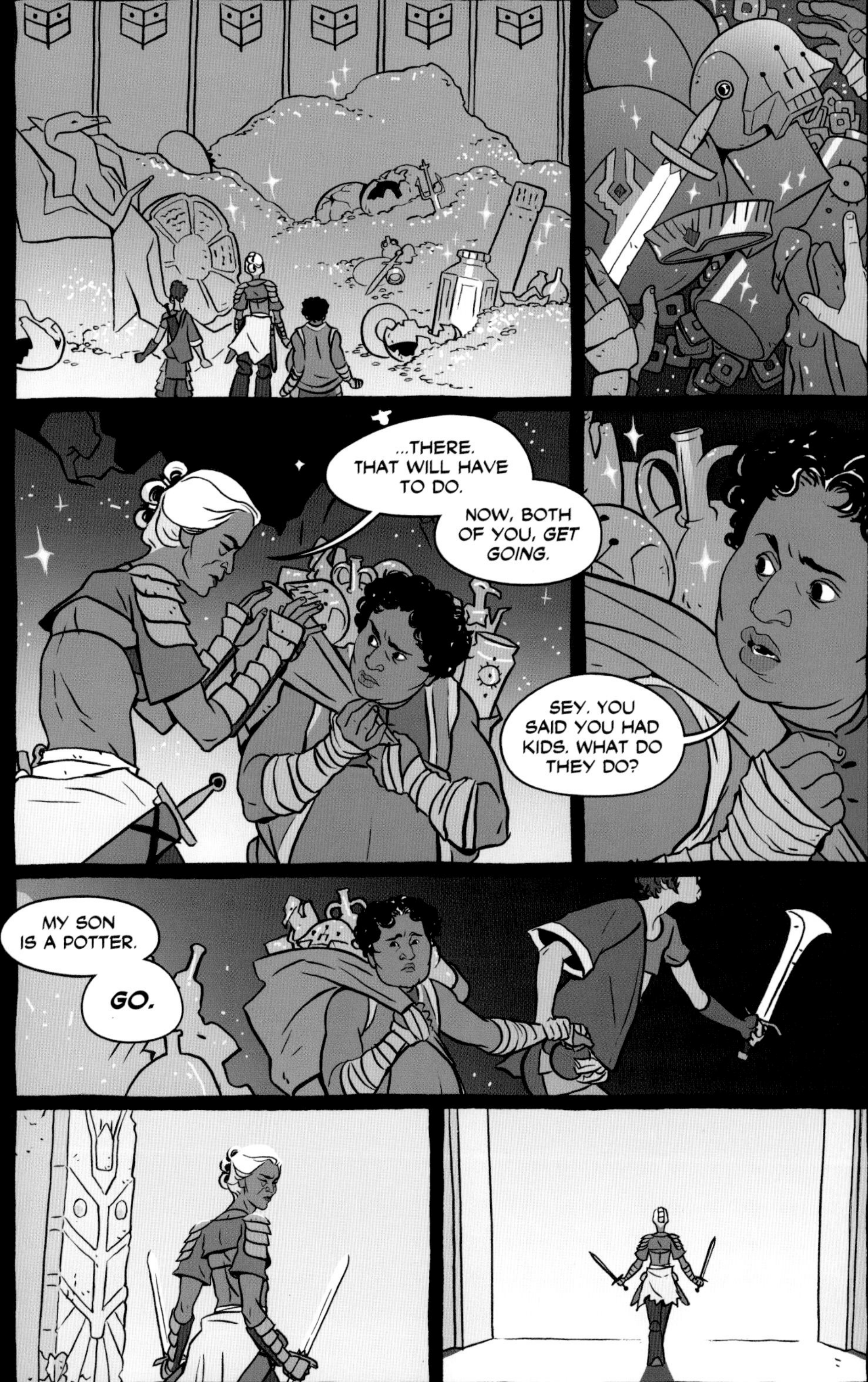
...THERE. THAT WILL HAVE TO DO.
NOW, BOTH OF YOU, *GET GOING.*
SEY. YOU SAID YOU HAD KIDS. WHAT DO THEY DO?
MY SON IS A POTTER.
GO.

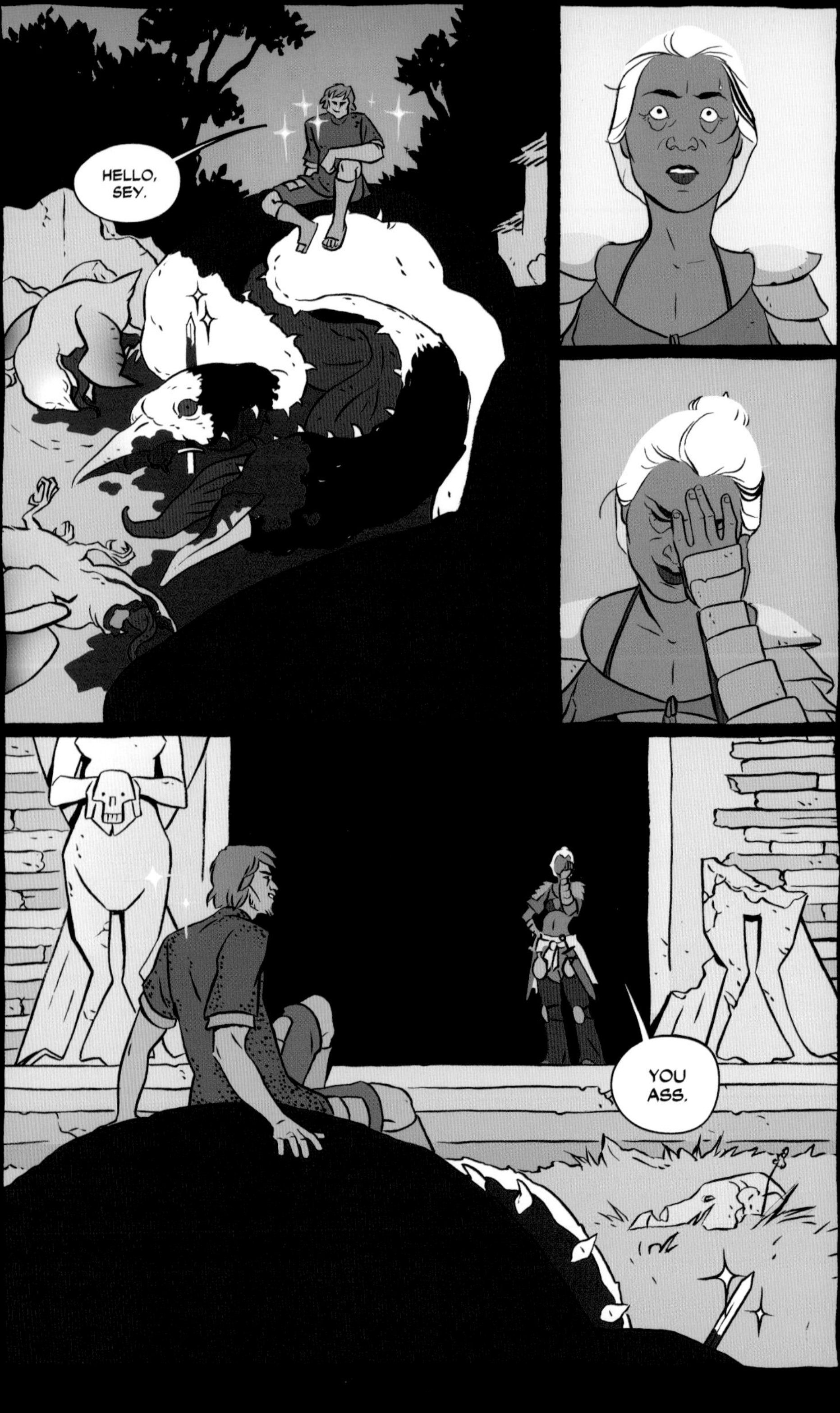
HELLO, SEY.
YOU ASS.

BEASTS AND DEMONS

BY DEVIN KRAFT

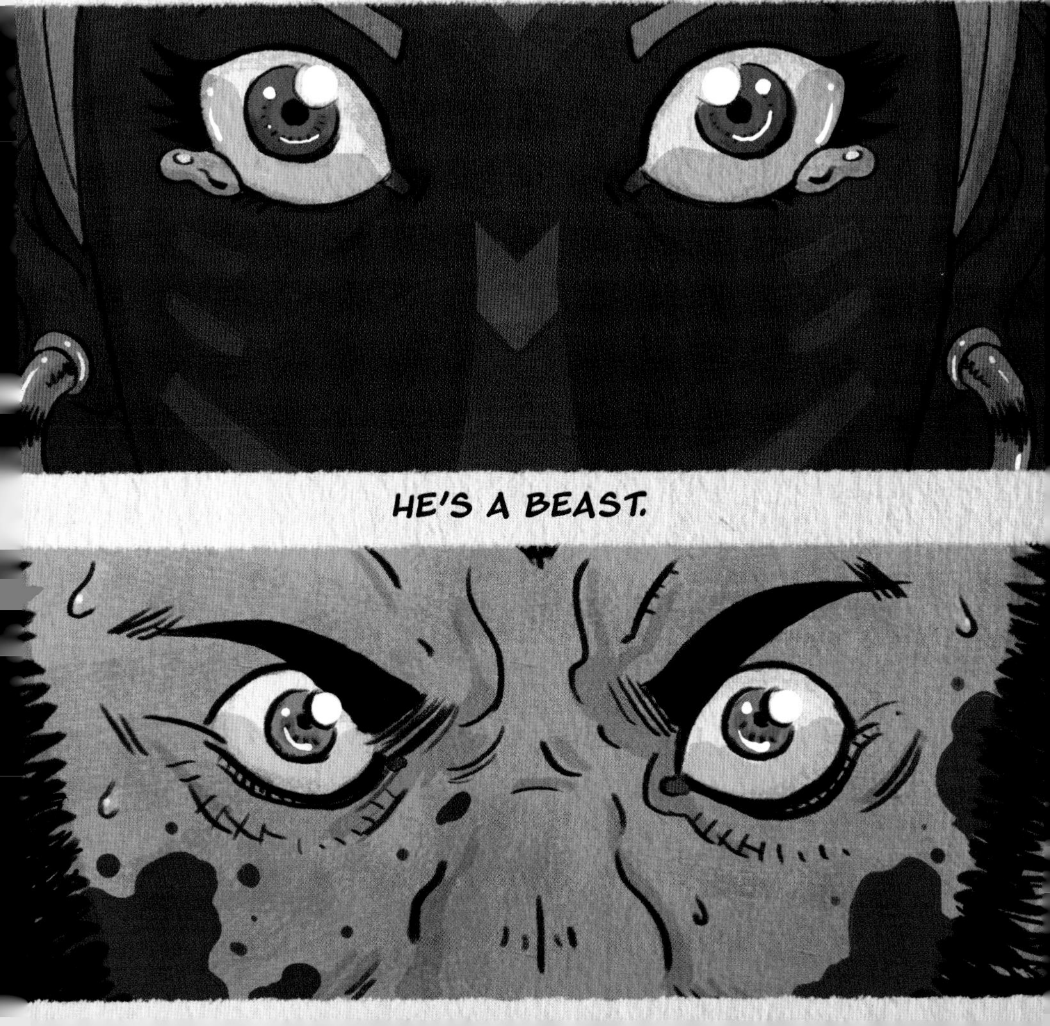
HE'S A BEAST.

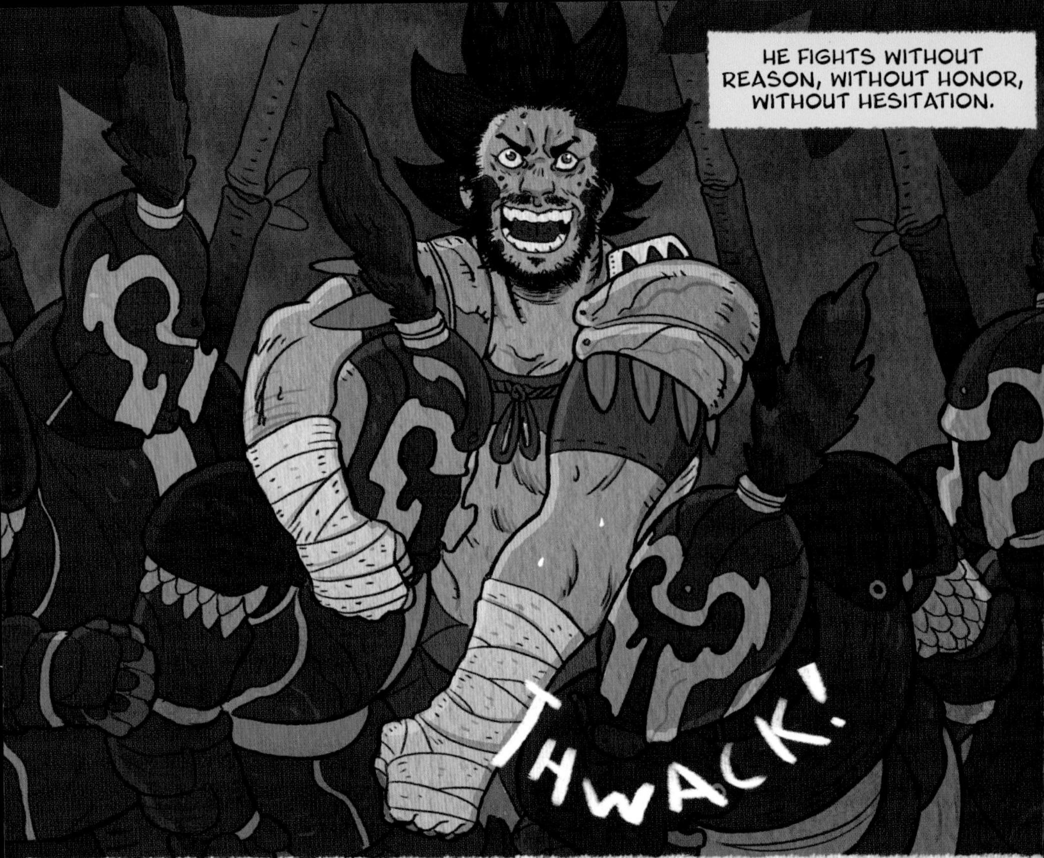
HE FIGHTS WITHOUT REASON, WITHOUT HONOR, WITHOUT HESITATION.
THWACK!

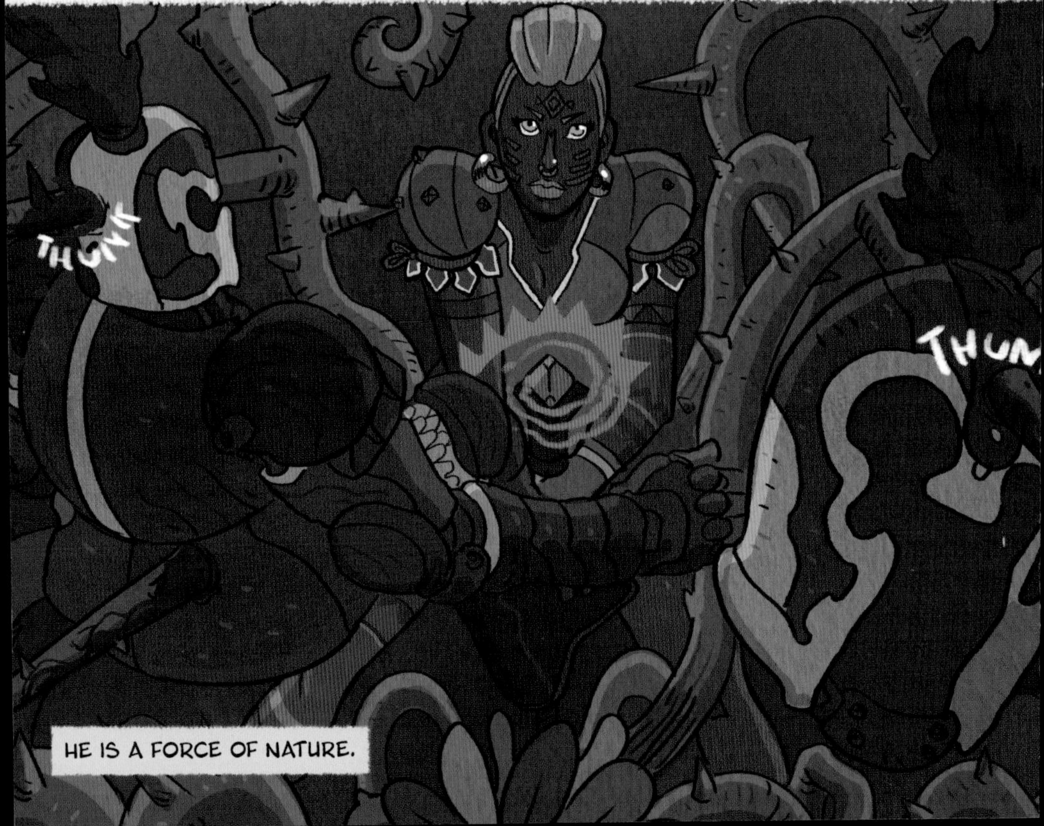
HE IS A FORCE OF NATURE.

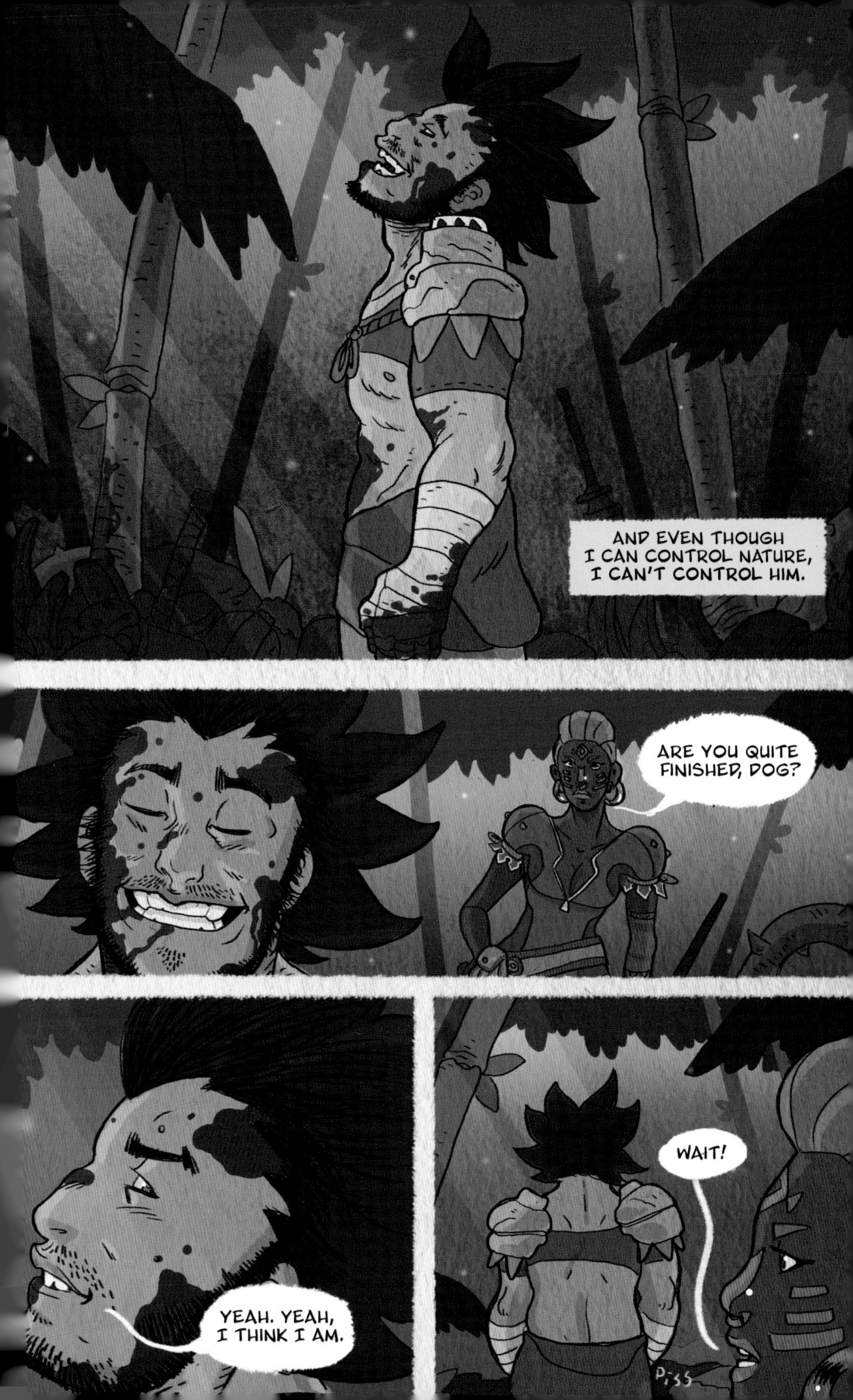
AND EVEN THOUGH I CAN CONTROL NATURE, I CAN'T CONTROL HIM.
ARE YOU QUITE FINISHED, DOG?
YEAH. YEAH, I THINK I AM.
WAIT!

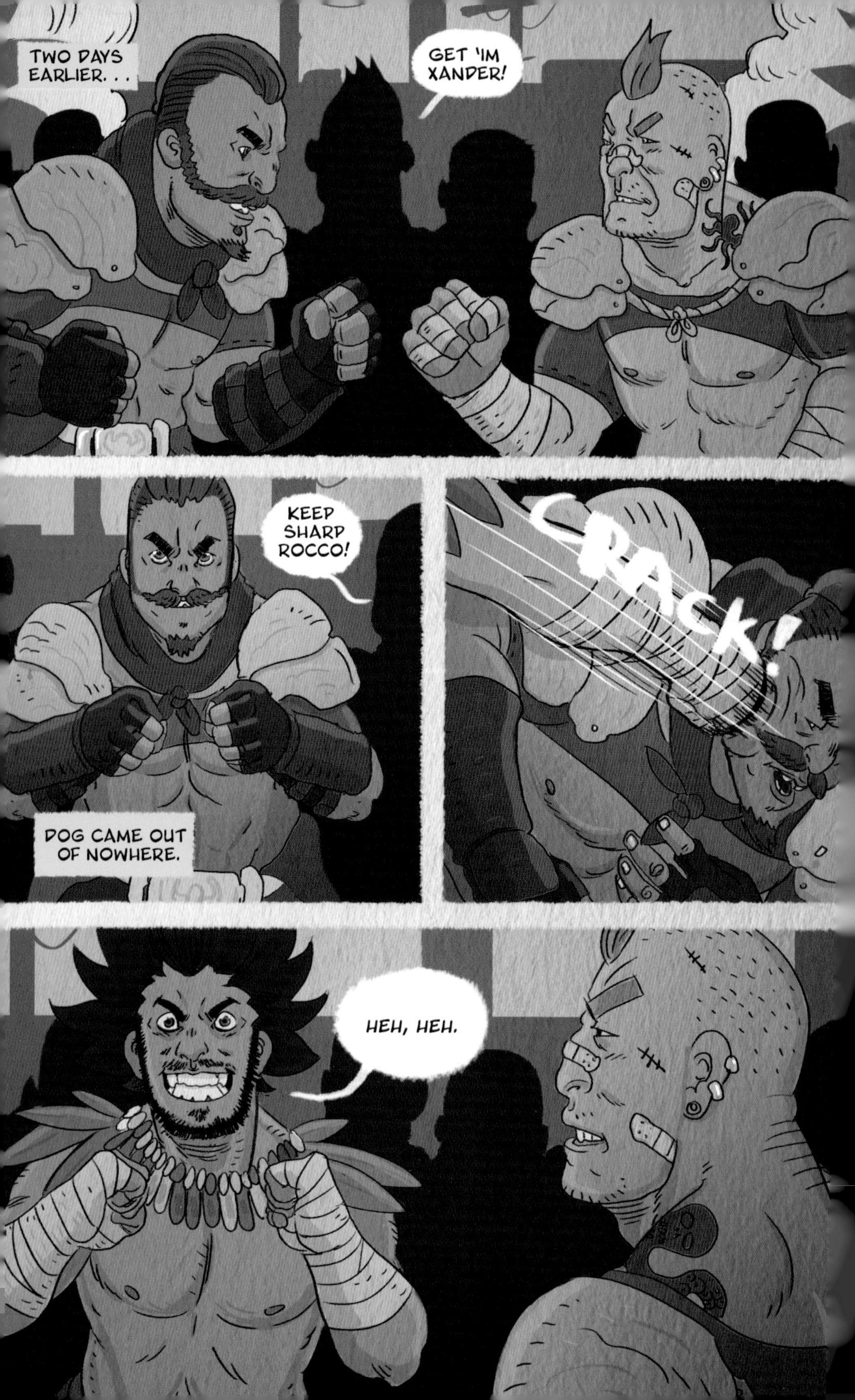
TWO DAYS EARLIER. . .
GET 'IM XANDER!
KEEP SHARP ROCCO!
DOG CAME OUT OF NOWHERE.
CRACK!
HEH, HEH.

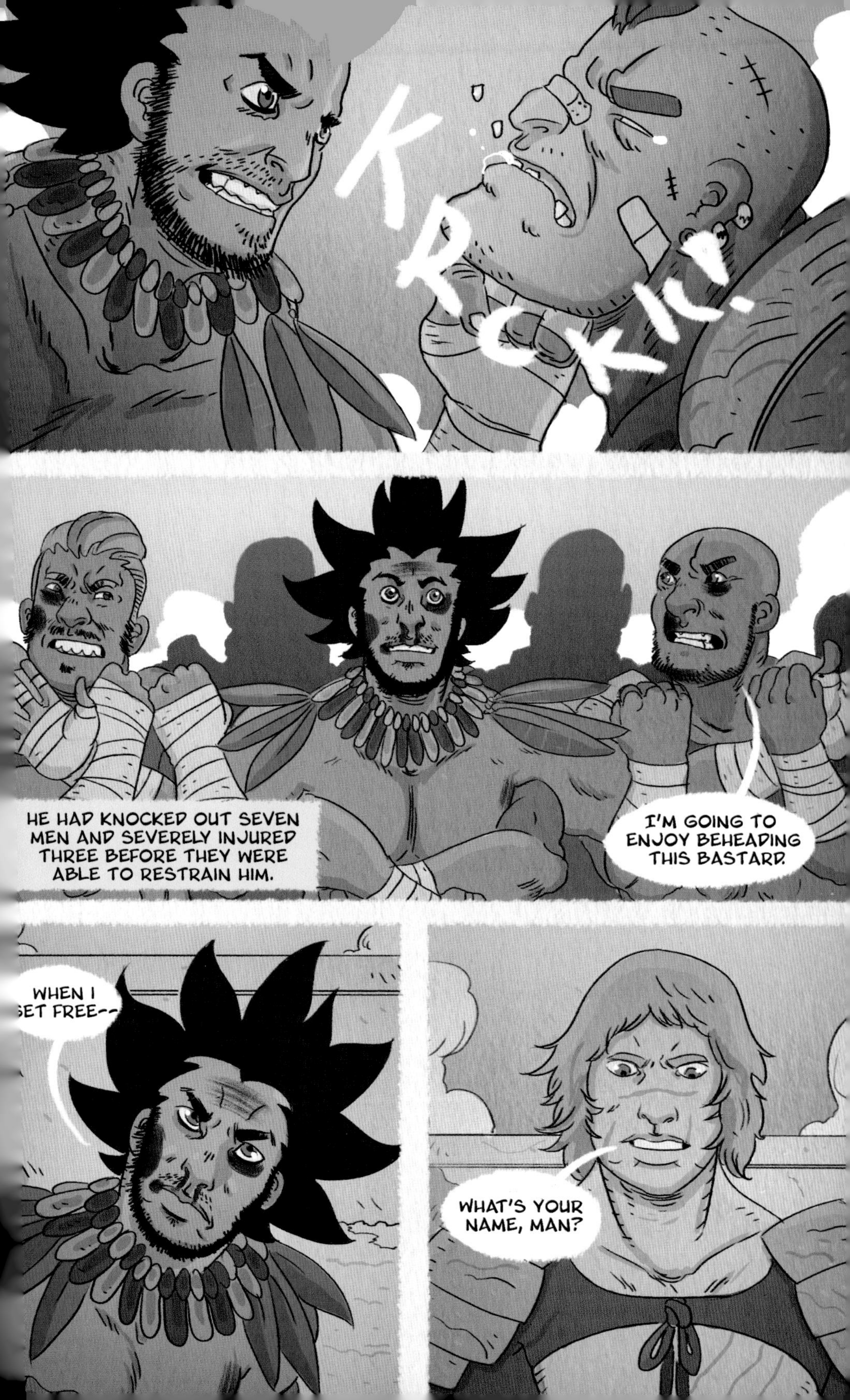
KRCK!!
HE HAD KNOCKED OUT SEVEN MEN AND SEVERELY INJURED THREE BEFORE THEY WERE ABLE TO RESTRAIN HIM.
I'M GOING TO ENJOY BEHEADING THIS BASTARD.
WHEN I GET FREE--
WHAT'S YOUR NAME, MAN?

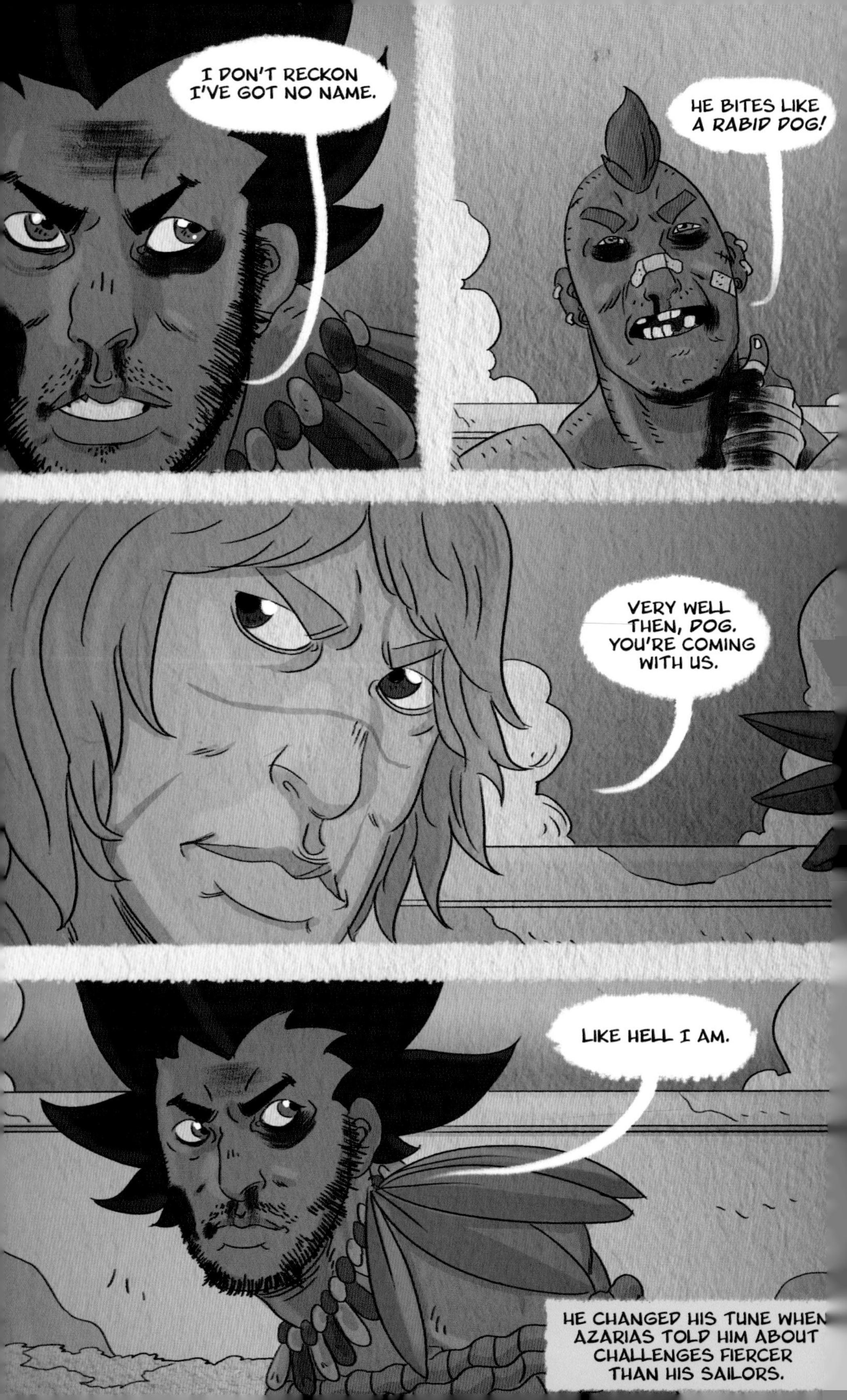
I DON'T RECKON I'VE GOT NO NAME.
HE BITES LIKE A RABID DOG!
VERY WELL THEN, DOG. YOU'RE COMING WITH US.
LIKE HELL I AM.
HE CHANGED HIS TUNE WHEN AZARIAS TOLD HIM ABOUT CHALLENGES FIERCER THAN HIS SAILORS.

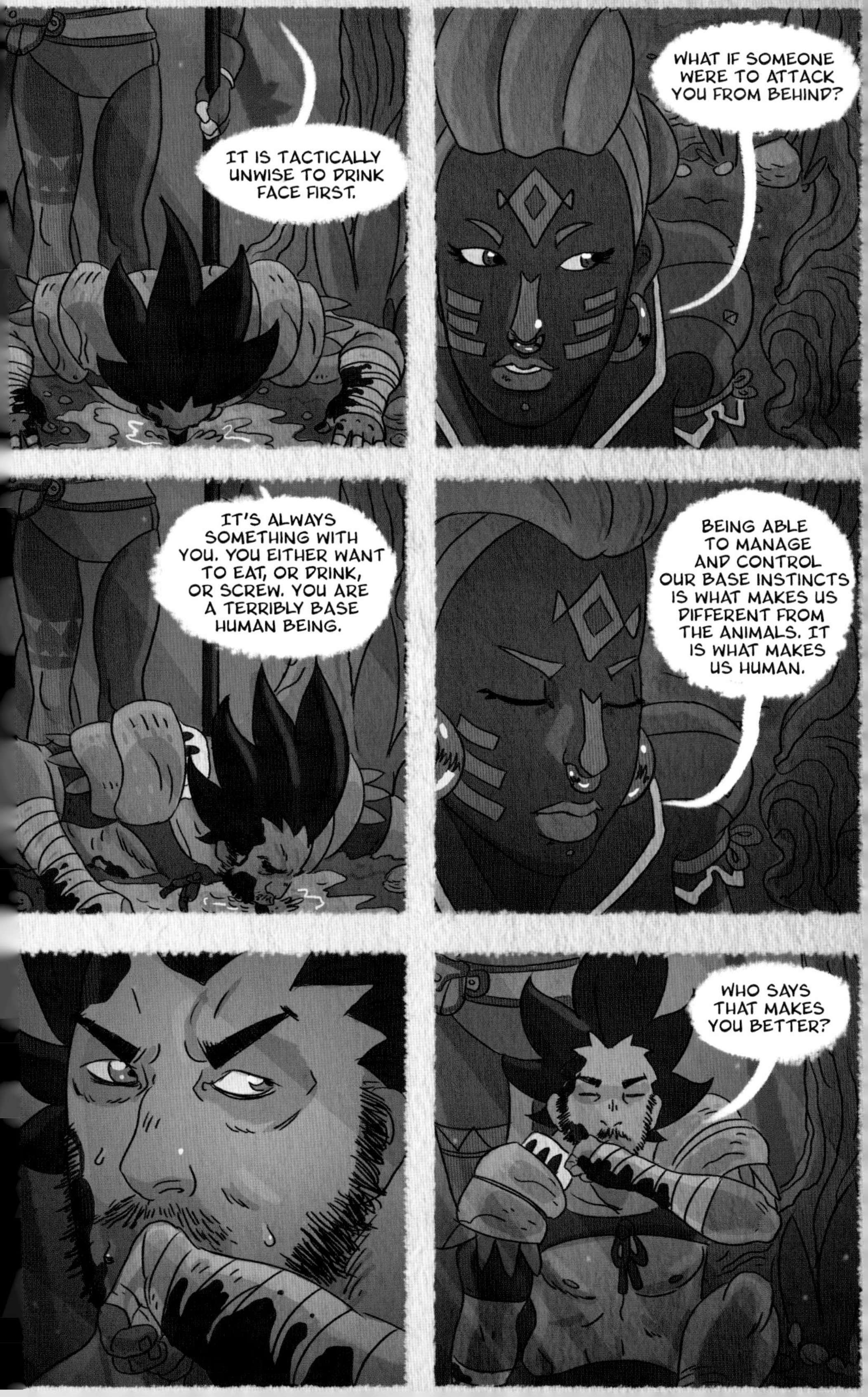
IT IS TACTICALLY UNWISE TO DRINK FACE FIRST.
WHAT IF SOMEONE WERE TO ATTACK YOU FROM BEHIND?
IT'S ALWAYS SOMETHING WITH YOU. YOU EITHER WANT TO EAT, OR DRINK, OR SCREW. YOU ARE A TERRIBLY BASE HUMAN BEING.
BEING ABLE TO MANAGE AND CONTROL OUR BASE INSTINCTS IS WHAT MAKES US DIFFERENT FROM THE ANIMALS. IT IS WHAT MAKES US HUMAN.
WHO SAYS THAT MAKES YOU BETTER?

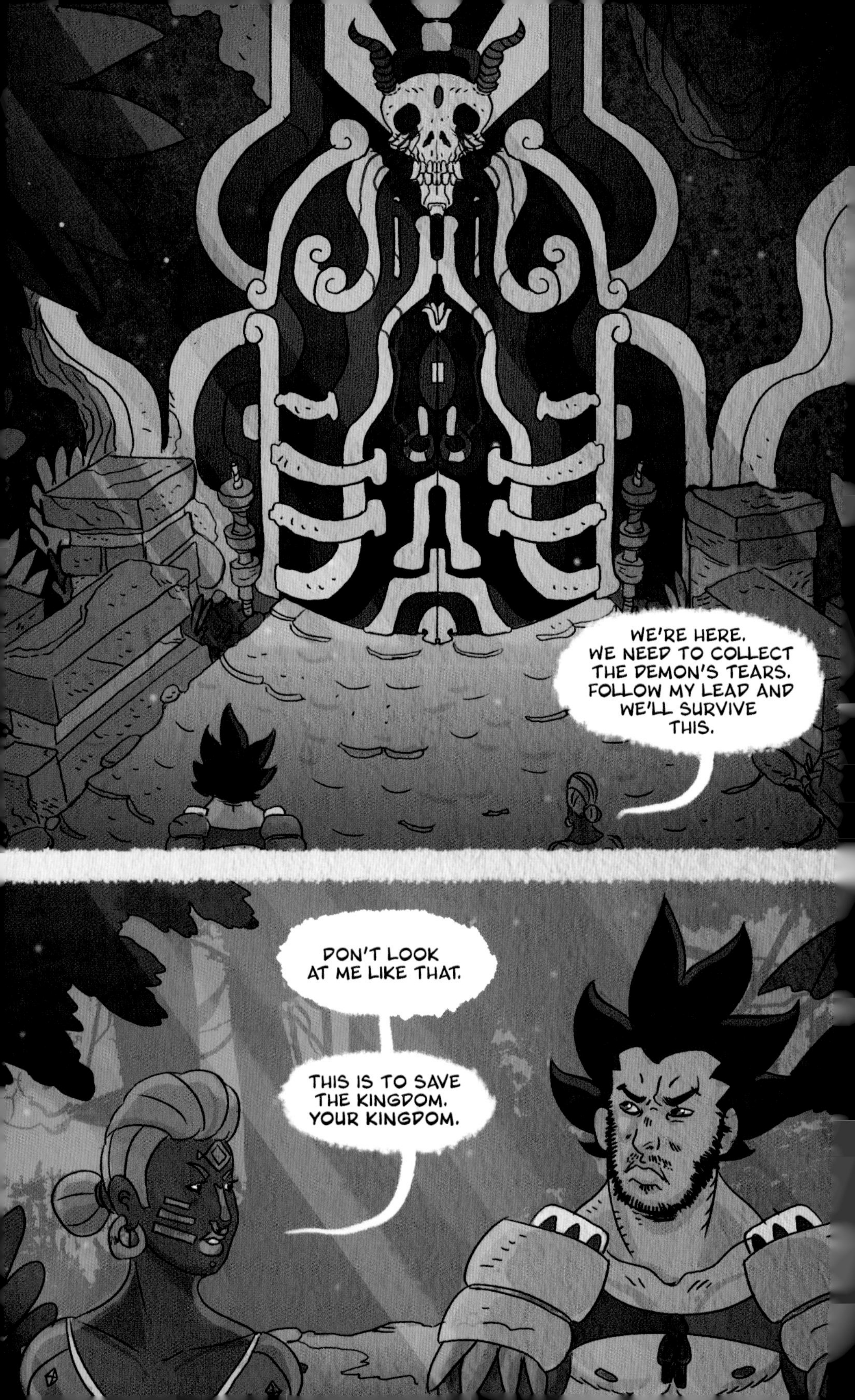
WE'RE HERE. WE NEED TO COLLECT THE DEMON'S TEARS. FOLLOW MY LEAD AND WE'LL SURVIVE THIS.
DON'T LOOK AT ME LIKE THAT.
THIS IS TO SAVE THE KINGDOM. YOUR KINGDOM.

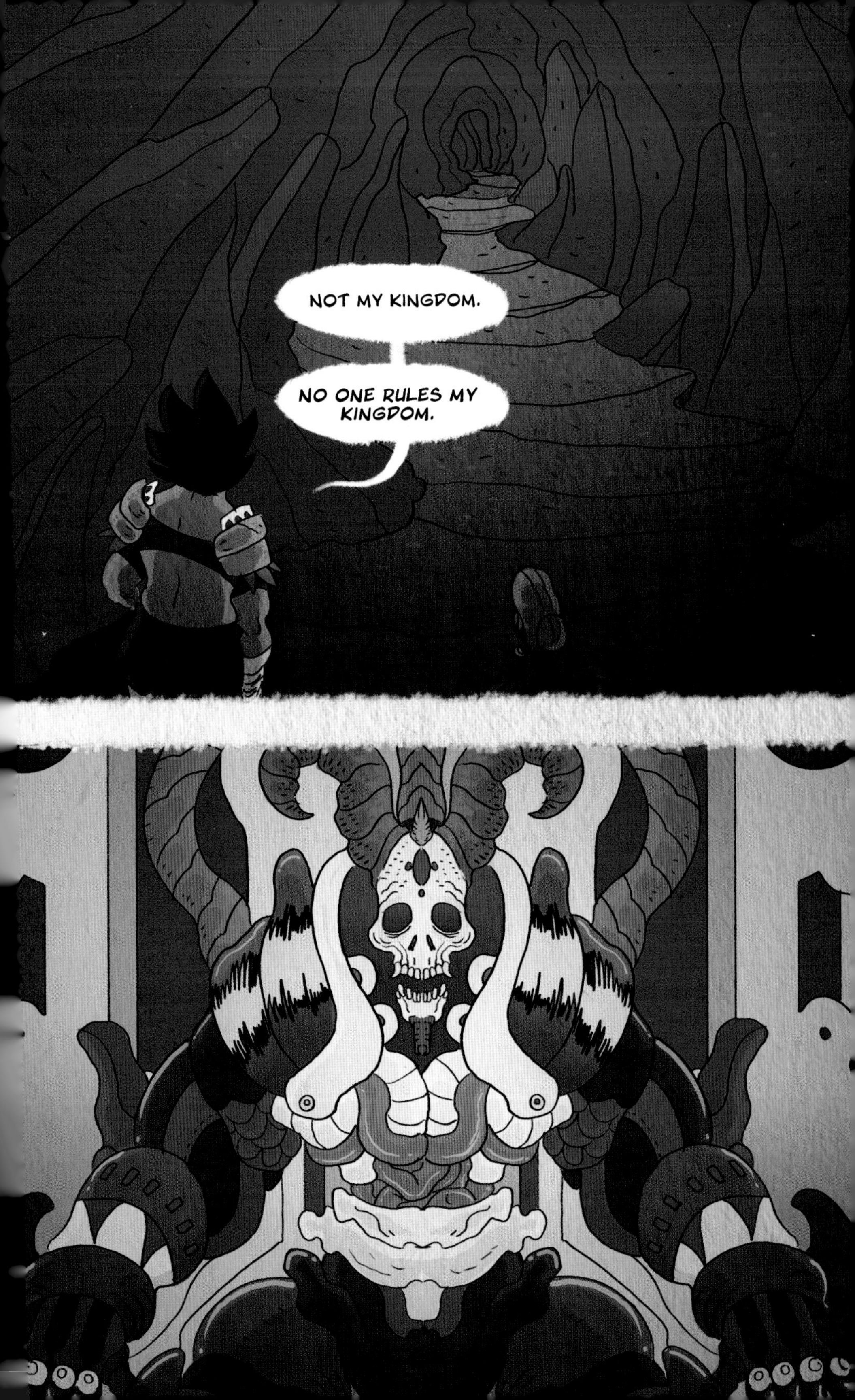
NOT MY KINGDOM.
NO ONE RULES MY KINGDOM.

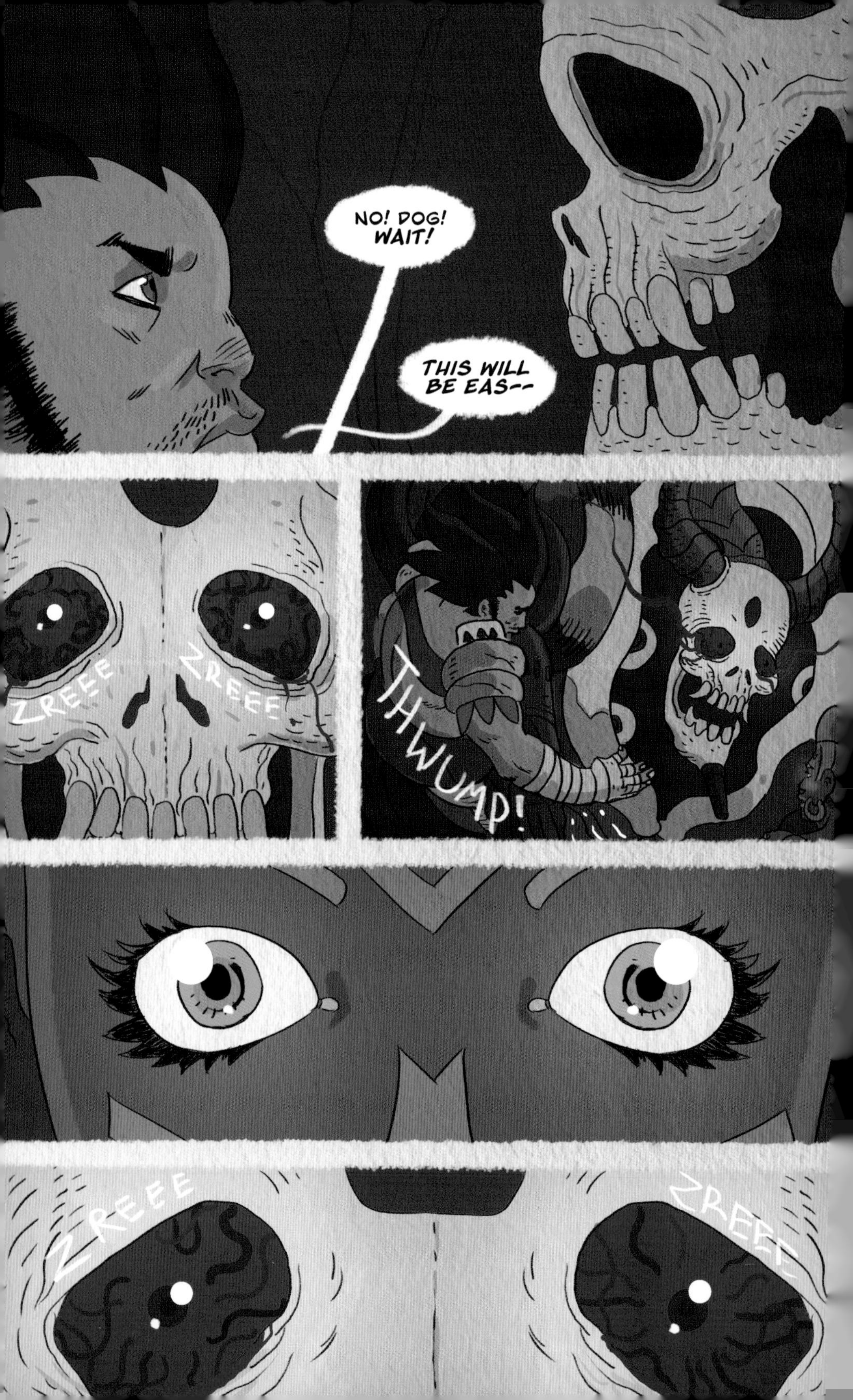
NO! DOG! WAIT!
THIS WILL BE EAS--
ZREEE
ZREEE
THWUMP!
ZREEE
ZREEE

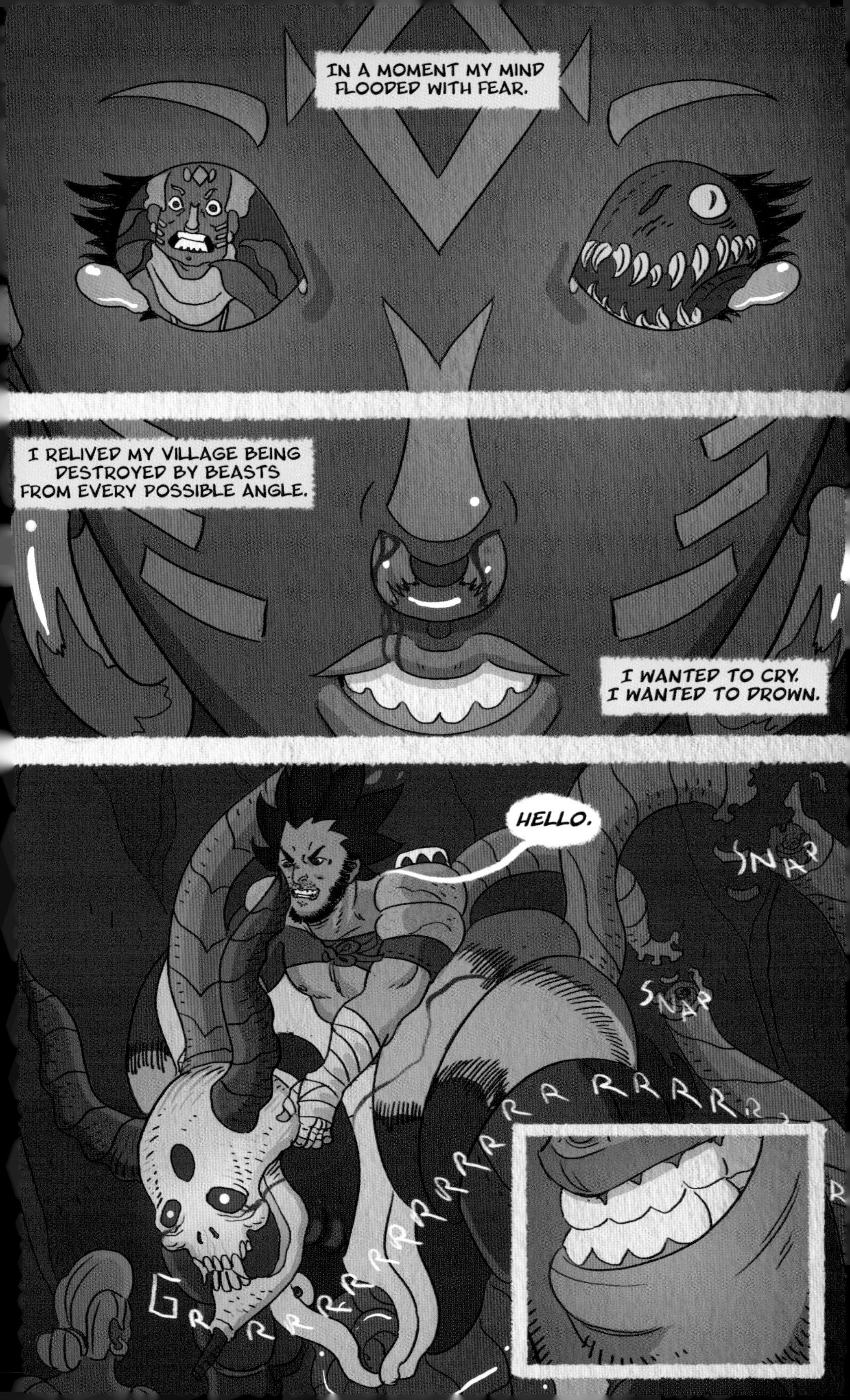
IN A MOMENT MY MIND FLOODED WITH FEAR.
I RELIVED MY VILLAGE BEING DESTROYED BY BEASTS FROM EVERY POSSIBLE ANGLE.
I WANTED TO CRY. I WANTED TO DROWN.
HELLO.
SNAP
SNAP
GRRRRRRRRRRRRRRRRRRRRR

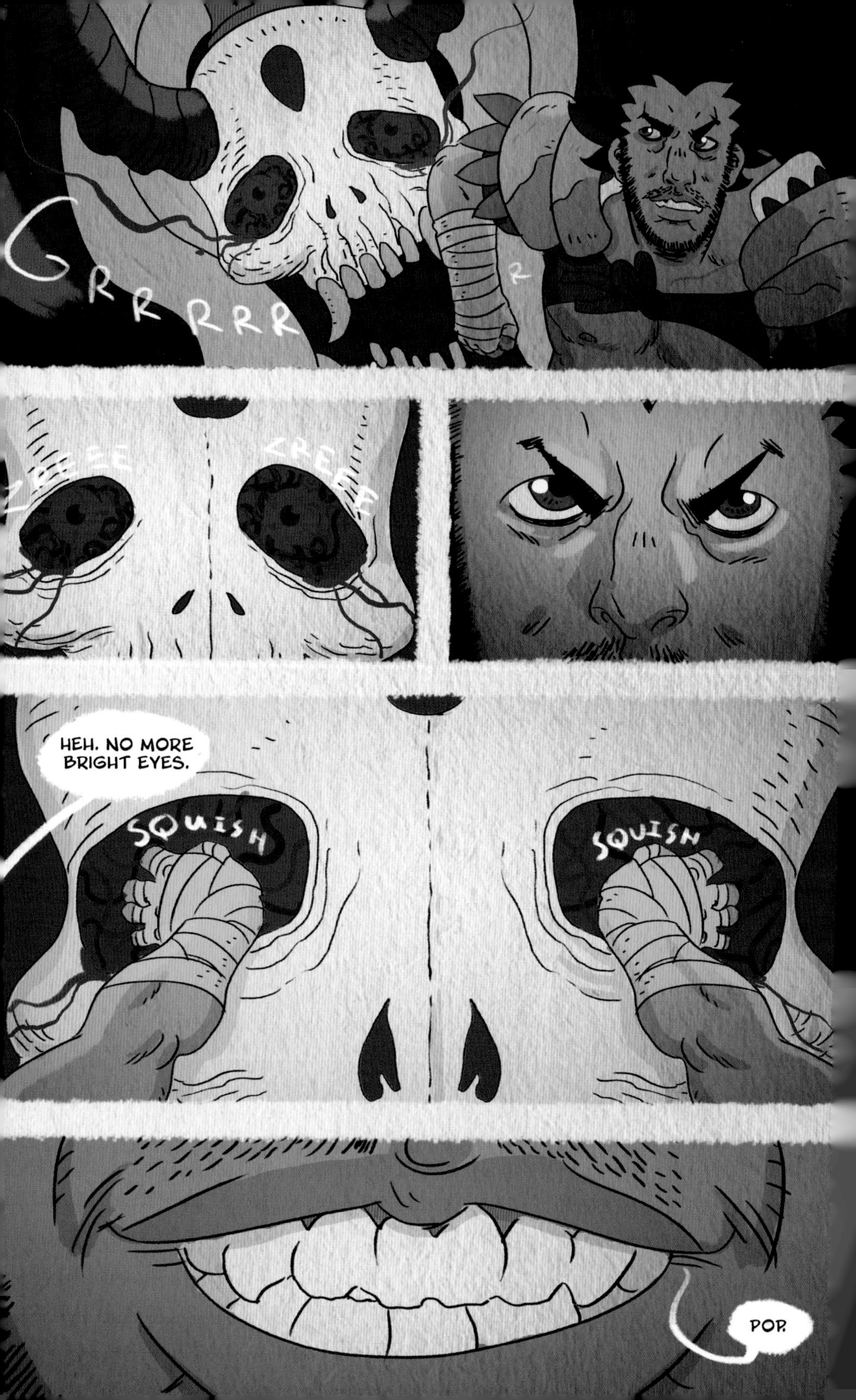
GRRRRRR
CREEE
CREEE
HEH. NO MORE BRIGHT EYES.
SQUISH
SQUISH
POP.

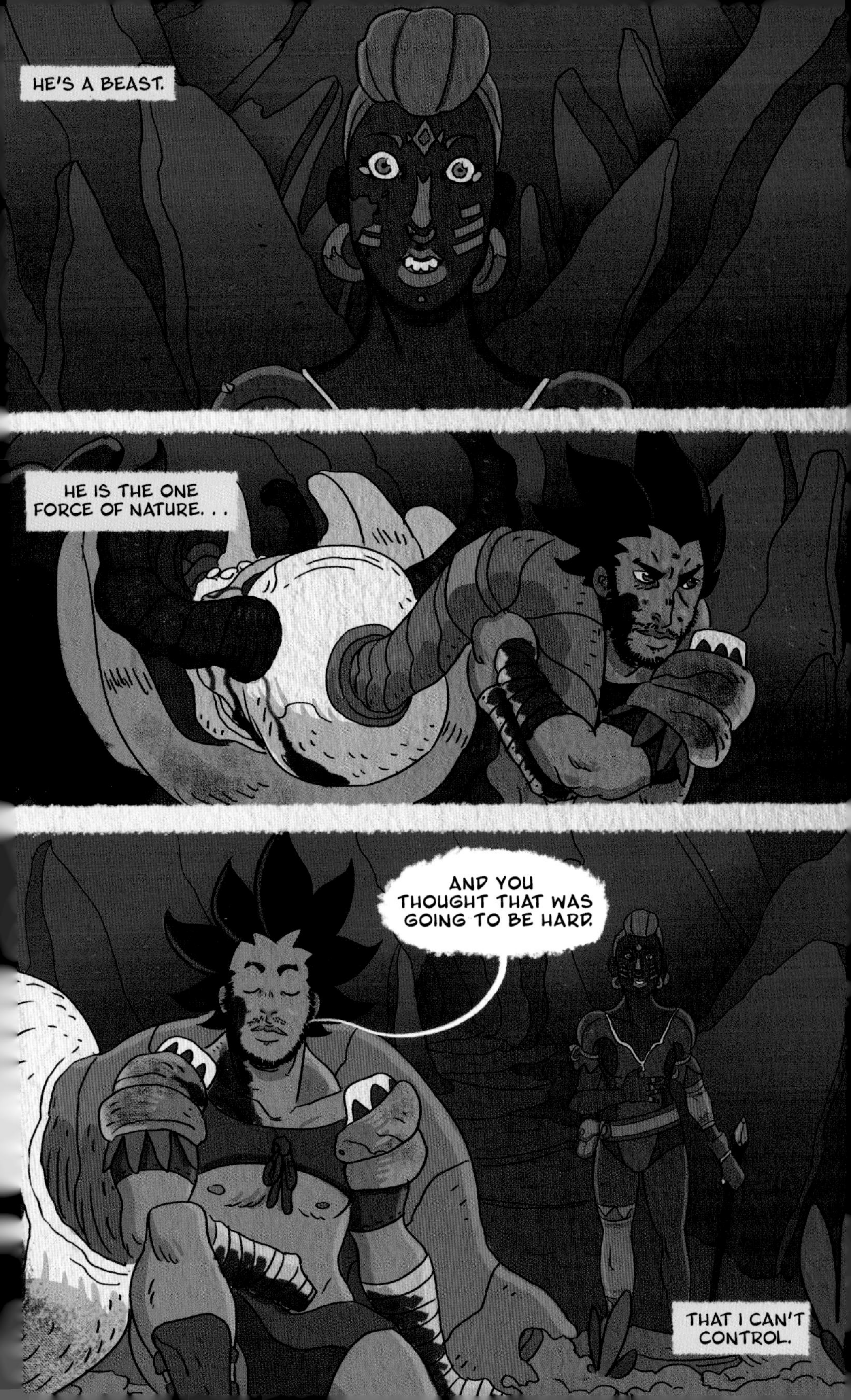

HE'S A BEAST.
HE IS THE ONE FORCE OF NATURE. . .
AND YOU THOUGHT THAT WAS GOING TO BE HARD.
THAT I CAN'T CONTROL.

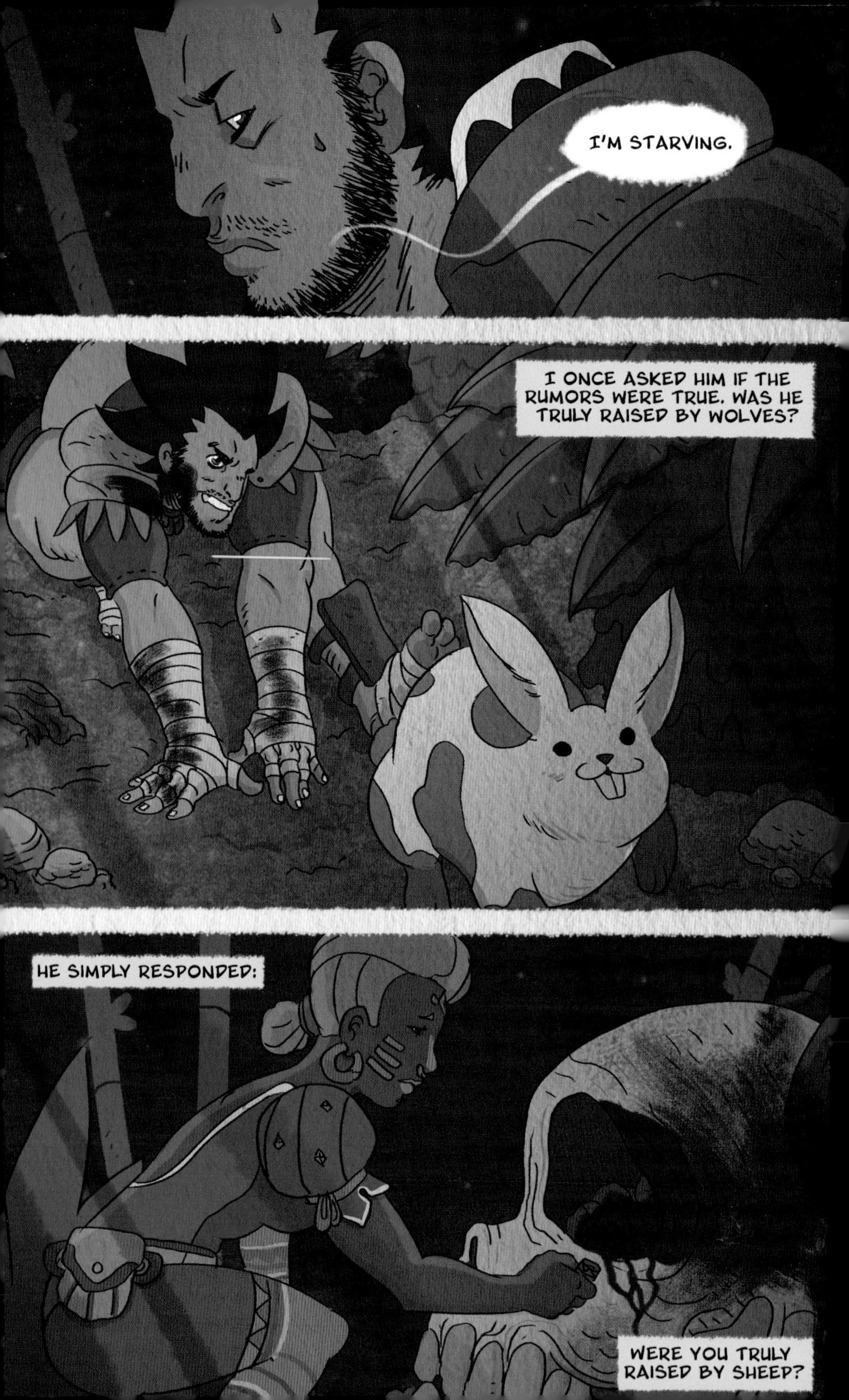
I'M STARVING.
I ONCE ASKED HIM IF THE RUMORS WERE TRUE. WAS HE TRULY RAISED BY WOLVES?
HE SIMPLY RESPONDED:
WERE YOU TRULY RAISED BY SHEEP?

HUNTERS

-THE RETURN-

JOSH TIERNEY - MIGUEL VALDERRAMA

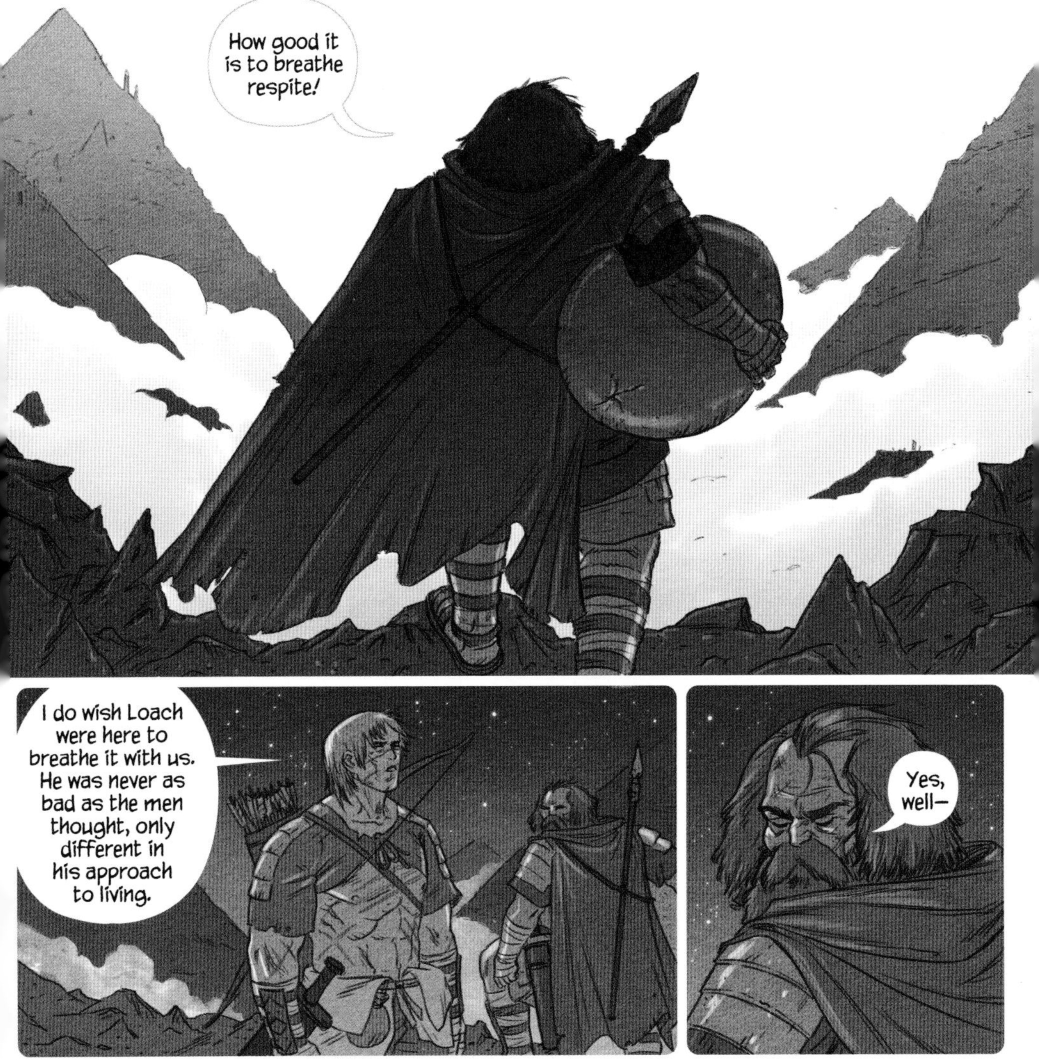
How good it is to breathe respite!
I do wish Loach were here to breathe it with us. He was never as bad as the men thought, only different in his approach to living.
Yes, well—

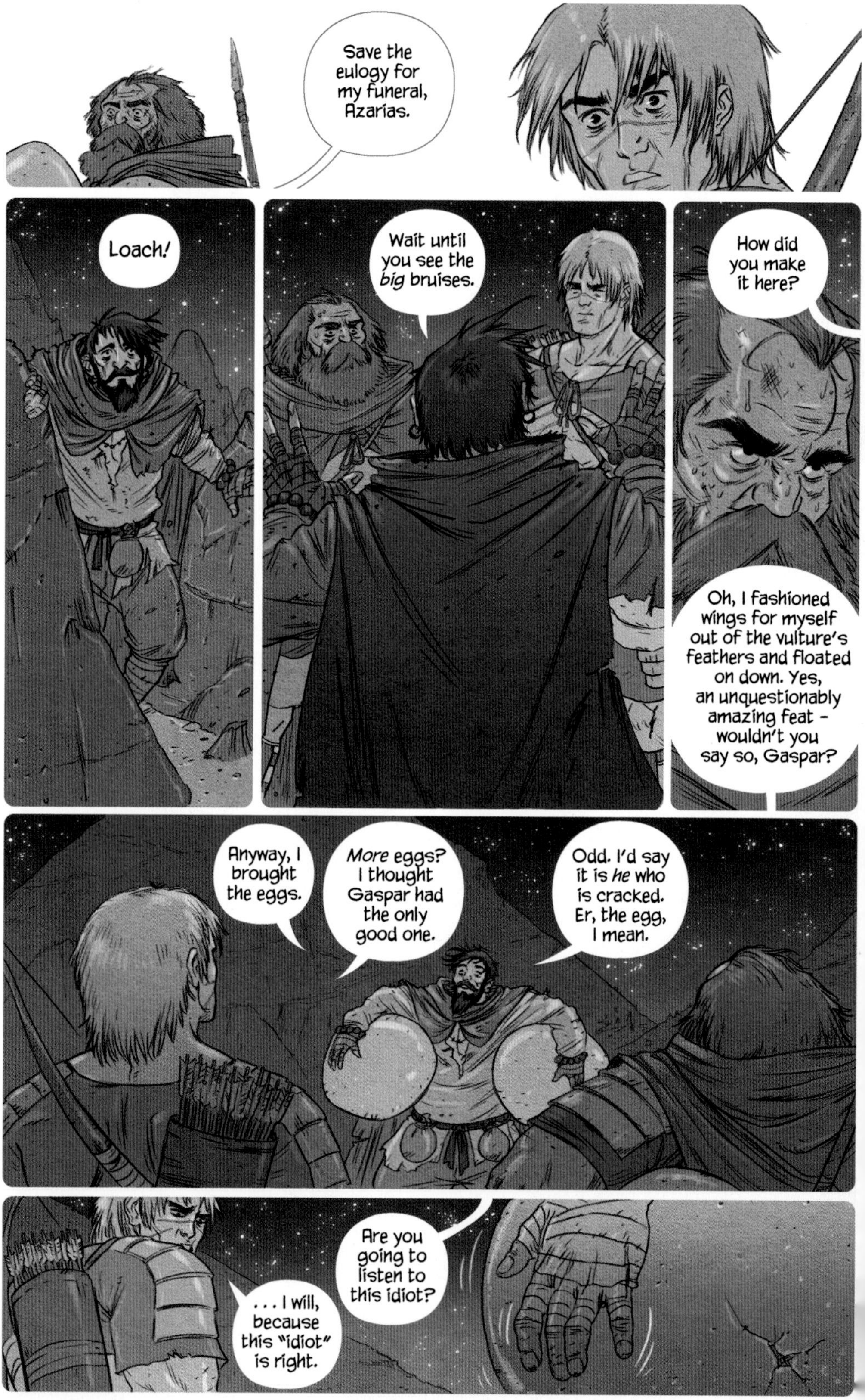

Save the eulogy for my funeral, Azarias.
Loach!
Wait until you see the *big* bruises.
How did you make it here?
Oh, I fashioned wings for myself out of the vulture's feathers and floated on down. Yes, an unquestionably amazing feat - wouldn't you say so, Gaspar?
Anyway, I brought the eggs.
More eggs? I thought Gaspar had the only good one.
Odd. I'd say it is *he* who is cracked. Er, the egg, I mean.
Are you going to listen to this idiot?
. . . I will, because this "idiot" is right.

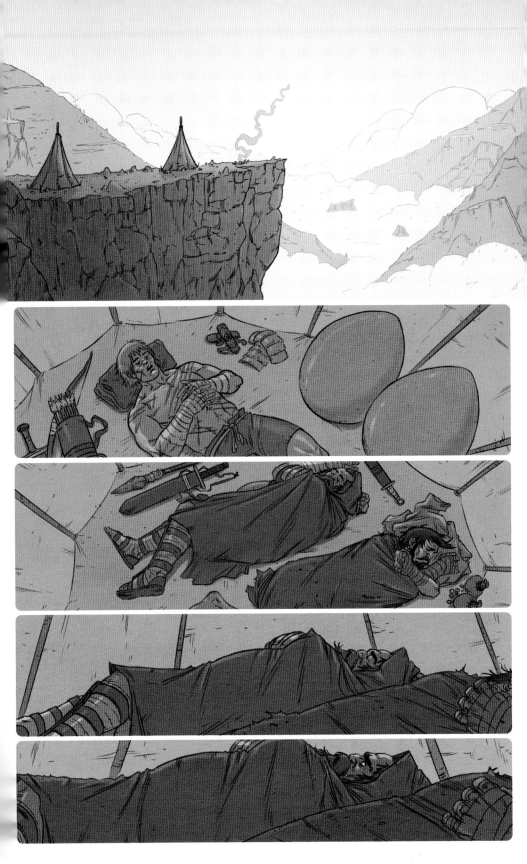

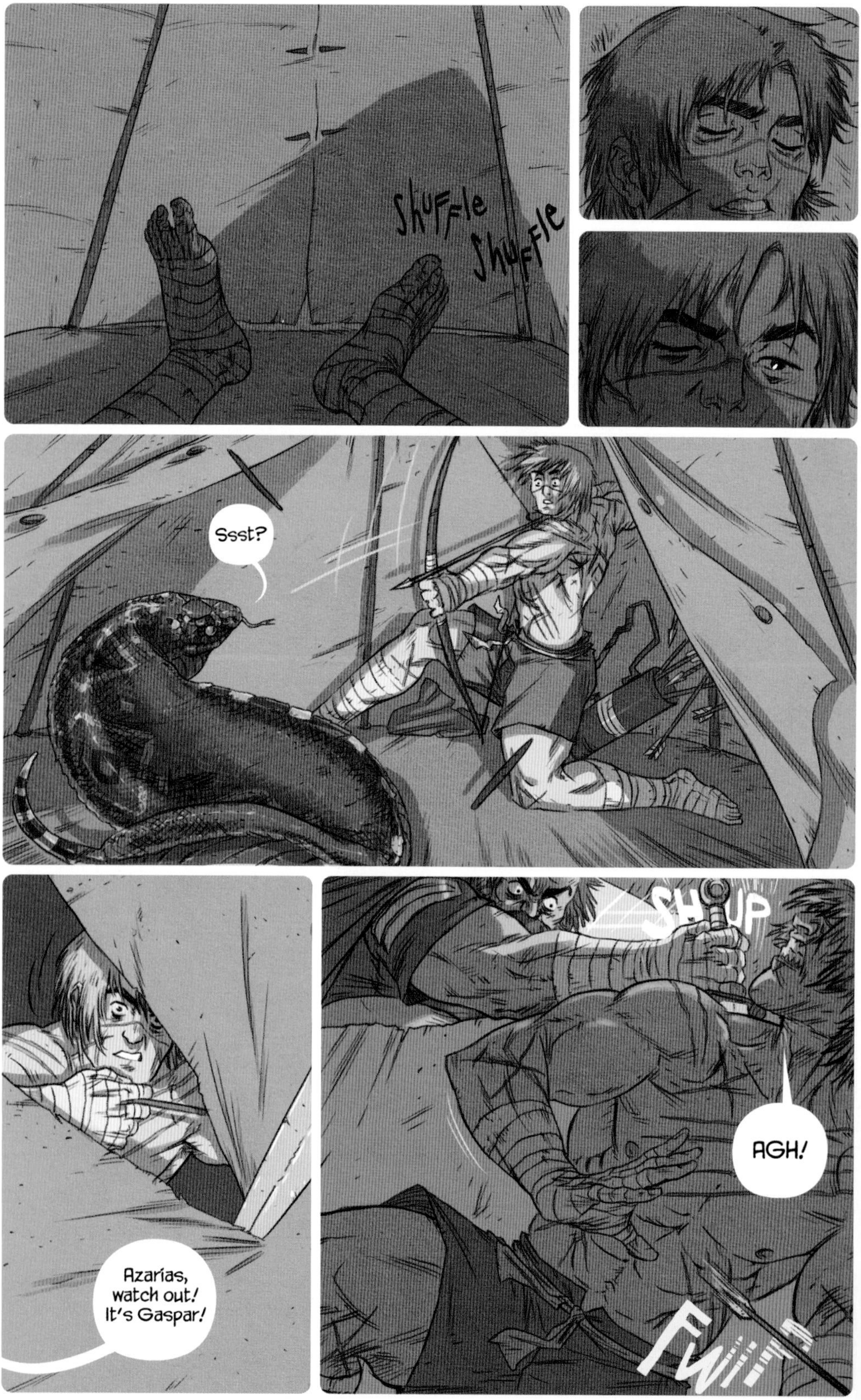
SHUFFLE SHUFFLE
Ssst?
SHUP
AGH!
Azarias, watch out! It's Gaspar!
FWiiii

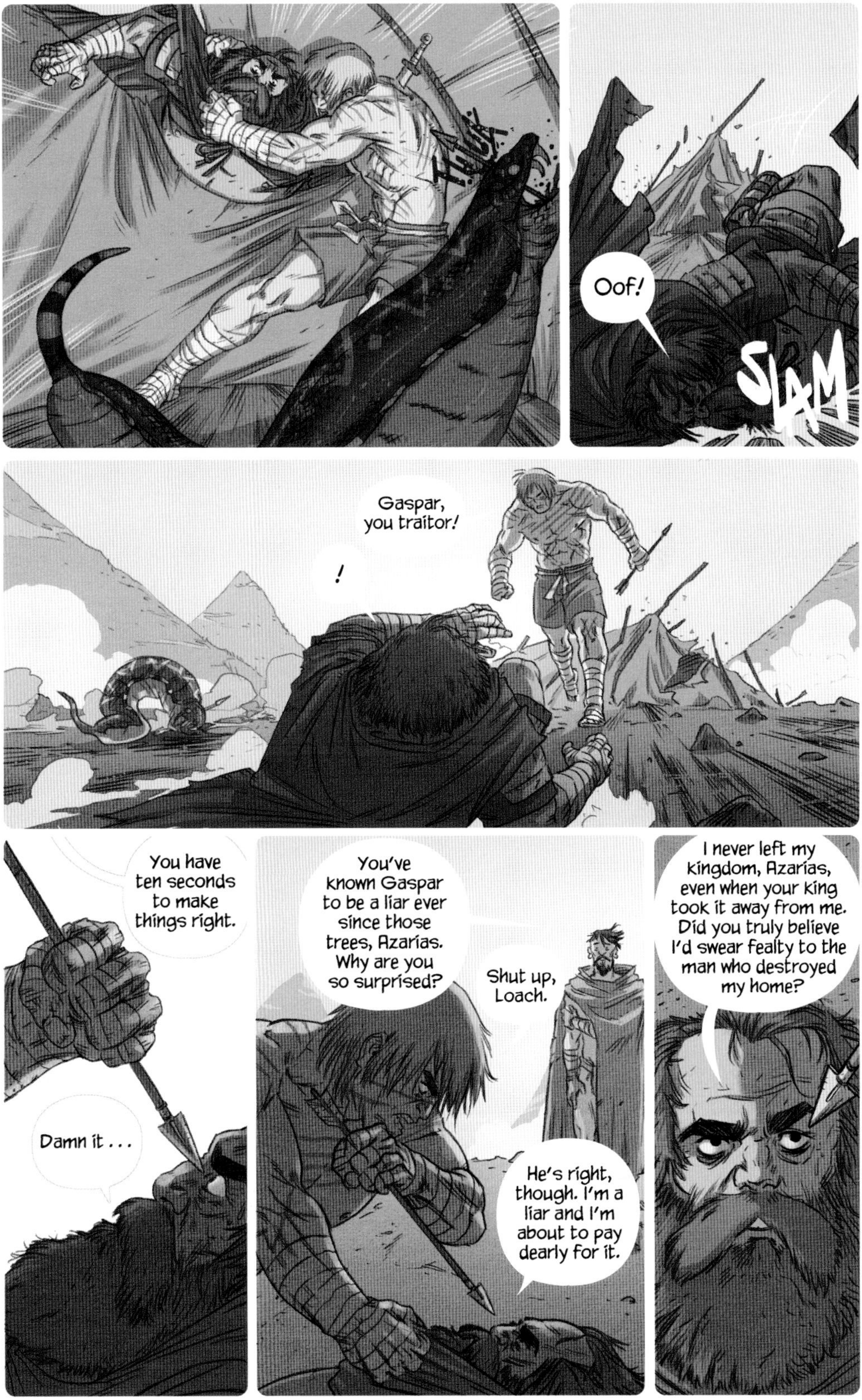
Oof!
SLAM
Gaspar, you traitor!
!
You have ten seconds to make things right.
Damn it . . .
You've known Gaspar to be a liar ever since those trees, Azarias. Why are you so surprised?
Shut up, Loach.
He's right, though. I'm a liar and I'm about to pay dearly for it.
I never left my kingdom, Azarias, even when your king took it away from me. Did you truly believe I'd swear fealty to the man who destroyed my home?

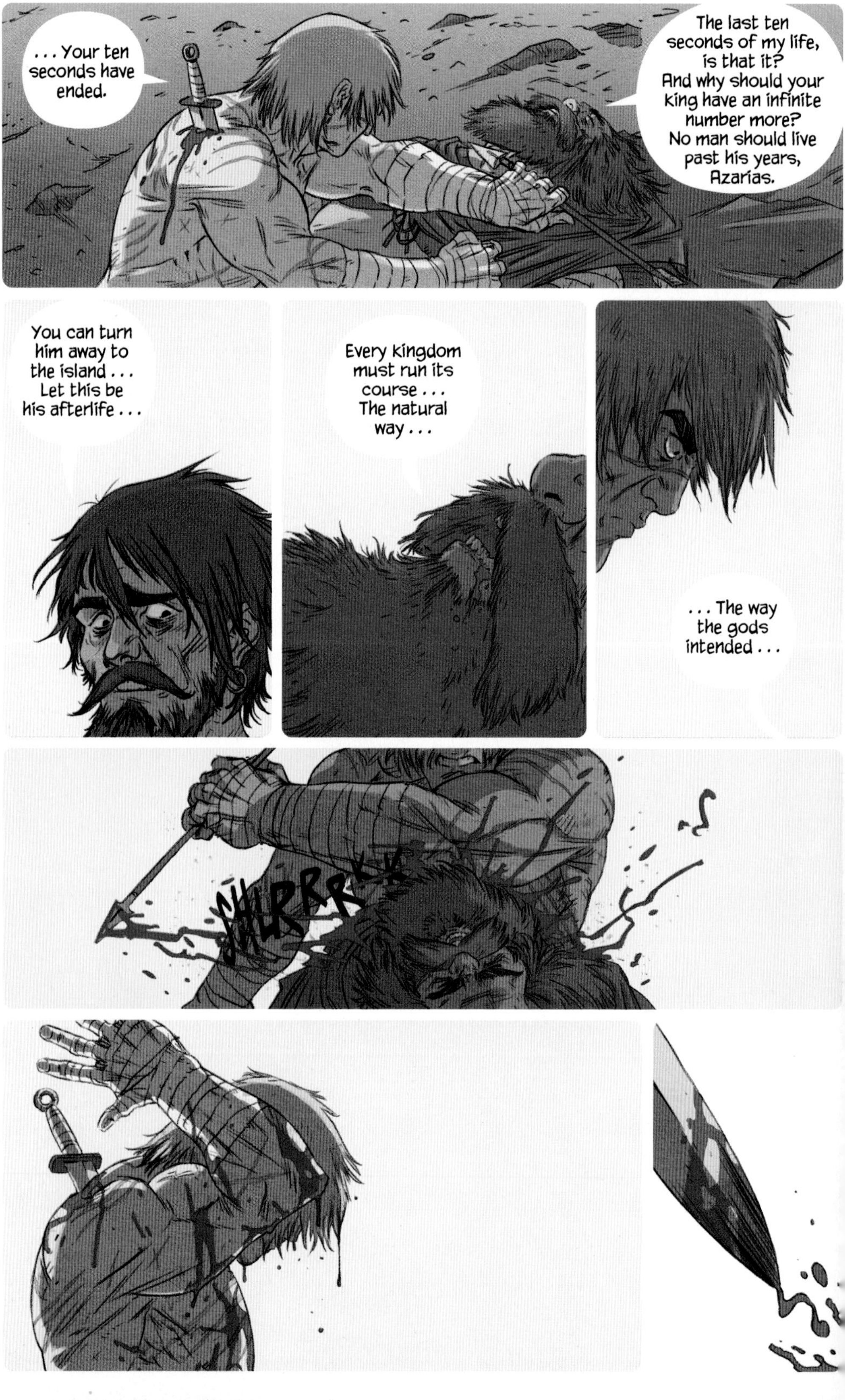
. . . Your ten seconds have ended.
The last ten seconds of my life, is that it? And why should your king have an infinite number more? No man should live past his years, Azarias.
You can turn him away to the island . . . Let this be his afterlife . . .
Every kingdom must run its course . . . The natural way . . .
. . . The way the gods intended . . .
SHLRRRKK

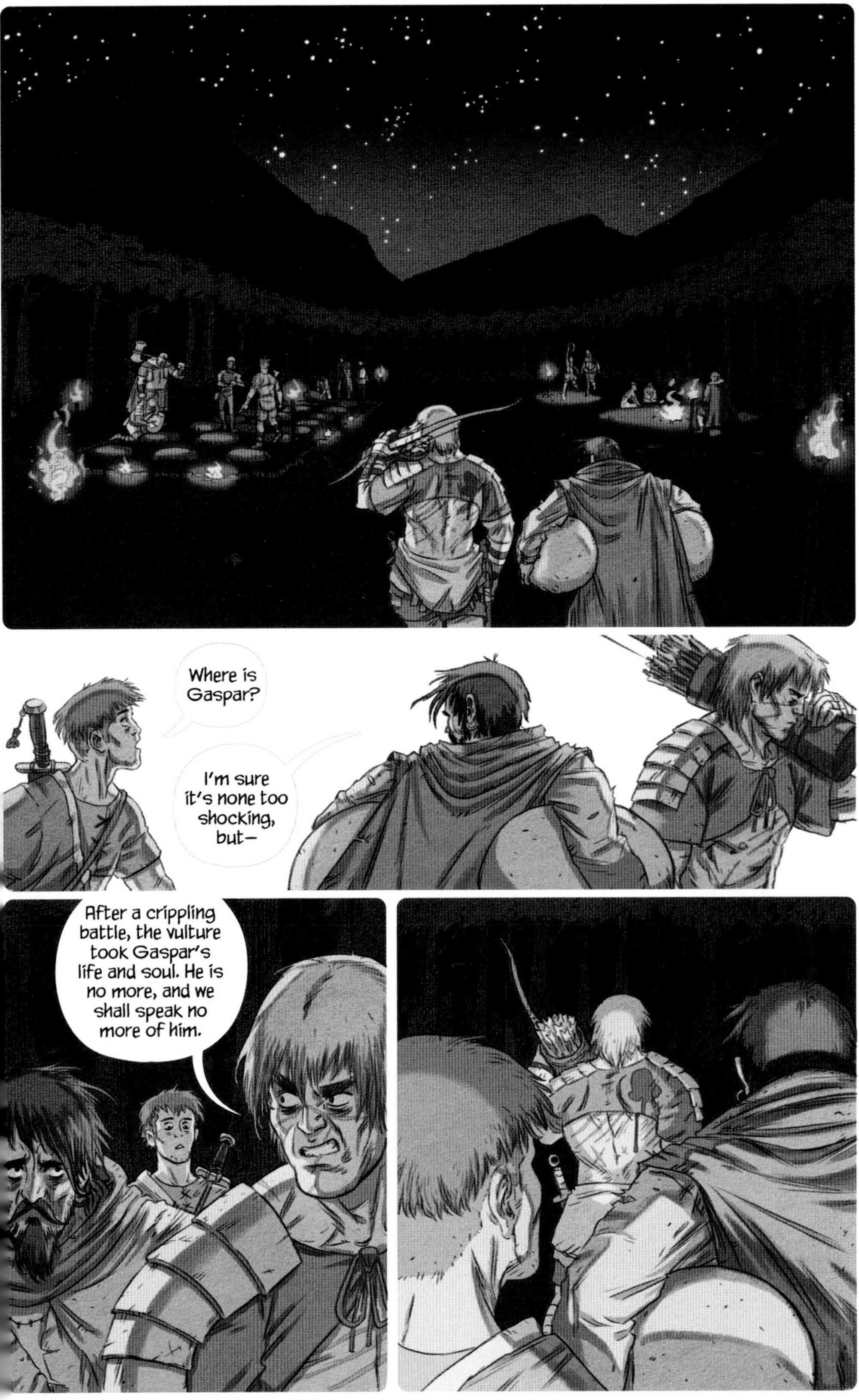
Where is Gaspar?
I'm sure it's none too shocking, but—
After a crippling battle, the vulture took Gaspar's life and soul. He is no more, and we shall speak no more of him.

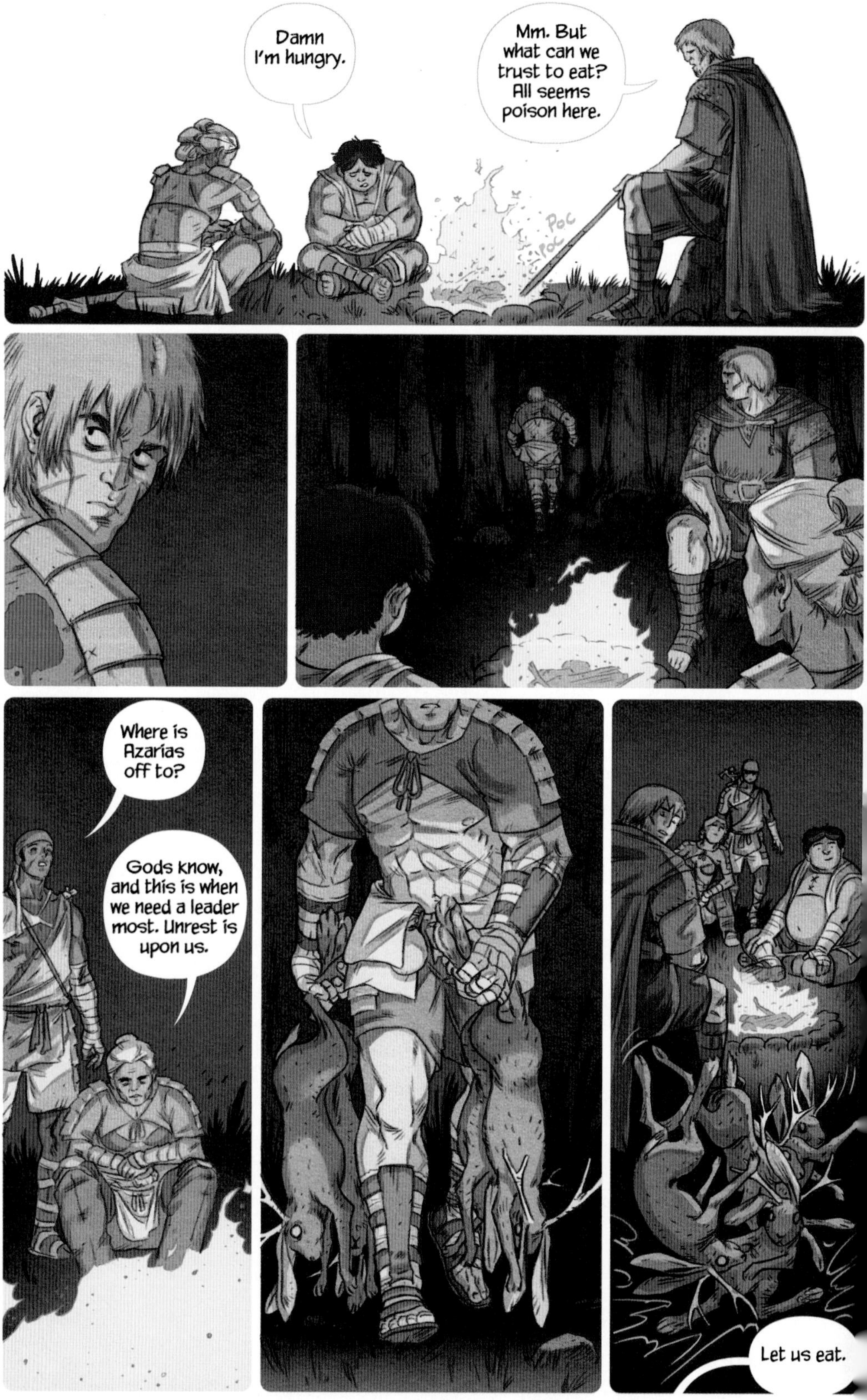
Damn
I'm hungry.
Mm. But what can we trust to eat? All seems poison here.
POC
POC
Where is Azarias off to?
Gods know, and this is when we need a leader most. Unrest is upon us.
Let us eat.

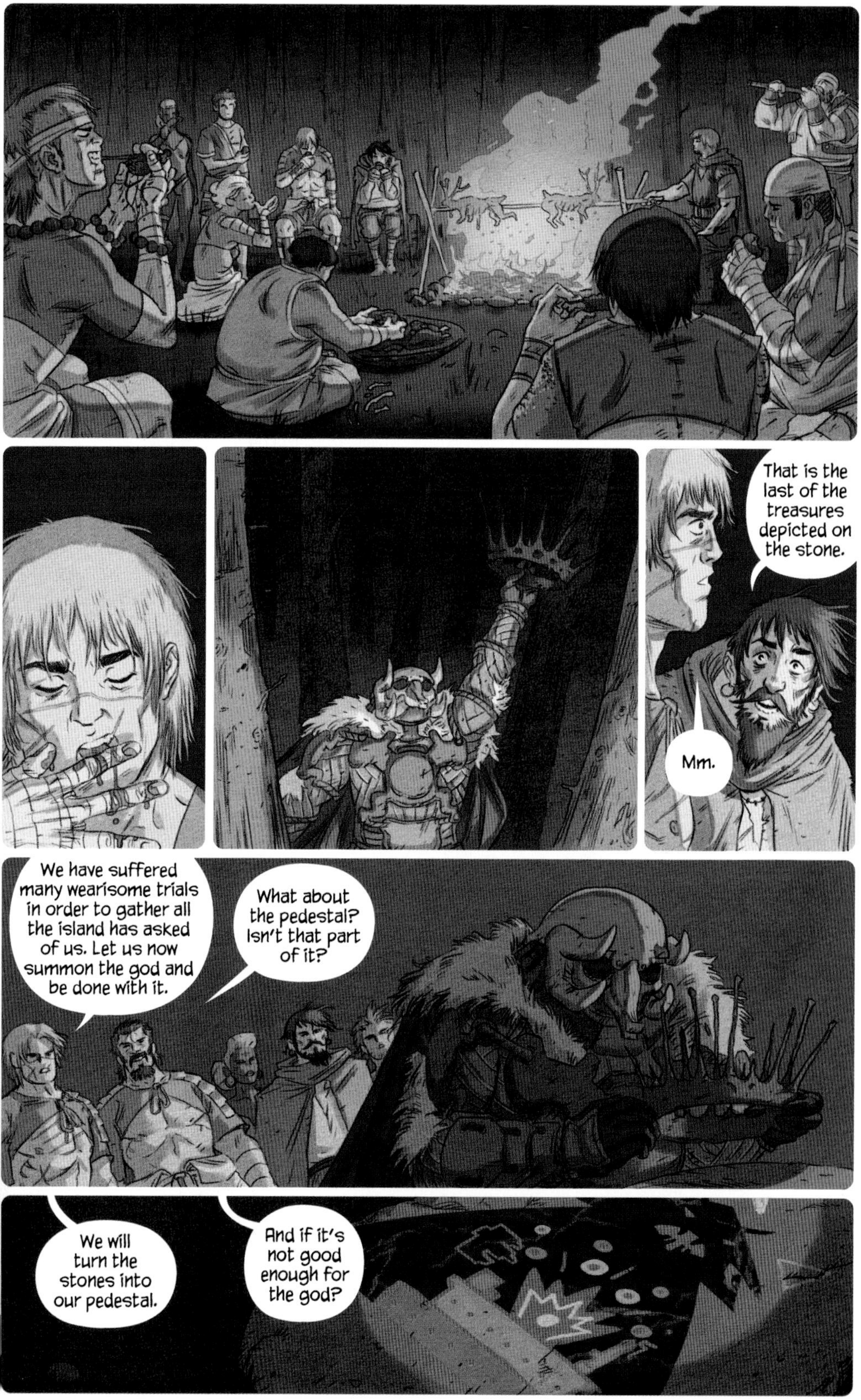
That is the last of the treasures depicted on the stone.
Mm.
We have suffered many wearisome trials in order to gather all the island has asked of us. Let us now summon the god and be done with it.
What about the pedestal? Isn't that part of it?
We will turn the stones into our pedestal.
And if it's not good enough for the god?

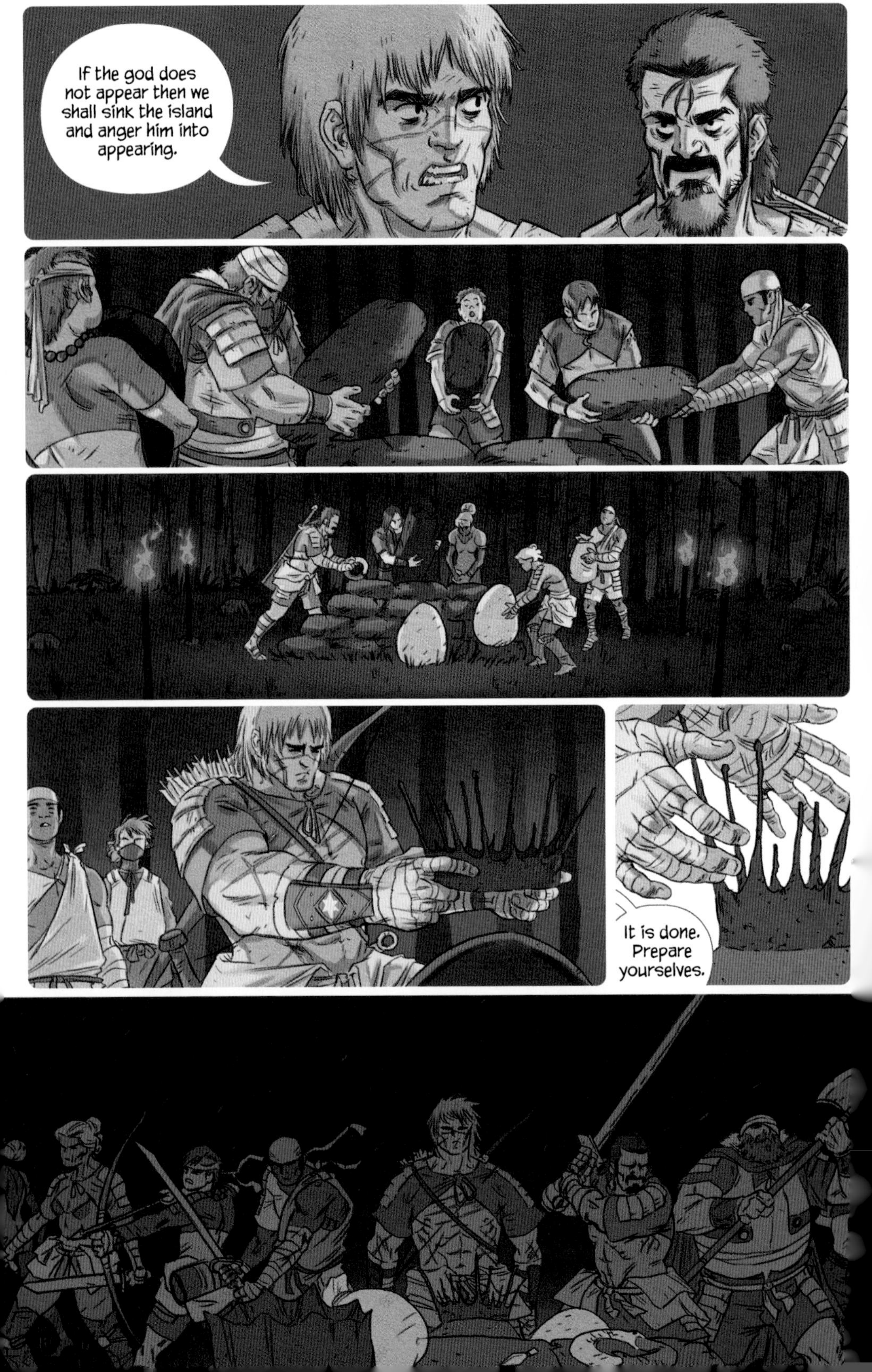
If the god does not appear then we shall sink the island and anger him into appearing.
It is done. Prepare yourselves.

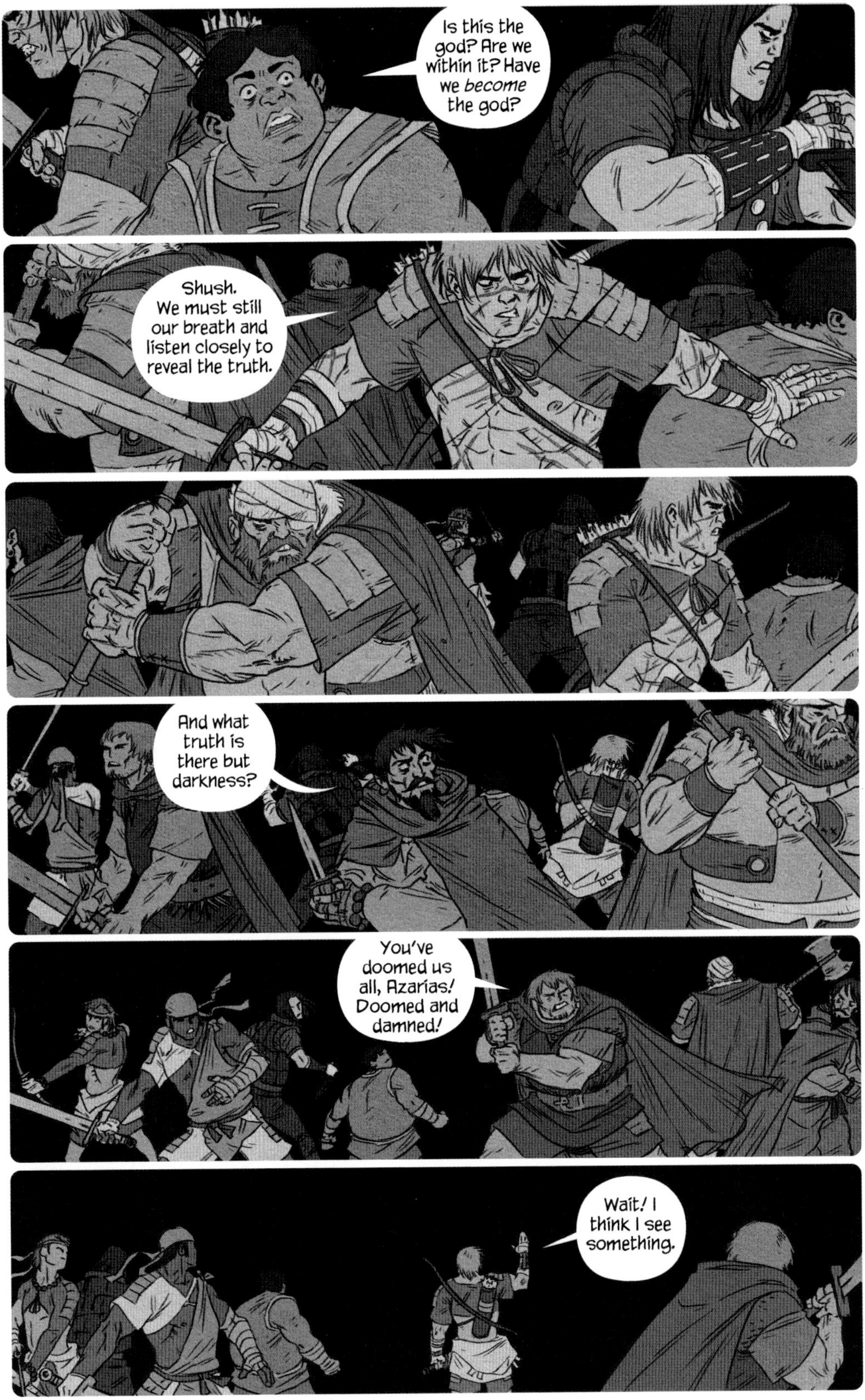

Is this the god? Are we within it? Have we *become* the god?
Shush. We must still our breath and listen closely to reveal the truth.
And what truth is there but darkness?
You've doomed us all, Azarias! Doomed and damned!
Wait! I think I see something.

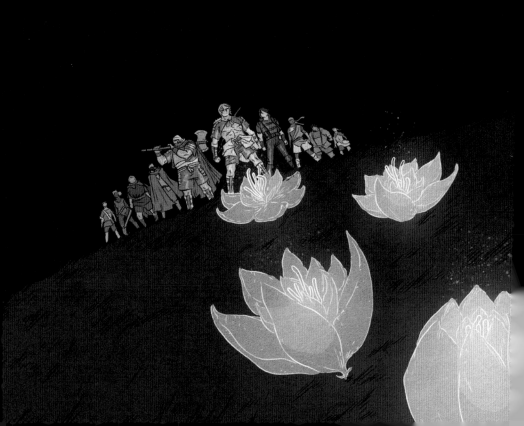

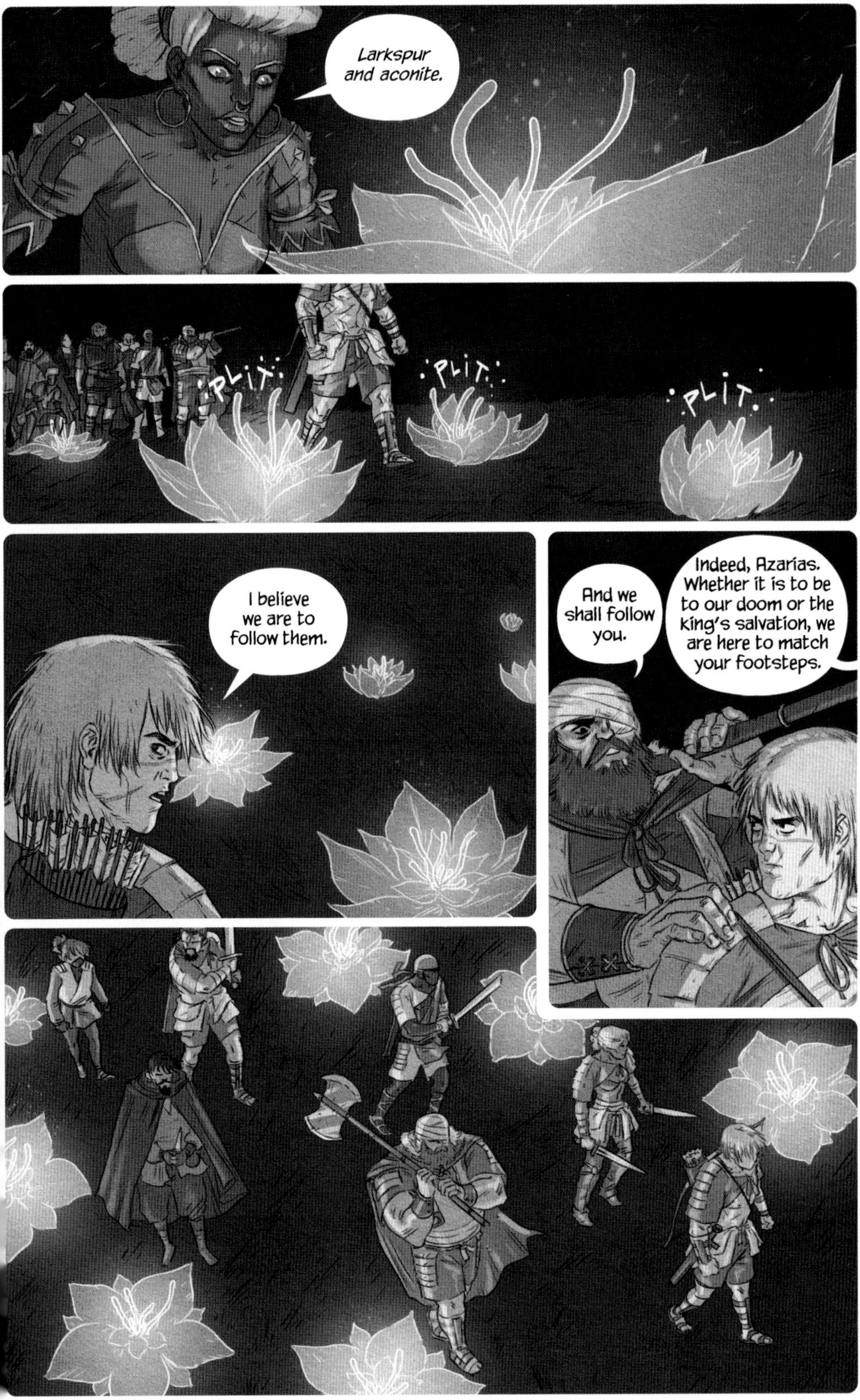
Larkspur and aconite.
PLIT
PLIT
PLIT
I believe we are to follow them.
And we shall follow you.
Indeed, Azarias. Whether it is to be to our doom or the king's salvation, we are here to match your footsteps.

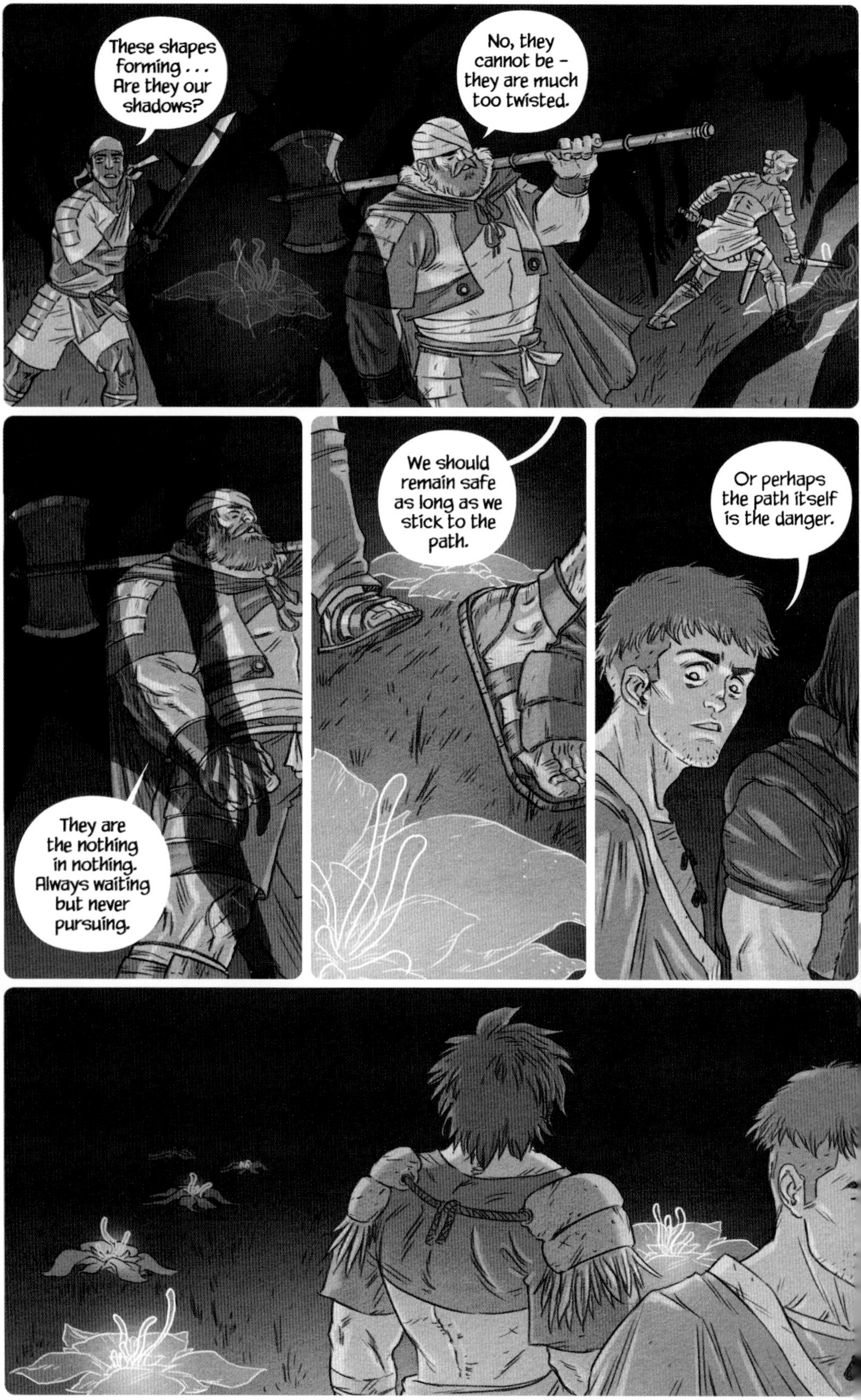
These shapes forming . . . Are they our shadows?
No, they cannot be – they are much too twisted.
They are the nothing in nothing. Always waiting but never pursuing.
We should remain safe as long as we stick to the path.
Or perhaps the path itself is the danger.

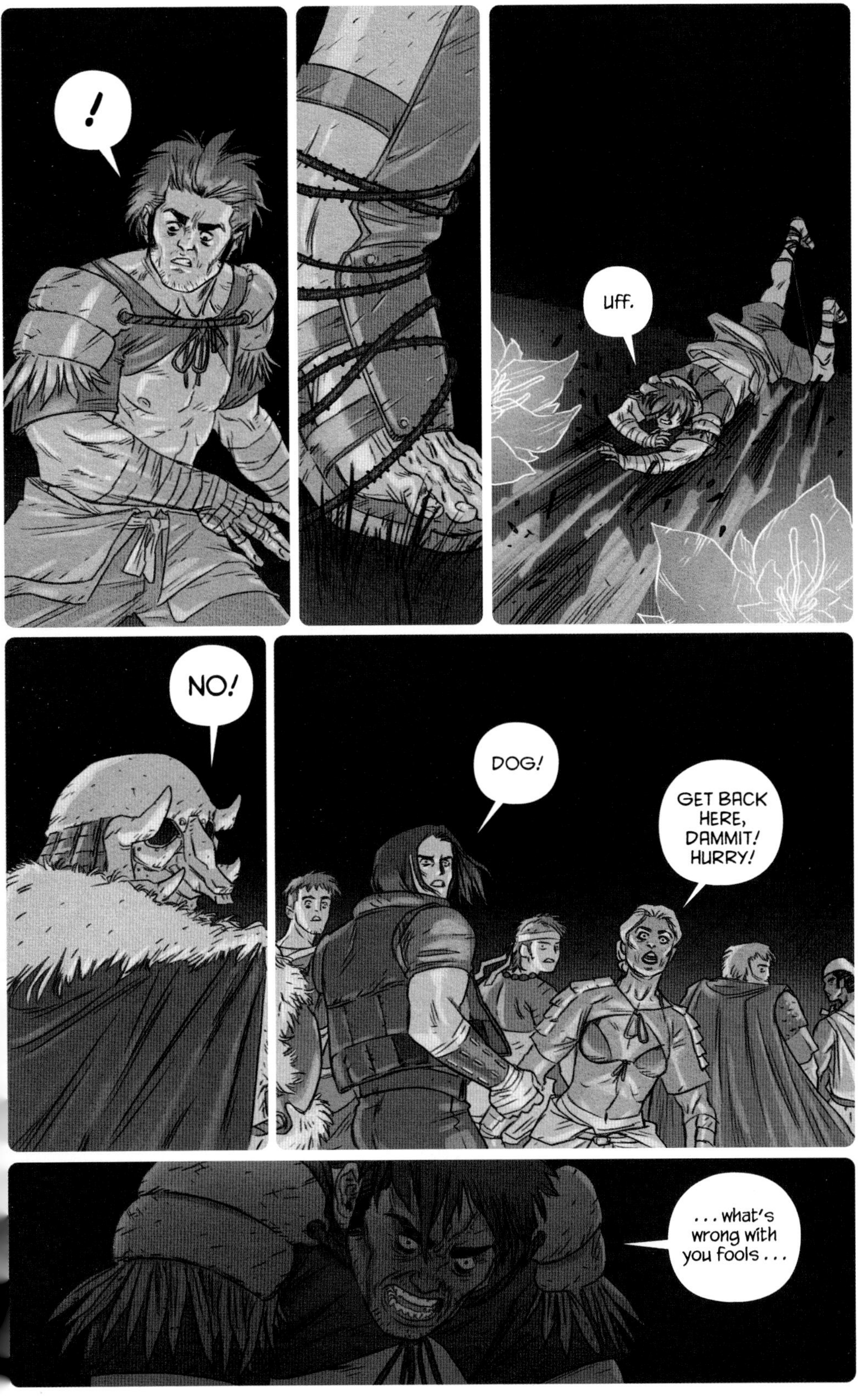
!
UFF.
NO!
DOG!
GET BACK HERE, DAMMIT! HURRY!
. . . what's wrong with you fools . . .

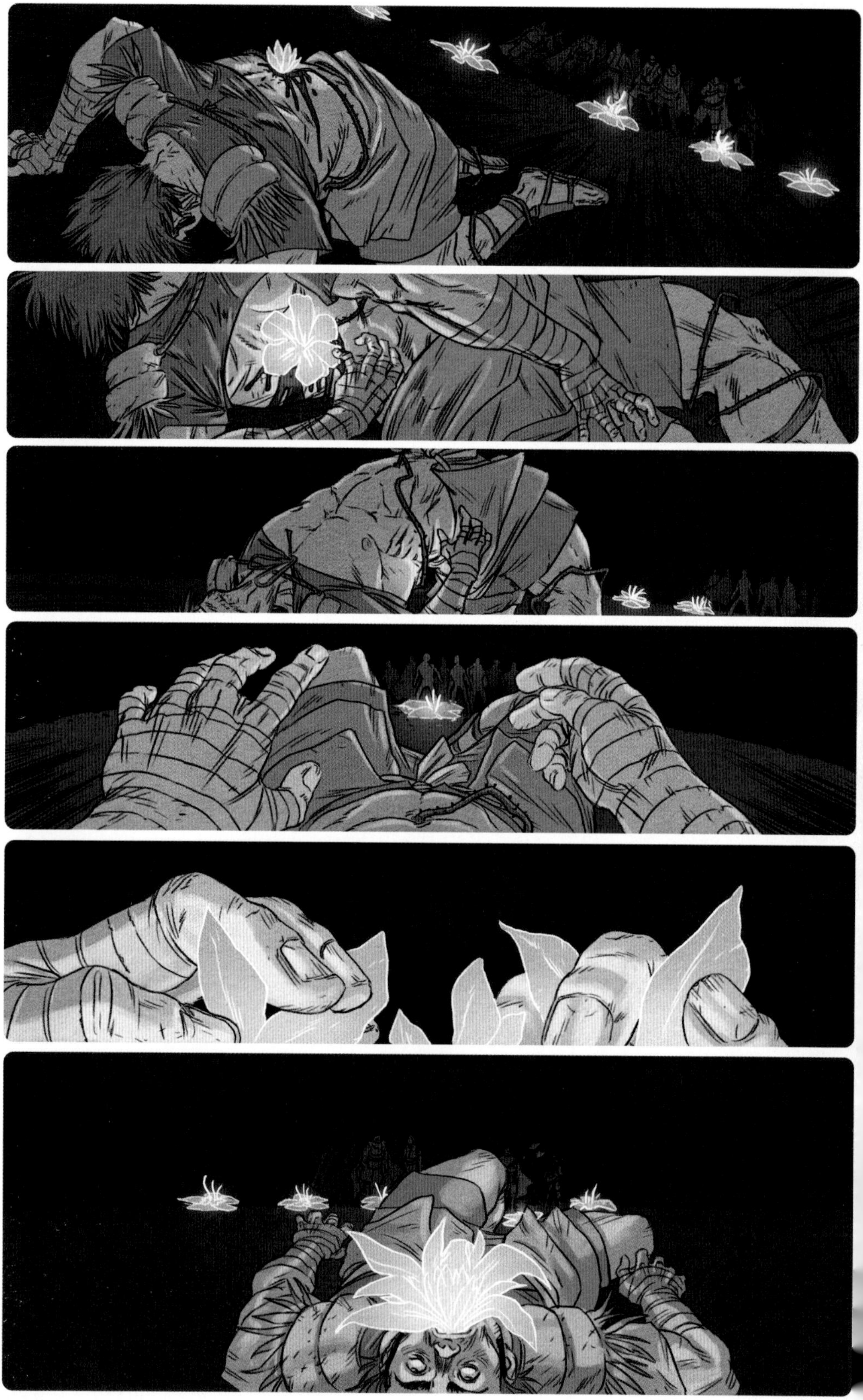

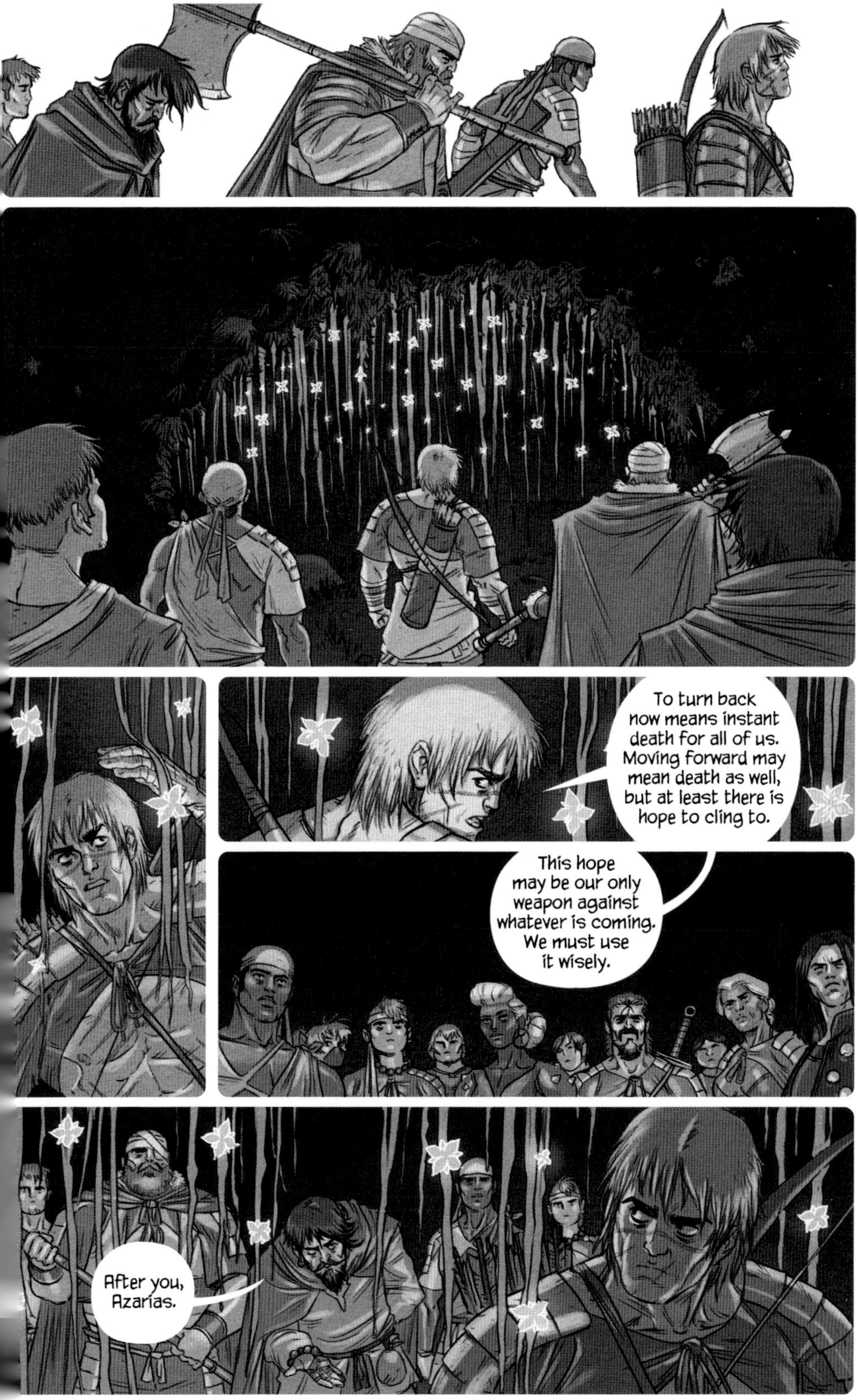
To turn back now means instant death for all of us. Moving forward may mean death as well, but at least there is hope to cling to.
This hope may be our only weapon against whatever is coming. We must use it wisely.
After you, Azarias.

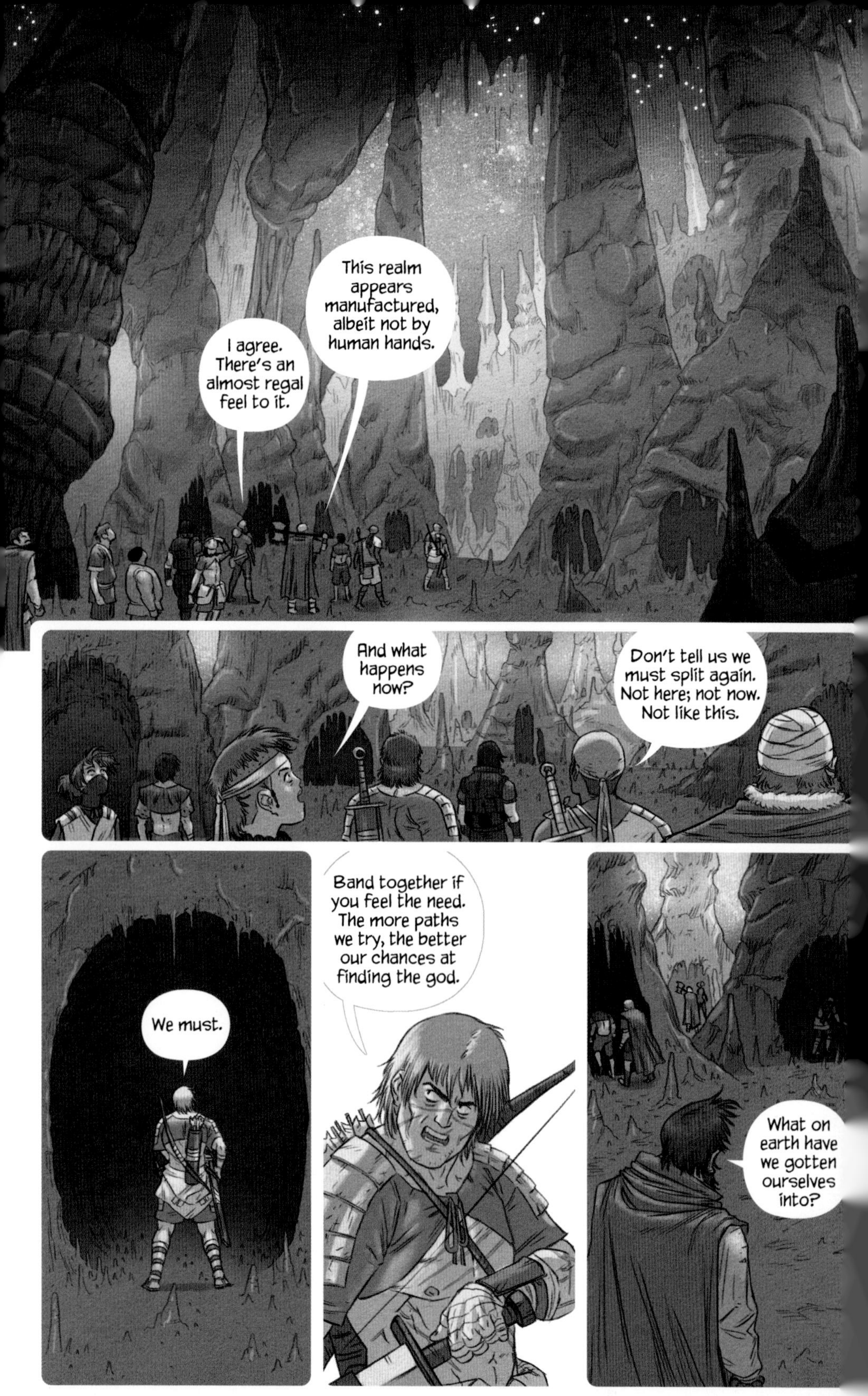
This realm appears manufactured, albeit not by human hands.
I agree. There's an almost regal feel to it.
And what happens now?
Don't tell us we must split again. Not here; not now. Not like this.
We must.
Band together if you feel the need. The more paths we try, the better our chances at finding the god.
What on earth have we gotten ourselves into?

IN THE BRIGHT DARKNESS

CARLOS CARRASCO AND VLAD GUSEV

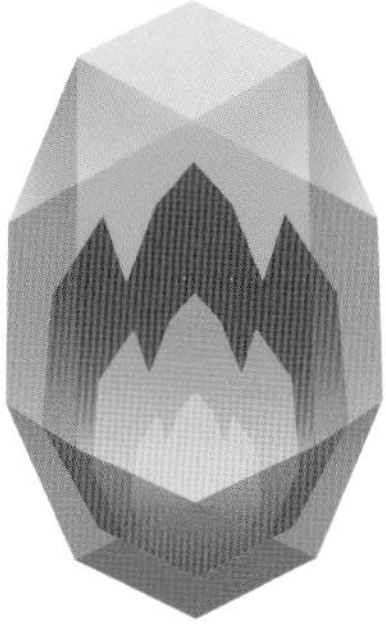

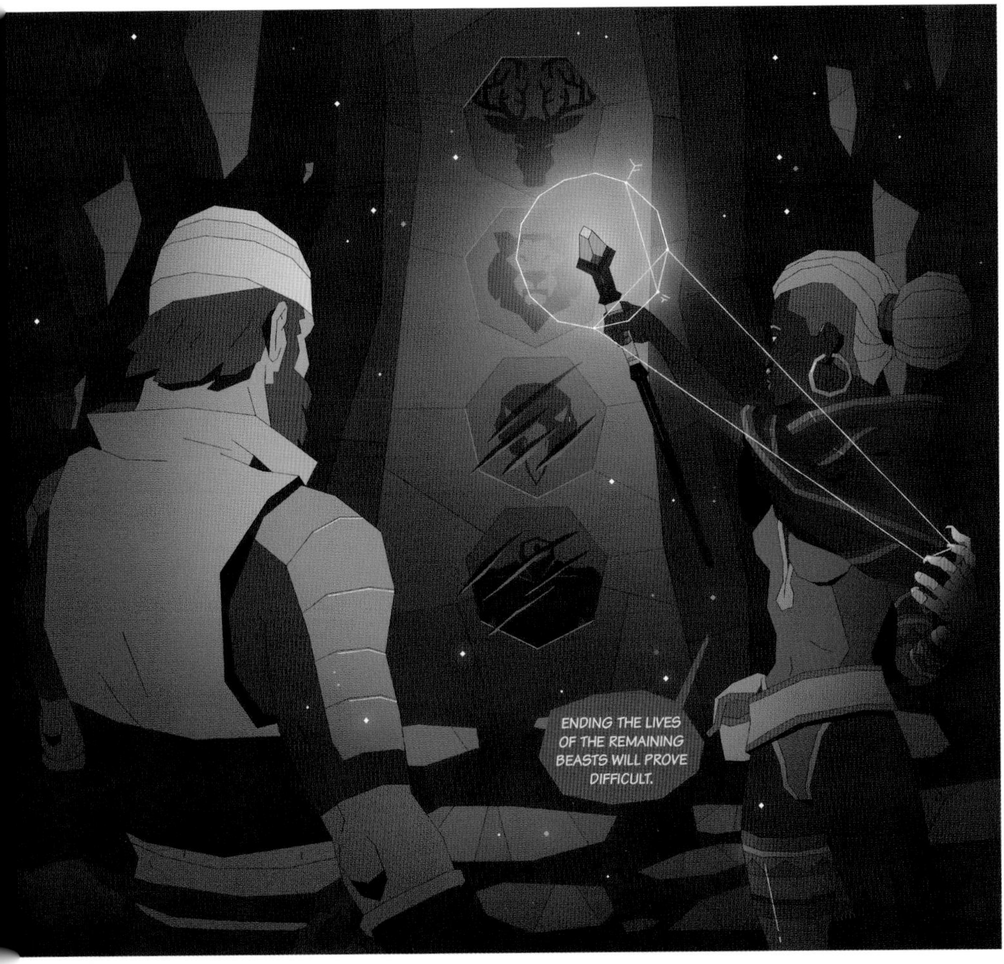
ENDING THE LIVES OF THE REMAINING BEASTS WILL PROVE DIFFICULT.

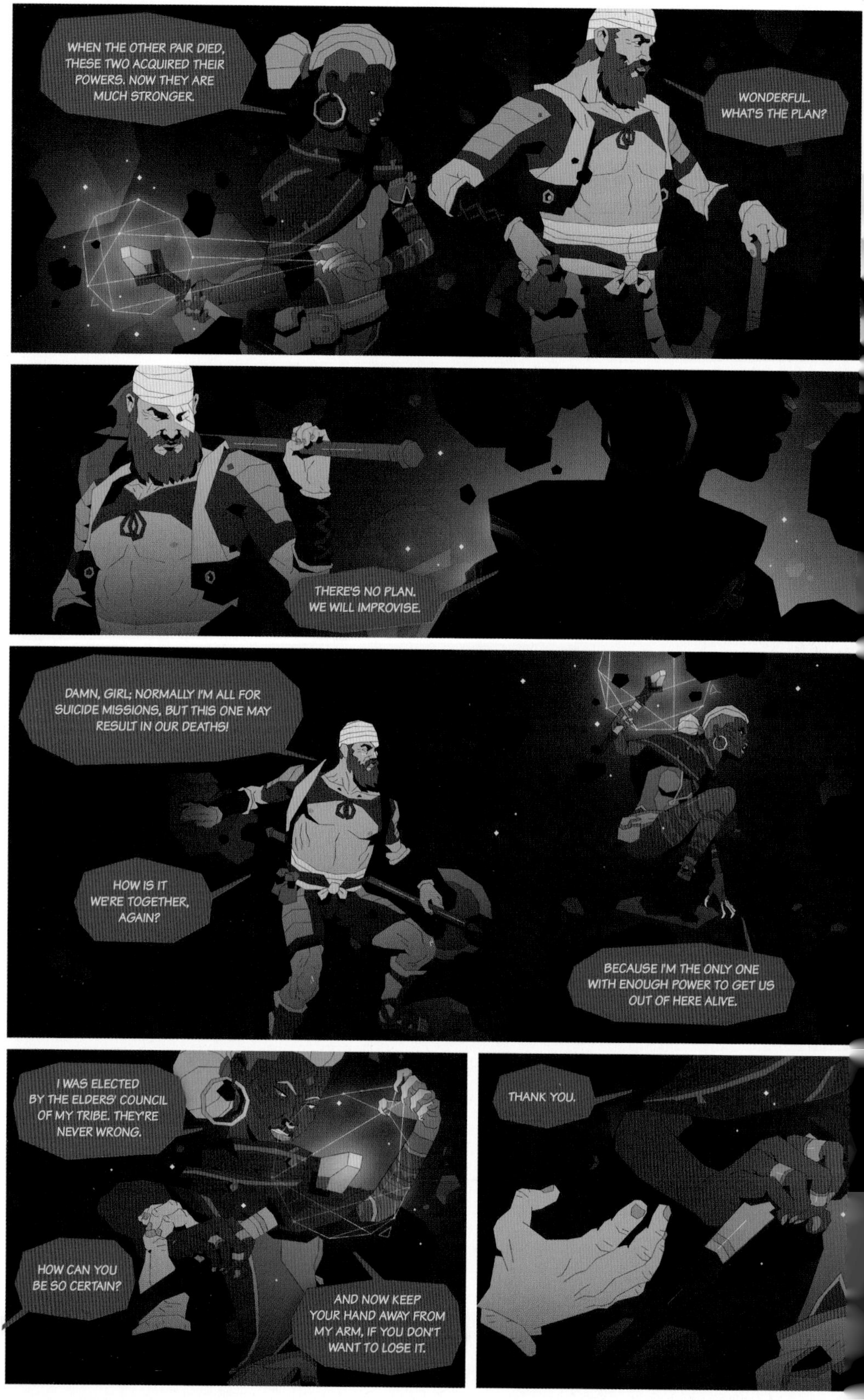
WHEN THE OTHER PAIR DIED, THESE TWO ACQUIRED THEIR POWERS. NOW THEY ARE MUCH STRONGER.
WONDERFUL. WHAT'S THE PLAN?
THERE'S NO PLAN. WE WILL IMPROVISE.
DAMN, GIRL; NORMALLY I'M ALL FOR SUICIDE MISSIONS, BUT THIS ONE MAY RESULT IN OUR DEATHS!
HOW IS IT WE'RE TOGETHER, AGAIN?
BECAUSE I'M THE ONLY ONE WITH ENOUGH POWER TO GET US OUT OF HERE ALIVE.
I WAS ELECTED BY THE ELDERS' COUNCIL OF MY TRIBE. THEY'RE NEVER WRONG.
HOW CAN YOU BE SO CERTAIN?
AND NOW KEEP YOUR HAND AWAY FROM MY ARM, IF YOU DON'T WANT TO LOSE IT.
THANK YOU.

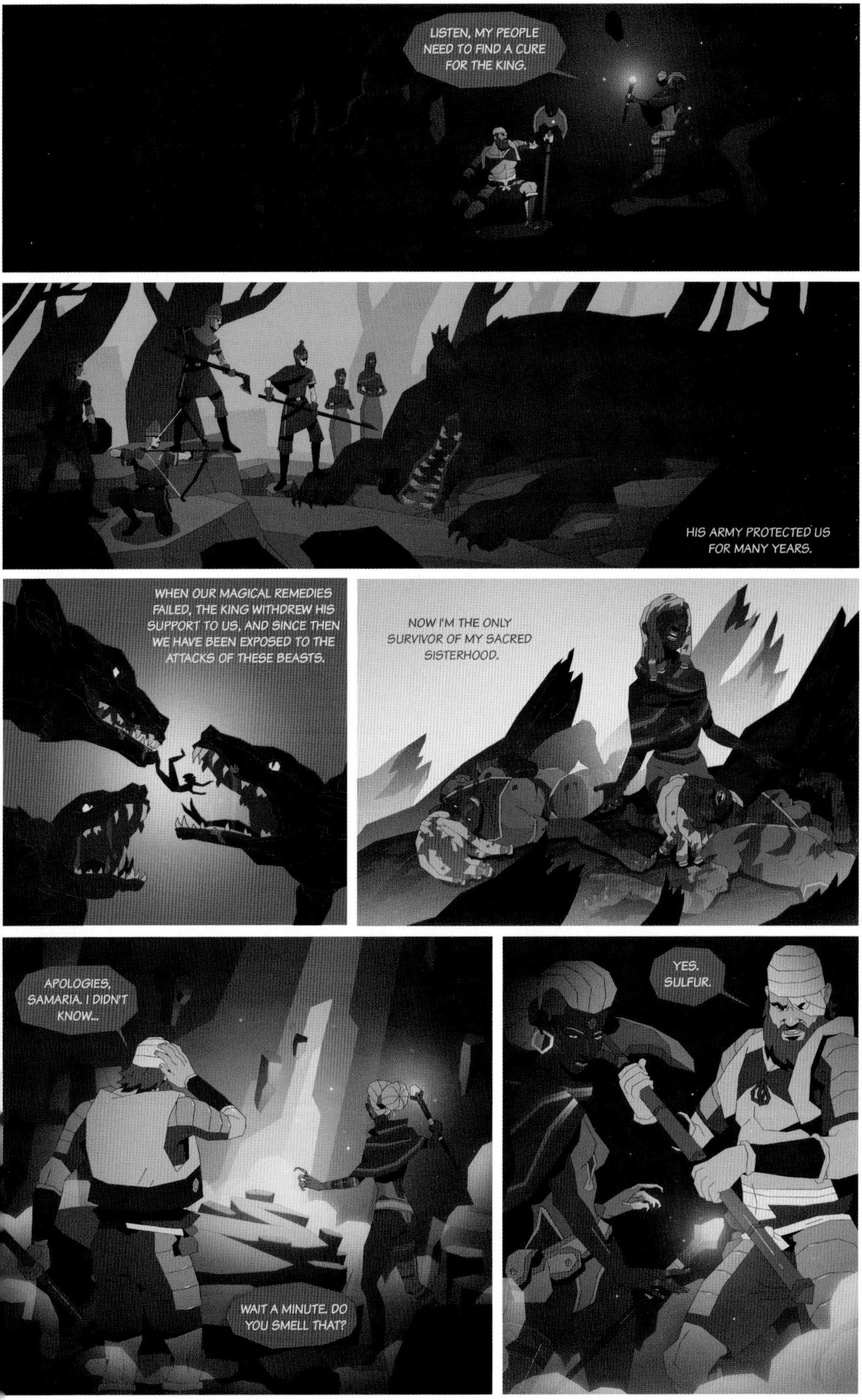
LISTEN, MY PEOPLE NEED TO FIND A CURE FOR THE KING.
HIS ARMY PROTECTED US FOR MANY YEARS.
WHEN OUR MAGICAL REMEDIES FAILED, THE KING WITHDREW HIS SUPPORT TO US, AND SINCE THEN WE HAVE BEEN EXPOSED TO THE ATTACKS OF THESE BEASTS.
NOW I'M THE ONLY SURVIVOR OF MY SACRED SISTERHOOD.
APOLOGIES, SAMARIA. I DIDN'T KNOW...
WAIT A MINUTE. DO YOU SMELL THAT?
YES. SULFUR.

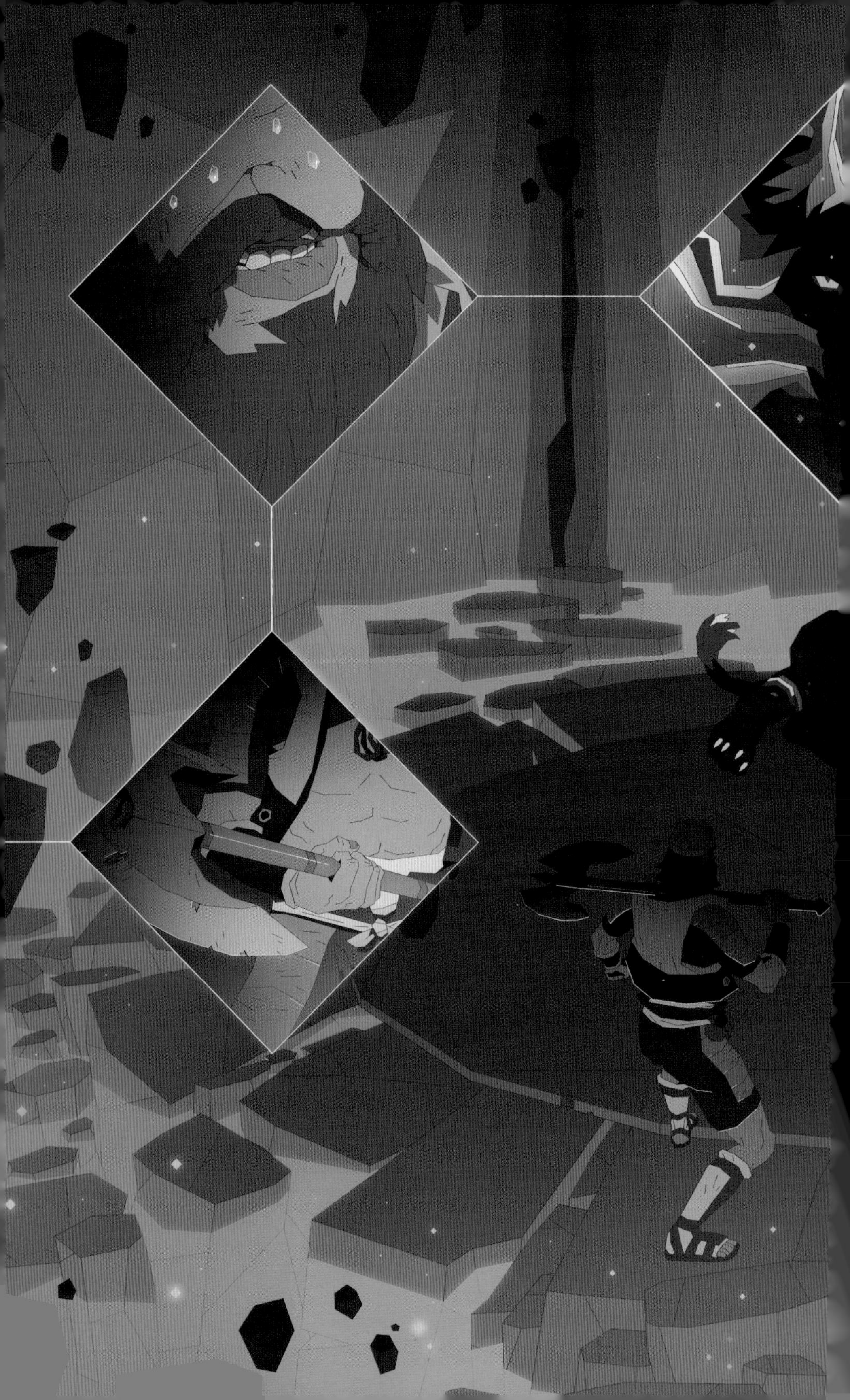

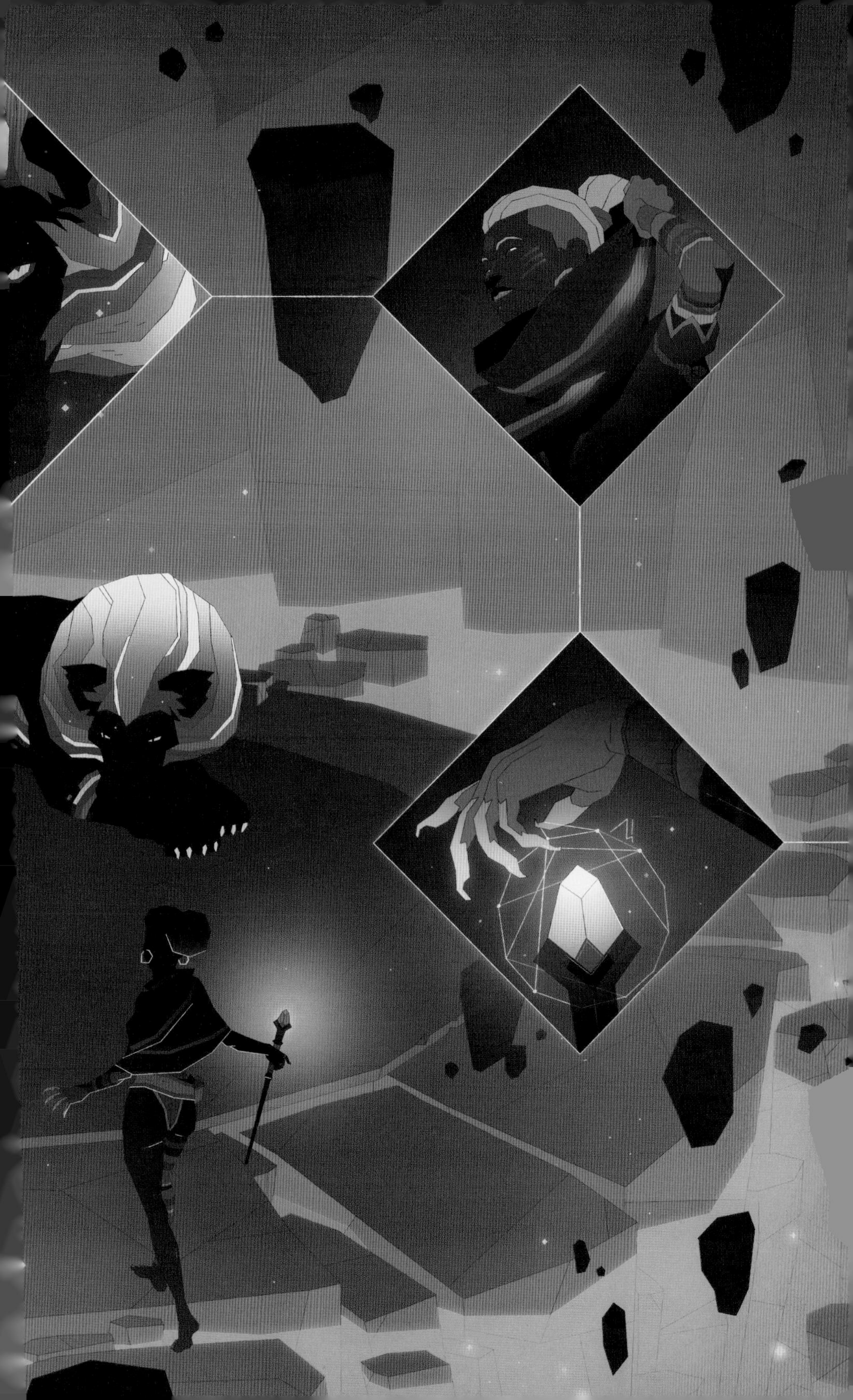

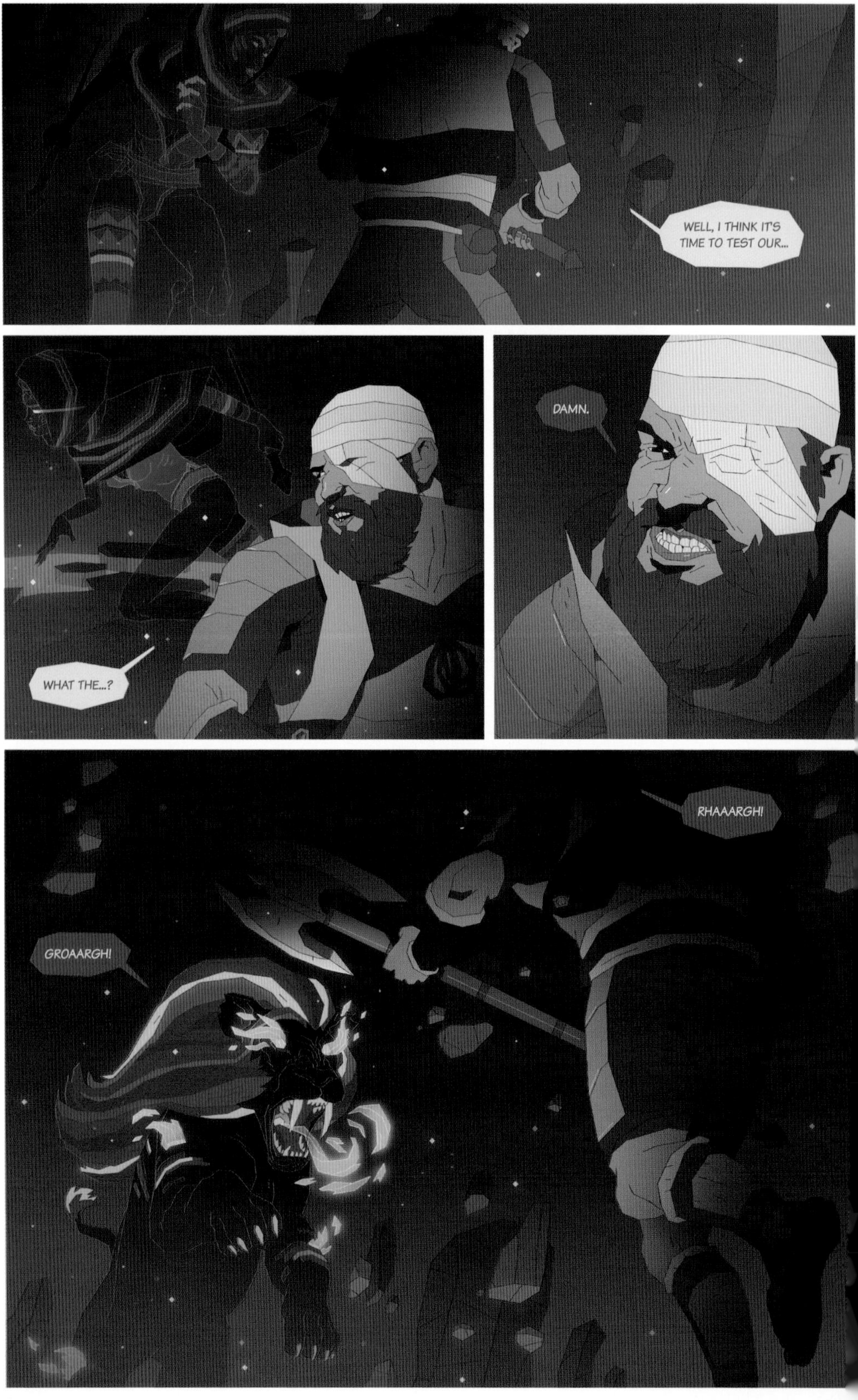
WELL, I THINK IT'S TIME TO TEST OUR...
WHAT THE...?
DAMN.
RHAAARGH!
GROAARGH!

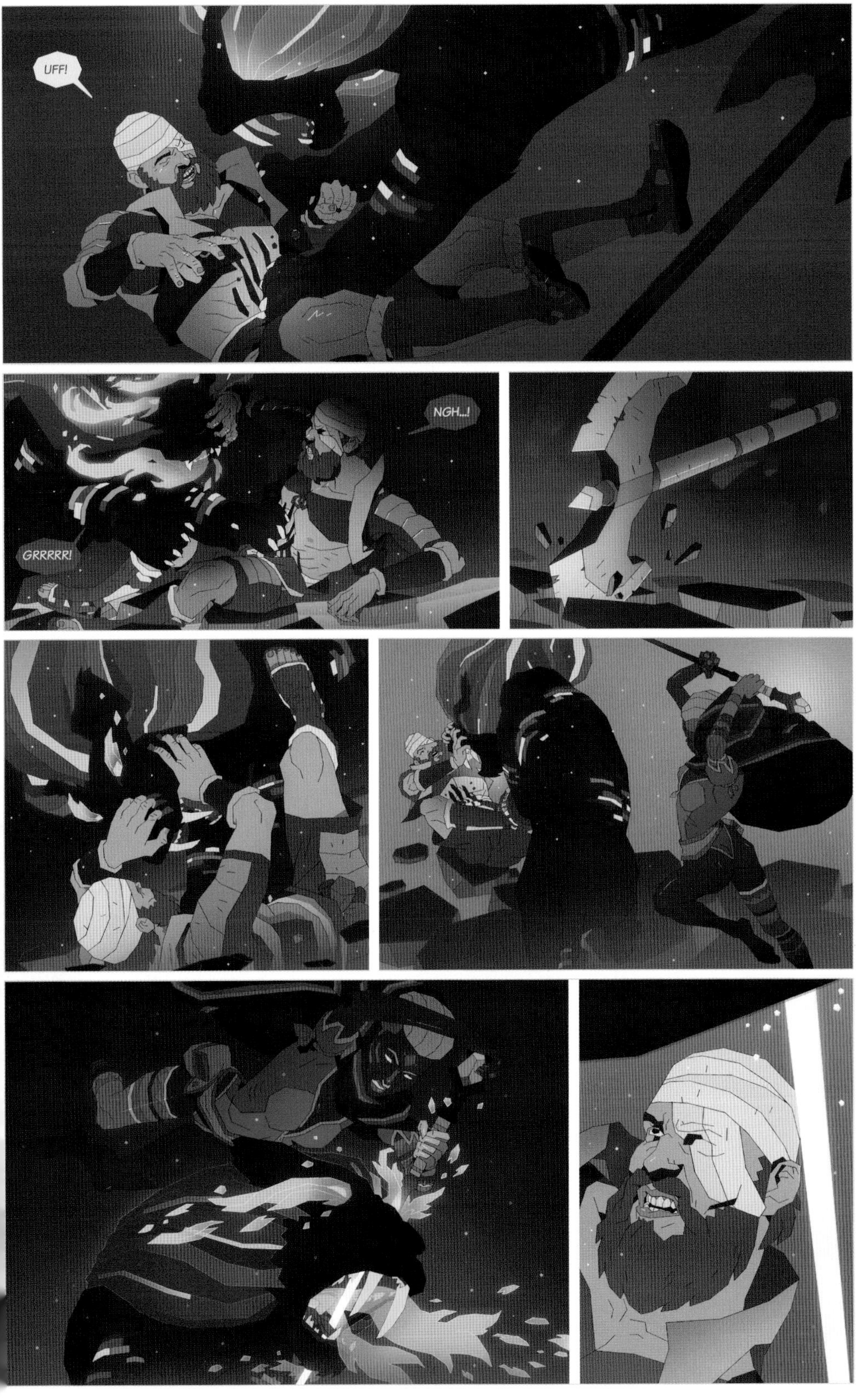
UFF!
NGH...!
GRRRRR!

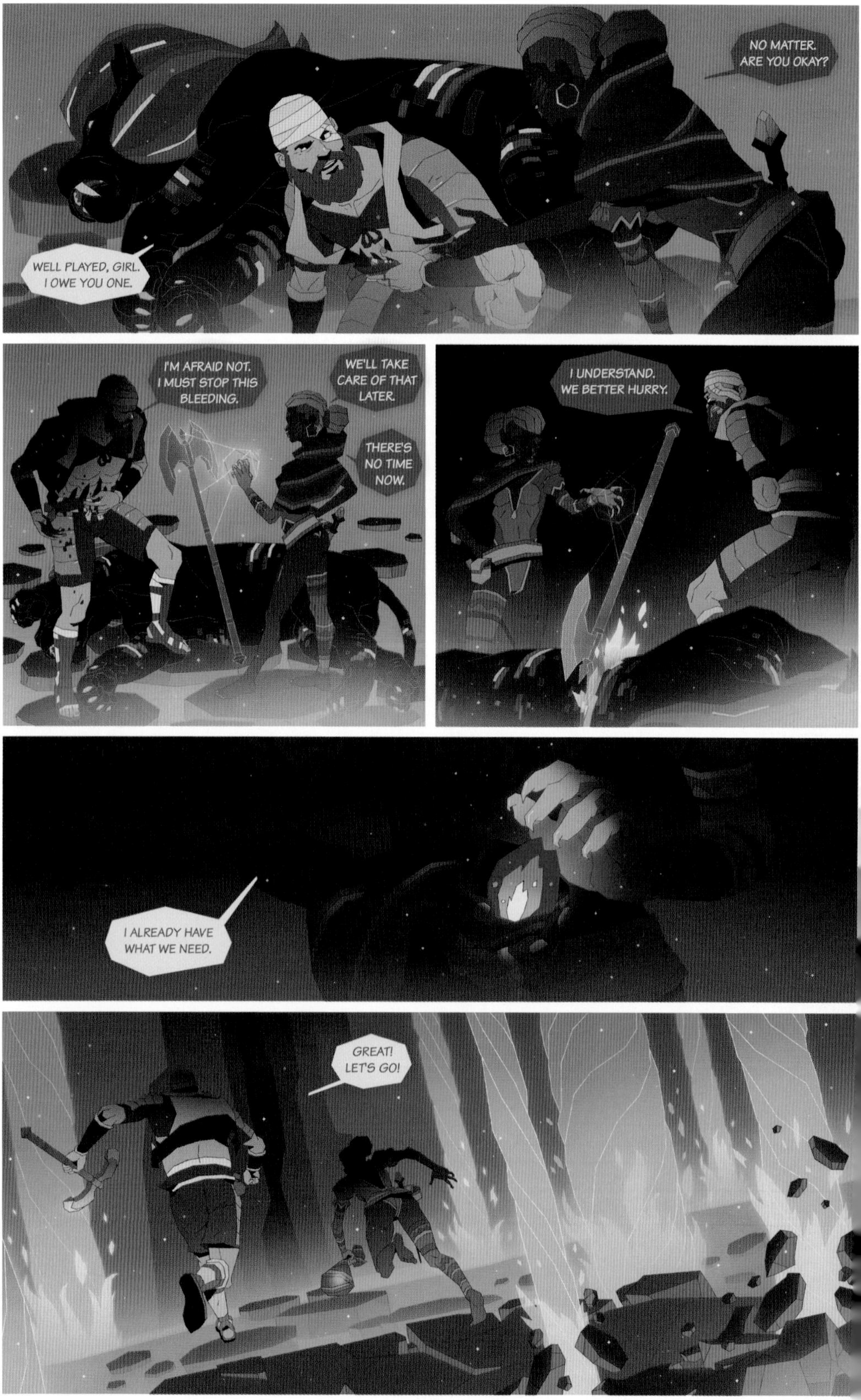
NO MATTER. ARE YOU OKAY?
WELL PLAYED, GIRL. I OWE YOU ONE.
I'M AFRAID NOT. I MUST STOP THIS BLEEDING.
WE'LL TAKE CARE OF THAT LATER.
THERE'S NO TIME NOW.
I UNDERSTAND. WE BETTER HURRY.
I ALREADY HAVE WHAT WE NEED.
GREAT! LET'S GO!

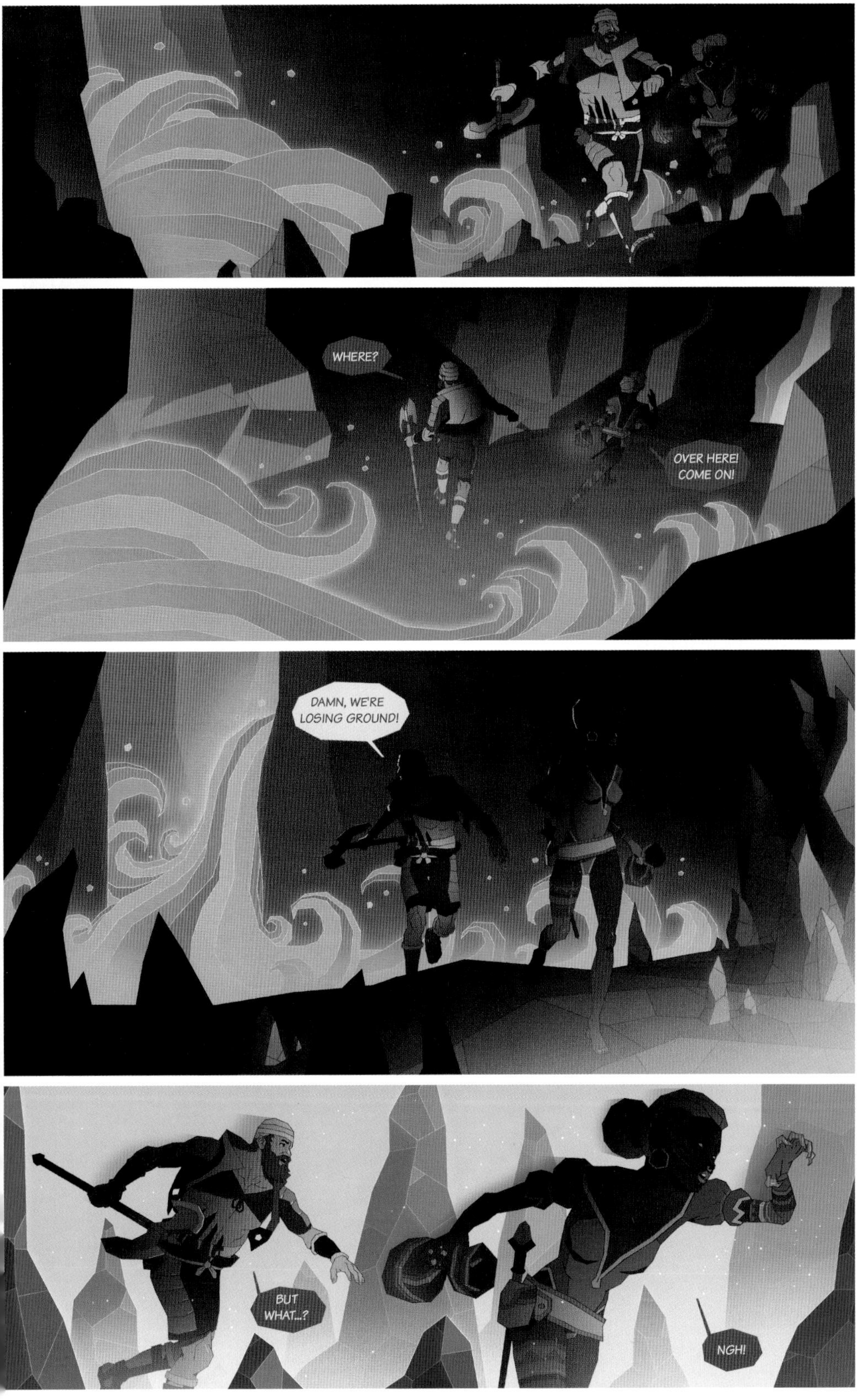

WHERE?
OVER HERE! COME ON!
DAMN, WE'RE LOSING GROUND!
BUT WHAT...?
NGH!

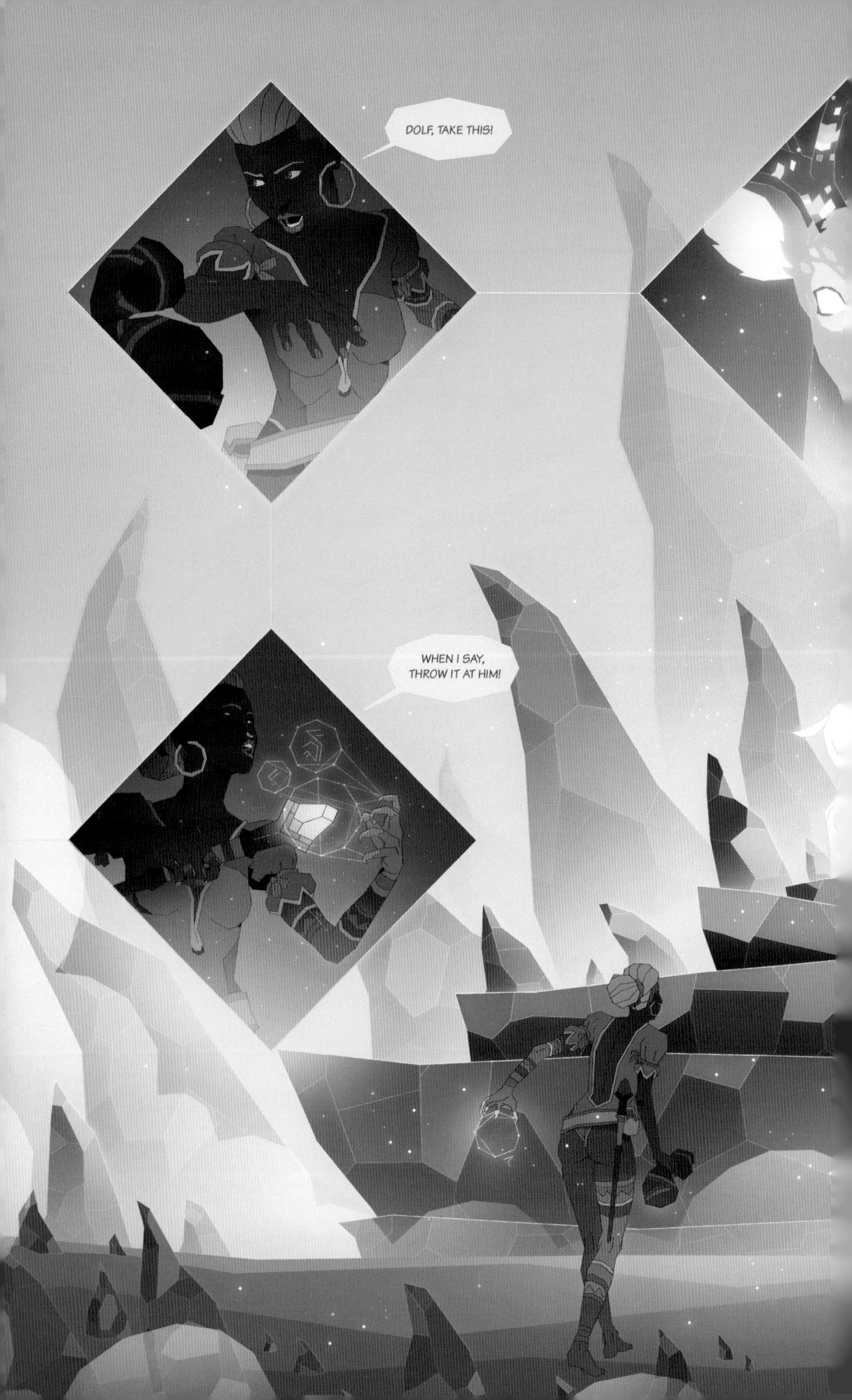
DOLF, TAKE THIS!
WHEN I SAY, THROW IT AT HIM!

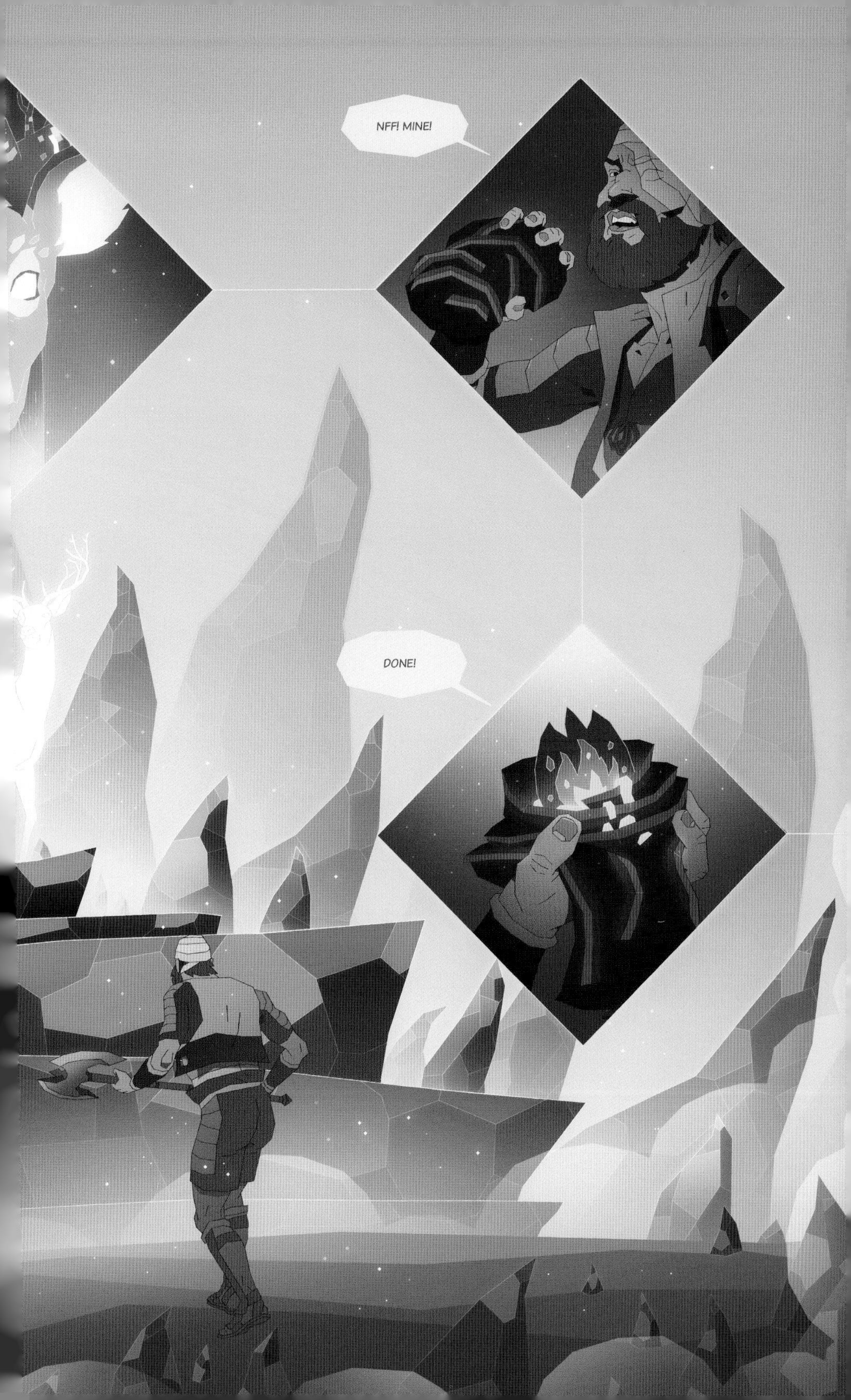
NFF! MINE!
DONE!

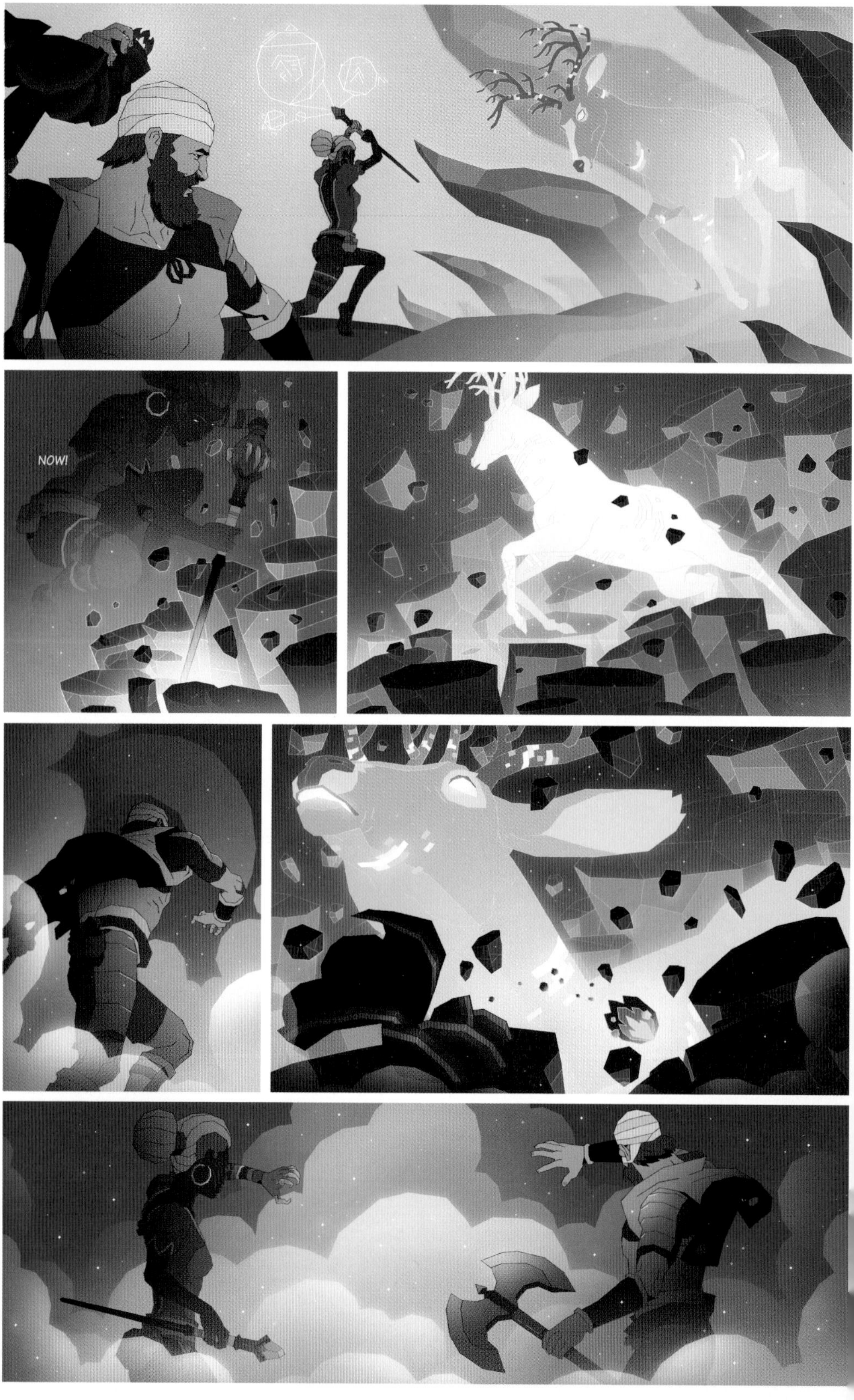
NOW!

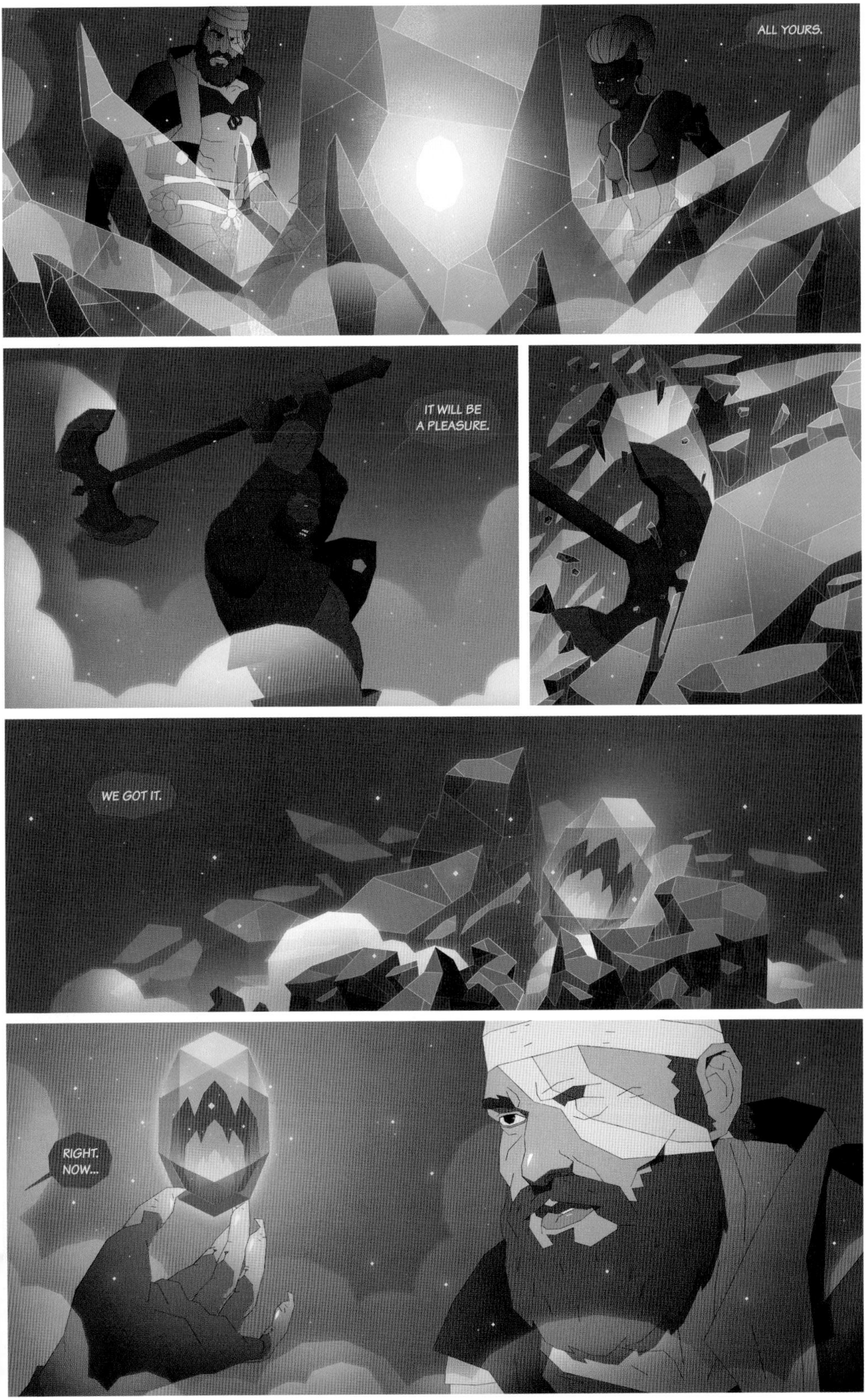
ALL YOURS.
IT WILL BE A PLEASURE.
WE GOT IT.
RIGHT. NOW...

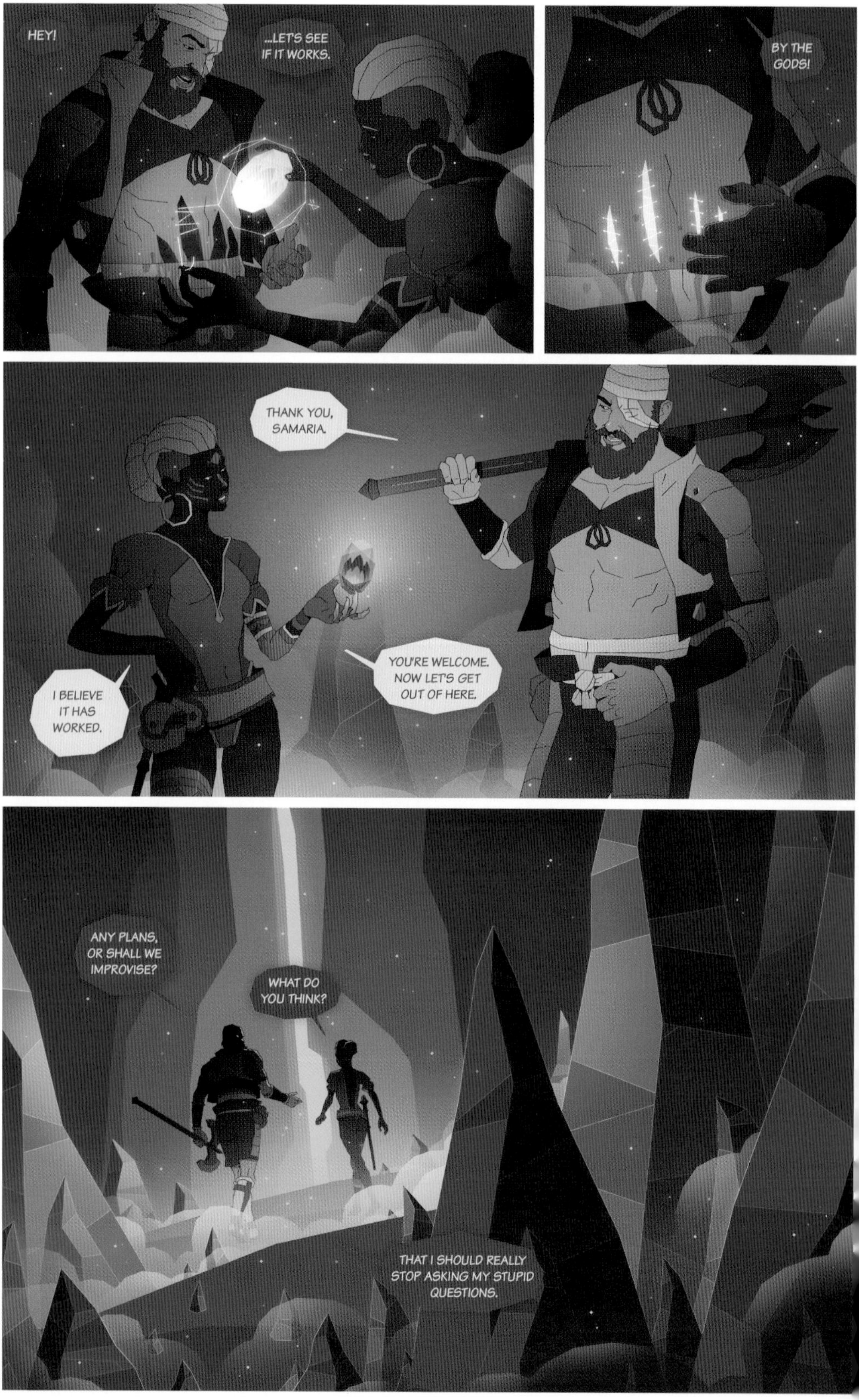
HEY!
...LET'S SEE IF IT WORKS.
BY THE GODS!
THANK YOU, SAMARIA.
I BELIEVE IT HAS WORKED.
YOU'RE WELCOME. NOW LET'S GET OUT OF HERE.
ANY PLANS, OR SHALL WE IMPROVISE?
WHAT DO YOU THINK?
THAT I SHOULD REALLY STOP ASKING MY STUPID QUESTIONS.

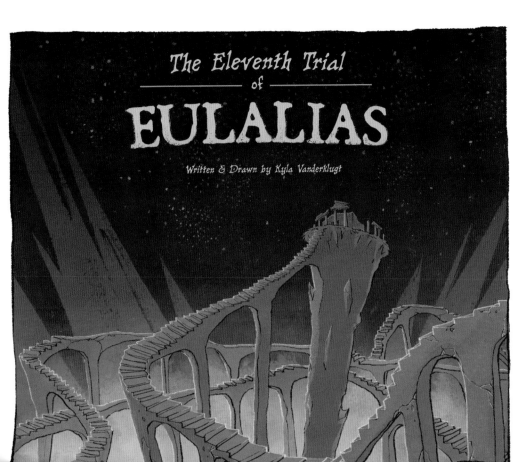

The Eleventh Trial
of
EULALIAS

Written & Drawn by Kyla Vanderklugt

THAT PILE OF RUBBLE UP THERE – IS IT REALLY WORTH ALL THESE STAIRS?

INVITING AS IT LOOKS, AND ALL.

THERE'S NO PLACE ELSE TO GO. BESIDES, I RECOGNIZE THE PLACE – STRANGE AS THAT MAY SEEM.

BEEN HERE BEFORE, HAVE YOU?

DON'T BE SMART, BRAUN; IT DOESN'T SUIT YOU.

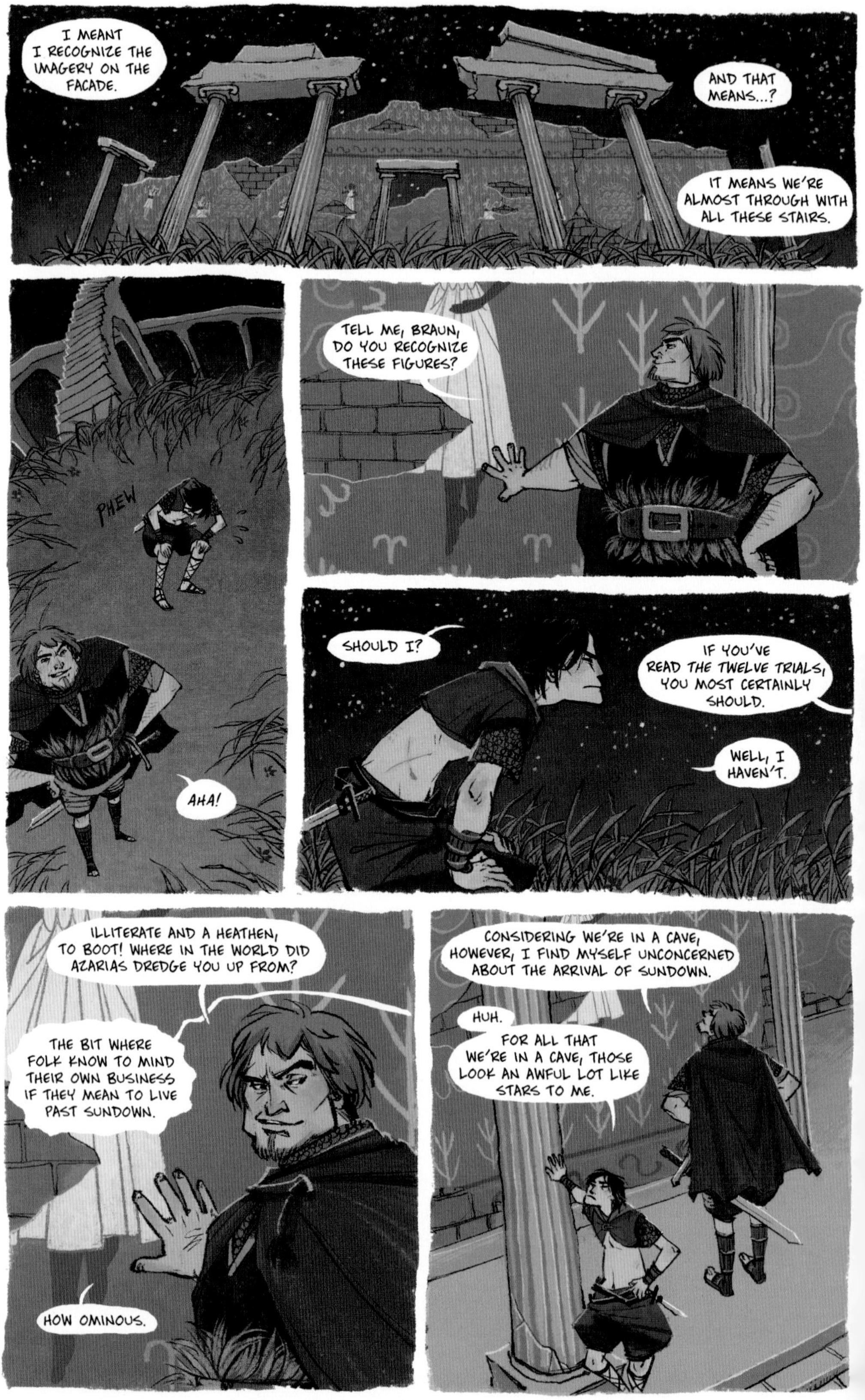

I MEANT I RECOGNIZE THE IMAGERY ON THE FACADE.
AND THAT MEANS...?
IT MEANS WE'RE ALMOST THROUGH WITH ALL THESE STAIRS.
PHEW
AHA!
TELL ME, BRAUN, DO YOU RECOGNIZE THESE FIGURES?
SHOULD I?
IF YOU'VE READ THE TWELVE TRIALS, YOU MOST CERTAINLY SHOULD.
WELL, I HAVEN'T.
ILLITERATE AND A HEATHEN, TO BOOT! WHERE IN THE WORLD DID AZARIAS DREDGE YOU UP FROM?
THE BIT WHERE FOLK KNOW TO MIND THEIR OWN BUSINESS IF THEY MEAN TO LIVE PAST SUNDOWN.
HOW OMINOUS.
CONSIDERING WE'RE IN A CAVE, HOWEVER, I FIND MYSELF UNCONCERNED ABOUT THE ARRIVAL OF SUNDOWN.
HUH.
FOR ALL THAT WE'RE IN A CAVE, THOSE LOOK AN AWFUL LOT LIKE STARS TO ME.

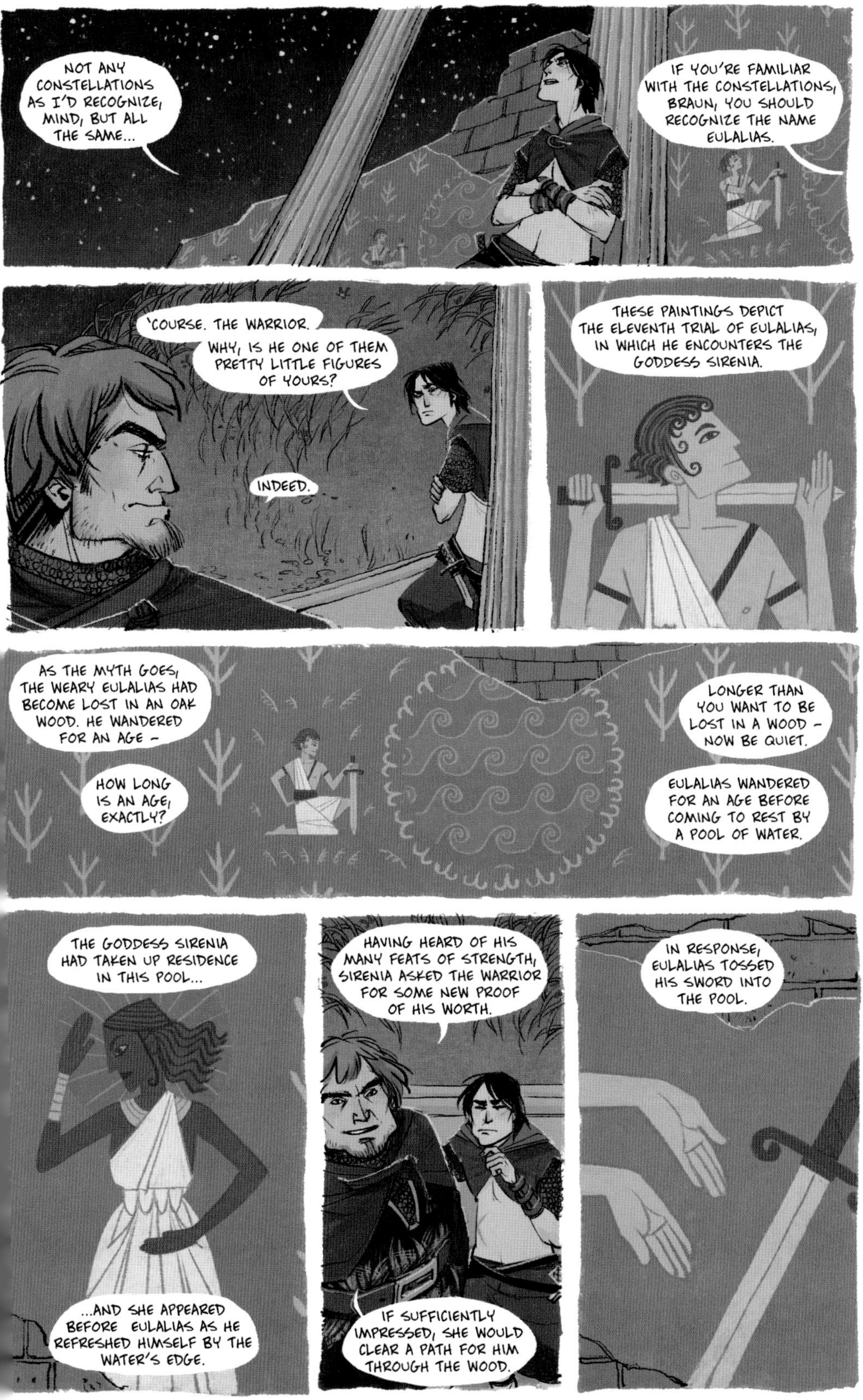
NOT ANY CONSTELLATIONS AS I'D RECOGNIZE, MIND, BUT ALL THE SAME...
IF YOU'RE FAMILIAR WITH THE CONSTELLATIONS, BRAUN, YOU SHOULD RECOGNIZE THE NAME EULALIAS.
'COURSE. THE WARRIOR.
WHY, IS HE ONE OF THEM PRETTY LITTLE FIGURES OF YOURS?
INDEED.
THESE PAINTINGS DEPICT THE ELEVENTH TRIAL OF EULALIAS, IN WHICH HE ENCOUNTERS THE GODDESS SIRENIA.
AS THE MYTH GOES, THE WEARY EULALIAS HAD BECOME LOST IN AN OAK WOOD. HE WANDERED FOR AN AGE –
HOW LONG IS AN AGE, EXACTLY?
LONGER THAN YOU WANT TO BE LOST IN A WOOD – NOW BE QUIET.
EULALIAS WANDERED FOR AN AGE BEFORE COMING TO REST BY A POOL OF WATER.
THE GODDESS SIRENIA HAD TAKEN UP RESIDENCE IN THIS POOL...
...AND SHE APPEARED BEFORE EULALIAS AS HE REFRESHED HIMSELF BY THE WATER'S EDGE.
HAVING HEARD OF HIS MANY FEATS OF STRENGTH, SIRENIA ASKED THE WARRIOR FOR SOME NEW PROOF OF HIS WORTH.
IF SUFFICIENTLY IMPRESSED, SHE WOULD CLEAR A PATH FOR HIM THROUGH THE WOOD.
IN RESPONSE, EULALIAS TOSSED HIS SWORD INTO THE POOL.

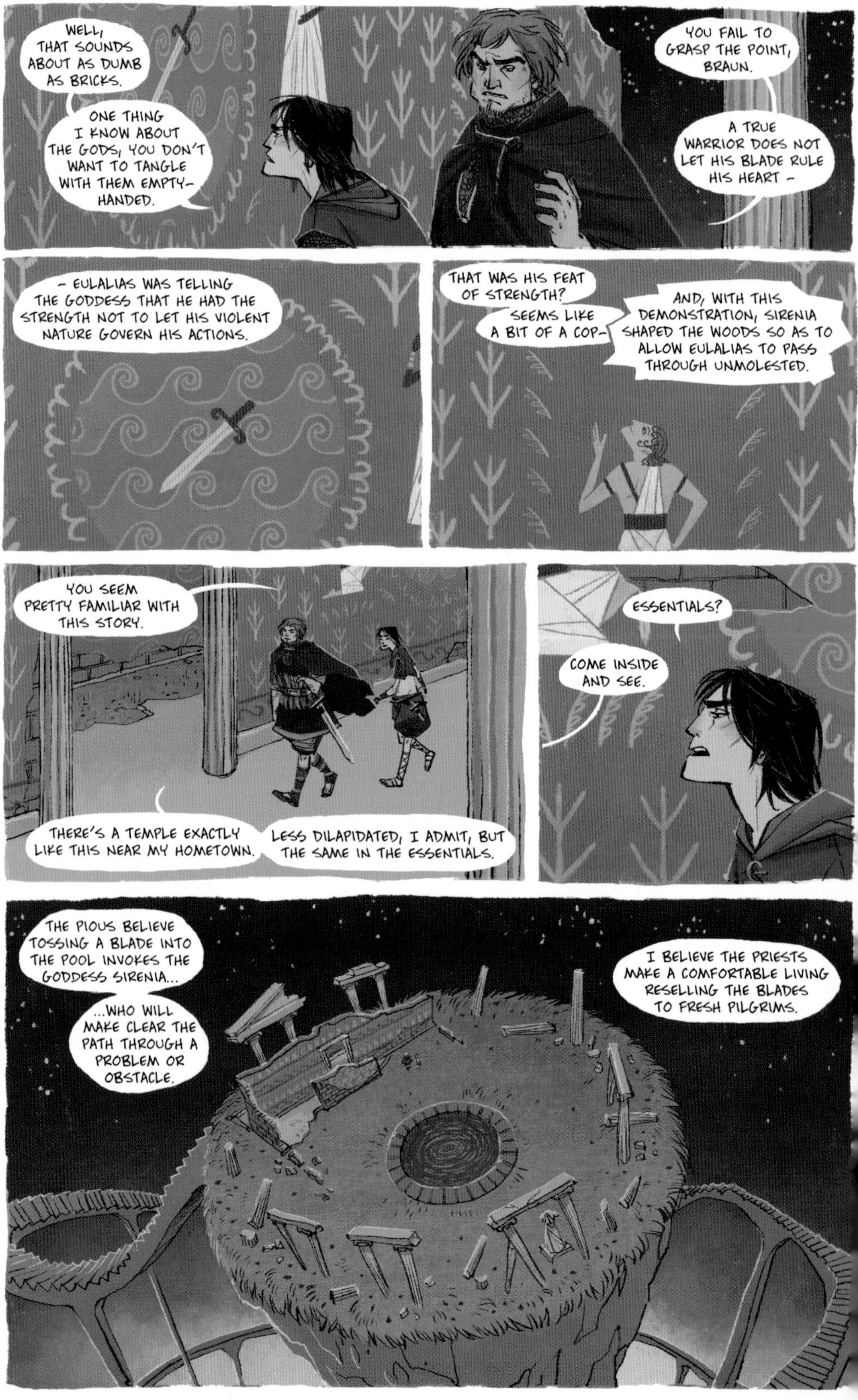
WELL, THAT SOUNDS ABOUT AS DUMB AS BRICKS.
ONE THING I KNOW ABOUT THE GODS, YOU DON'T WANT TO TANGLE WITH THEM EMPTY-HANDED.
YOU FAIL TO GRASP THE POINT, BRAUN.
A TRUE WARRIOR DOES NOT LET HIS BLADE RULE HIS HEART –
– EULALIAS WAS TELLING THE GODDESS THAT HE HAD THE STRENGTH NOT TO LET HIS VIOLENT NATURE GOVERN HIS ACTIONS.
THAT WAS HIS FEAT OF STRENGTH?
SEEMS LIKE A BIT OF A COP–
AND, WITH THIS DEMONSTRATION, SIRENIA SHAPED THE WOODS SO AS TO ALLOW EULALIAS TO PASS THROUGH UNMOLESTED.
YOU SEEM PRETTY FAMILIAR WITH THIS STORY.
THERE'S A TEMPLE EXACTLY LIKE THIS NEAR MY HOMETOWN.
LESS DILAPIDATED, I ADMIT, BUT THE SAME IN THE ESSENTIALS.
ESSENTIALS?
COME INSIDE AND SEE.
THE PIOUS BELIEVE TOSSING A BLADE INTO THE POOL INVOKES THE GODDESS SIRENIA...
...WHO WILL MAKE CLEAR THE PATH THROUGH A PROBLEM OR OBSTACLE.
I BELIEVE THE PRIESTS MAKE A COMFORTABLE LIVING RESELLING THE BLADES TO FRESH PILGRIMS.

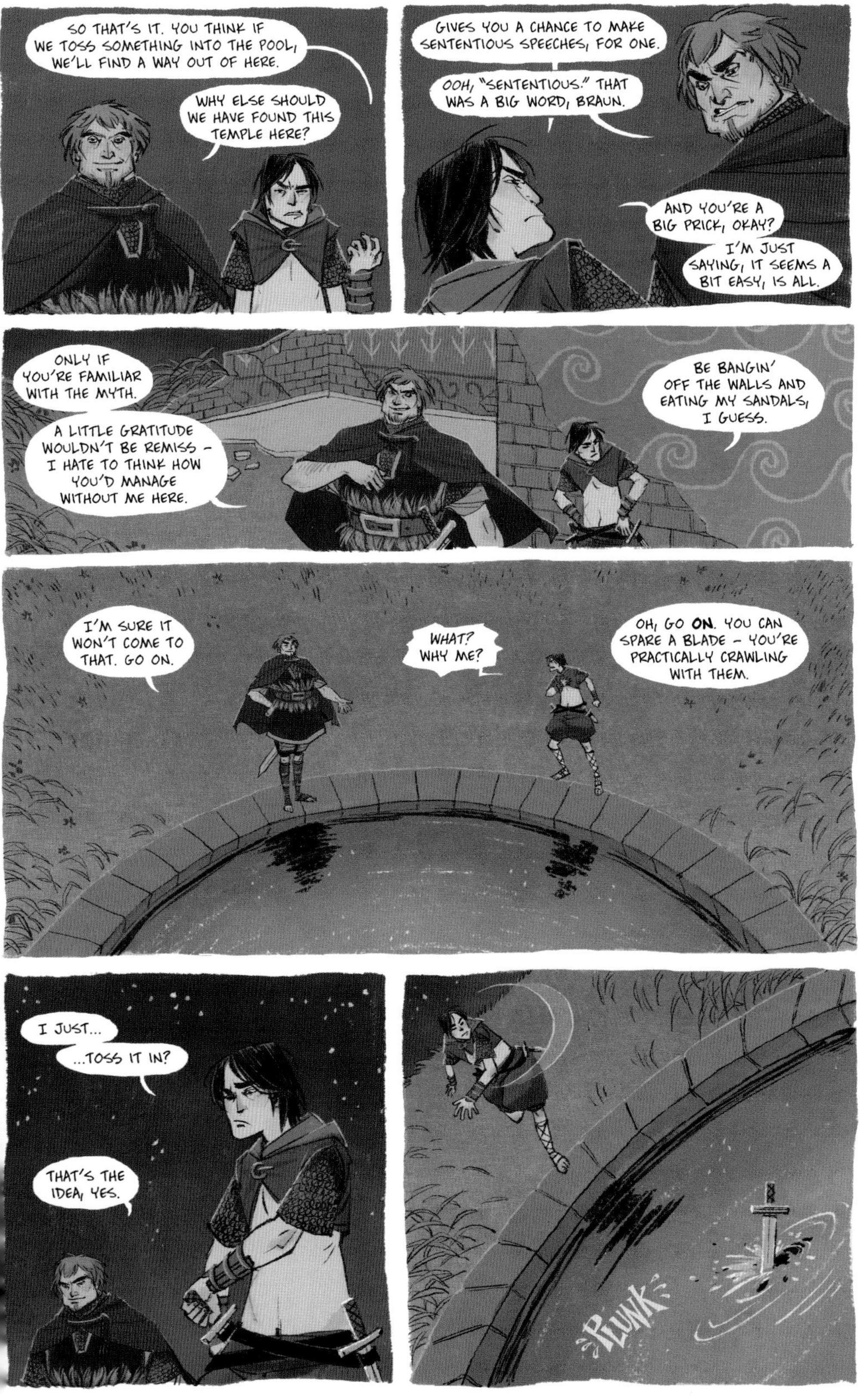
SO THAT'S IT. YOU THINK IF WE TOSS SOMETHING INTO THE POOL, WE'LL FIND A WAY OUT OF HERE.
WHY ELSE SHOULD WE HAVE FOUND THIS TEMPLE HERE?
GIVES YOU A CHANCE TO MAKE SENTENTIOUS SPEECHES, FOR ONE.
OOH, "SENTENTIOUS." THAT WAS A BIG WORD, BRAUN.
AND YOU'RE A BIG PRICK, OKAY?
I'M JUST SAYING, IT SEEMS A BIT EASY, IS ALL.
ONLY IF YOU'RE FAMILIAR WITH THE MYTH.
A LITTLE GRATITUDE WOULDN'T BE REMISS – I HATE TO THINK HOW YOU'D MANAGE WITHOUT ME HERE.
BE BANGIN' OFF THE WALLS AND EATING MY SANDALS, I GUESS.
I'M SURE IT WON'T COME TO THAT. GO ON.
WHAT? WHY ME?
OH, GO ON. YOU CAN SPARE A BLADE – YOU'RE PRACTICALLY CRAWLING WITH THEM.
I JUST...
...TOSS IT IN?
THAT'S THE IDEA, YES.
PLUNK

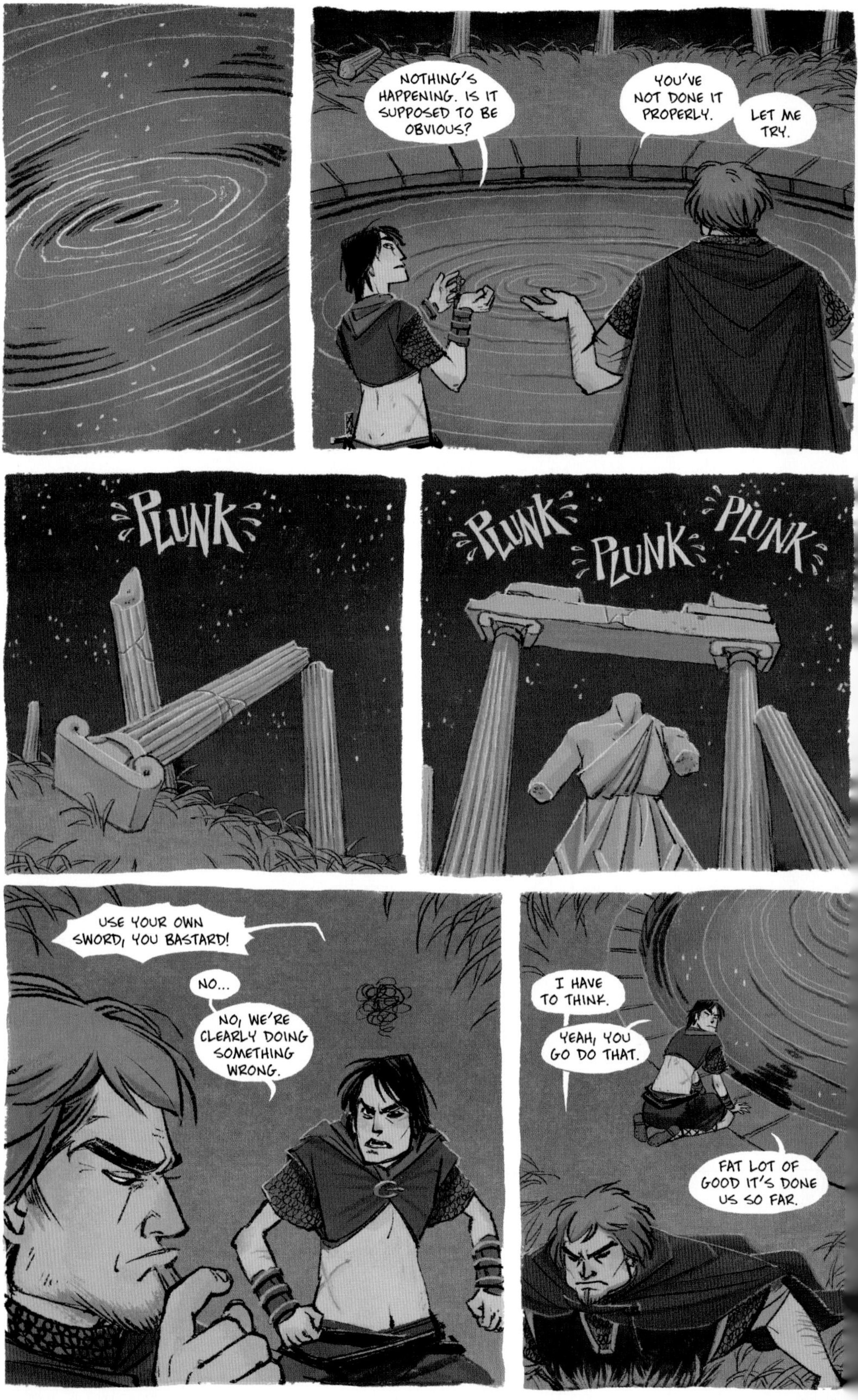
NOTHING'S HAPPENING. IS IT SUPPOSED TO BE OBVIOUS?
YOU'VE NOT DONE IT PROPERLY.
LET ME TRY.
PLUNK
PLUNK
PLUNK
PLUNK
USE YOUR OWN SWORD, YOU BASTARD!
NO...
NO, WE'RE CLEARLY DOING SOMETHING WRONG.
I HAVE TO THINK.
YEAH, YOU GO DO THAT.
FAT LOT OF GOOD IT'S DONE US SO FAR.

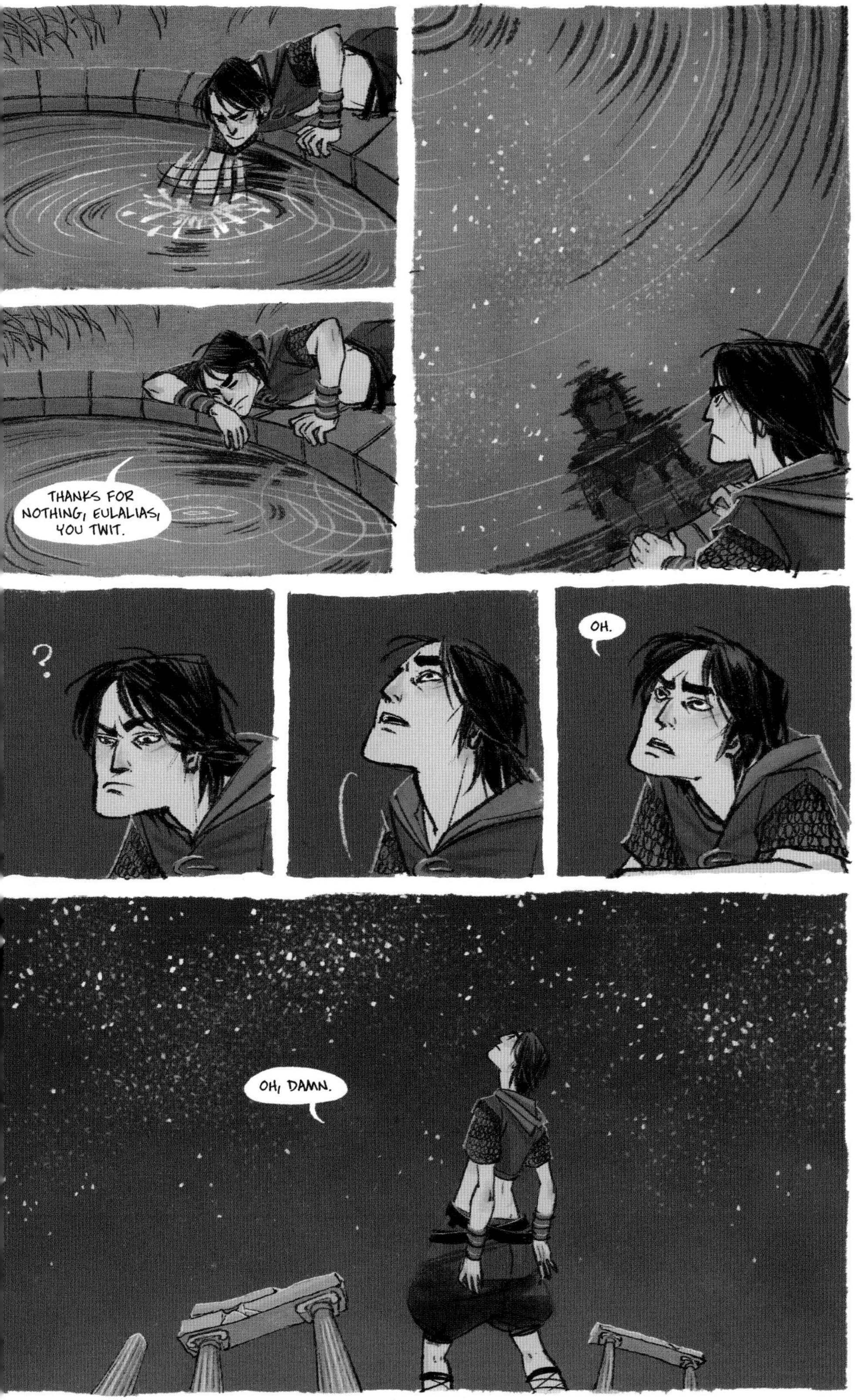
THANKS FOR NOTHING, EULALIAS, YOU TWIT.
?
OH.
OH, DAMN.

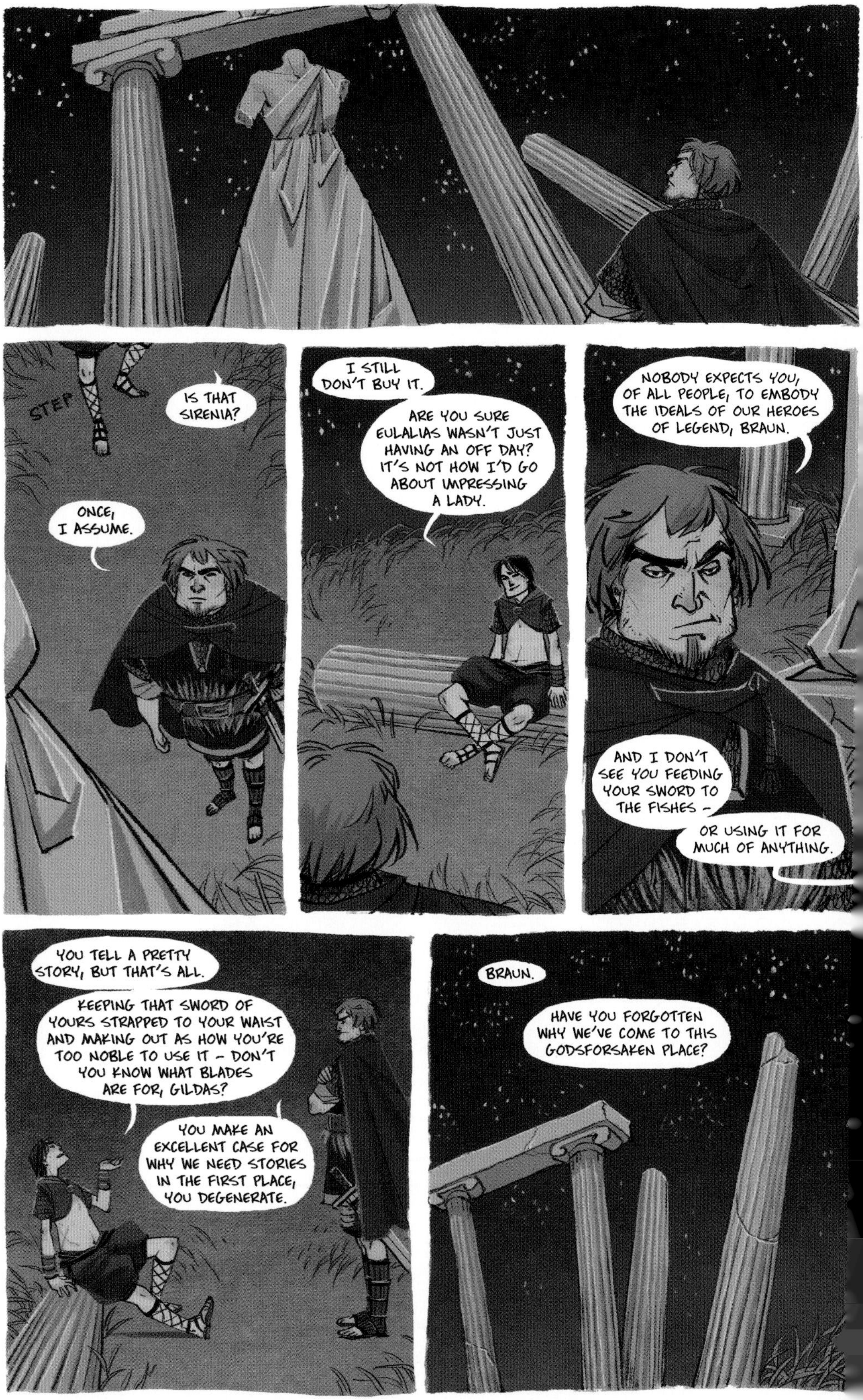

STEP
IS THAT SIRENIA?
ONCE, I ASSUME.
I STILL DON'T BUY IT.
ARE YOU SURE EULALIAS WASN'T JUST HAVING AN OFF DAY? IT'S NOT HOW I'D GO ABOUT IMPRESSING A LADY.
NOBODY EXPECTS YOU, OF ALL PEOPLE, TO EMBODY THE IDEALS OF OUR HEROES OF LEGEND, BRAUN.
AND I DON'T SEE YOU FEEDING YOUR SWORD TO THE FISHES –
OR USING IT FOR MUCH OF ANYTHING.
YOU TELL A PRETTY STORY, BUT THAT'S ALL.
KEEPING THAT SWORD OF YOURS STRAPPED TO YOUR WAIST AND MAKING OUT AS HOW YOU'RE TOO NOBLE TO USE IT – DON'T YOU KNOW WHAT BLADES ARE FOR, GILDAS?
YOU MAKE AN EXCELLENT CASE FOR WHY WE NEED STORIES IN THE FIRST PLACE, YOU DEGENERATE.
BRAUN.
HAVE YOU FORGOTTEN WHY WE'VE COME TO THIS GODSFORSAKEN PLACE?

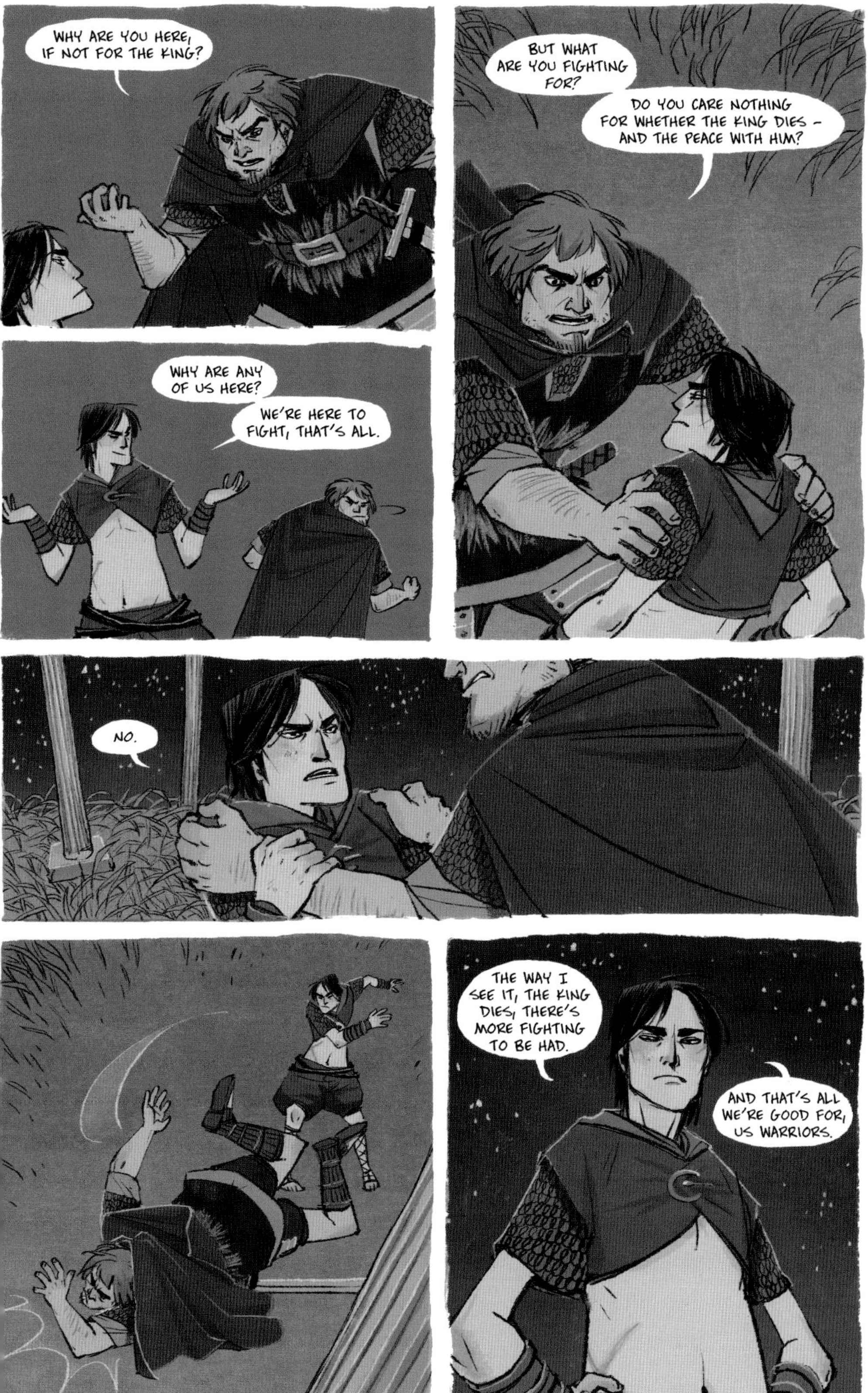
WHY ARE YOU HERE, IF NOT FOR THE KING?
BUT WHAT ARE YOU FIGHTING FOR?
DO YOU CARE NOTHING FOR WHETHER THE KING DIES - AND THE PEACE WITH HIM?
WHY ARE ANY OF US HERE?
WE'RE HERE TO FIGHT, THAT'S ALL.
NO.
THE WAY I SEE IT, THE KING DIES, THERE'S MORE FIGHTING TO BE HAD.
AND THAT'S ALL WE'RE GOOD FOR, US WARRIORS.

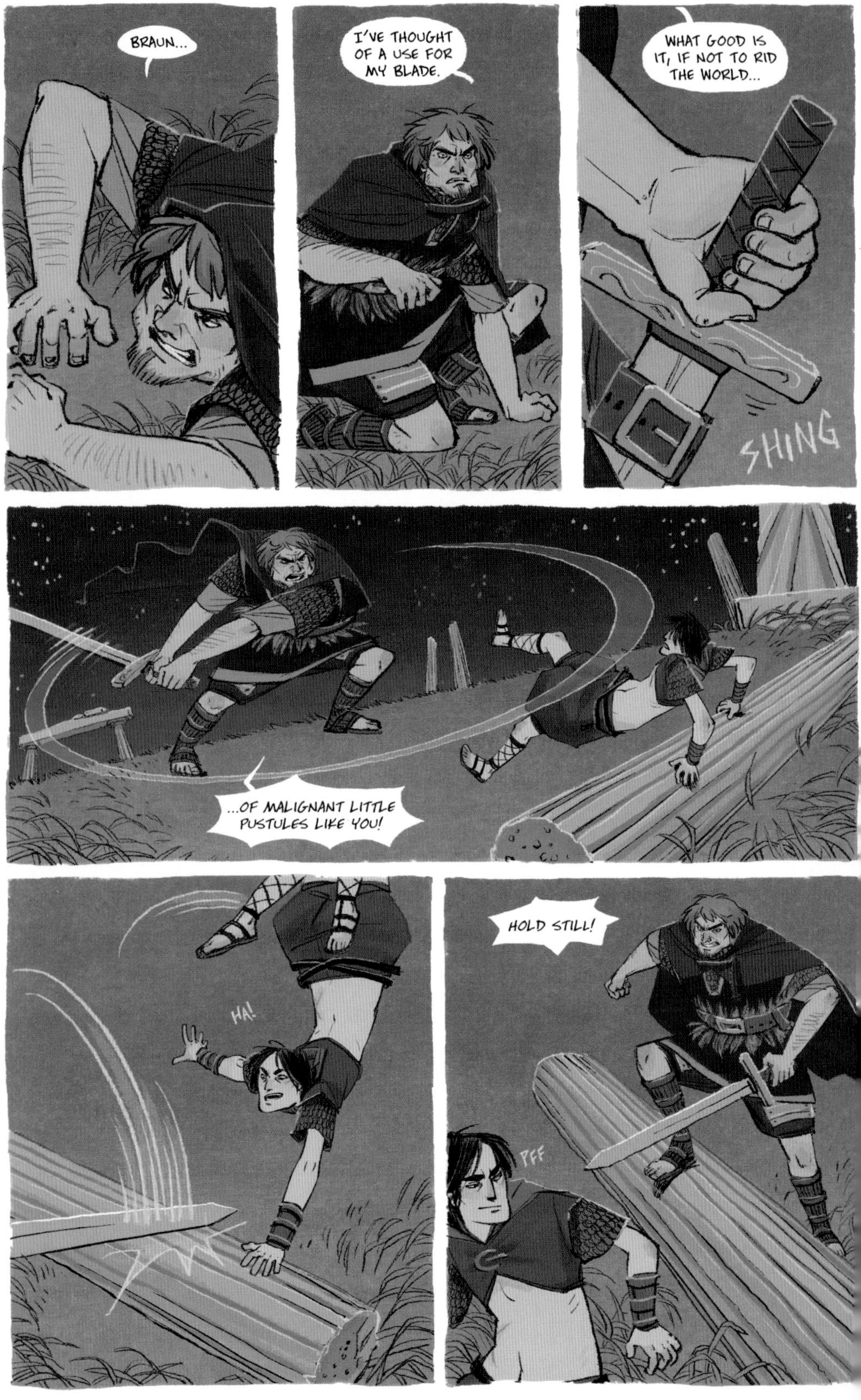
BRAUN...
I'VE THOUGHT OF A USE FOR MY BLADE.
WHAT GOOD IS IT, IF NOT TO RID THE WORLD...
SHING
...OF MALIGNANT LITTLE PUSTULES LIKE YOU!
HA!
HOLD STILL!
PFF

TRIP

WELL, BRAUN?

DO YOUR OPINIONS ON THE USEFULNESS OF SWORDS HOLD FIRM?

ANY CHANGES OF HEART?

NOT...

...ON YOUR...

...LIFE.

IT'S NOT **MY** LIFE THAT HANGS IN THE BALANCE.

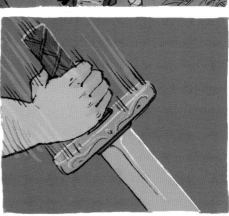

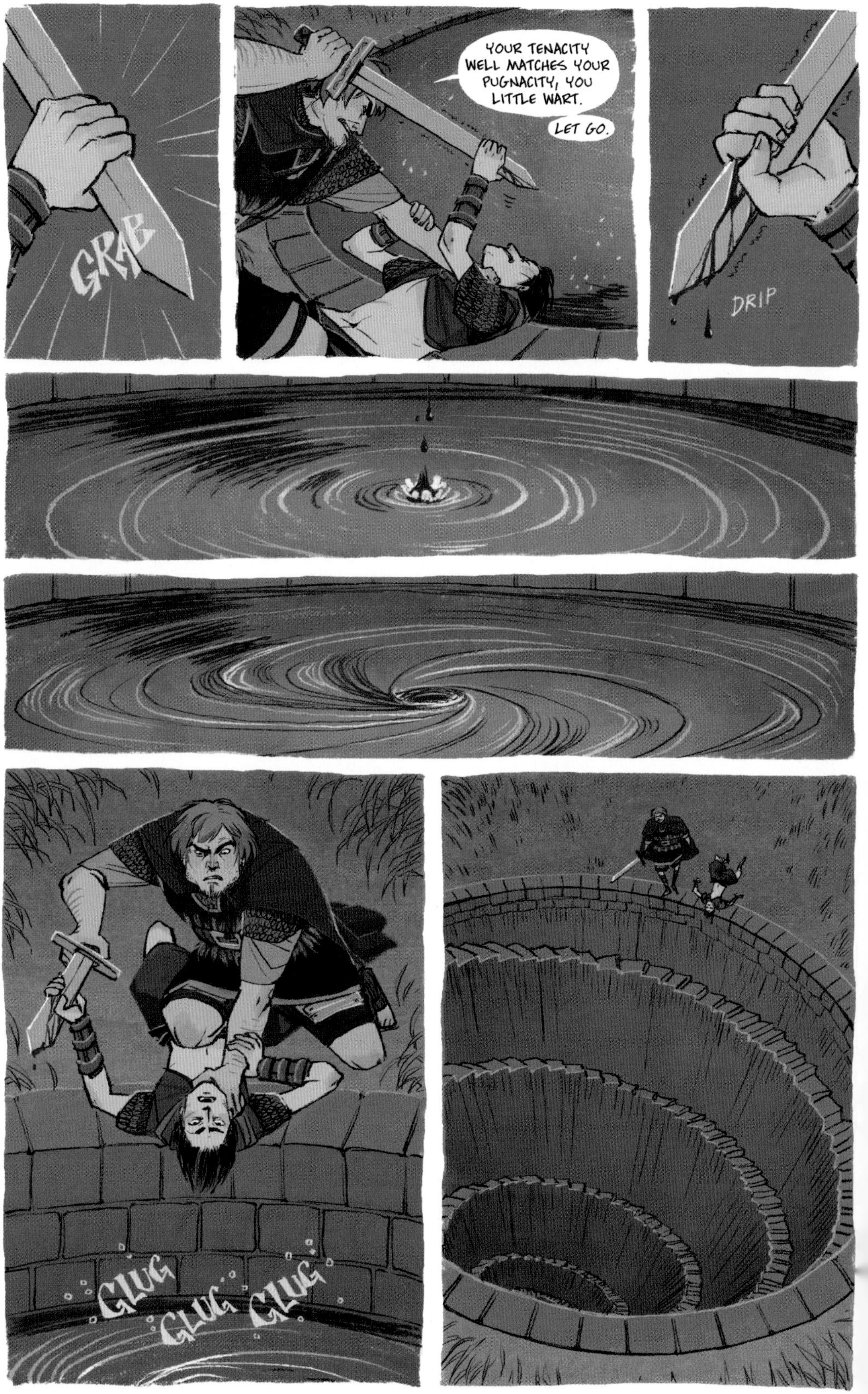
GRAB
YOUR TENACITY WELL MATCHES YOUR PUGNACITY, YOU LITTLE WART.
LET GO.
DRIP
GLUG GLUG GLUG

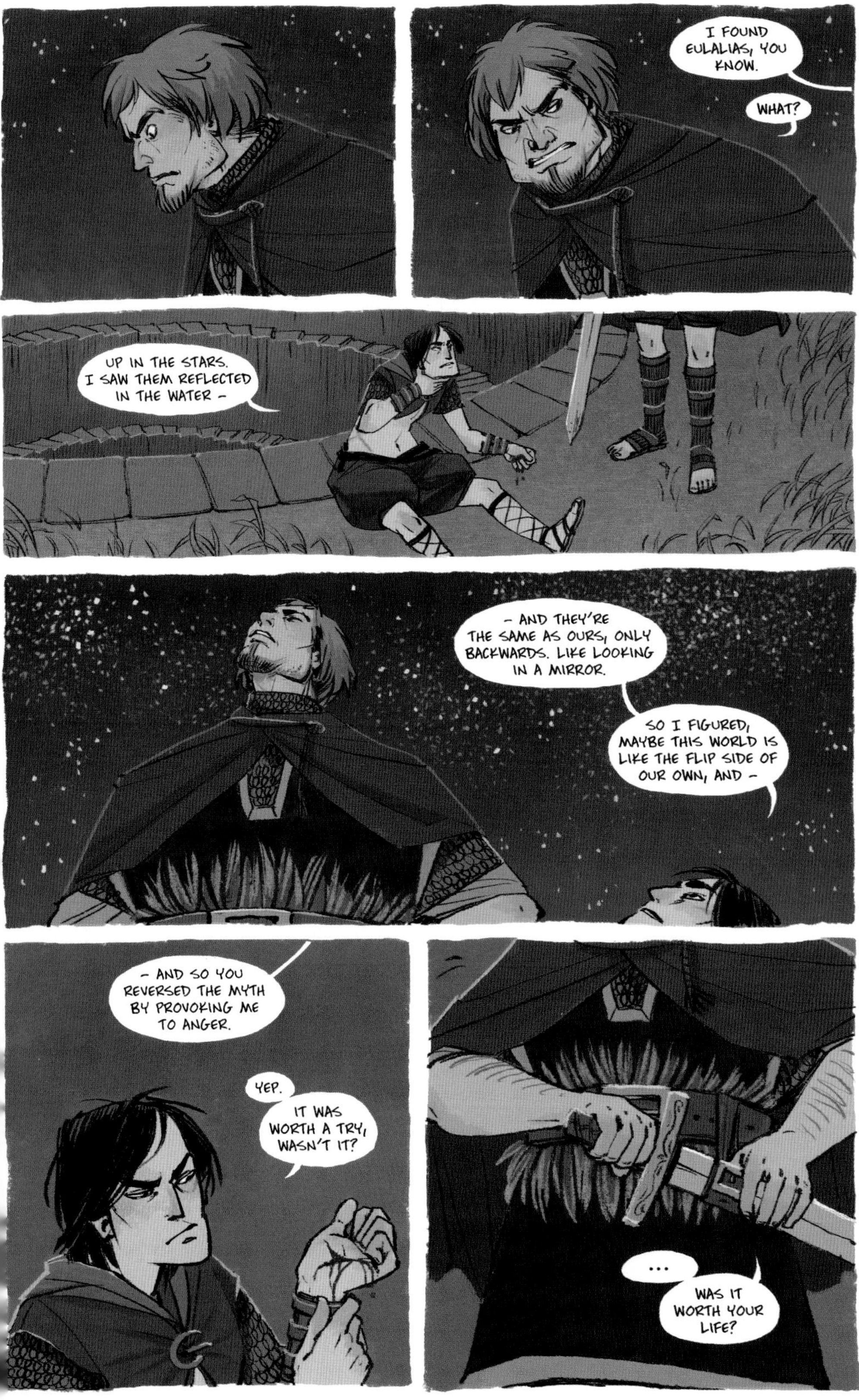
I FOUND EULALIAS, YOU KNOW.
WHAT?
UP IN THE STARS. I SAW THEM REFLECTED IN THE WATER –
– AND THEY'RE THE SAME AS OURS, ONLY BACKWARDS. LIKE LOOKING IN A MIRROR.
SO I FIGURED, MAYBE THIS WORLD IS LIKE THE FLIP SIDE OF OUR OWN, AND –
– AND SO YOU REVERSED THE MYTH BY PROVOKING ME TO ANGER.
YEP.
IT WAS WORTH A TRY, WASN'T IT?
...
WAS IT WORTH YOUR LIFE?

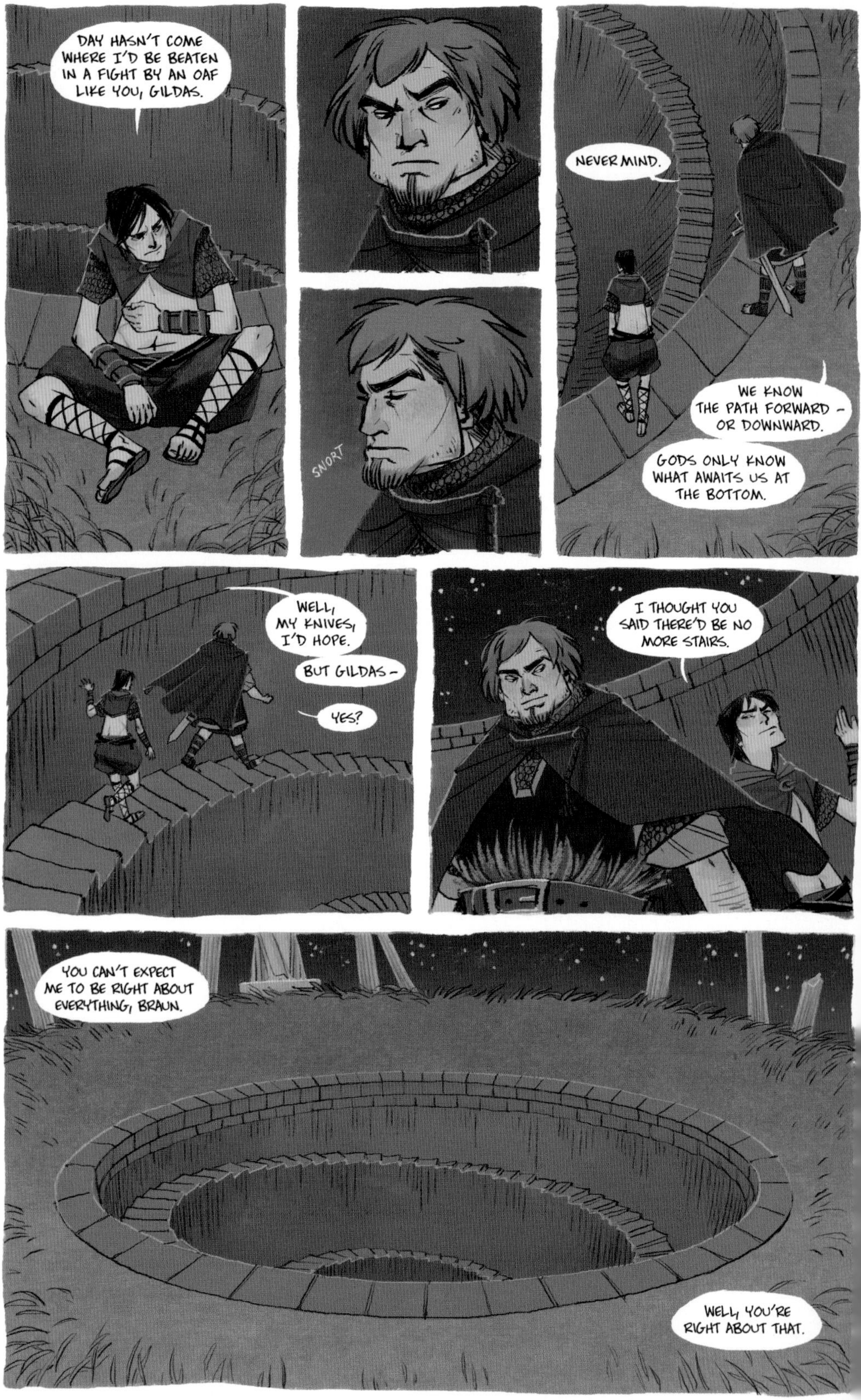
DAY HASN'T COME WHERE I'D BE BEATEN IN A FIGHT BY AN OAF LIKE YOU, GILDAS.
SNORT
NEVER MIND.
WE KNOW THE PATH FORWARD – OR DOWNWARD.
GODS ONLY KNOW WHAT AWAITS US AT THE BOTTOM.
WELL, MY KNIVES, I'D HOPE.
BUT GILDAS –
YES?
I THOUGHT YOU SAID THERE'D BE NO MORE STAIRS.
YOU CAN'T EXPECT ME TO BE RIGHT ABOUT EVERYTHING, BRAUN.
WELL, YOU'RE RIGHT ABOUT THAT.

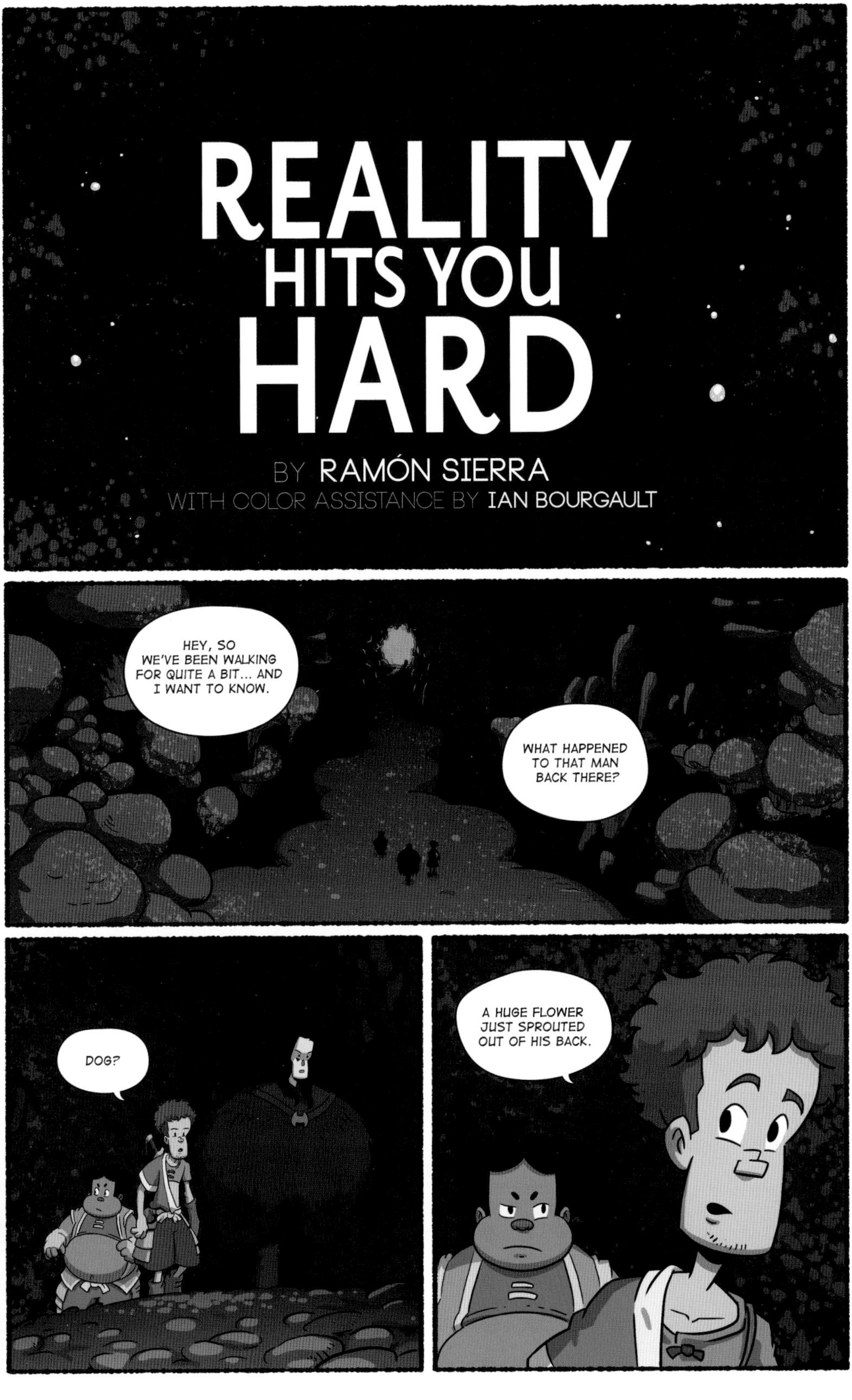
REALITY HITS YOU HARD
BY RAMÓN SIERRA
WITH COLOR ASSISTANCE BY IAN BOURGAULT
HEY, SO WE'VE BEEN WALKING FOR QUITE A BIT... AND I WANT TO KNOW.
WHAT HAPPENED TO THAT MAN BACK THERE?
DOG?
A HUGE FLOWER JUST SPROUTED OUT OF HIS BACK.

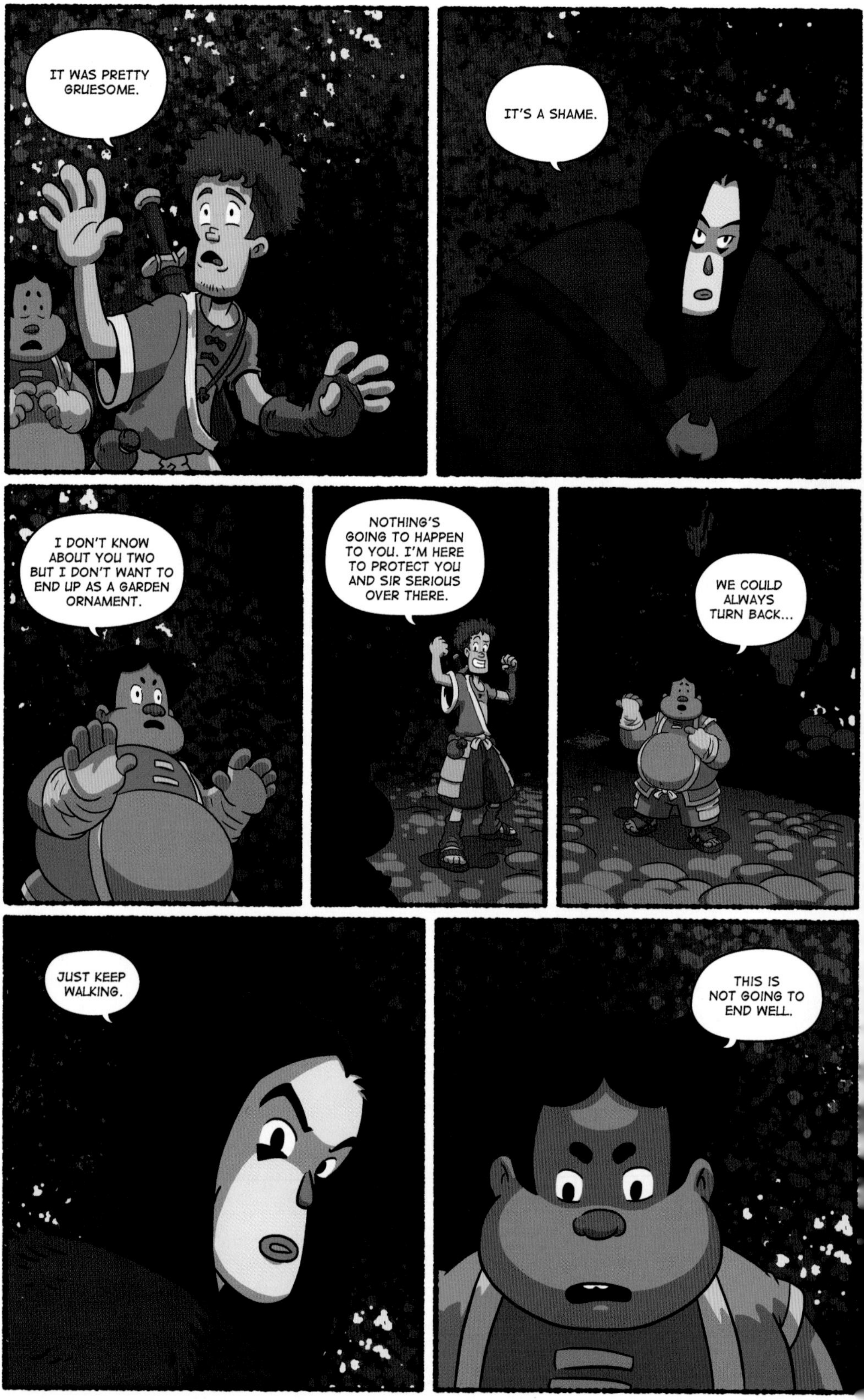
IT WAS PRETTY GRUESOME.
IT'S A SHAME.
I DON'T KNOW ABOUT YOU TWO BUT I DON'T WANT TO END UP AS A GARDEN ORNAMENT.
NOTHING'S GOING TO HAPPEN TO YOU. I'M HERE TO PROTECT YOU AND SIR SERIOUS OVER THERE.
WE COULD ALWAYS TURN BACK...
JUST KEEP WALKING.
THIS IS NOT GOING TO END WELL.

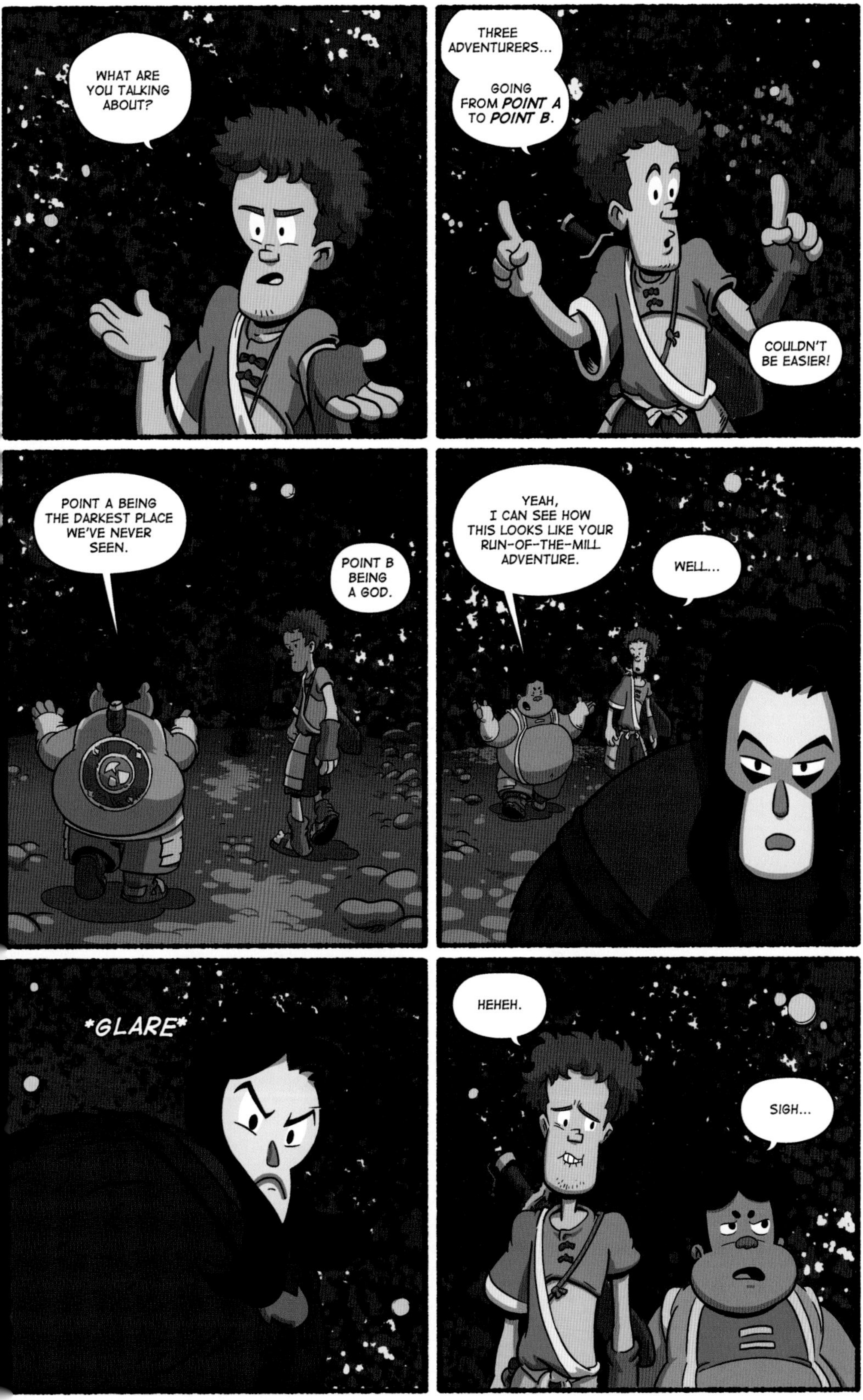
WHAT ARE YOU TALKING ABOUT?
THREE ADVENTURERS...
GOING FROM POINT A TO POINT B.
COULDN'T BE EASIER!
POINT A BEING THE DARKEST PLACE WE'VE NEVER SEEN.
POINT B BEING A GOD.
YEAH, I CAN SEE HOW THIS LOOKS LIKE YOUR RUN-OF-THE-MILL ADVENTURE.
WELL...
GLARE
HEHEH.
SIGH...

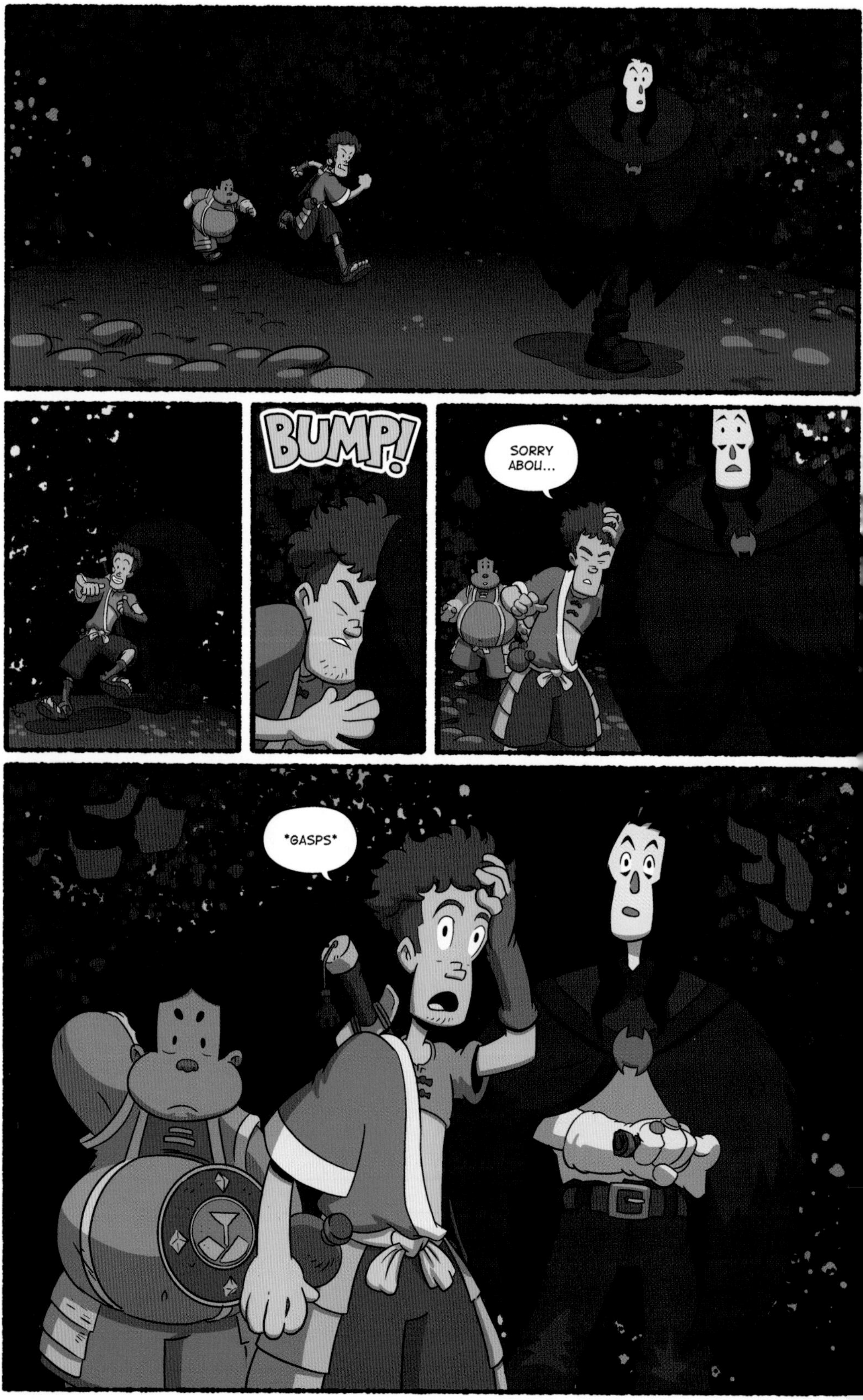
BUMP!
SORRY ABOU...
GASPS

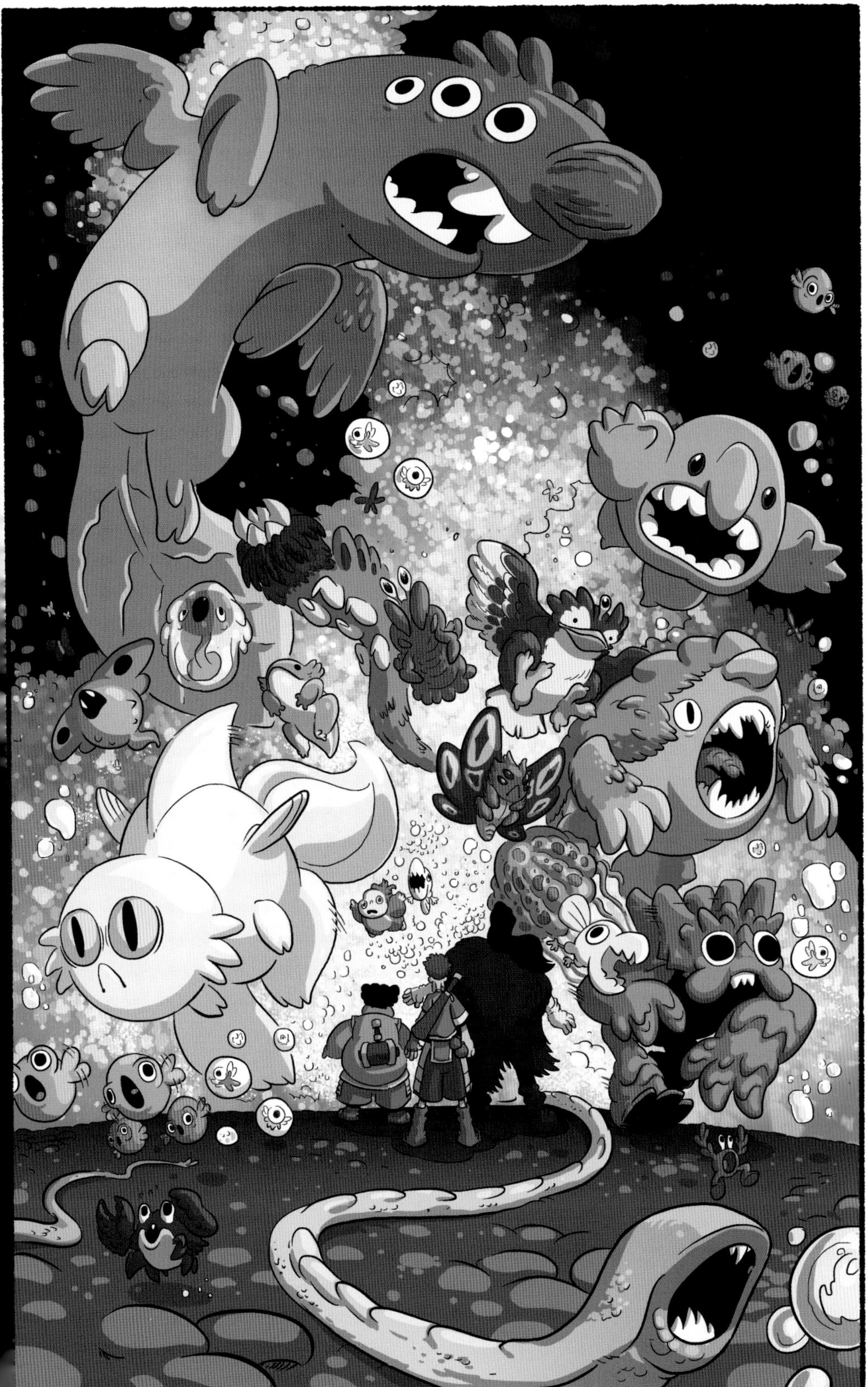

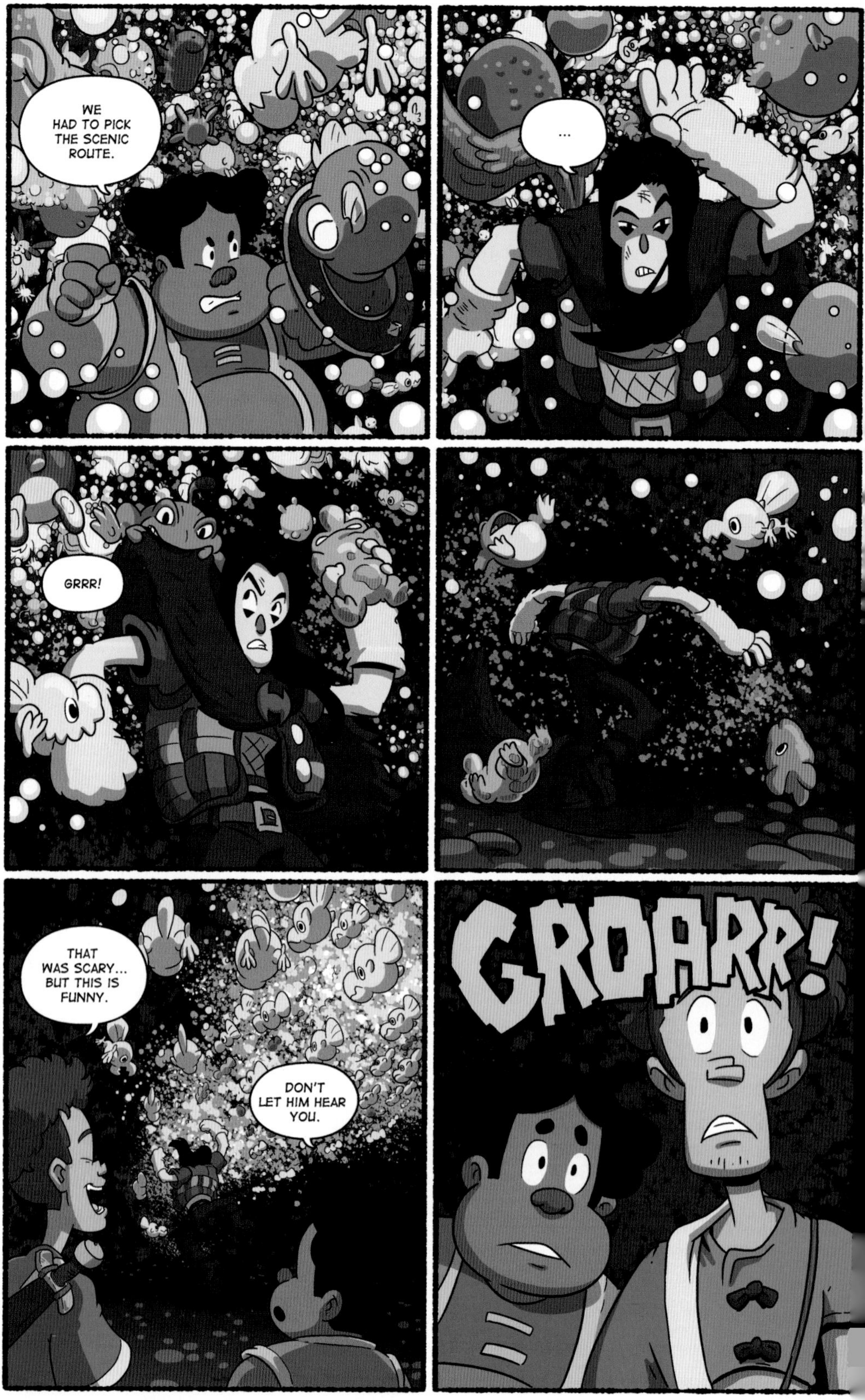
WE HAD TO PICK THE SCENIC ROUTE.
...
GRRR!
THAT WAS SCARY... BUT THIS IS FUNNY.
DON'T LET HIM HEAR YOU.
GROARR!

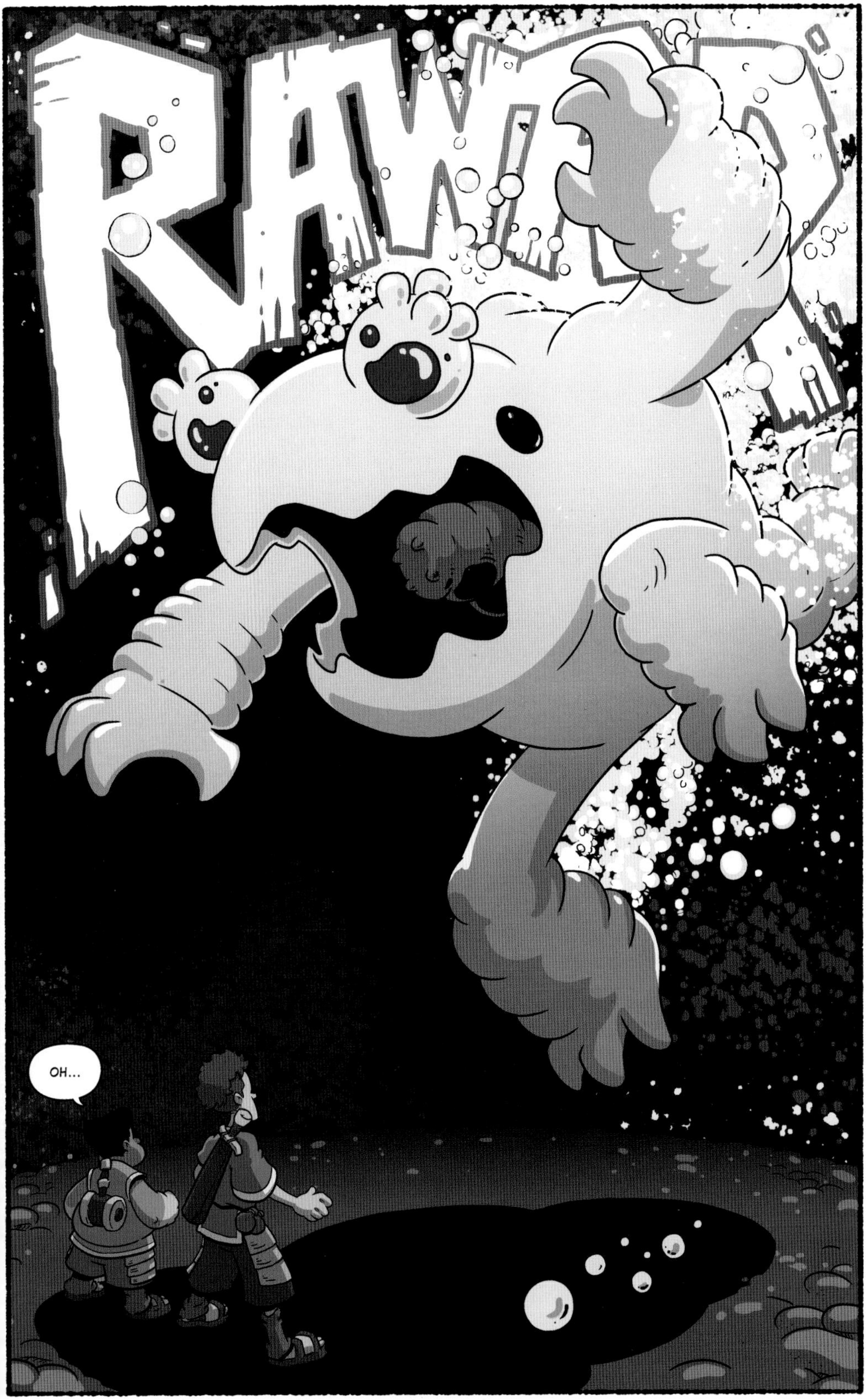
RAWR
OH...

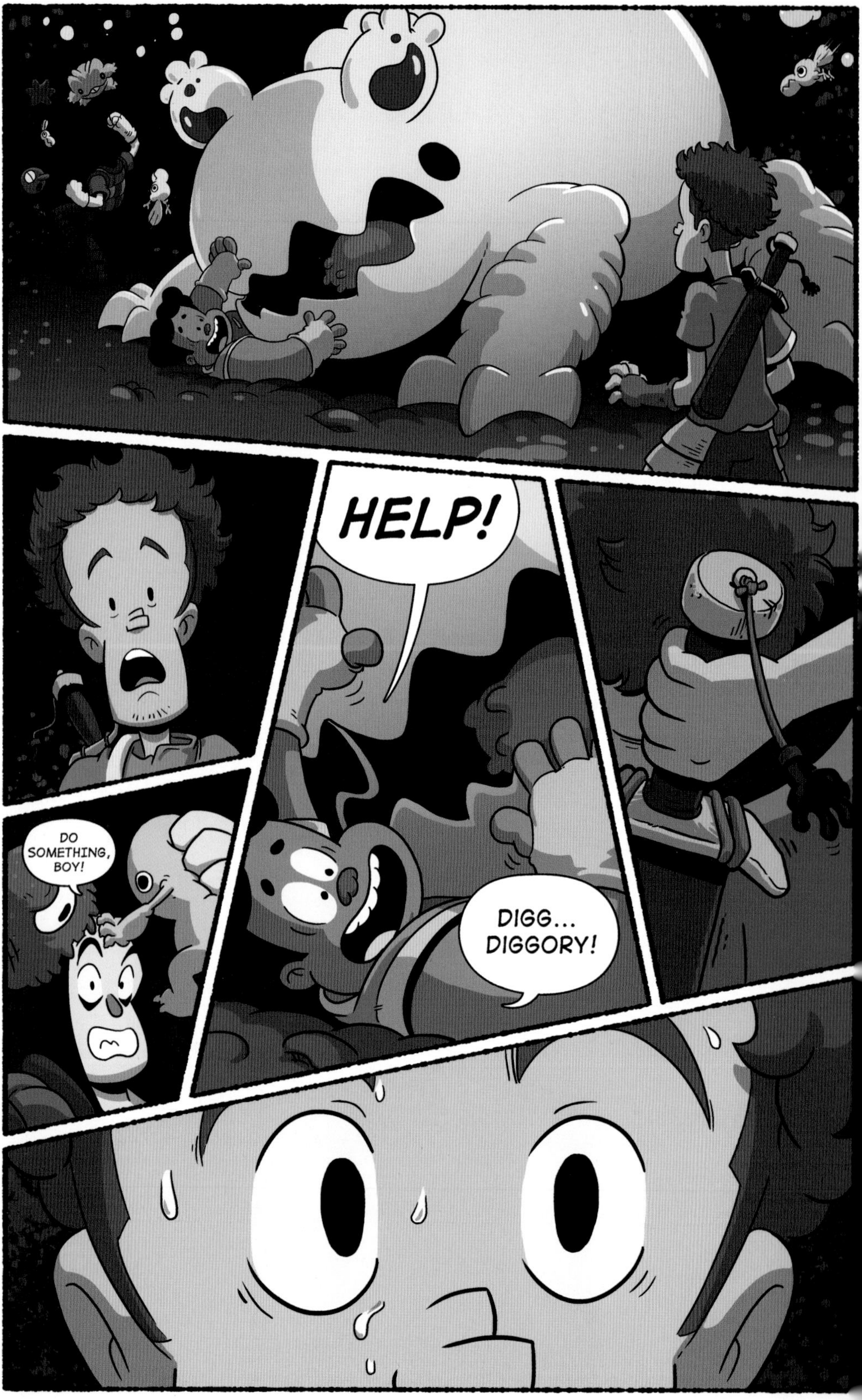
HELP!
DO SOMETHING, BOY!
DIGG... DIGGORY!

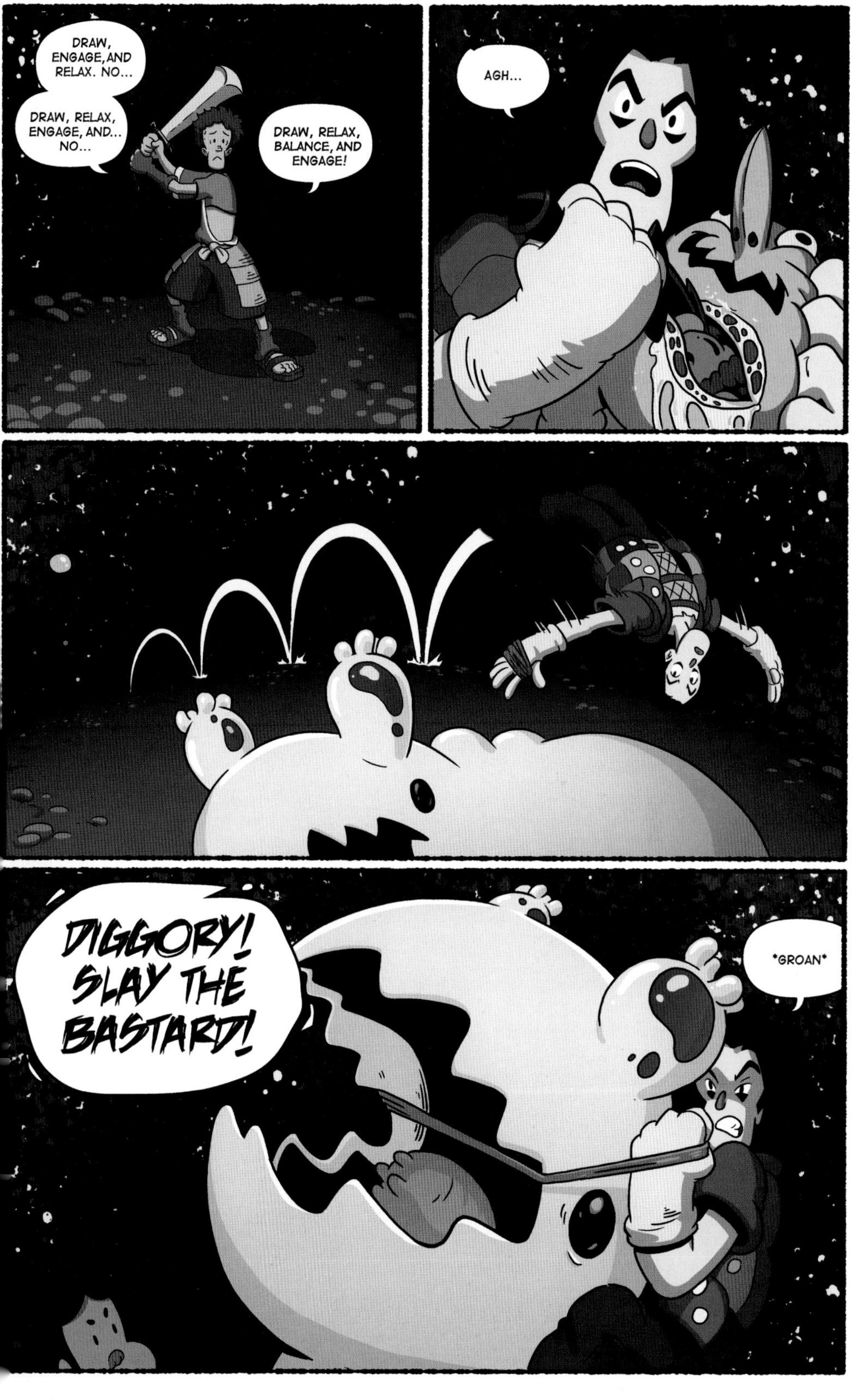
DRAW, ENGAGE, AND RELAX. NO...
DRAW, RELAX, ENGAGE, AND... NO...
DRAW, RELAX, BALANCE, AND ENGAGE!
AGH...
DIGGORY! SLAY THE BASTARD!
GROAN

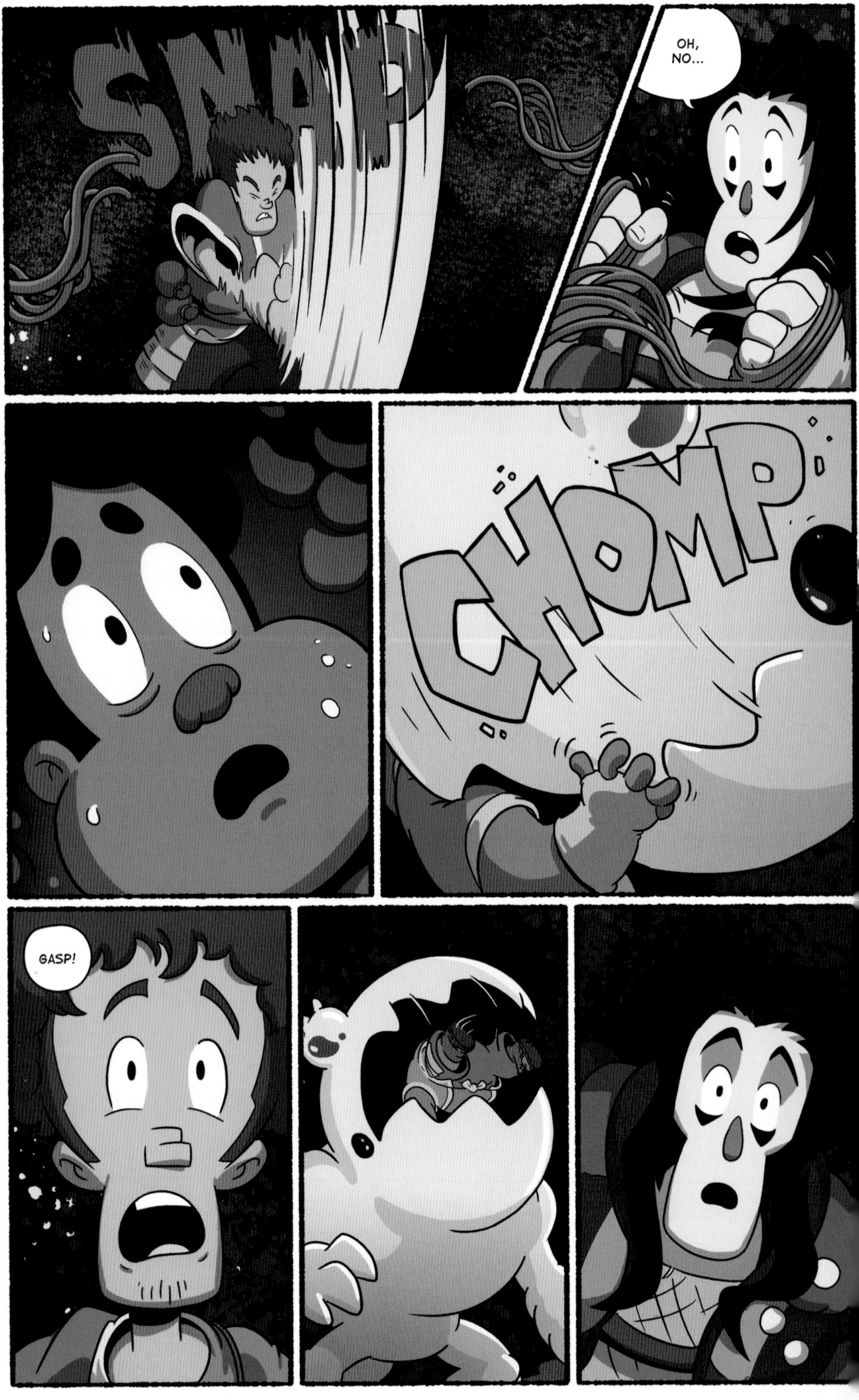
SNAP
OH, NO...
CHOMP
GASP!

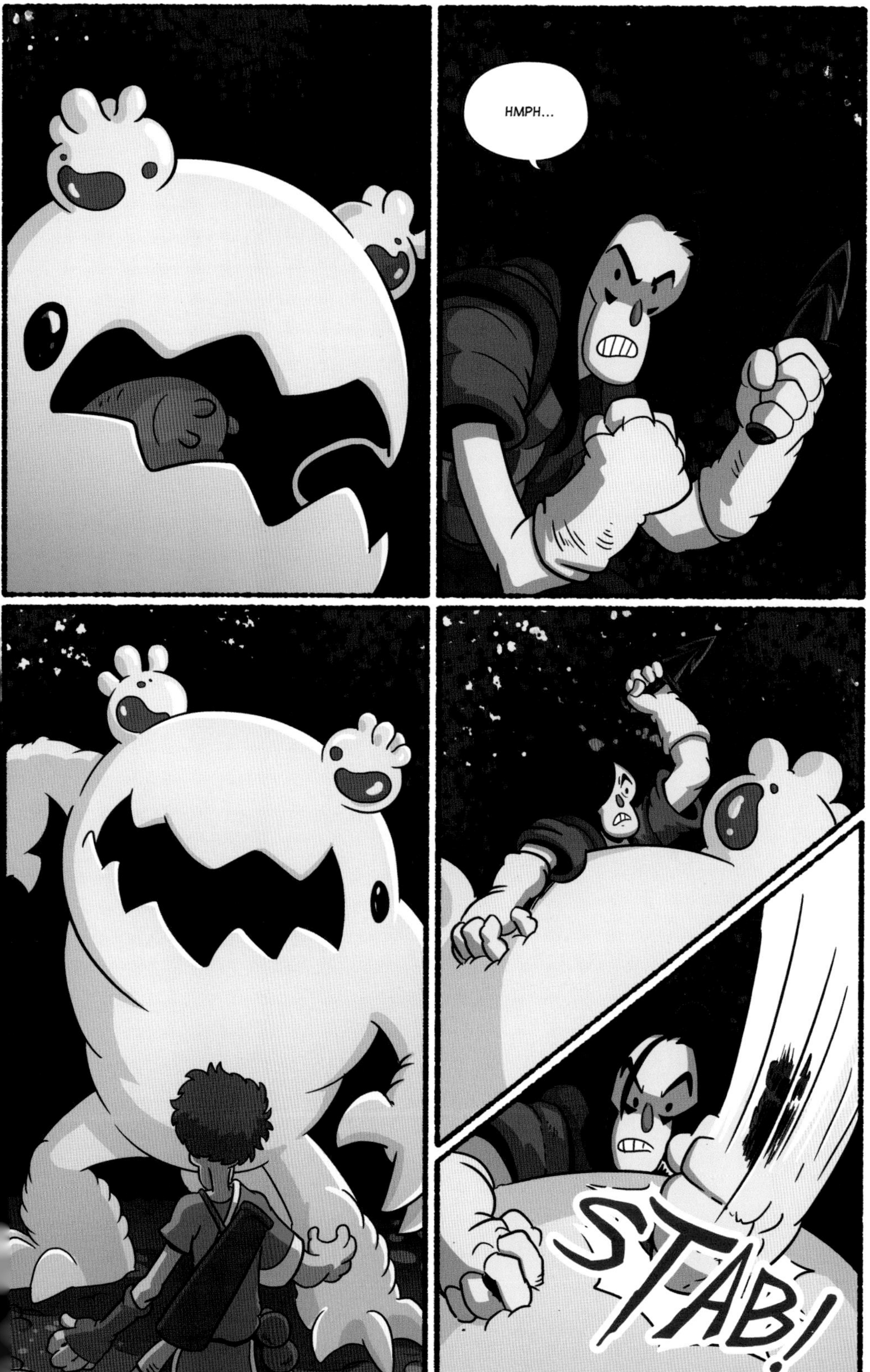
HMPH...
STAB!

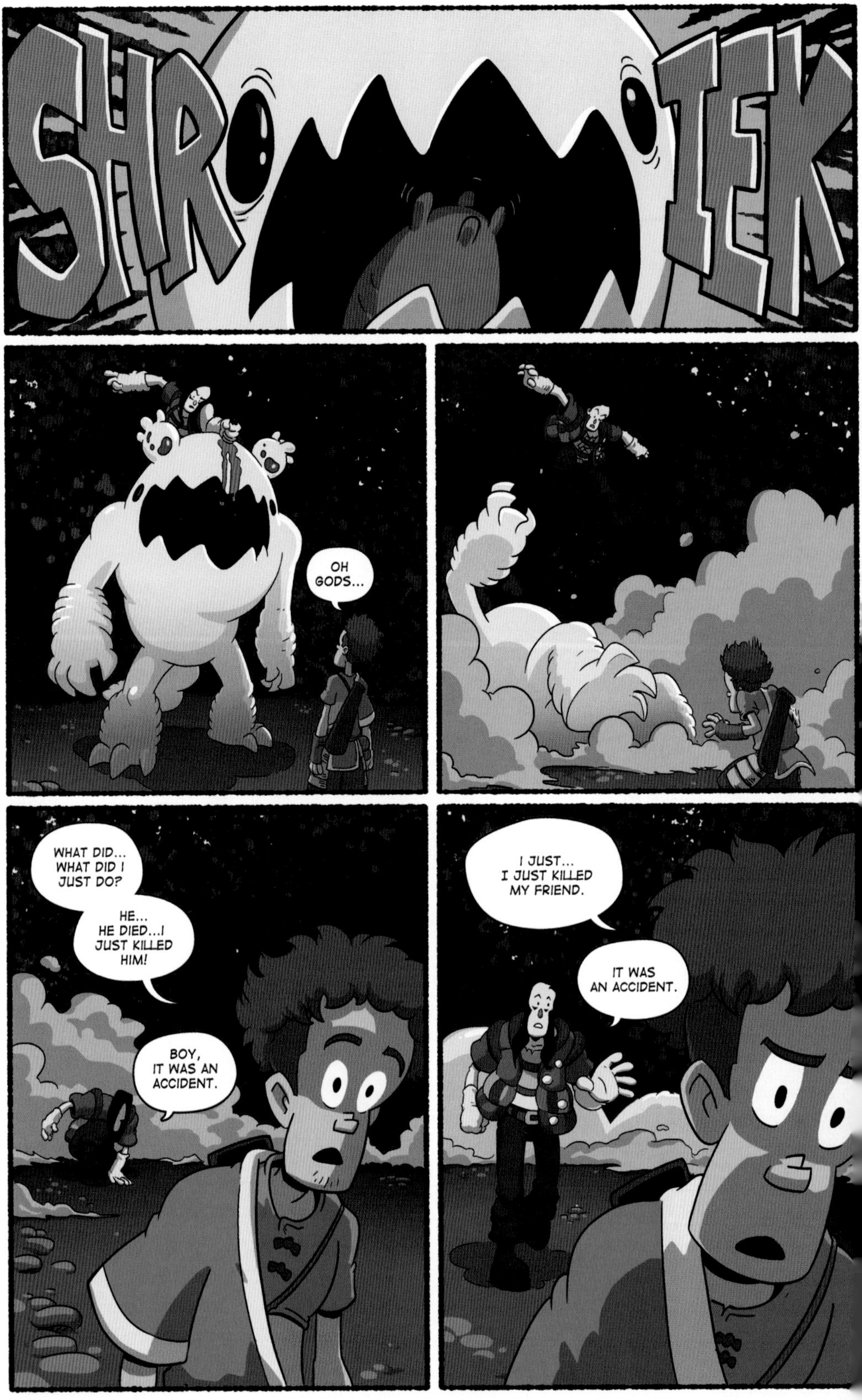
SHRIEK
OH GODS...
WHAT DID... WHAT DID I JUST DO?
HE... HE DIED...I JUST KILLED HIM!
BOY, IT WAS AN ACCIDENT.
I JUST... I JUST KILLED MY FRIEND.
IT WAS AN ACCIDENT.

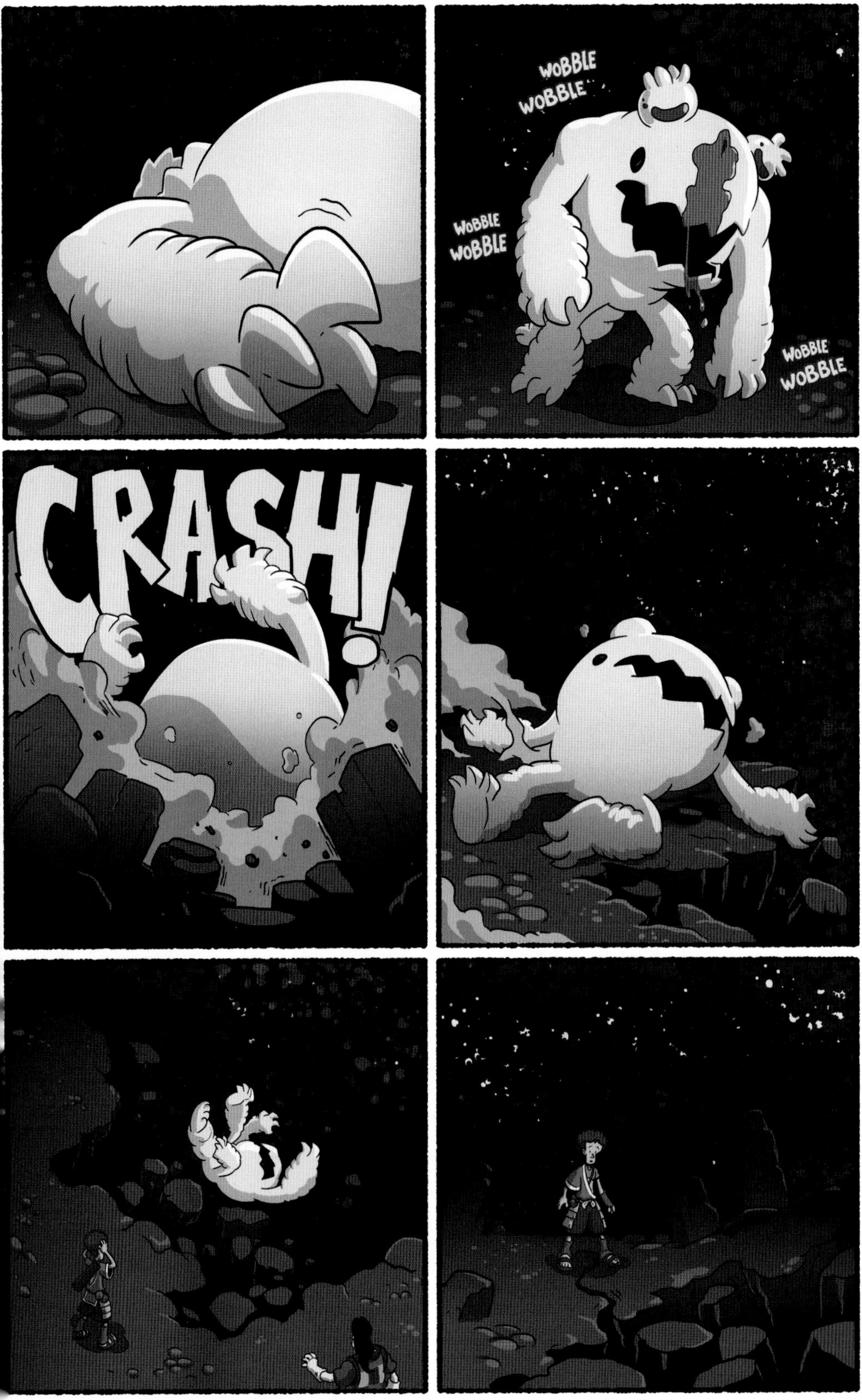
WOBBLE
WOBBLE
WOBBLE
WOBBLE
WOBBLE
WOBBLE
CRASH!

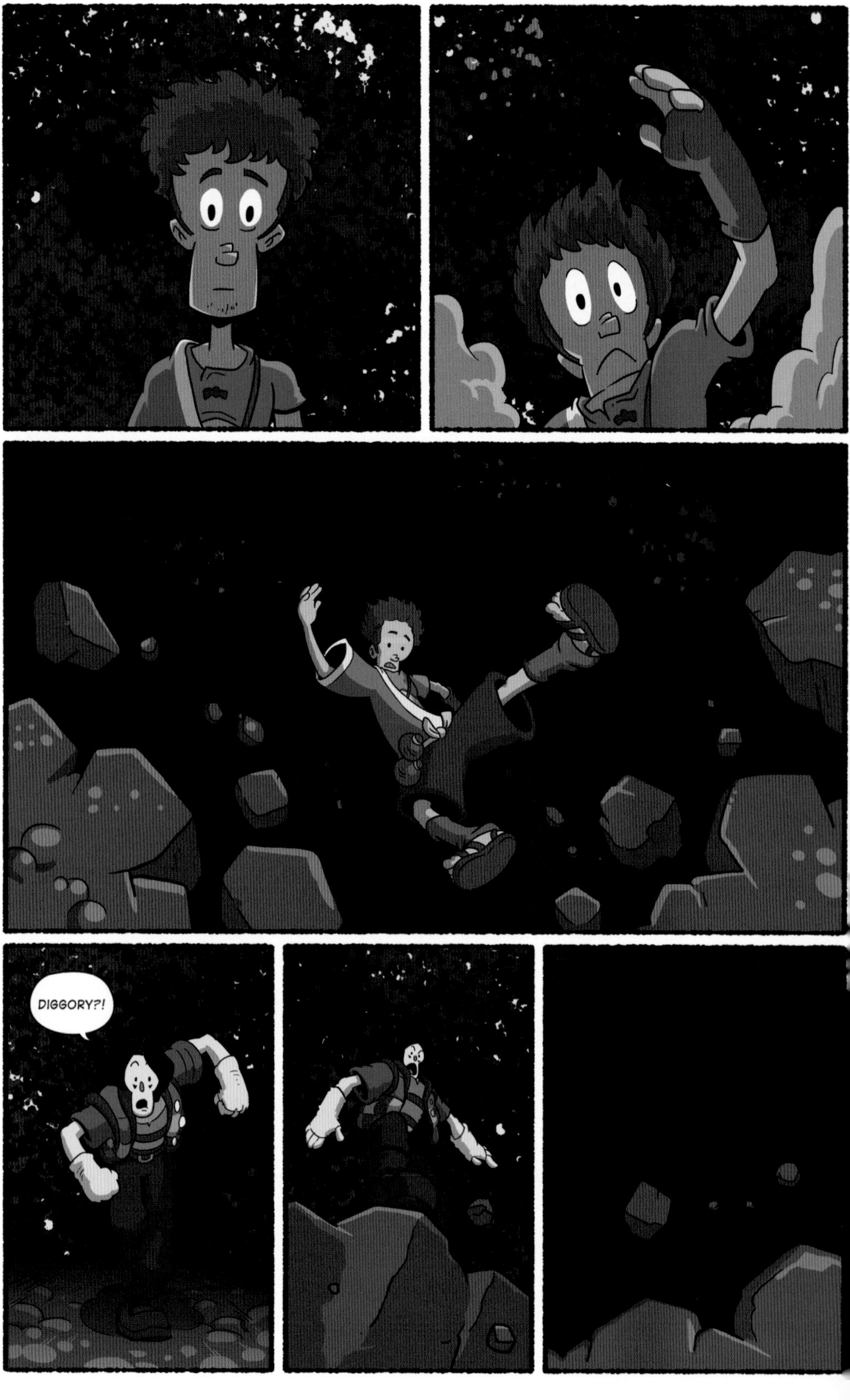
DIGGORY?!

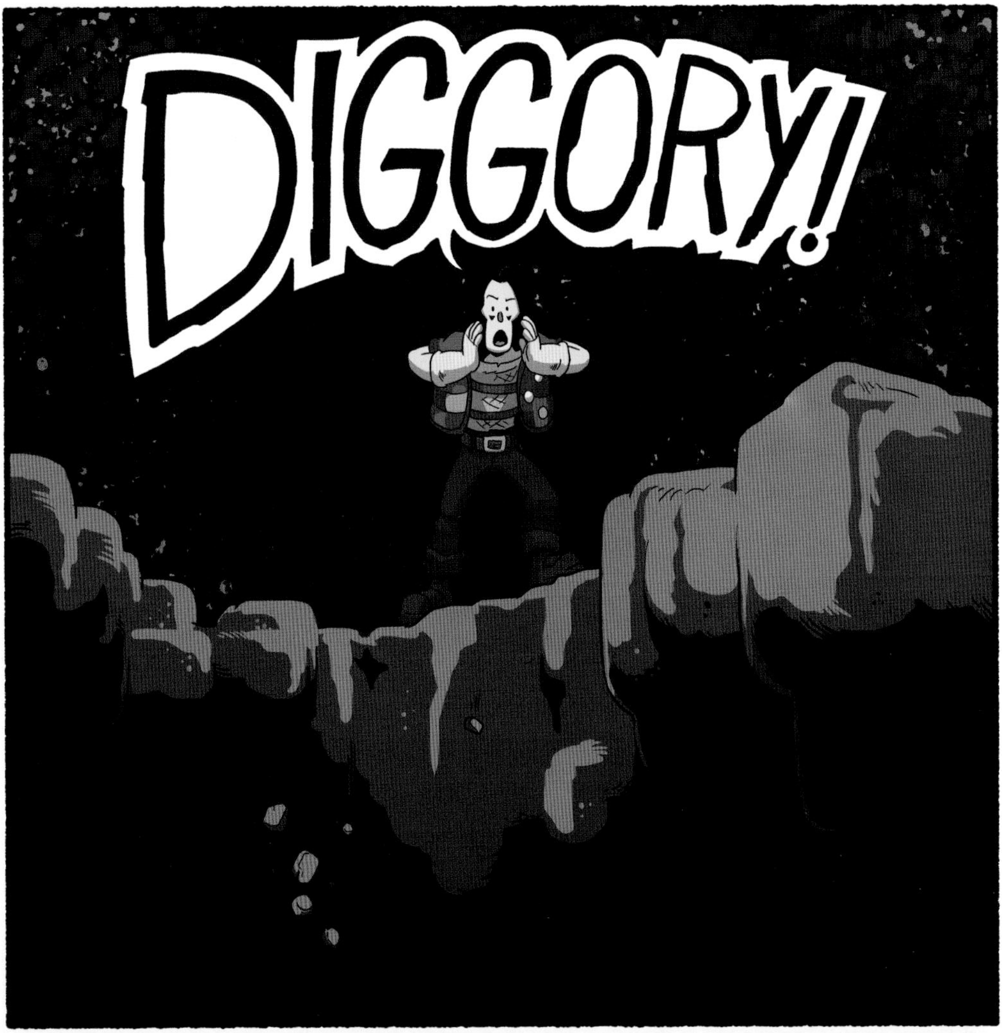
DIGGORY!
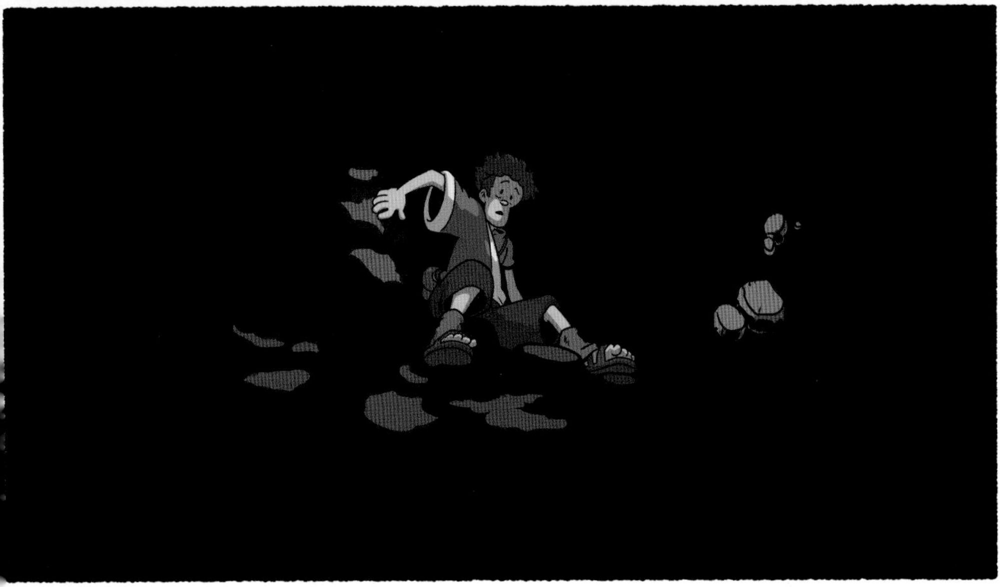

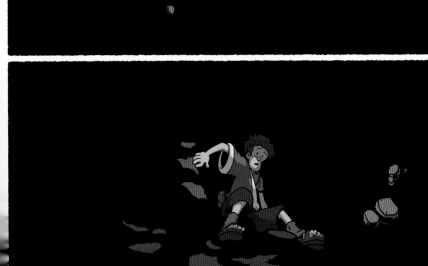

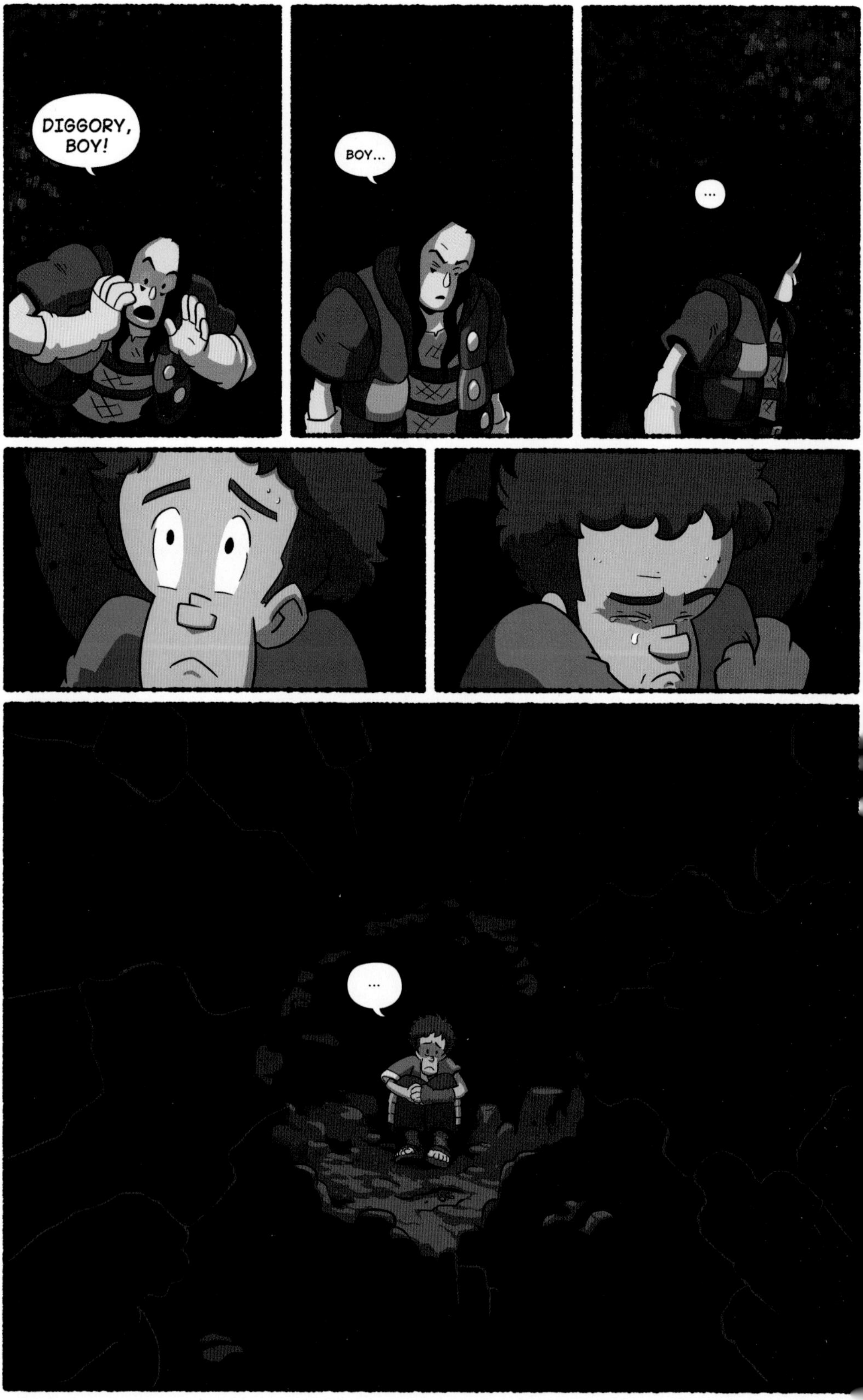
DIGGORY, BOY!
BOY...
...
...

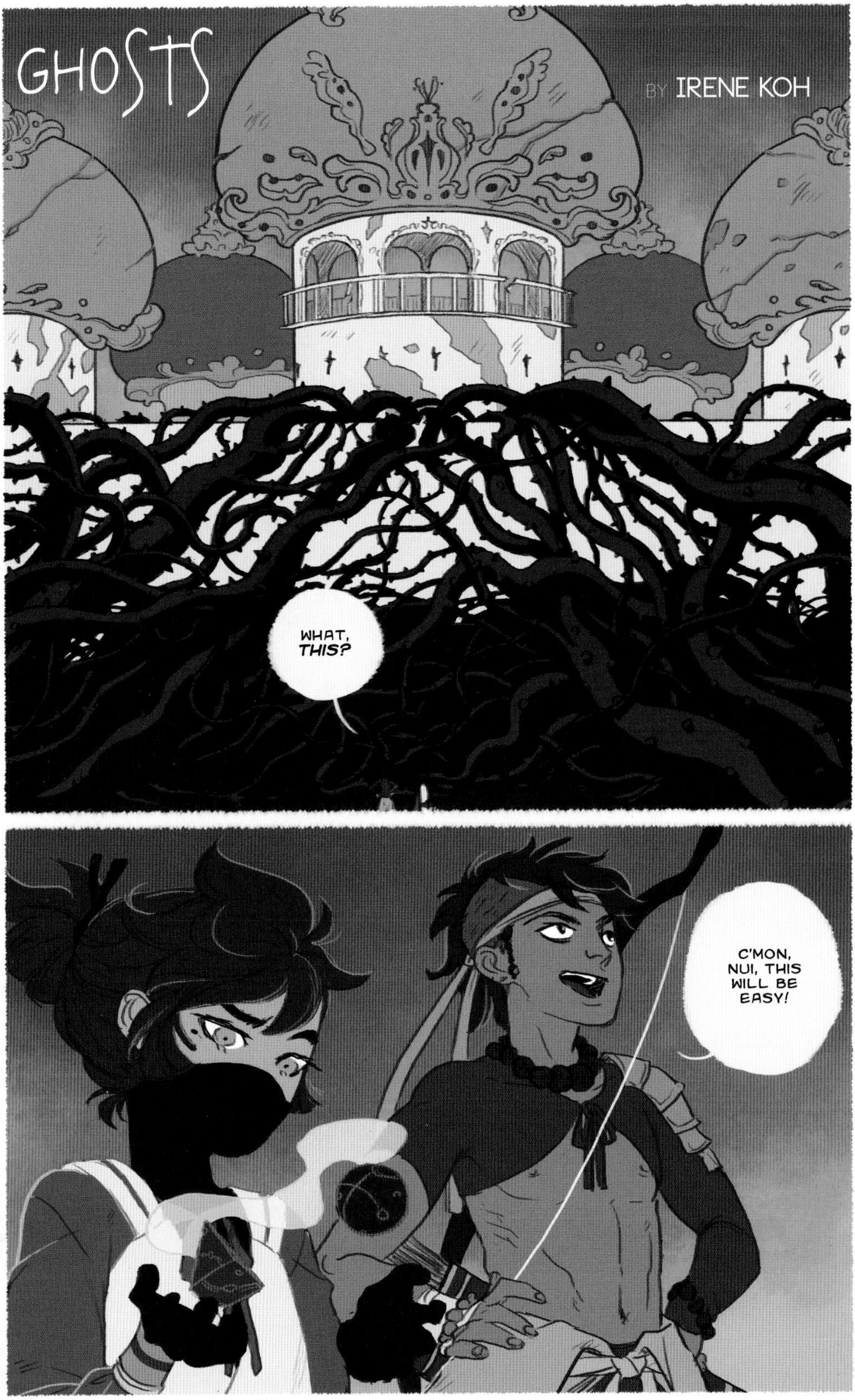
GHOSTS
BY IRENE KOH
WHAT, THIS?
C'MON, NUI, THIS WILL BE EASY!

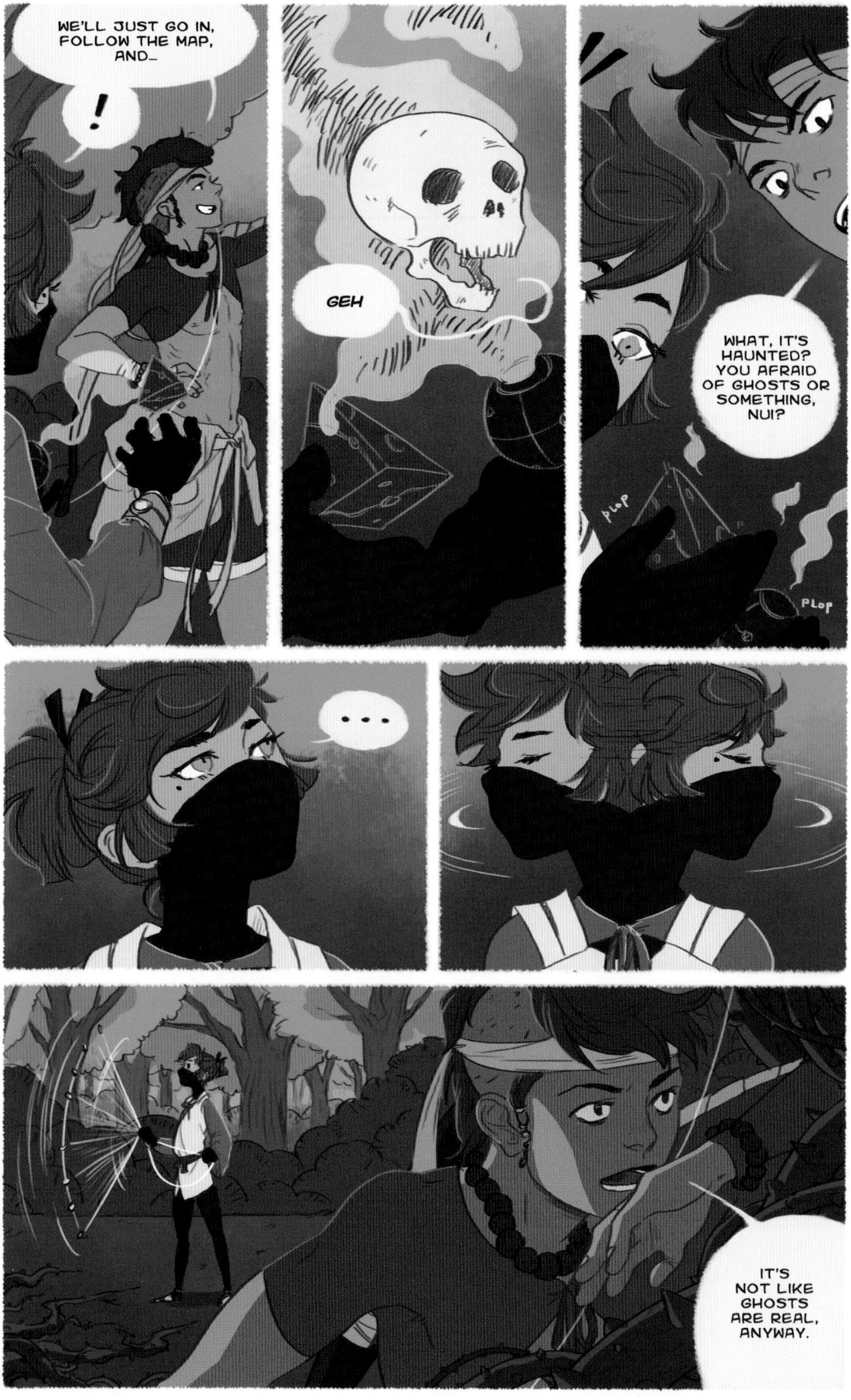
WE'LL JUST GO IN, FOLLOW THE MAP, AND_
!
GEH
WHAT, IT'S HAUNTED? YOU AFRAID OF GHOSTS OR SOMETHING, NUI?
PLOP
PLOP
...
IT'S NOT LIKE GHOSTS ARE REAL, ANYWAY.

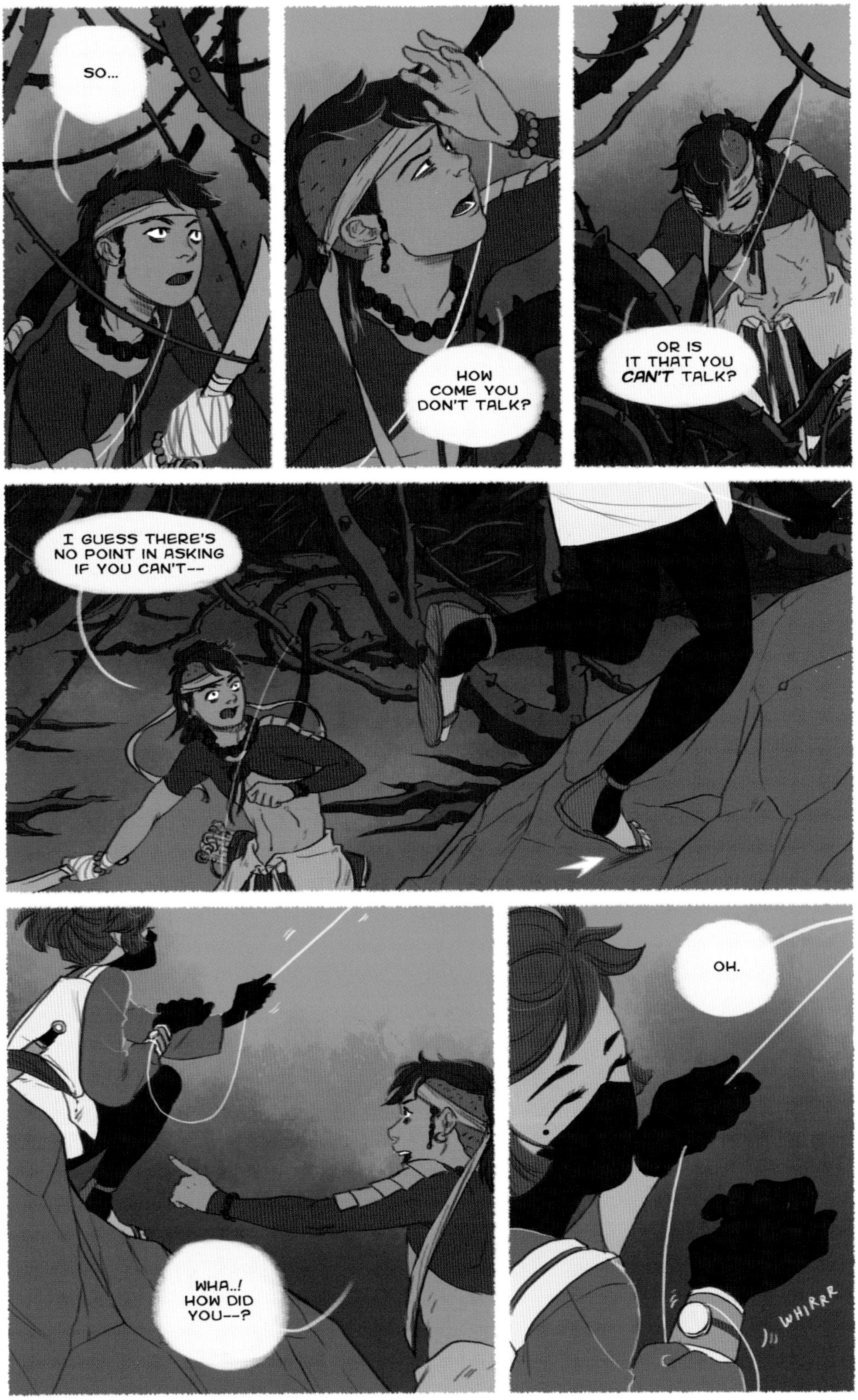
SO...
HOW COME YOU DON'T TALK?
OR IS IT THAT YOU ***CAN'T*** TALK?
I GUESS THERE'S NO POINT IN ASKING IF YOU CAN'T--
WHA..! HOW DID YOU--?
OH.
WHIRRR

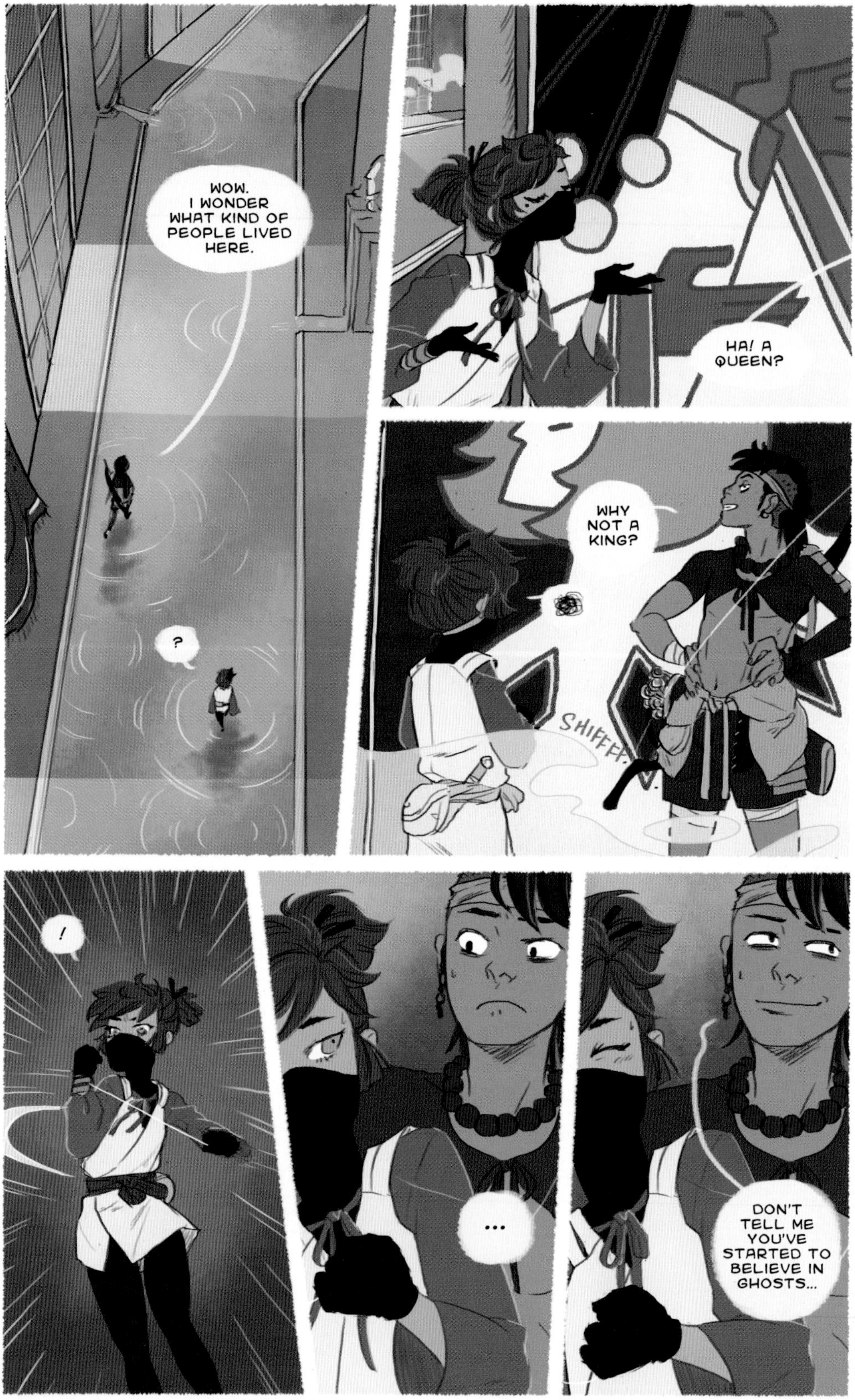
WOW. I WONDER WHAT KIND OF PEOPLE LIVED HERE.
?
HA! A QUEEN?
WHY NOT A KING?
SHIFFF.
!
...
DON'T TELL ME YOU'VE STARTED TO BELIEVE IN GHOSTS...

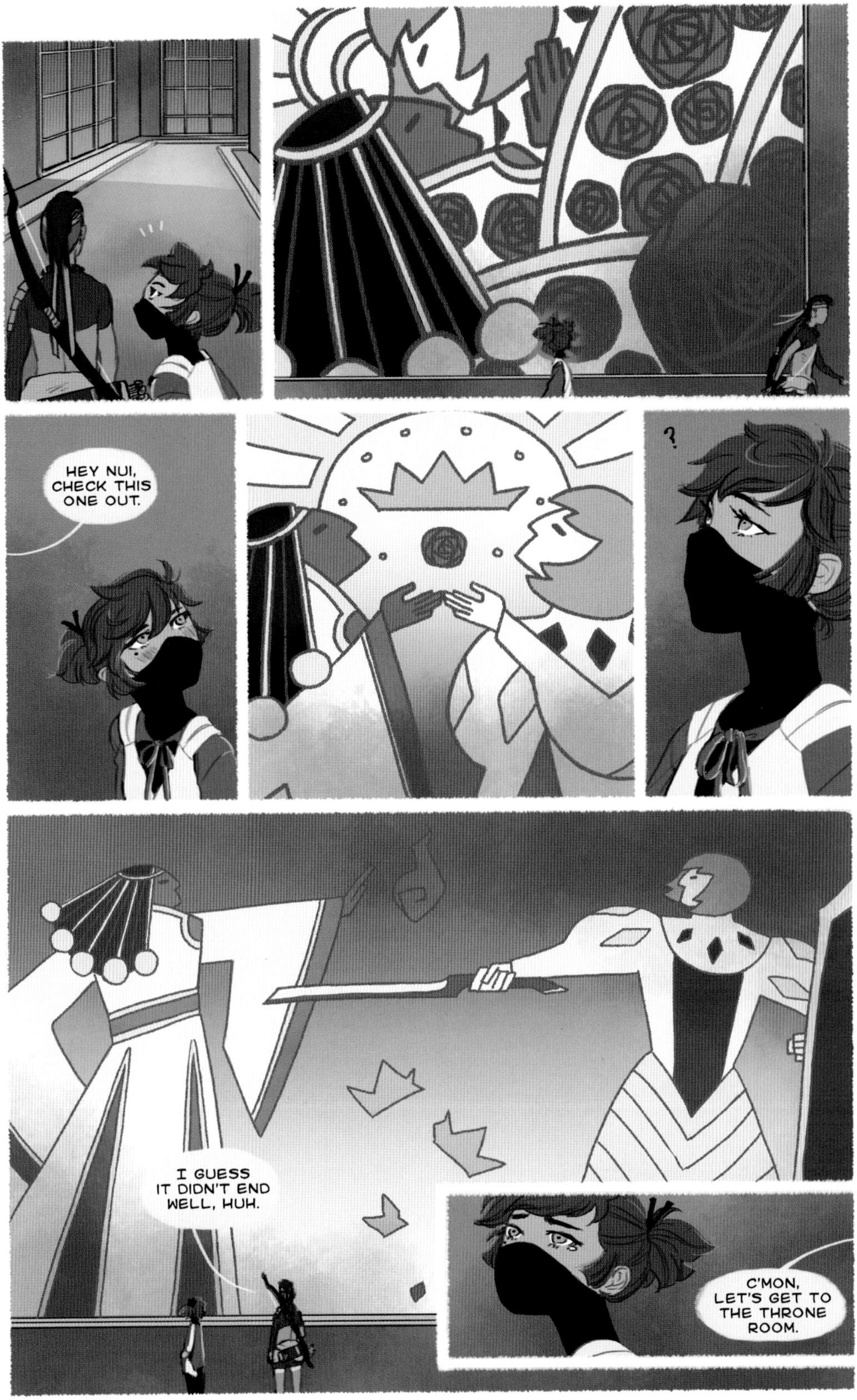

HEY NUI, CHECK THIS ONE OUT.
?
I GUESS IT DIDN'T END WELL, HUH.
C'MON, LET'S GET TO THE THRONE ROOM.

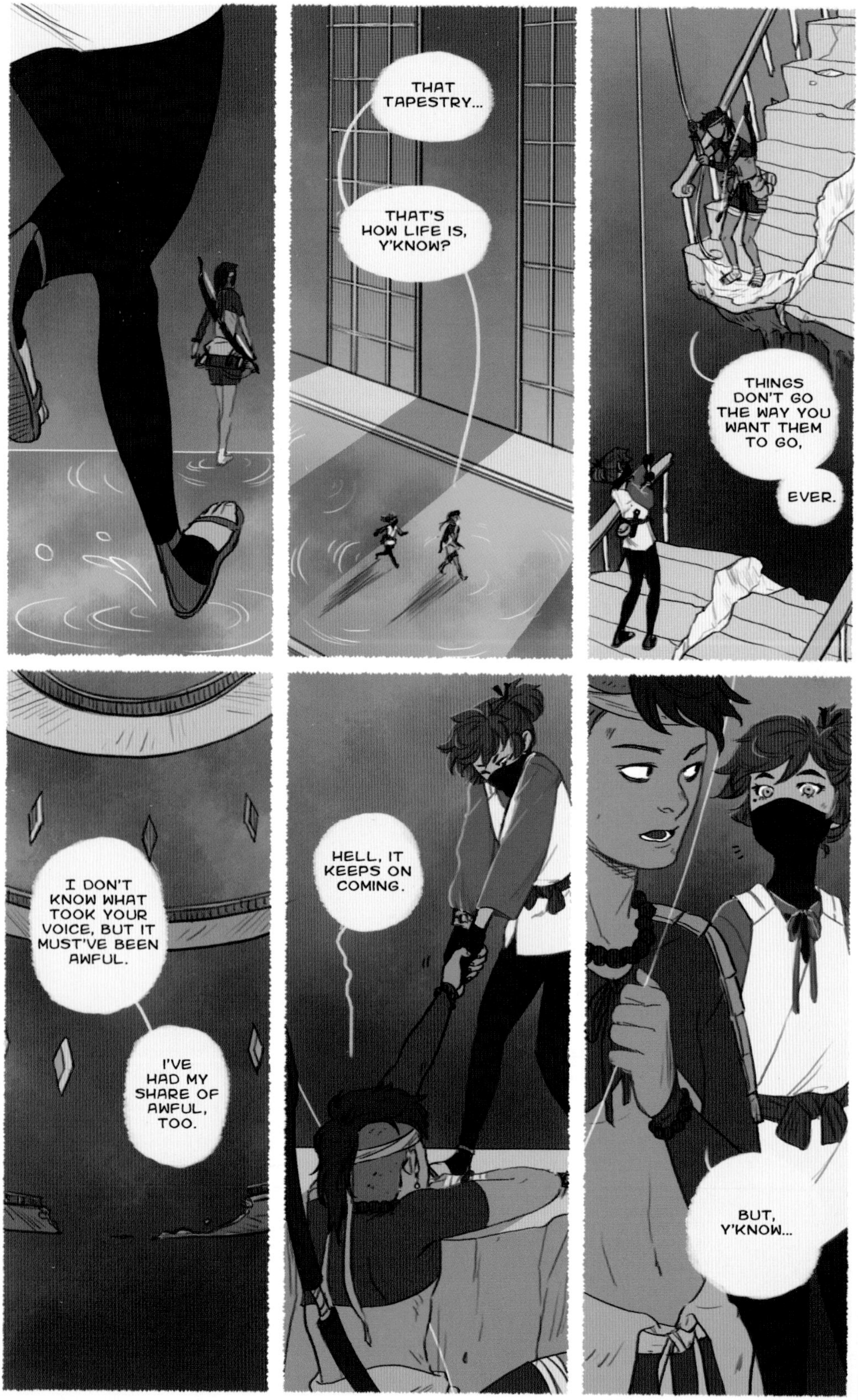

THAT TAPESTRY...
THAT'S HOW LIFE IS, Y'KNOW?
THINGS DON'T GO THE WAY YOU WANT THEM TO GO,
EVER.
I DON'T KNOW WHAT TOOK YOUR VOICE, BUT IT MUST'VE BEEN AWFUL.
I'VE HAD MY SHARE OF AWFUL, TOO.
HELL, IT KEEPS ON COMING.
BUT, Y'KNOW...

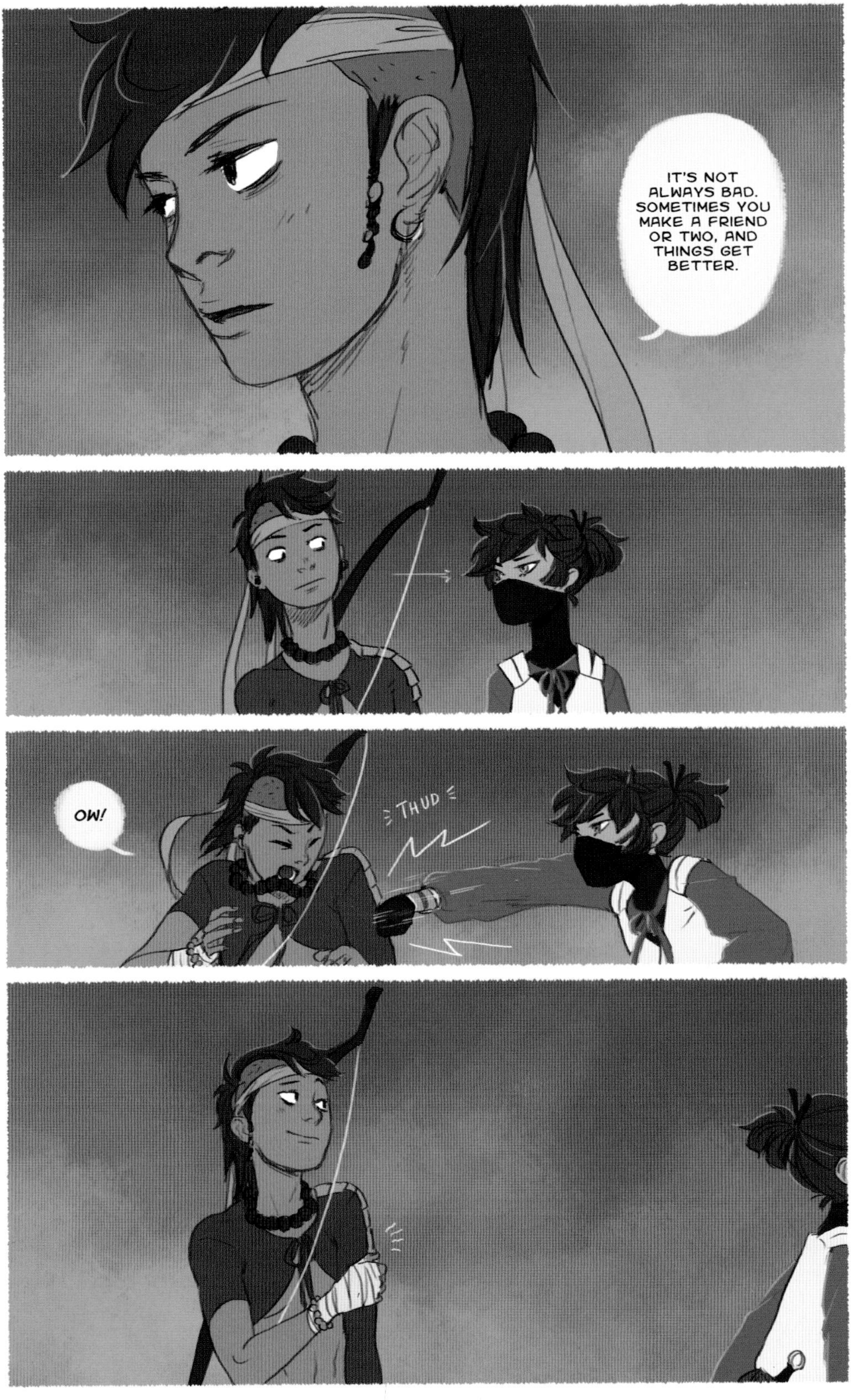
IT'S NOT ALWAYS BAD. SOMETIMES YOU MAKE A FRIEND OR TWO, AND THINGS GET BETTER.
OW!
THUD

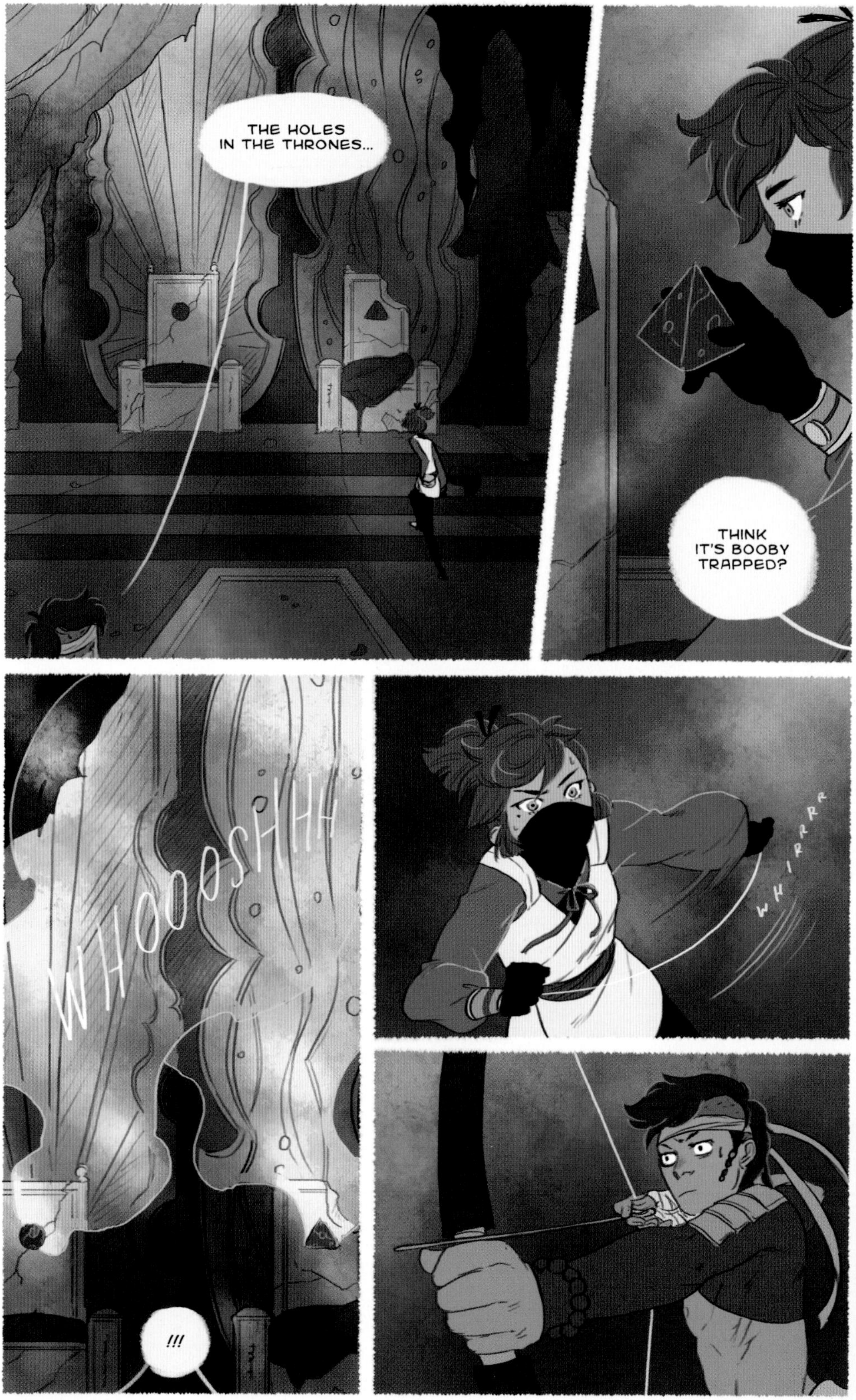
THE HOLES IN THE THRONES...
THINK IT'S BOOBY TRAPPED?
WHOOOOSHHH
!!!
WHIRRRR

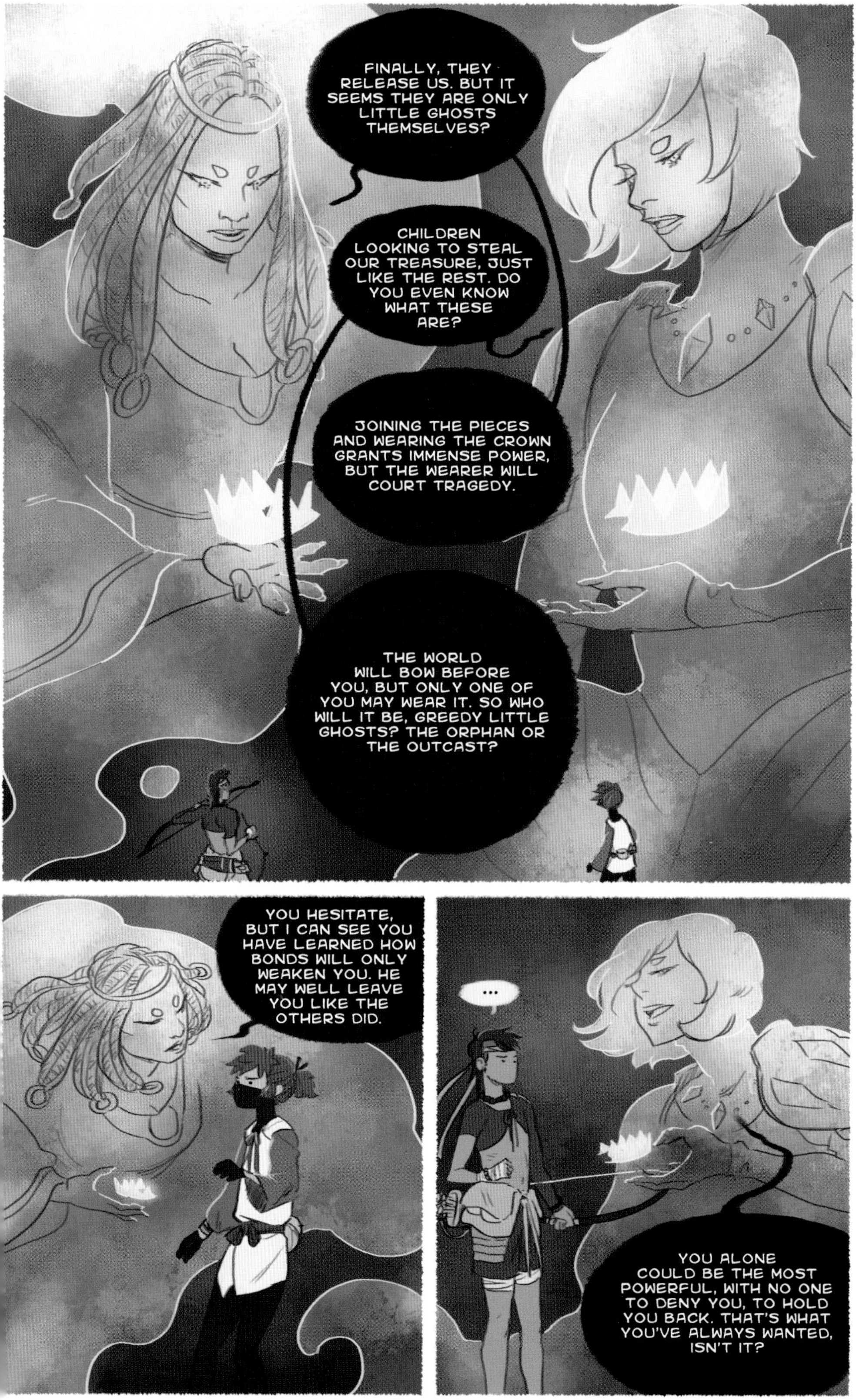
FINALLY, THEY RELEASE US. BUT IT SEEMS THEY ARE ONLY LITTLE GHOSTS THEMSELVES?
CHILDREN LOOKING TO STEAL OUR TREASURE, JUST LIKE THE REST. DO YOU EVEN KNOW WHAT THESE ARE?
JOINING THE PIECES AND WEARING THE CROWN GRANTS IMMENSE POWER, BUT THE WEARER WILL COURT TRAGEDY.
THE WORLD WILL BOW BEFORE YOU, BUT ONLY ONE OF YOU MAY WEAR IT. SO WHO WILL IT BE, GREEDY LITTLE GHOSTS? THE ORPHAN OR THE OUTCAST?
YOU HESITATE, BUT I CAN SEE YOU HAVE LEARNED HOW BONDS WILL ONLY WEAKEN YOU. HE MAY WELL LEAVE YOU LIKE THE OTHERS DID.
...
YOU ALONE COULD BE THE MOST POWERFUL, WITH NO ONE TO DENY YOU, TO HOLD YOU BACK. THAT'S WHAT YOU'VE ALWAYS WANTED, ISN'T IT?

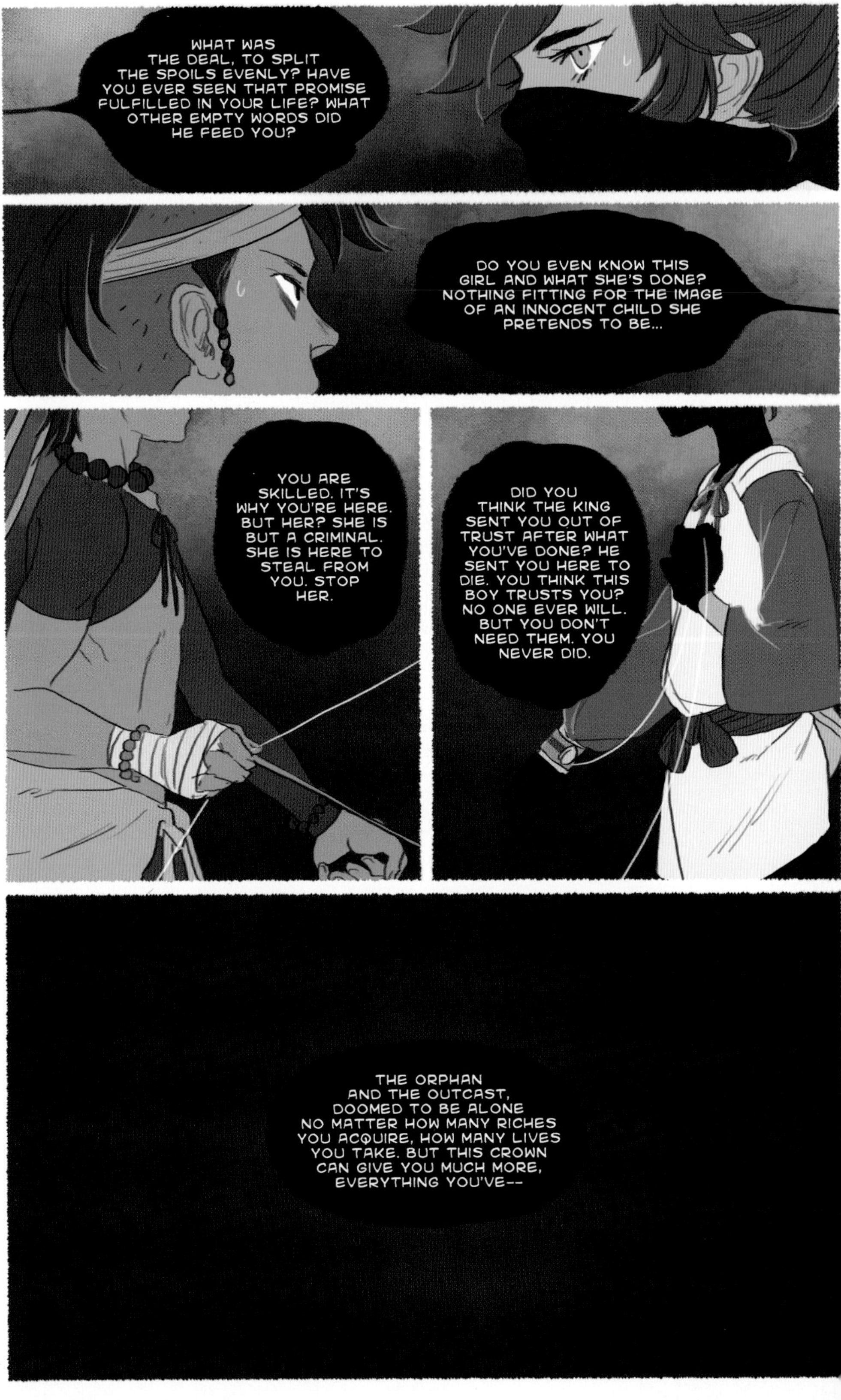
WHAT WAS THE DEAL, TO SPLIT THE SPOILS EVENLY? HAVE YOU EVER SEEN THAT PROMISE FULFILLED IN YOUR LIFE? WHAT OTHER EMPTY WORDS DID HE FEED YOU?
DO YOU EVEN KNOW THIS GIRL AND WHAT SHE'S DONE? NOTHING FITTING FOR THE IMAGE OF AN INNOCENT CHILD SHE PRETENDS TO BE...
YOU ARE SKILLED. IT'S WHY YOU'RE HERE. BUT HER? SHE IS BUT A CRIMINAL. SHE IS HERE TO STEAL FROM YOU. STOP HER.
DID YOU THINK THE KING SENT YOU OUT OF TRUST AFTER WHAT YOU'VE DONE? HE SENT YOU HERE TO DIE. YOU THINK THIS BOY TRUSTS YOU? NO ONE EVER WILL. BUT YOU DON'T NEED THEM. YOU NEVER DID.
THE ORPHAN AND THE OUTCAST, DOOMED TO BE ALONE NO MATTER HOW MANY RICHES YOU ACQUIRE, HOW MANY LIVES YOU TAKE. BUT THIS CROWN CAN GIVE YOU MUCH MORE, EVERYTHING YOU'VE--

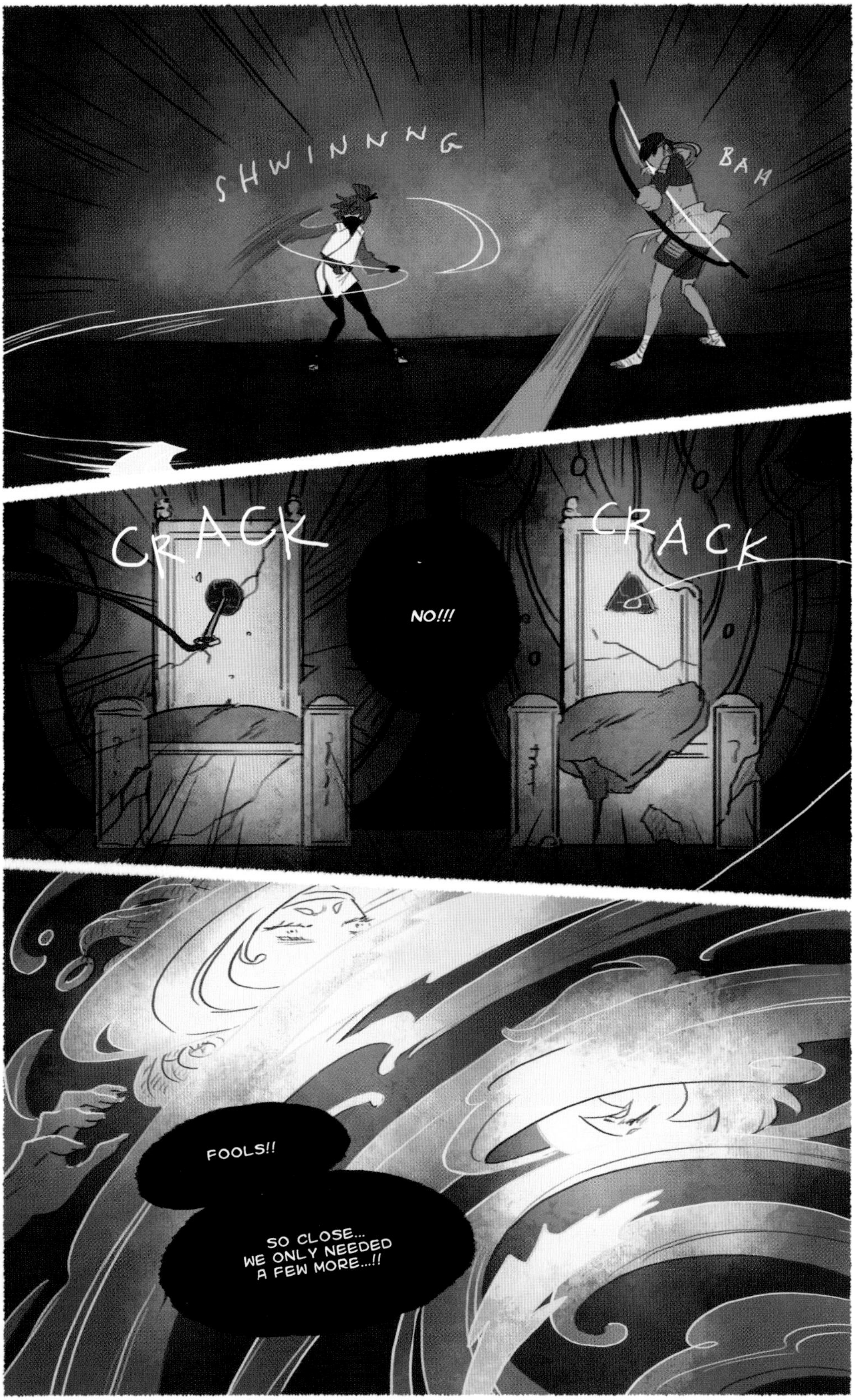
SHWINNNG
BAH
CRACK
NO!!!
CRACK
FOOLS!!
SO CLOSE... WE ONLY NEEDED A FEW MORE...!!

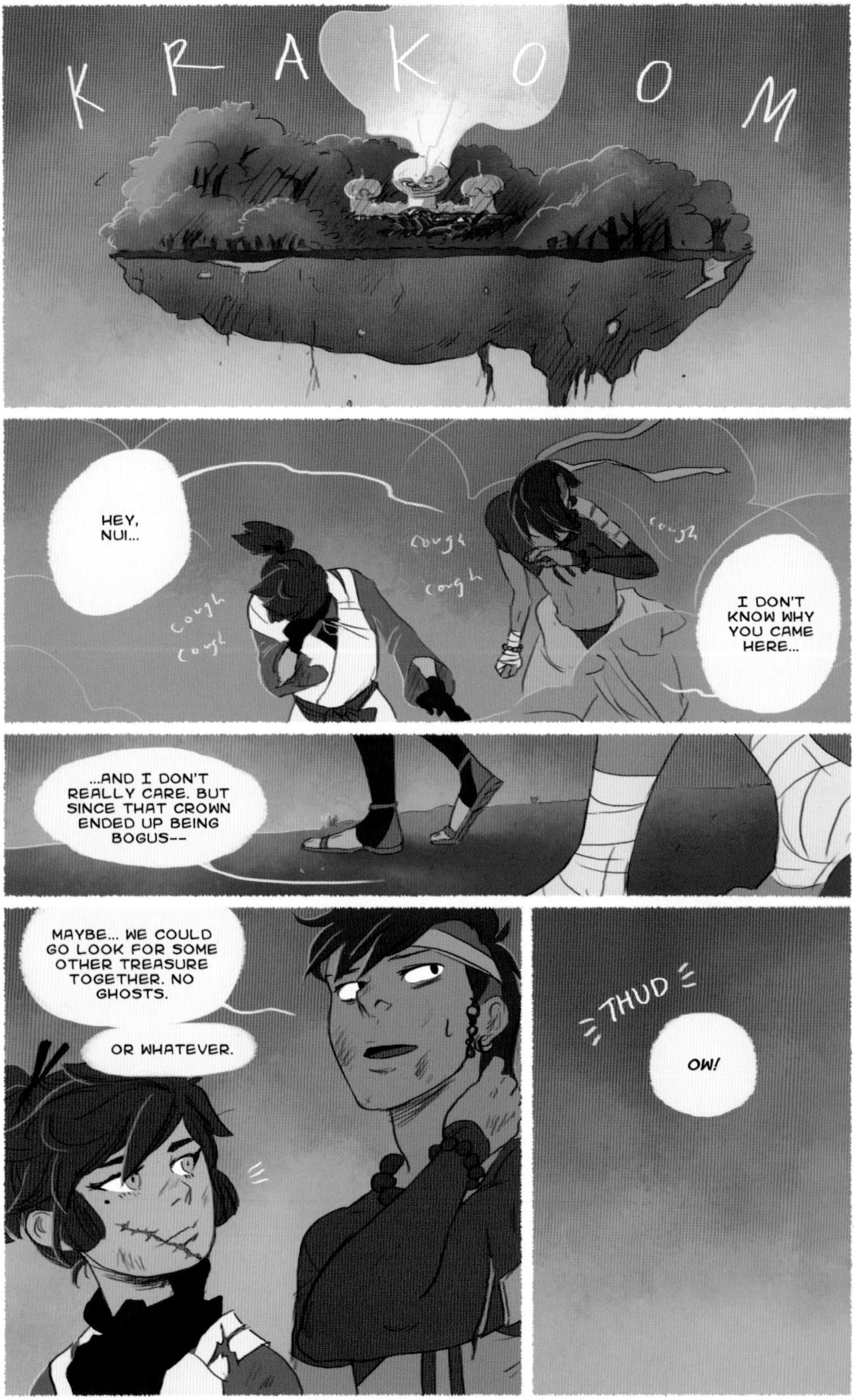
KRAKOOM
HEY, NUI...
cough
cough
cough
cough
cough
I DON'T KNOW WHY YOU CAME HERE...
...AND I DON'T REALLY CARE. BUT SINCE THAT CROWN ENDED UP BEING BOGUS--
MAYBE... WE COULD GO LOOK FOR SOME OTHER TREASURE TOGETHER. NO GHOSTS.
OR WHATEVER.
THUD
OW!

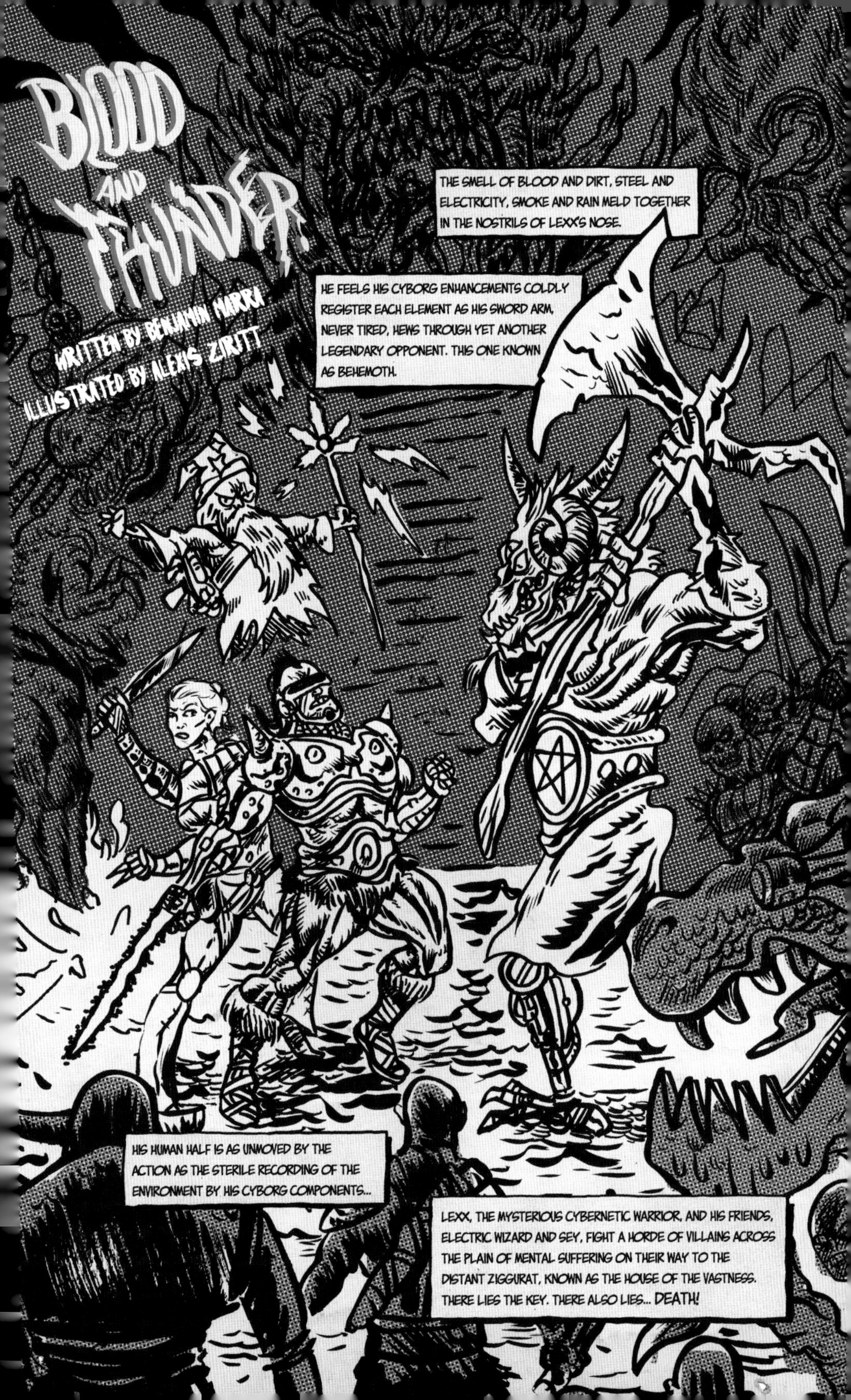
BLOOD AND THUNDER!
WRITTEN BY BENJAMIN MARRA
ILLUSTRATED BY ALEXIS ZIRITT
THE SMELL OF BLOOD AND DIRT, STEEL AND ELECTRICITY, SMOKE AND RAIN MELD TOGETHER IN THE NOSTRILS OF LEXX'S NOSE.
HE FEELS HIS CYBORG ENHANCEMENTS COLDLY REGISTER EACH ELEMENT AS HIS SWORD ARM, NEVER TIRED, HEWS THROUGH YET ANOTHER LEGENDARY OPPONENT. THIS ONE KNOWN AS BEHEMOTH.
HIS HUMAN HALF IS AS UNMOVED BY THE ACTION AS THE STERILE RECORDING OF THE ENVIRONMENT BY HIS CYBORG COMPONENTS...
LEXX, THE MYSTERIOUS CYBERNETIC WARRIOR, AND HIS FRIENDS, ELECTRIC WIZARD AND SEY, FIGHT A HORDE OF VILLAINS ACROSS THE PLAIN OF MENTAL SUFFERING ON THEIR WAY TO THE DISTANT ZIGGURAT, KNOWN AS THE HOUSE OF THE VASTNESS. THERE LIES THE KEY. THERE ALSO LIES... DEATH!

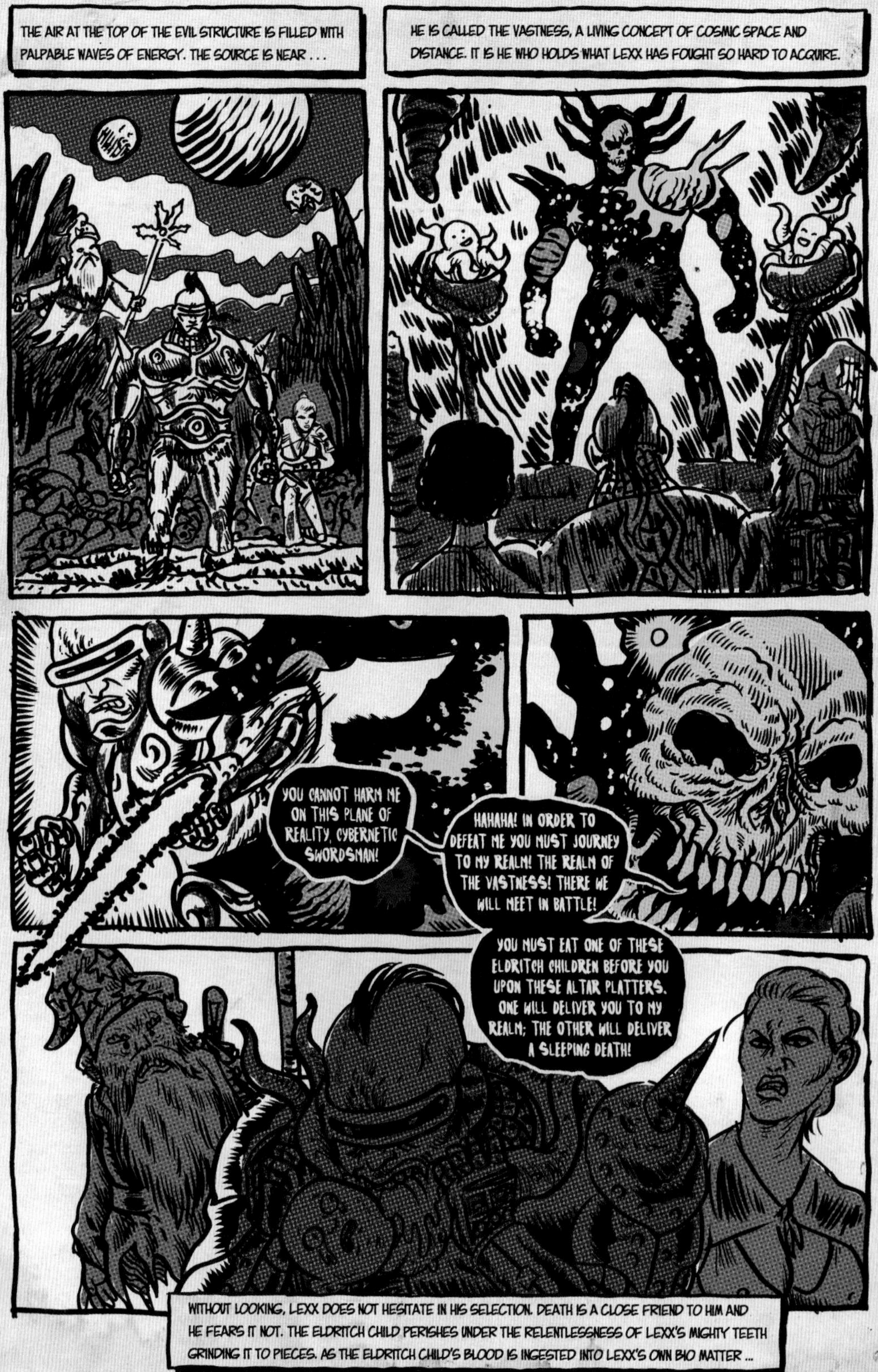
THE AIR AT THE TOP OF THE EVIL STRUCTURE IS FILLED WITH PALPABLE WAVES OF ENERGY. THE SOURCE IS NEAR . . .
HE IS CALLED THE VASTNESS, A LIVING CONCEPT OF COSMIC SPACE AND DISTANCE. IT IS HE WHO HOLDS WHAT LEXX HAS FOUGHT SO HARD TO ACQUIRE.
YOU CANNOT HARM ME ON THIS PLANE OF REALITY, CYBERNETIC SWORDSMAN!
HAHAHA! IN ORDER TO DEFEAT ME YOU MUST JOURNEY TO MY REALM! THE REALM OF THE VASTNESS! THERE WE WILL MEET IN BATTLE!
YOU MUST EAT ONE OF THESE ELDRITCH CHILDREN BEFORE YOU UPON THESE ALTAR PLATTERS. ONE WILL DELIVER YOU TO MY REALM; THE OTHER WILL DELIVER A SLEEPING DEATH!
WITHOUT LOOKING, LEXX DOES NOT HESITATE IN HIS SELECTION. DEATH IS A CLOSE FRIEND TO HIM AND HE FEARS IT NOT. THE ELDRITCH CHILD PERISHES UNDER THE RELENTLESSNESS OF LEXX'S MIGHTY TEETH GRINDING IT TO PIECES. AS THE ELDRITCH CHILD'S BLOOD IS INGESTED INTO LEXX'S OWN BIO MATTER ...

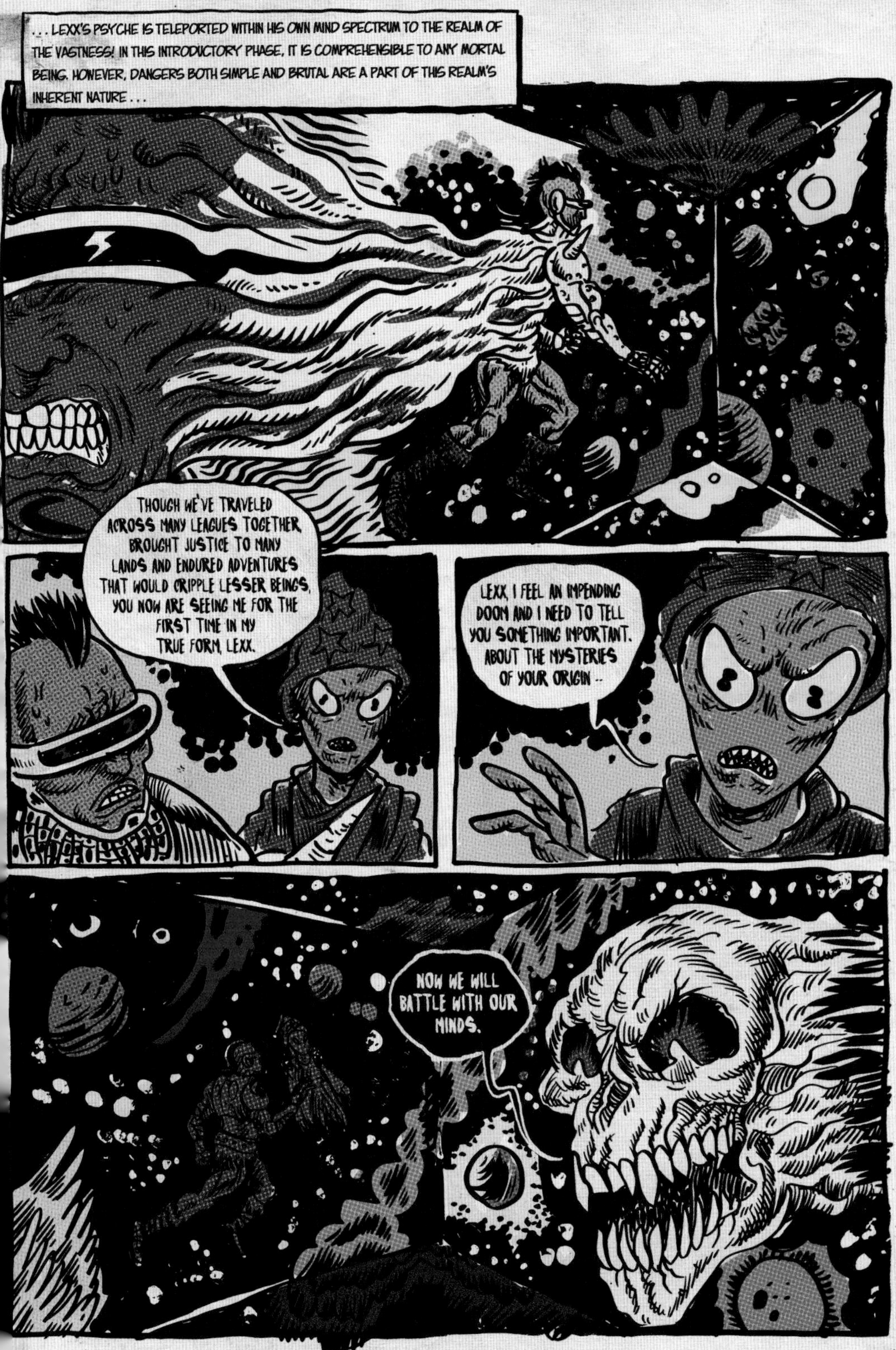

. . . LEXX'S PSYCHE IS TELEPORTED WITHIN HIS OWN MIND SPECTRUM TO THE REALM OF THE VASTNESS! IN THIS INTRODUCTORY PHASE, IT IS COMPREHENSIBLE TO ANY MORTAL BEING. HOWEVER, DANGERS BOTH SIMPLE AND BRUTAL ARE A PART OF THIS REALM'S INHERENT NATURE . . .
THOUGH WE'VE TRAVELED ACROSS MANY LEAGUES TOGETHER, BROUGHT JUSTICE TO MANY LANDS AND ENDURED ADVENTURES THAT WOULD CRIPPLE LESSER BEINGS, YOU NOW ARE SEEING ME FOR THE FIRST TIME IN MY TRUE FORM, LEXX.
LEXX, I FEEL AN IMPENDING DOOM AND I NEED TO TELL YOU SOMETHING IMPORTANT. ABOUT THE MYSTERIES OF YOUR ORIGIN --
NOW WE WILL BATTLE WITH OUR MINDS.

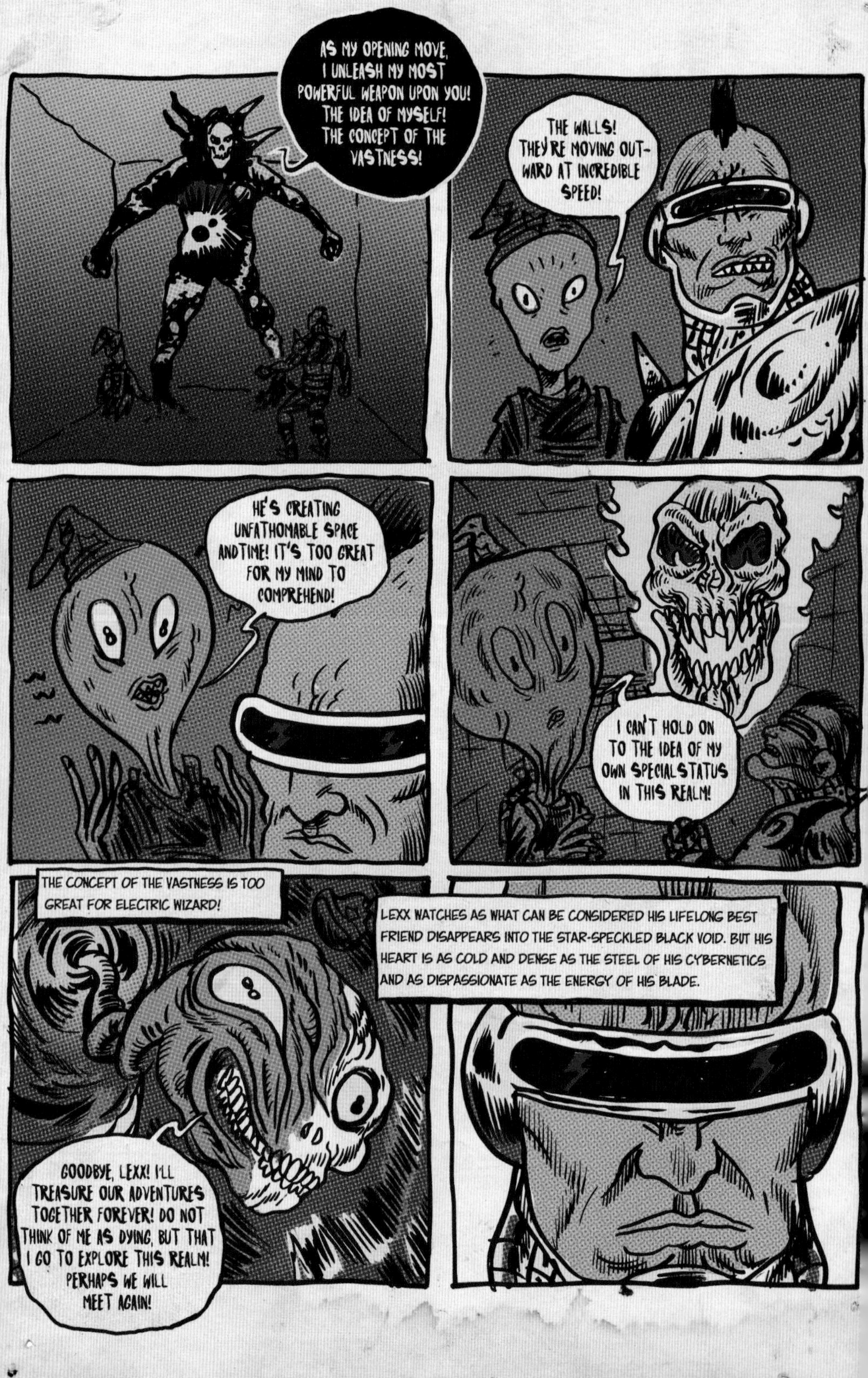
AS MY OPENING MOVE, I UNLEASH MY MOST POWERFUL WEAPON UPON YOU! THE IDEA OF MYSELF! THE CONCEPT OF THE VASTNESS!
THE WALLS! THEY'RE MOVING OUTWARD AT INCREDIBLE SPEED!
HE'S CREATING UNFATHOMABLE SPACE AND TIME! IT'S TOO GREAT FOR MY MIND TO COMPREHEND!
I CAN'T HOLD ON TO THE IDEA OF MY OWN SPECIAL STATUS IN THIS REALM!
THE CONCEPT OF THE VASTNESS IS TOO GREAT FOR ELECTRIC WIZARD!
GOODBYE, LEXX! I'LL TREASURE OUR ADVENTURES TOGETHER FOREVER! DO NOT THINK OF ME AS DYING, BUT THAT I GO TO EXPLORE THIS REALM! PERHAPS WE WILL MEET AGAIN!
LEXX WATCHES AS WHAT CAN BE CONSIDERED HIS LIFELONG BEST FRIEND DISAPPEARS INTO THE STAR-SPECKLED BLACK VOID. BUT HIS HEART IS AS COLD AND DENSE AS THE STEEL OF HIS CYBERNETICS AND AS DISPASSIONATE AS THE ENERGY OF HIS BLADE.

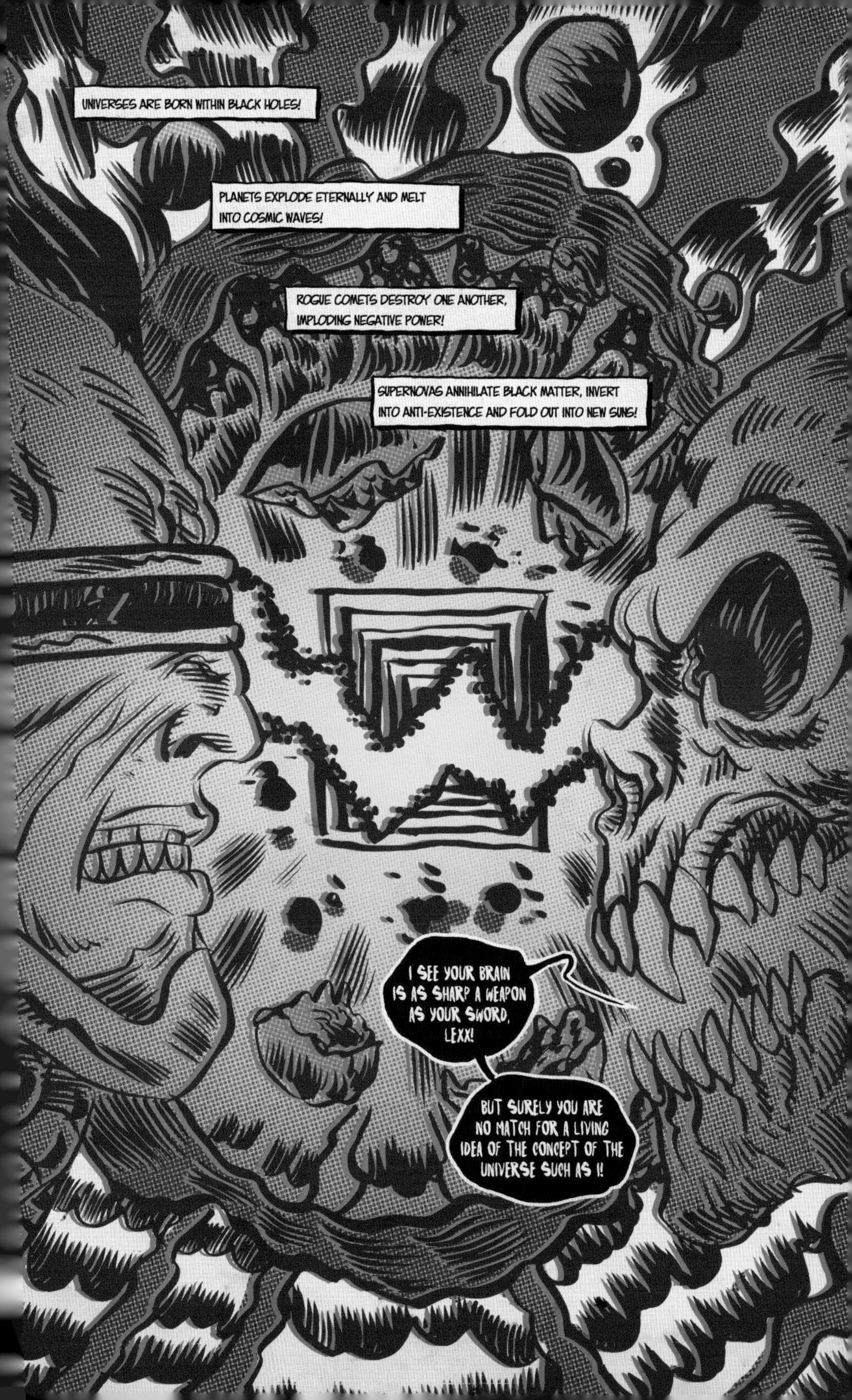
UNIVERSES ARE BORN WITHIN BLACK HOLES!
PLANETS EXPLODE ETERNALLY AND MELT INTO COSMIC WAVES!
ROGUE COMETS DESTROY ONE ANOTHER, IMPLODING NEGATIVE POWER!
SUPERNOVAS ANNIHILATE BLACK MATTER, INVERT INTO ANTI-EXISTENCE AND FOLD OUT INTO NEW SUNS!
I SEE YOUR BRAIN IS AS SHARP A WEAPON AS YOUR SWORD, LEXX!
BUT SURELY YOU ARE NO MATCH FOR A LIVING IDEA OF THE CONCEPT OF THE UNIVERSE SUCH AS I!

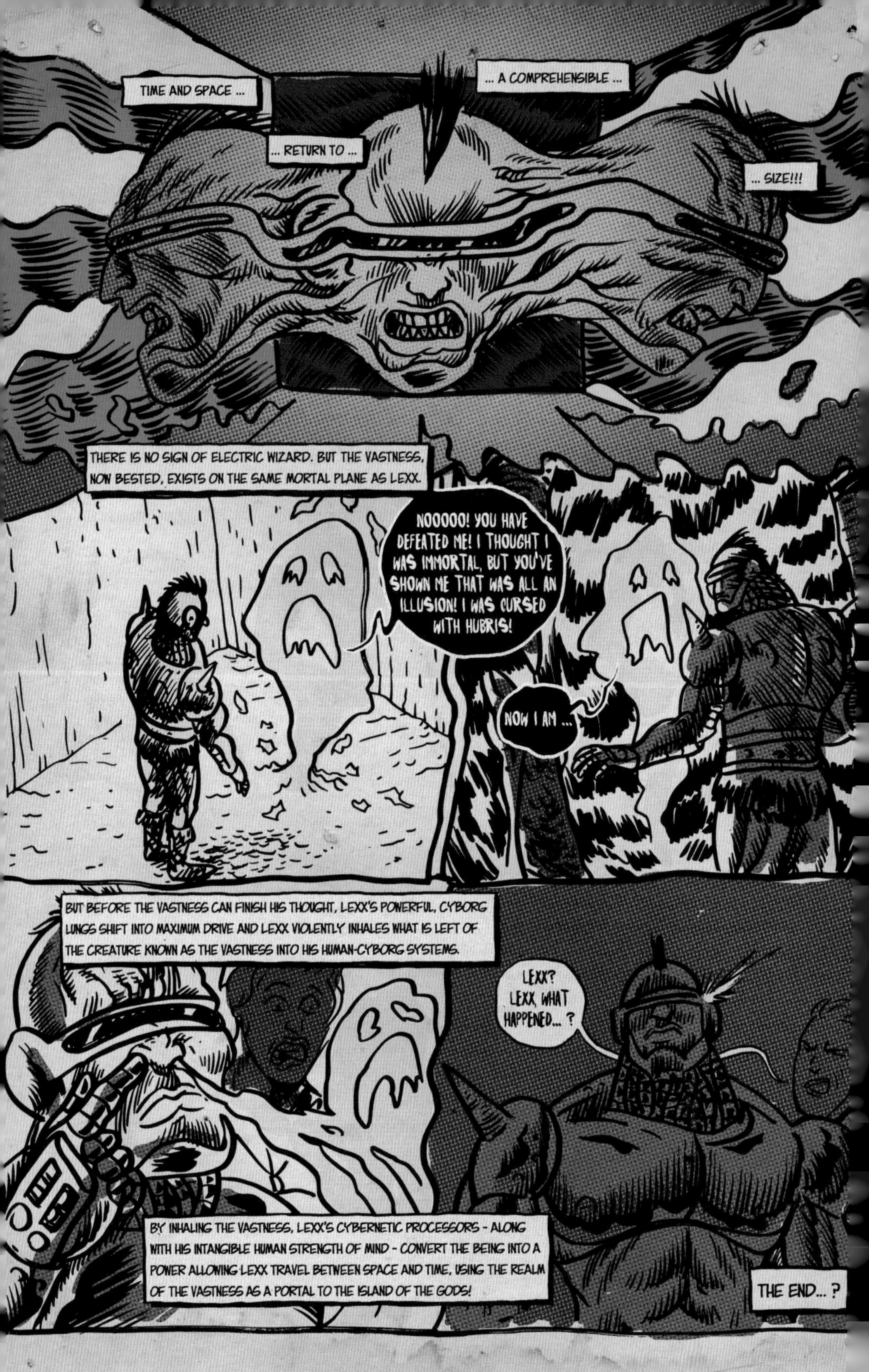
TIME AND SPACE ...
... RETURN TO ...
... A COMPREHENSIBLE ...
... SIZE!!!
THERE IS NO SIGN OF ELECTRIC WIZARD. BUT THE VASTNESS, NOW BESTED, EXISTS ON THE SAME MORTAL PLANE AS LEXX.
NOOOOO! YOU HAVE DEFEATED ME! I THOUGHT I WAS IMMORTAL, BUT YOU'VE SHOWN ME THAT WAS ALL AN ILLUSION! I WAS CURSED WITH HUBRIS!
NOW I AM ...
BUT BEFORE THE VASTNESS CAN FINISH HIS THOUGHT, LEXX'S POWERFUL, CYBORG LUNGS SHIFT INTO MAXIMUM DRIVE AND LEXX VIOLENTLY INHALES WHAT IS LEFT OF THE CREATURE KNOWN AS THE VASTNESS INTO HIS HUMAN-CYBORG SYSTEMS.
LEXX? LEXX, WHAT HAPPENED... ?
BY INHALING THE VASTNESS, LEXX'S CYBERNETIC PROCESSORS - ALONG WITH HIS INTANGIBLE HUMAN STRENGTH OF MIND - CONVERT THE BEING INTO A POWER ALLOWING LEXX TRAVEL BETWEEN SPACE AND TIME, USING THE REALM OF THE VASTNESS AS A PORTAL TO THE ISLAND OF THE GODS!
THE END... ?

WRITTEN BY JOSH TIERNEY

KLOE

ILLUSTRATED BY TRAVEL FOREMAN

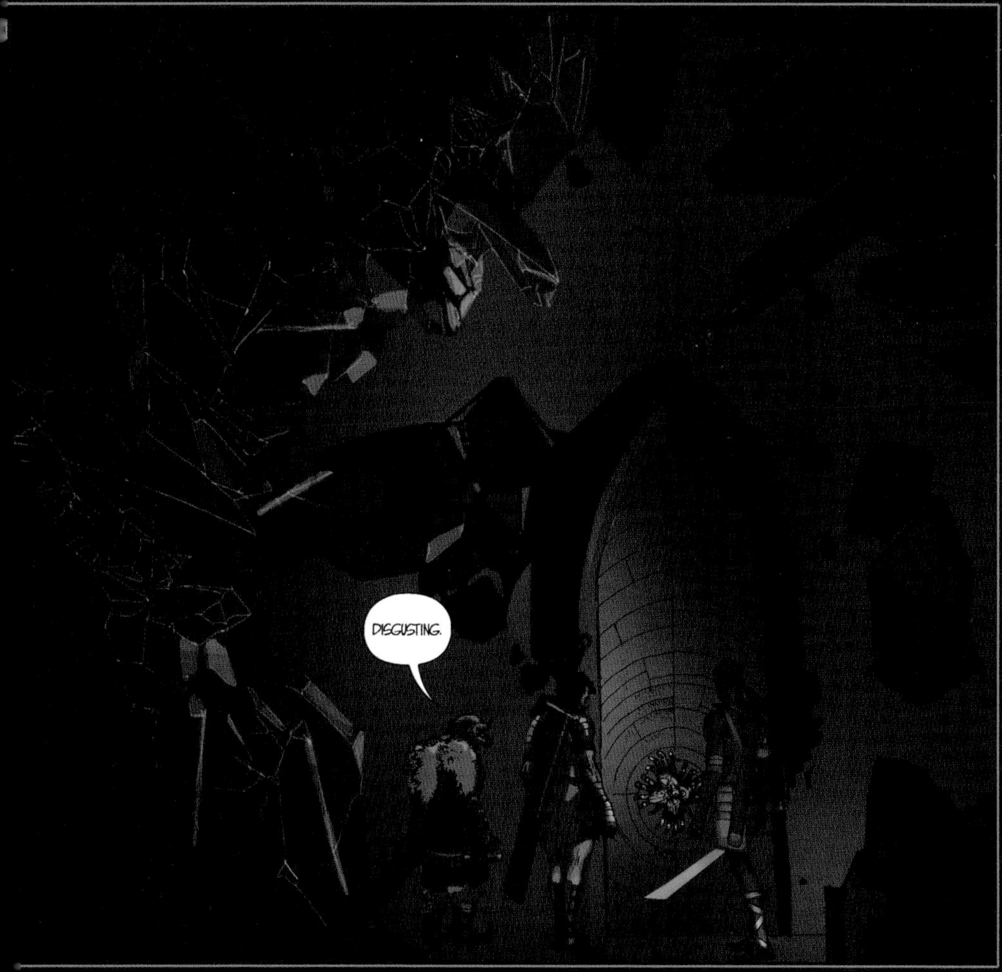
DISGUSTING.

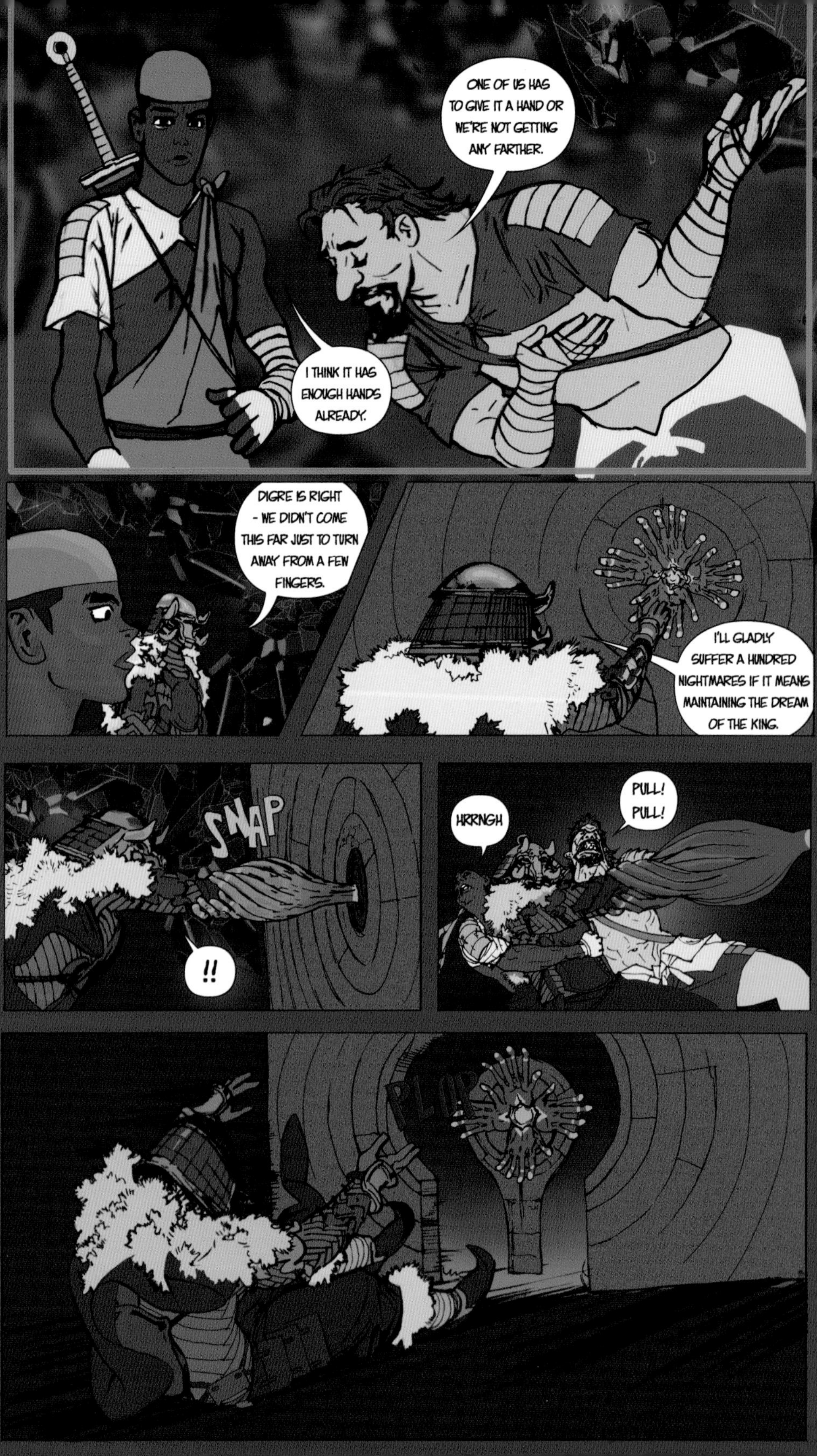
ONE OF US HAS TO GIVE IT A HAND OR WE'RE NOT GETTING ANY FARTHER.
I THINK IT HAS ENOUGH HANDS ALREADY.
DIGRE IS RIGHT - WE DIDN'T COME THIS FAR JUST TO TURN AWAY FROM A FEW FINGERS.
I'LL GLADLY SUFFER A HUNDRED NIGHTMARES IF IT MEANS MAINTAINING THE DREAM OF THE KING.
SNAP
!!
HRRNGH
PULL! PULL!

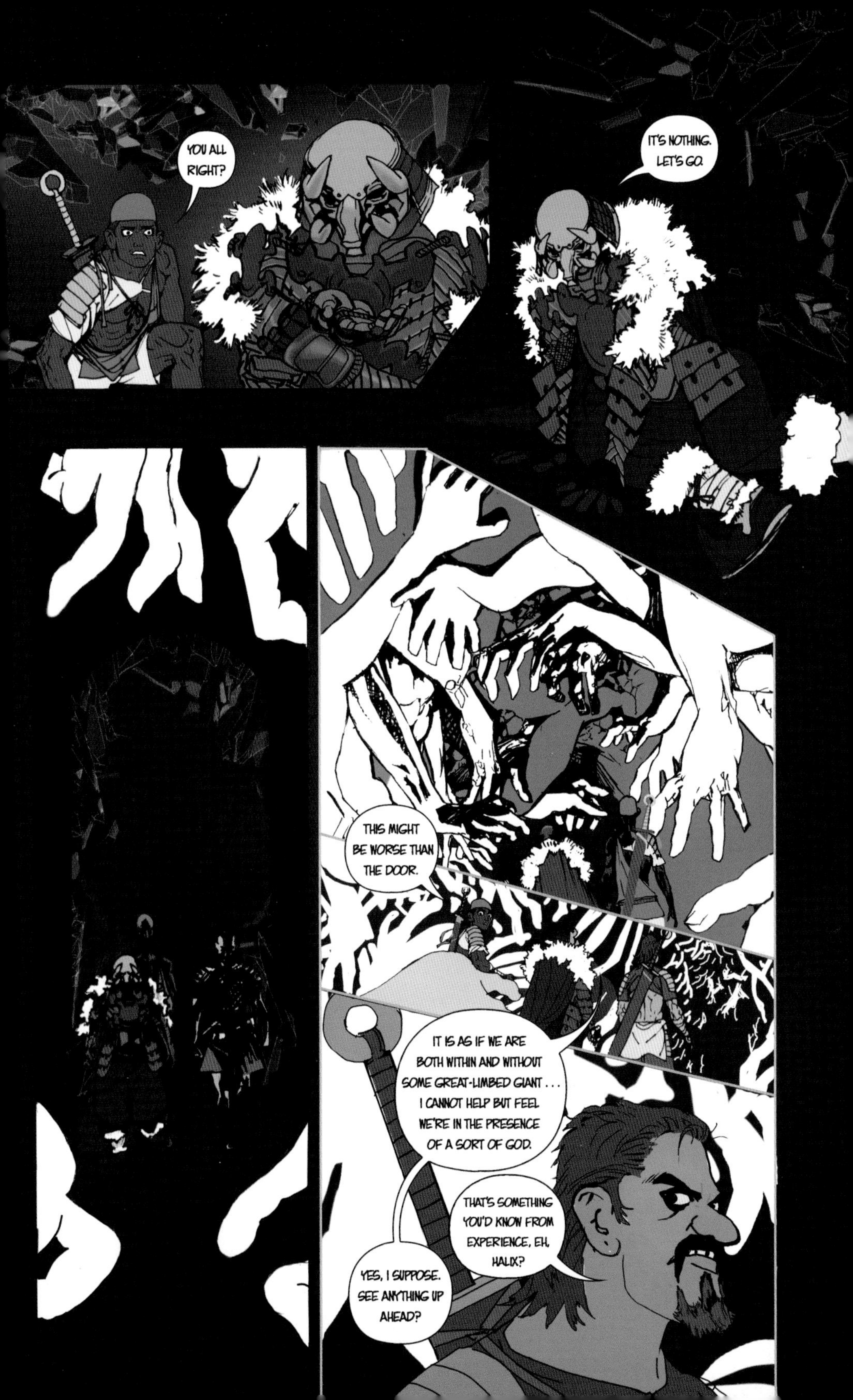
YOU ALL RIGHT?
IT'S NOTHING. LET'S GO.
THIS MIGHT BE WORSE THAN THE DOOR.
IT IS AS IF WE ARE BOTH WITHIN AND WITHOUT SOME GREAT-LIMBED GIANT . . . I CANNOT HELP BUT FEEL WE'RE IN THE PRESENCE OF A SORT OF GOD.
THAT'S SOMETHING YOU'D KNOW FROM EXPERIENCE, EH, HALIX?
YES, I SUPPOSE. SEE ANYTHING UP AHEAD?

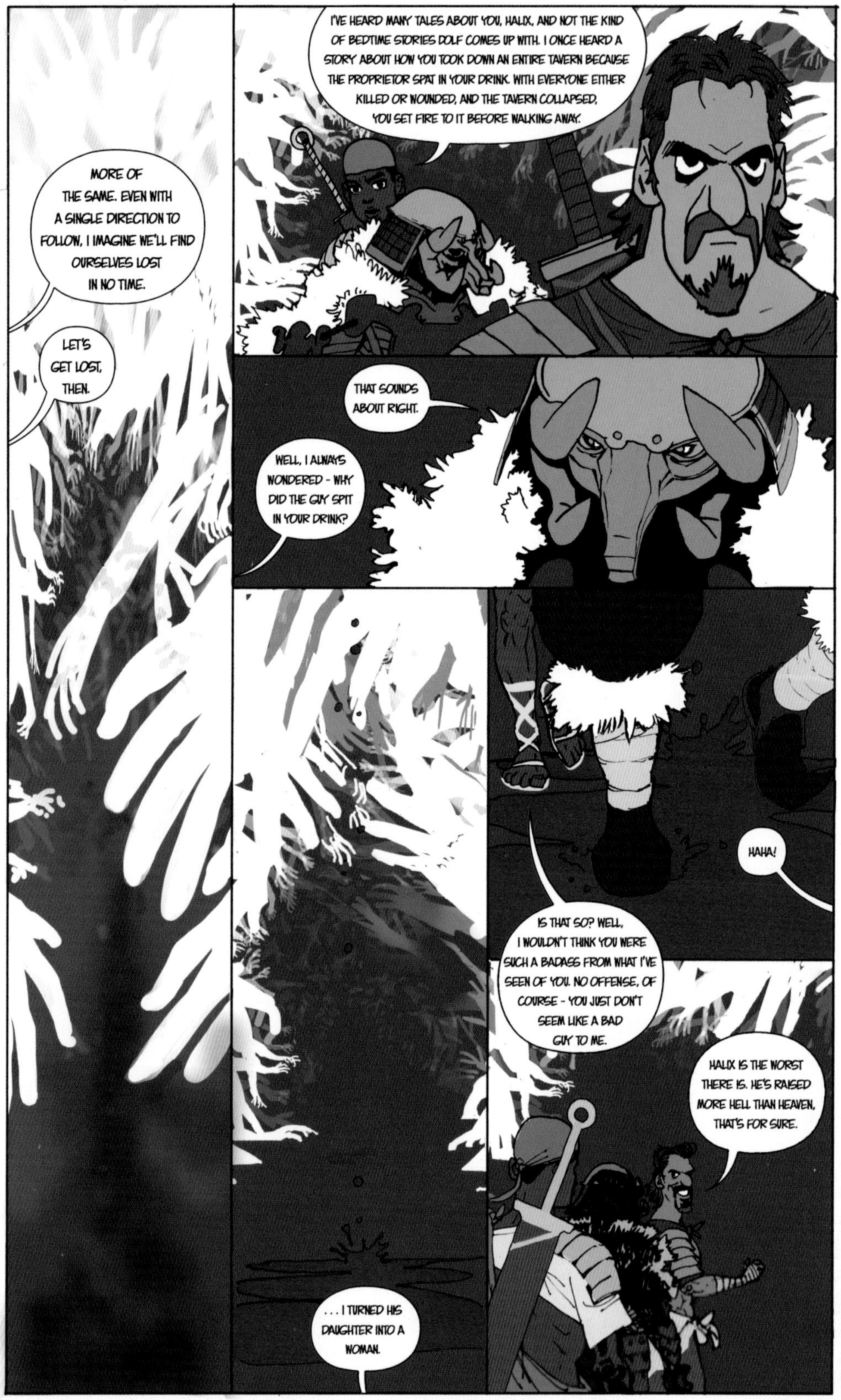
MORE OF THE SAME. EVEN WITH A SINGLE DIRECTION TO FOLLOW, I IMAGINE WE'LL FIND OURSELVES LOST IN NO TIME.
LET'S GET LOST, THEN.
I'VE HEARD MANY TALES ABOUT YOU, HALIX, AND NOT THE KIND OF BEDTIME STORIES DOLF COMES UP WITH. I ONCE HEARD A STORY ABOUT HOW YOU TOOK DOWN AN ENTIRE TAVERN BECAUSE THE PROPRIETOR SPAT IN YOUR DRINK. WITH EVERYONE EITHER KILLED OR WOUNDED, AND THE TAVERN COLLAPSED, YOU SET FIRE TO IT BEFORE WALKING AWAY.
THAT SOUNDS ABOUT RIGHT.
WELL, I ALWAYS WONDERED - WHY DID THE GUY SPIT IN YOUR DRINK?
. . . I TURNED HIS DAUGHTER INTO A WOMAN.
HAHA!
IS THAT SO? WELL, I WOULDN'T THINK YOU WERE SUCH A BADASS FROM WHAT I'VE SEEN OF YOU. NO OFFENSE, OF COURSE - YOU JUST DON'T SEEM LIKE A BAD GUY TO ME.
HALIX IS THE WORST THERE IS. HE'S RAISED MORE HELL THAN HEAVEN, THAT'S FOR SURE.

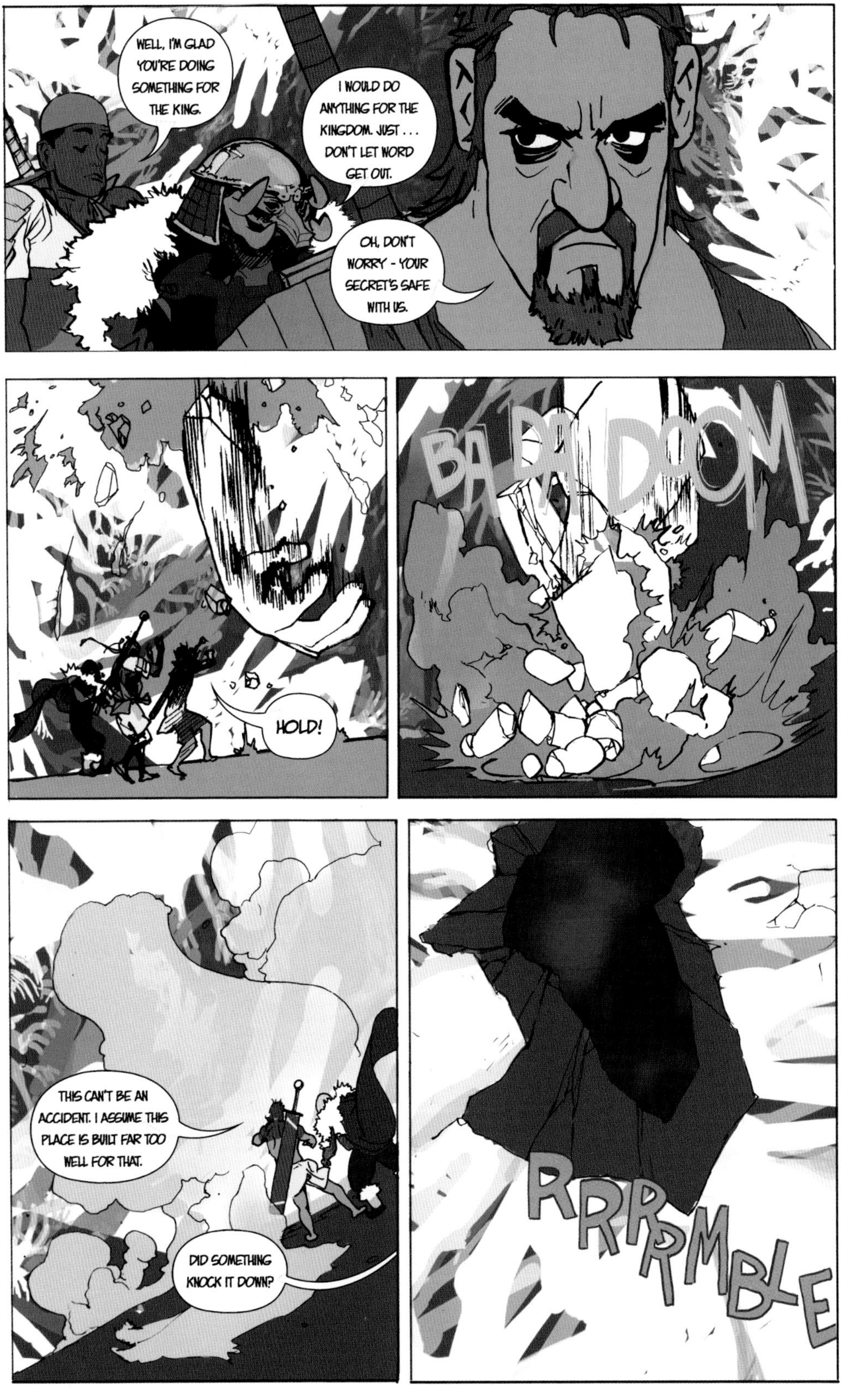
WELL, I'M GLAD YOU'RE DOING SOMETHING FOR THE KING.
I WOULD DO ANYTHING FOR THE KINGDOM. JUST . . . DON'T LET WORD GET OUT.
OH, DON'T WORRY - YOUR SECRET'S SAFE WITH US.
HOLD!
BA DA DOOM
THIS CAN'T BE AN ACCIDENT. I ASSUME THIS PLACE IS BUILT FAR TOO WELL FOR THAT.
DID SOMETHING KNOCK IT DOWN?
RRRRMBLE

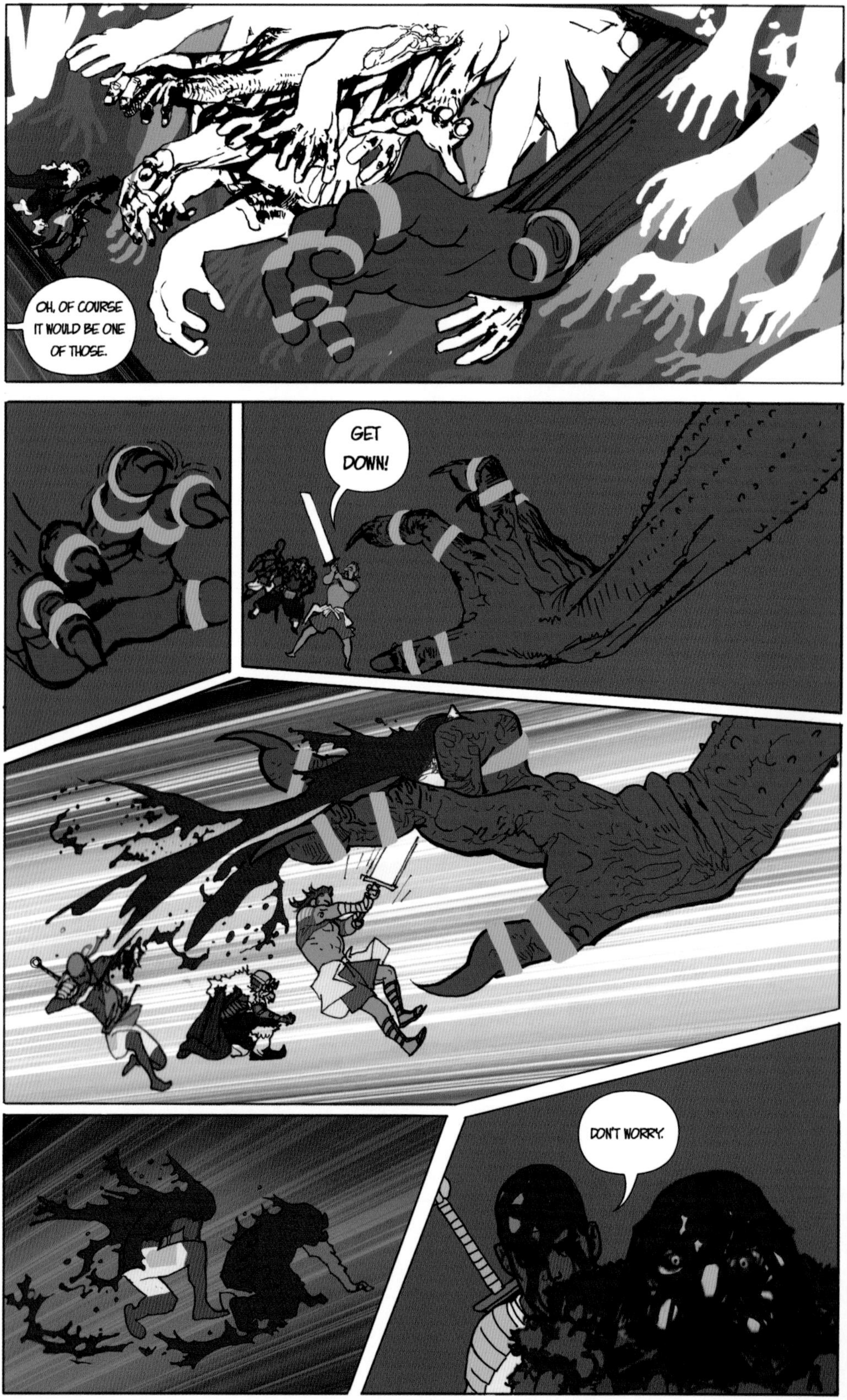
OH, OF COURSE IT WOULD BE ONE OF THOSE.
GET DOWN!
DON'T WORRY.

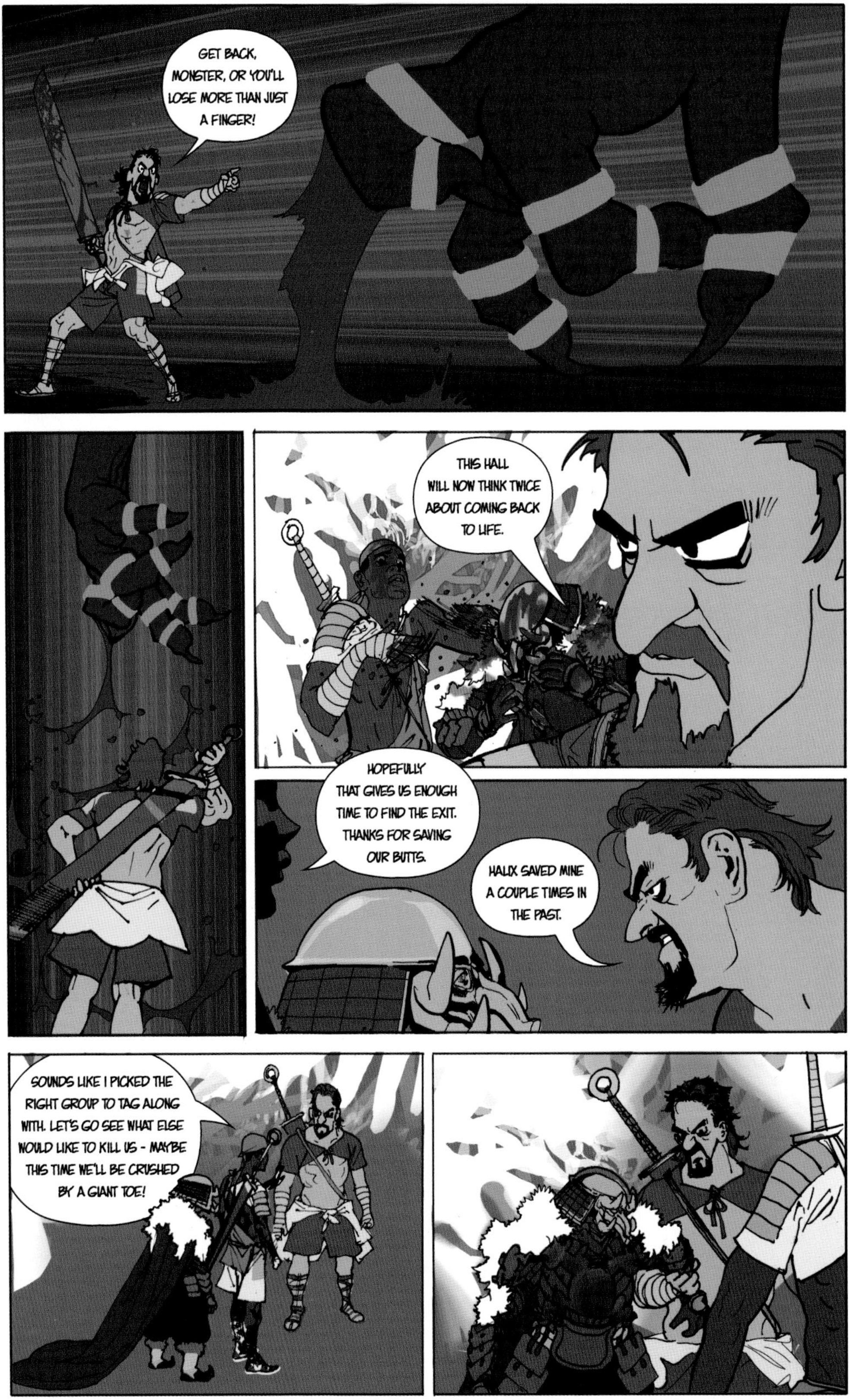
GET BACK, MONSTER, OR YOU'LL LOSE MORE THAN JUST A FINGER!
THIS HALL WILL NOW THINK TWICE ABOUT COMING BACK TO LIFE.
HOPEFULLY THAT GIVES US ENOUGH TIME TO FIND THE EXIT. THANKS FOR SAVING OUR BUTTS.
HALIX SAVED MINE A COUPLE TIMES IN THE PAST.
SOUNDS LIKE I PICKED THE RIGHT GROUP TO TAG ALONG WITH. LET'S GO SEE WHAT ELSE WOULD LIKE TO KILL US - MAYBE THIS TIME WE'LL BE CRUSHED BY A GIANT TOE!

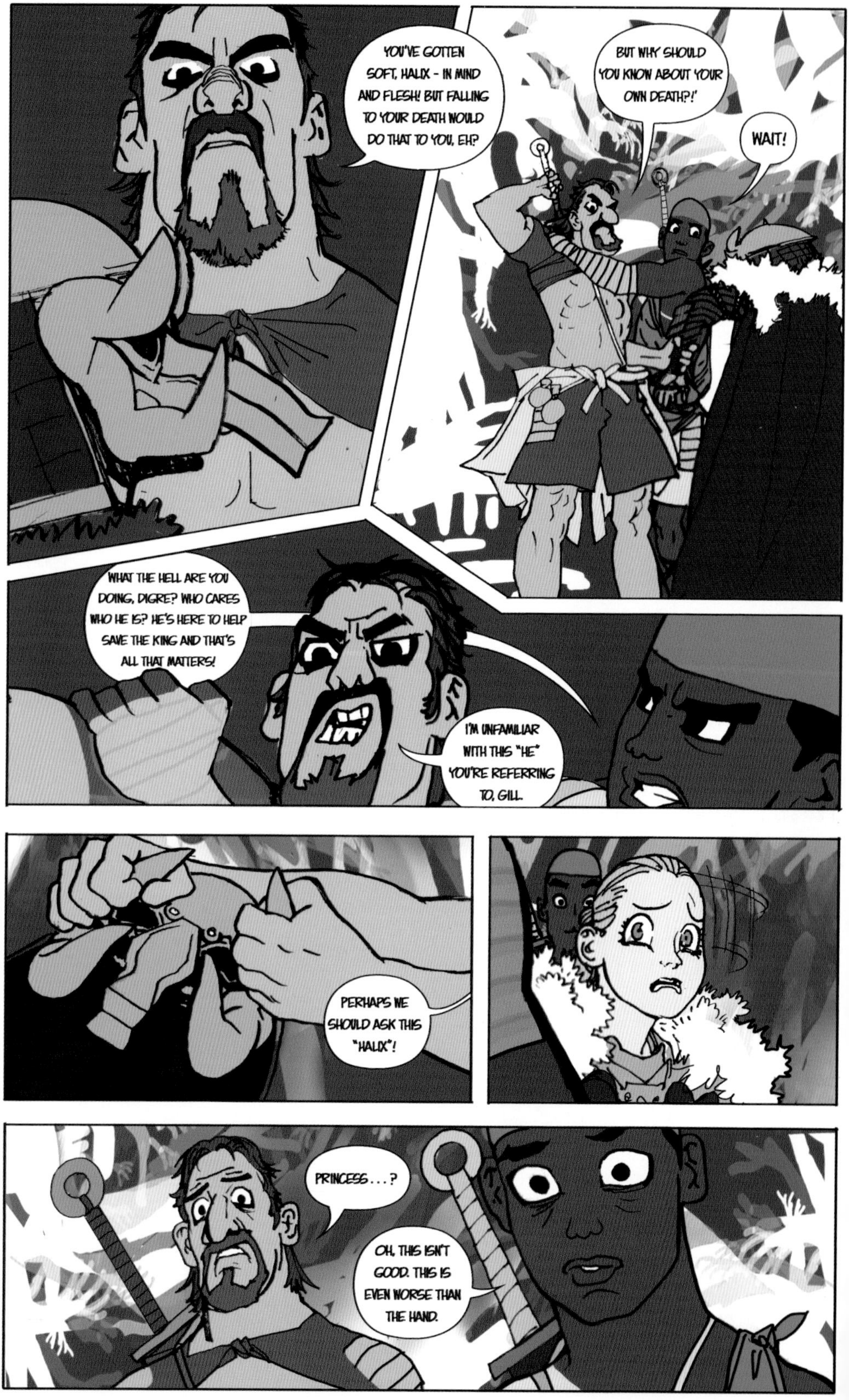
YOU'VE GOTTEN SOFT, HALIX - IN MIND AND FLESH! BUT FALLING TO YOUR DEATH WOULD DO THAT TO YOU, EH?
BUT WHY SHOULD YOU KNOW ABOUT YOUR OWN DEATH?!'
WAIT!
WHAT THE HELL ARE YOU DOING, DIGRE? WHO CARES WHO HE IS? HE'S HERE TO HELP SAVE THE KING AND THAT'S ALL THAT MATTERS!
I'M UNFAMILIAR WITH THIS "HE" YOU'RE REFERRING TO, GILL.
PERHAPS WE SHOULD ASK THIS "HALIX"!
PRINCESS . . . ?
OH, THIS ISN'T GOOD. THIS IS EVEN WORSE THAN THE HAND.

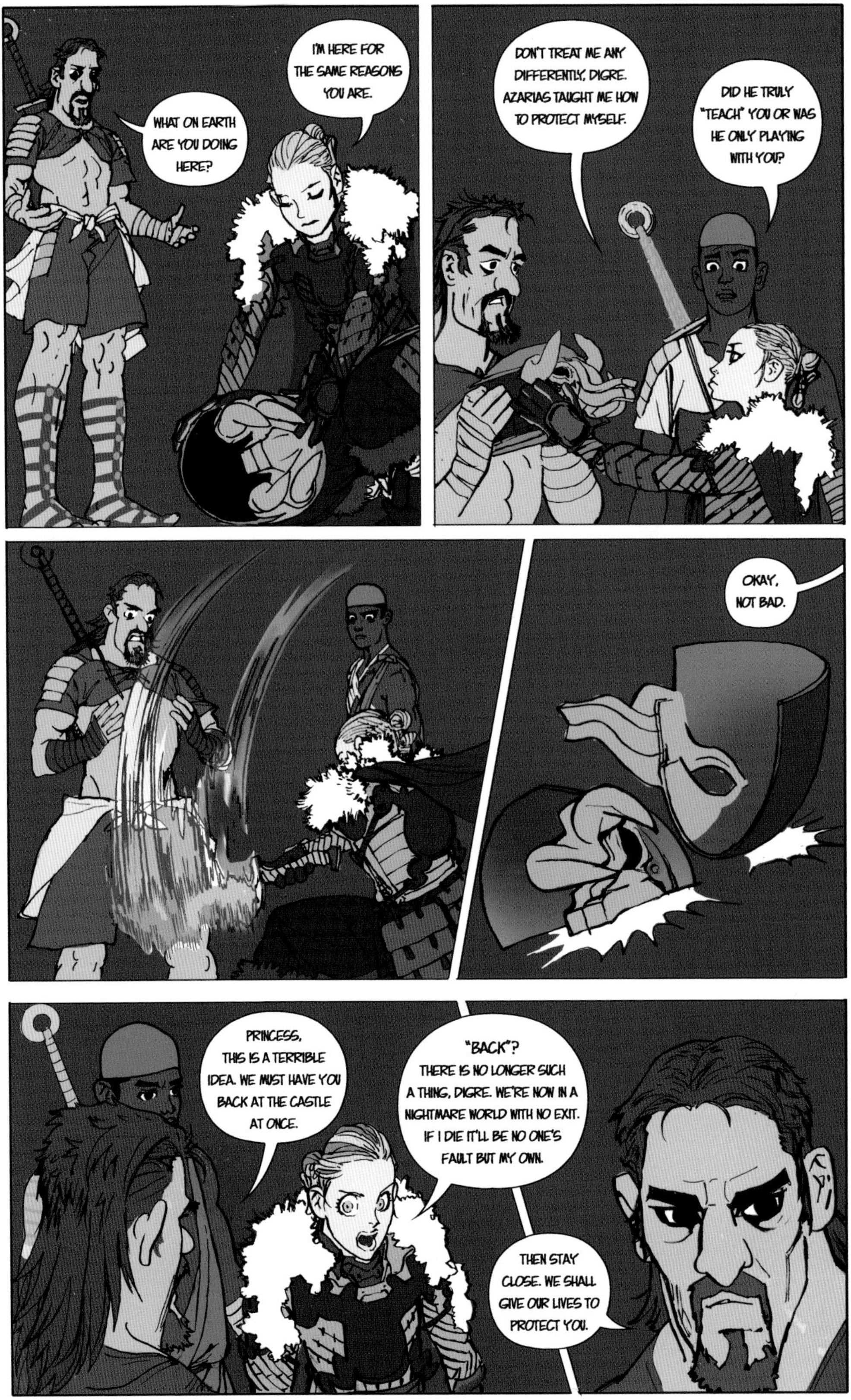
WHAT ON EARTH ARE YOU DOING HERE?
I'M HERE FOR THE SAME REASONS YOU ARE.
DON'T TREAT ME ANY DIFFERENTLY, DIGRE. AZARIAS TAUGHT ME HOW TO PROTECT MYSELF.
DID HE TRULY "TEACH" YOU OR WAS HE ONLY PLAYING WITH YOU?
OKAY, NOT BAD.
PRINCESS, THIS IS A TERRIBLE IDEA. WE MUST HAVE YOU BACK AT THE CASTLE AT ONCE.
"BACK"? THERE IS NO LONGER SUCH A THING, DIGRE. WE'RE NOW IN A NIGHTMARE WORLD WITH NO EXIT. IF I DIE IT'LL BE NO ONE'S FAULT BUT MY OWN.
THEN STAY CLOSE. WE SHALL GIVE OUR LIVES TO PROTECT YOU.

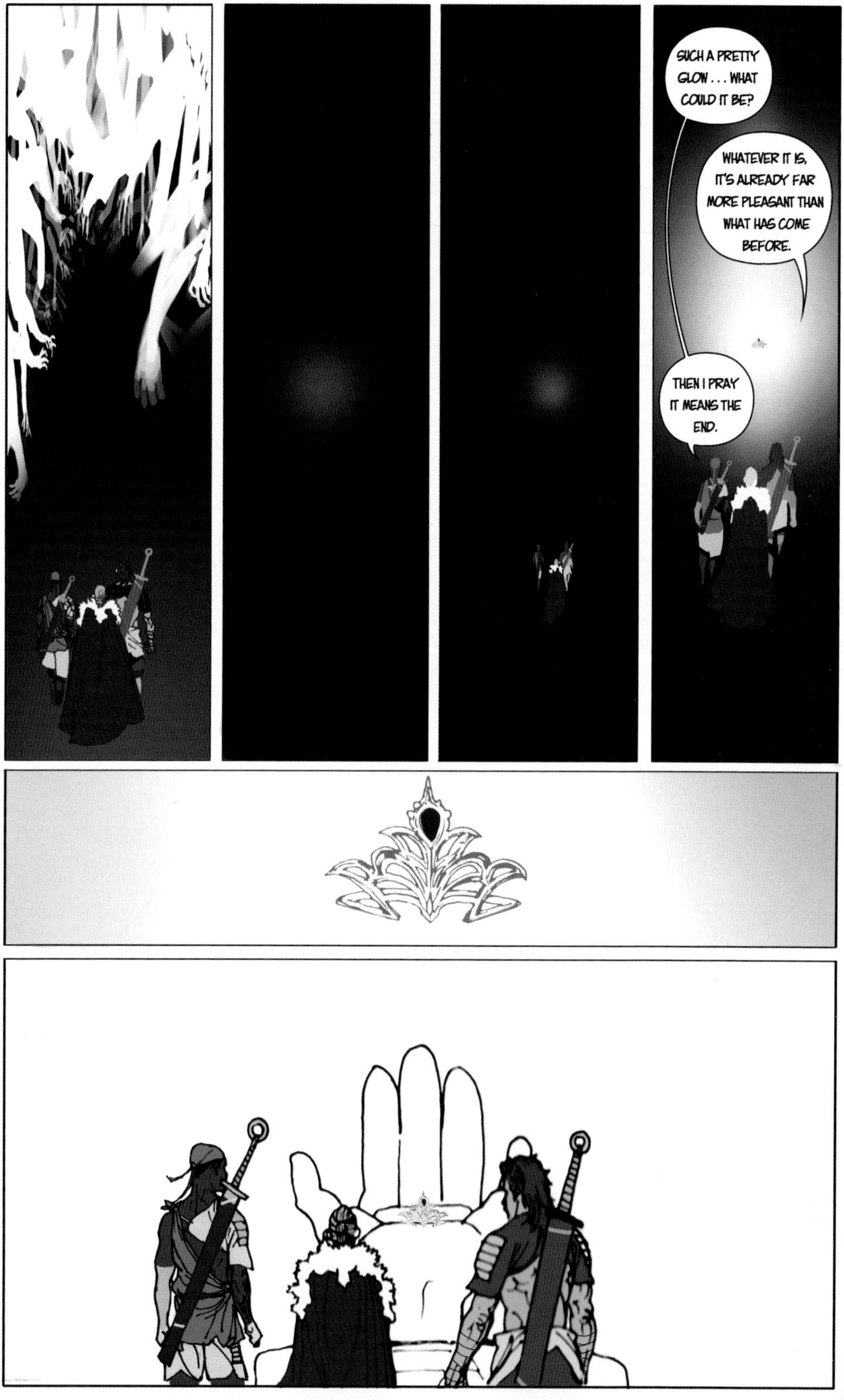
SUCH A PRETTY GLOW . . . WHAT COULD IT BE?
WHATEVER IT IS, IT'S ALREADY FAR MORE PLEASANT THAN WHAT HAS COME BEFORE.
THEN I PRAY IT MEANS THE END.

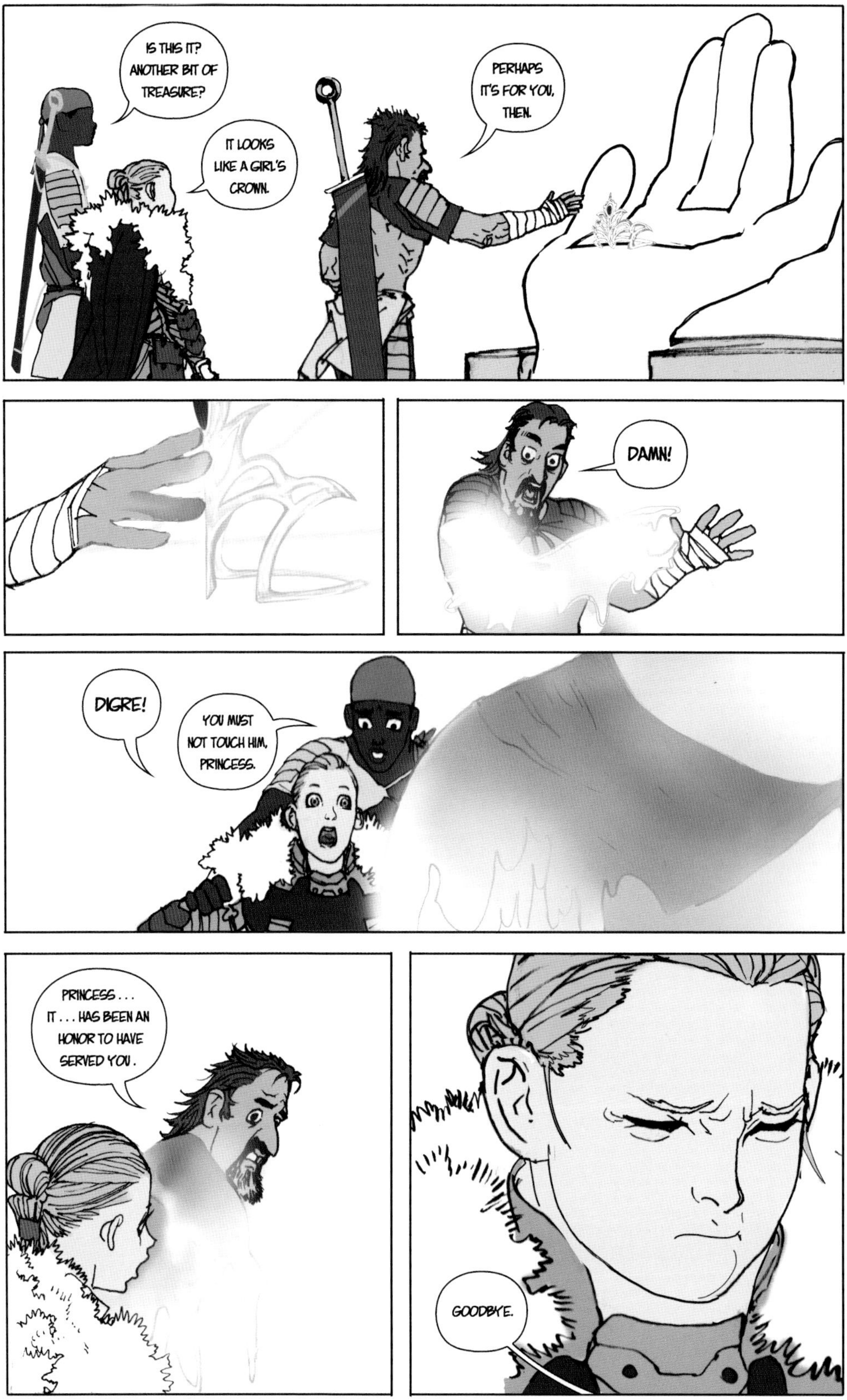
IS THIS IT? ANOTHER BIT OF TREASURE?
IT LOOKS LIKE A GIRL'S CROWN.
PERHAPS IT'S FOR YOU, THEN.
DAMN!
DIGRE!
YOU MUST NOT TOUCH HIM, PRINCESS.
PRINCESS . . . IT . . . HAS BEEN AN HONOR TO HAVE SERVED YOU .
GOODBYE.

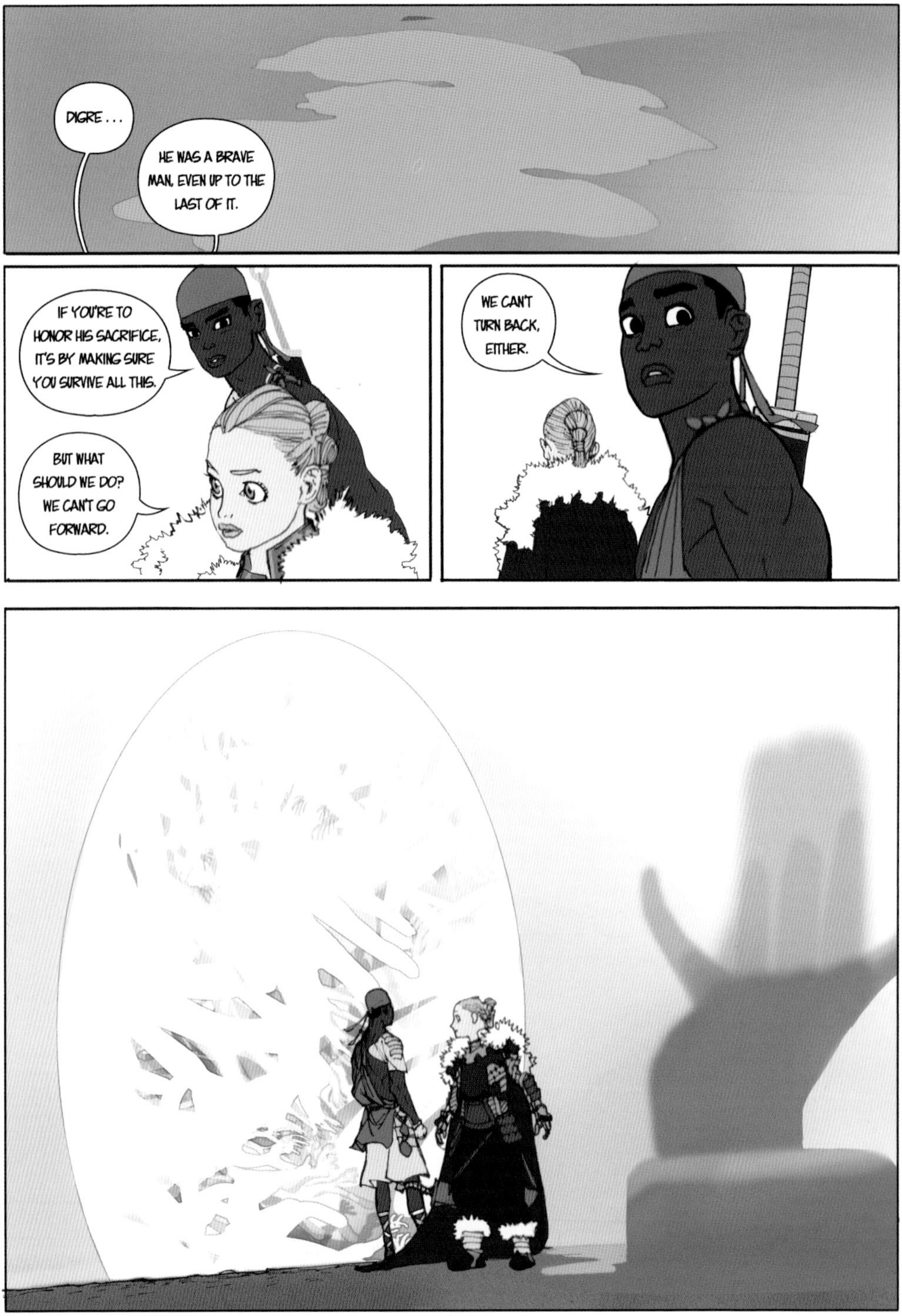
DIGRE . . .
HE WAS A BRAVE MAN, EVEN UP TO THE LAST OF IT.
IF YOU'RE TO HONOR HIS SACRIFICE, IT'S BY MAKING SURE YOU SURVIVE ALL THIS.
BUT WHAT SHOULD WE DO? WE CAN'T GO FORWARD.
WE CAN'T TURN BACK, EITHER.

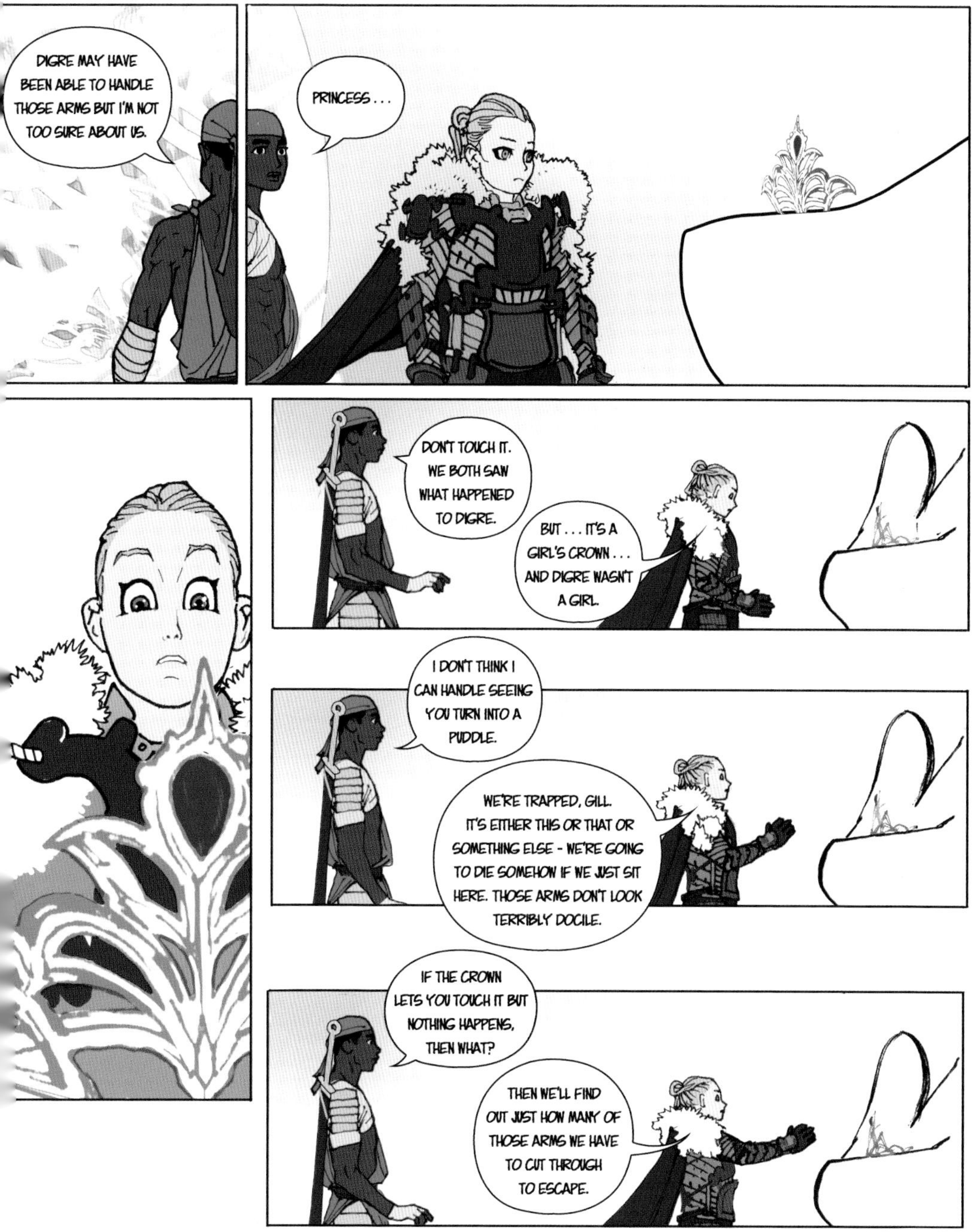
DIGRE MAY HAVE BEEN ABLE TO HANDLE THOSE ARMS BUT I'M NOT TOO SURE ABOUT US.
PRINCESS . . .
DON'T TOUCH IT. WE BOTH SAW WHAT HAPPENED TO DIGRE.
BUT . . . IT'S A GIRL'S CROWN . . . AND DIGRE WASN'T A GIRL.
I DON'T THINK I CAN HANDLE SEEING YOU TURN INTO A PUDDLE.
WE'RE TRAPPED, GILL. IT'S EITHER THIS OR THAT OR SOMETHING ELSE - WE'RE GOING TO DIE SOMEHOW IF WE JUST SIT HERE. THOSE ARMS DON'T LOOK TERRIBLY DOCILE.
IF THE CROWN LETS YOU TOUCH IT BUT NOTHING HAPPENS, THEN WHAT?
THEN WE'LL FIND OUT JUST HOW MANY OF THOSE ARMS WE HAVE TO CUT THROUGH TO ESCAPE.

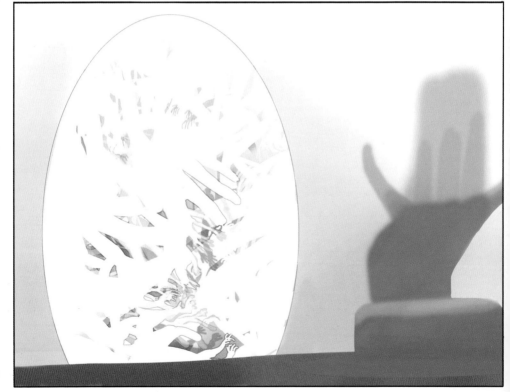

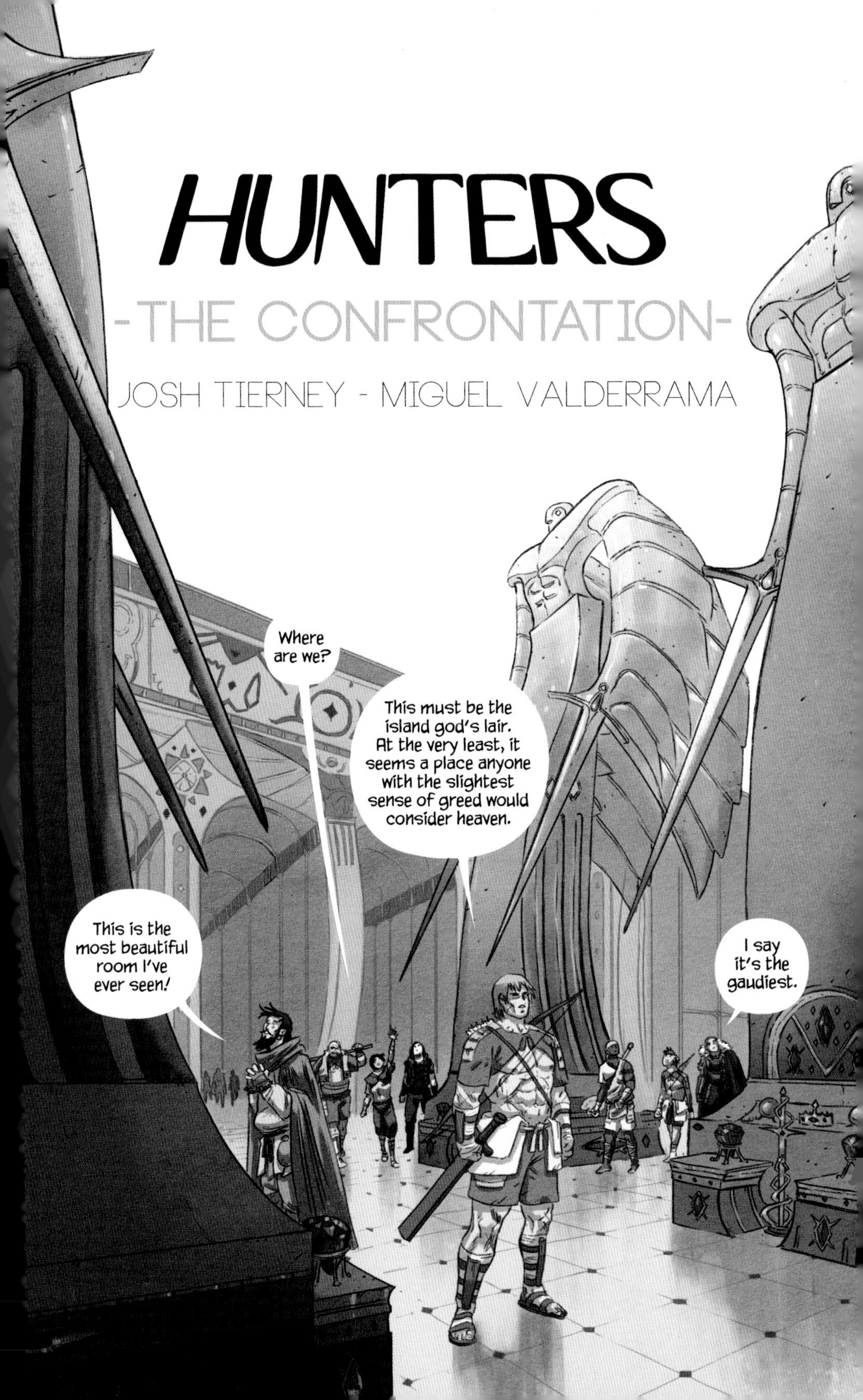
HUNTERS
-THE CONFRONTATION-
JOSH TIERNEY - MIGUEL VALDERRAMA
Where are we?
This must be the island god's lair. At the very least, it seems a place anyone with the slightest sense of greed would consider heaven.
This is the most beautiful room I've ever seen!
I say it's the gaudiest.

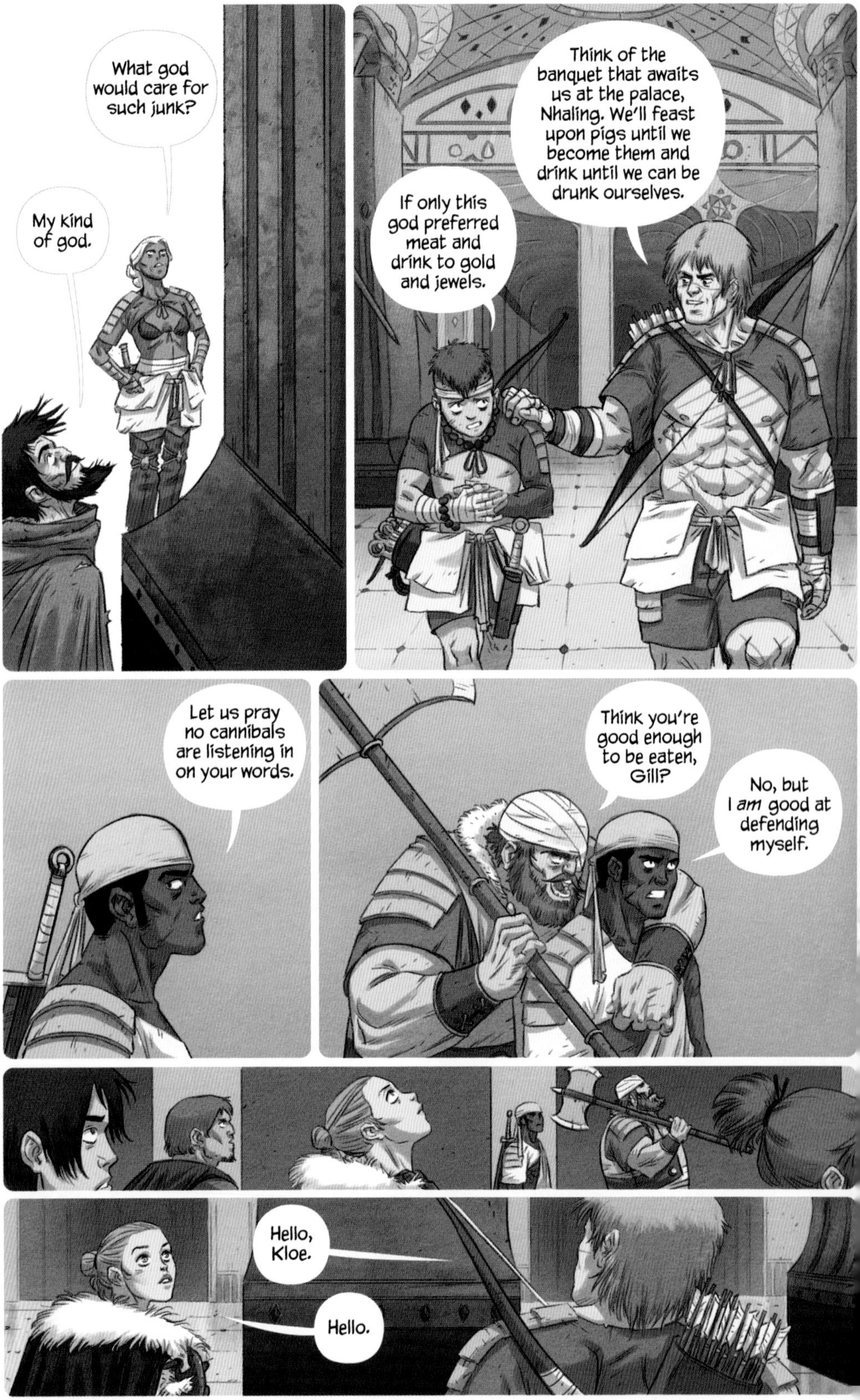
What god would care for such junk?
My kind of god.
Think of the banquet that awaits us at the palace, Nhaling. We'll feast upon pigs until we become them and drink until we can be drunk ourselves.
If only this god preferred meat and drink to gold and jewels.
Let us pray no cannibals are listening in on your words.
Think you're good enough to be eaten, Gill?
No, but I *am* good at defending myself.
Hello, Kloe.
Hello.

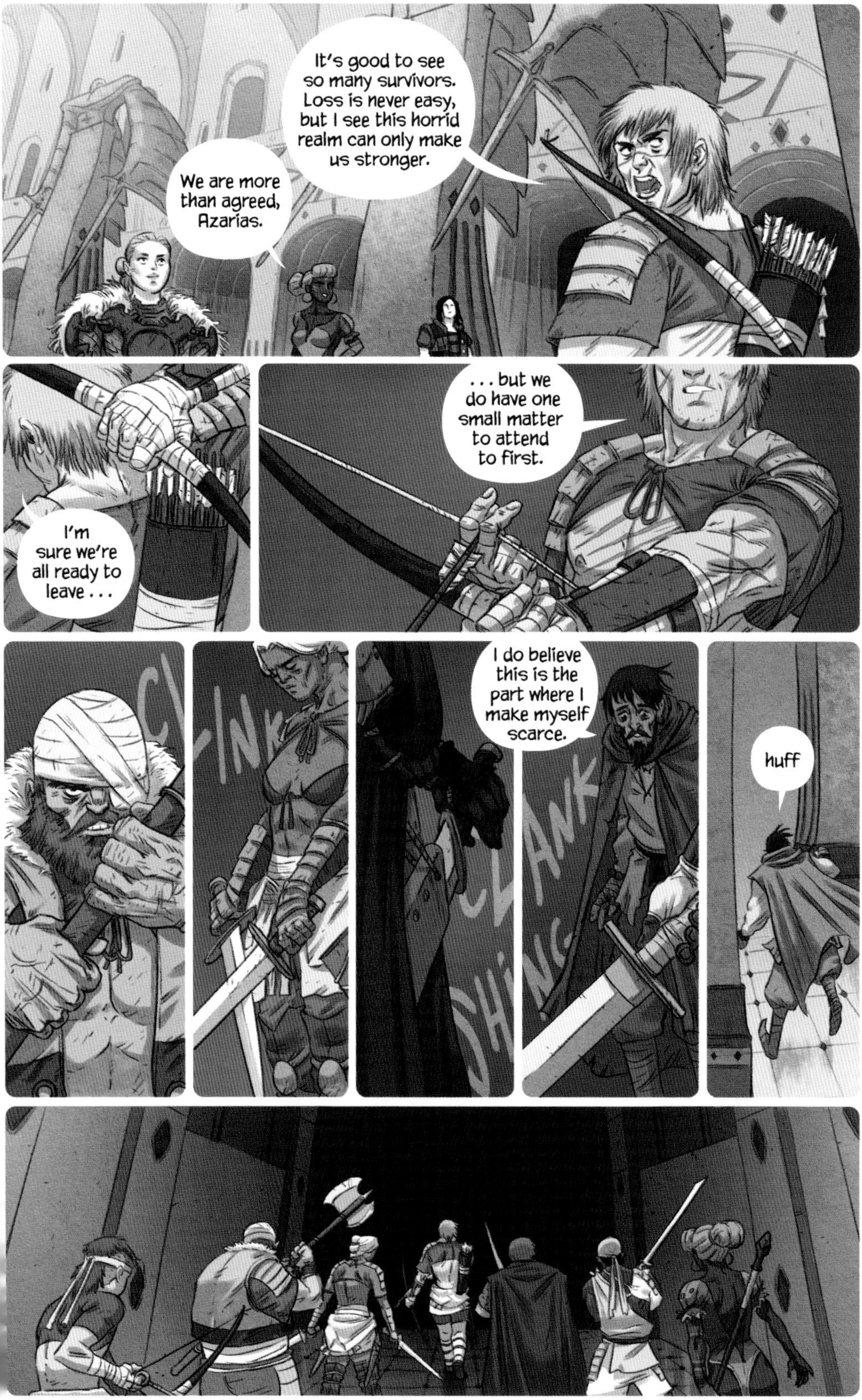
It's good to see so many survivors. Loss is never easy, but I see this horrid realm can only make us stronger.
We are more than agreed, Azarias.
I'm sure we're all ready to leave . . .
. . . but we do have one small matter to attend to first.
CLINK
I do believe this is the part where I make myself scarce.
CLANK
SHING
huff

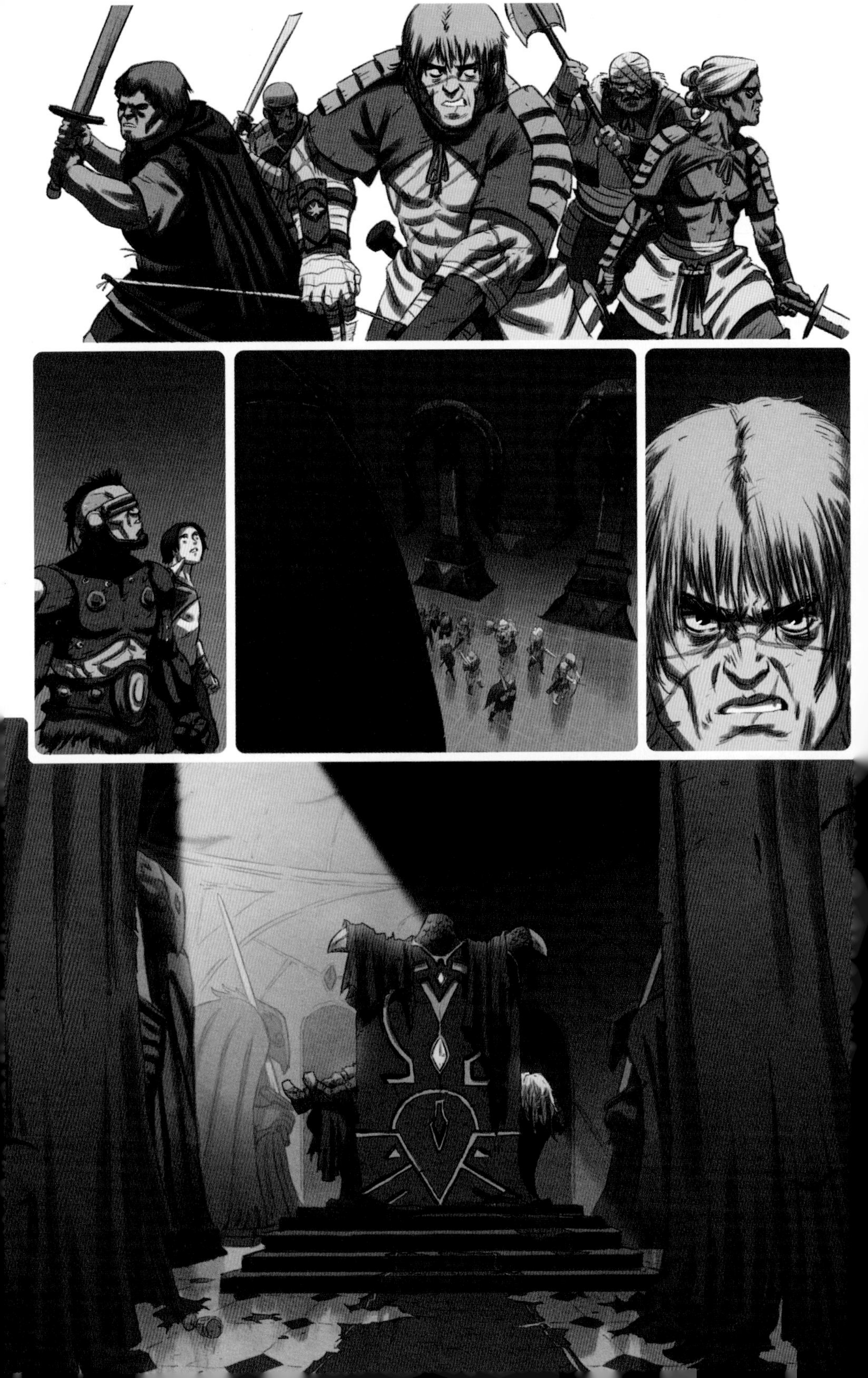

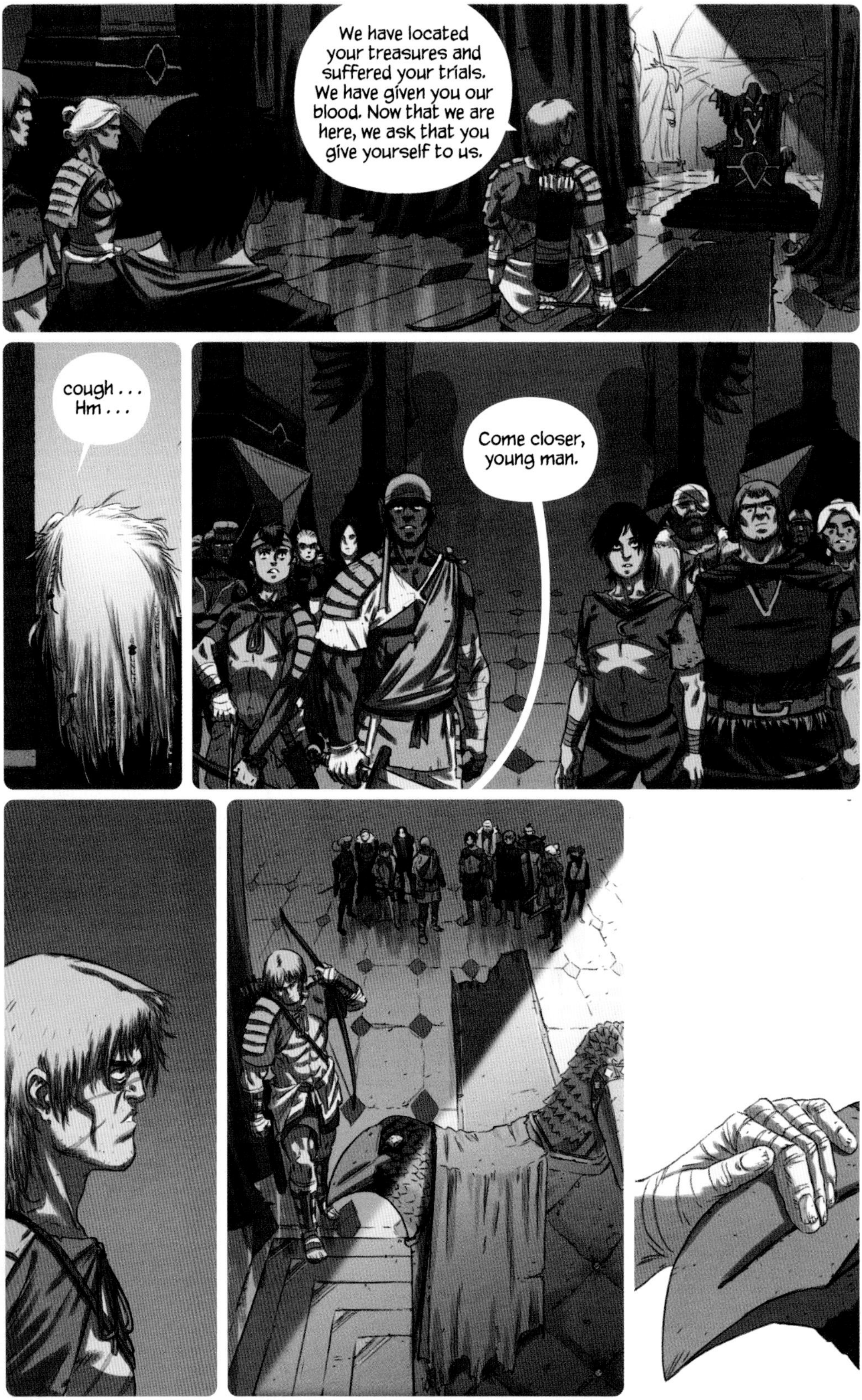
We have located your treasures and suffered your trials. We have given you our blood. Now that we are here, we ask that you give yourself to us.
cough . . . Hm . . .
Come closer, young man.

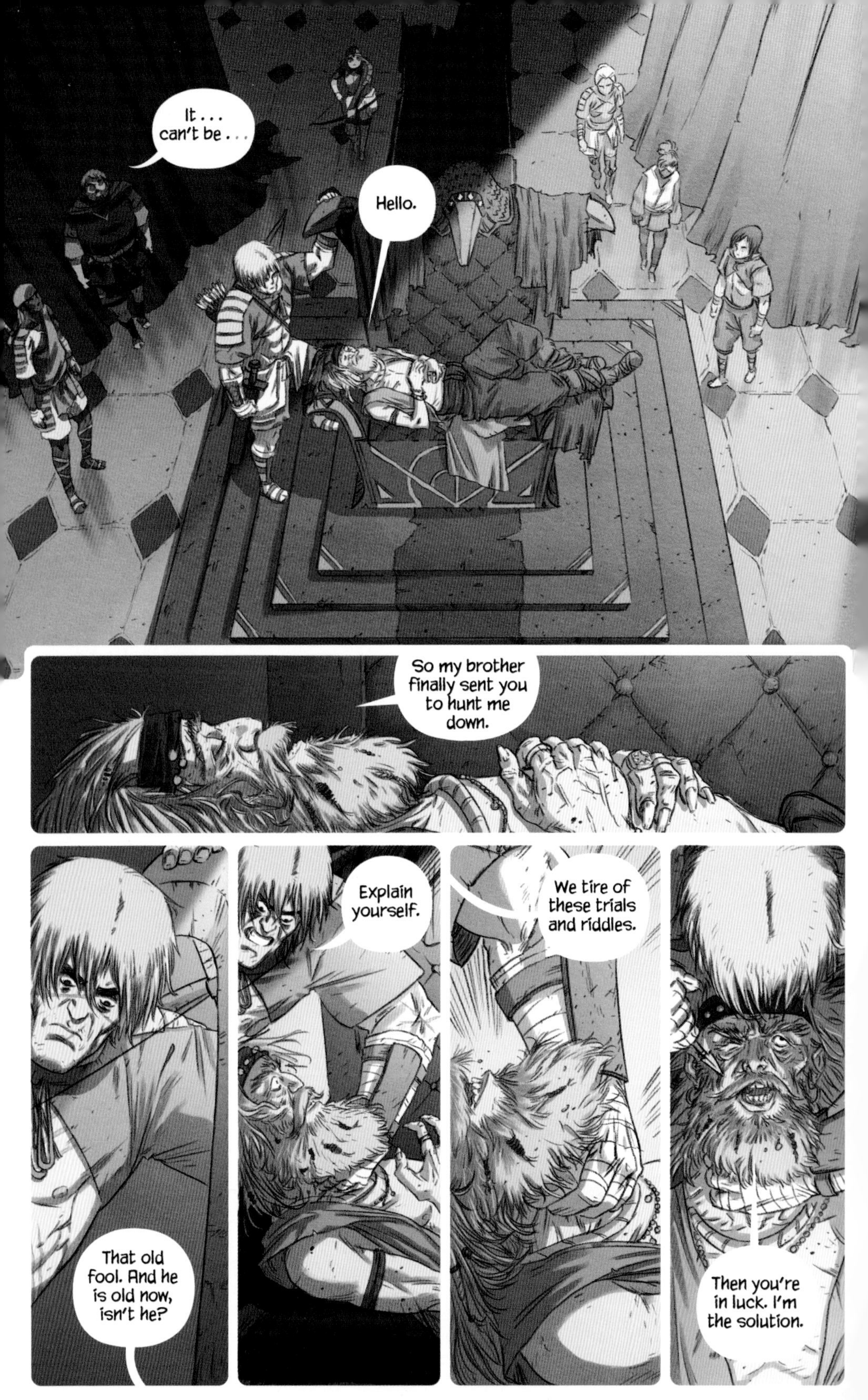
It . . . can't be . . .
Hello.
So my brother finally sent you to hunt me down.
That old fool. And he is old now, isn't he?
Explain yourself.
We tire of these trials and riddles.
Then you're in luck. I'm the solution.

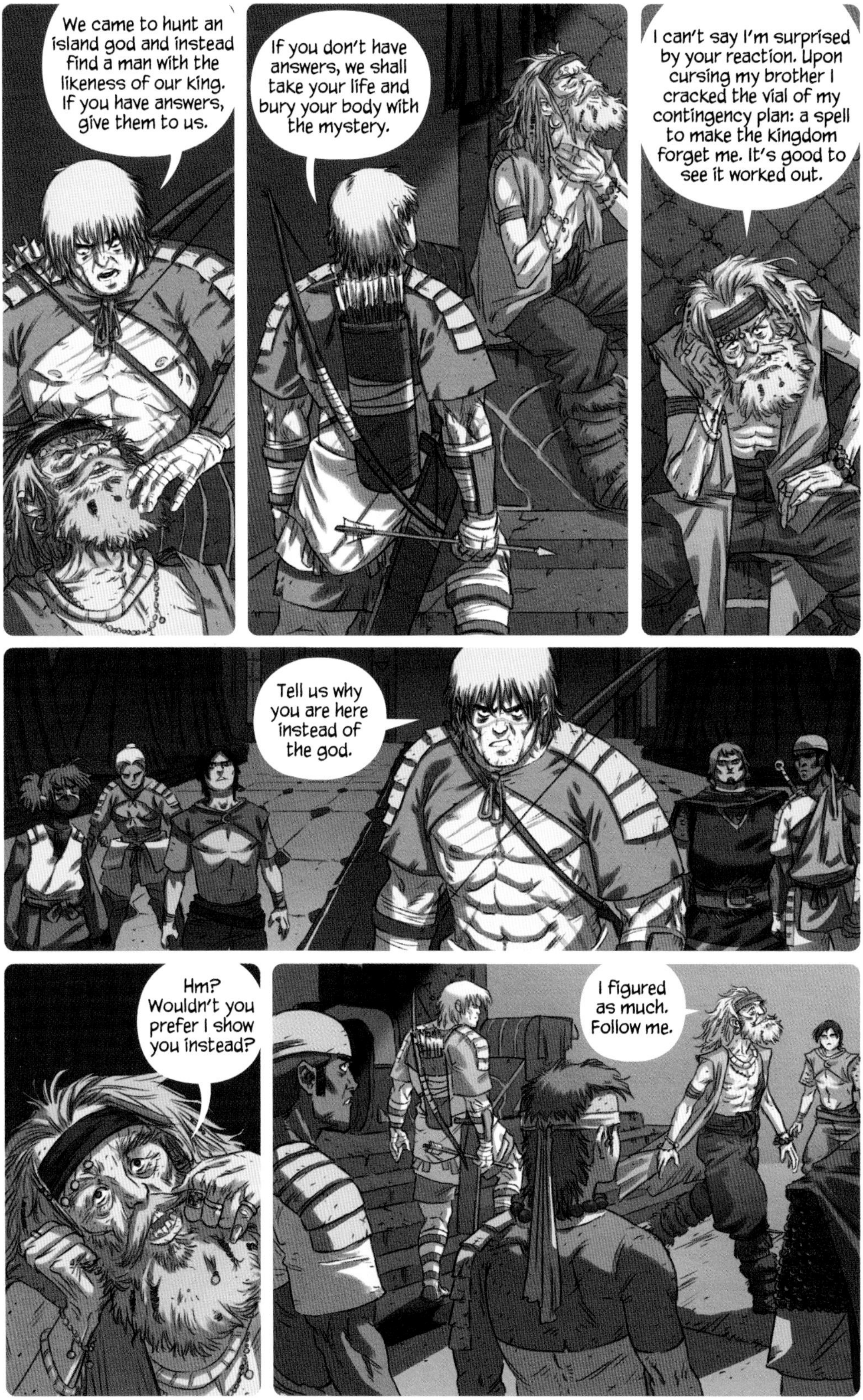
We came to hunt an island god and instead find a man with the likeness of our king. If you have answers, give them to us.
If you don't have answers, we shall take your life and bury your body with the mystery.
I can't say I'm surprised by your reaction. Upon cursing my brother I cracked the vial of my contingency plan: a spell to make the kingdom forget me. It's good to see it worked out.
Tell us why you are here instead of the god.
Hm? Wouldn't you prefer I show you instead?
I figured as much. Follow me.

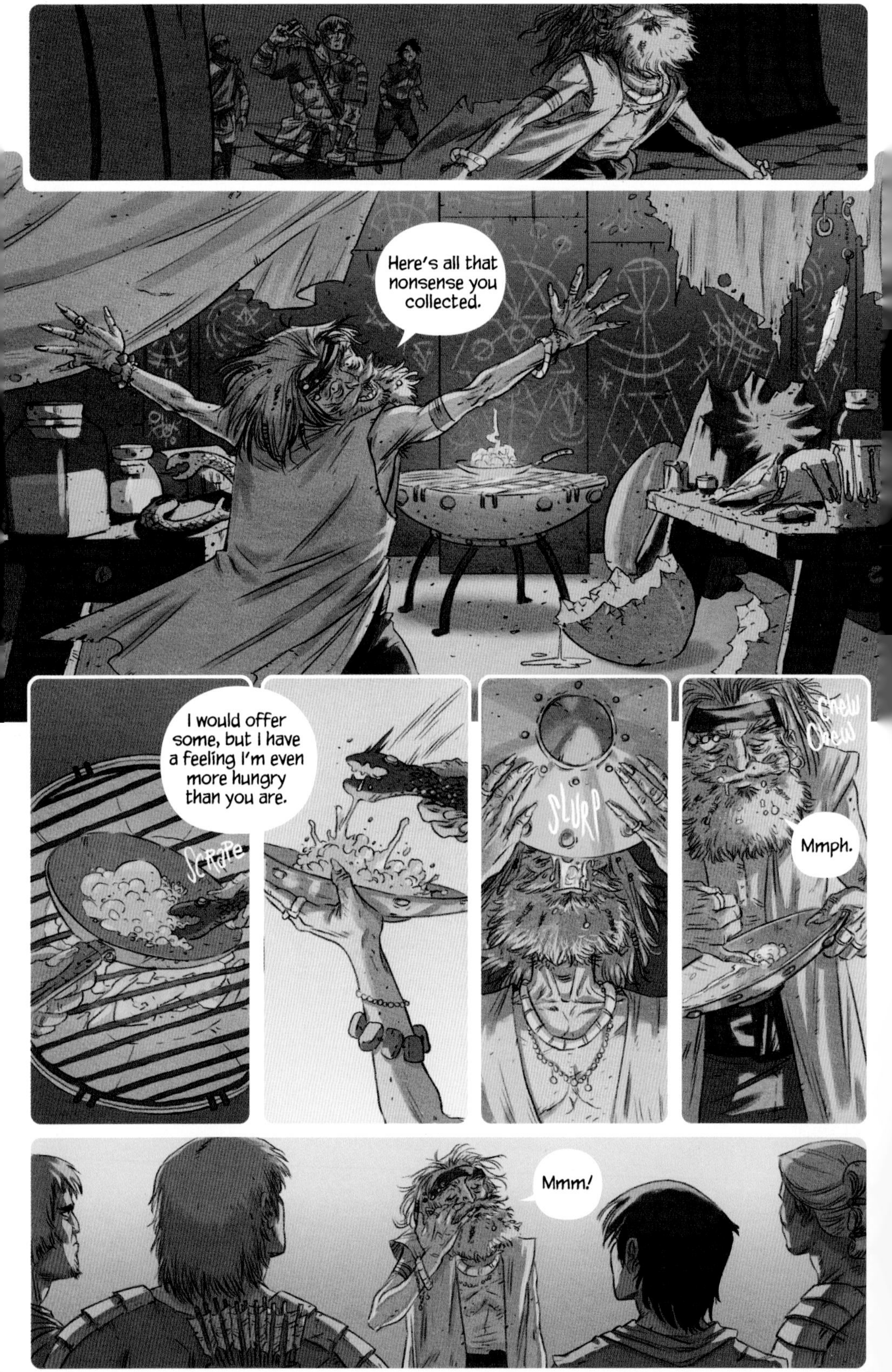
Here's all that nonsense you collected.
I would offer some, but I have a feeling I'm even more hungry than you are.
SCRAPE
SLURP
Chew Chew
Mmph.
Mmm!

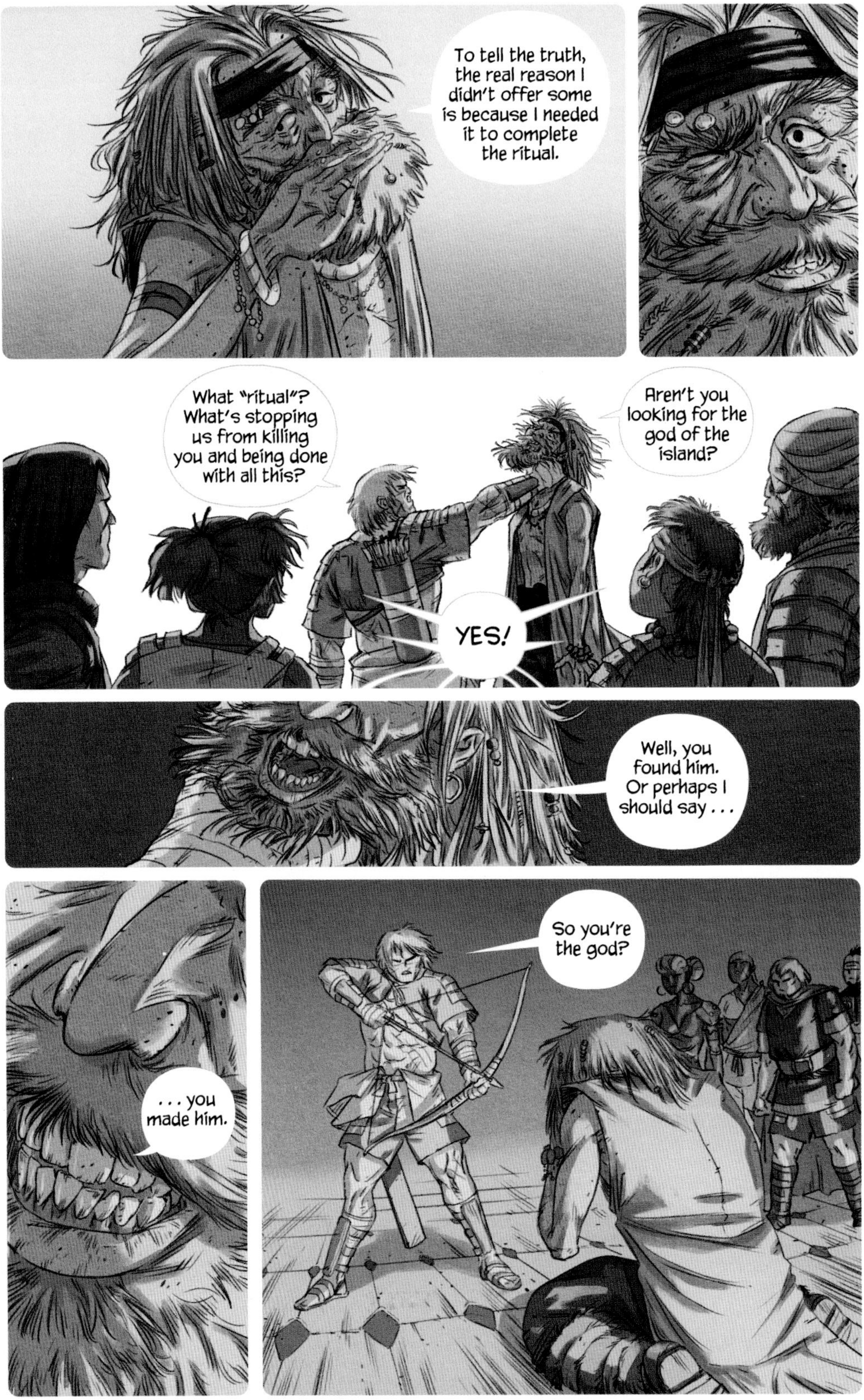
To tell the truth, the real reason I didn't offer some is because I needed it to complete the ritual.
What "ritual"? What's stopping us from killing you and being done with all this?
Aren't you looking for the god of the island?
YES!
Well, you found him. Or perhaps I should say . . .
. . . you made him.
So you're the god?

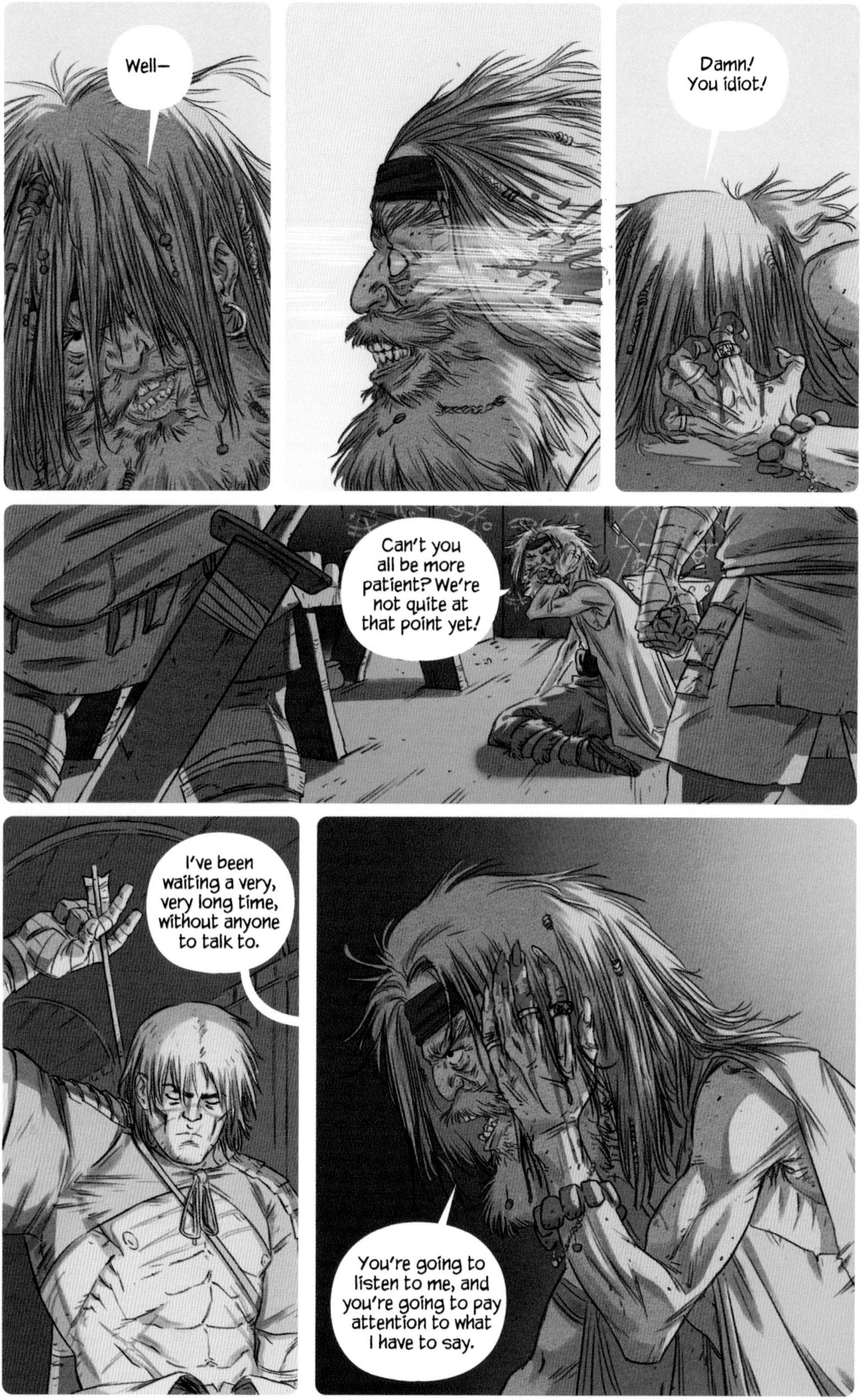
Well–
Damn! You idiot!
Can't you all be more patient? We're not quite at that point yet!
I've been waiting a very, very long time, without anyone to talk to.
You're going to listen to me, and you're going to pay attention to what I have to say.

Make it interesting, old one. These may be your last words.

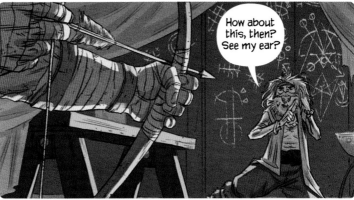

How about this, then? See my ear?

More magic?

Yes, in a way. Thanks to you.

You obviously found that mural the people of this island so desperately tried to hide from me. Without a discerning interpreter you must have thought it contained instructions on summoning a god. In a way that's true: the ritual is to give a person godlike powers.

This time I get to be that person. Last time it was a woman. Perhaps you've seen that white vulture flying around?

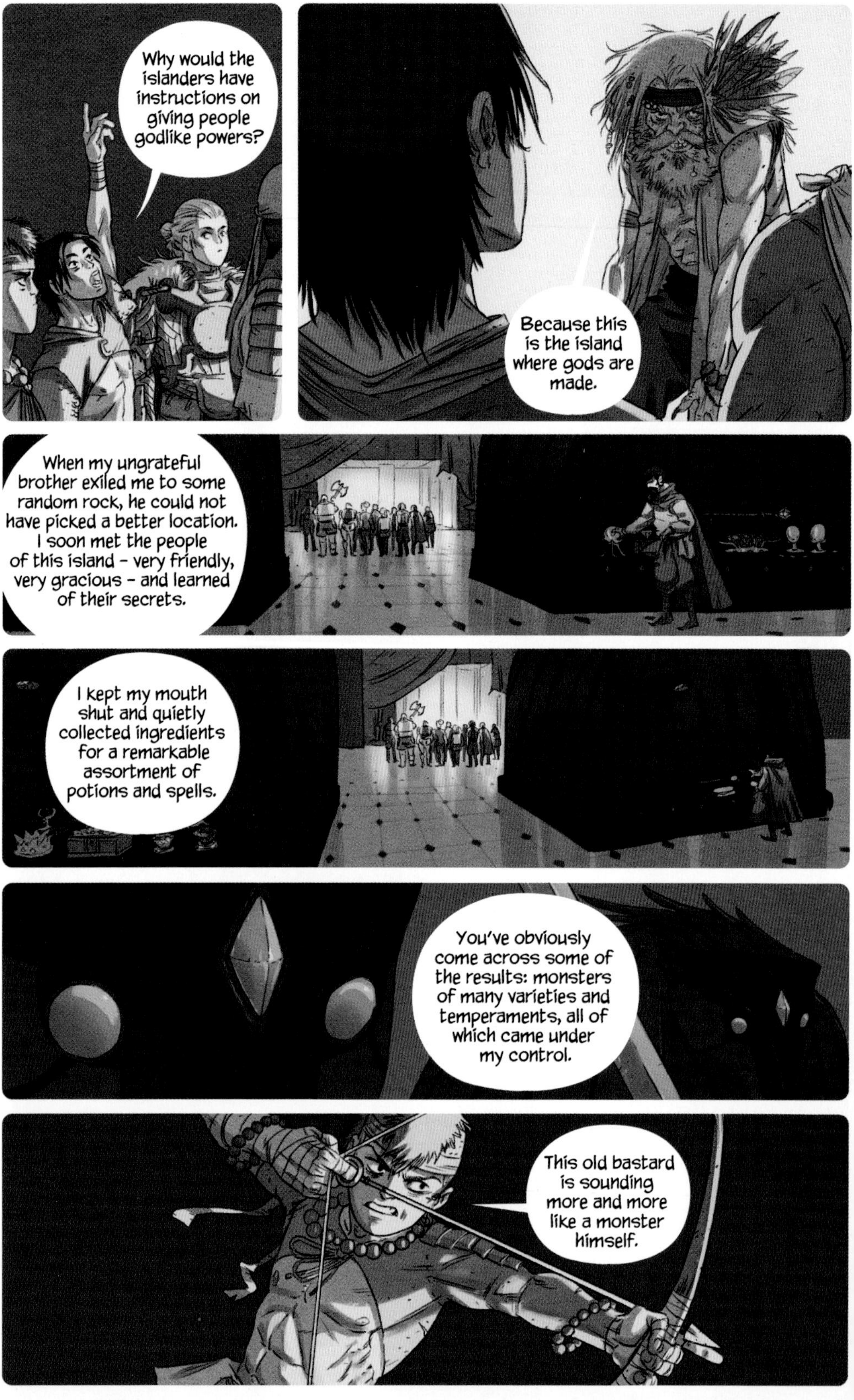
Why would the islanders have instructions on giving people godlike powers?
Because this is the island where gods are made.
When my ungrateful brother exiled me to some random rock, he could not have picked a better location. I soon met the people of this island - very friendly, very gracious - and learned of their secrets.
I kept my mouth shut and quietly collected ingredients for a remarkable assortment of potions and spells.
You've obviously come across some of the results: monsters of many varieties and temperaments, all of which came under my control.
This old bastard is sounding more and more like a monster himself.

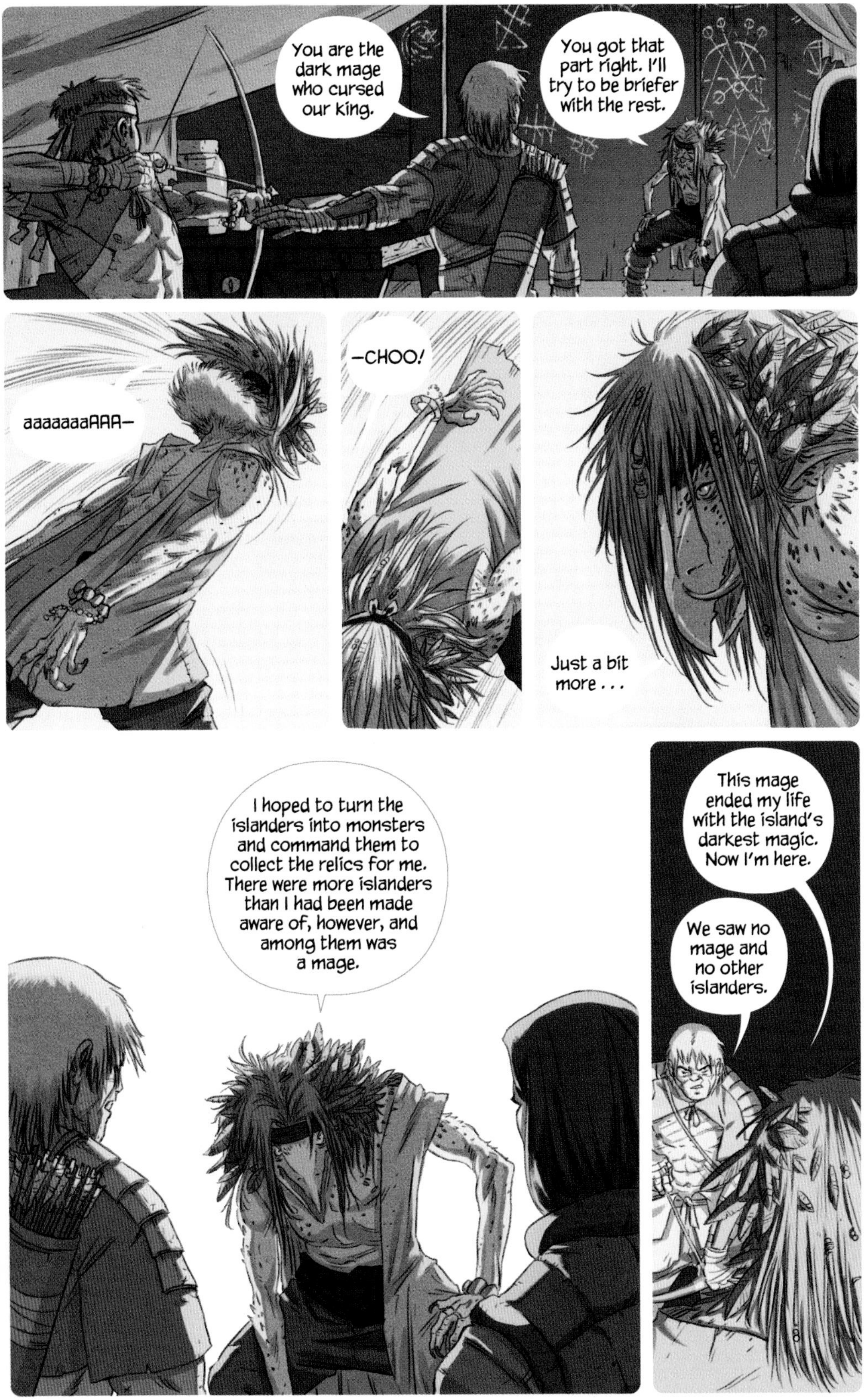
You are the dark mage who cursed our King.
You got that part right. I'll try to be briefer with the rest.
aaaaaaaAAA—
—CHOO!
Just a bit more . . .
I hoped to turn the islanders into monsters and command them to collect the relics for me. There were more islanders than I had been made aware of, however, and among them was a mage.
This mage ended my life with the island's darkest magic. Now I'm here.
We saw no mage and no other islanders.

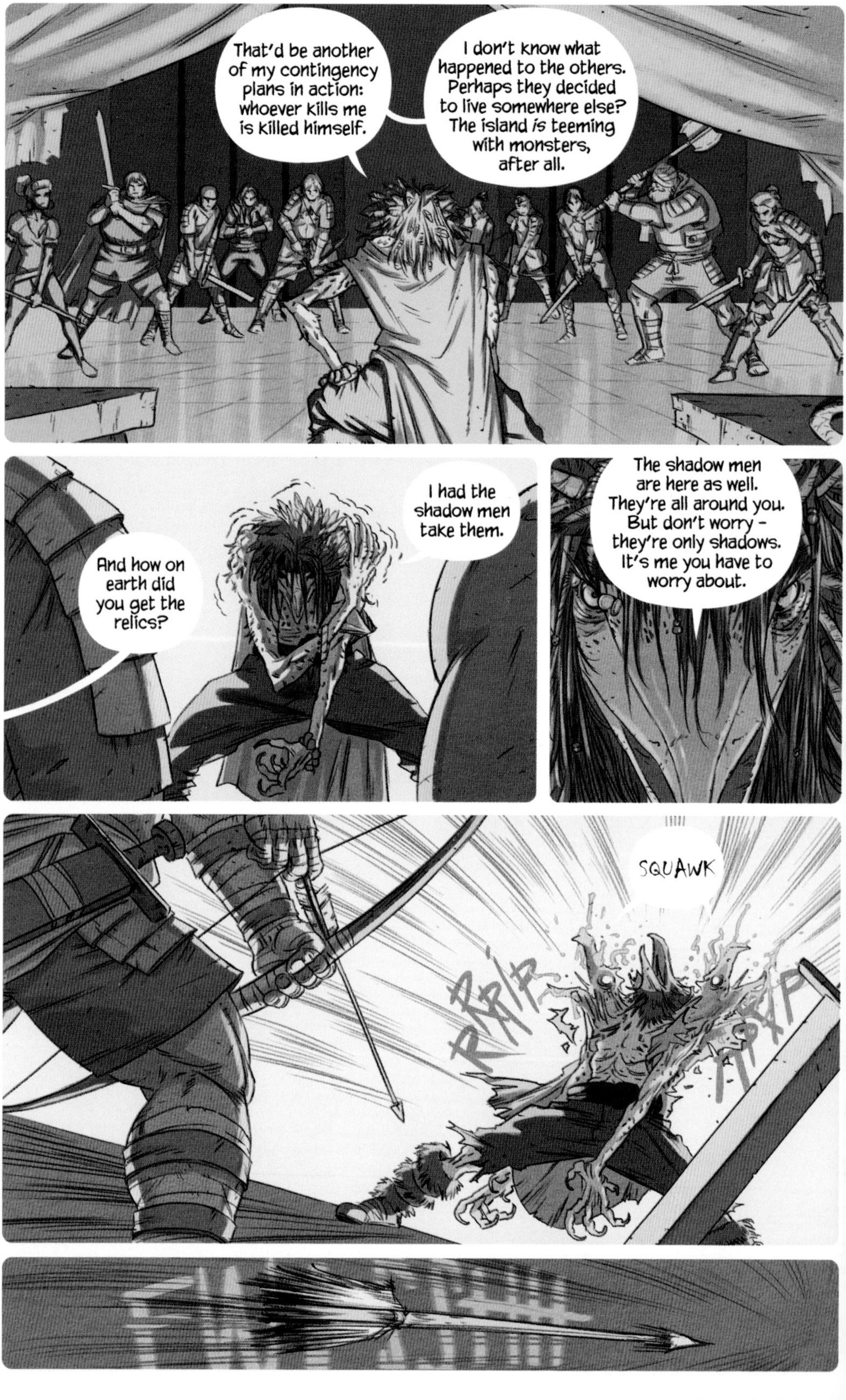
That'd be another of my contingency plans in action: whoever kills me is killed himself.
I don't know what happened to the others. Perhaps they decided to live somewhere else? The island *is* teeming with monsters, after all.
And how on earth did you get the relics?
I had the shadow men take them.
The shadow men are here as well. They're all around you. But don't worry – they're only shadows. It's me you have to worry about.
SQUAWK
RRIP

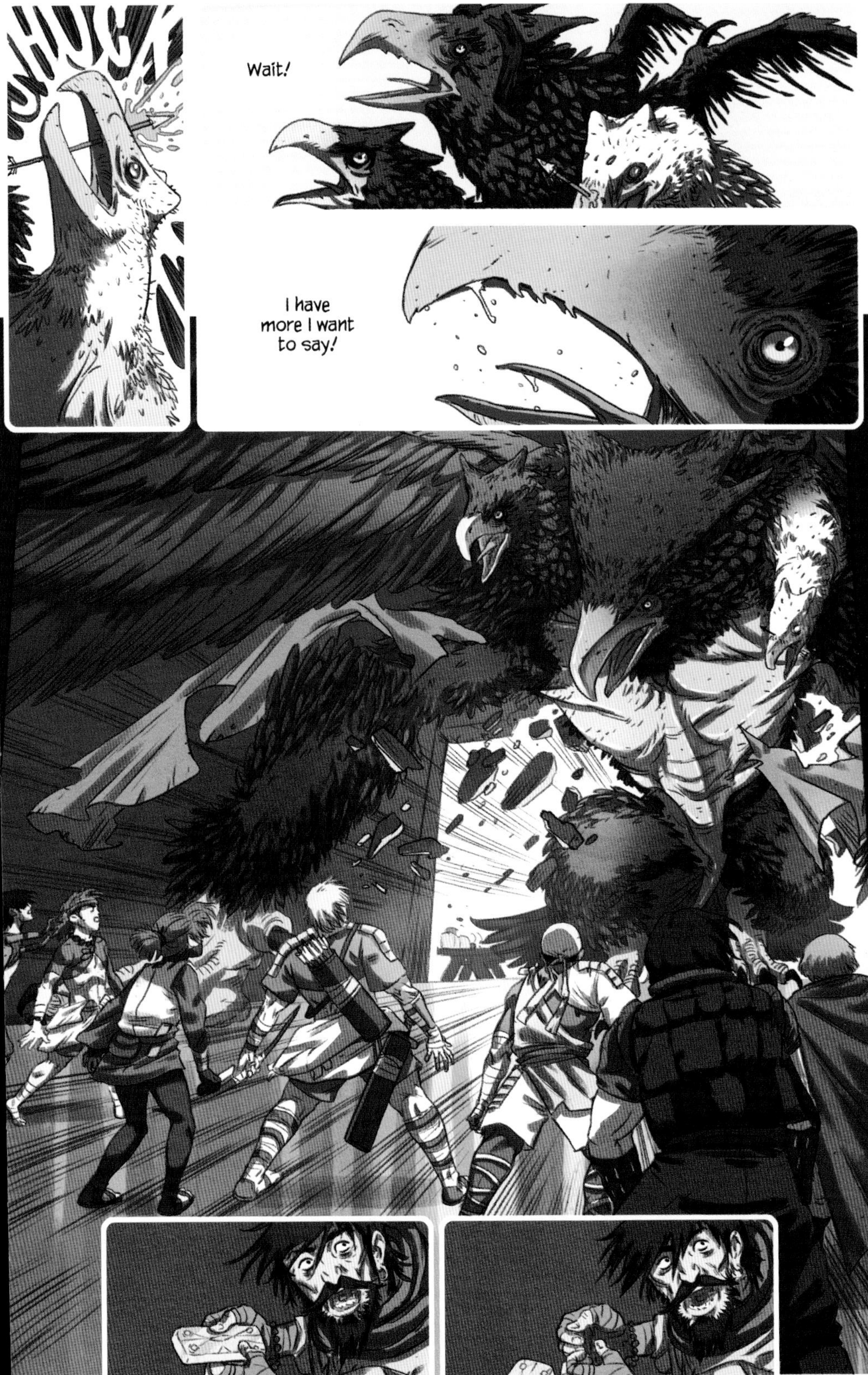
CHUCK
Wait!
I have more I want to say!

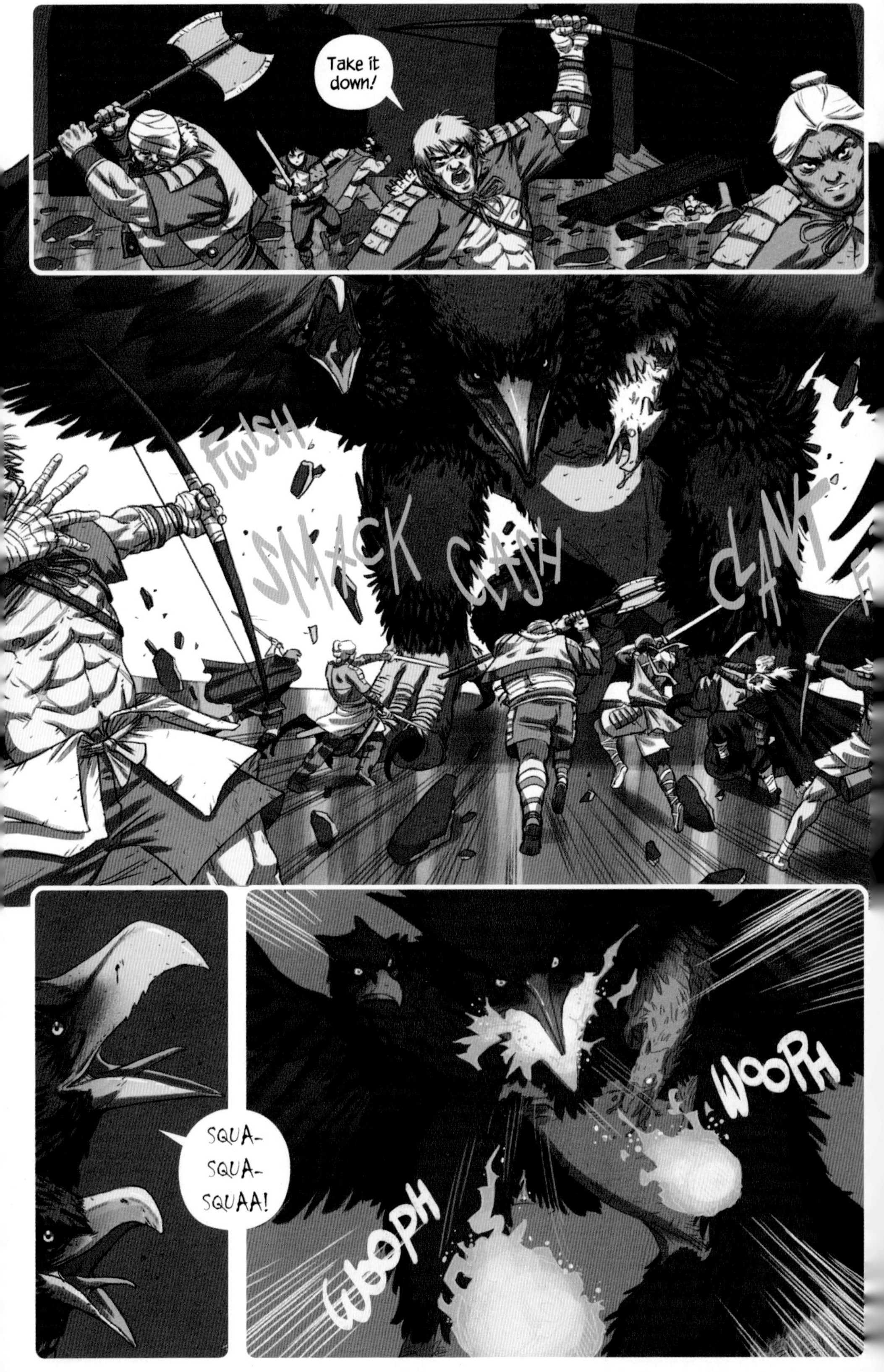
Take it down!
FWISH
SMACK
CLASH
CLANT
SQUA-SQUA-SQUAA!
WOOPH
WOOPH

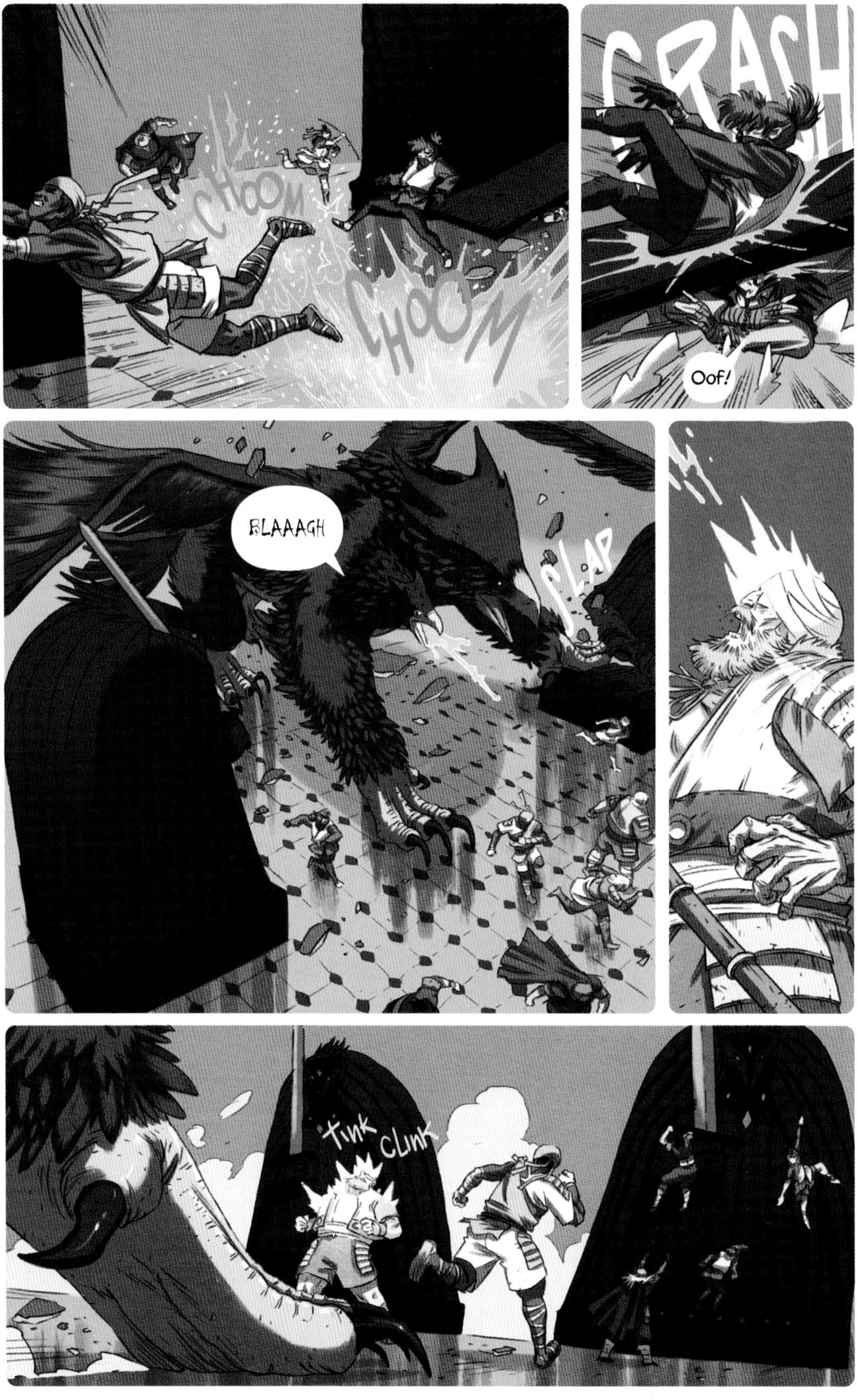
CHOOM
CHOOM
CRASH
Oof!
BLAAAGH
SLAP
TINK
CLINK

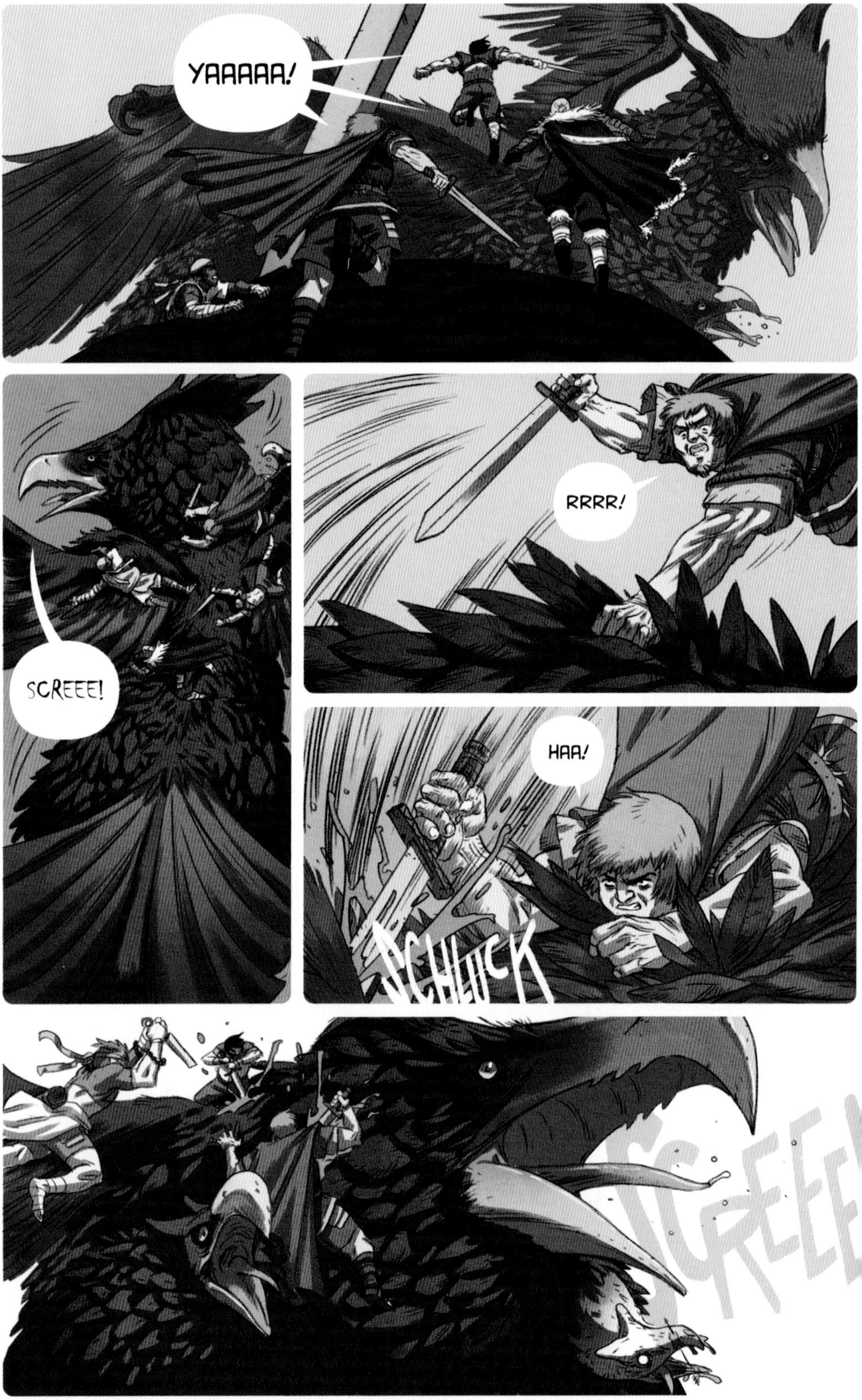
YAAAAA!
SCREEE!
RRRR!
HAA!
SCHLUCK

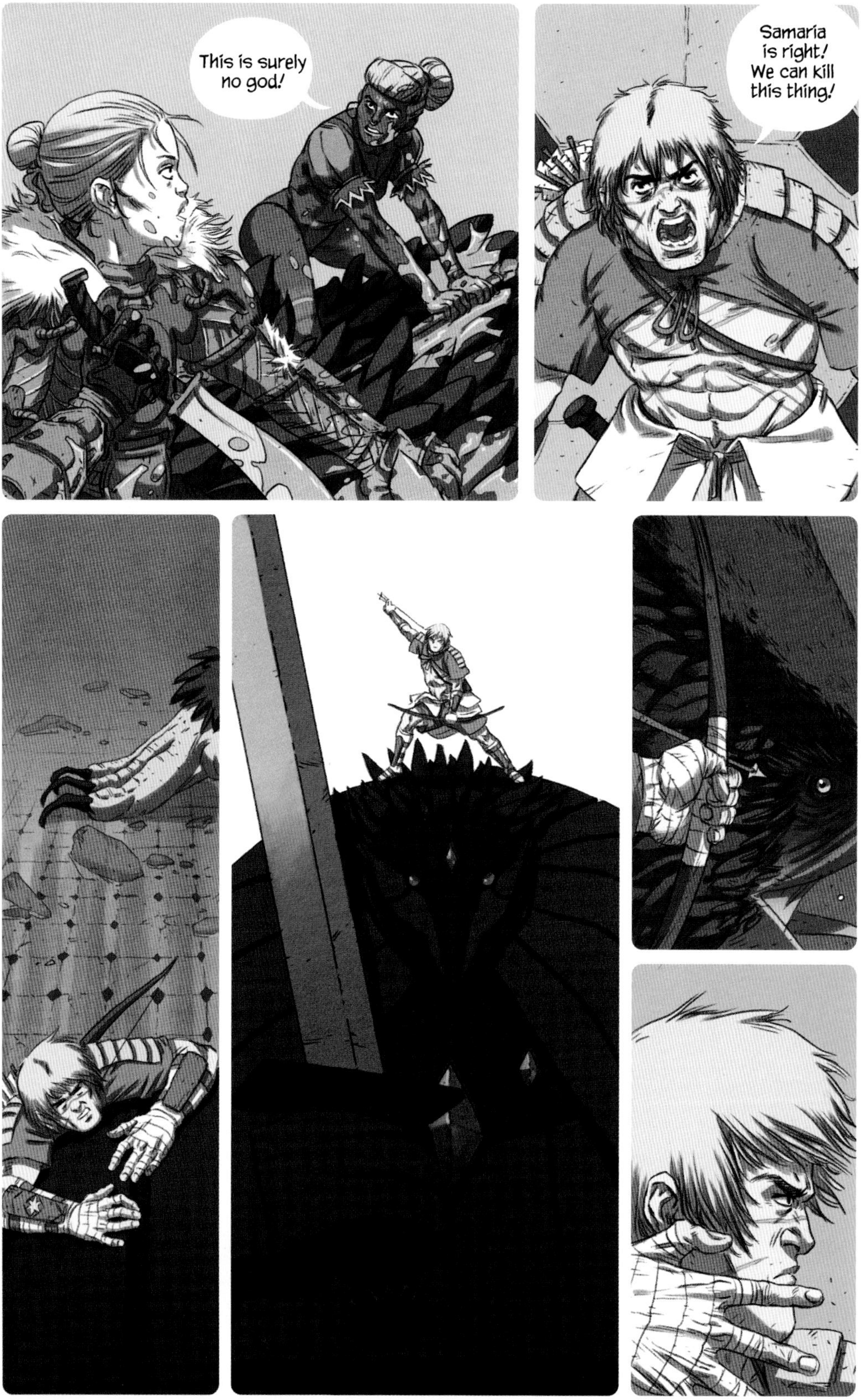
This is surely no god!
Samaria is right! We can kill this thing!

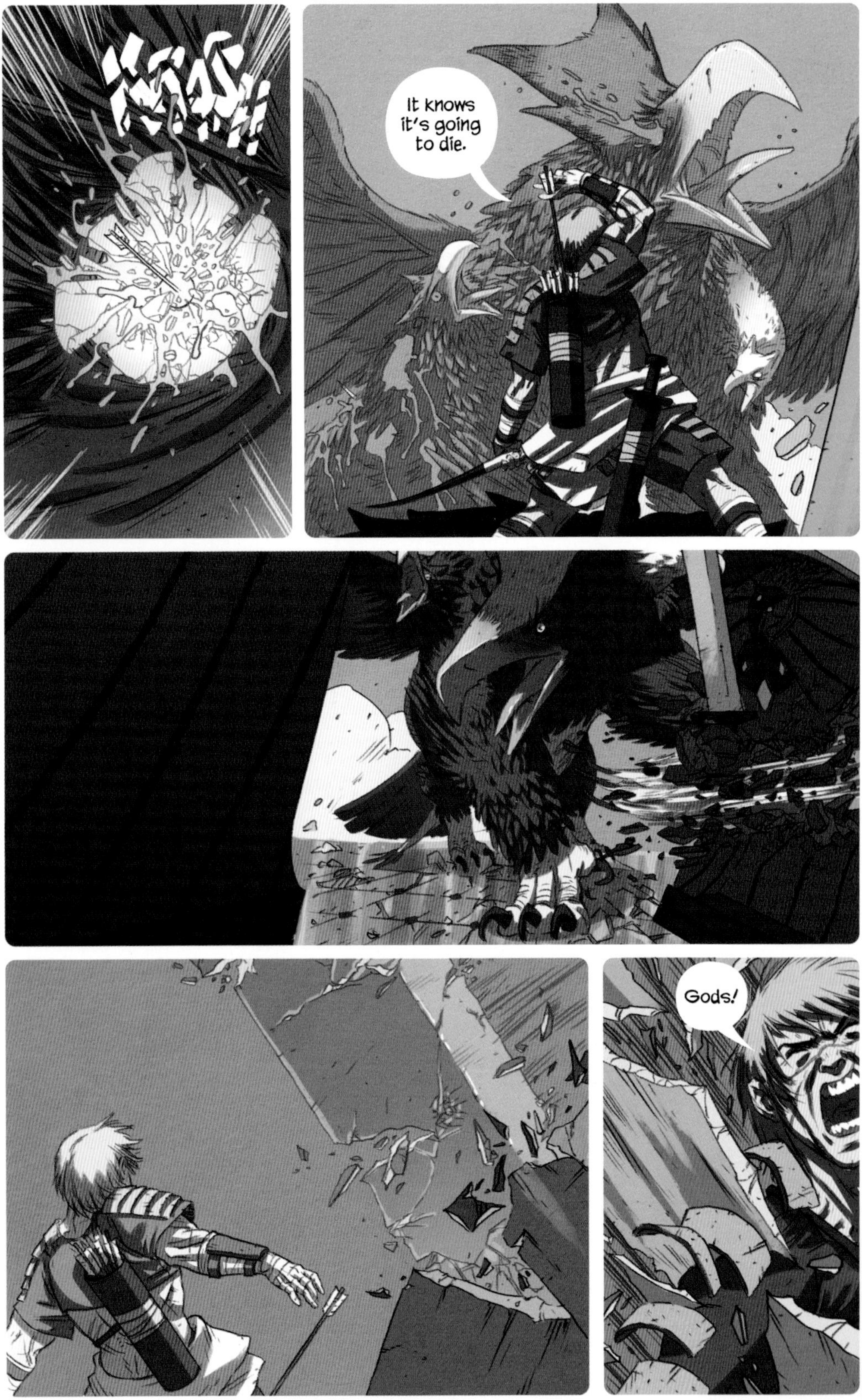
It knows it's going to die.
Gods!

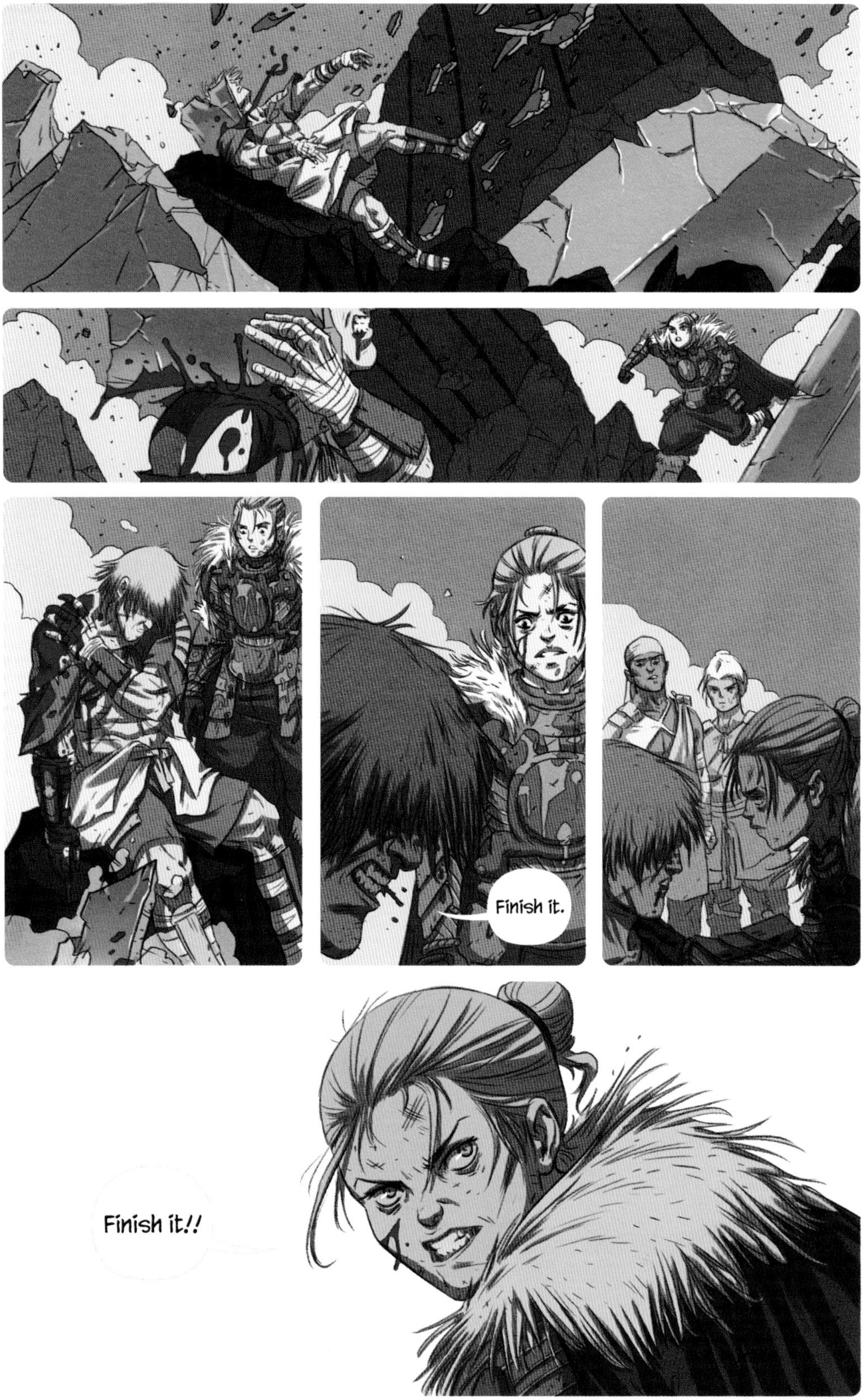
Finish it.
Finish it!!

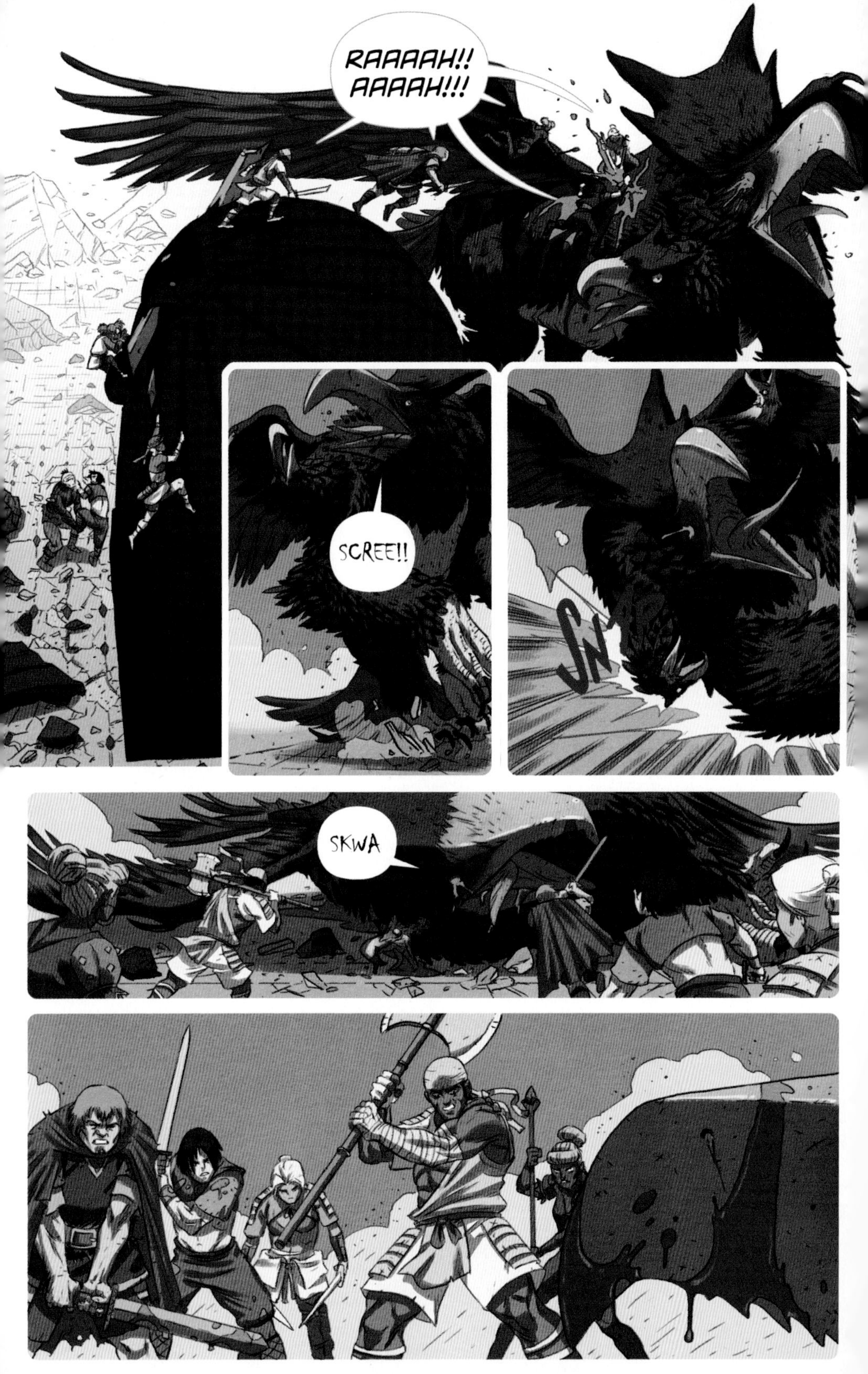
RAAAAH!!
AAAAH!!!
SCREE!!
SN
SKWA

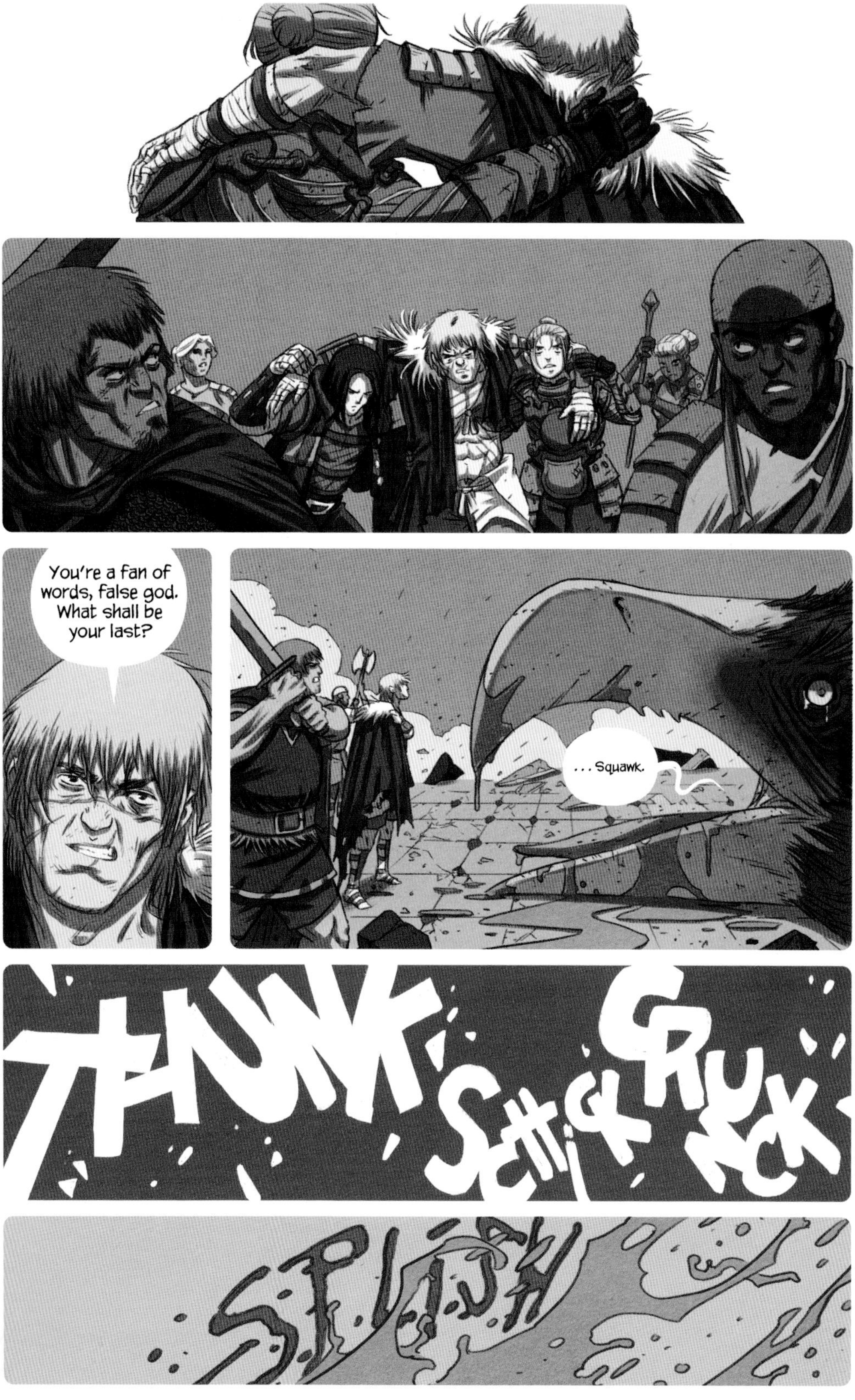
You're a fan of words, false god. What shall be your last?
... Squawk.
THUNK

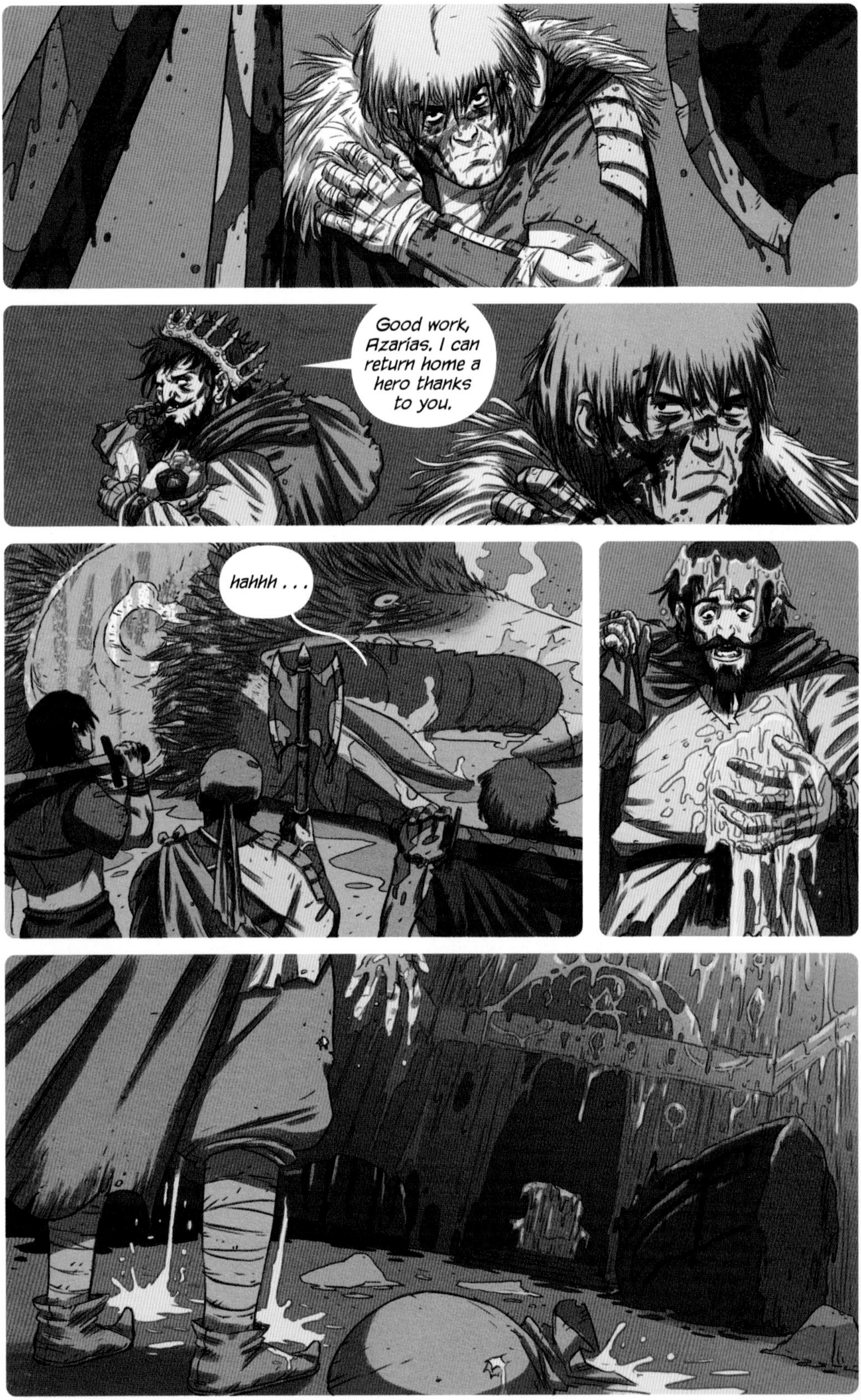
Good work, Azarias. I can return home a hero thanks to you.
hahhh . . .

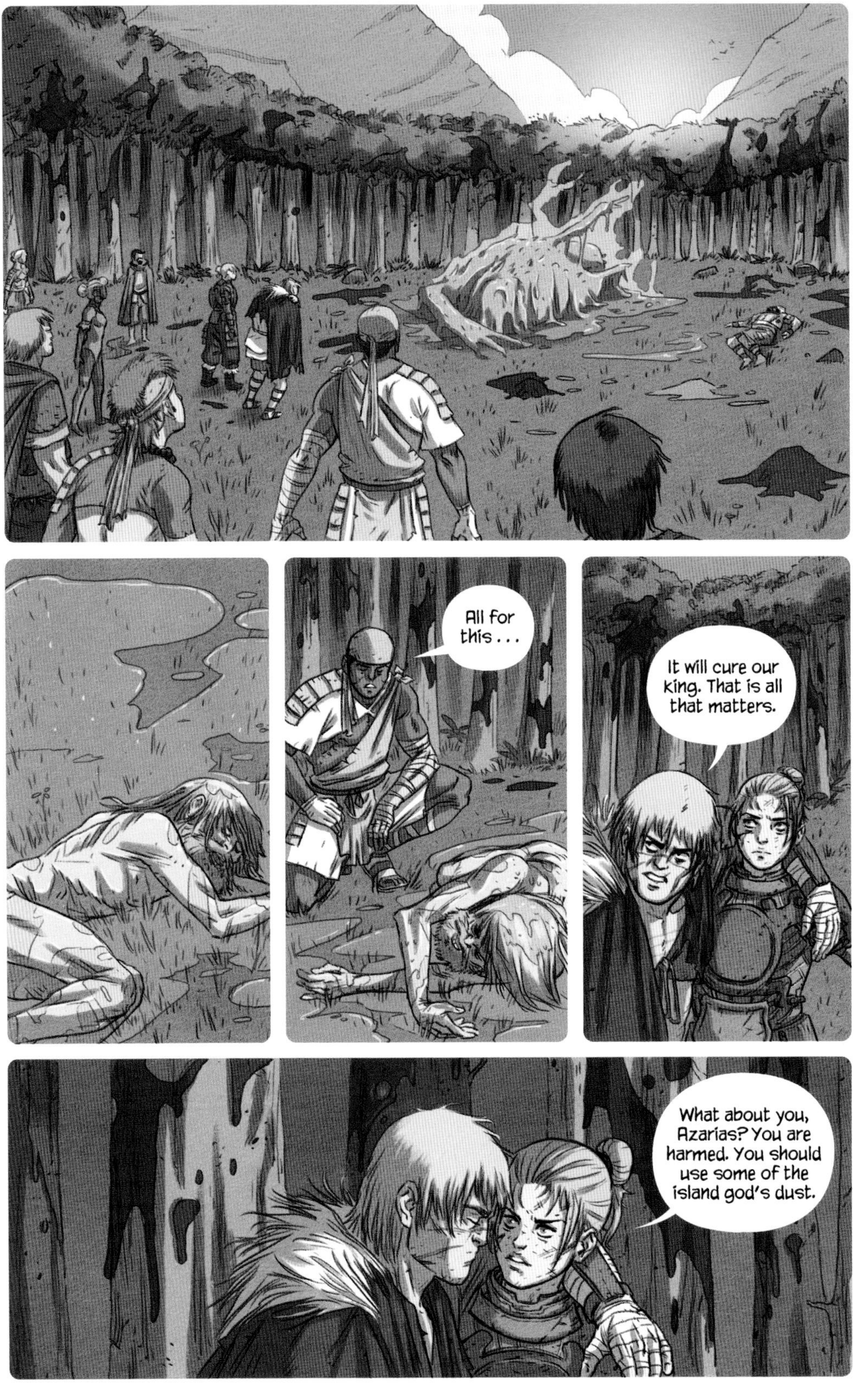
All for this . . .
It will cure our king. That is all that matters.
What about you, Azarias? You are harmed. You should use some of the island god's dust.

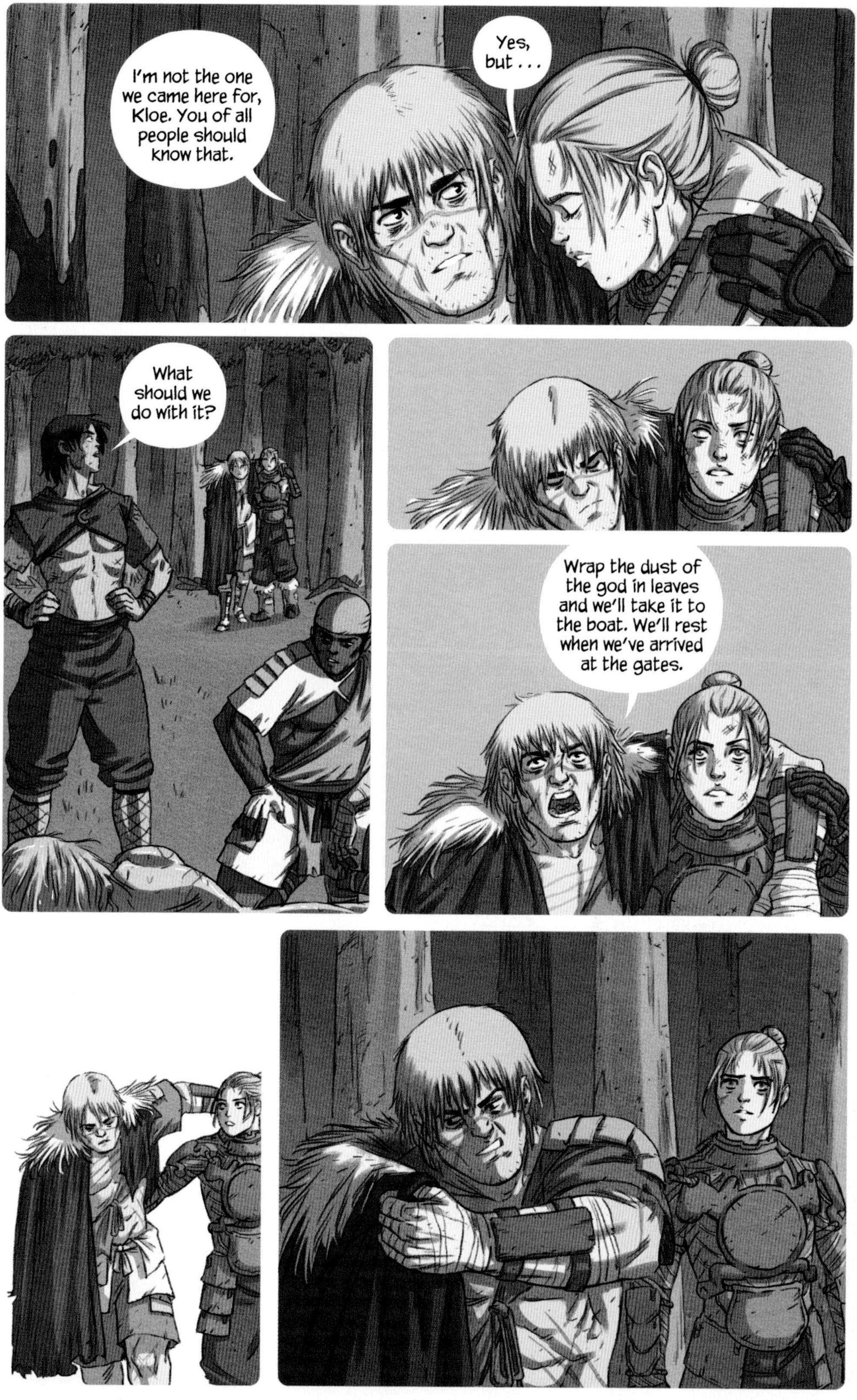
I'm not the one we came here for, Kloe. You of all people should know that.
Yes, but . . .
What should we do with it?
Wrap the dust of the god in leaves and we'll take it to the boat. We'll rest when we've arrived at the gates.

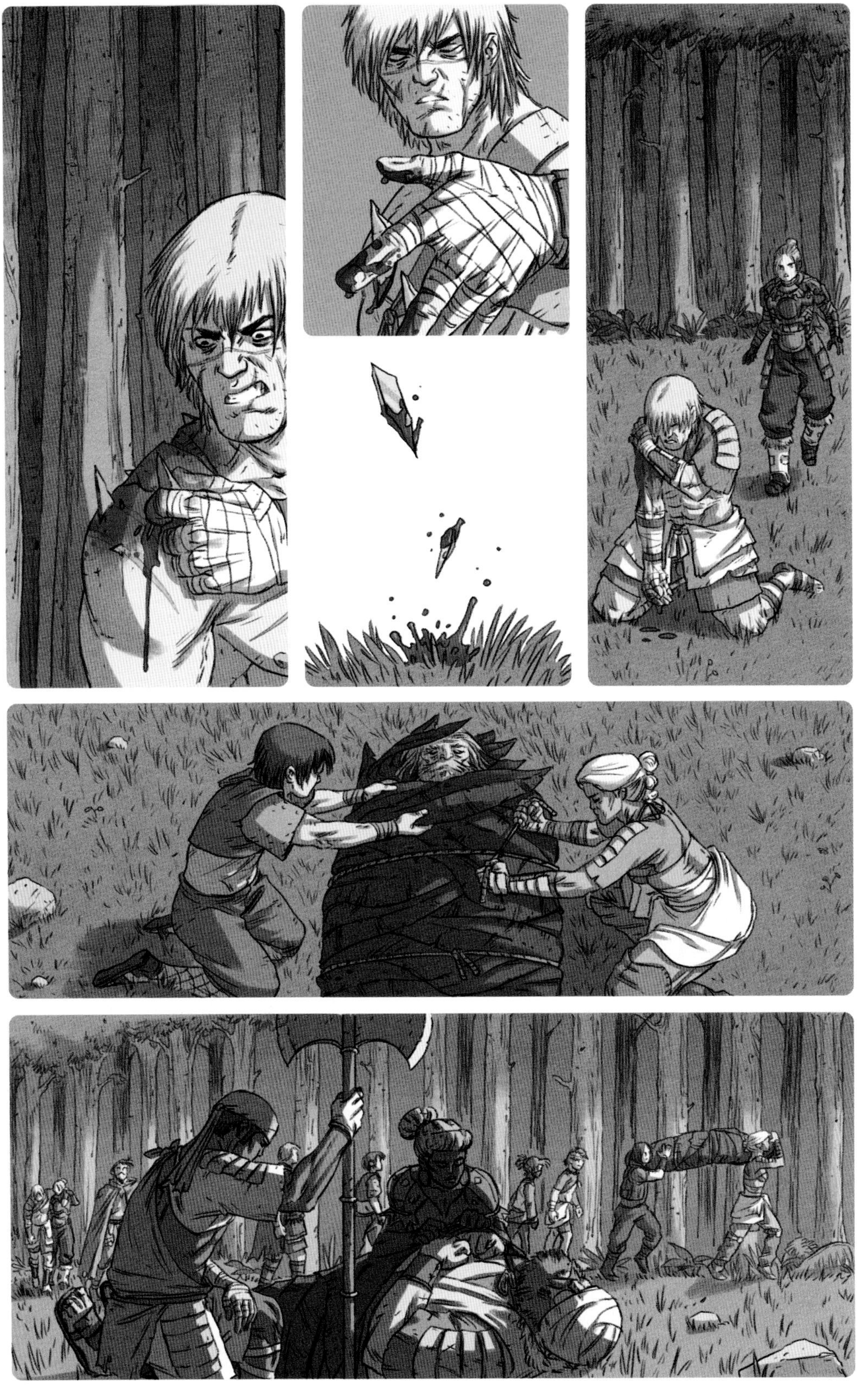

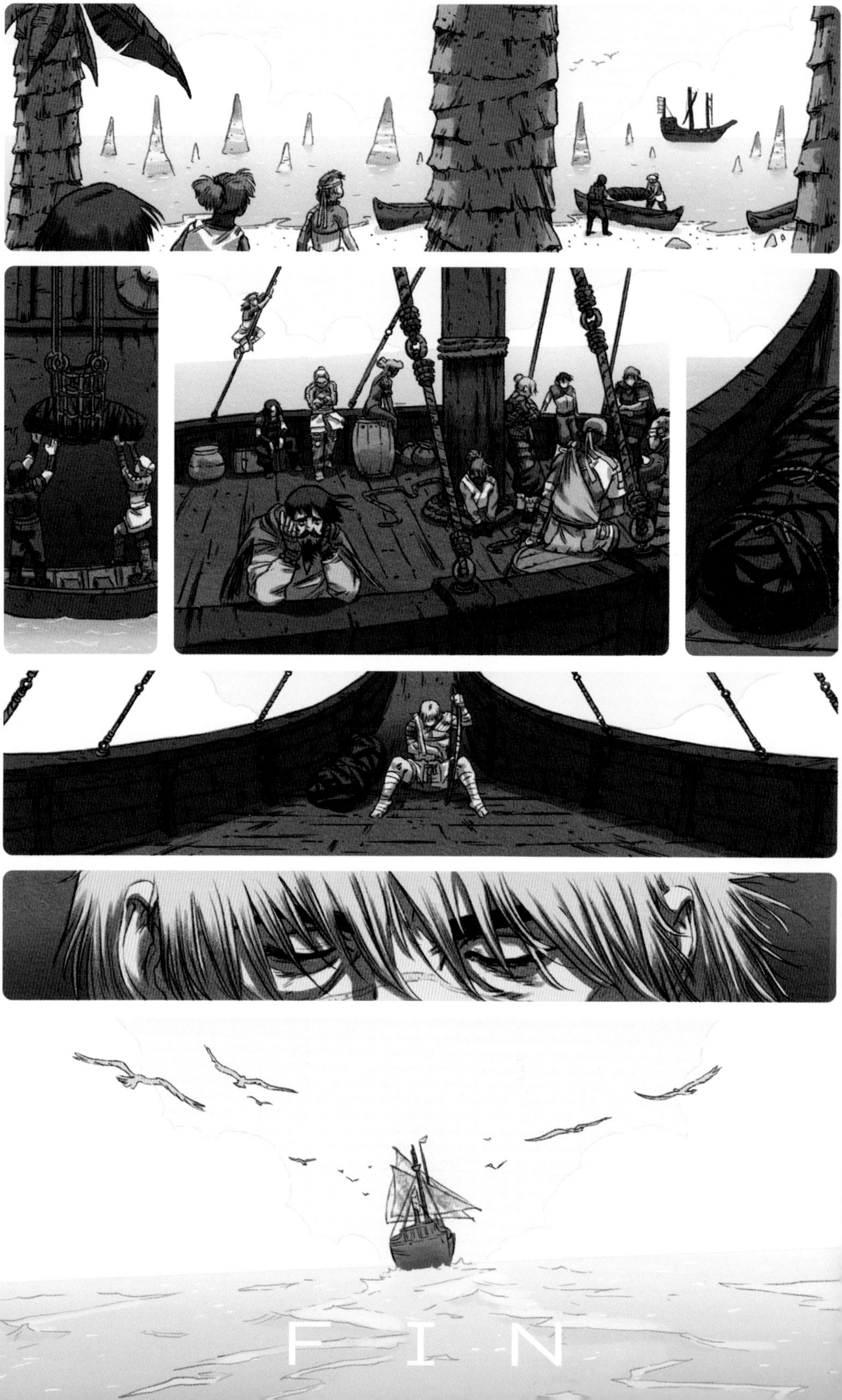
FIN

PAUL MAYBURY is an award-winning artist and writer best known for his original graphic novel *Aqua Leung* and his work on *D.O.G.S. of Mars*.

JOSH TIERNEY is the proud father of two very wonderful and silly children. He is the writer of the Eisner-nominated *Spera* fantasy series from Archaia/BOOM! Studios and the high school mystery webcomic *WarmBloodComic.com*.

MIGUEL VALDERRAMA is an artist born in Marbella, Spain. He currently lives in Madrid, where he teaches drawing to his students (and to himself) and makes comics with his brother Carlos, including *Giants* for Dark Horse.

AFU CHAN is a San Francisco-based freelance artist with a focus on comic books, illustration, character design, and concept art. He is currently working for Marvel as a comic artist. afuchan.com

NIAMI is an illustrator based between London, UK, Beirut, Lebanon, and Dubai, UAE. He graduated with a BA in illustration at Camberwell University of the Arts.

JARED MORGAN lives in Burbank, California, where he has fooled people into letting him work on cartoons and is occasionally asked to draw comics.

CARLOS VALDERRAMA was born and raised on the coast of Marbella, Spain. Now he is a teacher of digital concept art in Madrid where, alongside his brother Miguel, he is writing full-length comic books such as *Giants* for Dark Horse.

MEG GANDY is the co-creator of the webcomic *Godsend* (godsend.shatterlands.com), with other work featured in *Sleep of Reason*, *New World*, *Spera*, *Adventure Time*, and *Steven Universe*.

DEVIN KRAFT is a comic artist originally from Roswell, New Mexico. He is best known for *Dragon Slayer* and *Silence*, both self-published and funded via Kickstarter. He is currently based in Dallas/Fort Worth, Texas.

VLAD GUSEV is a Russian illustrator and graphic designer currently residing in Valencia, Spain.

CARLOS CARRASCO is a Spanish multidisciplinary artist living in Madrid. He recently collaborated with Vlad Gusev on *Anamnesis*.

KYLA VANDERKLUGT was born and raised in Toronto, Canada, where she graduated from OCAD University in 2008 with a Bachelor of Design. Her comics work includes contributions to *Flight*, *Nobrow*, *Spera*, and *Jim Henson's The Storyteller* series.

RAMÓN SIERRA is reading comics when he's not drawing them. A lover of old seinen, horror manga, and gekiga, he's been working on getting that same feeling of mystery in his own work.

IRENE KOH was born in Seoul, spent her childhood in Tokyo, and now resides in California. Notable works include *The Legend of Korra* graphic novels for Dark Horse and *Secret Origins: Batgirl* for DC.

BENJAMIN MARRA is the notorious and influential creator of many successful underground comic books including *Terror Assaulter: O.M.W.O.T. (One Man War On Terror)*.

ALEXIS ZIRITT is originally from Venezuela but has lived in Florida for the past decade. He's been published in *Complex* Magazine, *Heavy Metal*, and BOOM! Studios and Dark Horse Comics among others.

TRAVEL FOREMAN has worked on *Cla$$war* for Com.x, *The Immortal Iron Fist* for Marvel Comics, and *Animal Man* for DC Comics, and many more.

Designs by **AFU CHAN**

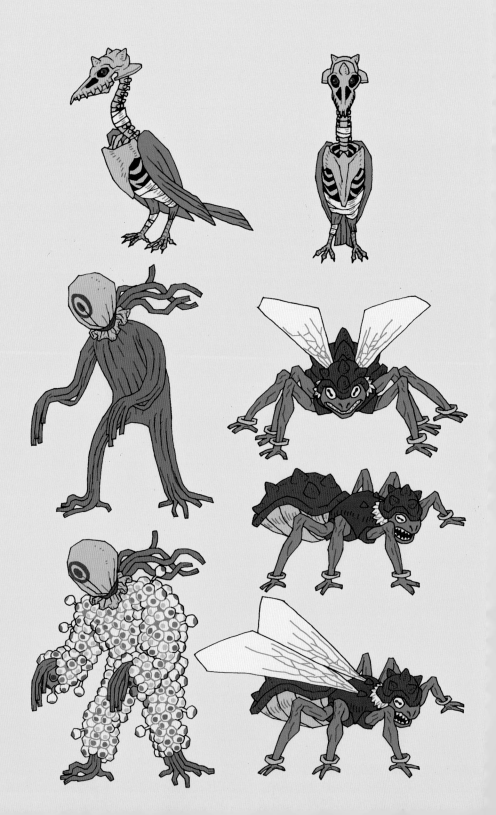

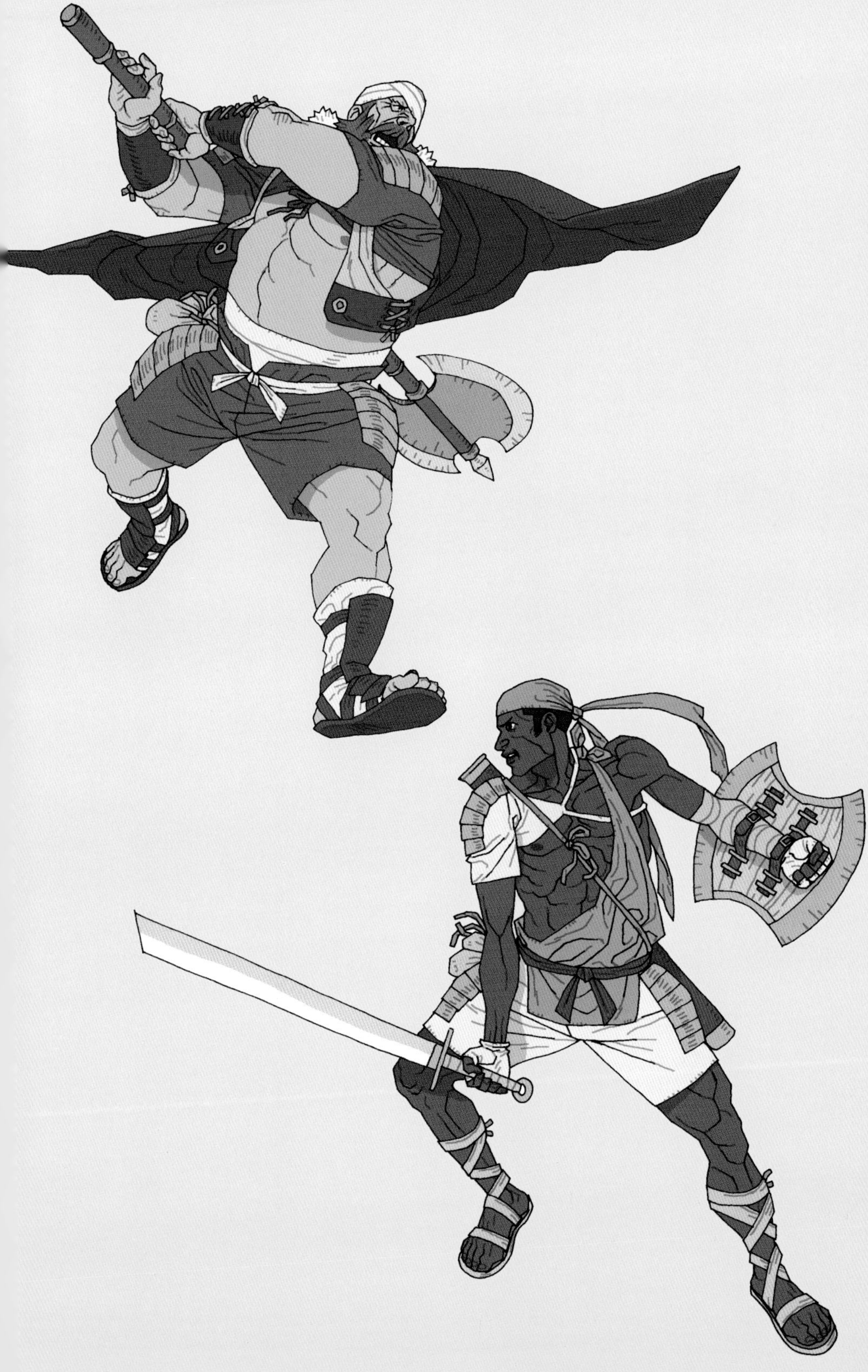

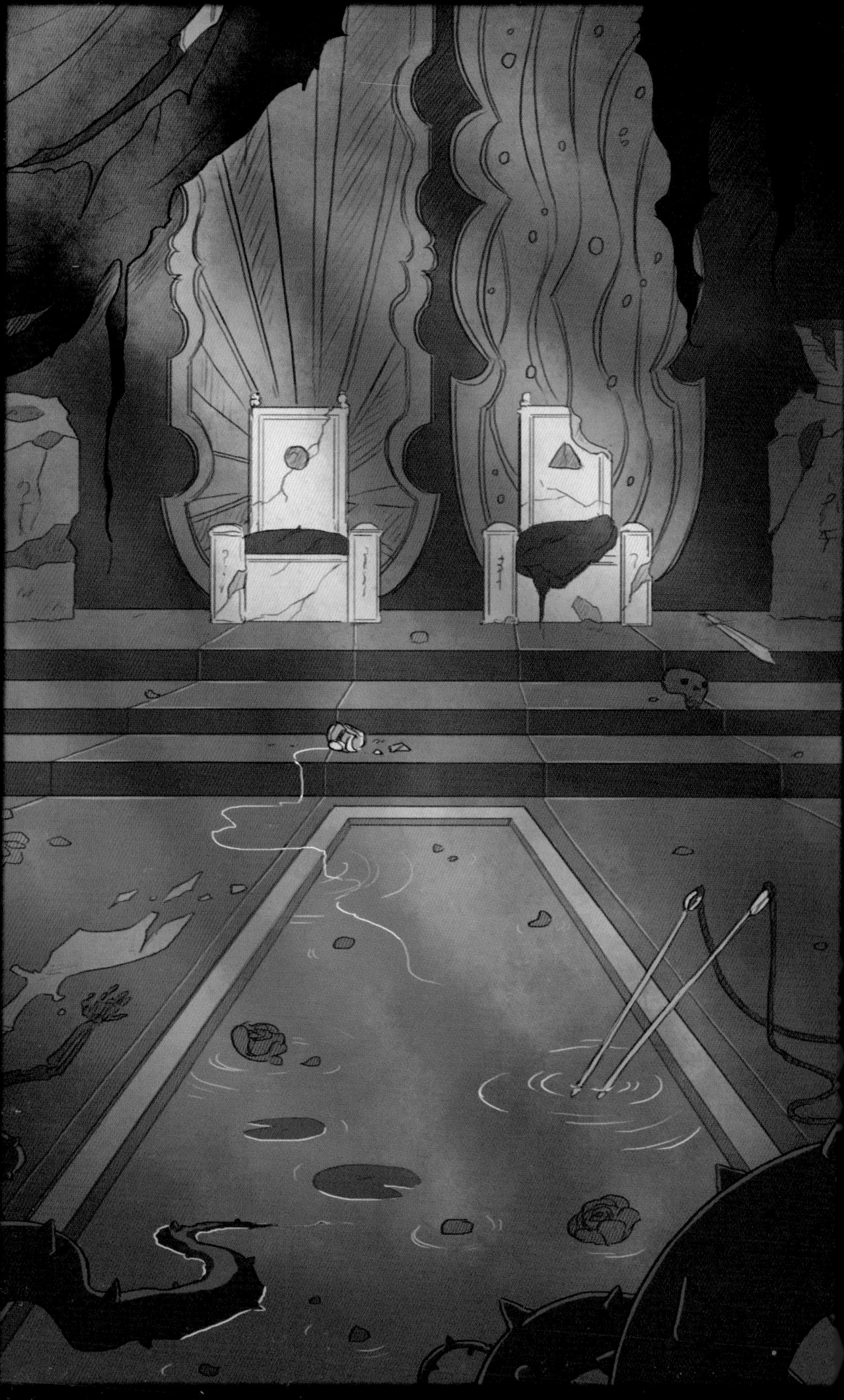